Alexander Mollin is the son of a miner and a cotton-mill worker. He works as an international commercial lawyer. He has been married for more than twenty years and describes himself as very happy. He and his wife have three children.

AUTHOR'S NOTE

I should make it clear that the inspiration to write *Lara's Child* came from the author's reading of *Dr Zhivago*. The book was not initiated by the Pasternak family nor did the latter have any involvement in its writing. The Pasternak family is in no way concerned in the promotion of *Lara's Child* and derives no financial or other benefit from the book. I would emphasize, too, that I have had no access to Boris Pasternak's private papers, memoirs or memorabilia, nor special knowledge of his intentions with respect to any further development of his masterwork. I accept full responsibility for the artistic choices I made in writing my book. Any failings in *Lara's Child* are entirely mine.

Lara's Child

Alexander Mollin

CORGI BOOKS

LARA'S CHILD
A CORGI BOOK: 0 552 13972 6

Originally published in Great Britain by Doubleday,
a division of Transworld Publishers Ltd

PRINTING HISTORY
Doubleday edition published 1994
Corgi edition published 1995

Set in 10/11pt Linotron Plantin by
Falcon Graphic Art Ltd

Corgi Books are published by Transworld Publishers Ltd,
61–63 Uxbridge Road, Ealing, London W5 5SA,
in Australia by Transworld Publishers (Australia) Pty. Ltd,
15–25 Helles Avenue, Moorebank, NSW 2170,
and in New Zealand by Transworld Publishers (N.Z.) Ltd,
3 William Pickering Drive, Albany, Auckland.

Reproduced, printed and bound in Great Britain by
Cox & Wyman Ltd, Reading, Berks.

Contents

BOOK ONE
Love and Contempt

1	KOMAROVSKY	11
2	THE WOMAN IN CORSETS	42
3	THE CAPTAIN OF CAVALRY	57
4	THE THREE SISTERS	85
5	THE TRAMP	102
6	THE MAN IN THE FOX-FUR COAT	123
7	LOVE AND CONTEMPT	152
8	VLADIVOSTOK	170
9	DISAPPEARANCE	191
10	PARTING	215

BOOK TWO
Reason and Romance

11	TONYA	247
12	THE WHITE COLONEL	274
13	THE DANCING JESUIT	303
14	THE KING OF ROME	336
15	DANCING IN THE SEA	360

16 VERA   392
17 RUBBISH AND NONSENSE   440
18 REASON AND ROMANCE   468

BOOK THREE
Life From Death

19 THE BUREAU OF NOTHING IMPORTANT   509
20 THE FOUNTAIN WITH CARYATIDS   537
21 DEATH BEFORE BREAKFAST   570
22 THE WORLD ICE THEORY   601
23 *EL NOVIO DE LA MUERTE*   635
24 THE LOST DOMAIN   662
25 THE FALL OF BABYLON   693
26 A NEGOTIATED PEACE   710
27 LIFE FROM DEATH   733

Principal Russian Characters

Russian names consist of a given name, a second name derived
from that of the father, and a surname. Diminutive or
affectionate names, here indicated in capitals, are very common.
In this list only Russian names used in the text are given, in
alphabetical order of surname.

Antipov, PASHA, *husband of Lara and father of Katya*

Antipov, Pavel Ferapontovitch, *father of Pasha*

Antipova*, Larissa Fyodorovna, LARA, *wife of Pasha
    Antipov and mistress of Yuri Zhivago*

Antipova**, Katerina Pavlovna, KATYA, *daughter of
    Lara and Pasha Antipov*

Galiullin, YUSUPKA, *a White general and boyhood friend
    of Pasha Antipov*

Golitsin, Maxim Yuryevitch, MAX, *a financier*

Gromeko, Alexander Alexandrovitch, *Professor and father
    of Tonya Zhivago*

Gromov, Semyon Maximovitch, *a cab driver*

Komarovsky, Viktor Ippolitovitch, *lawyer and lover of
    Lara Antipova*

Menshikov, *a White army colonel*

Mikulitsin, Avercius Stepanovitch, *friend of Lara and Yuri
    Zhivago*

Panov, Alexei Valentinovitch, *a friend of Viktor
    Komarovsky*

Petrova, Vera Mikhailovna, *a friend of Sasha Zhivago*

Samdevyatov, Anfim Yefimovitch, *a friend of Lara and Yuri Zhivago*

Shlyapin***-Nikolai Afanasitch, KOLYA, *a NEPman and husband of Katya*

Strelnikov, *an alias of Pasha Antipov*

TANYA, *daughter of Lara Antipova by Yuri Zhivago and half-sister to Katya*

Tuntseva, GLASHA, SIMA and AVDOTYA, *three sisters, friends of Lara and Yuri Zhivago*

Zhivago, Alexander Yuryevitch, SASHA, *son of Yuri Zhivago and Tonya Zhivago*

Zhivago, Antonina Alexandrovna, TONYA, *wife of Yuri Zhivago and mother of Sasha and Masha*

Zhivago, Marya Yuryevna, MASHA, *sister of Sasha Zhivago*

Zhivago, Yuri Andreyevitch, YURA, *husband of Tonya and father of Sasha, Masha and Tanya*

*   LARA is also known by the surname Komarovska

**   KATYA is also known by the surnames Komarovska, Shlyapina and Safronova

*** KOLYA is also known by the surname Safronov

BOOK ONE

Love and Contempt

CHAPTER 1

KOMAROVSKY

I am looking at him for the last time; saying goodbye in my heart for the last time because he cannot hear me. We spoke only a moment ago and already I cannot remember whether I said: I love you. Probably I did not. He said he would harness a horse and follow in the sleigh. He will be only a few minutes behind us, and, even if we miss each other in the dark, we shall meet again in Yuryatin before the train leaves. So I did not say: I love you. There was no need even to say goodbye. In a few minutes he will catch up with us.

I shall never see him again in my life.

The sun has not quite gone down. The sky is turquoise and amber. The snow is barred by the shadow of the trees. The sleigh shoots out of a dip and I can see the house. Yura is standing on the verandah with his coat draped over one shoulder. The sleigh stops by the last of the birches that border the road. Did I ask Viktor Ippolitovitch to stop? 'What now?' he says crossly. 'Don't lean over so far, you'll fall out.'

'He isn't moving. He hasn't gone to get the horse.'

Viktor Ippolitovitch strains to see. I think, at his age, he is a little short-sighted but his vanity does not admit it. Finally, he dismisses my concerns. 'We've been gone only a minute. Give him time to gather breath and arrange himself. Why shouldn't he come?'

'What's wrong?' asks Katya.

'Do I go on?' enquires the coachman.

'Yes,' says Viktor Ippolitovitch, and with a crack of the whip the sleigh starts again. Will I see him again? Will I see him again? I cannot remember the road – does it give another view of the house? Will the light last long enough?

We have reached the other side of the ravine across the field where the wolves were howling two nights ago. Looking back I can see him. And now even that moment is gone and there are no more. I did not say goodbye or I love you. From now they will sound strange to me: painful, then uncomfortable, and finally I shall not remember why. I shall hesitate over them and people will note it as a habit of speech; why is time like that?

According to Viktor Ippolitovitch, we shall meet again in Yuryatin. Look at him, sitting near me with only Katya between us. He has a pistol on his lap and his face is composed behind his red-brown beard. I cannot tell if he is lying behind that beard. How long has he had it? He must be sixty years old now, but I am not sure I can count the years. He came out of the room where he and Yura had talked, and announced that it was all agreed. There was not enough room in the one sleigh, and Yura would harness Samdevyatov's horse and follow. Yura said, yes, we must go; we cannot stay at Varykino now that Strelnikov is sought by the Reds. We must go for Katya's sake, and he will follow.

How strange it is to hear my own thoughts. How clear they are, as sharp as noises in the night, the howling of the wolves that kept Yura awake. I do not remember them like this before. My thoughts *are* me: they do not talk to me – never before.

'Is he following?'

'I can't tell,' says Viktor Ippolitovitch. 'We've the

advantage of the light to make a little distance. He'll have to travel the whole way in darkness. I'd stop and wait for him, but we're at risk from the wolves.' He pats the pistol and presses the coachman to make speed so the wolves do not catch us.

It is dark now and I cannot know if Yura is following. The trees are rustling with the night breeze and shedding snow invisibly fine against our faces. I can hear the runners slipping over the snow and cracking across the frozen pools. If this is a final parting, it is all over with. I should stop thinking about it. Tomorrow Yura will meet us at the station and joke about this journey. In any case, final partings are not like this. We are unconscious of them. People part and only years afterwards realize that they have never met again. Deaths are reported and we cannot recall exactly how it was that we last saw the deceased – probably we had talked about nothing and had expected to run into each other in a few days, and never thought that this was the end. So how can this be final, when I am thinking about it even now?

I shall see you again, Yuri Andreyevitch Zhivago, my beloved!

They reached Yuryatin at dawn and Zhivago did not appear.

'Perhaps he was delayed,' said Komarovsky. 'In the dark it would be easy for a horse to stumble and go lame.'

During the night Komarovsky had behaved considerately. He had made sure that the sleigh was well-provided with rugs and had kept Katya, the frailest of them, covered. And at the station, too, he made sure of food, some boiled potatoes and a piece of rye bread. But where Zhivago was concerned, the lawyer could not disguise his indifference.

He was concerned about the train. It was standing at the platform, three shabby regular coaches and three wagons-lits. The engine was bunkered and the boilers fired. The morning was sharp and the air still and blue. The plume of smoke from the engine rose in a straight column and the smuts rained gently down.

While Lara and her daughter stood on the platform clutching the warm potatoes in cupped hands, the stationmaster came from his cabin waving a telegram. He approached the group of men that Komarovsky had joined, men like himself, faded relics of the old regime, like oil paintings seen through layers of grime and varnish. Komarovsky took the paper, read it and interrogated the messenger. Then he turned to the other men and there was an animated conversation before the group broke up. He approached the two females.

'What's wrong, Viktor Ippolitovitch?'

Komarovsky's face was red and angry; the telegram was crumpled in his fist; he nibbled uncertainly at the ends of his moustache.

'We're not going east – at least, not yet.'

'Then where?'

'Some of the bridges are broken further down the line. The way things are it could take weeks to repair them. We can't go on as intended and we can't stay here in Yuryatin. It would be dangerous for you, with all this business about Strelnikov. And the authorities have asked that the train return to Moscow.'

'Can't you . . .'

'I can't do anything! I may be a government minister, but this train doesn't belong to my government. It's a Bolshevik train. Until we get to the East we have to do whatever the Bolsheviks require.'

'I see.' Lara understood something of his concern. In the East they would be beyond the immediate reach of Soviet power. But in Moscow she was the wife of the political criminal and terrorist Strelnikov, and the mistress of a doctor who was too imprudent to do other than describe things as he saw them.

'Well,' said Komarovsky glacially, 'we shall have to make the best of things as they are. I have friends and

14

contacts, and am of some use and importance to the Soviets. Strelnikov and Zhivago are for the time being of more interest to Yuryatin than to Moscow. Things may be arranged. But you must take your every direction from me – trust me implicitly.'

'Haven't I done that?' Lara responded with feeling and caused even Komarovsky to turn and scan the road in case Zhivago had arrived. 'How long can we wait?' she asked.

He was silent, watching the road. Cracking a pebble under the heel of his boot. And Lara felt within her a gnawing emptiness. She urged him: 'We have to wait for Yura! You promised!'

'The train is ready,' he answered carefully, even sadly. 'As I told you, there are limits to my power. And limits to the risks I can afford to take,' he spoke carefully and, it seemed to her, sadly, 'even for you, my dear.'

And so Lara and her daughter left Yuryatin. They had places in the day coaches and slept together at night in one of the bunks in the last of the wagons-lits. Zhivago did not join them. After the conversation on the station platform, Lara knew that he would not. But even now there was no admission that the parting was other than temporary; and Komarovsky, whether from pretence or otherwise, continued to maintain that Zhivago's delay was accidental and a temporary thing. Lara and he agreed this story as if it were a treaty between them. The imminent arrival of Zhivago created an armistice between their warring emotions and avoided the necessity of confronting openly the reality of their relationship. But inwardly? Lara was frightened of searching her own feelings. Yura *must* come! He *would* come! The alternative of being cast loose at the mercy of Komarovsky was too terrible to contemplate. So far as humanly possible she would not contemplate it. She would think only of the practicalities of life on the train.

Lara had forgotten the endless tedium of journeys

by train. She was aware only of a flight, pursued by regrets, towards a future that was shaped only by such trust as could be placed in Komarovsky. But the slow pace of the train seemed to reject her sense of panic.

The men, among whom the lawyer played a leading role, commandeered one of the day coaches as a smoking salon and there played cards and discussed politics. The politics were not those that Lara remembered. In her youth there had been a naive idealism – either the dreamy liberalism of the students and intelligentsia or the ruthless scientific socialism of working men like Antipov, the railway worker and Strelnikov's father. But these politics were in the world of the concrete. They talked of personalities and situations, not principles. They were concerned with the affairs of the Far Eastern Republic, and Outer Mongolia, and the delicate situation in the Maritime Provinces where the remnants of the Whites and the equivocal Japanese still held sway. Yet it seemed to Lara that for all their apparent concreteness, these Ruritanias were places of no substance, as transient as the snow which day after day was visible over the passing landscape.

The women and children occupied a second car. They lacked the apparent camaraderie and common political interests of the men, and for the first two days their differences held them apart. There were social distinctions – not that anyone would have dared to insist upon them in the dangerous atmosphere of the times, but they were visible in the dress and the language. The passengers were all officials of the Far Eastern Republic, and the meaning of that coalition was apparent in the wives: peasant wenches, bourgeois matrons, drawing-room ladies, and working women whose liaisons with their men were of doubtful legality. An odd motley of dress and manner went with and sometimes ran counter to this patchwork of humanity. So the wife of a former professor, a man of fearsome learning, was vacuous and withdrawn, and wore a made-up dress of coarse brown cloth and a pair of munition boots padded with newspaper to make them fit; while, in contrast, the mistress of a Bolshevik mining deputy, a woman of twenty or so who had lost several teeth and had eyes that were erratically arranged, proved to be a lively debater who had read widely, and, somewhere in the great reversal of things, had acquired a silk dress that would have graced the greatest of princesses and most splendid of harlots.

This medley of women and their fretting children travelled together. And bit by bit they came together to help each other and to lay down rules to control the men, particularly when the latter became drunk on the vodka that was in ample supply in the smoking carriage. In this respect Lara was grateful to Komarovsky. He was either abstemious or he held his drink well. The only sign he ever gave that he had been drinking was when he appeared from the men's quarters to lounge in the doorway smoking a *papirossa* and watch the women with his dark and saturnine gaze. Lara was grateful, too, to the other women. Katya was distressed at the sudden loss of Zhivago. Although she was not his child, Zhivago had treated her with a gentleness and fondness that had endeared him to her and, in the obscure way of children, she appeared to blame herself for his vanishing. Lara's assertions that Zhivago would soon rejoin them were disbelieved. Only the other women and their children could distract her. Lara watched Katya play with the greasy pack of cards that Komarovsky had provided, and saw in her intense blue eyes that she understood only too well the truth about parting. When she was three years old she was passionately attached to her father. But he had disappeared and was now probably dead.

And Yura is probably dead too, Lara told herself, not believing it, but testing the idea on her emotions, preparing herself for the worst – and then rejecting that preparation because it was too hard, too hard. She put Zhivago out of her mind. And for a time he was gone. Here I am, not thinking about him. Brushing Katya's hair like Yura used to do, and not thinking about him.

Playing with Katya and not thinking about him. It's an agony to think about him and not to think about him. I can bear it only because it has to be borne!

Day by day the snowbound landscape unfolded. Near Yuryatin the villages had been destroyed by the Whites during the civil war. Further west the devastation was less but never absent. The Reds had robbed the kulaks and the middle-peasants to feed the cities during the winter; the houses of the landlords and the rural gentry had been put to the torch in an earlier phase of the Revolution. These earliest ruins seemed reconciled to the land. Their chimneys stood like sentinels where the rest of the timber houses were burned away; but weeds and grasses and wind-blown rye had invaded these graves and reclaimed them for the earth. The fresh blackness of the more recent ruins was a brutal scar on the whiteness of the snow. Their acrid smell assailed the nose. In the corners of the gutted stations little wrecks of rapine formed bundles ambiguously hidden by the snow. Lara watched this and Katya played. The warmth of the carriage wore holes in the frozen window glass. She found herself saying: 'This is bearable. This is not too bad. I've seen worse,' as the next ruined station came into view. The train was travelling slowly; a man on foot could have walked with it. For long minutes she could see the roofless building. Inside a candle burned where the stationmaster worked. She thought how beautiful it looked in a dark and lonely night. 'This is bearable.' Would Yura have said that? Could he have hardened himself to this suffering? Already after a few days she was losing her sense of his reality, her instinct for how he would feel. She wondered if she were being corrupted by Komarovsky's worldliness and cynicism. Why had Yura left her to face this?

She thought that she was crying, but this was not the case. It was only that she had pressed her face against the mist on the carriage window as she studied the night and snow.

*　　*　　*

18

In Moscow Komarovsky arranged an apartment for Lara and her daughter. His own arrangements he kept secret. He told her only that, if asked, she was to give no personal details but refer all enquiries to himself, the Minister of Justice of a government friendly to the Bolsheviks.

The apartment consisted of a single room on the first floor of a house in Sivtsev Vrazhek. The house had once been the home of a banker and the former major-domo was now the chairman of the house committee and took a spiteful pride in the downfall of his masters. It was impossible to avoid him since the kitchen, pump and privies were used in common and he seemed to haunt the corners wearing his ancient livery and over it an army greatcoat and a dogskin cap.

'How wonderful! How spacious!' Lara cried, and she could have shed tears of thanks to Komarovsky. In her amazement at the size of the room, compared with the poverty of her life at Yuryatin, she ignored the dried excrement that had been daubed on the walls and the scraps of wood and brasswork that were all that remained of the fine mahogany and ormolu furniture that once graced the room.

'No beds, no bedding, no food or fuel,' said Komarovsky. In his most businesslike manner he added, 'I'll see what can be done.'

'Thank you, Viktor Ippolitovitch.' Lara felt some forgiveness for him.

When he had gone she begged a bucket from a neighbour and obtained water from the pipe in the yard, and almost lightheartedly commenced to wash down the walls. Katya sat for a while hunched in misery, and then decided this was a game she would join. And for two hours while the daylight lasted, mother and daughter sang songs and chatted and told each other that this was the first sign of a new life that was going to be happy.

It was the room. Its elegant proportions reminded Lara that there had been another life before pettiness and second-rate thought had seized hold of idealism and smothered it with their mediocrity. The stove was covered in faience tiles, chipped and marked with paint but still beautiful; and from the ceiling a chandelier still hung, and the candle-brackets were still on the wall. It had a pleasant haunted feeling of suppers with friends, of family parties on name days, of the none-too-serious subversive talk one could have among intimates, wishing damnation to the Tsar and looking forward to democracy such as the French had. And with that Lara remembered that she knew people who had lived in a house not distant from this one, in fact in the same street. Tonya had been brought up there.

Was she still there? No, of course not. Even if she were in Moscow, it would not be there. After Yura had returned from the war, he and his wife Tonya, their son and his father-in-law, Professor Gromeko, had left Moscow in the first winter after the Revolution and sought refuge and some land to grow food on at the Krueger property at Varykino. Old Krueger was an ironmaster and Tonya's maternal grandfather.

She had met Tonya at Yuryatin after Zhivago had been conscripted by force into the Red partisans and for all anyone knew was dead since he had simply disappeared. Tonya was pregnant with their second child. They had met at the library where Lara was working. Tonya had sought her out.

At first Lara did not know her and could not have guessed her identity from her appearance. It was still possible to have preconceptions, and the daughter of a professor and granddaughter of an industrialist should not have been wearing an old patched frock; and her poor diet and pregnancy had given her face a pinched look. Zhivago had been gone about a month; it was summer, and inside the library the bright sunlight which bleached the books had been softened by drawing the white goffered blinds so that one could see the dust motes layered in the shadows. The visitor examined the librarian and the other two assistants and then approached Lara.

'Am I speaking to Larissa Fyodorovna Antipova? I suppose from your expression that I must be. You look as Yura described you in his letters – he wrote to me about you when you and he were stationed together. Is there somewhere I can sit – somewhere we can talk in private? I get tired very easily.'

There was something in Tonya's voice that was appealing. Lara lost immediately any sense of being on the defensive, or of being the object of resentment. However, she had no time to think about this since the other woman was clearly about to faint. No-one else was paying attention since they had gone through a winter when people died unregarded in the streets and death had become no more than an administrative burden. Lara spoke to the librarian and was allowed to show her visitor into a small room where old books were gathered for re-binding. The air smelled of the glue used for the work. Tonya spoke first.

'Yuri Andreyevitch has disappeared. I had thought he was with you. Now I can see I was mistaken. But it seemed a reasonable assumption. Yura wrote in his letters that he admired you. And then I learned that there was an Antipova working at the library – Yura hadn't mentioned you. What was I to think?'

Lara's instinct was to say something tactfully evasive. What could it matter, now that Yura was denied to both of them? Yet tact could so easily become deceit, and Tonya had done nothing to deserve that injustice on top of all the others.

'I'd supposed that Yura had simply decided to stop seeing me,' she answered frankly. 'I was reconciled to that. It was understood that neither of us possessed the other – there were other considerations. He didn't treat them lightly. Love is difficult,' she said abruptly but softly. 'I thought it was exclusive – but it isn't. I don't claim to understand why.'

They did not discuss Zhivago's disappearance in any detail. It seemed odd afterwards but not at the time. It was a time of disappearances.

'You have a husband too, don't you?' said Tonya. 'I heard a story that Pavel Pavlovitch Antipov is the same man as Strelnikov, the military commissar.'

'I've heard that story too. I've never met Strelnikov. I lost trace of my husband during the fighting in Hungary in 1916.'

'Do you have any children?'

'A little girl – Katya – she's seven.'

'My Sasha is four.' Tonya seemed to draw some conclusion from this comparison of children. 'I came here to be angry with you. I was going to call you a thief. Now there doesn't seem to be any point.' She turned her eyes to examine her shabby dress. 'I don't know how I feel about that. It was easier to explain things when I had an enemy. Instead Yura has simply vanished. Only two years ago that would have been mysterious. Now people are disappearing and reappearing all the time and one has to accept it. When I was angry with you, it was all very clear and appropriate; I didn't even have to think about why I was angry since the response was so obvious. But I can see now that old standards of what is appropriate no longer apply. We've been given freedom to use our imaginations and things have become dangerous and confusing. Will you come to see me at Varykino?'

That summer Lara went several times to Varykino, taking Katya with her. Tonya's father, Professor Alexander Alexandrovitch Gromeko, was managing to keep a kitchen garden going in a haphazard fashion, but the family was otherwise living on the charity of Samdevyatov.

'We can't carry on like this,' the professor confided as they watched Katya and the little boy roll laughing in the weeds and wild grains under the hot sun. He brushed the gnats away and snorted at one more petty annoyance of country life. 'I can't grow enough food for us just with my own hands. And our occupation of this land is illegal, since we are informed by the powers-that-be that it all belongs to those same powers-that-be – or the people, which is the same thing, so they say. In fact, things could scarcely be worse. You understand that this was part of the Krueger estate – my father-in-law's estate. Do you follow me, Larissa Fyodorovna? People could say that I'm trying to assert some sort of right of inheritance, God forbid, just when we've got rid of that sort of nonsense. Assuming,' he added, 'that the Reds win this war.'

He was referring to the fact that the Whites were, for the time at least, again in control of Yuryatin. Lara knew that the Whites were even more capricious and dangerous than the Reds. They held religious processions and murdered Jews. Despite their recent military success they seemed bent on self-destruction. They claimed to hold to the old values of the tsarist days, but displayed nothing but an arrogant fury. They had nothing to offer – which was why they were losing the support of the peasants and why, in Lara's opinion, they would finally lose the civil war.

In the autumn Tonya gave birth to a little girl. Lara was there as midwife. Later, the family was forced out of Varykino by the Whites as part of a campaign against the Red partisans. For a while they lived in great misery in Yuryatin. Then, when the White army collapsed during the winter and the railway to the West was free again, the family moved back to Moscow. There they applied for exit visas. Tonya wrote to Lara and asked her to inform Zhivago if by some miracle he survived.

I must stop thinking of Yura!

Night had fallen by the time that they had finished cleaning. Katya complained that she was hungry and cried when Lara explained that there was no food. They sat in darkness on the bare floorboards in the middle of the empty room and embraced each other.

Komarovsky returned at eight o'clock. With him he had two gaunt labourers in puttees and army cast-offs. All three were carrying parcels. The lawyer produced a candle from the pocket of his fur coat. He lit it and placed it on the stove and dismissed the two porters. Then he leaned against the tiles, his hands behind his back under the skirts of his coat as if warming himself on an imaginary fire. In the candlelight his face was a patchwork of light and shadow.

'Do you have any news?' Lara asked.

'Of Zhivago? Be reasonable, my dear, we were on the last train to leave Yuryatin. It is difficult to suppose that any more trains will be coming from so far east until the line is repaired. Shall we turn to more practical matters?' He began to unwrap the packages. The first was a roll of bedding tied with string. 'For the present you will have to sleep on the floor. Furniture is a scarce commodity; so much has been used for fuel.' In the second parcel were a chicken, some potatoes, buckwheat, a bundle of tallow candles, putty to seal the window and a small bottle of kerosene. 'There's an epidemic of typhus in the city,' Komarovsky explained. 'I suggest you and Katya use this to keep away the lice.'

'How are we to keep warm?'

'Wear all your clothes and stay in bed. I'll return in the morning with some fuel. I'd suggest that you try to keep warm in the kitchen, if it weren't for the prying neighbours. If it's safe you may consider it. Be cautious when cooking the chicken – people talk.' Komarovsky opened the third parcel. It held clothes: two coats, two woollen skirts, frocks for Katya, knitted stockings, blouses, underwear; none of it was new but it had been scrupulously cleaned and repaired and Komarovsky had thought to include a sewing kit to enable any fine adjustments to be made. From a purely practical standpoint he was a shrewd observer of women. 'And also this,' he said and produced a light dress of cotton and muslin, figured with sprigs of flowers. Lara had seen nothing so lovely in years. Katya, stirring in her sleep, looked up and caught sight of the man holding the dress to the candlelight so that in the empty room it shone a rich creaminess against

24

the chocolate darkness. 'Pretty!' she said sleepily. 'Uncle Viktor brings us presents!'

They stayed in Moscow a week, confined to the apartment on Komarovsky's strict instructions. From the common kitchen there was a window with a view over the courtyard where pale children played among the rubbish and the rats. Katya watched them but could not join their cruel games.

Komarovsky visited every day, bringing food and fuel and a few small comforts. He provided books for Lara – Tolstoy and Pushkin – and even brought some toys for Katya. Although his manner maintained a distance, he displayed a care for them in his attention to detail, going so far as to allow the little girl to climb upon his lap and tug at his beard. On each occasion he stayed for about an hour. Most of the time he spent in the same pose, lounging against the stove and studying his charges in silence, the mother working with a needle on the clothes he had provided, the daughter playing with the toys; the small figures placed in the centre of the large bare room which took on the aspect of a stage. In his care and in his possessive attitude as he stood smoking a cigarette there was something paternal, but his face held always a shadowed look, as if he were inwardly puzzled.

There was no news of Zhivago. Lara asked Komarovsky daily when they were out of earshot of Katya. She was conscious of the supplication in her voice which masked her continuing terror. She sensed that she was losing Zhivago not merely as a physical being but as a person in her imagination. If I lose even that, she thought, I shall have lost everything.

When the report came through that the train was ready again for the journey east, Komarovsky had some words of caution.

'You must remember that, while where we are going to is safer than either Moscow or Yuryatin, it does not represent *safety*. Such security as we have is because the situation in the East is confused and fluid, and the writ of Moscow does not run out there in quite the same way. But you should bear in mind that the majority of my colleagues in the government are Bolsheviks, and that goes too for most of the passengers on the train.'

He had travel papers.

'It will be necessary for you to appear to be my wife. Katya, for present purposes, is my daughter. You must tell her that she is not to speak about Zhivago or about Strelnikov. Does she know about Strelnikov?'

'She suspects. But what does anyone know for certain about Strelnikov? Is there news of him?'

'His forces were stopped at Irkutsk. There was some fighting with the Reds. I don't know whether or not he's been taken prisoner.'

Two days after this conversation they left Moscow.

The world was still bounded by winter. The train moved with the same painful slowness through the bleak and devastated countryside. On board the same arrangements obtained as before, but the effect of the recall to Moscow had been to heighten the tension of the passengers. It reminded them of their vulnerability; that for all the miles behind them they were tied by an invisible cord to Moscow. Some of the original passengers had disappeared.

The halts were regular. The train took on supplies of wood and provisions. At the stations the men got off the train and delayed its departure for hours while they queued at the telegraph offices to send and receive messages. It was considered unsafe to allow the women and children to leave the carriages, since the effect of such an important-looking train was to bring out crowds of starving beggars who lined the track for miles on each side of the stations. Many of the beggars were demobilized soldiers and still carried their sidearms. And all this mass of humanity was haunted by typhus and dysentery.

Day after day in wearisome progression the train struggled across the plain and into the Urals. The random destruction of the Revolution and the Red foraging parties gave way to the fieldworks constructed and abandoned by the armies, lines of empty trenches and bomb-proofs, burnt-out waggons and artillery caissons, coils of wire from the field telephones, horse carcases.

One morning Komarovsky did not put in his usual appearance. That afternoon the train passed through Yuryatin without stopping. Lara saw a reception committee waiting on the platform. She recognized old Antipov standing with other members of the regional soviet. He did not register her presence. His face showed only ingrained ancient hatreds. She noticed that the placard which advertised Moreau & Vetchinkin, manufacturers of threshing machines, had been whitewashed over. Changes were happening over which she had no control, so that she scarcely thought of Yuryatin as a place she knew, and only afterwards did it come to her: *Yura was there!*

When Komarovsky reappeared to resume his habitual stance in the doorway between the men's and the women's coaches she challenged him.

'Why didn't we stop at Yuryatin?'

'No stop was scheduled.'

'I don't believe you.' she said fiercely. 'Yura was there. You knew that he couldn't leave Yuryatin! I saw my father-in-law and the other leaders at the station. They were expecting the train to stop!'

'Hush now!' Komarovsky retorted angrily and looked about the carriage where the other women were in frozen attention. He grabbed Lara roughly by the arm and dragged her into the passage linking the coaches. 'What have I told you about speaking of your personal affairs?' he asked accusingly. 'Are you a fool to your emotions? Have you no thought for your safety or that of the child?' He released her arm. The pain and confusion in her eyes affected him. He lowered his voice. 'Of course Zhivago is in Yuryatin – but what does it matter? Did you think he

27

was going to appear at the station?' He paused to light a cigarette. Lara remembered that he had once smoked cigars. He explained calmly: 'I've been making discreet enquiries about Zhivago. Whenever we've stopped at a station I've received answers to my messages. The Cheka in Yuryatin is taking an interest in Zhivago's case, as I predicted. If they find him, they'll arrest him and shoot him. Now do you understand why I had to ask the engineer not to stop the train?'

After Yuryatin, Lara stopped asking about Zhivago. She recognized in her heart that he was not going to come. I knew it all along, she told herself; and, this is bearable because it has to be borne. But why had he let her go? If there had been some doubt or reproach between them it would have been comprehensible. But this? Why did she feel bereavement, not betrayal?

She thought back to their last days at Varykino. They had fled there from the town after Komarovsky had given his initial warning of their danger. Zhivago and the lawyer had quarrelled. Yura had indicated then that he did not intend to leave. Only later had he appeared to consent to Komarovsky's scheme; and it was now evident that it had been only to save Lara and her daughter. But why stay? It was as if he had some presentiment of death. They had been so happy, but perhaps behind the limit of conceivable happiness Yura had felt himself slipping away because nothing more was possible and everything was complete. Was it an illusion that, recalling him now, she could see in his happiness a gradual dying? That night, escaping in the sleigh with Komarovsky, she had known that Yura would not follow. She had seen his figure pale and silent on the verandah of the house. He had been a ghost if only she had fully realized it.

After Yuryatin, Zhivago could no longer stand between Lara and Komarovsky. The truce that had been maintained by a fiction fell away. When the lawyer stood in the doorway, surveying the scene with his proprietorial air, Lara read in his expression the working-out of a plan of campaign. But still he seemed uncertain, as if surprised and puzzled by his own emotions and the risks he had taken. He began spending time in the women's carriage. He played with Katya. He tried to engage Lara in conversation.

When she had been a girl in her final year at high school – when she had first met Komarovsky – his speech had seemed urbane and sophisticated. In those days he had been something over forty years old and clean-shaven. His face was unremarkable, his clothing fashionable without being ostentatious. The only aspects of his person that might have attracted a girl on the verge of womanhood were the power of command in his low, unexpressive voice and the attentions that were paid to him in the salons and restaurants he frequented. She had been too inexperienced to recognize that his conversation – principally about politics and always careful and guarded – appealed only to his cronies in the law and the government, and that the attentions paid to him were those of women in pursuit of a financially eligible bachelor and the servility of waiters.

He talked about politics now. For her safety, he said, it was important that she understand the nature of the world they were living in.

'The Far Eastern Republic, of which I have the honour to be a minister,' he said ironically, 'is just a temporary device of Lenin's government to stabilize the situation in the East. The majority of my government is Bolshevik, and we must expect, at the appropriate moment, that a coup will be staged.'

He bored her. It seemed incredible to Lara that he had ever interested her, but the truth was that his words had once fascinated her. He had delivered them in the private booth of the restaurant they used. His eyes fixed hers over the winking rim of a wine glass.

'We should not be intimidated by the prospects for the future.'

29

Lara looked through the window. They were passing the wreckage of an armoured train abandoned by the Whites in their retreat. It had been shunted off the line and lay among broken saplings at the edge of the forest.

'The Reds themselves are changing. Cooler heads are taking command after the excesses of the civil war. There is a natural stability in the order of things, a tendency to drift towards the equilibrium of the middle ground. The Bolsheviks will use people like myself because of our expertise. And we shall suborn their system from within.'

Lara felt he had misunderstood. She knew the fire within revolutionaries like old Antipov, a hatred bordering on madness. They would destroy people like Komarovsky even at a cost to themselves.

She was indifferent. With each day she saw only the miles closing between herself and Vladivostok. From Vladivostok Komarovsky had promised to find a boat to take them abroad. And Yura, too, when he followed. And Strelnikov, if he were alive. How was it possible to believe him?

'Vladivostok?' he said. 'Yes, of course – in due time. But you haven't been listening to me, my dear. Vladivostok is in the hands of the Japanese. We may have a wait of several months at Chita.'

The train drove forward across the southern Siberian plain. Days of monotony in a landscape of snow bounded by forest of birch and aspen. Sometimes they halted for an hour or a day to test a bridge that had been destroyed and repaired, but these delays only emphasized their confinement in the close world of the carriages. Across this vast expanse the Whites had retreated the previous winter. Along the *trakt*, the beaten road that followed the line of the permanent way, the baggage of the fleeing army was scattered in mile after mile of broken waggons, piles of stores, derailed rolling stock and dead horses in their thousands. The world seemed a thing gutted of life.

Through the dead flesh of snow poked the charred bones of ransacked villages.

But all the while spring was near as if a pursuer. Sometimes, during daylight, there was a slight thaw; ice would clear from the windows to be replaced by a mist of breath and, as they paused to test a bridge at a river crossing, running water could be heard, rushes seen amongst the snow along the bank and buds on the branches of the trees. Birds appeared.

The snow cleared as they descended the depression into Irkutsk. The ice had almost gone from the river; chunks of it floated in the frost-haze. At Irkutsk the passengers were allowed to leave the train. The men disappeared to find the telegraph office. The women, holding hands like frightened children, ventured out of the station to stare at the river and catch glimpses of the cathedral and the white stuccoed houses of the town. They had become conscious that they were dirty and they felt embarrassed. 'Can we wash? Where can we launder our clothes? How pale the children are.'

In the station siding was an armoured train. The engine had been decoupled but the rolling stock formed a grey line trailing down a muddy length of track. Lara shared the inchoate fear that possessed the women; she held Katya tightly to her; her eyes were dazzled by the brightness of the daylight, the simple extent of sky which was something nearly forgotten. And there was the train in its dull brutality, a line of flat-cars, their sides built up with boiler plate, a row of sandbags at the top, machine gun emplacements, a heavy gun mounted in an open barbette, carriages for the men, and a command coach with Strelnikov's name painted on the side.

She took Katya's hand and together they walked along the tracks. The plating of the flat-cars was rust-streaked; some of it shattered by shell-fire; little piles of sand marked where the bags had broken. They reached the command coach, where a guard stood idly by watching them. 'You can't go in,' he said casually.

'I've heard of him – Strelnikov.'

The guard looked up and down, then silently placed the little girl on the steps to the carriage. 'Five minutes,' he said and walked to the end of the carriage and dodged under a coupling to the other side where he could not see them.

The interior of the coach was dim after the daylight, made dimmer by the slatted metal shutters that protected the windows. Papers were scattered across the floor – maps, manuals, scribbled notes. Pieces of equipment, a uniform jacket, a fur cap, an ammunition belt. At the end of the main compartment was a small cabin. It held a bedroll, a shaving set, a book of poetry with its pages shredded. Lara had expected that in some way these objects would be suggestive of Pasha, that they would quicken her memory and enliven him for her. Instead they kept a mute neutrality. My senses are deadening, she told herself, and only that thought stirred any emotion, a nostalgia for the times of real feeling. Her own photograph was pinned to the wall. Lara thought: so Pasha and Strelnikov were the same person. And I've lost him too. But she had lost him so long ago that to feel for him now was as if she were counterfeiting emotion; yet there it was, a pale tired shred of misery; does it go on for ever?

Komarovsky was standing on the platform with the other bourgeois politicians in their rusty frock coats. The men had been drinking; they were high-coloured and their conversation was excited. They noticed the woman and her daughter stepping down from the armoured train but passed over them as of no interest, except for Komarovsky who shaded his myopic eyes and stared intently. Lara returned to the station hall and waited for the lawyer to join her.

'That was foolish,' he said.

'Is Strelnikov here?'

'Of course not.'

'Isn't this where he was stopped?'

Komarovsky was impatient as if he felt her slipping

away from him. 'I shall satisfy your curiosity – this time,' he answered. Ten minutes later he returned, bringing with him a younger man with round spectacles and wearing a leather jerkin.

'Some of the traitor Strelnikov's men are prisoners here,' the latter explained.

'Can I see them?'

'I've arranged that,' said Komarovsky.

A small carriage was waiting outside the station. Their companion joined them and ordered the driver to take them to a tea warehouse that was not far away. He told them that the prison was full and the remaining prisoners were held at the warehouse; many of Strelnikov's men had been killed in the fight at Irkutsk and his senior officers had already been dealt with by a revolutionary tribunal. Strelnikov himself? It was difficult to say. No body had been found but where could he go, in winter, in the starving countryside still ravaged by soldiers and bandits?

The prisoners were in the warehouse as Lara had been told; but despite the guards it seemed to her that it was their demoralization that held them captive. The unheated building had been damaged in the fighting; the roof was holed, the walls cracked and fire-blasted. The prisoners were humbled in grey filth and disorder and racked by typhus, influenza and dysentery.

'These men should be in hospital,' she said. She listened to her voice and heard the absence of indignation. She had no faith that anything could be done for the prisoners. The thought came to her that her moral responses had been reduced to mere reflexes, to be disposed of in a few words. There was no help for it.

'No doubt,' answered Komarovsky as he checked his watch for the timing of their departure.

'Class traitors! Stand to attention!' shouted their companion.

Katya was frightened by the smell and the noise. She turned to her mother and buried herself in Lara's skirts.

A dry rustle passed among the men and from the huddled groups a handful stood up listlessly, their faces bowed to the floor and their caps clutched in their hands.

'Did any of these men know Strelnikov personally?' asked Komarovsky.

The question was repeated directly. One of the soldiers raised a hand.

'Name!'

'Podvoysky! – Podvoysky, Comrade Captain!'

'Here!'

Podvoysky looked to his friends and then came forward, shuffling and limping between the placid bodies. He was a short, stocky man with an intelligent face. He wore an Austrian army greatcoat and a woman's skirt. His feet were shoeless and bound in rags.

'Well?' said Komarovsky. 'Do you have any questions for him?'

Podvoysky was embarrassed in the presence of a woman. He could not look at Lara but cast his eyes about loosely.

'When did you first meet Strelnikov?'

'Summer of 1918, comrade. We was at Yuryatin, fighting Galiullin and the Czechos. The Comrade Commissar was our boss.'

'Did you know him well?'

'Not well, comrade. Nobody knew him well – except maybe Galiullin who, they say, used to be his friend even if he was fighting for the Whites. I don't know whether that story's true.'

'Did you know Galiullin?' Komarovsky asked of Lara. She nodded, but she did not want to think of Galiullin.

'And then?'

'And then – well, the Whites they retook Yuryatin, and then we took it again, and after that, we chased that lot clean across Siberia killing Whites and Czechos whenever we could.' Podvoysky was puzzled by his own explanation. 'I don't see how we got to be traitors, comrade. Not in my opinion, if you ask me. Nor Strelnikov neither, even if he wasn't in the Party.'

'When did you last see him?'

'Last year, comrade – round about January, I think. The main army was back down the line at Nizhne-Udinsk. This place was still occupied by Whites and Czechos, and they were fighting among themselves for some reason. Our lot pushed on ahead of the main bunch and helped the local Red Guards to clear the town. Then, when everything is peaceable, up comes our General Janin and announces that Strelnikov is a traitor. Well, we wasn't having any of that. There was a fight around the station and the upshot was that we lost. I still don't see how we got to be traitors,' Podvoysky persisted. 'I was a Bolshevik – lots of us was, even if Strelnikov wasn't. I took part in the strikes back in 1905. I was a railway worker.'

Komarovsky turned to Lara and asked distantly: 'Do you seriously think Strelnikov could have survived?'

She returned to Podvoysky. 'Did you see Strelnikov's body?'

'No, comrade. But no-one got away – there wasn't anywhere to go to – snow and bloody misery for hundreds of versts. Janin had the officers shot and the rest of us was locked up here. I haven't seen no body, comrade, but he's dead if you ask me.'

What was he like, Strelnikov? Lara considered the question but did not put it. Podvoysky's opinion could not help to define the intangibles: the mystery and passion that moved Strelnikov.

'Anything else?' asked the man in the leather jacket.

'Nothing.'

Podvoysky was dismissed and shambled back to his position at the far end of the hall. From there he turned. His face bore the same look of confusion. He shouted out: 'We wasn't traitors!' The other men took up the same cry so that the warehouse echoed with it, that and the banging of their wooden bowls.

On the way out, to Lara's surprise Komarovsky said,

'Poor devils,' and stared thoughtfully back into the gloom. She thought: he has done what people seldom do, he has stepped out of his own caricature and become real. But then he added, 'Of course, there's nothing to be done for them.'

It was too late to go on. There was a fault with the engine and they would have to stay the night.

'We don't have to sleep on the train,' Komarovsky said. 'I've arranged some rooms.'

'Can we have a bath?' Lara asked him wearily. She was conscious of the smell of her own body.

'Perhaps.'

The hotel was in one of the white stuccoed buildings of the town. It had escaped damage in the fighting and had a forlorn air of dirt and waste. Komarovsky showed Lara a room and an adjacent one for Katya. Again Lara was grateful for his foresight. Although the decoration was a shabby arsenic green and the bed appeared none too clean, there was a stove that gave a modicum of heat and a hip bath behind a papier mâché screen. Komarovsky ordered water for the bath and then retired to discuss things with his colleagues.

Alone again, Katya and Lara. She brushed her daughter's hair and then combed it carefully for lice eggs. Together they stripped to their shifts and turned the seams of their dresses, still hunting for lice. Katya thought this was fun. A grinning *muzhik* in an apron brought cans of water and filled the hip bath to the depth of a few inches. Lara made Katya bathe first and then dried her tenderly.

'My underclothes smell,' said Katya.

'I'll wash them after I've had a bath.'

'I haven't a change.'

'You can go without until they dry.'

'I can't go around with no knickers.'

'Yes, you can. Now go to bed, I'll tuck you in.'

Alone again, Lara stood before the spotted mirror trying to see who she was and what she had become.

36

She thought: the colour of my skin is bad; my hair is as brittle as mattress stuffing. She shovelled her hair into her hands and piled it in various ways to see how it looked. She practised smiles for Zhivago (I'm like a mad woman – here I go again, smiling like a mad woman!) trying to see herself through his eyes, and seeing his face in the mirror of her mind. No use, she decided sadly. My looks have gone. Not that it matters. Not that anything matters any more except Katya.

She slipped into a bath that was barely warm and washed herself with the gritty soap. She calculated the timing of her period and wondered what she would use for a towel. But, of course, I don't need one! Out of the bath she dried herself and bundled the underwear into the water. I won't be able to rinse it. Still, it'll be all right. How will I dry it? I'll solve that problem when I come to it. Naked she examined the scratched and broken furniture in the fading light. Once upon a time it had been of good quality. What a pity! She felt the bedclothes. They were rough blankets and smelled of other bodies. It was not to be helped. It would be wonderful all the same to have a good night's sleep.

As she felt the blankets there was a tap at the door and Komarovsky came in. He was smoking a cigarette. His waistcoat was undone. His face red.

'What are you doing here?' Lara asked acerbically. She had grabbed a blanket and covered herself.

'Where else am I to sleep?' he answered pointedly. He took a seat and began to unfasten his boots, all the while fixing his eyes on hers. They were old eyes, cloudy eyes in dark sockets. Unfathomable. Lara had to shake herself free of them.

'You can't sleep here!' she whispered forcefully, conscious that Katya was in the next room. Behind her fear there was a relief that Komarovsky had revealed himself in his true colours and released her from any gratitude she might have felt. But it was the fear that she had to deal with.

'You have another suggestion?' he said, apparently calm.

'You can't sleep here!'

He eased his feet out of his boots, hung up his coat and unfastened his tie. Then he said, sharply but quietly, 'I hope you're not going to be ridiculous. So far I've been tolerant, but don't count on my tolerance continuing.' His tone softened: 'I've tried to be your friend, Lara. I've always tried to be your friend.' He slackened the waistband of his trousers and sighed. His eyes dropped from hers and for a moment he appeared lost for what to do next. But Lara did not notice. She was thinking: no! Not again! Last time I was a child. Not again! I'll never become his mistress!

His voice became slyly affectionate. 'Let me brush your hair. You used to like it when I brushed your hair.'

Lara strove to be calm. 'That's all in the past, Viktor.'

'Because of Zhivago?' Komarovksy stood up. He was still struggling with how to address her, how to make his plea. 'Can't you see he's gone – that you're never going to see him again? I'm all there is, Lara. You knew that when you came with me. I'm not asking you to love me, but am I so unbearable? Aren't I entitled to – something?'

'I won't become your mistress,' Lara murmured.

'Why not?' he answered with a mixture of incomprehension and mute fury.

Because you'll never understand how much you disgust me, Lara thought. Because Yura has used up all the love I'm capable of.

She would have told him so, but at the thought of Zhivago tears sprang to her eyes and she was unable to speak. There was so much desperation to fight off that she had been trying to suppress for Katya's sake. She wanted to scream, to wail into the wall, tear her clothes – anything that would give physical relief to her suffering. She wanted to destroy this illusory character she had created in order to be able to go on from day to day as if her capacity to accept pain were infinite. It isn't me! It's just something I made so that Katya can survive. Can't you see that, Viktor?

In her tears Lara had sat down on the bed. Komarovsky was moved to approach her, muttering: 'There, there my dear,' and sit by her on the bed and take her hand, caressing it softly.

'You need a man to take care of you,' he ventured, dragging up the words from his stale images of women.

Lara looked at him coldly, thinking: if I were responsible only for myself, I should kill myself rather than accept you! You're talking to the illusion, not to the real me! But Komarovsky in his ignorance rejected that look. He held Lara's arm more firmly and pushed his bearded face close to hers, so that she could smell the tobacco smoke carried on his breath and lodged in every hair, and felt a sharp revulsion that overcame her fear of him and she was able to cry:

'No, Viktor! No!'

They left Irkutsk. Komarovsky now spent all his time with Lara in the women's coach. The other women, not knowing the truth nor recognizing the predatory gaze in the lawyer's eyes, commented that he was a dutiful and considerate husband.

Although Komarovsky's purpose might appear obvious at first sight, Lara found it obscure beyond her comprehension. When she had been a schoolgirl and Komarovsky a successful commercial lawyer and middle-aged roué, each had unintentionally bewitched the other in a mixture of disgust and attraction that was understandable with all its contradictions. But now? Lara was no longer a child confused by her own sexual awakening and offering a fantasy of possibilities to a jaded appetite. It was not possible that she held any fascination for Komarovsky in the way she had then. Too many years had gone by and changed their perspective. For Komarovsky most of his life was behind him and Lara could only represent his history. Was it that in a shaded corner of the lawyer's heart she had become a gnawing piece of unfinished business?

His presence oppressed her. Mentally he had stripped her of her defences except the illusion, the other Lara she had fabricated to endure whatever might happen. She was alone but for her child, and the future held no route to escape but only a species of imprisonment at Chita dependent on his bounty. Physically, she had been worn down by travel. The coaches smelled of stale bodies and stale food, and the drink and tobacco of the men. The cohesion of the women had begun to break down and they seemed to find each other contemptible in their dirtiness. The children had become a reproach instead of a source of pride. Lara combed Katya's hair; the greasy unwashed ringlets slid through her fingers; she found a louse that had escaped the kerosene.

The train circled Lake Baikal by the southern shore through miles of tunnels. It stopped briefly at Verkhne-Udinsk and then set out on the final leg towards Chita. On the following day horsemen appeared. They came in small bands, a tatterdemalion army riding behind ragged banners on their withered nags. But they kept abreast of the train which was labouring slowly after a mechanical breakdown at their last halt.

The women watched the riders indifferently. The men became tense and excited but would not talk. The horsemen increased their numbers until they became about a hundred. They wore a motley attire, as if every army that had ever existed had contributed its equipment to their dress. They carried lances, sabres, carbines. Their faces betrayed no pattern: Russians, Tatars, Bashkirs. 'Who are they?' Lara asked.

'Kappelevtsy,' was the answer. 'White bandits. If they can stop the train, they'll kill everyone on it.'

'Is that possible?'

'I should think so. We've only a few soldiers riding on the tender. Certainly not enough to win a pitched battle against these people.' Komarovsky spoke with a genuine indifference, and Lara realized that he was capable of a kind of heroism.

In the late afternoon there was an exchange of fire, but it seemed remote, coming as it did from somewhere towards the front of the train and outside of the carriages. It consisted of only a few shots like the snapping of twigs and had no effect. The Kappelevtsy pressed on and appeared unconcerned. They vanished only that night, when their mounts were too tired to continue.

The next day the train arrived at Chita. The passengers and their baggage were unloaded and carried to a line of waiting carriages. In the street outside the station a squadron of Red cavalry was performing evolutions in the mud. Lara and Katya watched them while Komarovsky arranged their further transport.

Later, as they sat in their ramshackle carriage to be taken to a house in the larch-covered hills above the city, he spoke:

'You should have told me that you were pregnant,' he said bitterly.

CHAPTER 2

THE WOMAN IN CORSETS

For nearly four years they lived near Chita. The house was the same one they had moved into that first day after a jolting drive into the hills by the town, a large cottage that had once belonged to a mine-owner, a wooden-frame house with carved shutters and a porch all painted green. At that time it had been abandoned and open to the weather, but Komarovsky was an important man and had caused the house to be repaired; and it was there that Lara gave birth to a second daughter whom she called Tanya.

During this time Katya grew and was no longer quite a child, nor yet a woman, even a young woman. But she was becoming beautiful because her mother had been beautiful, with light brown hair, blue eyes, a fresh skin, small nose, and a lithe skipping quality in her movements. Whether she was happy was difficult to say.

The squalor and nightmare of the journey east was long behind her. At Chita she had a room which she shared only with Tanya, who was still little more than a baby. Komarovsky had provided it with furniture (from no-one knew where) and toys. But Katya was becoming above toys. She dressed her doll, Ludmilla, and then found herself thinking: *this is silly!* Then another day she and Tanya, Ludmilla and Tanya's doll, Natasha, would play and Katya would not think *this is silly* at all.

Mother and daughter. Alike and unlike. When Lara studied her hands she saw thin fingers on which the knuckles had become prominent; her neck seemed somehow stretched, her skin muddied by an indifferent diet, her hair brittle and dull. And with all that Katya knew that her mother was still beautiful. Her fine eyes still enhanced her faded features, and her infrequent smiles, when they came, could still light her face. Lara busied herself around the house, and in Komarovsky's long absences chopped wood, repaired the byre, milked the cattle, delivered the mare of a foal, cooked, cleaned, sewed, and at most times, except in the evenings when tiredness might overcome her and she would pause over her dressmaking to stare into space, seemed content enough. And except when Komarovsky was there.

When Uncle Viktor was at home, Katya saw her mother become someone else. A dead weight of calmness hung from her, an unresponsiveness as if she were a servant, fulfilling Komarovsky's requests, answering his questions, meeting all her duties with a servant's anonymity. Katya hated these times because they cut her off from her mother; Lara became dull and distant even from her daughter, as if the strain of being two people at once were too great.

On her thirteenth birthday, Uncle Viktor brought Katya a present. It was a fine spring day and Katya was playing with her sister Tanya in the pasture on the hill behind the house. Here the dark mass of larches had been cut back and cattle grazed among the wild flowers dotted white and yellow in the grass, and the girls collected posies of stitchwort from the soft banks of the stream that divided the field.

From this elevation they could see the house and the road that swung in a muddy line from the valley and the direction of the town, following the contours of the land and little more than a forest track as it cut through the trees. A party making its way along the road could be seen a distance off, small figures on the lower slopes disappearing into the dark foliage and then re-emerging in the spaces cleared by the woodsmen only to disappear again.

As the figures grew closer Katya could make them out. Komarovsky was at the front, riding a small brown pony and wearing a large greatcoat with the skirts open and spread over his mount like a tent so that only the animal's head and legs were visible. On his head he wore a pointed soldier's cap with the earflaps down and a red cloth star stitched to the front, and the rest of his face seemed taken up by his beard which was longer than it used to be. Behind him followed a droshky with a driver and a passenger wrapped in rugs, and behind the droshky a heavy waggon drawn by bullocks, and finally another pony ridden this time by a boy who carried a rifle slung across his back. The driver of the bullock cart was lashing the beasts and a team of Buryat drovers heaved at the wheels and shinned over the waggon like monkeys. Whatever was in the waggon was covered by a sheet. The yells and cries of the teamsters broke the air, which was still but for the lowing of the cattle.

These days, Komarovsky's appearance had changed. He had shed his frock coat and city garb and exchanged them for a mix of worker's dress and uniform. Katya did not know the reason for this, but two years before, as he had predicted, the government in which he was a minister had fallen to the Bolsheviks and Komarovsky had neatly sidestepped the wreckage and discovered that he had all along been a Communist. He was now some sort of commissar with the administration in Chita and still an important man. He drank more than he used to, he had lost some of his suavity, and his temper was uncertain. He had conceived an unfathomable dislike of the younger child, and Katya had to shield Tanya from him.

As the rag-tag caravan struggled through the glutinous mud up the final slope, the curses of the drovers and the rattle of harness and creak of wheels grew louder.

Tanya, who had been sitting in the grass plaiting flowers and could not see the visitors, looked up and recognized Komarovsky. She shouted: 'Uncle Viktor!' in her thin infant voice and dropped her flowers, and in a blind panic gathered up her skirts and ran off across the pasture. Katya followed her and caught the child.

'Don't worry,' she reassured her, and stroked her hair.

'It's Uncle Viktor,' her sister complained and began to cry.

'Don't worry. I'll tell you what: you hide in the shed, and I'll come to you later.'

'Don't like the shed!'

'I shan't lock you in. Here – you can have my flowers. You can finish them for me.' Katya gave her the posy and took her by the hand. Behind the house was a stable and a woodshed. The woodshed was dark and fairly dry; Tanya would sometimes escape there and play among the shavings. Katya took her there and left the door open. Then she brushed down her own skirts and walked cautiously towards the house, pausing on the way to examine her appearance in the reflection of the small pool that formed the bottom of the field. The pool was often her mirror. It showed her against the sky with the light shining through her hair, and her still-forming features in soft shadow. Even when she was nervous of Uncle Viktor, Katya could pose by the pool and gather strength from the fairy image it gave her.

The visitors had stopped at the house; Komarovsky had tied his pony to the verandah post and was busying himself with the droshky; the bullocks had been unharnessed and the Buryats were watering them at the well. Katya saw her mother come out on to the verandah and survey the scene.

'I wasn't expecting you. I thought business would keep you in town.'

'And miss Katya's birthday?' Komarovsky replied cheerfully. He barked orders at his men and offered his arm to the swaddled passenger in the droshky. Catching sight of Katya he said, 'Aren't you going to give your Uncle Viktor a kiss?' Katya looked to her mother who gave a barely perceptible nod, then went forward and put her lips to Komarovsky's cheek. The lawyer continued meanwhile to help his guest.

The stranger unfolded into a tiny middle-aged woman in voluminous skirts over which she wore an oilskin waterproof. She stepped delicately from the cart and held a hand to steady her hat. Her face was apple-shaped, her eyes bright, and she wore some false auburn curls that might once have matched her hair, but the latter was now grey for want of dye. She gave directions in a foreign accent to the men with respect to the contents of the waggon. Then she took her carpetbag down from the droshky and stood facing the verandah as if for inspection, a tidy little person in elaborate, slightly exotic clothes like the contents of a child's dressing-up box. Katya immediately liked her.

'Larissa Fyodorovna,' said Komarovsky, leading the middle-aged lady up the steps to the verandah. 'May I introduce Fraulein Buerli.' He beckoned Katya and announced: 'This, my love, is your birthday present. Shake hands – curtsey – whatever you've been shown.' He was slightly drunk. Fraulein Buerli dropped a curtsey and beamed. Katya wondered what one did with middle-aged ladies – what they were for, that she should get one for her birthday? 'Fraulein Buerli is going to teach you music, and also French. She is from Geneva, which is in Switzerland. She used to be governess to —'

'One of the princesses Bagration,' Fraulein Buerli completed.

'You'd better come in,' said Lara uncertainly.

They went inside, Katya and the two women. Komarovsky remained with the waggon, cajoling the Buryat crew as they strove to unload the mysterious object that lay covered on it.

'Can I offer you refreshment – some tea? Have you come far? From Chita?' asked Lara.

'From Vladivostok,' said the 'present'. 'Your husband

46

found me there when I was near destitute,' she added frankly. She removed the oilskin. Beneath it she wore a short jacket of grey shot-silk with sleeves that ballooned above the elbows and frogging down the front, and above the jacket peeped the linen collar of a man's shirt. Her carriage was very stiff above the waist and Katya could have sworn she creaked as she sat down. She waited patiently while Lara busied with the samovar. Katya placed herself opposite and examined this curious creature.

Her mother asked: 'Have you been in Russia long?'

'Twenty years. I was a governess to —'

'One of the princesses Bagration – I'm sorry,' Lara apologized for interrupting. She ran her fingers through her fair hair. 'I don't mean to be rude. I was taken by surprise. I hadn't expected you.'

'I know,' came the mild reply. 'Nowadays there are so few foreigners in Russia.'

'Weren't you able to leave?'

'I was imprisoned. After the Tsar's abdication the idea seemed to get around that I was a German spy – and then that I was a White. There are so many ignorant people. They seem to have only the vaguest idea of where Switzerland is.'

From outside came curses and grunts and someone yelling for more rope. The shadow of a large object blocked out the daylight.

'Your husband —'

'Viktor Ippolitovitch isn't my husband.'

Fraulein Buerli dropped her eyes.

'Katya isn't Viktor's child. He's a – friend of the family. He gave us assistance during the difficult times.' Lara paused. 'I don't know how to ask this – is it Viktor's idea that you live here?'

'I understand so. He must be a very kind man – Comrade Komarovsky,' the visitor said hesitantly. She was now casting her eyes about the room, taking in the furnishings that the lawyer had procured from the various merchants' houses in Chita. 'Did he provide all of this?'

She had focused on a number of little ornaments and conveniences – all Komarovsky's doing – that made the light, airy room pleasant to live in. 'He seems to be very thoughtful, attentive to detail. As I said, I was destitute – do you mind if I talk about this? I've scarcely been able to credit my good fortune. Do you find that when good things happen you have to talk about them in order really to believe in them? I had nothing when Comrade Komarovsky —'

'Viktor Ippolitovitch.'

'– Viktor Ippolitovitch found me. He provided everything, but he was very considerate of my wishes. You know –' she said brightly '– I'd almost forgotten what it was that I had lost: the little things that we need if we are to feel like women, I suppose. Viktor Ippolitovitch was very sensitive and delicate in those matters.'

'He's very knowledgeable about women.'

Fraulein Buerli seemed slightly shocked by that idea; however she continued: 'It makes one bound to him in gratitude, don't you think?'

Katya thought her mother showed a flicker of distress. She found herself feeling uncomfortable. It was too disturbing to talk about Komarovsky. Analysis of people and their relationships somehow made them less secure; it suggested that the way things were was the result of chance. Then Lara said: 'Yes, that's probably the case. And now I think we should have some tea.'

Katya volunteered to pour tea. She prepared the glasses and the sugar, and meanwhile watched the two women curiously. She could not remember their receiving any female visitors before and had no idea what people talked about under those circumstances. Was this what they called 'conversation'? It struck her as oddly tense: she could not imagine anyone did it for pleasure. She supposed she must learn how to do it. The noise outside was very distracting – creaks and grunts and cries of 'Heave!'

'I was given to understand that there are two children.

Katya is aged thirteen, and there's another one?' asked Fraulein Buerli.

'Tanya is three – nearly four.'

Fraulein Buerli halted over some mental reckoning. 'The father of the child —?'

'— isn't Viktor.'

'I hope I'm not offending you,' the visitor said quickly. 'But one wants to understand one's situation.'

'I was taught to be honest,' Lara answered calmly. She turned to Katya and asked softly: 'Where is Tanya?'

'Oh, I forgot!' Katya blurted out. 'She's in the woodshed!' She saw Fraulein Buerli raise an eyebrow. 'I'd better get her.' She put down her glass of tea and left quickly by the rear door. A glance at the sky said it would rain; the wind was rocking the dark treetops and patterning waves in the long grass. She reached the open door of the shed and saw Tanya in the shadows, hunched forward with her arms wrapped about her knees, rocking and crooning to herself. Katya went inside quietly so as not to surprise her, and, as the child turned and smiled, picked her up and rested her in the hollow of her hip.

'Viktor gone?'

'Not yet, my love.' Katya thought of the time. 'He may stay all night. You wait here and I'll bring you some food later – and your doll, do you want your doll?'

'Katya stay with me?'

'Yes –' Katya hesitated. She wanted to return to the house and discover the rest of her mysterious present – whatever it was that the men were labouring under. But she could see that Tanya needed her. 'I'll wait. You play.' She placed her sister on the ground among the wood shavings and the twigs and saw the necklace of white stitchwort that had gone limp in the way of wild flowers. Outside the cows were complaining to be milked, something which her mother normally did; but this time she noticed the boy who had accompanied the waggon. He came up the slope, his rifle still strapped across his back, a wooden pail in one hand and a stool in the other. He approached the nearest cow and, in an easy fashion, began to milk her.

She stayed with Tanya for an hour. The boy finished the milking. The sky clouded over and it began to rain in large drops that fell on the ground like watery plates. In the meantime, out of the dust and dirt Tanya constructed something in her imagination and talked to it. While she was thus preoccupied Katya slipped out of the woodshed in time to see the gang of Buryats disappearing down the road and the bullocks, covered to their flanks in mud, dragging the empty waggon. Then they were lost in the mist and trees.

She entered the house by the rear door and took off her dirty boots and smoothed her hair in the glass. She practised a smile and a look of concentration. She could not suppress her sense of delight at the arrival of the eccentric little stranger; it seemed to her as if the world were opening up. Music and French! She was going to learn them both. A vague picture came into her mind of a world of elegant women and grave men that had once existed but for some unfathomable reason had gone. These images had come to her out of remarks that Uncle Viktor had dropped from time to time, and, although she did not fully understand them and Komarovsky appeared to regard them as of no interest, they seemed to her inexpressibly attractive; and somehow the learning of music and French fitted with that other world.

'You'll understand that the child is lonely and has few opportunities to play with children of her own age,' Komarovsky was saying in his usual weighty phrases. 'But her intelligence is precocious – both naturally and perhaps from so close an association with adults. She can be self-willed, but if you succeed in engaging her interest, then I think you'll find her responsive.'

'Is that your opinion too?' Fraulein Buerli asked; and Katya heard her mother say: 'She responds to affection.'

Komarovsky was standing, warming his back against the stove. He had removed his topcoat and boots and wore a peasant blouse and breeches, and his face was morose; but he dropped this expression when he noticed Katya's entrance and in a lively fashion said: 'Katya, my love, come in and see the rest of your present!' He pointed out a large wooden object positioned against one wall.

'What is it?' Katya asked. It appeared to be an oddly shaped box, but the wood was varnished like furniture and, in the oil lamps that had been lit against the coming evening, it glowed with the rich pattern of the grain.

'What is it?' Komarovsky chuckled. 'Do you hear that, Fraulein?' He poured himself a glass of vodka, drank it in one swallow, and gave a smack of satisfaction. 'This –' he said '– is a piano!'

Fraulein Buerli gave a kindly smile. 'Shall I show it to you?' she asked. Katya approached the piano. The word 'piano' was of course familiar to her and a picture of an instrument was attached to it; but it was not this picture, and in a second it was gone and never again in her life would she remember what 'piano' had once meant. She ran her fingers over the smooth surface, paying no attention to the waterstains that disfigured the varnish. She noticed the two brass candle-holders on their brackets. She lifted the front and gave a small gasp at the sight of the yellowed ivory. She saw the maker's name in gold lettering but the script was unfamiliar and only added to the mystery. Fraulein Buerli was beside her.

'You shall hear how it works,' she said. There was a stool with the piano; Fraulein Buerli arranged herself on it and began to play a light melody. After a few bars she started to sing in German, a melancholy song that sounded at counterpoint to the music. Outside it was dark and the rain could be heard drumming on the shutters.

The visitor played several of the sad German songs and then invited Katya to try. She gave a laugh of excitement, thinking that immediately she was going to be wonderful. She sat at the piano and spread her fingers across the keys as her teacher showed her, and to Fraulein Buerli's prompting struck the first few notes, a loud discordant sound that made her laugh this time with embarrassment. She looked around for Komarovsky's approval and saw him by the door. His hair was wet as if he had stepped outside for a moment. She looked to her mother. Lara was still in her chair, but her face was pained and distant. Katya had noticed before how her mother seemed to abstract herself whenever Uncle Viktor was around. Katya could not understand it: except where Tanya was concerned, Uncle Viktor always tried to be kind and considerate – yet her mother responded as if his presence hurt her; and then Uncle Viktor drank and his manner changed and held a note of dangerousness.

'Shall we eat?' Komarovsky proposed. 'I've brought rations from the town.' A supper of cold meats and pickled vegetables was quickly prepared and they sat down to it.

'Doesn't your other child eat with us?' asked Fraulein Buerli.

'She's too young,' said Komarovsky.

'Asleep, I suppose?'

'Yes – asleep.' He drank more vodka. 'Let's talk about other things. Tell Larissa Fyodorovna about yourself, Fraulein.'

'Oh, I'm not a very interesting person. I suppose interesting things have happened to me – after all, we've lived through interesting times – but that doesn't make me an interesting person. Someone who is dull sees nothing and understands nothing; and his or her account of even the most exciting events will seem dull and – small. I suppose I must be a dull person.'

'I'm sure that isn't the case. And if you're to stay here, then Lara will need to know more, won't you, my dear? Lara?'

'Yes,' Lara agreed sluggishly.

'Well,' said Fraulein Buerli, overcoming her reluctance. 'I came here in – 1903 I think it was. I'd never been abroad before, but one of the princesses Bagration was taking a cure in Switzerland and advertised for a

French-speaking governess to teach her children, and I applied for the position. We stayed a year in Switzerland and then returned to the family home in Tbilisi. Half our time was spent there and the rest was divided between Moscow and St Petersburg as it then was. And there were occasional excursions to the family's other estates. What can I say? Although our life was privileged and, as I realize now, *wrong*, it was very pleasant.'

'How did you come to be in Vladivostok?' Komarovsky prompted.

'That's the most confusing part. We were touring the estates in Siberia when the Tsar abdicated. I think the princess had a premonition that the cities were likely to prove dangerous, and thought that we should be safer with the loyal peasants around us. Yes – well – my employer returned to St Petersburg to be with her husband and we, the children and I, stayed on in the country. This was before the fighting at home started; the government had changed, but we were still at war with Germany. However, the atmosphere was different – panicky, I should say. I was arrested as a German spy and held in prison for several months; I don't know what happened to the children.'

Fraulein Buerli had the well-bred habit of dealing with tragedy through a short sad smile that suggested embarrassment more than anything else: as though telling a joke of uncertain effect or discovering that she was holding a wet baby. Rid of this inconvenience, she went on: 'Then the civil war broke out and the place where I was held was captured by the Whites. I was released, but there was nowhere I could go since all the roads west were barred by the Reds. So I moved with the army and was caught up in the terrible winter retreat when we were almost trapped by General Strelnikov. We fell back eastwards and I was able to find space on one of the Czech trains; and one way and another I found myself in Vladivostok, where I was arrested by the Japanese. They also thought I was a spy,' she added wryly, 'as did the Reds when the Japanese had left. So I was arrested again. And that's how things stood when Viktor Ippolitovitch rescued me.'

She concluded almost gaily. 'I told you it was confusing. It seemed to me at times that I was the most arrested person in the world. But what was the point of it? That I can't tell you. I never truly understood why I was considered to be a spy, or why the Whites were where they were or the Japanese where *they* where; I met no-one important and I saw very little: the inside of gaols and interminable stretches of snow. It seems to have been a wasted experience. That's why I suppose I must be dull.'

With that Fraulein Buerli was finished. She looked down at her plate and avoided the others' eyes. Katya thought how sad she was behind the gaiety and how nice. She had understood little of her visitor's story, but she remembered her own winter journey to Chita even though she had been much younger and the recollection was painful. She also caught the name Strelnikov. She was sure that it meant something, but could not recall what except that it was something she had lost.

Fraulein Buerli looked up from her plate and made conversation. 'Isn't your other daughter going to be hungry?' she asked Lara. 'I'm sure she'll wake up once she misses her supper.'

'The child is well enough!' Komarovsky interrupted abruptly.

'I'm sure I didn't mean to intrude.'

'Not intrude . . . It's . . . Damnation!' He was fuddled by the drink; not that his speech was slurred but as though it had opened a door through which he could only see obscurely. He stood up and turned on Lara. 'Don't think you women can make an alliance against me! I can always reconsider my decisions.'

Katya did not understand. She saw her mother turn pale and heard her mumble: 'Viktor . . .'

'People haven't forgotten Strelnikov,' he said. 'Nor Zhivago!' And his hand reached out to steady himself on the table. Katya was frightened. She distracted herself by suddenly remembering that Tanya was still in the wood-shed. Quickly she gathered a plate and some remnants of food and rushed from the room.

Outside it was raining. The water was streaming down her face, but she knew too that she was sobbing. The incomprehensible but terrible way that adults talked had shaken her and she wanted to escape them. Even Fraulein Buerli now seemed sinister. The talk about Strelnikov! It was her birthday and suddenly it was ruined!

In the darkness she made her way to the woodshed. The door had been closed and she found a padlock closed around the hasp. She shook it in frustration. So that was where Uncle Viktor had been! She rattled and banged at the door without thinking and then to her dismay heard Tanya waking up in the darkness.

'Don't worry!' she shouted over the noise of the rain. But Tanya had been surprised by the noise, her hunger and the darkness. The child was screaming in terror.

Komarovsky spent most of his time away, kept busy in the town or travelling. He was engaged by the government in Chita as an emissary to Mongolia and went there on unspecified business. Whenever he returned he endeavoured to be pleasant except for his aversion to Tanya. Katya observed her mother's civility towards him, but was now experienced enough to detect Lara's hostility, even if she could not interpret it. The realization disturbed her. She had memories of kind Uncle Viktor who had always taken care of them, and on the surface that was still the case; but she now had to bring into consideration her mother's reaction. It was a mystery to her: how could her mother maintain the appearance of friendliness when there was this deep undertone of antipathy? And how did Uncle Viktor regard it? Sometimes Katya could see his distress and dissatisfaction, but these too only puzzled her. With such forces of emotion driving the two apart, Katya had no idea what attraction it could be that sustained the façade of closeness. It contradicted her notions of adult freedom that her mother and Komarovsky should behave as if they were in some way enslaved.

In the nearest village a school had been started in the house of the former priest. The teacher was a barely literate ex-soldier. He taught reading from the only material he had to hand, some political pamphlets and a military manual. In addition the children spent the afternoons digging a garden in the church grounds, since the teacher said that they were all workers and peasants now and had better get used to what it felt like.

For her real schooling Katya relied on Fraulein Buerli. With her pleasant manner she had fitted easily into the family and proved very adaptable and quite willing to chop wood, milk the cows or clean the house as occasion demanded. In her long skirt and queer jacket she could even be seen with a hammer and a mouthful of nails fixing the wooden shutters.

She taught Katya French and some German and geography. They also spent time each day at the piano. Katya learned her scales and a few simple tunes and gradually the inexplicable sensation came to her that the old instrument had life in it: it seemed to respond to her as if she were encouraging rather than playing it; the notes began to flow out of the piano in sympathy with the movement of her hands. Fraulein Buerli was pleased.

CHAPTER 3

THE CAPTAIN OF CAVALRY

One Sunday in autumn Katya took her sister to go mushrooming in the forest. Katya searched out the fungi; Tanya sat by the basket and picked out the pine needles and the grubs. It was a bright day with a damp haze, but among the trees the light was softer, a brown shadiness between patches of mist.

Katya hunted mushrooms. Tanya sat and talked to herself. The silence was broken by the cracking of twigs, the trickle of water in the streams that divided the forest, and the soughing of the treetops in the light breeze. The sight of a horseman took Katya by surprise.

She was in a clearing. It was overgrown with decaying bracken and edged by birch trees. A stream ran down the middle and a number of cut logs had been laid as a crossing. The horseman was on the far side of the stream testing this makeshift bridge.

He was a tall man with fair hair and a long face. His clothes were drab and military-looking and he was dismounted and leading his horse by the reins. The horse was a bony nag that trembled continuously; its flanks were covered with sores and it was heavily troubled by flies. It carried a bundle on its back, slung over both sides like a

57

sack. Only as she held her breath and studied it did Katya see the bundle move, and she realized that it was a second man who appeared to be injured.

The stranger looked up from his examination of the bridge, shielded his eyes against the sunlight and saw Katya. His face registered nothing. He patted the horse's muzzle and led it across the logs to Katya's side of the stream; but all the while his blank eyes remained focused on hers. Then he put his fingers to his mouth and gave a piercing whistle; and in answer three more men, mounted and leading a spare horse, came out of the cover of the trees on the far side of the clearing and trotted idly towards the stream.

Katya remained frozen by the stranger's gaze. She was dimly frightened, but also fascinated by the apparition. She wanted to run, and she wanted to find out what happened next. The stranger approached her without any appearance of urgency; he continued to stroke the horse in reassurance. Behind him the rest of the party crossed the bridge. In contrast these were small, black-haired men with sallow faces and ragged moustaches, Tatars Katya supposed, though she could not be certain. Their horses were loaded with blanket rolls and various satchels and bundles, and Katya saw that each man carried a carbine.

'How far are we from the nearest village?' the fair-haired man asked. He had stopped a few metres away; his horse dropped its head and was gnawing the grass. 'Quiet, Kurt,' he said, apparently to his injured companion who was moaning softly. 'Well, little girl?'

Katya told him.

'You haven't walked so far to come mushrooming here, have you?'

'No, sir.'

'So you live nearby?'

'Yes, sir.'

'With your parents?'

'With my mother, Fraulein Buerli and Uncle Viktor – oh, and my little sister.'

58

'Is Uncle Viktor at home?'

'No, sir.'

'And Fraulein Buerli – who's she?'

'She lives with us and teaches me. French and music,' Katya added.

'French and music,' the man repeated. Then he laughed a long sad laugh. The others picked it up. They giggled in an uncontrolled way like children, so that when they were finished they had to settle their horses.

'All right,' said the fair-haired man. 'Lead on. I think you should take us to your mother. What are you called?' She told him. 'Katya? That's a nice name.'

They walked a short distance and collected Tanya where Katya had left her. She seemed undisturbed by the newcomers and took the fair-haired man's hand when he offered it to her. Katya began to feel pleased with herself: here was company to enjoy. The fair-haired man began to hum a tune. 'I can play that,' Katya told him. It was a German *Lied* that Fraulein Buerli had taught her.

At the edge of the pasture, from which the house was visible, the party stopped. The leader released Tanya's hand and unstrapped the carbine from the side of his horse. He broke open the magazine and checked the bullets. His companions did likewise. He asked Katya again whether Uncle Viktor was at home and she reiterated that he was away.

The children and their new friend crossed the pasture with the other horsemen fanned out on either side. Katya saw Fraulein Buerli busy with a pitchfork by the byre. She was going to call out to her, but was suddenly frightened again. She could sense the tension and caution in the men. And then Fraulein Buerli spotted them, dropped her pitchfork and went scuttling to the house. A moment later her mother appeared on the verandah, followed at an interval by Fraulein Buerli carrying a shotgun.

'Stay there!' Fraulein Buerli shouted.

At that same moment, when Katya felt a wave of terror

about to break over her, the fair-haired man relaxed and let the barrel of his carbine fall to his side.

'That won't be necessary!' he shouted back.

'Who are you?'

'Just soldiers. We're looking for food and rest for the night and then we'll be on our way. One of my friends is injured – do you have any medicines?' He stooped to one knee so that he could speak to Tanya closely. 'Now, sweetheart, there's your mummy waiting for you. Go and tell her that we are nice and don't mean anyone any harm.' He let her go with a pat on the bottom and the child ran across the field into Lara's waiting arms. Lara scooped her up and for a moment their faces were buried together while Fraulein Buerli, her own fierce little face pointed at the stranger like a weapon, kept guard. Then Lara put Tanya down and with one hand she pushed the shotgun slowly away so that it no longer threatened.

For several seconds the two small groups stared at each other and then the fair-haired man stowed his carbine away. With his back to the determined Fraulein Buerli and her shotgun, he fastened the clip that held the carbine to his mount. He tousled the hair of the wounded man and whispered to him and afterwards called to his colleagues and asked them also to put away their weapons and dismount. They obeyed. One by one they got off their horses and arrayed themselves like a bunch of beggars, small bandy-legged men beside their tall leader.

'Good day to you, comrade.' They stood at the foot of the verandah. The fair-haired man removed a dirty forage cap and swept it in front of him with exaggerated courtesy. 'Captain Brenner of the Red Army at your service. May we water our horses and share in your hospitality for the night? My men and I are tired. We've been chasing bandits – perhaps you've heard about them?'

'That man is seriously ill,' Lara answered, pointing at the soldier slung across the captain's nag.

'My thought exactly,' said the captain. Although his words were flippant, his manner was serious. Politely he asked again if he might water and graze the horses and whether there was food, 'bread, *kasha*, whatever you can spare. We don't want to impose. And if you could do anything for my friend, that would help.'

'Bring him in,' said Lara.

The captain signalled two of his men to dispose of the mounts and he and the third bandy-legged Tatar unstrapped the wounded man and helped him gently from the horse. Katya could not tell what was wrong with him, he was covered by a greatcoat; but he had lost a quantity of blood and there was a dark stain across his breast. Lara and Fraulein Buerli had gone into the house to prepare a place for him, leaving Katya to watch the two men carry him on to the verandah. She was struck by their tenderness, their smiles and murmured encouragements. The wounded man's face was waxy and inexpressive.

'There's a sweetheart, open the door for us,' said the captain. They carried the body into the house and through to Katya's room where the bed had been stripped and covered with an old blanket. The man was placed there and his greatcoat opened revealing a dirty blouse and a large chest wound.

Katya uttered a gasp and stifled a cry. She turned away and noticed Tanya, but Tanya was not bothered; she was uncomprehendingly licking the palm of her hand to no purpose. Then their mother was speaking.

'He's going to die.' Lara had scanned the wound with her practised eye and then turned her frank gaze on the visitor. Although she spoke bluntly and without particular emphasis, her unstated sympathy affected the captain, and Katya – from being shocked and revolted – began to share it.

The captain said: 'I thought you'd say that,' as though she had granted him a favour; and then he looked away and commented how pleasant the room was, so light and airy.

'Well, we shall have to make him comfortable, shan't we? I don't suppose it'll be long. It would be good to clean him up, though, don't you think? That at least.'

Lara prepared some hot water; Fraulein Buerli checked the larder; Katya and her little sister followed the captain outside where he took down his bedroll from the horse. 'I'll sleep on the floor in the same room as him,' he told Lara, 'if you don't mind.'

The two women cleaned up the dying soldier and dressed his wounds. A bullet had pierced his chest and come out of his back. The man was beyond paying any attention to their ministrations. They left him alone with a candle to light the darkness and busied themselves preparing bread, onions and dried fish to eat. Meanwhile, the captain and his three other companions assembled by the well, where they stripped down to their ragged breech-clouts and washed themselves. Katya watched them from a distance and saw that the captain wore a cloth wrapped around his body. He unwound this and, taking one edge each, he and one of the Tatars stretched it open and shook it before folding it carefully. Katya could see that it was white, with its edges trimmed with a toothed design of various colours. On one side was a black eagle; on the other the picture of a woman in a pale blue robe holding a baby.

The men exchanged their boots for bast shoes and returned to the house where everyone gathered for a meal. Katya took a seat with them, Tanya on her right, facing the Tatars who, though smiling broadly, had a barbarian look to them that unsettled her and distracted her from the questions she was otherwise eager to ask. The oil lamps were lit, the atmosphere dim and muted; only Fraulein Buerli attempted conversation.

'I'm surprised that there are still bandits about. I thought we were finished with all that nonsense.'

The captain put down the piece of bread he had been eating and composed himself for an answer. Watching him, Katya thought that he was really quite ugly: in repose his face was long and bony, hollow-cheeked and hollow-eyed, his eyes troubled and wandering. But he had a sweetness of expression and an engaging smile.

'There are still a few Kappelevtsy about. They call themselves an army, but they're really no more than a bandit gang. We've been chasing them for weeks and had a brush with them yesterday. You're fortunate they haven't paid you a visit. What does your man do?'

'He's an official with the government in Chita.'

'Well, there you are. The Kappelevtsy hate the Reds. If they knew this was the house of a Communist, they'd have no mercy. Isn't that right?' he addressed his comrades. The three Tatars interrupted their feeding to grin back. He continued: 'So you may have reason to thank us for your security.'

For a while there was silence except for the click of spoons on bowls. Katya, still tongue-tied, swapped smiles with the youngest of the Tatars. They were nervous smiles, hesitantly exchanged as if offering strange money. She heard her mother ask quietly: 'Why do they continue this struggle? Surely it's hopeless? They can only be killed. Couldn't they just give up? Here in Siberia everything is so open and disorganized, they could slip into the background.'

The captain put down his spoon, wiped his mouth on his sleeve – but in a slow almost gentlemanly way – and replied: 'Some of them are foreigners – Czechs and Hungarians, prisoners who were stranded here after the war. They can't melt into the background and they've nowhere to go to. And then –' he said, with a hesitation as if this were a new idea come to him '– perhaps some of them act out of ideals.'

'I've known people with ideals,' Lara answered. 'But when faced with hard choices, they compromise. Perhaps to save someone – a family perhaps. I don't regard such people as evil; they retain their ideals; but they remain compromised. I haven't met anyone who has taken ideals as far as the risk of death.'

'Death is just a matter of circumstances. Most of the time we think it's important, but then something happens and it's not so important. There are times when people are a little crazy. They want to be heroes. They want to stand outside themselves and look at their own bodies and cry at the tragedy of it all. And then, in a hopeless situation, some people get inspiration from simply doing their duty. It clarifies the mind. Or so I suppose.'

'You're a foreigner yourself, aren't you?' said Fraulein Buerli suddenly in the silence that followed the captain's last remark. He smiled indulgently.

'Und Sie auch, Fraulein, but does that make you a bandit? My family are Volga-Germans. Which makes us Russians after a fashion.' The food finished, the captain's eyes drifted to the piano. 'Who's the musician?' he asked.

'I am!' said Katya eagerly. The captain chuckled.

'Of course – it would be,' he said, and Katya thought he was about to mock her and felt a moment of panic that she would not know how to react. But instead he asked gently: 'Will you play for me?'

'I'd love to!'

'What do you play?'

Katya was about to answer but then forgot the names in her excitement. 'Tunes!' she exclaimed.

'Tunes, eh? Then play me a tune.'

Katya excused herself from the table and took her position at the instrument and opened the lid. She could feel the captain's eyes on her. How unfamiliar the keyboard looked! She spread her fingers and began, but the melodies competed in her head and she jumbled the notes. She tried again – and a third time, but only a discord came out. In frustration she banged the keys and stared defiance at the visitor.

'A valiant attempt,' he said charitably; and, guessing her thoughts, added: 'Now I think you're angry with me. Playing to an audience is different, isn't it? But don't worry, you'll learn. Who is your teacher – ah, Fraulein Buerli, of course. Will you play for us?'

Fraulein Buerli stood up cautiously and exchanged places with Katya. 'What would you like?' she asked.

Waiting for an answer she began playing a Schubert *Lied*. After a few bars the captain started to sing in a sentimental tenor, and when the song was finished he asked for another and again until he had sung four times, after which he lapsed into silence. Everyone's eyes were on him, including those of his three Tatar friends, who sat bolt upright in their chairs and restrained their urge to scratch, which had been evident at supper.

'I'd better see to Kurt,' the captain said at last, and he quit the room, leaving the women and children and his three companions who remained in their stiff pose.

'He's dead,' the captain announced calmly on his return a few moments later. He directed a few words to the Tatars in their own language and they stirred, picked up their caps and followed him back to the bedroom. Lara took one of the oil lamps and also followed, with Katya behind her and Tanya frightened and hanging to her sleeve.

In Katya's room the men had gathered around the bed. Katya saw her mother stoop to listen for any trace of heartbeat, pulse or breathing and then shake her head, but Katya found it difficult to believe that the adults could be right. He didn't look dead. His face was beaded with moisture which gave it a fresh appearance, and he seemed so young, barely older than Katya herself, though she knew that couldn't be true. She had an idea that he was the captain's son, which was equally improbable: despite the same fair hair and long pale face, he was beautiful unlike the captain. Prince Ivan from the fairy tales. A sleeping prince who would wake up if he were kissed.

The captain covered the face and informed Lara coldly: 'I'll bury him in the morning. Do you have any spades?'

'In the woodshed.'

'We'll take him to the forest – he'll be out of the way there. The ground will be hard; we may need a mattock to break it.'

'I think we have one.'

'Good.'

'Yes –' Lara answered distractedly.

Katya had not thought of the practicalities of death. It was brutal to think of them. They should be crying for the dead boy – but no-one had cried.

Her mother said: 'Will you need a winding sheet? If I look, I'm sure I can find something.'

'There's no need. You've been very kind to us, Larissa Fyodorovna. I don't want to trouble you any more. We'll bury Kurt in the morning and then be gone.'

Katya returned with her mother to the other room where Fraulein Buerli was clearing the table. The little woman looked up and asked: 'Does this make any difference to their plans for leaving? He's a dangerous man, that Captain Brenner, and the sooner he goes, the better.'

'They'll leave in the morning,' Lara told her.

Fraulein Buerli nodded and produced the cap that the visitor had removed when he entered the house. She indicated some unpicked stitching at the front. 'Someone's taken the badge off. I don't say that it means anything, but to be careful I suggest that we all spend the night in this room and let the men have the rest of the house. If all we lose is our food then we'll be lucky.'

Katya glanced at the door as if the captain would enter, then said: 'I don't understand. He's a nice man. How can you be frightened of him?' It seemed to her that Fraulein Buerli had missed something. Whoever the captain was, his kindness towards them was obvious.

Fraulein Buerli gave a half-smile. 'Don't upset yourself, my love. We're only being cautious without Uncle Viktor here to protect us.'

'Where's the gun?' Lara asked.

'In the kitchen.'

'I'll get it,' Katya said hastily. She had a dim notion that the women would do something foolish. Adults behaved that way. She rushed out to the kitchen, but when she got there she found that one of the soldiers was in possession. He was sitting at the table peacefully oiling his carbine, and when he saw Katya he gave her a friendly wink.

Not wanting to return without the shotgun, Katya went to her bedroom to wait until the kitchen was free. The door of the room was open and she could hear the captain inside. Nervously she peeped around the opening but at first could see only the bed, from which the cover had been removed and replaced by the strange cloth that the captain had earlier worn about his body. Now it was draped over the corpse with the image of the woman and child uppermost, and the captain was kneeling on the far side of the bed. Katya thought for a moment that he was praying, as she had seen old women doing in the village. He looked up and saw her.

His eyes were open and his hands were resting apart on the side of the bed in a position more suggestive of meditation than prayer. He seemed unconcerned that Katya was watching him. From one of his pockets he took some tobacco and proceeded to roll a cigarette, all the while studying the body. The candle that burned at the bedside was dying; it guttered as he picked it up, and went out leaving only a coil of smoke and the smell of melted tallow. 'Can you bring me a light?' he asked.

Katya went to the kitchen and disturbed the Tatar to find another candle. Then she returned to the other room where the two women and Tanya were waiting as she had left them. She lit the candle from one of the oil lamps and shielded the flame with her hand.

'Where are you going with that?' her mother asked.

'Where's the gun?' demanded Fraulein Buerli.

'The captain needs another candle,' Katya answered. She knew immediately that it was an answer that would not satisfy them. She had to say something that would make them realize that the captain was just an ordinary person – why couldn't they see it? She said: 'He seems so sad because of his friend.' She had an image of the room. 'He's put a cloth over him. It's got a picture of a lady and a baby on it. Is that the Virgin?'

Fraulein Buerli looked sharply at Lara, but to Katya she said pleasantly: 'That sounds interesting. Let me see.' She took the candle from Katya's hand and left the room without noticing that she was followed. They went to the bedroom where Fraulein Buerli paused to tidy herself before tapping the door.

'Come in,' said an answering voice.

The woman pushed the door open and entered. She advanced on the bed and briefly held the candle where she could see the design painted on the cloth. Then she passed the candle to the captain. 'I understand you asked for this,' she said.

'Thank you, Fraulein.'

'It's nothing.' She gathered her voluminous skirts and turned. Seeing Katya she ushered her quickly away but not before Katya had noticed the look of fear on her teacher's face. Together they returned to Lara.

'Is it a picture of the Virgin?' Katya asked.

'Yes, my love,' said Fraulein Buerli. She addressed herself to Lara and her face was serious. 'He's covered the body with a flag. It isn't one of ours. That captain was no more born in Russia than I was! He's an Austrian prisoner of war – a Kappelevtsy – a bandit!'

Katya thought her mother seemed confused by this information, as if she too had difficulty in accepting that the captain and his men posed a danger.

Fraulein Buerli had no hesitation. 'I'm going to get the gun,' she announced. She was back a moment later. 'It's gone,' she said. 'And so have the three toughs. The captain's still in Katya's room. What are we going to do?' In her hand she had three kitchen knives. 'At least we have these to protect ourselves.'

'What good would those do?' Lara asked. Fraulein Buerli now looked doubtful too. Lara said, 'If we can get out of the house, we can hide in the forest until they leave. The weather's still mild. We can take coats and blankets.' Her voice still lacked urgency and conviction. It was difficult to believe in an enemy one had eaten with and spoken to. Katya had heard stories of the terrible Kappelevtsy, but they had always sounded like fairy-tale robbers. She had never imagined that reality could be so confusing.

Katya was despatched to spy on the captain while the two women tip-toed about the house getting clothes to keep them warm. The captain was still in the room with the body of his friend, but he had closed the door and only the creaking of boards could be heard as he paced the floor. Katya wanted to break in on him and tell him to stop frightening them; that it was not fair after they had been so kind to him and his men! She was poised with these thoughts when she heard Fraulein Buerli whispering and she turned to see the little woman half-buried in coats, waiting for her, and Tanya by her side, shivering and fretful.

Huddled together they went to the back door. Carrying the least, Katya slipped the wooden latch and pulled the door ajar. Directly outside the door one of the Tatars was sleeping on the verandah, nursing his carbine. The noise disturbed him and he turned his head lazily and gave a sleepy smile. Katya closed the door. They went to the front of the house and tried that door too. Again, one of the captain's men had made himself comfortable in front of it.

'We must stay, then,' said Lara.

'We can barricade ourselves in,' said Fraulein Buerli. They returned to the main room and Katya helped the women to move furniture to form a barrier by the door. Katya still felt that this was all pointless, and she realized that she was not afraid: in fact it all seemed to be a game. She knew that Fraulein Buerli was terrified beneath her self-control, and yet she could feel only her own excitement.

The barrier was made and they all settled to pass the night behind it. Nothing happened to disturb them, and in the morning they felt slightly foolish and tried to dismantle their handiwork before the captain appeared.

His knock on the door interrupted them. He came into the room and took in the scene, understanding it at once.

'It seems you're afraid of me,' he said regretfully. There was nothing more to be said on the point but he noted the anticipation on the women's faces, as if they were expecting to be victims of his resentment at their doubts. 'I'm going out now to bury my friend,' he told them. 'When I come back, we'll pack and leave. If you have some food to spare, we'd be grateful, but I don't want you to deprive yourselves on that account.' He did not wait for a reply, but left them alone.

Katya watched the burial party cross the pasture towards the trees. The dead man, wrapped in the flag, was slung across one of the horses led by the captain. His companions carried spades and a mattock. An hour later they returned and towards noon they left without speaking further.

That afternoon Katya found the grave. It was a fresh unmarked mound about a hundred metres into the trees and loosely camouflaged by a scattering of pine needles. She stood by it for some time, feeling at first a distress for the boy who had died, the loneliness and sadness of him with no-one to care about him except the captain. Then this passed and was replaced by puzzlement, a longing to understand why he had died and what it might mean. She had heard about God from some of the village women and one of the old priest's books that was passed as contraband around the school. But God meant nothing to her and she had only a vague notion of how He might explain anything.

Later, while she was playing with Tanya in the pasture, the silence was interrupted by distant gunfire in the west. There were only a few shots, enough to unsettle the cattle and set the crows flying.

Two weeks later Komarovsky returned. He came alone on horseback leading a packhorse and followed by a dog. The dog was a lanky brown cur, a slobbering animal that was infatuated by its master and dangerous to everyone else.

Komarovsky kept it chained to the verandah and took it for long solitary walks.

The lawyer's manner, too, had become more solitary and unsociable. His conduct towards Fraulein Buerli was friendly and confiding and he was civil towards Lara; but in the evenings after supper, when Komarovsky had assumed his usual position warming himself by the stove and smoking, Katya saw a look of coldness and suspicion in his hooded eyes and knew that his sociability was a fraud. His manner towards her had also changed. Outwardly it was the same show of affection. Inwardly it was something different. Katya had no idea what this might mean.

One day while Komarovsky was away in the town, Katya overheard Fraulein Buerli approach her mother. They were cleaning the house; Katya had been tending to the needs of the cattle and had just returned. She could hear the two women in the kitchen. Fraulein Buerli spoke with little pants and sighs because of the stays which she insisted on wearing, and used her formal schoolmistress way of talking which belied her kindly nature.

'Larissa Fyodorovna – Lara, forgive me if I ask you a question – ah – do you want me to clean that pot? Forgive me if I ask you a question. The situation between yourself and Viktor Ippolitovitch – I admit it puzzles me. May I talk about this?'

'Yes, of course.'

'Are you sure? I don't want to interfere where it's none of my business. But here I am, living with you. I can't help noticing things. Then again, perhaps the subject is indelicate? Is Viktor Ippolitovitch a relative?'

'No.'

'No, I thought not.'

'Please clean this pan.'

'This one? You're right, it's filthy, but we haven't used it lately. So Viktor is just a friend? I see. Hmm – odd.'

'Why odd?'

'Well – it's just that I get the impression that you don't like him. For that matter I'm not convinced he likes you either. That's what I find strange. You're not his mistress.' Fraulein Buerli giggled nervously. 'You know, I never thought I'd be able to say that – but times have changed.'

'No, I'm not his mistress,' Lara answered. 'But I used to be.'

They had stopped cleaning the pots. Katya could hear her mother drying her hands. She felt guilty at eavesdropping like this, but she knew that the conversation would cease if her presence were known, and she was fascinated to learn the solution to mysteries she had never clearly formulated in her own mind.

'Do you want to talk about it?' Fraulein Buerli asked gently.

'It's difficult to talk about. No, I don't mean because I'm embarrassed, but because I don't understand why things are as they are. Rationally I tell myself that they could be different. For a while I tried to make them different. Then Viktor and I were flung together again as if in some way we are fated to be together. This is silly, I know,' Lara apologized. 'It contradicts everything we're taught about freedom. At one time I would have told you that I stay out of gratitude. Viktor saved us when we were in difficulty at Yuryatin after the civil war. That explanation at least made a sort of sense.'

'But you don't believe in it any more?'

'No. In any case it doesn't explain why Viktor stays with us. He isn't under any obligation to us.'

There was a pause and Katya felt at a loss. She could not see the two women and watch the interplay of expression and gesture that filled out the silence; and the door, too, filtered out the finer tones so that the conversation seemed curiously flat.

'I've never married,' Fraulein Buerli began again with a note of sadness. 'I can hardly claim to understand. I've suspected for a long time – this is from observation and I admit I could be wrong – that people are too tenacious of others; that they keep on when there is nothing to hold on to any more. Partly it's a habit of mind, a lack of imagination, and partly a fear of the alternatives. And partly, too, we're not pursuing a real person or some other thing that's really there, but, instead, something that's in our own heads. Perhaps that's what Viktor is doing? Perhaps he wants his youth back – and that's something you have no way of giving. Forgive me if this sounds obvious and unhelpful; but even obvious things are difficult when applied to oneself.'

After this the discussion changed. They talked about cleaning again. But later Katya thought that the relationship between the two women had changed. They seemed closer. As they worked of an evening, sewing, mending, bottling vegetables in the kitchen, trimming the wicks on the lamps, they exchanged smiles in a way they hadn't before. Katya noticed it and thought that Uncle Viktor did too.

When he was at home Komarovsky used to take the dog and the gun and go hunting. On these occasions, when his location was unpredictable, Katya had to keep an eye out for him in order to keep Tanya out of his way. Sometimes they played in Lara's room.

They possessed very little that predated their arrival at Chita. Katya had clear memories of Moscow and Yuryatin but she had never strung them into a story that explained them. She had a vague recollection of Strelnikov's existence and could recall Zhivago when he returned to live with them after his release by the partisans. But, since these were the only realities she knew, it was self-evident to her that her history was the normal way of things and she supposed it was much the same with other children. There was nothing to question.

Rummaging in drawers and cupboards in her mother's room, hoping to find something new to amuse her sister, she found a thin bundle of old letters tied with ribbon. Most of them dated back to a time when she had been a small child, no older than Tanya. The envelopes were marked with rubber stamps showing how many hands they had passed through, and sections of the letters were heavily scored-through by an unknown censor; but enough was left for her to read, and she did so now without any embarrassment since no-one had told her differently.

Most of the letters were from a soldier who signed himself 'Pasha'. He was writing from a place called Galicia (wherever that was) where he was serving with the army. Much of what he wrote concerned army life, his comrades, the countryside around him; and he wrote observantly, humorously, even affectionately. But in each letter there was a passage addressed to Lara. It said unaffectedly how Pasha thought of her so often that she was scarcely out of his mind; how he missed her presence, her touch, the feel of her body; expressing emotions that Katya had never heard adults express before and in a language that seemed remote from them. Katya realized that these must be love letters, but she had never previously thought what they would be like. It seemed odd to her that they were at variance with the way that adults spoke and behaved towards each other. And then it came to her, from references to 'our child', that Pasha must be her father!

Her father! The thought made her dizzy with excitement. And he had loved her mother! And he had loved her – his 'little Katya'! She swept the letters to her breast and laughed in her excitement so that she set Tanya laughing too and in a second they were dancing around the room, Katya swinging her sister by the arms. It was too wonderful!

But then – what? Where was he? What had happened to him? She could not make the connection with Strelnikov, a name she had heard once or twice, a memory of a train she had once seen. What had happened to him?

She put Tanya and the letters down and turned to the last letter which had not been tied in a bundle with the others.

It was from a woman called Antonina Alexandrovna

Zhivago. She was writing from Moscow and said that she was expecting to leave with her family for Paris; would Lara pass on the enclosed letter to her husband? It was a short letter and Katya thought the wording was stiff and uncomfortable as though the writer had difficulty composing it. Who was her husband? Was it Katya's own Zhivago – Uncle Yura of her infancy? But in that case, what was *her* Zhivago doing living with her mother and not with Antonina Alexandrovna? In an uncertain fashion Katya knew that Zhivago was the father of her sister Tanya, and she wondered whether that meant that there were other brothers and sisters.

She looked for the other letter that should have been enclosed with the one from Moscow. At first she picked over the contents of the drawer in which she had found the others. Then, not seeing it, she felt that it must hold the solution to the mysteries. She began to turn out the drawers on to the floor and root furiously among the clothing and the trinkets. Tanya, who had been playing peaceably, stopped and asked cautiously what she was doing; and then she too joined in the game and attacked the furniture and the bedding, piling pillows and blankets and clothing in a disordered heap which Katya worked over in anger and frustration until tears started in her eyes and she cried out: 'Stop it! Stop it!' and struck out at the child.

The blow missed, but Tanya was frozen by it. She began the slow animal wail that she gave whenever Komarovsky locked her away in her room or the woodshed. The pitiful sound brought Katya to her senses and she took hold of her sister and tried to pacify her. 'I'm sorry, my love – sorry – sorry.' She saw the chaos in the room and could hear her mother's footsteps.

Lara came into the room. She halted with a cry of anger on her lips and saw Katya furtively holding something.

'What do you have there?' she asked.

'Some letters,' Katya answered. 'We were playing. I found them.' The answer had a deadening effect. Lara seemed to forget about the mess and close in on herself. With a child's immediacy Katya also forgot about what she and Tanya had done. But she remembered the blow that she had wanted to give to her sister, and it forced a question to her lips:

'Why doesn't Uncle Viktor love Tanya?'

Perhaps her mother was going to answer truthfully. But then Tanya was sobbing: 'Uncle Viktor – Uncle Viktor,' and Lara answered as if the question were foolish: 'Of course Viktor loves her,' and moved to take hold of the child.

Katya wanted to say, 'That's not so,' but the answer would have been pointless since she knew that her mother knew this and that the lie was shared between them. Instead Katya remained puzzled by the dishonesty of adults towards children; by the obviousness of their lies. It did not occur to her that the lie was the only thing that Lara herself clearly understood: that the truth might be complicated or hidden; or that the truth is often dangerous only when expressed.

In any case there was no time to think about these things. Her mother was standing by the window, holding Tanya to her. Katya heard her murmur: 'Dear God, he's found the body.'

Through the window Komarovsky could be seen coming out of the woodshed carrying a pick and spade, with the scampering dog at his heels. Without looking at the house he directed his footsteps towards the forest. At this time of year the first snow had fallen, and in his bulky clothes the lawyer appeared dark and monumental. He crossed the ground towards the forest and disappeared leaving behind him the white empty field, the pearl-grey sky and orange sun.

Lara gathered the children and took them to the main room where Fraulein Buerli was darning stockings. The little woman saw Lara's alarm and asked: 'What's happened?'

'Viktor has found the soldier's body,' Lara told her.

Fraulein Buerli put her needlework away. She did this slowly, with small deliberate gestures as she gathered her thoughts. The socks, the bodkin and darning wool went carefully to their appointed places, then Fraulein Buerli smoothed down her dress and tugged the sleeves of her jacket into neatness before speaking.

'We should have explained things to him,' she said. She distracted herself by tending the stove. 'Still, that can't be helped. We must make the best of the situation.' One side of her lips tugged in one of the pretty little smiles that expressed her seemingly limitless hope and endurance. 'I suppose we must tell him the truth. I can't think of anything else to do. How do you think he'll react? You know, I can't think now why we didn't tell him in the first place. We were, after all, quite innocent. I don't see how the arrival of those uninvited men made us guilty of anything.'

Lara answered bluntly: 'Viktor's actions are unpredictable. That's why we didn't tell him.'

'Yes, I suppose you are right.'

They composed themselves to wait. Noticing Tanya fiddling with the knitting wool, Fraulein Buerli said: 'Do you think the child should be here?' The question pulled Lara out of her thoughts.

'I'm not thinking clearly. Katya, take Tanya to her room.'

'Should I come back?'

The women exchanged glances. Fraulein Buerli said: 'He's very fond of her. Her presence may have a restraining effect.' Lara nodded silently.

Katya hurried to take her sister away. Tanya was confused and moaned and whimpered so that Katya wished she would be quiet. 'Hush!' she told her sharply. 'You don't want Uncle Viktor to hear you!' This had the opposite effect to that intended and Katya was forced to stay to comfort her. In her tension, she sat rigidly on the edge of the bed with Tanya wriggling against her so that she had a feeling of physical revulsion against her sister and this, in turn, upset her because she was unused to it, and she cried: 'No! You mustn't!' and tried to pinion the child at the same time that she was trying to love her. It came to her then that it was all Tanya's fault: Uncle Viktor's moods, her mother's distress, the terrible secrecy that seemed to have invaded their lives – all Tanya's fault. The idea made no sense to her, but it had a brutal, insistent force as if this wriggling creature were an incubus that had attached itself to their lives.

And then Tanya fell asleep. Katya felt her relax and carefully she laid her on the bed, where she curled up and her face assumed a peaceful smile. Katya stood back and the strange emotions she had just experienced melted away. But not the recollection. She had hated Tanya – little Tanya! It was horrible to contemplate. And frightening, so that Katya was near to tears. She went to the window. The day was fading beyond the sea-grey snow. The edge of the forest was black and menacing. Komarovsky was coming from that direction and looked as black as a magician.

In the main room an oil lamp had been lit. The women were sitting quietly, both of them stiffly erect with their hands folded on their laps. Lara asked about Tanya and accepted Katya's assurances that her sister was now calmly asleep. Fraulein Buerli even smiled as if in painful amusement. They could hear the outside door open and Komarovsky unhurriedly removing his boots.

He knocked before entering the room, came in without speaking, and went directly to the stove to warm himself. He had put on a pair of red, elaborately embroidered slippers that he had picked up somewhere on his travels. Rocking on his feet he turned and said in an even conversational tone:

'I take it you know about this.'

He unfurled the flag with the Virgin and child exposed and the image besmeared with earth.

Without waiting for an answer he said, 'And I assume also that you are aware of the dead man around whom it was wrapped. Would you care to enlighten me?'

This time he gave them the opportunity to reply. He draped the cloth to dry upon the stove and studied the image in silence. Lara said:

'While you were away a band of robbers – called.'

'Did they?'

'One of them was wounded. He died during the night.'

'A gang of Kappelevtsy was run down and killed near here,' Komarovsky informed them neutrally. 'Would this be the same gang?'

'I suppose so.'

'Did they steal anything?'

'We gave them food,' Fraulein Buerli interjected. 'If we hadn't given them food they would have stolen it.'

'But nothing else – they stole nothing else?'

'No,' Lara admitted.

'Destroyed nothing?'

'No.'

'Molested you?'

Lara shook her head. Fraulein Buerli said: 'We protected ourselves. We were barricaded in here with the gun.'

Komarovsky must have caught the half-truth. He asked Katya: 'Is that so, my love?'

'We tried to get the gun but one of the soldiers had taken it.'

'And the barricade?'

'We made one out of furniture.'

The fact of the barricade might have stopped the drift of Komarovsky's suspicion if he had not reached the point where suspicion could exist independent of any facts. Instead of testing the significance of that last remark he said distantly: 'This gang of Kappelevtsy raided a station on the line to Verkhne-Udinsk. They killed the stationmaster and his wife. I knew him. And his wife, too. She was an inoffensive woman, fat and ugly, and she had a number of children. They also robbed some waggons taking supplies to the miners and murdered the family of the head of the village nearby. He was a Communist. There were three children in that case, I believe. All murdered.'

'We were left unharmed,' said Lara.

'I can see that,' Komarovsky answered. He sat down heavily on one of the chairs. 'Do we have some vodka?' he asked, and while Fraulein Buerli searched for it he continued: 'Did they know that I was an important official in Chita?'

'I don't know.'

'Didn't they ask?'

'I can't remember. I think they asked where you were, and I told them you were away on business.'

'It doesn't matter. The house is full of my papers – they did search the house, didn't they? – and it would be obvious from those that I was a Communist. You do take my point, don't you? These were desperate men. Why did they spare you?'

There was no answer. Komarovsky's manner indicated that he did not expect one and that in a perverse way this gave him satisfaction. In his eyes his pedantic cross-examination, delivered with the same deliberate tedium he had used as a lawyer in Moscow, had established the truth. But to Katya it appeared otherwise: that there was no answer because everything was based upon a misconception such that Komarovsky's questions were words without sense. Finding her mother still silent, she blurted out: 'But they were *kind*!'

Komarovsky smiled indulgently. 'Were they –' he asked Lara '– kind?'

'They were tired,' Lara answered him. 'People have to be angry in a special way in order to kill other people. It isn't a state of mind that exists all the time. The men were tired and concerned about their friend. If circumstances had been only a little different perhaps they would have killed us.'

'Your vodka, Viktor Ippolitovitch,' offered Fraulein Buerli. She distracted him by pouring the glass of spirit.

He drank it quickly but refused a second. Then for a space he was silent and let his bearded face fall so that it rested heavily on his chest. Katya thought how hurt he looked, as if some great tragedy had happened to him. He raised his head again and focused his myopic eyes dully.

'Why didn't you tell me all of this?' he asked.

'You were preoccupied by business,' Lara answered, 'and tired from travelling. And, in the end, nothing had happened.'

He looked to Fraulein Buerli.

'It was too distressing to talk about. It was best forgotten.'

'Katya?' he asked.

Katya felt his vague eyes plucking at her for a response, and any explanation fled her. But the fact was that it had never occurred to her to tell him about the bandits. Without discussion it had become a secret among them. Obviously Komarovsky was not to be told. Or so it had been. But now the reaction, which had seemed so unspokenly natural, appeared strange. And yet nothing *had* happened. Nothing that had not been explained to him. How could it be then that there still was a secret? Unless – and Katya came to this only with difficulty – unless the secret was not in the things that had happened, but the things that might have. The things that happen in the soul.

That night Katya was woken by a snuffling sound at the door of her room, a wet, animal sound that intruded on her sleep as if something unclean were too close. She opened her eyes and saw from a faint candle light beyond the door that it was open, and as her eyes adjusted she recognized Komarovsky standing there in the lounging position he assumed when he was in deep thought. The noise came from his dog, which he had let into the house.

He said nothing. Katya could not tell whether he knew she was awake or not. Without reason she held her breath and remained unmoving. He lit a cigarette, holding the match for some seconds after the cigarette was lit and staring through the flame so that his eyes each picked up the reflection and for that brief moment burned. He snuffed the match as it reached his fingertips, but otherwise remained still, moving only to smoke the cigarette in a leisurely fashion and finally extinguish it and slip the stub into his pocket. The dog meanwhile stayed by him, circling his legs and begging his favours like a familiar spirit.

The following day he left before first light and without warning. His travelling clothes and the horse were gone and his trail was visible on the track through the forest. The women felt an unspeakable relief that his dangerous presence had become an absence. They moved about the house with furtive lightness like survivors from the sack of a city, touching objects softly as if inspecting for damage.

They breakfasted together over bowls of *kasha*, Katya, her mother and Fraulein Buerli. Tanya had not appeared and they were disposed to leave her to sleep on. By this time Lara and Fraulein Buerli had already milked and mucked-out the cows, which always left them with a rich clinging smell of straw, earth and warm udders. Katya had come to associate that smell with breakfast when they were together contemplating the day, totting up the tasks to be performed, deciding who would do them. The cows, the horse, the water to be brought from the well, the washing of clothes, hot water – never enough hot water. What was the state of the woodpile? Who would hoe the vegetable patch and pick the greens? Was there a clean pinafore for Tanya? Uncle Viktor had hinted that the women were bound together in a conspiracy, and perhaps they were.

They finished their breakfast and Fraulein Buerli washed the bowls. Lara went to dress Tanya. She came back a moment later and asked:

'Where is she?'

'Isn't she in bed?' answered Katya.

'No. Was she there when you woke up?'

'I didn't notice. I thought she was asleep.'

'She's probably gone out to play,' said Fraulein Buerli, and offered to look for her, but Katya volunteered instead. She put on warm clothes against the morning chill and went outside to search the meadow. There she called for Tanya and got no reply; so she pressed on to the trees to their favourite mushroom spots and again called and again got no answer but her own voice sounding small and lost in the deadening blanket of snow. She began to feel uneasy.

She returned to the house and from the door heard high voices: Lara saying tremulously, 'Her clothes are gone'; and Fraulein Buerli answering, 'Viktor probably thought she would enjoy going into town with him'; and again Lara, this time snapping at her friend in a way Katya had never heard: 'Don't be ridiculous, Lotte! Viktor would never take Tanya into town, not just for the fun of it!'

The bedroom door burst open and Lara strode out and stared coldly at Katya as though she were an impediment, and then disappeared into the main room followed by Fraulein Buerli. Again voices – familiar – unfamiliar – the tone so high and pained. And the curious repetitiveness of the words: 'Viktor wouldn't take her for fun!' Katya had not realized how obsessive fear is. 'She wouldn't go with Viktor – what does he want? Oh, God, Lotte, what does he want?'

Katya remained excluded by the door, beyond which was the incomprehensible world of adults. She wanted to break in and take her mother and shout: 'What about *me*? *I* love you!' In her fear she had forgotten about its original cause, the disappearance of Tanya. What now frightened her was her own exclusion and the revelation that, beyond the limit of her understanding, adults lived as much in a world of chaos as of order. Chaos was what she heard, not Lara's desperate cries for Tanya.

Fraulein Buerli came to the door. Probably it was instinct that brought her there, since Katya was making no sound. The elderly woman's tender face looked at

Katya's and she said softly: 'I think you should go to your own room. Your mother's upset. It's for your own good.'

For her own good that she be excluded! For her own good that she should be consigned to ignorance and fear! No! She cried out: 'Mother!' and in response caught a glimpse of Lara's face that was so desolate and terrifying that she could not bear it. 'Mother!' she cried again, and tried to push into the room, but Fraulein Buerli had grabbed her arm and was forcibly leading her away, still saying it was for her own good, she should be a good girl, she should stay calm and help her mother. And so she was taken to her own room and left to fling herself upon the bed and sob.

Alone. Dreadfully alone for the long wearisome day. From the rest of the house the noise subsided. Then, after an interval, there would be a reprise – garbled words – an animal cry. Only once did Fraulein Buerli come to see her and sit on the bed, saying nothing, but holding Katya closely. And the day grew dark. And Komarovsky came home.

Katya had been sleeping fitfully and did not hear his arrival. But again came the sound of voices. Again chaos and exclusion. Lara: 'What have you done with her?' Again and again. Komarovsky: '. . . Zhivago's bastard!' Cries, tears, banging – madness. 'No! No! *No!*' all from Lara. Again and again. And a piercing scream that was so painful, so terrifying that Katya was caught up in it, it seemed to pluck at her own voice, seize her breath and drag it out, let it out! Let it out! And the scream grew louder and louder – deafening – horrible – let it out! Let it out! Whose voice is that? Whose scream can I hear? It's mine – and I can't stop it!

CHAPTER 4

THE THREE SISTERS

During the journey Lara's conversation was of Glasha Tuntseva and her sisters, old friends from the time she had last lived in Yuryatin. Though unmarried, Glasha gave the appearance of being everybody's mother. Lara could scarcely mention her without wanting to laugh at some story of the other woman's energy and good humour. 'I almost feel I know her,' said Fraulein Buerli enthusiastically. Lara had written to Glasha before undertaking the journey, but had not waited for a reply since she had been determined to leave Chita in any event.

The train passed through Torfayana, the nearest station to Varykino. It was a country halt, standing in dense birchwood, and the main-line trains did not stop there. Even so, the stationmaster in his battered red-topped cap came on to the platform to salute the train. And then it was gone as were thoughts of Varykino and that frantic escape by night and snow, and before long Katya could see the factories of Yuryatin, the marshalling yard and the red oil tanks and the train was slowing to glide to a stop along the platform.

The platform was crowded with peasant women trying to sell refreshments to those passengers who were continuing to Moscow. The railway officials tried to keep order and were laughed at by a gang of sailors who were joining the train. Behind these and pressing forward were more new passengers who were desperate to get on before all the seats were taken, and finally, forced against the wall by the crowd, a few people waited expectantly for visitors or loved ones. Katya wondered who was waiting for them.

Lara and Fraulein Buerli collected their belongings and the sailors helped them out of the carriage. After the long journey from Chita they might have expected a sense of urgency to find friends and shelter, but instead they felt an animal desire to stretch their limbs and blink in the sharp light, and then smile at each other to say: 'We're here!'

By degrees the platform cleared and their attention focused on a big-hipped, competent-looking woman who was standing near the exit and grinning. She wore her hair in untidy braids and had large shapeless features that looked as if they could be reordered on her face simply by chewing. She examined the arrivals and then stepped forward through a gap in the crowd ignoring a warning from the stationmaster that the non-passengers were not allowed to approach the train, and without a word she extended her arms to grip Lara and absorb her, and only after much hugging and kissing did she speak.

'I got your letter – not that I could understand it except that things hadn't worked out well for you out there. You look terrible.'

That last comment, for all its directness, was true. Katya looked at the two women together and saw how tired and wasted her mother looked.

'I've been ill,' said Lara.

'Well, now you'll get better. And who is *this*!' she said, turning to Katya. 'Katerina Pavlovna, and almost become a woman! You were so *small* when I last saw you. The food can't be so bad in the East if they're growing girls so big

86

and strong. Don't you remember me – Glasha – Auntie Glasha, you used to call me?'

Katya remembered Auntie Glasha, but she had been a child and so Auntie Glasha was someone different. But she looked nice enough, even if with her large gestures and loud voice there seemed somehow too much of her. Katya was more affected by the brightness of the day and the sense of freedom – not just the ending of the cramped uncomfortable journey, but the end of Chita and the nightmare that had followed Tanya's disappearance. She said something polite, but already Glasha Tuntseva was scrutinizing the third member of the party doubtfully.

Lara said: 'May I introduce Fraulein Buerli?'

The little woman added her own introduction in a deferential tone.

'Foreigner, eh?' said Glasha.

'Swiss.'

'Where's that?'

'Fraulein Buerli lived with us at Chita,' said Lara and began to explain her companion's peculiar position until Glasha cut her off and said: 'We can't talk here. There are some funny people hanging about railway stations nowadays. Let's get you to my place and settled in. Are you hungry? Did you tell anyone else you were coming? Have you got a job? We'll need to get you registered and also some ration cards, though things are easier on that score since they stopped robbing the peasants. We get traders in town selling food and all sorts of things – NEPmen we call them – did you have them out east? Here, let me take one of your bags. I'm afraid we'll have to walk.' She picked up the heaviest bag and together they left the station.

Lara quizzed her as they walked.

'Where are you living now?'

'Khokri. Me, Avdotya and Sima, we're sharing a room, still three old maids and likely to stay that way. You'll have to stay with us until we can sort out a place of your own. It'll be a bit cramped, but we'll manage. Housing is very short and there are many in a worse position: you'll remember that the Whites burned a lot of the town and there hasn't been time to rebuild. Also people are beginning to come here for work since the factories started up again. In fact the housing committee nearly stuck a family of five in with us – imagine that, eight of us in the same room with a bucket for the you-know-what – until Samdevyatov put a stop to it. He's still in town by the way, still trying to help people whenever he can.'

'How are your sisters?'

'Much the same, but older and thinner. Avdotya still works at the library and is as shy as always.'

'Is Sima still religious?'

'Worse, if anything. She regards everything that's happened as a visitation of God. But she's got enough sense to keep quiet except among friends. Her big problem is that they've closed all the churches. The priests have vanished – I don't like to think where to. St Tikhon's has been turned into a bakery. The old ladies like to buy their bread there: they think it's blessed somehow. Lord knows how they'll ever get rid of that sort of superstition. I buy my bread there, too, but only because it saves my legs; these days my legs are killing me.'

Katya had forgotten how hilly Yuryatin was. The tired women huffed and puffed up the slopes under their burdens. Lara had to stop frequently for breath and suffered the gentle encouragement of Glasha Tuntseva. Katya took another bag from her mother and in exchange got a look of gratitude.

'And you?' said Lara as they paused. The streets were empty of traffic except for the occasional handcart. The walls were plastered with bills, mostly of regulations referring people to the various administrative offices in October Street. Lara was looking not at Glasha but at the view over the familiar town, and Katya saw that her mother was smiling – the first untrammelled smile that Katya could remember since Tanya had vanished and Lara had been ill and, it

88

seemed at times, likely to die. Lara asked: 'How are you?'

'Me?' answered Glasha as if she did not figure in the scheme of things. 'Oh, apart from the shortages I couldn't be better. There's plenty of work around, so whenever I get bored I change jobs. You know I worked as a seamstress and then as a hairdresser? After that I did a spell as a railway crossing keeper, and for the last couple of years I've been at the postal sorting office. I get to open the letters. Before you say anything – I know it's disgraceful, but if I didn't do it someone else would; and I have to say that it's a lot of fun, keeping up with all the gossip. And I try not to do any harm: I make sure people get the important news. What about you? What are you going to do?'

'I haven't thought about it.' Lara answered falteringly so that Katya moved to her side; but Lara only shrugged her off and murmured that she was tired.

'You could go back to nursing,' Glasha went on. 'The hospital in Buyanovka Street is still in business. Or you could take your old job at the library. What job did you have, Fraulein?'

'I taught Katya,' said Fraulein Buerli.

'Viktor employed Fraulein Buerli as a tutor,' explained Lara.

'Ah. Well, I'd keep quiet about that. "Private tutor" sounds too bourgeois for safety. Stick to "teacher" – there's always a demand for teachers. Do you speak German?'

'Yes.'

'Well that should do. People want to learn German. There's a team of German engineers been brought in to make some machinery work at the old Krueger factory. Apparently we're friendly with Germany again.'

Khokri was the artisan quarter of town, full of small workshops, cobblers, locksmiths, glovemakers. A lot of it had been destroyed when the Whites shelled the town during the second occupation. Katya did not remember the attack, but Lara had told her of the nights spent sheltering under the stairs, the plume of smoke that lasted for days, and the gritty, waxy feel of the air when the tannery burned down. The Tuntseva sisters lived on the top floor of a building with a saddler's workshop facing on to the lane. The only other undamaged structure was a shabby commercial hotel where some broken-down horse-cabs were gathered with their bickering drivers. Glasha opened the door and led everyone inside and up the rickety stairs to the attic room, where her sisters were waiting, the samovar was ready, and on the table soup, *kasha*, rye bread and pickled cucumbers had been prepared.

The welcome was effusive, but Katya did not like it. She was tired of being called a 'big fine girl' and her compliments on her upbringing paid to Lara. They made her think of the little sister; and Katya had decided, when Tanya first disappeared, that she could live with that fact only by never thinking about it. For Katya knew in her heart that she had caused poor Tanya to vanish. She remembered that she had identified her sister as the source of all the misery at Chita and that she had wished, if only for a second, that Tanya were not there – and then she was not. And Katya wondered if that was why she had no father; and why Zhivago and even Komarovsky were gone.

Of Glasha Tuntseva's sisters, Avdotya was the prettiest, but so shy that in the presence of visitors she acted as if she were an unwelcome stranger in her own home. Sima wore spectacles and looked bookish, and her clothes were severe though her manner was open and friendly. Katya gathered from the conversation that there had been a fourth sister who married Mikulitsin, the manager of the Krueger properties and formerly an important man. She had a vague memory of Mikulitsin. He had lived at Varykino and turned a blind eye when Katya, her mother and Zhivago moved into one of the cottages. Katya had been happy then. Before Tanya.

They ate and the women talked. Mostly it was the

sisters who spoke, expressing their pleasure and telling stories of the people they knew and the events that had happened in Yuryatin during the previous five years. Lara was reticent, merely posing questions to prompt the others to continue, and expressing appreciation at points in the narrative. Katya felt their situation, like poor relations come from the backwoods. Yet they had not been poor. She could see now, from the cramped room with its sparse furnishings and the threadbare clothing of the sisters, how well Komarovsky had provided for them at Chita. She wished they would stop. She was tired and dizzy with names. Her mother was tired, too; Katya's young protective eye could see it. She wished they would stop.

And then they did. They had got to the point of repeating things they had said before and apologizing for the error, and after a couple of examples of this there was a sudden silence. They had reached the frightening pause between old friends meeting after a long time when, after a rehearsal of old history, the question comes: what do we really have to talk about? Do we even like each other any more? Fraulein Buerli saved the situation by telling her own story of exile and imprisonment, and, diverted by this, the embarrassment passed. Having heard it before, Katya was left with her thoughts and only then did it occur to her: they haven't asked why we have left Chita and come here. Don't they want to know? Or do they know already? She did not realize that the sisters might regard the subject as too delicate to raise in front of a young girl. She thought that they must know about Tanya and her own terrible secret.

They slept that night together in the same room, all six of them: Avdotya and Sima on a large straw mattress, Fraulein Buerli on an improvised bed under the table, Glasha and Lara under blankets on the floor and Katya on the supposedly comfortable sofa. They undressed together, only the nervous Avdotya seeking to hide herself as she stripped to her shift. Fraulein

91

Buerli's stays caused amusement, but Katya noticed how her teacher tolerantly maintained her dignity. Sima recited an old Orthodox prayer and then the candle was snuffed and they settled in the darkness, comfortable with their animal smells and noises.

In fact, the sofa was worn and lumpy and too narrow for real comfort. However Katya lay, she could not settle. Avdotya snored. Sima scratched. The building creaked of its own accord. Exhausted but restless, Katya's mind struggled in a twilight state. She heard Glasha and her mother talking in the darkness.

'I had another child,' Lara was saying.

No! thought Katya. Don't tell her about Tanya! Don't tell her how I got rid of Tanya! She wanted to sit up and speak out loud, but she found she could not. It occurred to her that she must be asleep. This was another nightmare about Tanya – about how Katya had wished her sister away and the wish had come true.

Then, after a long pause, Glasha replied: 'Did you now? And who was the father?'

'Yuri Andreyevitch.'

'Zhivago? The doctor?'

'Yes. We lived together at Varykino.'

'I know.' In her matter-of-fact voice Glasha added: 'He stayed on a few months after you and then left – or died. Zhivago, I mean. No-one knows where he is now. Why didn't he go when you did? Did you quarrel?'

'No.'

'No, I thought not. He didn't look the type for quarrelling. The milk-and-water sort in my opinion, if you'll forgive me. What's the explanation then?'

'I don't know. Or perhaps I do, but the reasons don't make sense; or not the sort of sense that lends itself to clear explanations. Yura was still attached to his wife, and one day Pasha might have come back to me – and to Katya. Our loving each other was a complication. It might have erased the love we felt for other people but it didn't. It added guilt.'

Katya must have dozed, for the subject changed.

'Why go with Komarovsky?' said Glasha. 'I didn't know him, but Samdevyatov did and thought he was a bad lot. And he should know since he's a lawyer himself.'

'I was his mistress. We became lovers when I was in my final year at high school.'

'That's terrible! I'd have thought you'd want to get away from him, not go back to him.'

Lara said wearily: 'It didn't matter. After Viktor, I could offer men my love but never my integrity.'

'I think that's an old-fashioned view. But then I've never been married.'

'I said integrity, not virginity. It didn't matter that I was Viktor's mistress. What mattered was that I never loved him. I gave myself to him and I never loved him!'

In the darkness, without the play of features to enliven the words, they sounded low and unexpressive. Katya could hear her mother's bitter confession and understood enough to grasp the pain that underlay the words. Yet how dead the words were as murmured sounds in the night. But, of course, Katya was asleep.

'What happened to Tanya then?'

Not that!

I wished her away and she vanished! thought Katya and she prayed that her mother would not reveal her crime, for she was sure that Lara knew. *Don't tell!* she urged her mentally, and scarcely was that thought out than another one took its place, *Forgive me! Forgive me! Forgive me!* The same thought drenching her mind in a cascade and she could hear herself crying.

But she was not crying. The sobs were from elsewhere. Her mother was saying:

'Viktor took her away – he gave her to another couple.'

There was a shocked silence.

'Gave her away? Just like that? Why did he do that? Was he jealous because she was Zhivago's child?'

'He gave her away and I became ill. It was a long illness. I thought I should die or go mad. Through all these last years it has seemed impossible that things could get worse. And then they became worse and the new state of affairs became normal and I would think that it couldn't get still worse. Then it did – and so on and on, everything falling away as if I had no claim on reality because I was too guilty and compromised, and that's how I managed to survive.'

'My poor love,' said Glasha soothingly.

'It doesn't matter,' Lara answered, and it seemed to Katya that her mother was talking not to Glasha but to herself. Katya could not imagine this conversation being conducted in the light of day; it seemed somehow dangerous to expose so much. How curious was the night. It jumbled one's own thoughts and other people's words. How could her mother tell another person about what had happened? Did Glasha have any idea of what it meant, those first days when Lara had raved at Komarovsky as though to kill him; then afterwards the weary months of fever and depression when Lara might be found at any time crying in the kitchen, the meadow or the byre? Could she picture the depths when Lara had fallen into filth and neglect and had fought Fraulein Buerli's attempts to wash her? Katya had seen all this. She had wrestled with her mother to help Fraulein Buerli. She had carried her mother limp and weeping to bed. She had faced at various times as the illness ran its course the indifference, the abuse, the loathing, the self-pity that went with being the survivor, and faced it all in the knowledge that she had cast the spell of hatred that had caused Tanya to go away.

Lara was speaking again:

'Viktor was my mother's lover before he became mine. Perhaps he wanted me because of his sense of possession. Mother – daughter. He was becoming too fond of Katya, though I doubt if he even realized himself where his feelings were leading him.'

'Dear God!' said Glasha in an appalled whisper.

'Katya must never know.'

During the next few days the administrative arrangements of their stay in Yuryatin were sorted out. Katya was placed at school, Lara took her old job at the library and Fraulein Buerli found work as a translator for the German engineers and did some teaching. The main problem was accommodation. The housing committee could offer lodging only at the barracks attached to the Krueger works. These barracks had been built thirty years before to house peasants who had left the land to work at the factory which produced mining machinery; and in their day they had been regarded as a model of their kind. They had escaped damage during the bombardment of the town, but had been abandoned by the workers who had fled to the countryside during the food crisis. The empty buildings were then taken over and used as stables by the various armies. The bunks, the latrines and cooking facilities were more or less destroyed and the soldiers had not cared when the weather broke through into the interior. Since the end of hostilities only the barest of repairs had been done, and the barracks now housed only the most miserable of people.

They returned home in a state of depression. Katya was frightened for herself and her mother. How could they live in the barracks? The mere recollection of the stench of raucous drooling poverty revolted her. The downtrodden women reminded her of her mother during her illness. Lara's recovery was too fragile to expose her to that horror.

Glasha spoke to her sisters when they returned from work. Katya noticed how she dominated them so that they sat like good girls, still wearing their headscarves, though Avdotya had taken off her socks and was easing her feet after a day standing in the library. Sima was picking threads from her clothes; she had a cough from the dusty atmosphere of the textile mill where she worked.

'We went to the barracks,' Glasha told them. 'It's a pigsty.'

There was a silence while each looked at the other.

Then, at last, Sima adjusted her glasses and spoke up reluctantly: 'In that case I suppose we'll all have to live here.'

'Avdotya?'

'I suppose so,' her sister agreed.

'Then it's decided,' Glasha confirmed, and added: 'Though God knows how we'll manage.'

Lara was moved by their generosity, and silently she hugged and kissed each of her friends in turn. Katya was grateful too, but she thought of the tight confines of the room, the mattresses, the furniture, the line that held drying clothes; and wondered how they could all fit. How would they eat? She guessed they would eat at work as much as possible. Bathe? She hated sponging herself at the zinc bowl in front of the others, and Glasha's lusty shamelessness only made her feel worse. Wash their hair? It was one thing, at this time of year, to use the trough in the saddler's yard, and another to face the prospect of winter, with hair thick and greasy, waiting for a chance of hot water or queuing at the public baths. Still it would all have to be managed.

One day during this period of settling in, Samdevyatov called. Katya learned afterwards that he was a lawyer who had been helpful in various ways when Zhivago and her mother had lived together at Varykino. For now she opened the door to a stately-looking man with greying curls and a moustache and goatee, who was well dressed by the standard of the times in a salt-and-pepper woollen suit, as if the owner of a small country estate. His manner was good-tempered but businesslike and he invited himself in a friendly fashion. Apart from Katya only her mother and Glasha were at home.

Accepting the offer of a glass of tea the visitor began: 'I've various forms for you to sign, Larissa Fyodorovna, to regularize your stay here. But that's all by the by: my real purpose was to check that everything was well with you. Is this your daughter Katya?' Katya was asked to say hello to Anfim Yefimovitch. 'She looks a fine girl and does you credit. The last time I saw you, you were living under difficult circumstances.'

'I never had the chance to thank you properly.'

'It doesn't matter,' Samdevyatov said modestly. He drank his tea and was embarrassed at being thanked. Wiping his moustache, he resumed: 'You left Yuryatin rather suddenly, probably wisely in the circumstances. I heard you went with that Moscow lawyer . . .'

'Komarovsky.'

'Komarovsky,' he repeated and seemed disconcerted at possessing the name. Katya had an idea – for which there was no obvious support – that he nursed an unrequited longing for her mother. But this did not disturb her since, despite his somewhat reserved manner, he was clearly inoffensive. He said: 'I gather that you're not still with him.'

'No.'

'Hmm. That may be for the best. People like Komarovsky are opportunists. They have their uses – no doubt he calls himself a Communist nowadays – but they don't fool anybody. One day his past will catch up with him.'

'Probably,' agreed Lara.

Katya could see that the brevity of Lara's replies made Samdevyatov uncomfortable. He was not a naturally sociable man and was uncertain what to say next. So by way of reaction to mentioning Komarovsky, and thinking that another name might be more acceptable he said: 'Myself I prefer honest characters like Zhivago. At least he had integrity and didn't pretend to be what he wasn't. No-one could take him for a Communist.' He stopped short, recognizing yet another mistake, and retreated with: 'Or take an unredeemed White like Galiullin —'

'Who is Galiullin?' Katya interrupted. She did not want to be excluded from the conversation and was tired of being called yet again a 'fine girl'.

Samdevyatov was relieved at any interested response. 'Galiullin was a White general. He used to be a friend of your father a long time ago, before the war and the

Revolution. He was commander of the army here during the civil war.'

'What happened to him?' Lara asked.

'Who knows? He fled when the Whites retreated and disappeared somewhere in the East. I never heard that he was arrested. Did you know him?'

'Not well. But I thought he was a decent man. He tried to control the atrocities when the Whites were here.'

'I agree. Not everything was his fault. Most of his troops were Czechs and they only answered to their own commanders; they wouldn't take orders from a Russian.' Pedantically he added: 'Technically, of course, he wasn't a Russian – his father was a Muslim of some sort from the South – but that sort of distinction would have been meaningless to the Czechs.'

'I imagine it would.'

'Most certainly.'

He was over-polite, Katya thought; and this made him sound insincere, which she was sure he was not. She still associated virtue with a fine voice and manner, which made it difficult to grasp that this was the Samdevyatov whom Glasha and her sisters had praised for the help he gave to people. In the exchange of small talk she caught her mother saying:

'Do you know why we left?'

The visitor was cautious to admit that he did. He said: 'I suspect that Zhivago was too free with his opinions.'

'Yes, that was partly the problem.'

'There was something else?'

'My father-in-law. He resented the fact that I was living with Yura when Pasha might still have been alive. The fact that Yura wasn't a Communist only made things worse. I'm not upset by that – I can understand how he would see the matter. But it was a hard judgement that he made. If we had all been in control of ourselves then things wouldn't have happened as they did. But that is how things happened and there's no helping it.'

Samdevyatov nodded sympathetically and asked: 'Are

you worried that old Antipov may still be angry? I don't think you need to be. These days he's not so important with the local soviet. Have you heard about the New Economic Policy? You can certainly see it in action in the town. The peasants have started bringing produce to sell on the free market and every day we get traders arriving to buy and sell things.'

'You call them NEPmen – yes, I've heard.'

'Yes – well, that was old Antipov's problem. He said that it spelled the downfall of Communism and the restoration of capitalism. However, since it's official government policy, he's been forced to keep his mouth shut. And there are other things that have knocked the spirit out of him.'

'What are they?'

The visitor fell silent. He looked at Glasha Tuntseva and then sadly at Katya, who recognized angrily that he was hiding another grown-up secret.

'You can speak in front of Katya,' Lara said. Katya was taken by surprise at this admission that she was growing up. Then she thought of the night when Glasha and her mother had talked of secrets in their whispering voices. Adults were inconsistent.

'Frankly,' said Samdevyatov, 'the old man was shaken when his son died.' He waited for a reaction, but for a long time Lara seemed only to stare blankly. Then she said:

'Are you sure he's dead?'

'Haven't you talked about this?' Samdevyatov asked Glasha. She looked ashamed and shook her head.

'I'm sorry,' he said, 'but if your husband and Strelnikov were the same man, then he is dead.'

'I see,' Lara murmured and her eyes drifted off her visitor and had the distant look that Katya feared from the time of Lara's illness. 'Of course I always suspected that was the case. Viktor – Komarovsky – wanted me to believe that Pasha was dead. But Viktor wasn't to be trusted. How can you be so sure?'

'The body was found.'

'Ah – what happened?'

Samdevyatov moved uncomfortably. He had difficulty dealing with emotions and for a second looked annoyed, but then he explained: 'Apparently Strelnikov was arrested in Siberia; there were a lot of arrests of non-Party officers after the war was over. Anyway, it seems he escaped from gaol and somehow made his way back here. He went to Varykino and saw Zhivago.'

'He saw Yura?' Lara exclaimed. 'How can you know that?'

'There really isn't any doubt. Someone buried Strelnikov's body at Varykino. Zhivago was the only other person there – other than Glasha's brother-in-law, Mikulitsin, who didn't know Strelnikov. The only mystery is what happened between them.'

'What do you think?'

Samdevyatov hesitated. Katya could see that he was cautious of saying anything that would hurt her mother. He was a sentimental man, she suspected; and she felt somehow stronger than him because she had had to face her mother's mental collapse after the disappearance of Tanya, while he studiously avoided any real closeness. She failed to recognize her own piece of evasion. The visitor had said that her father was dead. And she had felt nothing.

'There are two opinions,' Samdevyatov began in a voice that was slightly off key with nerves. 'One is that they quarrelled and that Zhivago killed your husband. The other is that Strelnikov knew his situation was hopeless and that, once he was satisfied that you and Katya were safe, he shot himself. I prefer to think that the second version is true. I don't know which gives you the most comfort. I'm sorry to have to tell you this.'

As if he were frightened of Lara's reaction, Samdevyatov excluded it by continuing to praise Strelnikov and talk about Zhivago and such information as there was about him. Listening to him Katya still felt no space for grief. She registered that her father was dead, but the visitor was not going to allow that fact to intrude until he had beaten a retreat, covering it with words.

That evening Katya discovered how small the room was. It contained no space to cry. The space was crowded with other sounds and emotions. Avdotya saying coyly to Lara: 'I think he's sweet on you.' Glasha feeling bad-tempered and guilty at not having told Lara of her husband's fate. Sima, with the bad taste that sometimes afflicts the religious, murmuring prayers to herself that everyone knew were for the souls of the dead. Katya shouted: 'I'm going out!' and before anyone could answer she had left, though without any idea of where she was going.

She went into the shop of Sergei Mikhailovitch. The saddler was still working and spared her no more than a glance. Katya stood against the doorpost at the entrance to the yard and struggled with the turmoil of her feelings. Her father was dead. What did it mean? The man who wrote love letters from Galicia was dead. Do I really remember him? I must – everyone remembers their father. I ought to be crying for him. Is that a tear?

Katya wrestled at once with the frustration of memory, her guilt and the burning integrity that could not allow her to mourn for a mere shadow. She had lost her father. But more than that, she had lost even the memory of her father, suffered a bereavement that in its totality was beyond even death. And she suffered as an animal suffers, that knows its loss but cannot find words to express it so that it can be comprehended. No tears – no understanding – frustration – guilt – loss upon loss – no tears – upon loss – no tears – loss – tears.

'The air in here doesn't half make the eyes sting, doesn't it, love?' said the saddler cheerily.

CHAPTER 5

THE TRAMP

That summer they went several times to Varykino. They took the train to Torfayana and walked through the wood and picked posies of yellow celandines which grew in the damp places.

The Krueger estate was being cultivated in a ragged fashion and this had allowed the goosefoot and willow-herb to creep into the fields, but the feeling was not one of decay, rather that nature had rounded off the sharp edges of man's handiwork and established a mutual harmony. Mikulitsin, the former manager, was still living in one of the houses, though, being an engineer, he was often in town working with the Germans. Samdevyatov had cautioned them that Mikulitsin was not in official favour. Firstly, he had been a plant-manager, which was doubtful enough in itself; and, secondly, his politics – he was a Social Revolutionary – while they might have been acceptable a few years before, were now a drawback. He was protected because his son Liberius had been a leader of a band of Red partisans. Glasha Tuntseva also thought that Samdevyatov himself had a hand in the matter: during the previous year there had been a sweep of arrests of leading SRs which Mikulitsin had escaped – though Samdevyatov never suggested that he had helped.

'So you're back!' said Mikulitsin in his sharp manner, which disguised his kindly nature. 'I knew you would be; these last few years have seen people coming and going like the tide. Is this your daughter? She looks a big fine girl. Well, what brings you here?'

'I wanted to remember things,' said Lara.

'I can't think why. Times were hard.'

'Yes, they were hard,' Lara admitted. 'But they would have been harder without the help of friends. I couldn't come back to live in Yuryatin without thanking you for your part. When Katya and I left, it was so sudden . . .'

'There's no need to thank me,' Mikulitsin said curtly. 'I don't know that I did all that much.' To divert any reply he asked: 'What do you propose to do today?'

'Go for a walk.'

'You've got plenty of choice. Nothing much is being done in the way of work; you won't be walking across crops.' He glanced to the house where his wife was watching from the verandah. She had not come to welcome the visitors, and that struck Katya as strange.

Mikulitsin announced that he had things to attend to, but relented from dismissing them altogether by suggesting that later that afternoon they might care to call at the house, by which time his wife would have tidied and prepared some refreshment. With that they were left to wander, which they did without any particular direction.

They had not gone very far when Glasha drew attention to the behaviour of her former brother-in-law's wife. 'Did you see her? Standing on the porch she was, as snooty as they come.'

'You shouldn't say things like that,' said Sima. 'It's un-Christian to impute motives to people when you haven't even spoken to them and don't have all the facts.'

'Excuse me for breathing!' retorted Glasha, somewhat

put out. 'What do you think?' she asked Lara.

'If Avercius Stepanovitch really has been in difficulties with the authorities, then they must all be nervous of visitors. My being here won't have helped. When Yura and I lived at Varykino we didn't have official permission. That may have been part of his trouble.'

'Well, I think that he's always been sour-faced, and that wife of his is a bit weak in the head,' was Glasha's conclusion, but she stated it mildly and clearly did not want to quarrel.

They found a spot to picnic and a mare with a foal, which Katya fed with handfuls of grass. For a while they sat and took in the stillness and sunshine and the dreamy contentment that can bring. Lara broke the silence.

She asked: 'Do you know where Pasha is buried?'

Standing as she was a little way off, the words, directed at Glasha, seemed remote to Katya, and she continued to tease the nibbling lips of the foal as the sense of the question bore on her; and then she felt a shudder. The question brought back that night of confusion when she had heard of her father's death and taken refuge in the saddler's shop. The conflict of memory and feeling remained unresolved except by forgetting. Katya prayed for silence.

Glasha appeared not to have heard. Avdotya, who had spoken scarcely a word all day, now began to cough her asthmatic cough, and hurriedly Sima volunteered to get some water and for a few moments they made a fuss of Avdotya. Only later did Glasha say thoughtfully: 'I don't know where Pasha's buried. We only heard rumours about the business because Strelnikov was famous. The authorities kept the story very quiet. Perhaps Mikulitsin knows.'

Mikulitsin did know. Lara asked him when they returned to the house. He said rudely that he did not want to have anything to do with the matter, but all the same he showed them. He took them to a gully called Shutma. The steep sides were covered in gorse and spindly birches.

At the bottom was a stream with flat marshy sides and a covering of aspens.

'Here,' he said pointing vaguely. 'I can't swear to the exact spot, but it was here more or less.'

'Who found the body?'

'I did. Zhivago buried him. I came across the grave when I was down here shooting wolves. You couldn't mistake it. He'd made a cross out of branches and it was sticking out of the mound.'

'Is Pasha still here?'

'No. As soon as I told the authorities they moved him. His father was furious about the cross; he broke it up and cursed Zhivago. But, if it's any consolation, I think the old man was in a position to see to a decent funeral – though naturally no-one knows where it was.'

As he told the story Mikulitsin softened. He put his pipe away and no longer talked between his teeth in his usual fashion. He glanced at Katya, saying nothing but with a deep understanding in his eyes.

Katya wanted to say, 'Well, that's it, now we know!' And that would be the end, and she could return to forgetting. Why did people have to go on about these things – about death, and all the suffering, horrible things that went on? She could hear her mother asking him:

'What do you think happened?'

'I don't know,' Mikulitsin answered seriously. He recognized that the answer was not enough, and Katya saw, with a feeling of wonderment, that death was no easier a matter for adults. He said: 'I'm fairly certain that Strelnikov shot himself. There was a bullet wound in the head just where you'd expect if he had. And Yuri Andreyevitch wasn't the type to go around murdering people. But I can't say whether they quarrelled or were friends.'

After a pause Lara said: 'I think they respected each other.'

'Yes – well, you would know, not me. I could only

judge from the business of the cross. I don't think that Zhivago would have put up the cross if he and Strelnikov had quarrelled.'

They stayed in the gully for a while until Katya became bored with it and annoyed by the swarms of midges that clouded the stream. She felt guilty about being bored; thinking that she must be wicked and have no feelings. Her eyes drifted to the top of the slope and there, along the rim of stunted thorns, she saw a face peering down at them intently.

At this distance she could make out only that it was a man and that he was wearing a rabbit-skin cap. He was definitely watching them and trying to hide himself, lying belly down and shielding his eyes from the sun. Catching sight of her he leapt to his feet. He was wearing rags and seemed scarcely to have a shape; and no sooner was he on his feet than he had vanished. Katya said nothing. She realized that the others had not seen him.

They returned to Mikulitsin's house. His wife, Helen, offered them tea and a plate of pickled mushrooms, and they sat in the shade where the flies were less irksome. A boy of five or six came out of the house and took his place on his mother's lap. She began to quiz him: 'How do you spell "pear"?'

'At least they haven't taken the good weather away,' said Mikulitsin. He was staring beyond them at the growing corn and the potato beds.

'What was the date of birth of Catherine the Great?' said his wife gaily to Katya.

Idiot! thought Katya. You'd think she was younger than me. She volunteered to take the boy and play hide and seek with him. He was eager to take up the offer and together they scampered off across the field.

'Do you want to hide?' Katya asked.

'Yes, please!' said the boy. Katya closed her eyes and counted to a hundred, and when she opened them found that she was alone among the green corn and the house not even visible. The air smelled of earth, a lark was trilling and the insects hummed and creaked. For a few minutes Katya searched for the boy and then simply wandered, enjoying the day. She took her shoes off and walked barefoot.

In this manner she stumbled on the tramp again. He was sitting at the edge of a small spinney, he had removed his rabbit-skin cap and bast shoes and was picking at the skin between his toes with little grunts of satisfaction. If he noticed Katya he paid her no attention. She sat down a little way off and examined him, a small-made man with a weather-beaten face and a slope about his eyes that suggested a Tatar ancestor. He continued to clean his feet and when he was finished, reapplied his cloth foot-bindings and shoes, took up his bag of belongings and ambled into the trees with a curt nod in the girl's direction. Katya had no time to consider him further. Mikulitsin's son was calling.

'I win!' he said.

Katya did not care. 'All right,' she agreed.

'Again!' proposed the boy.

'No – I'm tired,' Katya told him.

He was not too concerned. 'Look what I've got.' It was a broken egg-shell.

Katya said that it was lovely and then added: 'Did you know that there's a tramp living in your wood?' The boy was indifferent to this.

'It's only Yusupka,' he answered. 'He's always here. He used to be General Galiullin when he was famous.'

After the long day in the sunshine and the walk back to the station, they were all tired as they returned to Yuryatin. Avdotya, in particular, was exhausted after her attack of asthma and the others made a fuss of her. For the rest, they forgot about hardships and talked lovingly of the heat and smiled fat lazy smiles as people do when they are tired and have enjoyed themselves. This was true even of Lara, who seemed to derive contentment rather than sadness from seeing her husband's grave. They gossiped not too maliciously about Mikulitsin's wife.

'She's getting too old to keep up that girly act,' said Glasha. 'It makes her look ridiculous.'

Sima made a comment that Helen reminded her of the old Russian pilgrim-beggars, the Fools of God, whose childishness and innocence had been a feature of rural life; but Glasha was not convinced that Mikulitsin's wife was so innocent.

'It's an affectation or she's a genuine fool.' Glasha compared her with her own dead sister, who had been Mikulitsin's first wife. 'I don't think that Avercius Stepanovitch was as bad-tempered then, but he has to appear hard in order to keep Helen in line. They're a mismatch. I wonder sometimes if he confuses her with a daughter. That would make sense.'

No-one took up the point and they all closed their eyes and dreamed. That is, except for Katya, for whom the day had been confusing: first with the sight of her father's grave and then with her newfound knowledge of the tramp.

Walking back from the station, struggling up the hills, Katya said to her mother: 'I saw a tramp in Mikulitsin's wood. He's called Yusupka, but he used to be General Galiullin.'

'Don't talk silly,' Lara reproved her cheerfully. Katya decided that her mother did not want to listen and she was annoyed. She had an idea that it was important: Samdeyatov had talked about Galiullin. He's like my father, she thought. She had heard enough of his history to know that they were both outcasts.

A few days later, when she was helping her mother to wash clothes at the trough in the saddler's yard, she mentioned the matter again. Lara laughed and asked: 'Who told you that?'

'Sasha Mikulitsin.'

'He's only a little boy. He probably thinks that the tramp and General Galiullin are both bogeymen.'

'But I've seen him myself.'

'Oh, yes? And what does he look like?'

'He's old and he has slanted eyes like a Tatar.'

Lara did not respond to this, but her manner became cold and she attacked the washing.

For another week nothing more was said; then, one evening, when Avdotya and Sima were both out, Lara informed Glasha:

'Galiullin is alive. Katya saw him at Varykino.'

Glasha put down the sheet she was mending and answered: 'I know.'

'But how is it possible?'

Glasha shrugged. 'He came back about a year ago.'

'Who knows he's here?'

'Mikulitsin.'

'And Samdevyatov?'

'Probably. You can never tell what Anfim Yefimovitch knows or who he's helping. Let's say it wouldn't surprise me.'

'But Galiullin was a White!'

'You heard Anfim Yefimovitch talk about him. He thinks that Galiullin is mistaken, but he doesn't bear any hatred.'

'Is that everyone's opinion?'

'I shouldn't think so. Most of the time it's difficult to like even our friends. There's no policy of forgive-and-forget – or not that I've heard of. But Anfim Yefimovitch is a special sort of person. Mind you, I'm not saying that he does know about Galiullin. Only that it wouldn't surprise me. You saw Galiullin when he was in command here during the civil war. He seemed a decent enough man, even if he was on the wrong side.'

Glasha turned to Katya and said: 'You mustn't tell anyone else about this. It would be very dangerous.'

Katya asked: 'Are we friends with Galiullin?'

Glasha looked to Lara.

'I don't know,' Lara answered quietly.

'Are you his friend, Auntie Glasha?'

'It's none of my business, my love. I keep quiet

because of Mikulitsin, since he's a sort of relative. Galiullin is nothing to me, but it's none of my job to go around blaming other people. I suggest you forget about him.'

In fact it was not possible to forget about Galiullin. They saw Samdevyatov from time to time as he kept a sentimental eye on their well-being. On such occasions, the unstated question seemed to hang in the air: did he know? If he did, then he was too cautious to give any indication, though the direction of his thinking was clear enough from a story he told.

He suggested one day that they all go to Spirka's Dell. It was a place where people used to go walking on the fine summer's days that always existed 'a few years ago'. Important families like the Kruegers had villas there.

The day was beautiful; the trees were now in full leaf and the pale greens of spring had turned to the dark canopy of summer; the air hummed with insects. They walked in the dell and peered through the fences of the villas, and told stories of the families that had once lived there. Some of the villas had been taken over as recreation homes; others now housed several poor families; and one or two had fallen into ruin, with holes in the roofs and collapsed verandahs, and the melancholy debris of white garden furniture that suggested the interruption of a tea-party or one of those literary luncheons when people amused themselves by reading poetry aloud or the latest St Petersburg play.

Samdevyatov was affected by the mood of these decaying houses. He swung on a garden gate, staring at the unkempt grass and the parterres that were given over to dock and groundsel, as if he could step through the gate and into the past.

'I don't hate them,' he said, 'the people who owned these places. They weren't personally evil, no more than anyone else. They just found themselves on the wrong side of history. Think: if we'd been in possession of all this, would we have been willing to give it up? The temptation would have been too much! And in any case, our desire isn't to destroy the grace and elegance of these places. Our complaint is that it was all owned by a few and not by everyone.'

Katya was not touched in the same way since she had not known how things had once been. But it seemed odd to her to say that the intention was not to destroy, since clearly something had been destroyed.

They walked on along a country path. In a lazy thoughtful way, Samdevyatov juggled stones or took leisurely pot-shots at the trees. He said: 'A few years ago I was travelling on a train to Moscow. In the same carriage was a peasant called Susanin. He was going to see a lawyer and was all got up in his best clothes and polished boots and, when he discovered I was a lawyer, he pumped me for information in the way that strangers do of professional men – probably he was debating whether he could save the cost of his lawyer's fee. At all events we got on to talking about more general matters.

'He was nervous of the train. He told me it was the first time he'd travelled by train since the coronation of Nicholas Romanov in 1894. I said I was surprised he'd bothered for such an event. Ah, he said, but he hadn't gone to watch the coronation with the masses in the street; he'd actually been a participant, there in the Cathedral of the Assumption with the Tsar and the Tsarina, the grand dukes and duchesses and all the other noble ragtag and bobtail! He'd been there, standing in the congregation along with all his relatives, who were also peasants and more or less as poor as he was.

'Naturally I didn't believe him. After all, why should he be there? Well – he told me – it was because his ancestor had saved the life of one of the Tsar's ancestors; and, simply because of this, all the man's descendants were entitled to attend the coronation of the tsars.

'You can imagine that I was puzzled. What sort of

attitude would such a man have? I asked him, and he made no bones about it. He was a revolutionary. He hated the nobles and the landlords, the Jews and the money-lenders; and it wouldn't be too soon if the whole crew were shot. And the Tsar? Well, that was different. Because of the past, he owed a personal loyalty to the Romanovs, and he wouldn't have anything to do with any movement aimed at their overthrow.'

Samdevyatov studied the effect of his story and laughed. 'What can you make of such people? What did he do when the Revolution came? With those opinions he could have fought for the Reds, but it's just as likely that he sided with the Whites. So what are we to do with him? His heart's in the right place. Are we to shoot him because his political opinions are so naive and confused?'

Two days later the evening was broken by a thunderstorm and a sharp downpour of rain. The women were confined to the room. It was impossible to dry anything and clothes were hung everywhere. Fraulein Buerli was chopping sticks for the stove, which she had got from a foraging trip by the railway line. Sima and Avdotya were playing cards, Lara was patching a skirt, and Katya reading. Naked and standing in the zinc bowl, Glasha was washing herself down, straddling bow-legged as she sponged her crutch, while the others protected her modesty by affecting not to notice her (as if Glasha cared), though Katya could not help seeing her pendulous breasts, all blue-veined, and the hair on her legs, which was quite thick.

'Who wants the water after me?' Glasha asked. 'It's your turn, isn't it, Lotte?'

Fraulein Buerli nodded.

'God, but this place stinks!' Glasha went on.

Avdotya raised her eyes to ask quietly, 'Stinks? What of?'

'Meat.'

'We haven't had meat since last week. It must be from downstairs – all that leather.'

'Not leather! *Our* meat – you know, *us* – women's smells!'

They all sniffed this time. Katya found it embarrassing; but Glasha was only amused. Taking off her spectacles, as if it were a serious subject, Sima said stuffily: 'It's not as bad as the time you made soap.'

'That's true,' said Glasha. 'Which reminds me, we need some more. I'll have a word with Sergei Mikhailovitch; he can let us have some tallow. But you'd all better stay away when I boil it up!'

At this point Glasha burst out laughing and because of the noise they almost missed the knock at the door.

Katya answered to a bedraggled stranger, a crabbed old man in a railwayman's cap and wet clothes, who demanded abruptly to see Larissa Fyodorova Antipova and without waiting stepped into the room and proceeded to beat the rain from his clothes while Glasha leapt out of the zinc bowl, and, grabbing some clothes, retired out of sight behind the washing.

The newcomer immediately identified Lara and addressed her loudly: 'So you're back!'

His voice was explosive amid the stillness of low voices and the soft smack of cards on the table, as if he expected a violent reaction; and Katya, taking in his mood though not knowing what caused it, since the visitor had not identified himself, felt a shudder of surprise when her mother merely looked up and said calmly: 'Good evening, Pavel Ferapontovitch,' and to Katya, 'Say hello, Katya. This is your grandfather.'

Katya was stunned. Again she was surprised without notice by the complexity of life: unable to consider how she felt about the sudden stranger. Old Antipov was disconcerted. He glanced sharply at Katya, as if her presence were unwelcome, then looked at Lara but found his eyes returning to his granddaughter so that the two scrutinized each other. Katya was too inexperienced to read character from his face and registered only that he was wrinkled and, to her eyes, very old; but it took no experience to recognize his anger and frustration: the tight carriage of his body and the flicker of small grimaces and gestures like sparks from a fire told her this. But their reception gave his anger nothing to bite on, and, from a man who looked as though he wanted to break things, Antipov changed to someone who merely grunted, screwed up his cap and asked if he might have a seat. Sima, with a look of saintly forbearance, broke off her game of cards and offered hers, which he took without regard for where she might sit.

'So,' he began with a long exhalation of breath. 'How long have you been here?'

'Two months,' answered Lara. 'I thought you would know.'

'Of course I know! What does that matter? I don't know because of anything you told me. You've been hiding away. Frightened, I suppose. And what's brought you back? Has your lover thrown you out?'

It was a cruel observation and Katya was repelled by its crudity, but Lara ignored the barb. It missed its force in the old man's petty tone. She said:

'I thought you wouldn't wish to see me.'

'I don't!'

'But you're here.'

'I . . .!' the old man exclaimed; but, defeated by his own logic, he did not finish. Instead he said sorrowfully: 'I thought you'd be too ashamed to come back. After living like a whore with Zhivago and then taking off with that lawyer.'

'I didn't live like a whore,' Lara told him. Her eyes were fixed on her father-in-law and then slipped from the carapace of his resentment and focused somewhere in the air. 'It was different,' she said. 'Pasha would have understood.'

Katya did not know the meaning of 'whore', but she saw Avdotya blush and Fraulein Buerli bite her lip. Then her grandfather was speaking again.

'So you're not a whore? What have you done then, revolutionized morality?'

'No. But what I did may claim some understanding and forgiveness.'

'From me? From the father of the man you wronged?'

'If necessary.' Lara looked away. Katya saw the pain on her mother's face and her own must have shared it for Glasha intervened crossly from behind the washing:

'Watch your language, Pavel Ferapontovitch! Have some consideration for the child.'

'I should think that the child already knows too much for her own good from witnessing the carryings-on of her mother,' Antipov retorted, and then rebuked her: 'Mind your own business!

'Well?' he asked Lara.

There was a pause while Glasha struggled with a mixture of dumbfoundedness and contempt. Then Lara said quietly: 'He deserted me.' She spoke so softly that the old man asked her to repeat her remark.

'What's that? Come on – if you've got a story let's all hear it!'

And again Lara said: 'He deserted me.' Still the words were soft; and yet they came out as acute as a cry, as though the utterance were the lifting of a thin tissue of skin that bared a nerve. But Antipov was deaf to any pain that competed with his own.

'What did you expect? He was a soldier: first against the Austrians, and then fighting Galiullin and his White scum. How could he be with you?'

'When he was in Yuryatin he didn't come to see me, not once. Perhaps that doesn't matter. But he didn't visit Katya – not his own daughter!'

'He probably didn't want to upset her,' Antipov replied feebly.

'I'm not complaining.'

'No?'

Lara shook her head. She wanted to explain but

felt defeated as always by the explanation, the sense that language and thought itself were a descant to the reality they tried to grasp. She tried: 'Pasha was living at an elevated level. He was single-minded, inspired. But everyone can't be like that. Can't you forgive me for living at the level of ordinary existence?'

Antipov growled to himself, then looked up and his face was calmer, but it was a face from which anger had been robbed not appeased; and his frustration was greater not less. He sighed and groaned and stood up and sat down and finally said:

'I'm not here to make life hard for you. Don't look to me for forgiveness; but on the other hand I won't hurt you. There's the child to think of. She's blameless. She can come to see me sometimes.' He wrung his cap and fiddled in his pockets as if looking for words; then finding little he said abruptly: 'I'm going.' And equally abruptly he went, leaving behind him the women sitting silently in the darkening room, and beyond the window the summer storm, the dark empurpled sky and the roofs of the town washed yellow by the low sun.

Glasha spoke first. 'Silly old sod,' she said. 'How can a man expect to hang on to his wife if he never comes to see her?'

During the rest of that summer Katya saw her grandfather several times. She was taken by Fraulein Buerli to the shabby house where he lived. The first time he was surprised, his manner was surly and he treated her as an intruder, and she felt like one, something unwanted that appeared as a complication in the life of adults. This idea was tied to her confused attempts to understand what had happened to Tanya. By degrees she had grasped that the flash of hatred, which she had at first thought of as the magic spell that had caused her sister to disappear, was not something unique to her. She had the strange suspicion that it was part of adult make-up to hate their children as much as they loved them.

On the second occasion, old Antipov had prepared tea and some food and laid out photographs. He told her about his past in the strike of the Moscow-Brest Litovsk line in 1905, the war and the Revolution, and about the fighting afterwards against Galiullin and the Whites. Katya thought: he doesn't know I've met Galiullin! But she didn't tell him of the tramp since she knew it was a dangerous secret. Instead she noticed that he never posed her any questions about herself; and she supposed that was because to do so would reopen the closed subject of her mother, Zhivago and Komarovsky. So he preferred to lay down his resentments quietly and cement each one in place.

She went again to Varykino with her mother. The summer was nearly over, the grain ripe and the air filled with white down from the willowherb. Lara carried a basket but did not say what was in it. She avoided Mikulitsin's house.

As they walked among the fields and the outlying spinneys of birch Lara asked: 'Where did you meet the tramp?'

'I saw him near the valley where Father was buried.' It seemed strange to talk of her father: the subject had always before been subtly excluded and only now did Katya realize that the exclusion had not been natural but a device to avoid explaining the inexplicable. The realization made her feel grown up; she might not understand the currents of emotion that flowed between adults, but she knew now that they existed and she was alert to them and that they might lead to unknown shores. In fact her image of adults had changed. Before, they had been visible like the surface of a picture: good or bad, they were complete, evident and stable. Now she could see that they were as if half-hidden in shadow – dynamic but obscure even to themselves.

Lara did not take up the subject of Katya's father. Instead she directed her steps towards the valley, but the tramp was not there and all they could do was gaze down the slope towards the little stream and remember that Strelnikov had been buried there.

They picnicked a while. Lara broke open the basket and they each ate a piece of bread. The wind stirred the trees at the crest of the vale. A hare cut a rippling path through a field of rye. Beyond the valley, from the wood, a thin white plume of smoke rose and was scattered by the breeze. 'Shall we walk there?' Lara invited. And that was how they found Galiullin.

The tramp was sitting at a brushwood fire, gutting and jointing a rabbit and cooking a small piece on a skewer over the flame. As they approached, he broke off this activity and rose to his feet, threatening them with a bayonet. His appearance was ragged; despite the heat he was wearing a kaftan covered by an army greatcoat and his feet were swathed in filthy cloths. His Tatar ancestry showed in his eyes and the sparseness of his unkempt beard. He recognized Katya and said sourly: 'I know you. But who's that with you?'

'Have I changed so much? We knew each other years ago when I was little more than a girl . . . I was Pasha Antipov's wife. Katya is his daughter.'

Lara placed the basket on the ground. He did not react to the suggestion of an old friendship. It was, Lara suspected, immaterial to his animal – or perhaps spiritual – existence. 'Here – I've brought food for you.' She stood back and let him approach the basket with the crafty sniffing of a street-dog.

Galiullin removed the cloth cover and rummaged among the contents. 'Thanks,' he said briefly, and put away the bayonet by tucking it in his belt. He picked up the basket and returned to cooking his rabbit.

They remained like this, with a space the height of a birch tree between them. Lara squatted on the ground which was covered by an early fall of leaves; she beckoned Katya to sit with her. Galiullin ignored them, busied himself with turning the skewer and licking the juices from his fingers, stopping occasionally to check the treasures of the basket until he was satisfied and had brought them into his reality. Only then did he ask:

'What do you want?'

'To talk,' said Lara.

'About what?'

'About you – about Pasha.'

Galiullin laughed drily, as if spitting chips of wood.

'I am an Enemy of the People,' he said, 'a walking dead man.'

'Pasha became an Enemy of the People.'

'So I heard. I'm not surprised. Look –' Galiullin left off his cooking and gazed at Lara in a manner that might have been sorrowful except that Katya could not interpret the strangeness of his slanting eyes '– I got back here after Pasha was dead. If you want to know why he killed himself, or whether he had any last words for you, then I can't help, I don't know, I wasn't there. It's a shame he missed seeing his daughter, she's a big fine girl.' He paused, then said: 'I'm sorry he's dead. We found ourselves on opposite sides, but there was nothing personal. Now I remember, didn't I see you in Yuryatin when we occupied the town?'

'Yes.'

'I remember – I remember. It was Strelnikov who drove me out. He was a clever man. But there was nothing personal. Thanks for the food.'

'How will you get through the winter?' Lara asked.

'Maybe I won't. It was hard last year. I'd been down with typhus and still wasn't right. I thought I was finished.'

'Who helped you? Mikulitsin?'

Galiullin smiled. 'He doesn't recognize that I'm here; I'm invisible to him; he's never spoken a word. His kids put out stuff for me: food, a bit of bedding, this coat. I turn up at night and take it while they're all asleep. The kids must think I'm like someone out of a fairy story.'

'What about Samdevyatov?'

'I've never heard of him,' the man said neutrally.

'How long can you go on like this?'

'Not long, I imagine. But what does it matter?'

He turned again to his cooking, waving away the flies that buzzed around the small pile of rabbit guts. Watching him, Katya was taken by the image of him creeping in the starlight around the Mikulitsins' house like a nature spirit, murmuring blessings and enchantments before carrying away the offerings to his magic grove in the forest. She thought of those spirits and ghosts who were spellbound to a particular location and over time and change became thinned and finally disappeared. She believed him when he said that he could not continue for long.

Tentatively Lara began discussing the civil war. Katya recalled that Galiullin had held the rank of general in the White army, which she had imagined to be a gentlemanly thing; but Galiullin spoke not like a gentleman, not like Komarovsky, but in the folksy Russian of Sergei Mikhailovitch, the saddler who lived below their flat. Then she wondered why her mother wanted to go over this ancient history. But of course the answer had to be her father. 'He never came to us at Yuryatin. He was there fighting Galiullin but he never came to see us.' The thought would have upset her but for the fact that her father was so remote from her: more remote than the tramp who was not even a relative.

'You were a railwayman's son too,' said Lara. 'Why did you fight for the Whites?'

'Because I found myself on their side of the lines,' Galiullin said quite simply. 'I wasn't alone. It was the same for both sides – maybe for most of the soldiers. You were in the army because you were in the army. I didn't believe in all that God-and-tsar stuff that the Whites spouted, but I didn't believe in Communism either, still don't. Let me tell you what made me realize it was all rubbish. I used to work on the railway. I was just a spotty kid. I had this foreman. Now this foreman was a proletarian if ever there was one – an SR, a Menshevik, something or other, it doesn't matter. But whatever he was, all I know is that every day he was clipping my ear or kicking my backside for something I'd done wrong – or not even that, maybe just because he'd drunk too much or quarrelled with his wife. Day in day out, so that I could have killed him.

'So the managers and capitalists are bad? I'm not going to argue with that. But what does it matter to me if they get kicked out and my foreman becomes the boss? Don't tell me he's going to change because he's been "liberated"! He was a drunken lout and he was always going to be a lout. And I looked around and what did I see? Men who were just as bad, just as ignorant. *I'm* ignorant! And those who weren't ignorant were fanatics which, when it comes down to it and you cut out all the fine words, meant that they wanted to kill people.'

Galiullin halted. His face became pained. His lips fluttered over words he wanted to say, could not, and then could.

'Strelnikov was a fanatic,' he murmured at last. 'God forgive me for saying it, Larissa Fyodorovna, but it's the truth. He killed himself: doesn't that show how much hatred he had inside him? You want to know why he never visited you when he was in Yuryatin? I'll tell you. He was frightened that seeing the people he loved would have got in the way of his hatred. That's the truth, I swear it. I don't mean he wasn't a good man; but he couldn't see clearly. Now me, I'm a bad man. But I'm a *lazy* bad man. And sometimes that can be better.'

Galiullin finished there and his wrinkled Tatar face became an impassive mask as he shut them out. Lara waited a while longer and then began to collect her belongings, which consisted simply of the empty basket and her headscarf; but she patted herself and looked around as though something else were lost. Then, with a few words of farewell, she took Katya's hand and they began their walk back to the station, neither of them speaking to the other.

For as long as she could, Katya cast glances over her shoulder at the tramp as he mended his fire and resumed his cooking. She remembered that Mikulitsin's children called him 'Yusupka'. And that was how she, too, would remember him: not as Galiullin the general, but as Yusupka the spirit of the magic wood.

CHAPTER 6

THE MAN IN THE FOX-FUR COAT

Katya and her mother had been living in Yuryatin a year when a rumour went about the town concerning the occupant of a house in Suvorov Street that had formerly belonged to a railway director. The new arrival had come from no-one knew where, armed with a sheaf of contracts and letters of authority from Moscow, and had set up an office from which he was trading in all the agricultural products from Yuryatin and the surrounding region. It was impossible to ignore him: the queues of peasants waiting to sell their crops stretched down the stairs from his office into the street, and he could be seen in one of the few remaining restaurants entertaining the German engineers from the Krueger works and the local Party officials. He wore a fox-fur coat that scandalized everyone.

On her visits to her grandfather Katya heard him grumble about the stranger, whose name was Shlyapin. 'I told them what it would come to,' old Antipov said. 'This New Economic Policy has let the capitalists in by the back door. And not even the best type of capitalist. In the old days there were owners like the Kruegers who, with all their faults, had a stake in the place where they carried on business. They built factories and homes for the workers and created the preconditions for socialism. But these johnny-come-latelys are just speculators, here today and gone tomorrow.'

Samdevyatov in his measured way said much the same to Lara when he called to visit them, though he was more circumspect and less negative about something that was, after all, a matter of official policy.

Katya followed all of this with an uncertain under-standing of what it meant. Economic policy was not a subject of interest to a fifteen-year-old; and, had it been merely that, she would have ignored the matter. But there was Shlyapin himself to consider. As the stories came in, her picture of him filled out. He was young. He was hand-some. He kept a mistress. He had a store of wine from the Krueger cellars and access to imported luxuries through his friends, the German engineers. He had the use of a motor car. In short, he behaved like one of those figures from the past, the captains of industry, the noble boyars (the two were easily confused in her imagination), the mythical princes from mythical times. Of course, Katya had never met him.

Galiullin survived the winter. For a period he was ill and it was feared that he would catch pneumonia and die. He took shelter in Mikulitsin's stable where the family pretended to ignore him, and there he recovered. Twice Lara visited him, taking food and medicines. On the second occasion she ran into Samdevyatov on the platform at Torfayana station. The lawyer was surprised to see her and explained that he had been to see Mikulitsin on busi-ness. He never mentioned Galiullin, but Lara's suspicion was confirmed, that he too was secretly helping the other man. When spring came, Galiullin moved out of the stable and resumed life as a tramp in the woods and fields around Varykino.

In the last week of June the German engineers finished their work at the Krueger factory. It was the occasion of a public ceremony to thank them and a banquet which soon became reported about the town because of its extravagance in these hard times – whether this was true or not. Katya heard the stories at school where there was some boasting by those children whose parents had attended the dinner. Although the Germans had never been particularly visible in Yuryatin, their presence had been widely felt and had given people a certain confidence and optimism that the country was coming out of the isolated phase of the Revolution and joining the wider world which promised prosperity. When the foreigners left, this mood ceased and was replaced by silence and apprehension. It was as if they had been visitors to a bickering family, who had been polite for the time being and were now left to face the truth of their loneliness and conflict.

Meanwhile, the five women and Katya continued their life in the single room above the saddler's shop. Katya still attended school, but now there were no piano lessons from Fraulein Buerli since there was no piano. Instead, the succession of days went past with the women coming home wearily from work only to go out again to queue for food or fuel, or attend to the chores. The room was too small. No space for privacy. The perpetual smell of bedding, of bodies and washing, and, in summer, the stench from the saddler's stock of hides, his boiling fats and glues, and with them the swarms of flies. And the struggle to stay clean: washing clothes in the trough behind the shop; heating pans of water on the stove with rarely a chance to bathe in water that one of the others had not used; weekly trips to the public washhouse, grey scummy water and the power-ful odour of disinfectants used by the authorities to keep down disease. Katya was tired of being dirty, of wearing clothes that were threadbare and patched, and heavy boots that were kept in repair by appeals to the drunken good nature of Sergei Mikhailovitch, the saddler; of standing for hours in line for a piece of dubious meat. Boys had started to notice her and, although she dismissed them as lumpish boors, she wanted them to notice her. Trudging through the streets of Yuryatin in her scarf and mended coat she felt her own special ugliness; and the fact that it was not so special – in fact, that it was shared with every other girl – was immaterial. Among other rights (such as freedom from fear and want) is the right to be beautiful. At times this is wanted so intensely that we would cheerfully sell the others. Katya wanted it, not to excess, but a ribbon's worth, just now and again, would have made her happy.

On a sultry evening, a week after the foreigners had departed, Katya was opening the window to clear the air of the stuffiness that afflicted the overcrowded room. In the street she saw a closed horse-drawn van pull up outside the saddler's and two men get out. They were wearing city clothes and flat caps, but strapped around their waists they carried guns which they did not bother to hide. A few minutes later there was a knock on the door. Glasha broke off from washing her feet and answered it.

'Does Comrade Lotte Buerli live here?' enquired the caller, carefully blocking the door with his boot.

'Who wants to know?'

'Official business.'

'Like what?'

'Like don't cause trouble. Is she in – yes or no?'

With casual force, the two men shouldered their way into the room and examined the occupants. The first man spoke again. 'Comrade Lotte Buerli, step forward.' Fraulein Buerli put down the book she had been reading and asked what the visitors wanted. 'There are irregularities in your residence and work documents. You must come with us to answer questions.'

Fraulein Buerli looked at her friends and then, with her strange sweetness, said: 'Arrested again. Just like me!'

The two policemen were surly, but they made no fuss about allowing her time to prepare herself and find a coat, and they even permitted Glasha to slip a piece of bread into the poor woman's pocket. And then they were gone.

'It's probably something and nothing,' Glasha said with feigned cheerfulness.

But Fraulein Buerli did not return home that night.

It was Lara who was affected most. Without the comfort and help of her friend she would never have recovered from the terrible loss of Tanya. It was all she could talk about that evening. 'We must help her! We must!'

'Of course, of course,' said Glasha soothingly; but Katya could see that she was at a loss what to do, and Avdotya made the situation no easier by starting one of her asthmatic attacks.

'Oh God, are we going to have this every time something bad happens?' Glasha snapped at her, and told Sima to shut up praying, put on her thinking cap and come up with a bright idea.

They went to bed early. It was useless talking about the matter; it only made them more excited to no purpose. Katya crept into bed with her mother and felt the suppressed sobs that racked her even in her sleep. As for Katya, she was unable to sleep. Lara's continued vulnerability made her feel very lonely. Whom could she look to, to lift her own burdens?

In the end they decided that they must go to the police station to seek information. Out of nervousness it was resolved that they all go together, even Avdotya, provided that she was not to be asked to speak. So they put together a small parcel of food and appeared at the station, where they were kept waiting for two hours before finally being admitted to the office of one of the investigating officers. He proved to be a small, bald, thickset man with stubby worker's hands and a heavy accent not from those parts. His manner was indifferent rather than offensive, and Katya had the impression that he must often receive people like themselves and was bored by the stale repetition of complaints. He gave them time to explain their business and then, after checking his file, spoke.

'She is a foreigner, your friend?'

Glasha stepped in with an answer before Lara could reply. 'Yes, but what's that to do with anything? She's lived in Russia for the last twenty-odd years.'

The officer stared patiently at his desk. 'Her papers are not in order.'

'What do you mean? She got papers when she came here.'

'Ah, yes. *Here* – in Yuryatin. But what about Russia?'

'I don't know about that. Twenty years is a long time. The papers may have got lost. There was a war – you probably heard about it.'

The officer looked up at this piece of sarcasm, studied Glasha, and in an intimidating way began to make notes on the file. Lara intervened, praying for understanding.

'Is it a problem, the fact that she's a foreigner?'

'Not necessarily. Merely a factor in her case. Our country is hemmed in by antagonistic capitalist powers. Any foreigner is obviously an object of caution.'

'But she's been here twenty years!' Glasha repeated.

'And she's a vagrant,' the man continued.

The women were nonplussed by this remark until Lara realized his meaning. 'It's true,' she said, 'that Fraulein Buerli lost her job translating for the German engineers; but I'm sure she'll find another one shortly: it isn't as if there weren't plenty of work to do. And she's got a place to live. Surely that means she isn't a vagrant?'

'At present she has no job,' the man emphasized quietly. 'And the fact of her being a foreigner means that she's rootless. Do you want me to write down here that you will be fully responsible for her actions? Tell me, and I'll write it.'

But it was obvious that no-one would want him to write *that*. When one might be arrested at any time without good cause, it was dangerous to be responsible for others.

The women abandoned this fruitless interview after first arranging to get a food parcel to their friend, which the officer agreed to with the same leaden civility he had shown throughout. Glasha proposed that they call on Samdevyatov, which, she said, was what they should have done all along. 'He'll help us,' she affirmed confidently.

They found him at his office, where a crowd of supplicants was waiting to see him. Encouraged by this show of faith, they joined the queue, and at the end of an hour he saw them.

'My dear friends,' he said, rising from his seat and offering them places. 'I'm sorry you had to wait, but just at the moment there's so much happening that I scarcely have time to think. What can I do for you?'

Katya had never been to Samdevyatov's office before and she was surprised now that she saw it. Although a little shabby, it had an air of faded gentility about it with its books and array of pens, blotters, rubber stamps and other clerical gadgetry. She had an idea that a nobleman's study must have looked something like this, and the description 'like in the olden days' flitted across her mind. Samdevyatov was sitting across the desk attentively, but tugging with evident nerves at strands of his goatee beard. Glasha began:

'Our friend, Fraulein Buerli, has been arrested. It's something to do with her residence and work papers, we can't believe it's serious.' She went on with her account of the visit by the police and their own visit to the station.

Samdevyatov let her finish and then said simply: 'Another one.'

'What do you mean?' asked Lara.

'I mean,' he answered, 'that Fraulein Buerli isn't the first.'

'I don't understand,' Glasha interrupted. 'There can't be many people in her situation, not foreigners with problems about residence and work permits.'

Samdevyatov laughed. Katya was surprised since he was normally so unexpressive. But it was a sad laugh. He said: 'Dear, dear Glasha, you don't suppose for a moment that this business has to do only with your poor little Fraulein and her problems?'

'I don't understand? It's what we were told.'

'Told!' Samdevyatov replied with a sharp irony, then hesitated as though picking up and discarding an idea

129

before going on: 'The Cheka has been waiting only for the Germans to leave town before arresting everyone who had dealings with them. The entire management of the Krueger works is under lock and key together with several Party officials. Small wonder then that our dear Lotte has also been detained since she both speaks German and was acting as translator.'

'It was her job.'

'Irrelevant.'

'I don't see how – what are the charges against these people?'

'Corruption, if they're lucky. Otherwise the charges will be sabotage or espionage, it all depends.'

'On what?' Lara asked him.

'On whether the plant can be made to work; on whether the expected level of production can be achieved; on other considerations that you can't even imagine. The world has become very complicated, but people are still looking for simple explanations.' The lawyer's tone had become exasperated, to the point that Katya thought he regarded them as fools. It was so unlike him that she did not know what to make of it. Then her mother was asking:

'How do you know all of this? Do you work for the Cheka?'

To Katya's eyes Samdevyatov looked suddenly ashamed. He did not answer the question. Instead he said: 'Mikulitsin has been arrested.'

That put an end to curiosity about the lawyer's relationship to the authorities.

Glasha exclaimed, 'Oh my God!' and Sima crossed herself.

'I don't want to worry you,' he went on, 'only to indicate the extent of the problem. In Mikulitsin's case, he'll probably be all right. His son still carries some influence and he should be able to secure his father's release. Don't mention to anyone that I told you this. It's also dangerous even to know an arrested person.'

Despite his warning, Samdevyatov smiled one of his

comforting smiles, which in the past had meant that he could help. But since he had offered nothing specific, Katya suspected that the smile was more from habit than confidence. It upset him to see people unhappy. Her mother had apparently drawn a similar conclusion since she asked:

'Can you do anything for us?'

Samdevyatov answered reluctantly. 'I don't know. Please understand: as long as this crisis lasts, my own position is very difficult. I can't explain why.'

'Is there nothing you can do?'

'Not directly.'

'But indirectly?'

'Perhaps.' He picked up a pen and a scrap of paper from his desk. He hesitated and then, as an exercise of will so it seemed, wrote a few words and passed the note to Lara. He asked: 'Do you know the NEPman, Shlyapin?'

'I've heard of him.'

'Yes. Well, he has a certain reputation; but he also has some influence. Perhaps he'll use it on your behalf, though I make no promises. Take this letter and go to see him. I can't meet him personally.'

Lara read the letter, folded it carefully and placed it in her pocket. She said: 'I don't understand. I thought Shlyapin also worked with the German engineers. Everyone has heard the stories. Hasn't he been arrested, too?'

Samdevyatov smiled again but this time ironically. 'Shlyapin knows how to please everybody. All the time he was entertaining the Germans he was spying on them for the Cheka. And, for all I know, the other way round, too. Do you understand me now about the way things are going? At all events he's safe for now and there are a lot of people who owe him favours. I scarcely need tell you that he's not to be relied upon — his sort never is — but he may offer you help, and there's a chance that he'll keep any promise he gives you.'

By now Samdevyatov was checking his watch. He said: 'I'm afraid I can't allow you any more time. There's so much to do.' This sounded rude to his ears and he buffered its effect with some enquiries about their health, but his impatience to be rid of them remained evident. Only at the end, opening the door, did he linger, and then only to say: 'Don't think too badly of me.'

As they walked back to their home in Khokri, Glasha could hold herself no longer.

'Who would have thought that Samdevyatov was a police spy!' she said indignantly. The lawyer was no longer 'Anfim Yefimovitch'.

Katya was stung by the remark and blurted out: 'He never said that he was!' She had never before felt close to him with his cool, diffident manner, and she did not know why she felt so now; but, Mikulitsin apart, he was the only man she knew well who was of an age to be her father.

Glasha looked at her curiously, but, instead of rebuking her as she might have done a child, let the matter pass and they walked on a while in silence. Then she said: 'Did you see the look on his face? That look when Lara put it to him? I call it guilty.' Sometimes Glasha was a gossip and made remarks about people not because she particularly believed them to be true, but to get something off her chest. She went on: 'I don't believe that he really was helping Galiullin. After all, we've never seen any evidence. I know that he was at Varykino that time; but he said he was calling on Avercius Stepanovitch, and who's to say he wasn't?' Then: 'Oh, my God!' she exclaimed suddenly. 'Now that Mikulitsin's been arrested, he could tell them that he's been sheltering Galiullin and that we know all about him!'

'I don't think he'd do that,' Lara answered. But of course she was in no position to know.

Back home Glasha explained the situation to her sisters. Then she said to Lara: 'Are you going to see Shlyapin? I don't like the sound of him. He sounds like a villain.'

Avdotya interrupted: 'They say he's very handsome.'

She was taken aback by her boldness and blushed.

Glasha ignored her: 'What do you think? I can't see his type helping anybody unless there's something in it for him. And I don't know what we've got to offer. It's taking us all our time to feed and clothe ourselves.'

Pursuing her own train of thought, Avdotya continued blindly: 'He's got a mistress, so they say.' As the prettiest of the sisters she had been attractive to men but too shy to do anything about it. This left her with a sense of wonderment at anything to do between men and women.

'I'd take Katya with you,' Sima suggested. When the others expressed surprise, she explained: 'A woman and child may make him sympathetic. After all, we don't know that he's as bad as he's made out. It could be a matter of appearances.'

'He's little better than a gangster,' Glasha said scornfully.

'We don't know that,' Sima persisted. 'People are often better than we first think.'

'Or worse,' Glasha answered sceptically. But Sima was not to be put off.

'Are you thinking of Samdevyatov? I don't understand why you suddenly think he's so bad. What has he actually done? We know of lots of people he's helped, but who has he harmed? Perhaps he is co-operating with the police. I don't think that's very wrong. If he weren't close to the authorities, he wouldn't be in a position to give help to others. What do you think, Lara?'

In fact, no-one knew what to think. From one point of view Sima's suggestion sounded like a piece of religious innocence. From another it might be shrewd psychology. Who knew what might appeal to the NEPman? They talked some more about it and in the end decided that that was what should be done.

Shlyapin conducted business from a private room behind a restaurant near the Giant cinema. Formerly the restaurant had been regarded as luxurious, and even under reduced circumstances it was still the best in town. Glasha volunteered to spy out the lie of the land and take Samdevyatov's letter of introduction to arrange an appointment with the NEPman. She did this partly because she had the boldest spirit among them, but largely out of curiosity; and she came back excited with stories and descriptions.

'There's nothing much to be seen in the bit that's open to the public,' she told them, 'in fact it's much shabbier than I expected – a bit of a disappointment really. But the characters who go in and out of that back room!'

What had particularly impressed her were the prostitutes, as she supposed them to be. At all events they were smart and attractive women, and their existence was a shock to Glasha's memory and caused her to go off at a tangent and talk about how things had been before the war, when the Cherry Tree had been frequented by the town's businessmen and their splendid mistresses.

'Did you arrange for Lara to see him?' Sima interrupted.

'Tomorrow,' said Glasha, 'at twelve o'clock.'

Though no-one mentioned it, the prospect frightened them.

In the meantime, there was the question of what to wear. Glasha put the question, but Katya was glad she did. Part of her fear was the shame of appearing at the Cherry Tree looking like beggars – or, in Katya's case, a child. At the back of her mind Katya had a romantic image of the NEPman, which had been reinforced by Glasha's description of the restaurant. Unwittingly, Glasha had painted a picture of a demi-monde of courtesans and their lovers. Katya could not match them, and indeed never thought in exactly those terms. But she wanted to be – pretty. She wanted Shlyapin to think: that's a pretty girl!

'Well, there's no chance of you looking all dressed up like a tart!' said Glasha to Lara when she had made everyone turn out their stock of clothes. 'Not that that's the idea, but you couldn't even if you wanted to. God, haven't we got *anything*? Here, Katya, here's a piece of ribbon you can do something with. Well, Lara, anything to say?'

Lara shook her head. She stared listlessly at the clothes. Glasha tried to cheer her up. 'It's for Lotte, remember?'

Avdotya had found a metre or so of calico. It was the end of a bolt that had been bought to make a sash, a scarf – or something. Avdotya had paused to pick it up and was rubbing a corner of the cloth musingly against her cheek.

'Did you know,' she said, 'I used to make all my clothes?'

'You still do,' said Glasha shortly.

Avdotya ignored her.

'We used to get patterns. They were French fashions. Or the library had ladies' magazines. If anything was too complicated I could always get Natasha Nikolayevna to make it up. Whatever happened to her?'

'She's dead,' Glasha told her.

'What do they wear in France now?' Avdotya dreamed on. 'I haven't a clue.'

Sima giggled. 'Maybe they just paint themselves and wear feathers!'

Everyone laughed except Lara.

Glasha said: 'If we start heating the water now, you two can scrub yourselves and wash your hair. The new lot of soap isn't too bad – better than the last lot, which smelled like something had died. Avdotya, put that thing down and do something useful, will you?'

Then Avdotya found the muslin dress, which was folded and creased.

'This is nice!' she exclaimed, and unfolded it. 'Where did you get it?' She put it to her nose and sniffed the faint odour of camphor.

Lara examined the dress dully. 'Viktor bought it for me.'

There was a pause and Glasha picked the dress up and held it against herself. 'Well, it's nice all the same.'

'I can't wear it.'

'No? No, I suppose not.'

Glasha looked at Katya, who felt her heart leap. The dress was beautiful! She could say nothing, but she was longing for Glasha to complete the thought that was forming in her head. Glasha eyed her speculatively.

'It's a bit full – you know – up here.' She cupped and lifted her bosoms. 'What do you think of the length?'

'We could pin it and tack it; gather it up here and there,' Avdotya suggested. 'It would be a shame to cut it.'

'Try it on,' said Glasha.

Katya looked to her mother. *Please don't say anything!*

Lara said nothing.

Katya put on the muslin dress. There was no mirror, but she could see admiration reflected in the eyes of the sisters. She glanced down at her boots.

'I've got some shoes,' said Sima. 'We could pack the toes. They'd be all right.'

And that's what they did.

Promptly at noon Katya and her mother presented themselves at the restaurant. Katya wore the muslin dress and Sima's shoes packed with straw that rubbed her toes until they were sore. Lara wore a clean woollen skirt and a cotton blouse and her hair was pinned and tidied. In any case, what did it matter when she was beautiful? That seemed to Katya to be of itself enough. She still associated beauty with goodness, and it did not occur to her that it might mean anything else. The stranger would see her mother's beauty and recognize goodness. Hardship had sculpted rather than withered Lara's face, and the firmness of her features and clarity of her eyes still arrested the attention of anyone who looked at her. How could they fail to appeal to Shlyapin?

The sign of the Cherry Tree was still there, in need of a repaint but with the gilt lettering visible. These days there was a standing queue and no menu – the customers accepted whatever was available. Lara attracted a waiter and explained that she was expected by the occupant of the back room, and this sufficed to get her through the press of people to the rear of the restaurant and a green baize door at which the waiter knocked and was admitted. The door was closed and a moment later opened again and she and Katya went in.

At first, Katya's impression was of darkness. The room had no windows and was lit by brass oil lamps mounted in brackets on the wall, and the walls themselves were papered in a dark claret that shimmered as if it were satin. The atmosphere was oppressive with smoke and, instead of restaurant furniture (there was only one table), most of the space was taken up by a chaise longue, some comfortable armchairs, a side-table with a tantalus on it and an upright piano. The decoration was finished off with several pictures, some hunting prints, and, near the stove, a large painting of a reclining nude, an odalisque lying on a bed of studied drapery, a picture that was no doubt erotic in its intent but in fact oddly prim and cold in its effect. Lounging on the chaise longue was a man.

He was short.

He was, however, strikingly handsome with black hair, a fine nose with flaring nostrils, a well-formed mouth and a ready smile that disclosed flawless white teeth. He was probably in his middle twenties but his face was the open, eager face of an adolescent; and as Katya and her mother came into the room he sprang energetically to his feet and treated them to a careful examination through dark liquid eyes. He spoke first.

'You must be Larissa Fyodorovna Antipova. And you,' he addressed Katya kindly. 'Someone gave me your name. I remember – Katya!' In contrast to his appearance, which was light and youthful, his voice was deep and rich, full of attractive resonances. It carried an immediate suggestion of understanding and past intimacy so that one could relax into it as if meeting an old friend.

Katya was not disappointed. She was ready for him to be romantic, and he was romantic: the hair, lips, eyes, the quickness of him.

Shlyapin offered his visitors a seat and rang a bell to summon the waiter. He proposed that they should have a bite of food while they talked, and, without waiting for a response, ordered the waiter to bring in some *zakuski* and a jug of apple juice. This done, he sat back attentive and sympathetic.

'We have a friend,' Lara began. And she told him in simple words the history of Fraulein Buerli so far as she knew it down to the time of her arrest. Shlyapin allowed her to take her time, merely giving encouragement with small gestures until the story was finished.

'I understand your problem,' he answered at last.

'But can you help us?'

'I don't know,' he said in a way that implied 'yes'. He paused to offer Katya something from the plate of food. 'I won't make promises to you, Larissa Fyodorovna. Maybe I can help you, but I don't want to raise your hopes. It's my general rule not to disappoint people since my business depends on trust and confidence. I'll try to help you. But I can't promise any results. I've only a certain amount of credit with the authorities and I have to be careful with it.'

'You're being kind to us,' Lara said sincerely. Shlyapin was neither smug nor embarrassed by her thanks. The matter was disposed of; Katya was surprised how easy it was, how painless this man had made it. He indicated there was nothing more to say on the topic and turned to other things.

'You must know Anfim Yefimovitch Samdevyatov well.'

'Yes, I do. I gather you know him, too.'

'Slightly – I mean in a business sense. He works closely with the local soviet, helps them to write their decrees and so on, using the correct legal terms. But I don't know him personally. What sort of a man is he?'

'Very kind.'

'That doesn't tell me very much,' Shlyapin replied. But it was a gentle rebuke with a note of humour in the voice. He relaxed back in his seat. 'You don't have to tell me,' he went on. 'It won't make any difference. I'm not some sort of spy. But I am curious about people – aren't you curious about people, Larissa Fyodorovna? I should think you were very curious about what sort of person you were going to meet today.' And with a smile: 'Well, Katya, weren't you?'

Katya found herself responding to the warm familiarity that Shlyapin assumed as natural. Her mother's reserve seemed ungracious. But then Lara smiled and said: 'Anfim Yefimovitch is a kind man, but his manner often seems cold and gives a different impression. He doesn't like to be thanked, though there are a lot of people who owe him a great deal.'

'Who, for example?'

Lara named several people for whom the lawyer had done favours. Katya listened for a while but found her attention wandering to the furnishings. On re-examination she saw that the gloss of luxury was gone from them: there were water stains on the deep red wallpaper; the carpet was worn, the upholstery frayed; a chip flawed the glass decanter held in the tantalus. On reflection, she found the decor of the room unpleasant and wondered why such an attractive man as Shlyapin should use it.

This last thought was interrupted by the sound of her mother laughing. Lara rarely laughed. Shlyapin's eyes were bright as they chatted. Their conversation confirmed his interest in people: Samdevyatov, Mikulitsin, old Antipov, all sorts of people they knew. He was as happy as Glasha to gossip and learn their history and foibles; and for a while they carried on like this until the waiter returned and announced that there was someone else who required to see the NEPman on business.

'Then I'm afraid we must stop,' Shlyapin said regretfully. He picked up Lara's coat and helped her to put it

139

on. 'I hope we'll meet again, Larissa Fyodorovna,' he told her. 'Perhaps next time you'll let me call you Lara?'

To Katya he said: 'That's a pretty dress you're wearing.'

A week later Fraulein Buerli was released without warning, delivered at night as a bundle on the doorstep, like something left by children who have run away.

Lara answered the door. She opened it on a pale figure with hair that was ragged and dirty. Each of them looked on the other as if at a stranger, and then there was a wordless gasp and they embraced each other, hugged, kissed, rested their heads on each other's shoulder, rubbed cheeks. Lara took both Fraulein Buerli's hands and drew her into the room and family. Lara's face was a picture of relief and radiant happiness.

How are you? How have you been? Was it awful? Oh, Lotte, it's so wonderful to see you again! God be praised! The women clamoured around their little friend, so eager to ask questions that they could not wait for answers. And in fact the answers were few. Fraulein Buerli did not want to talk about her ordeal. She strove to treat her arrest as a matter of no consequence, as though she had merely gone out for a few minutes and been caught unprepared in the rain. She knew nothing of Shlyapin nor of why she had been released. Indeed, she was uncertain why she had been arrested: she had not been charged nor had anyone interrogated her; too busy, she supposed; the prison was full and many people were in the same situation; when one caught sight of the interrogators they looked tired and sleepless so that one was almost sorry for them. Really she preferred not to talk about it.

'Still, we've got to celebrate!' said Glasha. 'What do we have?'

'Bread and potatoes,' said Sima.

'Grapes and wine!' said Glasha. 'It doesn't matter. I've got something. Something I've been saving!' She rummaged in a corner of the room and produced a plain bottle of clear liquid.

'What is it?' asked Avdotya. 'Vodka?'

'Sort of.'

'Sort of?'

'I got it from a porter at the hospital. It's not quite vodka, but it's all right to drink with water.'

'Are you sure?'

'Positive!'

Katya got some cups, and after some initial reluctance the women sipped at the clear spirit. 'After all,' pronounced Glasha, 'why should men have all the pleasure?'

It was agreed that they should not.

They drank, and although Katya did not join in she became bright-eyed and intoxicated simply by watching them drink. They were unfeignedly happy. They talked of food, clothes, holidays, festivals, schools, friends, memories – before the war – when everything was real and magical at the same time – old friends, dead friends, real colours, real smells, memories – before the war. Oh Lotte, it's good to have you back! Let me kiss you! Sima, you're crying! Glasha, do you have to use the pot in here! Am I laughing or crying? Glasha, you're disgusting! Lotte, I can't believe it's you! Another drink? Tell me that story again. Before the war.

I shall have a headache in the morning.

For a while none of them saw anything of Shlyapin. Occasional stories were heard about him: most of them unflattering. Glasha picked them up at her work at the post office because people writing to their friends and relatives about conditions in Yuryatin could not help mentioning the NEPman. From being his detractor, Glasha became his defender. Katya had noticed that Glasha held strong likes and dislikes and found it necessary at the same time to have people that she liked and those she hated; and since the dethronement of Samdevyatov there was a space which Shlyapin could fill for the time being.

Then, one day, Katya was walking down the street

with her mother, returning home after a long queue at the bakery in St Tikhon's church, and they were passing the commercial hotel on the other side of the road when a voice hailed them. They looked round and saw that it came from Shlyapin, who was sitting in a small carriage and wearing his famous fox-fur coat and a slouch hat. They crossed the road to meet him.

'Are you well, Larissa Fyodorovna – Lara?' he asked. 'And you too, Katerina Pavlovna?' A slovenly peasant in a filthy kaftan was holding the door of the carriage open. Shlyapin dismissed the man but himself remained where he was, borrowing the height of the carriage so that he could look down on the two females. 'How's your friend – Fraulein Buerli, was it? Is she in good health?'

'We're very well,' Lara answered him. 'And very grateful to you.'

'It was nothing,' he said. 'Really. Or does that make me sound too modest?' This thought made him laugh his rich warm laugh.

'I would have thanked you before if I'd seen you.'

'You could have seen me,' Shlyapin reminded her. 'I can be found at my office or at the Cherry Tree. Why didn't you call on me?'

Lara hesitated. Shlyapin recognized that he had struck a false note, but passed it off brightly with: 'Never mind. Here you are now with nothing to do but go home. This place,' he indicated the hotel, 'actually has coffee for its favoured customers. How long is it since you drank coffee? Have you ever drunk coffee, Katya?'

'I don't think so,' Katya told him.

'Well, then! Lara, I think you owe your daughter the experience.' He was already descending from the carriage. On foot he was only the woman's height and could look her levelly in the eyes. Katya thought how nicely made he was, his movements compact and well balanced. There was no denying his request, put as it was so cheerfully and treating Lara's reluctance as a joke. Together they went into the hotel.

The interior of the hotel heaved with a crowded mass of railwaymen, drovers, soldiers, peasants come to market, leatherworkers, craftsmen, and their women – all drinking, bargaining and bickering in a heavy atmosphere of smoke and sweat. Here and there little tables had been set up, and behind them other NEPmen were doing business, but they seemed makeshift types by comparison with Shlyapin. The latter pushed his way through, ignoring the many calls on his attention, and with a word in the ear of one of his colleagues displaced him from his table and made space for Katya and her mother to sit down. He summoned a waiter and ordered coffee for the three of them, then turned to his guests.

'What shall we talk about?' he asked. 'This is a social occasion, a getting-to-know-you occasion. Let's put business aside. You know, you haven't even called me by my proper name.'

'I don't know it,' Lara said.

'You never asked. In fact it's Nikolai Afanasitch, Kolya to my friends. You can call me Kolya, too,' he confided to Katya. 'I don't mind.'

'Thank you – Kolya.'

'Don't mention it. Well?'

Katya looked at her mother. Shlyapin, wearing a patient smile, was doing the same, so that Katya found herself on his side, sharing his embarrassment at Lara's hesitations, his wonder at what she was thinking. Katya had never seen her mother in such an external way before: never viewed her as a woman like other women and a relative stranger. The sensation made her feel insecure. She felt a thinning in the bond of affection that prevents parents from being merely people. To regain her balance, she turned her eyes on the man and pushed him away with her gaze; and now that she was outside the two she could see the unfathomable tension between them.

'Where do you come from?' Lara asked at last.

'From here, Yuryatin,' said Shlyapin. 'My father worked on the railway. I was a travelling salesman for

Moreau & Vetchinkin – I was little more than a kid.'

Thinking of her father, Katya asked: 'Were you in the war?'

'After a fashion,' Shlyapin answered laconically, and did not elaborate.

Katya blurted out her next question. She knew she should not ask, but felt an overwhelming desire to know.

'Are you married?'

'Katya!' exclaimed her mother.

'No, it's all right,' said Shlyapin with amusement. 'No, I'm not married. I believe you are – or were, Lara?'

'Yes.'

'To a general.'

'Yes.'

'The wrong sort of general – or so I heard. I don't mean to be offensive. Put my question down to curiosity between friends. Yes? Someone also told me that you were very close to another man, a doctor who got into trouble with the authorities.'

Lara did not answer. Perhaps her mother was surprised that Shlyapin should be so frank. But the question did not appear to Katya to be offensive; Kolya was a friend. The coffee came. Katya sipped hers and the novelty of its bitterness and spice shocked her. Between tastes, Shlyapin said:

'It sounds dangerous to me, your history. You don't make it any easier for yourself by associating with the likes of Fraulein Buerli.'

'She isn't dangerous. She's just a poor innocent woman.'

'I imagine you're right. I didn't mean that she was dangerous in that sense, just dangerous to know. People judge from appearances, and hers is – I don't know the word,' he said with a smile. 'I wish sometimes that I'd had a better education. Anyway, you know what I mean. The point is that she could easily be arrested again; I shouldn't be at all surprised. And then who's going to help you? Samdevyatov? I don't think so. He's a good man, but

144

his own position is tricky. Believe me,' Shlyapin urged, 'I don't want to frighten you, but you have to face up to realities.'

If there was a purpose to Shlyapin's comments he did not spell it out. After this incident Katya did not see him again for several weeks, and then only briefly. From the window of their room she could see down the street to the commercial hotel, and one evening she caught sight of the NEPman in his fox-fur coat escorting a woman into the premises. It was the woman who attracted Katya's notice. She was blonde and at a distance seemed very beautiful. Her clothes were colourful and appeared luxurious. They were mismatched, but the clash of style and material lent only an air of the exotic and mysterious. Mentally Katya contrasted her with her mother in the severe poverty of her dress. Lara was older than the stranger, her former beauty fined down into handsomeness, but masked by stress and weariness. Against that contrast, Shlyapin's interest seemed charitable.

In the evening two days later, the police called again. Fraulein Buerli sat as still as a frozen bird while they banged about the room like poltergeists, searching every item of furniture, every book, every crevice. They asked no questions, found nothing, and left. The following day Sima and Avdotya were stopped and searched in the street. The police called on Glasha as she worked at the post office and went over her papers and interrogated her in front of the manager.

On the following Saturday Lara received an invitation to have dinner with Shlyapin. She accepted and returned home very late without talking of what had passed between them. In Lara's absence Glasha was bad-tempered. She snapped at her sisters and found fault with everything that Katya did.

The summer and autumn passed and winter came with snow and cold dry days. Harassment by the police stopped. Lara continued to see Shlyapin and occasionally

Katya met him too, when he was always cheerful and polite and gave her a small present.

Samdevyatov disappeared.

It was three days before they learned of this. No-one knew for certain what had happened to him, though it was generally supposed that he had been arrested. From the saddler came the story that Samdevyatov had been lifted straight off the street in broad daylight and taken in one of the vans that the Cheka used. Glasha was told the same story at work, with details of the street name and exactly what the lawyer had been doing and what he was wearing. No-one claimed actually to have witnessed the event, but they knew someone who knew someone who had seen Samdevyatov, so the account was generally accepted.

'What are we to do?' Glasha asked. In the forefront of her mind was the fact that Samdevyatov knew about Galiullin's presence at Varykino and might tell; and if Galiullin were caught, it was impossible to say who might be implicated. For some time the town had been riven with rumours of a White conspiracy; the authorities had been using this panic to whip up enthusiasm for various of their projects. Katya noticed that Glasha made no reference to their former friendship with the lawyer. She was unrelenting in her conviction that Samdevyatov had become a police spy, and saw no contradiction between her present concern and the fact that he could have betrayed Galiullin at any time if he were an informer. In Glasha's opinion, the fact that one was a spy did not mean that one told one's masters everything. A piece of information held in reserve was a stored morsel of power. When Lara tried to voice her fears for Samdevyatov himself, Glasha cut her short with: 'You're being sentimental!'

'I don't suppose Avercius Stepanovitch knows what's happened,' she went on, thinking of her brother-in-law. Mikulitsin rarely came to town since he had lost his job at the Krueger works, been arrested and released. His family lived quietly at Varykino, relying on help from the son, Liberius. 'He ought to be warned, for all our sakes.'

The problem was how to warn him. Suddenly there seemed to be spies everywhere, and if Mikulitsin had himself been arrested again – which was quite possible, though there was no way of knowing since these things were done secretly – then to turn up on his doorstep might itself be dangerous.

In this confusion, Katya saw what had to be done. There was clearly no alternative. She felt no fear.

'I'll go,' she volunteered.

'Don't be silly,' said Glasha.

'But no-one will suspect me. And I want to help.'

'Lara, can your NEPman friend, Shlyapin, help?'

Of course! Katya had forgotten about Kolya. Of course he would help. She looked at her mother, and to her astonishment saw a fleeting look of shame.

'No, I'm sorry. He warned me that something like this might happen.'

'And you didn't mention it?' Glasha said indignantly.

'There was nothing to be done about it,' Lara said resignedly. 'He said that if the Cheka moved against Anfim Yefimovitch, then he'd be beyond help. I don't know why.'

Katya noticed that, although Shlyapin was a friend, her mother still referred to him by his surname. The thought caused her to pass over the fact that he could not or would not help. She felt aggrieved for him: that his generosity was received so reservedly; but then she remembered that her mother often saw Shlyapin and accepted his invitations. It was not possible to make sense of adults.

Glasha was frustrated. She seemed angry with Lara. 'We still have to decide what to do!' she stated emphatically. And by degrees their eyes drifted uncertainly to Katya, who felt not fear but a sense of pride and the knowledge that another door had been opened into the grown-up world.

*   *   *

Maintenance crews shovelled snow from the line to Torfayana. It had snowed during the night, the sky was grey with cloud and a veil of snow hung in the air to a vaporous horizon of trees stained palely against a wash of grey. Katya travelled in her heaviest clothes and felt boots, feeling trapped by them in the warmth of the carriage. Outside, the labourers sang intermittently; the train moved so slowly that she could catch the halting words, the refrain to the grey haunted day.

At Torfayana, the stationmaster had more sense than to venture out into the cold, and Katya was left abandoned on the deserted platform, reluctant to leave it for the beckoning silence of the wood and the empty pathways that snaked away into uncertainty. For a few minutes she sat down on a bench, watching the train, which suddenly clanked into action and pulled away leaving her finally alone. I suppose I'd better go, she said to herself. She got to her feet and set off without looking back.

She kept as far as possible to the forest paths where the snow was thinnest. Where her way led across open ground there were deep drifts and level fields of white marked only by animal spoor. After a while she saw horsemen on the near horizon.

They were taking a different, more exposed road, and their mounts struggled breast-high in the snow. Katya paused to watch them. She remembered Captain Brenner and his Tatar band (now so long ago), but these men were Russians, big men on big horses, six of them leading a couple of spare animals, and all of them as black as spiders at this distance; and so physical, Katya thought, as she watched the thrashing of the horses and the men striving to maintain their balance while controlling and driving the beasts forward. Viewed from her position by the wood, and framed by snow and sky, the group acted out a little tableau of black and white movement, a shadow play; and in her detached way Katya saw how beautiful it was, and she keyed it into her memory where it would remain until unlocked, perhaps in twenty years, by a particular configuration of snow and movement or something as banal as a horse pulling a cart under the whip of its driver; and she would be drawn down a trail of memory to this day – and still further: on to the image of Captain Brenner crossing the bridge in the pasture above the house at Chita. And ultimately she would remember Tanya, with whom she had been playing. There it was and now it was gone; the horsemen had overcome the obstacle and the party trotted on into the dissolving light.

After that moment of beauty, Katya was forced back to the hard reality of her trek through the forest to Mikulitsin's house. The way was more difficult than she had anticipated, both because of the burden of snow and because she was unsure of her directions in the changed landscape. At one time she was uplifted by the sight of a cottage, but as she approached it she saw that, though familiar, it was not Mikulitsin's: it appeared disused, the porch had collapsed, the gingerbread woodwork was snapped like rows of gaping teeth, a broken water butt was split with ice. Yet so familiar.

She mounted the rickety steps of the porch and pushed her way through the warped and rotten door. By now she knew the house, though the realization brought curiosity not excitement. She had lived here with her mother and Zhivago. From here they had fled with Uncle Viktor. So this is what it was like. Smaller than she recalled. Distant and not intimate. Empty and loveless. She paced the rooms and studied the damp ruin of unfamiliar possessions, broken pictures, mouldering books, a doll (my doll? Tanya's doll, Natasha? No – Tanya wasn't even born. I don't want to think about Tanya! What happened to her doll? It had only one eye. Did Uncle Viktor take it when he took Tanya? Poor Tanya – she loved that doll!). The stove smelled of a recent fire. There was a pile of fresh newspapers and a few ragged blankets. Galiullin has been hiding here. This must be one of his dens, she told herself. But Yusupka the forest spirit was not there. He probably saw the soldiers. From the porch she saw a boot-trail going off towards the trees, and, at the margin of the woods, a man on foot, holding his horse and examining the ground.

Slowly the realization came to her that the soldier was hunting for the tramp. Yet he showed no urgency. His eyes turned from the particular footprint to the direction of the trail, and patiently he patted his horse and took a pistol from his belt. Only then did he set off in pursuit of his quarry; and, even then, slowly, leading the cautious horse and stepping carefully to avoid a fall in the snow. Gradually Katya lost sight of him in the saplings and brush.

She remembered that she wanted to save Galiullin. In the moody rhythm which had affected her while searching the cottage, she had forgotten. The thought jolted her and she hurried her pace, placing her feet in Galiullin's footprints until she, too, was at the edge of the wood. And then she heard a shot, followed at an interval by two more and a crashing and breaking of wood. She stopped. She was frightened. The heroic idea which she had held suddenly seemed silly and dangerous. And desperately futile.

For a while Katya stood miserably. The soldier returned, still leading his horse. But this time there was a body slung over its back and blood trickled down the animal's flank, and the horse, smelling it, was fearful. *Yusupka!* Katya cried to herself, but she could not recognize the tangle of rags and hair. The soldier's face was inflamed as if intoxicated. *Yusupka!* The man was talking to the horse, trying to calm it, but he sounded as if he hated the beast. His free hand held his gun; his finger was still on the trigger and his muscles were tensed and his manner taut with pent-up fury. He had killed Galiullin and it was not enough, Katya realized. The soldier's own fear and determination could not be as easily discharged as the bullets, three of them, fired at a fleeing figure. It was not enough. He would have to obliterate his enemy from Creation and then obliterate the memory before all passion was spent.

He saw Katya.

'Who are you?' he snapped. 'Whoa – easy, boy! Are you one of the Mikulitsins?'

'Antipova – Katerina Pavlovna,' Katya answered.

'Papers?'

'Here they are.'

'Hold them open for me. Can't you see my hands aren't free? Antipova? They look all right. Clear off then, and forget what you've seen.'

'Yes, comrade.' She looked at his face. He was only a few years older than herself, ugly and wearing a pitifully thin moustache. After his initial surprise he did not notice her; the shivering horse occupied all his attention. He pushed past her and took the path back to the cottage and beyond. Though he looked back several times and saw her following, it did not disturb him. In this way Katya reached Mikulitsin's house.

A group of people stood on the patch of earth outside the door where in summer they had often put out a table. Katya dared not approach closer and had to stand off, watching the dumbshow: Mikulitsin's wife and children in tears, a soldier on foot holding them at bay with a rifle and bayonet as if they were a riotous rabble, the other soldiers steadying the uneasy mounts. Mikulitsin himself was sitting bolt upright on one of the horses, his hands tied behind his back. The horse stood stock-still and quietly manured the ground.

CHAPTER 7

LOVE AND CONTEMPT

They lived in fear. The sound of the saddler bumping around his workshop, the rattle of his customers at the shop-front, the night-time visits of his drunken friends provoked surges of panic in the women, in case the noises signified the arrival of the Cheka. They could not look at vehicles in the street from fear that one of them was a police van. They avoided the gaze of strangers and the knots of rowdies who were always to be found near the commercial hotel, in case they would find the still eyes of a police spy.

The nervousness that this induced was physically wearing. But more taxing was the effect of their sense of guilt and evasion on their morale and cohesion. Openly, they maintained their joint support and responsibility for their predicament. Privately, they assessed their individual blame and the blame to be attributed to the others, and each of them struggled with a spirit of resentment.

This was allowed to come out, though still in a subdued form, when they spoke of Mikulitsin. He was no longer a friend or, in the sisters' case, a relative whose good nature had got him into trouble. It was as if he were a stranger from whom they had innocently bought stolen goods.

After all, it was he who had harboured Galiullin, and without a hint of warning allowed Katya to find him and thereby embroil them in the dead man's political crimes (and in her private version, Glasha blamed Lara for keeping up the contact, for speaking to Galiullin and taking him presents of food – which in retrospect had nothing to do with charity, but simply gave her the opportunity for conversation to satisfy her obsession with the past and her madman of a husband, Strelnikov). Apart from Katya only Sima did not participate in the veiled attacks on Mikulitsin. In her view it did no good to apportion guilt: they were all guilty before the glory of God, and whatever happened would be His will. Glasha thought that Sima held this opinion only because she felt personally innocent and therefore had the pride to be forgiving.

The change was destructive of their way of life. Hitherto, they had lived in the cramped conditions of their little room bound together against dirt and discomfort by solidarity and affection. The introduction into their world of private suspicions and resentments sapped their solidarity. Thinking of Galiullin, it was too easy to snap at each other about clothes left lying around; the time it took to wash, so that the water went cold; whose turn it was to join an interminable queue for food. What's happened to us? was the unspoken question.

A week went by after Katya's fateful visit to Varykino, and nothing happened. The tension became unbearable, and Lara therefore resolved to see Shlyapin, hoping that he would set her mind at rest. The NEPman's people claimed that he was out of the town.

That night Katya found her mother crying and Glasha comforting her. From the whispers she understood that Lara had given Shlyapin something, and now he would not repay her.

The following evening, coming home in the darkness, Katya saw an elderly man walking slowly down the street, scanning the doors and the ruined buildings and peering into alleyways as if he were lost. He wore a carefully preserved, expensive black overcoat and rubber overshoes, and his head was largely hidden by scarves and a fur hat; but enough was revealed to show that he wore a beard and that his hair was nearly white. He carried a stick and had a slight hand tremor.

As it happened, Katya and the man arrived together at the saddler's shop. The man was checking the address; Katya had her hand on the street door that led to the upstairs rooms. She was about to push the door open when her arm was arrested by the stranger's hand. He said one word.

'Katya?'

It was Komarovsky.

He pushed her into the shadow of the doorway and demanded forcefully: 'Is this where you live? Is your mother here?'

'Yes, Uncle Viktor.'

'Is she here *now*?'

'Yes, I think so.'

'Good – good!' he said eagerly and, shaking her out of her surprise, added: 'Take me up, then!'

They climbed the creaking steps. Katya heard Komarovsky wheezing behind her, and once he paused for breath. She was puzzled, as if he were still a stranger: she did not remember him so frail. She had a picture of his black fierceness as he used to be, striding about the pasture with his loping dog; but, though he had shocked her, he could not intimidate her in the old way.

'Are you all right, Uncle Viktor?' she asked.

'Well enough,' he answered and flashed a laconic smile. Distractedly he said: 'You've changed, too. You've become a big fine girl.'

Katya rapped at the door and it was opened by Avdotya, who did not recognize the visitor and turned pale, thinking he was a policeman. Katya found she had the confidence to ask Komarovsky to wait while she prepared her mother, and almost meekly he agreed.

'Who is he?' Avdotya whispered.

'A friend,' Katya told her, though she was not sure that the term was correct for someone as ambiguous as the lawyer.

'Who's that with you?' Glasha asked shortly. 'Is he going to stand there all night, letting in the draught?'

'It's someone who wants to speak to mother,' said Katya and she approached the chair where Lara was sitting, and in a low voice informed her: 'It's Uncle Viktor.'

Katya was not sure what she expected – a cry of 'My God!' – some show of emotion at least. In her surprise at meeting Komarovsky she had treated him politely, adopting him as a friend just as she had told Avdotya. Yet she knew that this was not true: that Uncle Viktor would always be something else. But she had allowed herself to be wrong-footed and could not now recover unless Lara gave her a cue as to what she should really feel. Instead Lara revealed little. She stood up stiffly and faced Komarovsky like a widow receiving condolences from a dead husband's disreputable relatives. Katya was left to watch and listen, and feel inside her the discordance of her emotions and expression. *I won't think of Tanya!* she told herself firmly as if lecturing a doll. *I won't!*

'Viktor,' said Lara calmly. 'I wasn't expecting to see you.'

'No. I imagine it is – a surprise.'

'Yes, a surprise.' Lara was forced to turn away from him. She introduced the sisters, using their formal names and patronymics. Komarovsky gave each of them an old-fashioned bow from the waist. The sisters said nothing, though Glasha returned a distasteful look which Komarovsky chose to ignore. In fact, his manner retained the faint air of a supplicant.

He looked around the room, then asked: 'May I rest my legs? I've been walking – the stairs.' Sima offered him her place. He took off his coat and revealed a neat but well-worn suit of clothes. He sat down heavily and sighed.

'Have you been travelling?' Lara asked.

Komarovsky appeared grateful for the question.

'From Vladivostok.'

'A long journey.'

'I arrived yesterday. I've been resting since.'

'Vladivostok? So you've moved from Chita?'

'Yes.'

'And you like it there?'

'Yes. Vladivostok is a different world – a great city, a port. It's altogether a more significant place.' Komarovsky's voice was a mix of genuine enthusiasm and a desire to be done with these formalities of conversation. He seized a pause to say: 'I've often thought about you.'

'I've never been to Vladivostok,' Lara said almost before he had finished. 'Are you enjoying life there?'

He was annoyed. 'Yes, it's a fine town.'

'So I've heard.'

'But it's impossible to forget the past.'

'The past,' Lara repeated lightly, banishing its painful reality.

'Would you like some refreshment?' Fraulein Buerli asked him despite Glasha's sour looks.

'No, thank you. And you, Lara, are you well? You look none the worse for wear, Fraulein. Katya I could barely recognize. She's grown.'

'Katya and I have made a life here. Thanks to our friends.'

'Good. At times I've been worried.'

'There was no need.'

'Ah,' Komarovsky sighed, and Katya detected in his saturnine eyes, which had formerly been pools of anger and obscurity, a pleading look at this dismissal of his concern for their welfare. There was a pause in which Glasha coughed uncomfortably.

'Are you here on business?' Lara asked.

'I have some affairs in Yuryatin,' he answered obliquely. 'This and that. It isn't often that I have opportunity to come west. My business is mostly in relations with Japan

– an offshoot of my interest in Mongolia, a subject which also occupies the Japanese, but I won't bore you.'

'You'll be here long?'

'That depends.'

To avoid the coldness of Lara's level gaze he was studying the walls. Katya began to see the room through his eyes: the poor attempts at decoration that the women had made. He sniffed the air, and Katya detected too the musky menstrual smell that was an inseparable part of their close world. She saw him mentally comparing the room with the fine house at Chita and reckoning them up as though about to make an offer, and then calculating that such an offer would be in false coin. The conclusion seemed to leave him bereft of what to do. He mused in silence, Katya could not say how long, but Glasha got out of her seat and began to perform some petty chore.

At last he said: 'Will you come for a walk with me, Lara?'

'Why? Where should we go?'

'I find that the cold air calms me. We don't have to go anywhere in particular. A stroll and a talk. Yes?'

Lara looked on the point of refusing, but there was in Komarovsky's unfamiliar modesty an appeal. And there was, too, a threat, simply in his presence and the fact of his journey from the East.

What happened next? Katya did not know until a year later when Lara told her. They were alone together in an upper room of an apartment house and outside there was a sea-fog and the stillness of the evening was broken by the horns of passing ships. It was dark, they had not lit a lamp, in the streets kerosene flares had been placed to guide the people, and the yellow-tinted fog was glued to the window. And Katya felt the dawning of an intelligence, the knowledge that at last, if she posed the question, she would understand the answer. So she did, and the answer came. Later, the story became incorporated into her memories: her feelings for it so lively and the images so vivid that she became confused as to whether she had not in fact been there and heard everything that was said between her mother and Komarovsky. By one of memory's ironies, it was the quiet evening spent talking to her mother that became the illusion.

Lara put on her heavy winter coat and went down with Komarovsky into the street. The saddler was closing his shop. The commercial hotel was open for business. They took the opposite direction, walking slowly because of the ice and snow and the absence of light except for such as leaked from the buildings, the glittering stars and the ice-haloed moon. Komarovsky walked with small shuffling steps and an old man's fear of falling.

For perhaps five minutes they walked this way, without speaking, without touching. Komarovsky relied upon his stick for support across the treacherous ruts. Lara did not look at him. She was at the same time frightened of him, which was why she had wanted to get him away from her friends, and contemptuous of him, knowing that at bottom she was a stronger person. And, too, she was astonished by him; that he had dared to make contact with her again. After everything! After Tanya!

And then he fell.

He went legs akimbo and landed on his back. The movement was so sudden and the sight of him so absurd that Lara involuntarily laughed before catching herself and asking: 'Are you all right, Viktor?'

'I'm all right,' he snapped, but he still sat there recovering from the shock. 'My clothing broke the fall,' he added. And then he too was laughing. 'Here, give me a hand up,' he said. Lara stooped to offer her arm. He took it and heaved himself to his feet so that he was facing Lara with scarcely space between them. His hand remained fastened around her arm.

She said brusquely: 'We'd better walk together to avoid accidents.' Standing so close, she could smell the stale tobacco on his beard. That smell was the talisman of her revulsion for him. It brought back images of his arrogance and treachery: Viktor the sophisticated city lawyer, dining in the best restaurants, parading a schoolgirl on his arm; Viktor lounging in the women's carriage of the train from Moscow studying the doctor's mistress and her child; Viktor planning his successive campaigns against her; each time a cigar or cigarette between his fingers; tobacco on his breath, stronger than the pomade in his hair and the toilet water that scented his linen; the physical summary of his vileness.

He slipped his hand so that they could link arms. The thick shoulders of his overcoat jostled hers. As they walked Lara felt the jogging intimacy of their bodies. She thought, against every rational wish: we are bound together, he and I. Like drowning slaves chained together. There's no point in being angry, whatever he may have done in the past. No sooner had the thought come than her intellect rebelled against it: reminding her of her freedom. And her anger did rise; but it was a weakly thing, like the anger we experience at being found out in our sins, which flares up, often at first more acutely than if we are innocent, only to die under the burden of guilt. It clasped her heart, but did not reach her lips. She searched her memories for how it could be so. He was my mother's lover before he was mine. Perhaps that was the confession that no exercise of argument could ever overcome.

She wanted him to say something cruel so that she could disengage any sympathy from him. She could feel his age and tremulous frailty.

'You're crying,' he said softly.

'It's nothing – the cold air.'

He apologized: 'I'm sorry to bring you out in this weather. But we needed to talk, and that wasn't possible in front of your friends. Lara –' he paused '– you must leave Yuryatin!'

'Why?'

'You know why! Your position here is dangerous – Mikulitsin – Samdevyatov – Galiullin – yes, I know about Galiullin. It can only be a matter of days before you, too, are arrested.'

He had said it – told her what they had all feared. But from him Lara was unwilling to accept it. Even the truth bore his taint.

'How do you know?'

'I have my informants.'

'Shlyapin?'

'Perhaps. Isn't it enough that there are people concerned about your welfare? You must come with me to Vladivostok.'

It was obvious that that was what had brought him to Yuryatin. Lara had known it from the moment he had stepped through the door. But to hear the words and contemplate the prospect appalled her, and in the shock of the idea she pushed him away and he recoiled against a wall and had to struggle to keep upright. Now he was angry.

'Don't be ridiculous!' he said sharply. 'Use your head for once instead of your emotions! Stop it! Stop that martyred look! It's nothing but selfishness!'

'Selfishness?'

'That's what I said! I'm not stupid! I can tell what you're thinking! But you should think of your friends. Do you think they can avoid arrest if you're here to compromise them? Think of Katya!'

'I am thinking of Katya!' Lara cried out, but he had no sense of what she meant. She hurried away from him, hearing him calling her name. 'I can go somewhere else!' she called back to him.

'You're being ridiculous!' he shouted back. 'Where would you live? How would you manage? You haven't the slightest idea how to hide yourself without my protection.'

A troika came along the street. The regular trot and jangle of the horses distracted and calmed them. Lara allowed Komarovsky to catch up with her.

'Why are you doing this to me, Viktor?' she asked him. 'Why can't you leave me alone?'

He did not answer immediately. Instead his face registered pain and his own inner shock that she should not have understood him.

'Because I love you, Lara,' he answered, and quickly went on: 'It's always been that. I know you don't love me – that you find me disgusting – but that has never made any difference except that I've tried and failed to put you out of my mind. God knows I've tried.' He seized both her hands. 'Do you think that I'd be here if I had any choice? I'm not blind! I can see that in your eyes I'm repulsive and pitiful. I've lived for twenty years with that hideous reflection. And it's made *no difference!*'

His hands were shuddering. His lips trembled and were rimmed with spittle. Under the force of his emotions his face seemed to crumble, leaving only the dark intensity of his eyes. He struggled to master himself.

'You took Tanya from me,' Lara said. She had thought that she would never be able to speak those words. And hearing them, they sounded weak. An accusation and an admission of her own shame.

'I was wrong,' he confessed tonelessly. He explained, as if she would see his reasons: 'I thought that it was Tanya who stood between us. And that if she were gone we could be – happy.'

Though his words recognized his crime, the explanation, as he saw it, relegated the subject to history: made it a matter for regret, but external to the present predicament. He had a dim appreciation of the distress he had caused her, but to his lawyer's mind she had also failed to see his point of view and this could be remedied by argument, overcome by words as if she could remain dispassionate.

'I tried to find Tanya again,' he said. 'I made enquiries. The people had moved on. It wasn't possible.'

'She was a child!'

'Children are more adaptable than we care to think,' he answered reasonably.

'You treated her as if she was a mere thing!'

This he did not understand. He had taken great care in finding Tanya a home.

Then he had an insight – Lara's attack on him was to assuage her sense of her own guilt. If he chose, it would be easy to reproach her with her past: betrayal of her mother, her affairs with himself and Zhivago while her husband was still living. At times he knew that he had felt a contempt for her as a woman who could not control her own life. Yes, it would be easy to reproach her!

However, he did not do so. He would forgo his advantage out of charity towards her. Out of the same charity that had brought him from Vladivostok.

'My dear,' he said kindly, 'you can't help thinking of the past. I've told you that I'm sorry. Whether you accept my apology is immaterial. You must think of your obligations to your friends.'

'I'll go to Shlyapin for help.'

'He won't help you,' Komarovsky answered with a finality that made Lara recognize that he was speaking the truth. He asked: 'Is he also your lover? I can see that he is. Poor Lara. You need me, even you must now see that.'

And already he was talking of the arrangements that would be necessary for her to leave Yuryatin, as if the fact of her leaving were already incorporated into reality. The force of that assumption overwhelmed her. She reflected that that was how choices were made: that that was the true nature of freedom. But she could still say 'no' to him – a simple word, easily enough spoken; she could feel it floating inside her head along with her fear of him, her sense of disgust. Thoughts floating about without roots, like the phases of a dream, at once so sharp and then so hazy as they are crowded out by new images. She could say 'no', but she would not. He might appal her, but he had had from the very beginning a moral superiority over her: his version of reality had always had more reason and solidity to it than hers.

Then she remembered Katya.

'I can't go with you.'

'Why not?' He was no longer angry; felt no need to point out her absurdity. Any objection she might raise now would be trivial, so sure was he of his ascendancy over her.

'Because of Katya.'

'Katya? What about her? Her school? Her friends? There are schools and friends in Vladivostok. I've already made arrangements for her to study music. Doesn't that prove that I care about her?'

'Not that,' Lara answered. She could not explain to him. She could hear his scorn at any attempt to bridge the abyss in the heart of his understanding of both himself and others, any attempt to reach the far place where his passions were darkly secluded from his powerful rationality. Mother – daughter – daughter's child: the syllogism which so terrified Lara would mean nothing to him; he would recoil from the idea and turn it against her; charge her with hiding her guilt for her mother and jealousy of her daughter behind a filthy accusation for which there was no evidence. Evidence – the lawyer in him would use that word and Lara was not equipped to answer it. She was innocent before it: left with a wordless animal panic.

Komarovsky believed that he had won. He suggested they return home, and there he accepted the sisters' hospitality.

The following day Lara went to see Shlyapin at his office. She had not been able to sleep, and she had to resist Glasha's resentful enquiries after her return with Komarovsky. These were contradictory except that in their contradictions they were all implicitly critical of Lara. On the one hand, Glasha disliked and feared Komarovsky, and blamed Lara for her past weakness towards him and for now bringing him down upon them all. But on the other hand, Viktor had convinced her of the danger facing them all and that his offer was the only solution, which Lara had no right to reject.

In fact the broken logic could be reconciled. Glasha's behaviour represented no more than the limits of friendship, which can resent as well as love: the two emotions being not opposed but expressions of each other. Still, for Lara it meant that the humble room in which they lived had changed from being a home to a temporary resting-place in which she had never been more than a guest. She could see now what had happened to them all and that the love and intimacy that had overcome so much could not be reconstructed. Ah, Glasha! she thought. If you only knew what you mean to me! If you only knew how you saved me after I lost Tanya! But without her having any choice in the matter it had become unavoidable that Lara and Katya should leave.

She forced her presence on to the NEPman, past the clerks and cronies who guarded him. She found him in his private room, working like a regular businessman on his papers. The room was a sharp contrast to Shlyapin's other haunts, with their louche characters and tawdry furnishings. Here there was a simple order: a desk, a couple of chairs – everything as clean and tidy as the times allowed; daylight from the window and a smell of freshly made tea.

'Hello, Lara,' he said. His mouth bore a priest's neutral smile. Innocent. Lara wondered at times if he had any sense of morality. Its absence would explain his lack of shame which was a kind of innocence.

'I need to speak to you,' she told him.

'I'm glad you could call.'

She was armed against any attempt to dismiss her, but there was no attempt. He offered to take her coat and pour her a glass of tea. She said:

'It was difficult to see you.'

'Was it? I'm sorry.'

'Why wouldn't you see me?'

'I didn't refuse to see you. I didn't know you'd called.

Please, Lara, don't look as if you don't believe me. In the nature of my business there are lots of people I try to avoid. I tell my people when I want to be left alone, but I hadn't intended them to exclude you.'

He put aside his papers and lit a cigarette. Lara followed his hands with unconscious fascination; they were so nicely formed. She still did not believe him. He was waiting patiently, presenting a smooth surface to deflect any anger or emotion.

'If I couldn't get to see you –' she said '– why didn't you try to see me? Have I done something to annoy you?'

'You mean – why haven't we had dinner together?'

'I mean – what have I done to deserve your rejection?'

'Nothing.'

'Nothing? Then why am I here like a beggar looking for favours?'

'Is that why you're here? To ask for help?'

Shlyapin probably did not intend to be sarcastic, but his manner could be interpreted that way. He had adopted the detached air with which the more civilized sort of men hope to rebuff what they see as the emotionalism of women. Its effect is often the opposite, and this time it was too. Lara cried:

'You know it is! You know what's happening in Yuryatin. Samdevyatov has been arrested and Viktor has come here from Vladivostok!'

'Why should I know about Komarovsky?'

'Because you're Viktor's spy!'

He was unmoved by the accusation. Lara thought: I sound like a cast-off mistress. It isn't what I wanted. But what else am I?

'You see things so simply sometimes, Lara,' Shlyapin was saying. His deep voice was fatherly, though he was the younger of the two. 'You're partly right. I do know Viktor. We have some business together. But I'm not his spy, unless you mean that we've spoken about you. But friends do that, as well as spies, don't they?' He waited until he had forced a nod of acknowledgement from her, then went on: 'I've been trying to help you in your own interest, whatever you may think. Because of my business I've got to stay in Yuryatin. But it must be obvious to you that you can't stay here under present circumstances. Who else is going to help you, if not Komarovsky? Tell me.'

I want to hate him, Lara told herself, but he won't allow even that. 'There has to be another way,' she said aloud. She thought: I'm not permitted even to dictate my own emotions, that's how powerless I've become. Only with Yura did I have any self-respect and that was because of his own weakness. Kolya is different. I don't even know if he is sincere or not.

'I haven't asked you about your past with Komarovsky,' Shlyapin answered her, 'and I don't want to know about it now. I know that you don't like Viktor, but you don't have to like him. You can see that he's old and weak now.'

'Then why does he still want me?'

'I can't answer that. He hasn't long to live; that must be clear to you. A year? Two years? Perhaps he's trying to make amends.'

He had never said that he loved her. Lara had neither wanted nor expected his love. In a way she respected him because he had never bothered to lie. That was why he could let her go with nothing more than a sentimental regard. What then had she bought with her sacrifice? A temporary cessation of police harassment? It was not a sufficient explanation. Or perhaps it was. At times she felt so worthless that she could spend herself for a trifle as if she were a piece of inflated coin. Thinking of Komarovsky she knew now what lay at the root of her contempt for him: that by taking her as a girl, without love but only from a brutal passion, he had reduced her to an object of manipulation so that she had never recovered her value in her own eyes. She had thought that she was stronger than him – and she was wrong. Even now, when she had twice contemplated killing him, twice left him, he exercised a moral dominance.

Shlyapin asked: 'So will you go with him?'

'I don't appear to have any choice.'

'I think it would be for the best.'

'Then I suppose I must.'

The NEPman began to talk of Vladivostok, the opportunities that a large city could offer, particularly to Katya who was of an age to take advantage of them. It was evident to Lara that he was trying to cheer her up. Whatever his motives or his doubtful honesty, he was not gratuitously cruel; and compared to Viktor he was in control of himself.

'I can't help you now,' he told her. 'But I'll know where you are. And who knows about the future?'

So they were to leave Yuryatin and go to Vladivostok. This time Lara took Katya aside to explain the move. 'It isn't safe for us to stay here. There's a chance we'll be arrested.' She went on to tell about Samdevyatov, Mikulitsin and Galiullin, all of which Katya knew about already. What Lara did not explain was: why go with Komarovsky? She might have said that they had no choice – an explanation which had a large element of truth in it – but in fact Lara chose to say nothing because she feared to be dragged into the only half-understood intricacies of her relationship with Viktor. Katya accepted the half-confidence for what it was: an attempt to recognize her as something more than a child. She was beyond being angry with her mother for continuing the deceit of childhood. On this day she was experiencing the moral elevation that allows children in their teens to feel tolerant towards their parents. On another day she might have been angry.

When Lara announced her decision to the sisters there was no real surprise. There was a moment of shock, but only because what had until then been merely a fear had become real. Glasha, of course, said that they could stay – and in her way she was sincere – but they all knew the way things were going to be.

Komarovsky came round again to confirm that the decision was made and to discuss arrangements.

'I've got tickets for the three of us. We can leave the day after tomorrow.'

'Three of us?' said Lara. 'What about Lotte?'

'She isn't in any danger. There's no reason why she shouldn't stay here.'

'No!' Lara cried. 'She has to come with us!'

'Be reasonable.'

'She's my friend!'

Komarovsky saw at once that Lara was not to be moved on this point and he shrugged and agreed tetchily that he would see what could be done. But the effect of what he had said destroyed the calmness that Lara had assumed to face her ordeal. And when he was gone, faced with the cold contemplation of her vulnerability, she broke into sobs.

On the last night they sat in the little room among the bundles tied in string ready for the journey. It was dark; the room was lit only by candles since the lamp-oil had run out. The air smelled of warm tallow and the wax used to seal the bundles. Glasha had provided another bottle of doubtful alcohol which she poured and said: 'So this is it! Who would have thought it?'

'I'll write,' Lara told her, striving to be cheerful.

'I don't write much; I never was much of a one for letters. It's more in Sima's line. Still, I suppose I could give it a try.'

'Probably it'll only be until all this trouble blows over,' Avdotya ventured. This evening she was finding breathing difficult. Poor Avdotya, thought Katya; it was no wonder that she had never married; so shy and all that coughing.

They were all agreeing that the parting was not final – but Katya did not believe them. The past could never be remade. Something had happened to destroy the security that underpinned their little ménage and it could never be recovered. Glasha thinks my mother is dangerous. She doesn't really trust her any more. Avdotya is so frightened she can hardly breathe. And Sima? What does she really think, sitting there smiling and playing with her crucifix? I've never understood what Sima thinks.

'This vodka doesn't seem to be working,' Glasha commented drily. In a flicker from the candle, Katya saw a tear rolling down her fat cheek. 'It's just making me more miserable.'

Lara crossed the room to sit next to her and put an arm around her.

'For you it's going to mean a new school,' said Sima pointlessly to Katya.

'And clothes,' said Avdotya. 'In Vladivostok there are probably better shops. Where is your muslin dress? Have you remembered to pack it?'

Sima pressed on matter-of-factly: 'The teaching opportunities are almost certainly better, Lotte.'

'Oh, stop it!' Glasha exclaimed and wiped her eyes. They fell silent. Glasha embraced Lara, pulling her head to her bosom, and over her shoulder said: 'Let's all have a good cry and go to bed.'

The following day they gathered at the station, each of the women carrying a share of the packages. Komarovsky, dressed in black and smoking a cigarette, stood a way off, idling with the station staff, but occasionally casting a wary eye. The women were red-faced from the cold and the last tears which sprang forth with the last hugs, the last kisses, and even the last appeals to stay, which were not meant but had to be said. And then they were on the train and Lara felt it leaving the station, clickety-clack, never again, clickety-clack, windows frozen and figures as pale as ghosts, steam blowing past so that the station was almost immediately lost to view. How do I feel? Never again. Clickety-clack.

CHAPTER 8

VLADIVOSTOK

Katya was sixteen when she, her mother, and Fraulein Buerli moved to Vladivostok to share a three-roomed apartment with Komarovsky.

Before Vladivostok, neither Lara nor Katya had ever seen the sea. Now it was unavoidable; the city rose in terraces over the Golden Horn Bay and the harbour was full of ships. 'The Naples of the East!' said Komarovsky's friend Panov, the marine engineer. He spoke like that – Leningrad was 'the Venice of the North', and Moscow 'the Third Rome'. Despite which, it was true: the city was beautiful – something which neither of them had expected – especially in autumn, when the fogs diminished and the maples turned yellow. Nothing in the shabbiness of the times could take that away.

In the two years that Katya lived in Yuryatin she grew to resemble Lara in appearance, beautiful to anyone's eyes but with something of her father, which might have been his haunted quality and passion – it was as yet too early to say. Her mind also expanded. The physical horizons of her world had been limited by poverty and oppression, but out of affection for Fraulein Buerli she pursued her studies and read avidly; and more than anything else she had her own history and that of others around her from which she wrested an understanding. She reached an age when she recognized at last that the facts of her life, her family's structure and relationships were not God-given and universal, but particular to her. She had become aware of the difficulty of human motivation: seeing how two people, her mother and Komarovsky, could be at once so driven and repelled by each other, at once so patent and secretive in their feelings. And, of course, there was the recollection of Tanya – her own burden of guilt that a girl should not have to carry – a memory of days spent playing happily in the pasture above the house at Chita, and of that single flash of hatred when, for a moment at least, she had believed her sister to be the source of the poison that spoiled their life there.

In this new condition of enlightenment, Katya saw that Komarovsky, even at his most deceitful, genuinely cared for Lara and in his complex way tried to make her happy. He provided the best accommodation and livelihood that could reasonably be arranged and as often as not deferred to her wishes. In particular, it was understood that Lara would share a bed and bedroom with Fraulein Buerli. Katya was given her own room. Komarovsky slept on an old ottoman in the largest room where both the piano and the makeshift kitchen were.

Then there were the clothes – and cleanliness – and space! To be able to walk in the parks without, as at Yuryatin, feeling an object of contempt because of her shabbiness and, instead, catch the eye of the boys. To feel her hair shining and free-flowing. To sit quietly on her bed, in her own small room with her own possessions (few, but her very own). Katya was happy – and, if she knew happiness to be fragile, it was the more poignant, the more intense.

Komarovsky was now in semi-retirement because of his age. He still had some administrative duties associated with his former government employment, but he spent much of his time in the apartment, wrapped in a shawl and working by the stove on his papers. He wrote monographs on aspects of Soviet-Mongolian relations, and his latest project, in which he tried without success to interest the authorities, was to compile from all the decrees and regulations issued by the local soviets and other administrative organs a comprehensive statement of socialist legal practice which, in his opinion, would be universally valid, since within the new Soviet Union all manner of peoples, economic conditions and social development existed.

Lara returned to work as a nurse. Fraulein Buerli found a job as a teacher and also taught the piano to Katya. As for Katya, she resumed her schooling and learned to sing: much of her time was taken up with choirs and learning solo parts since she had a fine voice.

With all these occupations the organization of their ménage changed. From work, school or choir practice the women often returned to the apartment late. It was Komarovsky who found himself at home, insufficiently busy with his maps and papers, and rejected as a shabby relic by younger men. He joined a coterie of similar old men: railway and marine engineers, retired naval officers and bank employees, many of them washed up in Vladivostok by the tide of the past. They walked the city's parks and waterfronts, where they could stare at the ships and glean thin entertainment from chess, cards, vodka and tea. They bored each other with their stories and their projects (Komarovsky's universal legal code and description of the economy of Mongolia; Panov's account of the design and function of the boilers of the vessels in the harbour and his suggestions for improvements). Sometimes Katya found them at home when she returned from school. They wore grizzled goatee beards, pince-nez, odoriferous suits, cracked boots; and chain-smoked *papirossi* while talking about strange places such as Mukden, 'the Manchester of Manchuria'.

The group broke up when one of its members was caught up in a sweep of random arrests, as periodically happened. After that they met in pairs and less frequently and Komarovsky was left much on his own. He took to doing the shopping and cleaning the apartment. He discarded his frock coat for a dressing gown and a shawl since his thin blood caused him to suffer from the cold, and he pottered around the apartment in slippers. When the women came home late, he checked the time from his turnip watch and reproved them like an old *babushka* for their unpredictable ways. In all of this his manner became more gentle, even ingratiating, like an old prisoner seeking remission of sentence for his past crimes.

One day a letter arrived from Glasha Tuntseva. It was addressed to Larissa Komarovska. It said:

Dearest Lara,

I am not much of a one for writing – perhaps it's because I spend so much of my time reading other people's letters. We are all well, Avdotya and Sima send their love. The room is as it always was. Thank our stars, the authorities didn't try to billet anyone else on us, and it now seems so spacious (Lord, how tactless I'm being! but that's your old friend).

After you left we did have some 'visitors', about whom I can't say very much. They didn't give much explanation, but they were looking for some old acquaintances. However, we didn't know where these acquaintances were, and after a while they lost interest and we have heard nothing since.

You will remember that some of our friends and relatives also left the area. Unfortunately, we have received little news of them, which is not good. Our friend the lawyer has disappeared entirely: his office is now used by the Party (which, of course, is a good thing), and his home has been let to a poor family – something which we must also approve of. Our relative has apparently been travelling and is unable to write. His son has taken over the house and is taking care of his mother.

Oh Lord, what times we are living in! Though I must say that things are getting better every day.

The reason that I am writing is to tell you that old Antipov has died. It was after a short illness and he did not suffer. When

173

I heard the news I went round to his place to see if he had left any messages or things for his relatives. Sadly, there was nothing. He was living alone and not taking care of himself and the things he had were mostly junk. However, I did find a photograph of his son and his son's wife on their wedding day. You will remember that the old man quarrelled with his daughter-in-law. So the fact that he kept her picture may mean that he had forgiven her in his heart.

That is all there is to tell, really. Please write to me and let us know how you are all getting on.

Your loving,
Glasha

The letter arrived in the daytime when everyone by chance was at home, and the initial reaction, perhaps because it was daytime and the sun was streaming through the window, was one of joy. Lara read the letter aloud and only Komarovsky commented sourly: 'She's naive if she thinks that coded way of writing about "visitors" and "acquaintances" will fool anyone. She should watch her step.'

That night they lit the oil lamp and settled around the stove to read the letter again. This time they recognized the reality of the sad news.

'Poor Anfim Yefimovitch,' said Lara.

'Do you think he's dead?' Fraulein Buerli asked cautiously.

Lara shook her head in ignorance. 'That's what Glasha thinks. Mikulitsin is obviously in prison or exile somewhere. I'm glad that his son is looking after the family.'

They talked a while about Samdevyatov and Mikulitsin, their different characters; yet both had given help to Lara in times of crisis. Then Fraulein Buerli said:

'I'm sorry to hear that your father-in-law has died. Even if you had your differences, he was a link to your husband.'

'I think we had made up our differences, even if we rarely saw one another. He was an honest man. I never had any ground for complaint against him. And he tried in his way to be kind to Katya.'

'You used to see him, didn't you, love?' said Fraulein Buerli.

Katya nodded. It had never been possible to be fond of the old man: there was always a ferocity about him, as if she carried a taint. But she had memories of the trips to his little room and the little treats he prepared for her. She was sad for him now. It was the first time that she had recognized the finality of our opportunities to make clear to each other the true nature of our feelings. And she thought how different things might have been if her grandfather had given her such an opportunity.

During this conversation they ignored Komarovsky. He had lost his power to terrorize and they were free to speak even about Lara's husband. Now Komarovsky was bumping and grunting to make them aware of his presence and annoyance. Finally, he interrupted to tell them he was going out.

'Where?' enquired Lara indifferently.

'I've just remembered that I agreed to play chess with Panov.'

'When will you be back?'

'It's late now, so I imagine I'll be very late. I have my key.'

While Komarovsky busied himself with his coat, the others continued to ignore him. They returned to conversation about Yuryatin, and the time when Komarovsky was not there. They did not notice him leave.

The overt text of the letter was exhausted, so they turned to other things, wishing that Glasha had written more. For example, what had happened to their neighbour, the saddler? Or to all the others they knew? The letter was examined like an old sheet. Having scanned the surface they checked it for tears and stains, and patched the holes from their imaginations, so that even its silences were eloquent. To take the saddler's case: they were certain he had not married. He had been on the brink of taking up with a street-porter's widow, but he had had reservations about the children. If the nuptials had taken place, surely Glasha would have told them? So in this case, the silence was a cause of relief since they had some liking for the saddler but knew very little of the widow except that she had a bad reputation. And what about . . .? There were so many 'what abouts' that they spent several hours in enjoyable speculation; departing from the letter to rehearse their most pleasant recollections of Yuryatin (temporarily forgetting the fates of Samdevyatov and Mikulitsin); taking the letter as a biblical text from which they could sermonize to their hearts' content, all sadness gone in the knowledge that there were friends still who thought and cared about them.

They did not talk about Shlyapin or his fox-fur coat. Glasha did not mention him and neither did they. Katya noted that fact. She could have raised the subject of the NEPman herself, but did not and did not know why. Perhaps Glasha's silence in this respect was also eloquent.

Komarovsky came home at midnight. He was drunk but sheepish. The fight had gone out of him.

Katya dreamt one night of Shlyapin. There he was, walking through the door of her dreams, a surprising stranger. She had never dreamed of him before; though she had thought about him often. In her thoughts he was not an individual. He was a mirror. She washed her hair for Shlyapin and wore pretty clothes for him – or someone like him. She was well aware that she did not really know him, but she attached his face and his eyes to that abstract spectator whose approval she sought for her appearance, who stood at her shoulder and whispered, 'Wear your hair like this,' who appreciated every little moue or courtesy. And at another level he represented her aspirations. He was the departure from the ordinary. He was the man who transformed everyday life and poverty and tedium with the magic cloak of his fox-fur coat.

In her dream, Katya was in a crowd of people and he

shouldered his way through them wearing his fox-fur coat and his sly attractive smile, pert, dapper and mysterious. What was he doing there?

Katya felt shy and embarrassed by his presence and had to explain him to her schoolmates. 'Nikolai Afanasitch is a friend of my mother.' Her schoolmates were unaffected by the news. They could see that Shlyapin was different from them. They were the sons of seamen and factory workers; clad in coarse jackets and heavy boots; rowdy and ignorant and threatening in their ignorance, so that she wanted to fly to Shlyapin for protection. She could hear them gossiping behind her back, that she was the daughter of a counter-revolutionary, and her mother was the kept woman of an old man.

They walked along the waterfront. The sea rolled grey and oily among the rusting ships. Shlyapin took off his coat and draped it over her shoulders and she pulled it across her so that she could be completely enveloped by its fur. Her schoolmates had turned into street beggars and followed them, yapping like stray mongrels.

'Who are you going to marry?' Shlyapin asked.

'I don't know. I don't like any of the boys at school.'

'I could help you. I've always wanted to help you and your mother.'

'Could you find my sister, Tanya?'

'Perhaps.'

'And Samdevyatov?'

'Probably, though he has only himself to blame.'

'And my father?' Katya blurted out.

'Almost certainly. He isn't really dead. That's just a story that was spread about to fool the Reds.'

Fraulein Buerli was playing the piano at the apartment. Shlyapin stood by her side and began to sing a melancholy German song in a limpid tenor voice.

'I didn't know you knew German,' Katya said.

He laughed his rich brown laugh and answered, 'You must remember that time at Chita!'

'When the Kappelevtsy called at our house?'

'Of course!'

Katya thought how stupid she was. She remembered now that Shlyapin had been there; she had seen him. She could still see him, on his knees at the bed of the dying boy whose body was covered by the flag of the mother and child.

In the morning the dream was forgotten, but afterwards Katya found herself looking at her schoolmates differently. They seemed poor and miserable. When one of the boys caught her in horseplay and gave her a kiss, she felt a flash of revulsion.

There was a children's home. Lara passed it every day on her way to the hospital. Attached to it was a yard where the able-bodied played. On the second floor was a series of barred windows, and pressed against these were the faces of the children who could not play, the sick and the crippled and the others whose eyes were dull with the light of idiocy. After she had first noticed it, Lara planned a new route to walk to work; but for one reason or another there was always occasion to walk past the building, and she could never put the fate of the children out of mind. She spoke about them to Fraulein Buerli.

'Whenever I go past, I think of Tanya,' she told her. Those simple words expressed her insupportable misery. 'I can scarcely bear to wonder what happened to her.'

'It wasn't your fault,' the little woman reassured her, and maintained her reassurance with an expression of almost angelic sweetness.

'You're too good,' Lara murmured. Although she meant the words sincerely, she could not disguise the fact that sympathy was almost as unbearable as guilt – in fact was a testimony to her weakness – and that was all that her companion could offer, this curious little person, this weary piece of flotsam who might have been Lara's mother.

What did I say? *I can scarcely bear to wonder.* I haven't wondered at all – not since . . . when? – I can't remember when I last thought of Tanya. The truth is that it's more important to hide my own guilt than to do anything to find her. And the only way to do that is not to think of her.

She remembered instead that there were women who conspire with men against their children; who allow them to be neglected and abused, not from hatred, but because their own lives are so empty of love that there is none to spare for others; women who face their men with a child's fear of abandonment; in whom the prospect of loneliness induces a panic that overrides every other consideration of duty or feeling.

Is this me? How else can I explain that I'm still with Viktor?

In a matter-of-fact way Fraulein Buerli sighed and said: 'Well, obviously this problem isn't going to go away. We need to think of something practical to do. I'm sure there are steps that could be taken. Have you talked to the authorities?'

'No.'

'No? I see. Then we could make a start there.'

'Viktor tried.'

'When?'

'After we left Chita. He tried to find the foster parents, but it wasn't any use. They'd moved. No-one knew where they were or if Tanya was still with them.'

'I find that hard to believe. In this country the authorities seem to know all there is to know about everyone. Just because Viktor couldn't find her doesn't mean that no-one can. In his heart he was probably glad not to.'

And was I glad too? Lara turned her friend's observation into another version of the same corrosive question: what does love mean?

Again the images of desperate women with faces as thin as shadows and voices as hollow as echoes arose in her. She had seen them often enough: a woman who lived below the room that Komarovsky had found in Moscow, who existed in a world of drunken abuse; the knife-grinder's widow who chased Vasili the engraver from next door to find herself rejected because of her children (would she keep them or abandon them?). Tired women who caught themselves staring at their mewling offspring and wishing, if only for a moment, that their children would disappear so completely that they had never existed. Women whose nights were filled with dreams of accidents and death to their children so that they could be spared the guilt of hatred and instead enjoy the luxury of tears over small coffins, and the virtuous knowledge that they were good mothers, freed from their burdens by the hand of God. Lara had had those dreams. Oh yes, she had had those dreams and knew that she had felt a despair as intense and hopeless as those other women. And though her conscious mind rejected the thought that she had not wanted Tanya and she could justify her actions, there came moments like now when she considered her situation and all reasoning became meaningless before the stark contemplation of her loss and the fact of her living with the criminal who had caused it.

Komarovsky came home from one of his long walks and chess games with his friend Panov. He found the womenfolk at home but no food prepared and without complaint set to work to prepare a meal and present it. He had had several drinks and was jolly and regaled them with amusing stories about his friends, their ideas and manners, which he studied with a lawyer's detachment and an old man's irony. On occasions like this he could be very droll. And afterwards, noticing Katya's listlessness, he volunteered to read aloud to them all, which he did well, in a fine round voice full of intelligence and expression. All evening he was at his most good-humoured and indulgent.

They went to bed. During the night Lara awoke. A faint mist had drifted into the apartment through the poorly sealed windows and ships' horns could be heard from the roadstead beyond the port. She found that she could not sleep and so got up and wrapped herself in a peignoir and sat for a while. The room was cold. She was restless. She went into the main room to steal warmth from the stove. A tallow night-light burned on the table and gave off a fatty smell. The cornices with their elaborate mouldings were shrouded in gothic shadow. Mice could be heard scurrying beneath the floor.

Komarovsky lay on the ottoman, covered in a cavalry blanket and an oriental rug, with his feet in their darned stockings protruding and his head resting on a cushion. She could see his white hair and beard and his old wrinkled skin; and, although his habits were clean, she could smell him, the sweat of his body, the exhalations of his breath, the meaty animal presence of him, his age and decay. She thought how disgusting he was in repose: so pale and flaccid without his manners and his fine voice to seduce and distract the senses. How appalling – not that she had ever loved him – but that she had ever been able to bring herself to live with him for any reason; upon any terms.

She stood at the head of the ottoman. Komarovsky's shrouded body stretched away from her like the carving on a catafalque. She was reminded of her mother's funeral; the sight of the powdered corpse laid out for inspection. She had expected then that the pitiful token of flesh would attract her affections, but she had felt only a cold repugnance, that the body was a sham which had nothing to do with all that was lively and had justified those affections. She remembered the other mourners. After a moment of piety and embarrassment in the immediate shock and presence of death, they had fallen to talking of everyday matters.

In truth, it was possible to say anything in front of a corpse.

'I hate you,' Lara said.

There – it was done! And it was not enough. Useless, useless, petty and useless! A child talking behind an adult's back. What else can I say or do that will lift this burden from me? In the quiet of the room it was not even possible to be sure that she had spoken aloud above the clamour of her thoughts.

'I know,' said Komarovsky.

No! He hadn't spoken! How could she be sure? His eyes were closed and he said nothing more. From lying on his back, he turned on to his side, but still gave no recognition that Lara was there. She would tell him again. She would say nothing. The words were as complete as she could make them and to repeat them would be to add to her sense of futility. She did not want to discuss this with him. It was enough that he knew. She found a chair and sat in it, tightening the grip on her peignoir against the cold.

After some moments she heard a noise. A muffled animal sob. It was coming from Viktor. He was still lying on his side with his face turned away. He was crying in his sleep!

Never before had she known him cry; even believed it were possible. But now it was there, scarcely more than a whimper, and she felt the reflex that pulled at her sympathy and made her rise from the chair before she could consider; and she would have gone to him and taken his head in her arms and comforted him as if he had been Tanya. And then she caught herself, and told herself that it was Viktor, and that the tears were of drink, guilt and self-pity.

She froze. She was angry. How dare he cry! Having stripped her of everything else, how dare he try to strip her of her hatred? She wanted to scream at him, even at the cost of provoking his violence, so that she could regain her focus and see him as he was. Not tears, Viktor! Please God, not tears!

She stood for a while, shaking her head and muttering to herself, sounding in the darkness as though she were casting conjurations over him. 'I'm losing my mind,' she whispered aloud. 'What can I do that will stop him?' But in fact he had stopped; he had lapsed into a deeper sleep and rolled on to his back so that now he was snoring. And Lara felt a calmness descend on her.

I must put an end to this, she told herself. It can't go on. She had no idea of how that was to be accomplished; only the overwhelming need for finality. She thought: I shall kill him. I tried to kill him once before, at the Sventitskys' party when I was little more than a child. This time I shall do it. There's a kitchen knife on the table. I only need to take it up and kill him.

Quite coolly she picked the knife up.

He was still asleep. She had the knife in her hand, and it was not uncertainty that stayed her. She was mentally rehearsing all the reasons that led her to killing him, so that each of these ghosts could be summoned and laid by her act; and it would be complete; and she would be absolved. She thought: I don't need him. It was never an emotional necessity that drove me to him, just the accident of circumstances that left me without any choice. From that conclusion it followed that she had not subconsciously conspired with Viktor to get rid of her daughter. That crime had all along been his. Killing him would prove that she did not need him, and exorcise that portion of her guilt. And then afterwards, tomorrow, she would set about finding Tanya.

She stepped forward. It was time to get the matter over with. One blow to the heart and he would be dead. She studied the rug that covered him. Amid the folds she tried to locate the point where she would cause the fatal wound. It vaguely occurred to her that she would inevitably be caught; but that would be so unjust an outcome that the possibility could be dismissed. She thought: now I shall do it!

'Mother?' said Katya.

'Just a moment.'

'What are you doing?'

Sleepy-voiced, Katya was standing in the doorway of her room, naked feet entwined and her arms embracing herself for warmth. And then little Fraulein Buerli was also there, taking in the scene with one shrewd glance.

'Come back to bed,' she said gently.

On her next free day Lara went to the children's home. She asked to see the principal. She was shown to a dull office and introduced to a woman of her own age who wore severe braids and a washed-out blue cotton dress.

'I'm looking for my daughter. She's seven years old.'

'This is a home for orphaned children,' said the principal. 'If it's a case of a lost child, it's a matter for the police?'

'Tanya isn't lost. She was taken from me.'

'Oh?' said the woman, and Lara realized that in the other's mind the thought had passed that she was a hysteric, unreconciled to the death of a child. Lightly, Lara said:

'She was placed with foster parents. I've got the names. It isn't a story I've made up.'

'I didn't suppose you had. But a foster child would hardly be here. Where was she taken from?'

'Chita. My – my husband was working for the government there.'

'Perhaps you should apply to the authorities there.'

'I could write, I suppose,' Lara answered mechanically. She was proud of her control and detachment, but disturbed that the woman in front of her was examining her so curiously. *But perhaps she isn't and I'm overwrought.* 'Unfortunately I don't know anyone there. Is there a children's home? Could you tell me to whom I should talk?'

'I can give you an address. And you should also contact the police.'

'Yes, of course.'

Lara waited while the principal dipped her pen into the inkwell and wrote out the address on a slip of paper. She asked: 'Isn't there some form of register of all orphaned and fostered children?'

'There are so many. Ever since the war. Perhaps

184

there's a list in Moscow, but I've never heard of it.'

'Do you have a list?'

'Of our children – yes. And photographs. We take photographs of the children as they come into our care. Would you like to see them?'

'Please.'

The woman moved from her desk to a cupboard, and from the cupboard took out two old albums bound in worn buckram. She laid these on her desk and said to Lara: 'Look if you like. But please excuse me if I leave you alone to get on with it. I've some other things to attend to.'

'You're being very kind,' Lara said.

'Whatever I can do to help.'

Left alone, Lara opened the first of the books. Each page held four photographs and, with each photograph, a gummed card with a name and date of birth, entry to the home and leaving, written in sepia ink. Lara flicked urgently through the pages and then more slowly until she stopped at random before a picture of a little boy and found herself wondering what had happened to him. She chided herself for her own eagerness. There was no possibility that Tanya had passed through this orphanage. Indeed Lara had not come there with that expectation, but merely to gain information to allow her to pursue her enquiries. The existence of the photographs was just an occasion for false hopes: one of those moments of folly when she allowed herself to think that there was some principle of order and justice that would fulfil those hopes.

A tap on the door and it opened, and the principal of the orphanage returned. In the passage behind her, two unshaven men in slovenly approximations to uniform waited. The principal made no allusion to them, but enquired in a polite tone whether Lara was finished.

'Yes, I am,' Lara told her. To herself she said: I was right; she does think I'm mad. She's brought those two men to restrain me if I become violent. But I haven't done anything to make her think this.

Lara left quietly and, back at home, tried to explain to Fraulein Buerli. The latter listened patiently and then said: 'Well, to be frank, Lara, your behaviour is a little peculiar.'

'In what way? I've been very careful to contain my emotions and approach the problem rationally.'

'Yes, I can see that.'

'Then I don't understand.' Lara matched her friend's calmness with her own. She knew that she was consciously taking cues. It was like learning to dance: watching a partner's feet to avoid any possibility of embarrassment. She was sure her behaviour couldn't be faulted. In a way she was proud of it; this ability to overcome any hint of trouble and tackle the world in exactly the right way.

'You sound too rational,' Fraulein Buerli answered. 'Too detached. That's how you sound now; but friends don't talk to each other that way. Someone thinks you're mad, and you can discuss it coolly as if it were the most normal thing in the world. Well, it isn't.'

'Do you think I'm mad?'

'That's what I mean. What you've just asked isn't a normal question.'

'But am I mad, Lotte?' Lara asked, feeling the cracking of her external self. 'How am I supposed to ask? Don't you think I want to know?'

'Oh, my love, of course you're not mad!' Fraulein Buerli exclaimed, and she held her arms out and folded Lara into them and then caressed her hair while Lara's head rocked against the little woman's shoulder. 'The burdens have been too much for you, that's all. You have to put some of them down.'

'But I must find Tanya!'

'Of course you must. But there are other ways. If you insist on calling on people, then they'll only make you disappointed or angry. You must begin gently. Write some letters. Find out what you can from the library or the newspapers. Yes?'

Lara accepted her friend's advice. She wrote to the

police authorities in the Maritime Provinces and in Chita; and to Party officials and the various organs that for one reason or another registered the population. None of these letters bore fruit, but the fact that she was doing something about her daughter helped to settle her and avoided the hostility that personal encounters might have caused until she was in a calmer frame of mind.

What did Katya make of all this? She was in a period of retreat from her mother, Viktor and Fraulein Buerli, self-absorbed in adolescence and resentful. Who am I? What do I want? Standing in front of the mirror playing languidly with her hair, touching the blemishes of her skin. Am I beautiful?

Lara frightened her. That night when she had disturbed her mother over Viktor's supine body, she knew that Lara had intended to kill him. Lotte had ushered her back to bed, but Katya knew. Or did she? The following morning no-one talked about the night's events, so they could have been a dream. Well, if they could keep secrets, so could Katya! Tell them nothing! Steal small coins and bits of ribbon – I need them! Steal a half-hour after school to meet with the other girls and laugh at the boys. The boys shout back: 'Show us your knickers!' The younger teachers look at her curiously. Sailors on leave leer and make gestures. *Am I beautiful?*

Who can I talk to? No-one. What is wrong with my mother? She seems as brittle as when Tanya vanished. Lara is apparently calm. She has calmness painted on her. All surface. Not to be touched. Lotte is absorbed only in Lara. Viktor is ridiculous – maybe he's going crazy.

One autumn day they all took a walk in one of the city's parks. Komarovsky, for the occasion, was wearing a linen jacket and a battered panama and in his elderly flat-footed way was ahead of them, striking out at patches of grass and stones with a malacca cane. Katya walked by her mother and listened as Fraulein Buerli spoke about Katya's musical education.

'I've done what I can,' said her tutor, 'but I was only trained to teach young gentlewomen – if that expression doesn't seem too bizarre – enough so that they could accompany their husbands with a song. Katya needs to study somewhere where she can hear greater music and receive better tuition than is available here.'

'Do you mean Moscow?' Lara asked.

'It would certainly be best.'

Lara put it to Katya: 'Would you like to study in Moscow?'

'I don't know.' But Katya knew very well, and did not want to say so. She was able to avoid an immediate answer because Uncle Viktor had suddenly turned and was coming at her in the stooping gambolling way he had sometimes adopted when she was smaller, when he would pick her up and swing her round. Really his behaviour was becoming odder as he grew old.

'Ho! Ho!' he cried.

'Stop it, Viktor!' snapped Lara, and Komarovsky stopped and retreated sulking to hack again at the grass. Lara turned again to Katya. 'You don't want to leave your friends? Is that it?'

'I don't have any friends,' Katya answered impatiently. She hated being interrogated, and lately it seemed to her that no-one ever spoke normally: everything was a spoken or unspoken criticism. 'I don't want to leave you or Fraulein Buerli.'

'But your music?'

'It isn't important.'

'How can you say that?'

'Because it's true.'

'Lotte doesn't think so.'

Katya shrugged. Adults were blind sometimes. She had already realized that although she could play the piano and had a good singing voice and enjoyed music well enough, she had no passion for it. She knew that she was competent, not gifted. If she completed her musical education, she might qualify for the orchestra or the chorus, but never as a solo performer. It was not enough. It could not fire her enthusiasm.

Seeing her sullen answer was unwelcome, Katya left the other women and joined Komarovsky. He seemed pleased enough with her company. Behind her she could hear them talking. About me, she thought touchily, which in fact happened to be true.

'A girl of her age should have dreams,' Lara said to her companion.

'She's experienced too much,' Fraulein Buerli replied sadly.

Lara heard the echoes of her own passionate nature, now faded. Ashes and disillusionment. And Katya knows, she thought. She can see every day where my own feelings and ambitions led to. When did I last have any true joy in life? With Yura. Never since. Viktor was only able to take Tanya because I was dead to her and never really fought for her. I'm dead inside.

These days, when she looked at Katya, her daughter seemed so calm, so studied. Even the awkwardness of adolescence was muted. She has learned to accept, was Lara's conclusion. She learned that from me. Is that a good lesson or not?

Physically, Katya was maturing into a woman; and Lara knew that her sexual awakening was only a matter of time. And what then? Where would that detachment leave her? From ignorance and indifference she might take the first man who brought a measure of security. Or, without preparation, her emotions might become unlocked and she would commit herself headlong and unreasoning to the man who had found the key.

And with everything I know about Katya, I can't predict which way she will go.

Moscow – Moscow. Katya could learn music there. If there are any records of Tanya, that's where they'll be. They don't reply to my letters. Katya could learn to sing – or play the piano – I think singing. Yura used to sing. Or perhaps I only think he used to sing. Perhaps it was Pasha who sang. In Moscow they'll definitely know about Tanya if anyone does. And now, thanks to Lotte, I can face people again. Months of writing letters, and no replies, none that help. I know when to become angry and when not to. That really is the test of a rational person. Singing would be best.

She watched Komarovsky still ahead of them. As mothers walked past him, he sprang playfully at their children, his fat rump going waggy-tail like an old dog.

He's becoming senile, Lara thought and smiled to herself. It isn't what I expected. I thought that he would be a devil to the end. It will finish with him incontinent and childish and I shall have to take care of him like a mother. It isn't what I expected.

'What will you do?' Fraulein Buerli broke in as if from a distance.

'I'm going to Moscow,' Lara told her.

CHAPTER 9

DISAPPEARANCE

One day in September of that year, 1929, Nikolai Afanasitch Schlyapin found himself walking down Kamerger
Street in Moscow past the Arts Theatre. It was a bright day
with a cold snap in the air and he was wearing a grey felt hat
and his fox-fur coat. He walked with the wandering slouch
of a man who has other things on his mind, he gave way
to other passers-by, and waited patiently while a gang of
labourers unloaded some theatrical flats and carried them
into the building. While he waited, he finished gnawing the
core of an apple and fed the remains to the horse that pulled
the workmen's waggon. His eyes drifted about the street
and lit upon a woman in neatly turned clothes, who was
coming out of a door that led into an apartment house. He
focused on her briefly and was then distracted by two men
carrying a huge, gilt papier-mâché urn, who asked him to
make way; and only afterwards did his eyes return to the
apartment house, and he realized that he had seen Lara.
But by then she was gone.

In the afternoon, Shlyapin went back to Kamerger
Street to the house where he had seen the woman he
had taken for Lara. He enquired of the *dvornik* whether
Comrade Antipova lived there. The old man did not

recognize the name. Shlyapin tried Komarovska, but still elicited no identification; nor when he tried a description. But the old man was a drunk who would hardly know his own name. So he tried some of the residents, but had no luck there either. He began to think he was mistaken.

That might have been the end of the matter. Shlyapin told himself that, in any case, he had no real interest in Lara. But as a relief from the tense meetings that occupied his days in Moscow, he found himself inadvertently thinking about her, and about their time together in Yuryatin. They were quite sentimental thoughts. He remembered their dinners together and their lovemaking; and, if he recalled at all his part in returning her to Komarovsky, he felt no shame about it. It was obvious that her continued presence in Yuryatin would have been a danger both to herself and her child. He had done her a favour.

He had got into the habit of walking in his free time while he considered the business that had brought him to Moscow; and, a few days later, wandering in the area of Kuznetsky Lane, he was again in Kamerger Street. It was a mild evening, people were in the street and, over the heads of a group of gossiping women, he again saw Lara: this time walking away from him. He pushed past the women and set off at a run, and just before she turned the corner he caught her and placed his hand on her shoulder.

'Lara!' he said breathlessly.

She turned with a mixture of shock and incomprehension, and only slowly did she fix his identity. She said: 'Oh – it's you. You took me by surprise.'

'Yes, I suppose I did.' Shlyapin was still breathless. Lara added nothing more and he was placed for a moment in the situation of being unable to speak, and at the same time felt the oddity of the fact that he had had to chase her, which was not the way things used to be.

'I wasn't sure it was you.' Now his voice sounded hurried as he caught up with his breathing. 'I saw you a few days ago, but I wasn't sure. I thought you were in the East somewhere?'

'Vladivostok.'

'Yes. Are you still with Komarovsky? Is he here?'

'No.'

'No,' Shlyapin repeated. He took the opportunity now to study Lara's face. She looked – not happy, but composed; as if a problem had been resolved for her: there was an air of assurance about her. 'We must have a meal together,' he proposed without knowing why. 'I'm at a little hotel, the Hotel Lublin, do you know it? It has a different name nowadays, but everyone still uses the old one. Where are you staying?'

'I've found a room. I'm sharing with a family. Thanks for the invitation, but I'm really very busy.'

Despite her obvious reluctance to continue the conversation, Shlyapin was equally reluctant to let her go. Her new manner excited his curiosity. And perhaps too, his present difficulties made him want to remember their common past, which in his recollection was pleasant enough. He asked: 'Have you been here long?'

'Several weeks.'

'And when are you leaving? Is your daughter with you?'

She paused, and Shlyapin thought that for a moment she was contemplating a convenient lie to dispose of him; but in her new confidence she said:

'Katya is still in Vladivostok. I don't know how long I'll be here. I'm trying to find a place for her at the Conservatoire, in which case we'll move to Moscow.'

'Surely it hasn't taken weeks just to do that?'

'No.'

'So you have other business?'

'Yes.'

'Official business? If you tell me I may be able to help.'

'I don't think you could help.'

Shlyapin ventured a chuckle, not really knowing if it was appropriate. 'Well, you'll never know unless you tell me.'

Again Lara hesitated as though weighing up how much to tell him, and then came down in favour of honesty. 'I've another daughter – do you remember? Tanya.' Shlyapin had a vague recollection of being told, but the fact had never interested him. 'She was taken from me by Viktor. And now I'm trying to find her again with the help of the authorities. But you know officials. They can be very slow.'

She waited. He wanted to help her and was disappointed because the problem was outside his experience. It was his habit to help people when it was not too inconvenient, a habit that went with his image of power and built up the stock of favours owed. Yet he could not help her, and it annoyed him the more because she was apparently not expecting help. Instead she was studying him. He could not know that Lara had recognized the trace of softness in his manner and was thinking how different men were from women: that women nurtured relationships whereas men cultivated them only by occasional gestures and, instead of true feeling, experienced merely flashes of sentimentality such as now, like this man, who was ordinarily so rational and calculating.

'How are you getting on?' she asked.

'Very well.'

'Your business is successful?'

'Excellent. Is your room here in Kamerger Street? I tried to find your address.'

'No, it isn't.'

'You've got friends here then?'

'Someone I used to know lived in one of these houses.'

'Isn't he still here?'

'He died.'

'I'm sorry. Do I know him?'

'I may have mentioned him. Zhivago. I only found out after my arrival that he was here in Moscow. It was a surprise. I haven't seen him in years, and I had no idea where he was. He was a doctor.'

She looked – Shlyapin was not sure – not sad, which

suggested an immediacy of pain. Her face registered pain overcome but remembered calmly. Over this Zhivago? He had a memory of the name, a hint of a story he had picked up when he had learned Lara's history before taking her as his mistress; or perhaps she had told him and he had not listened. She was saying:

'He had a weak heart and he died one day in the street. We were within days of meeting again – and he died.'

But Shlyapin did not want to hear about Zhivago. He said: 'Maybe there is something I can do for you. They've re-introduced meat rationing. Do you have a card?'

'No.'

'I'll get you one. Just tell me what name you're going under: Antipova or Komarovska?'

'Antipova – but it really isn't necessary. I'll get by.'

'I'll do it all the same.' He was rummaging in his pockets for pencil and paper. 'I come this way quite often. Isn't the house back there the one you were visiting? I'll leave the card with the *dvornik*; he can give it to you.'

'Please . . .' Lara said, but stopped. She looked at the sky and the stars in a clear heaven and the moon passing over the rooftops. 'It's late,' she finished, 'I must go.'

'Call at my hotel.'

She nodded in acknowledgement and then turned and walked away, leaving him alone. And only then did he reflect on her coolness towards him and feel resentful because he did not deserve it. He tried to shrug her off as he returned along the street and halted by the apartment house. He examined its shabby nondescript façade and then let his gaze slip with his wandering thoughts until he was looking across the street at two workmen lounging against a wall, about whom there was nothing remarkable except that their hands were clean and white.

The truth was that Shlyapin's affairs were worse than

he had told Lara. Most of his business had been as a middleman trading in the peasants' surpluses. But during the previous year, under pressure of a grain shortage, the Government had reverted to requisitioning the crop as it had done during the hated period of War Communism before the New Economic Policy. In 1928 there was no surplus to sell. Shlyapin had survived on his reserves and by opening a small shop to sell soap, paraffin and nails.

This year the peasant was again allowed to sell his grain to the market; but he had no faith that it would be worthwhile or safe. There was a lot of propaganda in the countryside against the supposed exploiting kulak class; and the richer peasants that Shlyapin dealt with – and they were a pretty poor lot – had been selling or giving away their livestock and property to relatives and neighbours, and, in some cases, had decamped to the towns to avoid the attentions of the troikas of Communists who now controlled the villages. Under these conditions Shlyapin had decided that his days as a NEPman were numbered. He had come to Moscow in the hope of finding employment as an official.

After meeting Lara, Shlyapin returned to his hotel. The encounter had left him feeling both confused and a little foolish. It was not his custom to spend much effort in pursuit of women. With his good looks and the glamour of his power, they had come to him. He had not previously considered Lara to be different from any of the others, except that she had had a certain attraction of reluctance. What galled him now was the knowledge that she had never in any real sense been his; and never less so than at present when his power was diminished. It galled him and at the same time made her mysterious and therefore desirable.

It was nine o'clock in the evening. He was tired and irritable; yet there was still business to be done. He set about tidying the dirty room with its cracked ceiling, leaking window and broken furniture. He placed a small, stained deal table in the middle of the room, covered it with a sheet and set four chairs around it. He went to the hotel kitchen and came back with a plate of bread and pickles for which he had bribed the cook. He put these on the table and from his pocket took a pack of greasy playing cards which he also set out. Around his waist he wore a money belt. He took it off and checked the wallets, counting his reduced wad of banknotes and the stock of wedding rings and jewellery he had collected from the villages. Finally he sat on the edge of the bed studying the effect of his arrangements, and prayed silently to no-one in particular that his efforts would be rewarded.

At ten o'clock there came a knock on the door. Shlyapin opened it and let in a fat man with a smiling face who looked at him and said: 'It looks like I'm the first, Kolya. Where are the others? Are they coming? You don't happen to have a drink about you, do you?'

The visitor took off his topcoat and slung it on the bed, smacked his red hands together for warmth and flexed his fingers. 'Thanks,' he said, accepting the drink. 'So this is where you're hiding. Not bad, I've seen worse. Pickles! Can I have one? Have you got any cigarettes or do I have to smoke my own?'

Shlyapin took a gun-metal cigarette case from his jacket and offered a cigarette. 'Here, Sergei.'

'Nice,' said Sergei, fingering the case.

'Keep it,' said Shlyapin casually. 'I can get another.'

A few minutes later two men arrived together. They greeted Sergei warmly and without any ceremony helped themselves to a drink and food from the plate. The taller of the two was a stooping middle-aged man with thinning hair and the weather-beaten face of someone who has worked in the open air, but for now he was wearing the baggy pants and jacket of different suits. The smaller, younger man was slim, with a goatee beard and long pale fingers. He had on a pair of woollen trousers and a military jacket without insignia. Dangling from the breast pocket was a pince-nez. His name was Solovyev.

'So what are we going to do tonight?' he said curtly.

'I thought a game of cards,' Shlyapin answered.

'Okay by me,' said the fat man.

'What game?' asked his companion.

'Skat.'

'Don't know it.'

'It's a German game. I learned it from some German engineers in Yuryatin.'

'You're a real internationalist, Kolya!' said Sergei playfully.

'All right,' assented Solovyev. 'You can teach us the rules.'

'We'll play a few practice hands.'

'And then what? We play for money?'

'If you like.'

'Money?' chimed Sergei. 'Oh, I don't think there's much interest in money. I could paper my room with *money*. It's not as if you can buy anything worthwhile with it.'

'No, that's true,' Shlyapin agreed with heavy-handed humour. He heard his own torpid voice, and thought: this is a bad idea; I'm not in the mood. He had not selected his visitors for their ability to amuse him. That was a custom he had so long ago got out of that normally he scarcely noticed their tedious conversation. Friends were selected because they were useful. Everyone did the same, didn't they? But tonight he was distracted; and by a woman moreover who appeared to have no idea of the effect she had had on him, no more than he had expected it.

'Since it's a friendly game,' he proposed, 'we could play for vodka.' On top of the wardrobe was a suitcase. He took it down, laid it on the bed and took out four bottles of vodka and four glasses. 'The winner gets a drink from the losers' bottles. Anything you don't lose, you keep.'

Makarov, the older man, the former peasant, who had so far said nothing chose this opportunity to speak. 'It doesn't seem fair.' The others looked at him sharply and he explained: 'If Kolya is providing the stakes, and we lose, we don't really lose anything.'

Since that was the point of his suggestion, Shlyapin said: 'Then call it a loan. Pay me back some time. All right? Let's play then.'

They took their places. Shlyapin explained the rules, dealt the cards, and they played three practice hands in concentrated fashion without talking, at the end of which Sergei announced: 'It doesn't seem so difficult. It's okay by me. We'll play skat. Yes?'

The others agreed – Solovyev in an offhand way as if granting a privilege, and old Makarov reluctantly, still troubled by qualms.

Once they had begun in earnest, Shlyapin took the first two hands in order to persuade his visitors that he was playing seriously. He drank his winnings with a show of eagerness, but the vodka felt as fiery as bile. He needed to keep his head. He prayed he would not get drunk. Then, using the excuse that the others had beginners' luck, and pleading the effect of alcohol, he started to lose steadily and, as the others felt the effects of the vodka, they ceased paying attention and were content to congratulate themselves on mastering the new game. And so they went on.

Since he did not need to attend to his game, Shlyapin could allow his thoughts to wander. He watched Makarov. The man worked at the Commissariat of Agriculture. He was Sergei's friend. The fat man took him everywhere as a foil for his own joviality, in the way that a pretty girl will often have a plain friend. Nowadays Makarov worked on production statistics and would, with nervous pleasure, recite the figures for pig meat production as if that were a winning way of conversation. Shlyapin had no particular hopes of the old peasant.

Solovyev was poring over his cards, occasionally putting his pince-nez to his nose then letting it fall. Drink had not caused him to slacken his attention, but a peevishness crept into his voice when he lost. 'Damn! Let me look at that card again – whose card was it – yours, Sergei, yours?'

Shlyapin had checked him out as far as he could. Solovyev had been a bookkeeper in a linen factory, a petty clerk who sweated his days over his employer's ledgers and his nights studying Marxism. Since Shlyapin cared for Marx as much as for Buddhism, he had only a passing curiosity as to what people found in it, but when he came across the real article, a genuine Communist, he sometimes experienced a detached fascination, as if he had stumbled across an aging bonze mumbling in his temple before a row of gilded idols and offerings of decaying fruit.

Between hands Solovyev tried to silence Makarov by lecturing him on the merits of the collectivization of agriculture and the threat posed by the kulak class.

The fat man broke off from singing under his breath to comment: 'What kulak class? In our village the only kulaks were moneylenders, and we got rid of them not long after the Revolution. I don't follow all this talk of a kulak class.'

'That's because you're a political ignoramus,' Solovyev rebuked him.

'Maybe. I'm not a know-it-all, that's for sure. What do you think, Kolya?'

'Me?' Shlyapin had not been paying attention to the words, only noting Solovyev's pince-nez. It said that, whatever the clothes, the man considered himself an intellectual. 'Oh, I'm no theorist. If the Party says there's a kulak class, then there must be.'

'What sort of answer is that? You frightened to discuss politics? Is this a democracy we're living in or not?'

'Really, I don't understand anything about kulaks. They're none of my business.'

'You go into the villages, don't you? You've seen more of what's going on than we have.'

'I just traded in grain, that's all,' Shlyapin answered in the hope of closing the subject. He noticed Solovyev hanging on to his reply, and felt like telling him, I agree with Sergei: the only kulak I ever knew was a wealthy peasant who lent money to help his neighbours – and we shot him in 1919, God forgive us. But it was obvious Solovyev would not agree, so he said nothing.

The other man adjusted his pince-nez, setting himself up for a speech.

'The kulaks are the bourgeois elements among the peasantry who will cling to private ownership of land and use their petty accumulations to re-introduce capitalism into the countryside.'

'Marx save us!' interjected Sergei ironically.

'They're the people you've been dealing with,' Solovyev said coolly to his host. 'Give them a couple of horses and ten *desyatins* of land and they think that's socialism. And the devil with the needs of the State as long as they can sell their surpluses to the NEPmen. You should watch your step, Kolya. How does Article 107 go? Something about causing rises in prices and failing to offer goods for sale? That's what you've been doing, isn't it? There are people in the camps at Solovky for doing exactly the same thing.'

'Probably,' Shlyapin answered. He had another answer prepared, a little piece of piety about the New Economic Policy being advocated by the Party and therefore something which, for a time at least, all good Communists were obliged to go along with. But he rejected it. What was the point? Solovyev knew who he was and what he did. If he had the power and the mind to have him arrested, then nothing Shlyapin could say would stop him. In fact, he was not sure he cared any more. He put his cards down and asked: 'Are we playing or discussing politics?'

'Playing,' said Sergei.

'Whatever you like,' said Makarov cautiously.

'Okay, we'll play cards,' Solovyev agreed after a moment's pause.

'Good. Then I propose we change the stakes for this round. Sergei, can you get me a meat ration card?'

'The way you're playing I shan't need to.'

'But you can get one?'

'Sure. But what do you want one for?'

'Someone I know is in Moscow on a visit and doesn't have a card.'

'Man or woman? Knowing you, I bet it's a woman. Am I right?'

'She's just a friend.'

'I'll bet she is!'

'Whatever you like. Is the bet on?'

'Okay.'

In the next round of play, Shlyapin won the meat ration card.

The game of cards finished at midnight when the vodka ran out and Shlyapin's visitors, tired and drunk, retired to their own homes. The NEPman cleared the mess from his room, smoked a couple of cigarettes and emptied the dregs of alcohol alone. He checked his funds again. He checked his suitcase again as if there might be another bottle there, in the absurd way that people repeatedly go over the same places when they have lost something, and with the same futile result. Mentally he calculated how long he could remain in Moscow at his present rate of expenditure. He calculated the effect of the evening's entertainment, whether it had gained him any influence or advanced his case at all. He knew from experience that the cultivation of influence was the cultivation of an intangible, but it was human nature to try to weigh such imponderables and he wrestled with the problem for a while, until finally he gave up and went to bed.

The following afternoon Sergei came round to Shlyapin's hotel. He was ashen-faced and feeling terrible, and asked for a drink to fight his headache.

Subsiding into a chair, he told Shlyapin: 'I've brought the ration card,' and asked, 'Who is it really for?'

'A woman I know.' Shlyapin fingered the card as if it were of no importance.

'Is she beautiful?'

'Not particularly. She's an old friend, that's all.'

The fat man lost interest. He went through his pockets to no purpose, then enquired: 'Did I do anything stupid last night?'

'Not especially.'

'What did we talk about?'

'All sorts. Solovyev went on about the kulak menace.'

'Did he now? What did I have to say on the subject?'

'You didn't believe there was a kulak class.'

'Christ.'

Shlyapin offered another drink from the bottle he had acquired that morning. Sergei accepted it gingerly. 'Did I really say that?' he asked.

'Yes. Why not? Is it important?'

'Of course it is!' the fat man answered sharply.

'Why?'

'Because it's obvious to anyone that next year is going to see a big drive towards collectivization. And the Party expects resistance from the better-off peasants, so something will have to be done about them. We can all look forward to a big campaign against the kulaks. The last thing to be saying is that they don't exist. Hell, what a mess! What about you, what did you say?'

'I kept my mouth shut.'

'Lucky you.'

Lucky me, thought Shlyapin, remembering also Solovyev's tirade against NEPmen. Warning or threat? He said soothingly: 'It doesn't matter. We had a few drinks and were talking among friends.'

'You don't know Misha.'

'Solovyev? What's wrong with him?'

Sergei tapped his nose. 'What do you think?'

'He's a spy?'

'I didn't say that. But who started all this kulak talk? He was sounding out other people's opinions. His kind do it all the time: keeping tabs on anyone who isn't toeing the line.'

'I'm sure you're mistaken,' Shlyapin answered. But, in fact, he was not sure.

By chance, Solovyev also called that afternoon. He had left behind a parcel of food and came to collect it. It took only a moment to find, but instead of leaving Solovyev indicated he wanted to talk, and began:

'You know I'm your friend, Kolya?'

'Of course,' Shlyapin agreed. As a matter of routine he offered his visitor a drink, but Solovyev refused it: he was not ordinarily a drinking man; he drank only when he was nervous in social situations. He more or less explained this, in his thin flat voice.

'I'm glad we're friends,' he went on, 'because I want to give you a friendly warning.'

'About what?'

'About Sergei.'

'Really? I don't follow? I thought he was your friend too.'

'Oh, don't mistake me! He's all right. But you know he has connections with the OGPU?'

'I didn't know. Are you certain?'

'As certain as anyone can be. I thought you would recognize the style. When we were talking last night, remember? He said he didn't believe in the existence of a kulak class. That was to find out whether anyone was going to agree with him. That's one of their tricks. Why do you think I got on my high horse? I was protecting myself.'

'I had wondered.'

'You can't be too careful of who you talk to – I mean, we're all right, but – do you have a cigarette?'

Shlyapin gave him one. Solovyev smoked it in a prissy way, putting it to his mouth as if rouging his lips.

Where did you learn that? Shlyapin wondered. He began to have doubts about his visitor's intellectual credentials. The man was a bag of tricks, using half-learned mannerisms in order to impress; Shlyapin had seen the sort of thing before: bad actors impersonating aristocrats in cheap theatres.

Between puffs Solovyev said: 'You know there's a list? The secret police have a list of all the NEPmen. It's only a matter of time before they start making arrests.'

'I'm not in that business any more.'

'That doesn't matter. Once a class enemy, always a class enemy. That's the way they think.'

'What are you trying to tell me?'

'You need to get abroad.'

Shlyapin did not reply at once. He was staggered by the other man's audacity in making a proposal that was as near to treason as made no practical difference. And he had made it after warning Shlyapin about the untrustworthiness of friends.

How am I different? he wondered. He asked:

'Why are you warning me?'

Solovyev bridled: 'I was trying to be a good friend to you.'

'I'm sorry,' Shlyapin apologized. He saddened the tone of his voice in order to placate. 'I thought – well, I thought that Sergei was my friend too.'

'Oh, he probably is,' answered Solovyev with an airy ambiguity. 'Last night probably doesn't mean anything. Most likely Sergei won't do anything about what was said. Provoking people like that just gets to be a habit. Now isn't the right time for action. But what about in six months, or a year? When things get a little difficult for people in your position, then perhaps Sergei will remember. Do you follow me?'

'I follow you. But it's a shock. Leave the country? I've never thought about it.'

'Then forget I said it. Really. I was just trying to be a friend.'

'And I'm grateful, honestly.'

Solovyev was satisfied.

He then accepted a drink and opened up. He began to talk about his family and his past life, and the circumstances that had caused him to become a Marxist. Shlyapin could not keep up with the oddity of the other man's tone. At the same time Solovyev was keeping the conversation almost skittishly light, and yet revealing a great though unspecified bitterness about his family and the past. He drew comparisons all the time as he spoke. 'I bet you didn't have to put up with that, Kolya, did you?' or 'You probably had it easier.'

He's jealous of me, was the only way Shlyapin could explain it. But for some reason he admires me.

The conclusion left him puzzled.

He returned to the house in Kamerger Street, taking with him the meat ration card. Entering the street he felt a sudden reluctance to continue. He paused and lit a cigarette and studied the thin traffic of horse carts. The strain of his stay in Moscow was telling on him. There was information to digest and he had important decisions to take, against which this business with a former mistress was a distraction.

He tried to consider his situation in a clinical way. What did she have to offer him? She was a middle-aged woman, he told himself brutally, with a daughter and a dangerous history. Her feelings for him, now that he considered them, were at best equivocal. The whole pattern of her behaviour was a mystery. What did he want of her?

He decided that he would at least deliver the ration card. That much seemed reasonable, and did not commit him to anything. And if she were there? Well, they would chat a little as old friends do. None of it need signify anything.

While he was thinking of this, he was at the door and knocking, and the old *dvornik* had answered.

'Yes?'

'I'd like to see Comrade Antipova. Is she in?'

'No.'

'Does she live here now?'

'No.'

'But she calls?'

The old man grunted and admitted that she did

sometimes, but not tonight; he hadn't seen her for a few days.

Although he had persuaded himself that he was indifferent to Lara, that the call was merely to fulfil a promise, Shlyapin was disappointed. Although he expected only frustration and confusion from any interview with her, he had wanted to see her if only to – what?

He told the old man sharply: 'I've got something for her,' and handed over the envelope containing the ration card. 'Give it to her. You understand?'

He turned on his heels to leave, but his anger stood in front of him like a barrier. He returned to the *dvornik*.

'Have you got a family here named Zhivago?'

The old man rocked his head expectantly. Shlyapin rummaged in his pocket and produced some money which he pushed into the *dvornik*'s hand.

'Well?'

'Second floor. Green door. There's nobody living there. Nothing to see except books and papers. The place has to be re-let. The Antipova woman has been making enquiries about taking it. Are you looking for a room or a corner? I could put in a word if you made it worth my while.'

Shlyapin ignored him. He was mounting the stairs.

The door to the flat was open and someone was inside, an old woman on her knees, picking through an untidy heap of books. There was no furniture, not a stick. Stolen, Shlyapin supposed. But no-one had been interested in the books except the old lady; and she probably wanted to burn them for fuel.

Shylapin joined her, standing over her and stirring the pile with his toe. Medical textbooks, some poetry, one or two religious works. Shlyapin was personally uninterested in books and curious only as to what they told him of the dead man: which was nothing much, only that his contempt was justified if Zhivago lived on books and poverty.

'Did you know him?' he asked. The old lady ignored him. 'What were you? A friend, a neighbour? Did he have a family?'

A younger, bold-eyed woman came in. She had a hip-swagger, red forearms, and wore a skirt cut short over labourer's boots. She let her glance glide off the stranger. 'Take the thin ones,' she told the old lady. 'The others don't burn so easily. Who are you?' She turned to Shlyapin.

'An acquaintance. You knew Zhivago?'

'Not much,' the woman said straightforwardly. 'The thin ones!' she repeated to the old lady. And to the NEPman: 'He kept to himself. I don't think he was quite right in the head. This place was a pigsty.'

'He lived alone?'

'There was a wife. They were separated. She turned up for the funeral. I say "wife", but I don't think they were married. There was talk of another one somewhere abroad.'

'Do you know where?'

'None of my business.'

Her indifference was total. Shlyapin felt uncomfortable in interrogating her when his own interest remained unexplained. He enquired:

'The wife who came to the funeral was called Larissa Fyodorovna?'

'No.'

'No?'

'I saw the one you mean. She's trying to get this room. The wife was called Marina – Marina something or other. And the other one, his proper wife – Tonya?'

So there were three women in Zhivago's life. And the third had come on the scene after Lara. What had they seen in him? He seemed insignificant. He had lived in this room alone at the end, with his life falling to pieces. It made no sense.

'What's your name?' he asked.

'Who's asking? Marfa – if you must know.'

'Married?'

'Widowed.'

Shlyapin looked at her more closely. He guessed her

age at twenty, more or less. A good face but ugly with poverty except for the insolent eyes.

'Children? Do you have any children?'

'Two, and one that died.'

'How do you get by?'

'I work in a cigarette factory. My mother takes care of the kids. Who are you really? Police? You don't look like a Chekist; more like a – I don't know. Not a Chekist, anyway. What do you want to know about Zhivago for? He was a nobody. He lived on his own in this filthy room like something going mouldly. He was sick. A bad heart. And a bit crazy. Well?'

Well? What sort of a question was that? Shlyapin offered her a cigarette and she said:

'I don't mind if I do,' like a shop-girl being polite, in the days when shop-girls were polite. She waited for a light, and, when he gave one, cupped the match in her red hands.

'You look like a man with money,' she went on with a nonchalant confidence. 'Look at that coat!' Her tongue clicked with admiration. 'I've got it! You're a NEPman! I can see it now. I've met your sort before. It's not Zhivago you're interested in, it's that Lara woman! What do you want her for? She's a bit old for you and carries her nose in the air like a duchess. And I bet she's got kids too.'

'That's enough!' Shlyapin snapped at her.

Lara thought very little about Shlyapin even after their meeting. Between trying to place Katya at the Conservatoire and arranging accommodation for them in Moscow, what time she had left was spent mostly in thoughts and recollections of Zhivago. Of course, she sometimes thought of Tanya, but not often: because thinking of Tanya was painful – even if her guilt had lessened – and she substituted activity in the form of enquiries of the various authorities who might aid her search. The pounding of streets, the long waits in gloomy corridors at the behest of bureaucrats became an anaesthetic.

Once in a while the image of Komarovsky intruded. But even here she felt that the crisis had passed. She had ceased to hate him.

She was able now to contemplate that evening at Vladivostok when she had come close to killing him, and recognized how much self-hatred had been within her. It seemed to her that the hatred itself was merely one more thing that Komarovsky had willed on to her, since it arose only because she had accepted his definition of their situation.

By rejecting that hatred she had freed herself from the shackles by which he bound her. His darkness had obscured her own ability to think, just as his will had overridden hers. But now, with a task before her that had nothing to do with Viktor, she experienced a heady clarity and a confidence in her own freedom. Komarovsky was no longer the hated magician. He was an object of contempt – even pity: for his mediocrity and his enslavement to his base nature. It was an illusion, from which she was now free, to think that his power was ever greater than the heap of moral dross that underlay it.

In her freedom Lara achieved a sort of happiness. It was fragile and perhaps temporary and liable to upset as it had been on the day of Zhivago's funeral. But it was real enough.

On the day of the funeral, after her conversation with Yura's brother Yevraf, she had despaired of being able to carry on. Standing among the mourners over the body, she had at first felt an elation almost to madness at the recollection of their love. That she was in the presence of his perishable remains meant nothing. The transcendence of love over everything that was material or temporal had hit her with a force that made her dizzy. But of course there was a reaction.

Yura and her past were consigned to the earth. Love seemed more earthbound and ephemeral when the practical problems of life presented themselves. For one thing there was the insistent need to find accommodation. Yura's room perhaps? It would do.

After the funeral she found herself thinking of Yura and calculating the floor area of the room. Like a poor relative picking over the belongings of a rich man. She remembered Sonya Sergeyevna, who had been their laundress in better times. When her father died, Lara attended the funeral as a courtesy. Afterwards she recalled her disgust as the poor woman rifled the dead man's pots and pans for anything usable. And that's me!

The thought cast her into deep depression. Love was reduced by need. It had to live with measuring the floor and looting the pots and pans. It had to become immanent so that every thought or action became its expression.

She would never get over the strangeness of her life. There was no logic to it, nothing capable of sensible explanation. Nor for Yura. He had married again – or, at least, lived as a husband with Marina and fathered her children. Lara accepted this without resentment and had even expected as much. Their parting at Varykino had truly been final, and life in some fashion had to continue.

But still it was inexplicably strange that they had ever been willing to recognize that finality. How had they managed to abandon the spouses they loved in order to love each other and then throw away that for which they had sacrificed so much?

Yet for all its inexplicable qualities, Lara understood that there was a natural pattern to what had happened. It troubled her reason, but not her ability to accept its reality. These days the mystery in the heart of life forced itself upon her.

Once she had thought of life in terms of the explained. The mysterious was at the margin of things. But now it appeared that it was the explanations that were marginal. She had taken the naturalness of mystery into herself.

Their sacrifice was, she supposed, at the heart of the pattern she and Yura had created of their lives.

Viewed from outside she could see that it would

appear meaningless, even contemptible. But it was there and they had done it. And it had meant *something*.

Sacrifice was at the heart of religion, bound to love and creation. If it were contemptible, then it was because of man's small and contemptible place in the scheme of things and his humorous efforts to rise from his condition.

Lara woke one morning from sleeping in a bedroll in the rented corner she had taken from a poor family whilst she stayed in Moscow. She had been thinking these thoughts, and, hearing the stirrings of the family and seeing the patch of morning light that fell on the blanket that divided the room and masked the window on the other side, she smiled at her own folly. And for half an hour she dozed contentedly and the thoughts faded away with the ragbag of her dreams.

Two days after her encounter with Shlyapin, Lara returned to Kamerger Street, meaning to work through the mound of papers that Zhivago had left behind.

Outside the Arts Theatre she was stopped by two men dressed as labourers. In fact they were OGPU operatives and they arrested her.

She was taken in a closed van to one of the Moscow prisons. She was held there for several months. From time to time she was interrogated in such a way that made it difficult for her to identify herself with the criminal whom the authorities thought they held. Then one day she was told that she had been tried and found guilty of certain offences and sentenced to ten years' corrective labour. She was taken from prison and sent to the first of a series of camps.

No-one heard any more of her. She met other women and told them her story. But they did not know Zhivago, Strelnikov, Komarovsky, Katya or Tanya – or, if they did, the news never came out; these women in turn died, or they never passed the story on because it was the story of only one woman among millions and of no particular importance. She was raped on several occasions and became pregnant once, but miscarried because of her age and poor diet.

What did she feel? Very little that was human. She forgot about her attempts to find the higher meaning behind what had happened to her. Instead she concentrated on her animal existence. She fought for food, clothing, warmth and shelter; and, as long as her strength held out, was prepared to use violence, deceit and treachery against others to obtain them. Her very thoughts were ground out of her until she was left with little more than her instincts for life and happiness, however impossible the reality seemed.

One spring day at a logging camp in the taiga, at a time just after the melt, she woke in the cabin she shared with a hundred others. Her eyes were sticky. Her joints were stiff and swollen. She breathed in shallow gasps because deep breaths brought on a racking cough. Outside the sun shone.

From the leader of the work brigade she begged the right to join the water-carrying party. These were women like herself who had barely survived the winter. They worked in groups of two to cross the marshy ground tangled with rotting brush to the stream. Each supported the other, taking turns to carry the cans. The stream had not completely shed its ice. In shadowed pockets it lay glassy-thin and transparent.

At the water's edge Lara sat down to recover her strength. Staring at the water, she was reminded of another stream at a time and place she could not fix; and, although it was a mad thing to do, she unwound her dirty footcloths and exposed the purple flesh of her swollen feet. Gingerly she dipped her toes into the water, and then the whole foot, gritting her teeth against the cold. She washed her feet thus for a half a minute, and, for that brief time, experienced a sharp pleasurable sensation.

Then she dried her feet roughly, bound them, filled the water cans and limped back to the others, leaving no trace except a flattened piece of grass and a few blood smears where she had sat.

That night she thought how wonderful the sensation of being alive had been; how clean her feet were for once; how pleasant it was to waggle her toes freely, to smile at her toes as children do – as Tanya did, lying on her back – hands, feet, plump bottom in the air – ten toes, ten little men waving back at her as if sharing a joke.

But the result had been that she had felt cold all day. She decided that it was too risky to repeat the experiment.

CHAPTER 10

PARTING

Katya had a single clear memory of the Civil War. One day, while she and her mother had been trying to get provisions in Yuryatin, a White artillery battery rushed through Kholodeyevo on its way to the front. The pedestrians, such as they were, pressed themselves to the wall or sheltered in the doorways of the artisans' workshops as the guns went by, each pulled by its team of horses, urged on by the crack of the drovers' whips and the cries of the crews: gun after gun, limber after limber; a line of horse-drawn caissons, a mobile blacksmith and farrier; so many horses that the air was filled with their sweat and the jolting racket of hooves, harness and wheels.

In itself the memory had no particular significance except that Katya could put a date to it. It came to her in Vladivostok. She was watching a line of waggons drawing away from the harbour and the sight of the heavy horses brought back that day in Yuryatin; and, after a moment's reflection, she said to herself: that was ten years ago.

Of course she had earlier memories, small snapshots stretching back almost to infancy. But these were private memories that did not fit into any larger world; that, in a way, had no date or time to them since dates relate to history, and children have no place in history. So, though

Katya had occasionally thought about her childhood, she had never thought: that was a long time ago, or, it must be ten years since . . .

There was the difference. When Katya said to herself that it was ten years ago that she had seen the White soldiers in Yuryatin, she felt a sense of shock. It was the first time that she had become aware that life was finite and that she had already lived a sizeable piece of it. The awareness of long spans of time was a characteristic of adults. Their conversation was larded with comments like: 'I haven't seen him in ten years,' or 'We lived there about ten years ago.' Now, suddenly, she felt herself transformed from a child for whom time was infinite, into an adult with a history that could be related to other histories and cut up into the great lumps of time that constitute decades.

After her mother had gone to Moscow to make arrangements for their move there, as well as to search for Tanya (though she did not care to think of Tanya), Katya was left in the care of Fraulein Buerli. They continued to live in the apartment with Komarovsky, who was increasingly old and frail and paid them little attention, spending his days drinking tisane or vodka with his friend, Panov, the marine engineer, and his sleepless nights working on correspondence for his great project, the compendium of socialist law.

In his old age Komarovsky had become simpler. This did not mean he was a better, more virtuous person. He was still occasionally drunk, and argumentative like a fretful child. But he had lost his dangerous quality. In the past his slightest gestures, such as his habit of smoking while lounging by the stove, always alert and on his feet, had seemed overburdened with hidden motive. Now his manner was readily explicable in the pains and weariness of an old man. It was not, however, that the dark places of his soul had been illuminated – he had not acquired wisdom – rather they had been extinguished. The complexities of his character had been reduced to the fussy mannerisms of age. Katya found that she did not fear him, and had almost forgotten that she ever had.

She continued her schooling and her musical studies, joining choirs but making few friends. Whom, then, did she dress for? Whose eyes studied the shine on her hair as she combed it? Whom did she smile at in the mirror? Not the boys with downy lips and spotty faces, that was certain. Nor the teachers, who these days were careful never to be alone with a single female pupil. Nor Uncle Viktor's friends, who were gentlemanly or repellent – and often both, depending on whether they had been drinking. In the evenings Fraulein Buerli was her company, taking care never to leave Katya alone with Komarovsky.

After more than two months, letters for each of them arrived from Lara.

'Would you like to read mine?' Katya offered. She was pleased to receive the letter, but was annoyed and disappointed at its blandness. Lara had tried to give reassurance. Everything was going well, though slowly. She was hopeful that the spring would allow them to move to Moscow. And Uncle Viktor? Katya wondered. But the letter avoided difficult issues. Behind the caring words there was little information. She's still treating me like a child, Katya thought sorrowfully.

Fraulein Buerli put down her own letter to read Katya's. 'It's nice,' she concluded.

'What about yours?' Katya asked.

'Oh, it's much the same.' The little woman put it away in the reticule she had bought in the flea market to complement her quaint wardrobe. Katya found it later. Fraulein Buerli had reread it and must have been disturbed by a caller (probably old Panov), since she had left it open on the table.

Dearest Lotte,

I have neither good news or bad. It isn't even possible to be angry. Although I make almost no progress, there is nothing I can focus on and blame. Even the officials try their best to be helpful (I never thought I should write this). The worst I have experienced is indifference.

Such news as there is is inconclusive. The Conservatoire would in principle be prepared to receive Katya. That means no more than that there is space available. She would have to be auditioned for her talent – though I think that neither of us have fears on that count. The problem is one of accommodation. Moscow is desperately crowded. Even a shared room is hard to come by – in fact, I have found only a corner in a room with a family of six. How we shall find space for the three of us I don't know? Particularly since, at the same time, we have to show that we have work.

When I was looking for a room, someone told me of a vacancy in Kamerger Street, a place I used to know well. Someone had died. I went there and found that the room had belonged to Yuri Andreyevitch Zhivago. It was he who had died.

I don't know how to write about this. Yura was the writer. I have told you that I loved him so much. I can't think of any other way to put it, but the words seem so brief and put like that don't seem to say a great deal. People are always claiming to be in love, so I can't claim that we were in any way special or different. But when we fell in love it seemed unique to us. Isn't that ridiculous?

On a separate sheet Lara wrote:

I have been out all day and just resumed this letter. After writing about Yura I had to stop. I could not go on. You may think that I am sad, but I am not sure that that describes how I feel. Since I heard the news I have felt both despair and elation. The despair explains itself. The elation I find difficult to understand, except that I have been forced to think of Yura; and the memory of the joy that we had together has helped me. Perhaps my life has not been entirely pointless?

I should not have written to you about this, but there is no-one to talk to.

* * *

Lara had continued later, in a different ink.

I can't find any news of Tanya. There are no records or they have been lost and destroyed in the confusion of the last few years. I doubt that I shall find her. It is difficult to admit this. I won't say anything more.

Are you well? How is my darling Katya? Does she miss me? I have hated every moment of being away, but I tell myself that it is necessary for Katya's education, and to try to find Tanya – and if we are ever to be free of Viktor. Please, dearest Lotte, be careful of him! Make sure that he is never left in control of Katya. You know my reasons.

There is nothing else to write about. I miss you both terribly, and send you all my love.

Lara

When Katya had finished reading the letter she replaced it as she had found it. She was ashamed at reading something that was not addressed to her; but she also felt a dull anger – not so much at her mother as at all adults – at the things that were kept hidden from her, the dishonesty of adults. She picked the letter up and studied it again, this time reading the passage about Zhivago, the Uncle Yura of her childhood. She had known without thinking about it that Zhivago and her mother had been lovers and, indeed, that he was Tanya's father; but that was not the same as imagining their being in love. She was a child when Lara and Zhivago were together and, as a child, accepted the relationships of adults as given, as much a part of the stable universe as the trees or the sky, in which people were placed not by emotion but by decree, as if by act of God. But to be in love meant that it was all the product of fragile human feeling – passionate and changeable. Her mother was a creature of such emotion.

And then there were the references to Viktor. Katya understood them well enough and also how absurd Lara's fears were. They took no account of Katya herself. They described a Komarovsky who was long gone, not the shambling old man who was more to be pitied than feared. Recognizing her mother's blindness to the present, Katya felt in this small respect superior to her. She was still too young to understand regrets or obsessions about the past. With all her ten years of coherent memory, she had no sense of life and time lost beyond recovery.

When Fraulein Buerli returned to the apartment she found the letter where she had left it. She examined Katya for clues, but finding none silently put the letter away and never mentioned it again. Komarovsky came across the envelope and recognized the handwriting.

'I see that Lara has written,' he said. 'Is she well?'

'Yes,' Fraulein Buerli told him.

He was not interested and did not press the matter.

Later, both Katya and Fraulein Buerli wrote replies to Lara and sent them to the address in Moscow.

Lara never wrote again.

Winter came, and again the fogs and the wailing of ships' horns during the night. Katya returned home one evening and found Fraulein Buerli in a distressed state waiting for her by the door.

'What's wrong?' Katya asked.

'It's Viktor. He's ill.'

'Is he here?'

'No. At the hospital. He's had a stroke.' Fraulein Buerli explained that he had been at his friend Panov's flat when he was stricken. Panov had called a doctor and transferred him to the hospital, and then informed her.

'Have you seen him?' Katya asked.

'No. I couldn't go and not tell you first. I didn't want just to leave a message.'

'No, I suppose not,' Katya answered calmly. In fact, it occurred to her how calm they both were and she wondered whether it was the effect of shock, a delayed realization of what had happened, or because it was Viktor.

Knowing this she was still calm. 'I shan't take my coat off,' she said. 'We should go to see him now.'

'Is it still foggy?'

'A little, but we shouldn't have any difficulty.'

Fraulein Buerli put on her coat.

They found Panov at the hospital.

'They wouldn't allow me to see him on my own,' he said with a catch in his voice. 'Because I'm not a relative.'

He was a large man with an expansive paunch, grey hair and a beard, and a rocking way of walking caused by stiffness in his hips. His manner was ordinarily bluff, though deferential to Komarovsky. He looked as though he had been crying.

'Has there been any change, Alexei Valentinovitch?' Fraulein Buerli asked him.

'The doctor says he's still the same. He's paralysed. He doesn't recognize anyone.' He turned to Katya and said: 'We were playing cards and talking,' as if this were significant and would affect the prognosis.

'It must have been a terrible shock to you,' Katya answered sympathetically.

'Terrible.'

They were waiting in a corridor. The fog had leaked in and the dim lights under their green shades glowed through a haze. The walls were pasted with warnings on the notification of infectious diseases – typhus and cholera. Small movements caused a hollow sound in the empty space.

'You haven't seen him?' Fraulein Buerli sought confirmation.

'I hate hospitals,' Panov said. He was nervous of silence, the sort of person one meets on trains who will tell his life story for a grunt of acknowledgement and then thank the listener for the interesting conversation. Recognizing belatedly that he was being addressed, he answered: 'No. I asked, but they wouldn't tell me. I was worried that you wouldn't get here in time.'

'In time?' Katya queried. Then she realized that Uncle Viktor was expected to die.

'This is the best hospital in the city,' Fraulein Buerli said. 'I've heard lots of people say that they work miracles here.'

Katya had difficulty taking this message in. Viktor dying? Whom she had known since a child?

'I had a friend,' Panov was saying. 'Do you know Martov – Innokenty Semyonovitch? It was something to do with the kidneys. Viktor knew him. He was part of our little circle until he moved to live with his daughter.'

'Was he the instrument-maker?'

'That's him.'

'Don't you remember, Katya? He called once or twice.'

'No, I don't remember him.'

A nurse came out of the ward and told them they might see the patient. He was in a general ward, his bed screened off from the others. Two chairs were placed, one on each side. Panov elected to stand.

'Talk to him,' Fraulein Buerli suggested. 'He may recognize your voice.'

Katya looked at Komarovsky. He was lying with one eye open and one closed. Only his head was visible. His hair and beard appeared greasy with sweat.

'Uncle Viktor,' she said. It was a struggle to pitch her voice. Was she asking a question? Could he understand her? 'Uncle Viktor, it's me – Katya. I'm here with Fraulein Buerli and Alexei Valentinovitch. Can you hear me?'

'It's a pity that Larissa Fyodorovna can't be here,' said Panov.

'Uncle Viktor?'

'Yes, it's a pity,' said Fraulein Buerli.

'Uncle Viktor?'

'Have you heard from her?'

'She's written once. Perhaps she wrote again. You know how slow the mail can be.'

'*Please*, Uncle Viktor!'

'Don't upset yourself, Katya. Yes, the mail can be a problem.'

If Uncle Viktor could not hear, how could he respond? How pitiful he looked. Perhaps he could hear. What should she say? That she loved him? That he was forgiven? She did not love him. Only her mother could forgive him. What would Lara have said? Katya felt tears on her cheeks from the frustration and pity of the thing.

'There, there,' said Panov innocently. 'You were fond of him, weren't you?'

Komarovsky died the following night and was buried two days later. Katya was surprised how many people attended the funeral, a dozen at least, most of them old men like Viktor. Tactfully, Panov provided refreshment afterwards in his own small room crowded with models and prints of ships. Katya found herself treated as the bereaved, though of all of them it was probably the marine engineer who was the most upset.

'He was a great man.'

'Was he?' Katya asked out of genuine curiosity.

'One of the finest legal minds of his day. You knew that he was working on an encyclopedia of Soviet law? No-one else could have done it.'

'I suppose not.'

'And he was very widely travelled. Did you know that he was an expert on Mongolia? The Government was always consulting him.'

'I didn't know that.'

The room smelled powerfully of unwashed clothes and tobacco. The day was damp and the room warm. Panov felt he could confide as a friend of the family.

'You've grown into a fine young woman,' he said emotionally. 'And beautiful too, like your mother. It's a shame she couldn't be here. Does she know? No, I imagine she doesn't – of course not. He was very proud of you. Very.'

'Please . . .' Katya did not want to talk. She felt

223

hypocritical. Were she and her mother mistaken in Viktor? It was not possible to doubt Panov's sincerity.

'He was a wonderful friend,' said the marine engineer. 'The Lion of the Law!'

One day, about a month after he had last seen Lara, when he was at the end of his resources and near to abandoning his hopes of Moscow, Shlyapin received a visit from Solovyev, his card-playing partner from the Commissariat of Foreign Trade. This was at the Hotel Lublin, where Shlyapin was still trying to keep up appearances. He had a last bottle of vodka. He offered his visitor a drink.

'I hear you're leaving town,' Solovyev began.

'Who told you that?'

'Is it true?'

'I'm considering it. My business here is finished and I need to take care of things in Yuryatin. Why should you worry?'

'It's a pity.'

'Well, all good things must come to an end.'

Shlyapin found himself sounding abrupt, was sorry, and then decided that he did not care.

'We've had some good times,' said Solovyev.

'Yes – one or two. That's the way it goes in business.'

Solovyev asked for another drink and sat morosely on the edge of the bed. Shlyapin took his own glass to the window and stared into the narrow interior court which was full of crates and general rubbish. He glanced at Solovyev and noticed, not for the first time, his over-neat appearance: the clipped beard, the pince-nez, the uncreased uniform jacket. He wondered, with a shade of annoyance, what sudden attack of sentimentality had made the other man want to say goodbye. In the ordinary way he would not have considered Solovyev a sentimental type, rather the other kind. He did not have the mannerisms of a man of real feeling; his manner was stiff and his conversation that of a committed Marxist.

Solovyev asked: 'Have you got family in Yuryatin?'

'Not to speak of. I have an uncle somewhere, assuming he's still alive. You?'

'My mother. And I've got two married sisters.'

'You're not married yourself?'

Having asked, it struck Shlyapin as funny that these basic questions had never been asked before.

'I've never had the good fortune,' answered Solovyev. The tone sounded at once regretful and superior; Shlyapin could not fathom it. 'Most of my time has been taken up on Party work. There hasn't been much left for anything else.'

'Not much fun.' As a sort of consolation Shlyapin proposed: 'Here, let's knock a bigger hole in that bottle!'

They poured another couple of drinks. Solovyev felt obliged to tell a bad joke which did nothing to relieve the atmosphere. Shlyapin was bored with his companion, but as reluctant to let him go as the other man was to leave. He was aware that his craving for company was just a symptom of his depression at the state of his affairs. And Solovyev? It occurred to Shlyapin then to wonder if his friend were a homosexual? Probably not, and in any case what did it matter? Old man Feldstein, who used to be chief accountant at Moreau & Vetchinkin, was one: and he was all right once he knew where you stood. And generous, too, towards the younger clerks, even when there was nothing in it for him. An emotional type.

'Did you know,' said Solovyev out of the blue, 'that we're recruiting for our trade missions to the West?'

'A nice job if you could get it. Is it on the cards for you?'

'Oh, I couldn't go. Personal reasons.'

'But good for someone.'

'Undoubtedly.'

Shlyapin examined the other man again. Like a little boy whose present has broken. Shlyapin had an idea that homosexuals were clean-shaven. Solovyev wore a beard.

'The problem,' said Solovyev, 'is that so few people are of the right calibre.'

'What does that mean?'

'They have no experience of business. Party members haven't generally been in trade.'

'I'm a Party member. I've been in trade.'

'There are exceptions.' Solovyev was musing. His voice had softened. 'If only you weren't so *compromised*.'

'I suppose I am,' Shlyapin admitted.

In his disappointment he fell silent, and it was a moment before he looked up and caught the longing in the other man's eyes.

My God, it's true! he thought. He's like a moonstruck lover! What do I do?

'If you want the job,' Solovyev murmured, 'I could help.'

Lara did not write. She had been gone six months and winter was turning into spring.

'I don't know whether we should make enquiries or not?' Fraulein Buerli said. 'Surely if there had been an accident we'd have been told?'

They were taking care not to panic each other about Lara's absence. The fact was that they had got used to her being away. They were concerned, but there was nothing on which to focus. Lara had not suddenly vanished or met with an accident or died. There was no report or event to shock them: no day different from any other day, on which they could say, 'We'll never see her again.' Only a gradual unease for which they made excuses, blaming the mail or, in a nebulous way, the authorities for the lack of any news. Just now and again Katya blamed herself for callousness, but she was wrong. She had not understood the effects of time.

She left school and did clerical work in a shipping office. Her music was behind her; nowadays she did no more than practise occasionally and sing duets with Fraulein Buerli. In response to the stirrings within her, she went out sometimes with boys, clerks from the office and, once, a music teacher five years older than herself who tried to romance her with flattery about her voice; but there was something unsatisfactory about them all. They had no vision, even the music teacher. What that vision might be she had no idea, but she wanted to reach out to something larger.

She remembered her dream of Shlyapin – Kolya! – his dark handsomeness, his mysterious past and glamorous present. If there was someone she looked to it was him. She felt him as a shade hovering about her, a promise whispered in her ear – *Kolya!*

Spring came. In the evenings Katya walked home from work through streets filled with sailors on leave and stevedores returning from the docks. They often whistled at her or made quips in her direction. She ignored them, but they made her conscious of the changes that had overcome her; not merely the changes to her body, but to the sense of who she was. The transition to adulthood was marked by the opposition of adults; when the child cast off childhood and shouted: 'Look at me!' the adults remained blinded by fear and disbelief. For a time at least. But for Katya that time was passed. Her mother was not there to voice any concern. Uncle Viktor was dead. Fraulein Buerli never laid claim to authority, and at best or worst offered only a few comments and an amused tolerance. Katya felt that she possessed herself, and had the feelings that went with any property: pride in its possession; fear of its loss.

Out of the jostling crowd one evening, a man accosted her. He was a slight figure in a quilted cotton jacket and a workman's cap. He stood in her path and confronted her with a dark good-looking face and a look of curiosity.

'It is you, isn't it, Katya?' he said. 'I hardly recognized you; you've grown so tall.'

Katya was surprised but not frightened. She was aware that she knew the man, but the context was somehow remote. And then it came to her.

'Nikolai Afanasitch!'

He smiled. 'You used to call me Kolya. For an awful moment I thought I'd made a mistake. I've caught sight of you a couple of times, but this evening is the first time I felt sure enough to talk to you. I'm astonished by how much you've changed – I mean you still look the same person, but, well, you've changed. There's something of your mother about you.'

'What happened to your fur coat?' Katya asked, and then thought the question was gauche, but she was still shocked. This wasn't Kolya! This was a man, a reality and not a dream. Katya was astonished, as though a reflection had stepped out of a mirror and spoken to her.

'I sold it,' said Shlyapin and gave her a smile in the old ironic style. 'It wasn't as fashionable as it used to be. But you, how are you? You look fine.'

They walked together. He was eager to talk, which was as well since Katya was still suffering the paralysis of a dreamer. He asked:

'Are you living with old Komarovsky still?'

Katya knew she had to reply.

'No. Didn't you hear? Uncle Viktor died a few months ago.'

'I hadn't heard. I'm sorry about that. I suppose it was to be expected, given his age.'

'He had a stroke.'

'Ah.'

Katya paused a second to look at him. She thought he was tense and careworn, something he had never been before – or so she thought, still trying to sort out dreams from memories, and thinking: he was always so self-assured.

'What are you doing in Vladivostok?' she asked.

'Business – nothing special.'

'Are you still a NEPman?'

'No,' he answered briefly, 'that's finished with. There's no work for NEPmen any more. Do you live close by?'

'Fairly close. We can hear the ships.'

'The sea – do you know that this is the first time

I've seen the sea?' A hesitation. 'How old are you?' He excused himself. 'Isn't it easy to lose track of time?'

Katya was disappointed. The question indicated that he had never previously paid much attention to her. That couldn't be right. *Her* Kolya was always attentive, subtly aware of her thoughts, infinitely sympathetic and responsive. But she said:

'I'll be eighteen on my next birthday.'

'Good Lord!'

'I've got a job now, as a shipping clerk.'

He was uninterested in her job, but affected by her age. 'Eighteen! It's incredible – it seems – well – eighteen!' He was smiling, an inward-directed smile, wistful, ironic, self-mocking. Katya was charmed by it.

They were at the apartment house, standing in the street. A ship chandler's van rattled by with the driver labouring the horse. Shlyapin watched it. He displayed no inclination to go, and Katya saw that he expected to be invited in. She was pleased. It meant that he wasn't completely indifferent to her. She couldn't have borne it if he had been.

'Would you like to come in?' she asked him. 'I'm sure we can offer you a glass of tea.'

'I should like that,' he answered in his resonant voice which up till then had been absent, so that Katya recognized what it was about him that was different – not the fur coat. With the voice, *her* Kolya was coming back.

Fraulein Buerli was at home. She was surprised to see the visitor, whom she did not know, having heard only his reputation related by Glasha Tuntseva and having caught the occasional glimpse of him in the street at Yuryatin. Shlyapin introduced himself in his old style, courteously; delighting Katya, confirming his remembered kindnesses. He gave a brief explanation of how he happened to be in the city on business and had encountered Katerina Pavlovna. The little woman was immediately reassured and set about making some tea. This done, they chatted politely.

229

Now that they were relaxed, Shlyapin fell into the easy gossiping manner that Katya remembered. He had an instinct for charming women, not with the fictitious charm of the demon lovers who figured as heroes in the second-hand romances, Katya had picked up, but from a pleasure in talking that seemed unforced. So he was not a dream character. Katya did not care. Now that she had grasped the fact of his reality, he was still wonderful!

His news, however, was not all good.

'It's true about Samdevyatov,' he told them. 'I know people and they tell me he was shot. The story was that he was a German spy; but of course we know that isn't true. There were problems at the Krueger works with the machinery that the Germans installed. The truth is that it broke down because no-one knew how to repair it, but it was more convenient to blame the failure on sabotage by spies.'

'How terrible,' said Fraulein Buerli. 'And what about Mikulitsin?'

'He was sentenced to ten years for economic crimes. His son was arrested about a year ago.'

'And the family?'

'They left Yuryatin – I don't know where they went. But you needn't worry about your friends, the sisters. They're all right.'

'We were worried. It's a long time since they wrote to us.'

'People don't write much any more.'

'Thank God they're safe.'

Katya shared Fraulein Buerli's sadness and relief, but there was nothing for which they were not prepared from the hints in Glasha's letter. Perhaps, she thought, that was why their sadness was muted. Had they received the news earlier or under different circumstances there would have been tears. But such was the effect of distance in time and place that even tragedy became banal.

'What are you doing nowadays?' Fraulein Buerli asked. 'Are you still a NEPman?'

'The New Economic Policy is finished,' Shlyapin answered. He laughed. 'I've had to get a proper job!'

'In Yuryatin?' asked Katya. Shlyapin stared at her, not unpleasantly but as if still surprised that she could speak. What did you expect? Katya thought to herself. I'm not a child any more. But it's still *me*, Kolya!

'In Moscow. I've got a job with the Commissariat for Foreign Trade.'

'Is that good?'

'I think so.'

'I'm glad.'

He was looking around the room. Katya had the impression that he was an observant man, although she had no specific reason to think this was so. He was able to examine people and things in the most direct way without giving offence.

'By the way,' he asked at last, 'when do you expect Larissa Fyodorovna home? I can't stay long, but it would be a shame to go without saying hello to her. What's wrong? Have I said something?'

'No – no,' Katya murmured.

'I thought I'd upset you?'

He had. He had reminded both women that they could not continue to ignore the fact that Lara had been gone too long. Katya spoke for both of them.

'My mother isn't here. She's in Moscow, trying to arrange for us to move there. I'm sorry to disappoint you. There wasn't any reason for you to know.'

It was Shlyapin's turn to be surprised.

'Hasn't she written? Didn't she tell you that we met there?'

'In Moscow?' Katya asked excitedly. 'When?'

'It must have been September. She told me why she was there. But when I didn't see her again I supposed she must have returned to Vladivostok.'

'Was that the last time you saw her? September?'

'Yes, I'm afraid so.'

The women pressed for news, and Shlyapin told them

briefly of his meeting with Lara outside Zhivago's flat. How was she? Was she well? Did she seem worried? They tried to convert Shlyapin's story into good news – which it was, if only they could forget how old the news was and that there had been none since except for Lara's letter to each of them, which must have been written after her encounter with Shlyapin, although she had not mentioned him. Katya caught him looking at them curiously – wondering, she supposed, how they could have let her mother be absent so long without enquiry – not realizing that fear of the worst had paralysed not just their actions but their thoughts.

In the end Shlyapin said he must leave them. He seemed cheerful and unperturbed again. Katya thought he was about to go then and there without any formality except a mild display of thanks, as if they were only slight acquaintances who might not meet again. But then he grasped their hands warmly, and kissed them both.

Shlyapin had come to Vladivostok looking for Lara. He had business there, but it was of the manufactured sort that merely excused him from confronting the unpalatable truth. He was chasing a woman ten years or more older than himself, whom he had once picked up and then discarded as a mistress.

After their parting in Yuryatin, Shlyapin had scarcely thought of Lara until their meeting in Moscow. He liked her well enough and wished her well; but after the arrest of her friends her personal life was becoming too complicated in a world that was difficult enough. But for that accidental encounter he would have quietly forgotten her.

So what had changed?

The truth was that, at a period when his affairs were going badly and he had time on his hands in his miserable hotel room for brooding introspection, he had become fascinated by her. Fascination was an accurate description of a feeling he could not rationally explain. Lara was a mystery to him and in interpreting her that way he did not realize that a mystery, being blank, is like a mirror in which are reflected images of ourselves – reversed, inverted or distorted – but still of ourselves. So, she was honest and he was dishonest; she was straightforward, where he was evasive; loving where he was selfish. And, at a point in his life when he was vulnerable, she had what she had never had in Yuryatin, an air of confidence and, finally, of self-possession, as if aspects of her existence had at last made sense to her and she had an intelligible mission.

And perhaps the real Lara was like that – although what he had seen in her were the omissions in his own character; and, even then, imperfectly. For the truth was that he was not wholly dishonest, evasive or selfish. He had enough of their opposites to think, under the stress of his current circumstances, that the rest was worth having. So, in his idealized image of Lara, he was partly in love with himself. And, since self-love is normally more powerful than the love of others, the strength of his feeling was perhaps accounted for.

At all events he felt an emptiness inside him at the realization that Lara was in prison or worse.

For several days after seeing Katya and Fraulein Buerli, Shlyapin remained in his hotel. Specifically he was avoiding any chance of meeting them again.

After learning enough to guess Lara's fate, he thought that, whatever he might feel – the anguish of knowledge – it was only a matter of a short time before he put the aberration of his infatuation with that strange woman behind him. He had left the apartment of the daughter and the elderly tutor in the belief that he would never see them again. He had got to the point of arranging a booking on a train back to civilization.

Then had come the crux. He was afflicted with a lassitude he could not account for. He made one or two expeditions to settle his business affairs, but otherwise he stayed in his room and drank. He lay on his bed and stared at the door. On it was hung the coat he had bought after

233

selling the fox fur. It reproached him with his failure. He wanted a way of escape both from this constricting country which frustrated and terrorized him when he tried to make a living, and from the mire of depression and self-doubt. Where was it? Through the route given him by Solovyev? The recollection of Solovyev filled him with disgust.

While Shlyapin speculated about his own position, Katya also suffered. She found her thoughts penetrated by him whenever she had an idle moment or was off her guard. At times he was again the figure of her dreams, the strong, romantic stranger, the man of mystery and vision. At other times she saw through her fantasy to the image of a man like other men – attractive, yes, but no more so than others. Katya was not stupid. She could tell the difference between dream and reality. But Kolya stood at the borders of both. The fact of his sudden reappearance seemed to have a providential meaning, as though Fate or God or whatever it was that structured lives was offering her an opportunity. Katya could not simply ignore the miracle.

A week after his first encounter with Katya, Shlyapin waited for her on the route he knew she took home from the shipping office. Katya saw him first. He was reclining against a wall in his quilted cotton coat and pulled-down cap, smoking a cigarette, and at first she took him for a plain-clothes policeman, since the latter could often be found idling around the harbour. She was about to cross the street to avoid him when he looked up and, seeing her, called her name. She hesitated and then approached him.

'Hello, Kolya,' she said. 'You took me by surprise. I thought that by now you'd have gone back to Moscow.' She was more surprised by her own tone of voice. So calm when she wanted to cry out with joy that her fears that he had vanished were unjustified.

'Another few days.'

'Isn't your business finished?'

'Nearly. I have things to tidy up and then trains to

arrange; you know how difficult travelling can be. Are you well?'

'Yes.'

'And Fraulein Buerli?'

'She's well too.'

'Good.'

They walked side by side in the crowd of workers. Shlyapin spoke only occasionally to ask questions about her work, which were of no particular importance. Katya did not care. He was there with her and that was enough. He was tangible without being touched. He was a promise and a danger – but above all, a promise!

'Didn't you want to carry on studying?' he asked.

'It wasn't possible after Uncle Viktor died. There was no money. Fraulein Buerli doesn't earn enough to support both of us.'

'But would you like to study?'

'I don't know. Perhaps when my mother returns, she'll have news.'

At the thought of her mother Katya stopped.

'Yes?'

'I don't think I want to study music.'

'Why not?'

'I haven't really got the talent. Or perhaps it's just that I'm not dedicated enough. I should like to help people. Did you know that my mother was a nurse? She became a nurse during the war. Maybe I'll become a nurse. Or does that sound naive and adolescent? Aren't all girls of my age supposed to want to become nurses?'

'I don't know.'

'I think so. It isn't a very original idea; so perhaps it isn't me.'

Katya told herself that she was mumbling; saying nothing very much. What did she want to say? I love you? Stupid! She did not love him. She hardly knew him. Stupid – stupid! She was unsure how far Shlyapin was listening; his responses were largely meaningless, but his face had a look of concentration. What does he want? she wondered. His presence embarrassed at the same time that it fascinated and excited her. She was not used to talking to men other than to take orders at work. But Shlyapin's manner seemed to suggest an equality between them that Katya did not really feel. She was aware that he was ten years older than her and infinitely more experienced. Then, to her surprise, she noted that she was now slightly taller than him so that when they spoke they looked levelly at each other. His brown eyes were of searching intensity. She thought: he's remembering that last time I was just somebody's daughter. The frankness of his gaze unsettled her. She thought: it isn't me he wanted to see. It's my mother. The thought was bitter to her and for the rest of the journey home she was deliberately silent.

'Lotte, I'm home!' she cried with relief as she opened the apartment door. 'Nikolai Afanasitch is with me! Will you come inside?' she asked Shlyapin. He nodded and closed the door behind him.

Fraulein Buerli was preparing some *kasha*. At home they ate only lightly. It was easier to get rations at work. The little woman looked up and bade Shlyapin a cautious welcome.

Katya took off her boots and her coat. She was more comfortable now that she was in the apartment. She was its mistress and this gave her the confidence to volunteer a smile at her visitor.

Still in his coat, Shlyapin had accepted a seat. 'I don't want to trouble you,' he said.

'It's no trouble,' Katya answered generously and was aware of her sense of control, which gave her a slight feeling of pride. I'm not going to be silly. I know what this is all about.

Finished with her chores, Fraulein Buerli sat down and began to put the same polite questions that Katya had asked earlier. How was Shlyapin's business? And so on.

'By the way,' she said to Katya. 'I've had some unfortunate news from the house committee. Now that

Viktor's no longer here, they want to put another family in with us. They came to look over the flat today. The name is Kuznetsov. He's a railway traffic controller, whatever that is. I forget what his wife does. They've two children, but I didn't see them. We talked about arrangements. The only practical solution seems to be for the Kuznetsovs to have your room. You'll have to share with Lara and me. I imagine the children will sleep in here. They seem very nice people,' she ended hopefully.

'When are they coming?'

'Next week. Forgive me, Nikolai Afanasitch –'

'Kolya.'

'— but I wanted to tell Katya before I forgot. No – that sounds silly. I was hardly likely to forget, was I?'

'I understand,' Shlyapin answered and did not appear to mind; as if, Katya thought, he did not know why he was there, which puzzled her until, with difficulty, he said:

'Katya – I don't know how to put this. I don't believe that your mother will be coming back.'

He spoke so slowly, so flatly that the words registered just so, as words, things that had to be assembled into a meaning.

My – mother – is – not – coming – back.

'No!' Katya cried.

'I'm sorry.'

'I don't believe you!'

'Listen to me,' he said calmly. He looked to Fraulein Buerli, and so did Katya; but the little woman sat in stone-faced silence and Katya felt the agony of realization that her friend agreed with Shlyapin.

No! But this time the word would not come out. She looked to him and her expression said: please don't tell me, Kolya! Even if it's true I don't want to hear. What do we have left if hope is taken away? I shan't cry.

'Don't cry.' Shlyapin was offering her a handkerchief, a lady's handkerchief with embroidered edges. 'I wouldn't tell you this if it could be avoided, but we have to recognize reality. I saw your mother in Moscow last September. She was trying to find a room in Moscow. The room was free but she never went back. Do you understand me? *She never went back!* Have you heard from her?'

'We got a letter from her, four or five months ago,' Fraulein Buerli said.

'Did you reply?'

'Yes.'

'And did Lara write back?'

'No.'

What did I tell you? No, he didn't say that. He kept silent until Katya emerged from her own silence. Then he sprang to his feet as if the tension were too much for him and placed himself by the window, his back towards the women.

'We're on the brink of a catastrophe,' he said in a low monotone. 'I mean the whole country.'

Katya had seized a measure of self-control. She said, more sensibly than she felt: 'I don't understand you.'

'No, I suppose not. I'm not sure I know myself what I mean. But there is something – something waiting to happen. In fact, it may be happening now, but no-one tells us. Do you read the papers?'

'Yes.'

'You've read about the campaign against the kulaks?'

Katya nodded. But what did it matter? At the office they had received a political lecture. The kulaks were exploiters of the peasants. To people in the cities the campaign meant nothing as long as there was food.

'There are no kulaks,' Shlyapin said wearily. 'The real kulaks were wiped out in the civil war. All that are left are a few peasants who did well out of the New Economic Policy – if you can call owning a horse and a couple of cows doing well. Believe me, I know what I'm talking about, I made my living doing business with the peasants. I've seen how they manage.'

I can't listen to this, Katya thought. My mother has disappeared and he is talking about politics. But she could not think of her mother. She had to hold back her tears and listen to this man as if he were talking sense. There was probably some point to this story. She had heard Viktor dealing with problems in the same way. Trying to lift the particularities of suffering and place it in a general context, a larger explanation, as if that somehow made it better. If only, instead, someone would take me and hold me close like my mother used to! If only you could, Kolya.

But Shlyapin could not. And in his failure he abolished Katya's fantasy.

'The authorities have arrested the kulaks and exiled them.' He went on relentlessly in his distracted fashion. 'Thousands of them – who knows how many? And not for anything they've done, but for who they are. And they are whoever the authorities say they are. Whole families, including the children.'

At this juncture he seemed to recall himself, and that his story was wandering from any relevance to the two women. He asked for permission to smoke. Slowly he lit a cigarette. He resumed, this time more earnestly:

'When I was coming here from Moscow, the train was stopped for two days. We had to wait for a troop train to pass us. The soldiers were going to put down a rebellion in a village up the line. The villagers were objecting to being forced into a collective farm. Apparently it was the women who rebelled. They would lose their cows, and they needed the milk for their children. Later on we passed the village. It had been shelled and was burning. I saw soldiers burning the carcases of the cows to stop the spread of disease. So in the end nobody got the cows.' He paused, then asked: 'When did you last eat meat?'

'A week ago,' said Fraulein Buerli.

'I hear things are worse in the Ukraine.'

Even in her distressed state Katya understood him. They were not safe. But when had she ever been safe? Her life was a series of moves from one unsafe place to another. She had ceased to be frightened of insecurity because she had no experience of security. Still, to him it appeared important, and because he would not allow her to cry for her mother she kept up the pretence of rational conversation, though the words seemed to her to be detached things that she could walk around and observe. But within her she was empty with disappointment and desperate with her double loss – Lara – Kolya – both gone.

She asked: 'Are you saying we have to move again?'

'I'm going abroad,' he answered indirectly.

'Where to?'

'It isn't certain yet. But I have to go. People in my situation – former NEPmen – are being arrested.'

'Then you're lucky to have somewhere to go to.'

'Yes.'

'How did you arrange it?'

'I've been offered a position in the Commissariat for Foreign Trade. They need people with experience of business negotiations.'

'That's fortunate for you.'

'A friend was able to manage it for me.'

'You're very lucky.'

'Yes.'

From barely listening to him, Katya had a sudden insight. 'Is that why you came here? To ask my mother to go with you?' Of course! I'm not of any interest to him at all. I never have been. I was just an inconvenient child.

'It would have been possible,' he answered neutrally. 'And you could have come too.'

'And Fraulein Buerli?'

He did not answer. The little woman spoke up for him:

'I wouldn't want to go.'

'Lotte!'

'I'm too old and peculiar, dear. I've been in Russia too long. It's become home. Believe me, I'm not being unselfish. I could go back to Switzerland any time, and without the help of Nikolai Afanasitch. At my age I'm more of a liability than an asset. The authorities would be glad to let me go.'

'You have to think of your own safety,' Shlyapin said. Yet from the way he spoke, his deadly flatness, Katya could not fathom his desires in the matter, as if he did not know them himself. She thought: he rejected my mother and then wanted to take her abroad with him. He doesn't know why. How is it possible for people ever to understand each other when they don't even understand themselves? I can see him more clearly than he can see himself.

Shlyapin was staring intently at her, but she was sufficiently abstracted in her thoughts that she could bear his gaze unaffected. She looked at Fraulein Buerli again as if for the last time. How old, wrinkled and fragile she was. Her movements in her absurd corset so stiff and creaky. Oh, Lotte, how I love you! How good you've been to Mother and me!

Shlyapin was saying:

'It's still possible for you to leave, Katya. I can take you with me. There's a need for interpreters. You speak French and some German.'

'Without my mother?' she retorted.

And knew at once: but of course without my mother. She is in prison or dead. We both know that. Oh, God, she's dead, but I shall never know for certain. I said goodbye to her at the station and never knew! And now he wants me. I have to become whatever it was that he saw in her. That's how little I really am to him. I'm just an empty vessel into which he can pour his fantasies.

It was too much! She would stay in Russia and face whatever had to be faced rather than have this man impose his will on her in the way that Komarovsky had overshadowed her mother. How different he looked. In appearance he was modest and downcast in his shabbiness, and his face, still so young, was almost beautiful, just as she had dreamt in the dreaming time of her sexuality. Yet behind that he was hateful because he was trying to manipulate her without any real regard for her except the fiction of his concern.

It was too much, and she would have told him so; and perhaps Lotte suspected her because she too was waiting for her answer. Lotte, who had no care except for Katya's well-being and yet clearly felt that she should say yes.

What would Lara have advised?

When Komarovsky had died, Katya had come near to despising her mother for her association with him. Lara had gone with Viktor because he offered survival and a sort of security. Her reasons were as basic and weakly human as that. And they had seemed to Katya to be pitiful at best.

Now she was confronted with the same choice. She could reject Shlyapin and in the same breath reject her mother. The choice seemed to her as stark as that. If only she could understand why survival was now at all costs important, and then to be thrown away in a romantic gesture. Why did its value change? Had Lara tried to survive to some purpose? Was Katya that purpose? If only someone could tell her!

But no-one could. Poor Lotte – unloved by any man – had lived a governess's life, ignorant of passion, and was too used to being moved like baggage from one place to another. No help there. Was this what being an adult meant? Loss of illusion – compromise – the death of all feeling in order to live with a bleakness in the heart? Katya was faint with despair. To have passed so cruelly from hope to nothing in so short a space!

'The arrangements,' said Shlyapin blandly, 'will take about a month. You understand – paperwork. It isn't easy, but it's possible. But there is something you must agree to. It's only a formality – believe me, that's the only reason – but it's the only way I can get permission from the authorities.'

He stopped there, when Katya was expecting him

to go on. And she saw that he thought she was not listening, and needed a cue from her.

'What is it?' she asked and waited for him to tell her of a form to be filled or an oath to be sworn, in the way that even he did with the curious display of pedantry that seemed to afflict all men.

'You will have to marry me,' he told her.

BOOK TWO

Reason and Romance

CHAPTER 11

TONYA

During the winter after the Civil War Moscow appeared as the encampment of a retreating army. Demobilized soldiers shuffled through the streets, begging at doors or seeking news of relatives who had been uprooted and swept along in the tide of war and revolution. The cobbled streets rattled with ammunition waggons and trains of worn-out pack animals. Shots rang out at odd hours of the day and night as horses were killed for food or the Cheka engaged in gunfights with the lawless elements among the disbanded troops. It was a time of want and privation, of worthless money and loss of illusions, a time when people were ground into grit and mud, and the old feelings of decency and honesty seemed as ornamental as the trees along the boulevards or the fences around the great houses which could be torn down and burned for warmth.

Tonya and her family had been for some months in the city. She had found a room to house them – in truth, only half a room, but for a latecomer to Moscow it was a triumph of achievement. And it could be regarded as private, almost as a whole room if her family and the other occupants accepted that the blankets strung along a rope down the middle of the room represented a wall. This was an easy illusion, since the other residents wanted to be friendly and seemed to take comfort from the presence of the new arrivals.

The room was shared with a family called Liubishkin. Originally they had had possession of the entire room, but Ivan Lukitch Liubishkin needed the money and rations offered by Tonya if he were to support his wife and four children. He was a photographer's colourist. He worked from home, tinting the black-and-white portraits that were brought to him; and also painted watercolours of old Moscow, which he hawked around with indefatigable optimism and little success. Although he was no more than thirty, he had lost his hair and most of his teeth because of something in the paints he used. It gave him a frightening appearance that was quite contrary to his nature and a source of regret. His wife was consumptive and his children skinny and undernourished. Despite this, Liubishkin was a cheerful man and optimistic about the future: after all, the Revolution was about the future, wasn't it? And the future as dreamed of by the Bolsheviks was of science and progress – in which, naturally, photography would be at the forefront of technology; from which it followed that, after the triumph of Communism, there would always be work for a photographer's colourist.

In the meantime pickings were thin. Nobody much was taking photographs – you could pick up a camera for a bag of flour or a small chicken – and those that were taken seemed suited by the starkness of black-and-white as a badge of the revolutionary moment. The fat times had been when people stood for their portraits, planted solidly among the potted palms and painted backdrops; but for the time being this was a dangerously bourgeois fashion. So Liubishkin went out daily to peddle his wares and dragged himself wearily home, often carrying the same bundle up the cracked stairs where the rail had been taken for firewood. Tonya tried to encourage him by admiring the pictures he could not sell. The colours seemed so pale and washed out that the views of Moscow had an ethereal quality. She studied them and thought: yes, it was all a dream. We lived in a dream and didn't know it. Ivan Lukitch has captured it exactly. The truth, however, was that Liubishkin was running out of paints – no-one was making them and he could not afford them – and he had to water those that he had so that his pictures contained mere hints of colour.

His luck went when he had no more red pigment. A genteel photographer in a threadbare frock coat brought a large group portrait. Some Red Army officers wanted a memorial of their time together and had posed for this picture outside the Church of the Annunciation with their favourite cannon. Could Liubishkin colour it? The officers would pay with meat – horsemeat from the battery teams, but none the worse for that. Yes he could. He worked with a will for a day and a night to the coughing of his wife and the whimpering of his children until the red paint gave out and he had to supplement the flesh tones with yellow. The officers came to view the work, stomped up the stairs and stood on the other side of the improvised curtain drinking vodka and studying the result. In the end they rejected it. All those yellow faces – it made them look like Mongol invaders.

To increase their income and qualify for something better than the fourth-class ration, Tonya's father found work lecturing on agronomy. This took some courage on the part of Professor Gromeko; the streets were dark when he went out of a morning and when he returned, and robberies were frequent. Also, a change had come over the students he taught. Now they were former soldiers and peasant revolutionaries, and from their committee they had appointed a monitor to check the political leanings of their teacher. The professor had never realized before what a suspect science agronomy was: how a discussion on the correct root crop for winter fodder opened up the whole basis of the rural economy. And in these days, when estates were being broken up and farms appropriated, that could be very treacherous ground. 'To have land available to grow winter fodder supposes a certain minimum size of farm, does it not, Comrade Instructor?' said the sly class monitor. Well, yes, it does – but you won't catch me saying that. 'I am merely imparting information,' answered the professor; and as a nice afterthought which made him feel smug and cunning, he added: 'It is for the People to draw the correct political conclusions.' There! I'm getting an ear for the way they talk. 'And who are the People in this context?' came the retort. Oh, Lord, save me! Help me, Tonya! I only want to talk about turnips.

Between searching for food and fuel Tonya took in sewing. Needlework of a decorative kind was something she had learned as a child and, although there was not much call for it, she could take some orders for patching and mending; all Moscow seemed to be going about in rags and cast-offs. This way she felt that she was making some contribution to the family economy, and the work distracted her from the suffering of Liubishkin's wife, who was coughing out her life uncomplainingly on the other side of the curtain.

In the meantime she wrote letters to her Krueger relatives abroad, begging for their assistance.

That winter Liubishkin's wife died. Her body was carried off without a winding sheet and disposed of no-one knew where. Liubishkin was too poor to get drunk; he had no more paints and was confined to the room in order to take care of the children, though Tonya offered to help. As a result he could not sell even the small stock that he had, and his family starved quietly. Only at night did he leave the room to scavenge for peelings and scraps to make into a thin broth. Tonya spared him some food but her own children were hungry enough. Liubishkin accepted his suffering quietly: only his footfalls as he paced the room betrayed his distress. Sometimes he would punch the curtain or butt it with his head, and Tonya would see the bulge of a human form pressed into the blanket like a mummer's costume. If she pulled the blanket aside and intruded into his world Liubishkin would give a gummy smile and say, 'Things are looking up.'

'Would you paint me an icon?' she asked one day. She needed an excuse to give her neighbour a portion of some meat that one of Professor Gromeko's students had traded him for a good grade.

'I have no paints,' was the answer. But Liubishkin tried and found some somewhere. Then he set to and painted a picture of the Virgin with angels and an inscription in Church Slavonic, framed it and provided mounts for candles. It was a pale and suffering Mother of God, starved of paint and looking with compassion on the starving. Tonya cried over it when Liubishkin gave it to her, and called it Our Lady of Moscow, who had watched them and shared their misery. It became her talisman.

That same winter, two of Liubishkin's children died of whooping cough. Sasha caught the disease too, but his robust baby sister was spared. Perhaps it was a miracle performed by the wonder-working icon. In fact, Professor Gromeko called on an academic colleague, a doctor, who helped; though the Liubishkin children were beyond his skill. For a week Sasha hovered between life and death, then came down on the side of life; and Tonya's heart was filled with joy even as her neighbour's children were dying. She felt guilt at first about their unequal fates; but once she understood that it was fated, she acknowledged the miracle that had spared her children to life and knew she had to be joyful.

Then Liubishkin himself died in an accident. Or killed himself.

An old woman, Galina Mattveyevna, lived in the alcove at the bottom of the stairs on a diet of air and dust. Toothless and dressed in rags, she hammered at the door of the room and summoned Tonya. 'Quickly – quickly! Ivan Lukitch, he's dead!' Tonya grabbed her shawl and followed the old woman three flights down the unguarded staircase to the hallway where Galina Mattveyevna lived behind a piece of sacking underneath the last flight. At the same time, the other occupants of the house appeared from their rooms with their clamouring children. The chairman of the house committee yelled officiously for order and asked what had happened.

'He flew past my home,' said Galina Mattveyevna. 'Just flew like a bird. And not a sound – no scream or anything.'

'How would you know he flew?' said the chairman of the house committee. 'In your filthy hole you couldn't have seen anything.' He stirred the body with his foot as it lay spread-eagled on the tiles.

'Cover him up, for pity's sake,' said a voice, but no-one was prepared to risk the loss of a sheet.

'There'll have to be an inquest.'

'Those stairs are dangerous. What a terrible accident!'

'Or suicide – he didn't scream or anything, which isn't natural. He flew like a bird!'

'Sod him!' murmured the house chairman, who was thinking of the trouble of the inquest and his responsibility for the fact that the stairs had no rail.

In the end there was no inquest. The chairman and two of his friends carried the body away at night and left it in the street where it would look like a traffic accident. Party officials came and removed the two remaining children and Tonya's family was left in possession of the whole room.

He flew like a bird and didn't cry out! Oh Lord have mercy on us and in thy grace save us!

Salvation came in the form of a letter.

Old Krueger, the mine owner and ironmaster from the Urals who was Tonya's grandfather, had a younger brother who, finding no opportunities in the family business, left his homeland for France. He settled in Paris and founded his fortunes on trade between the two countries. From Russia he exported timber, iron and furs and on the return leg, his ships brought manufactured goods and luxuries for the Russian nobility and *haute bourgeoisie* who aped the language and manners of the French. He passed this business to his son, who by 1921 was an elderly invalid, and it was currently run by his grandson, Mikhail Alexeyevitch Krueger, a man in his mid-thirties. This youngest Krueger had been born and brought up in France and had changed his name during the war, at which time the firm branched out into the arms trade. Shrewdly he kept the surname, which had business value, but he gave out without expressly saying so that his family came from Alsace-Lorraine where German surnames were common. So from being a suspected alien, he became a lost Frenchman from the occupied provinces ground under the heel of the German invader and an object of pity and admiration. He changed his first name to Aristide and his company was called Aristide Krueger et Cie.

The letter from Cousin Aristide stated that he was moved by the plight of the family, as a result of which he was willing to arrange for their emigration and provide for their maintenance in France. He enclosed various forms and letters of recommendation that would assist in getting exit visas, and promised to send funds and tickets in due course so that they could leave in the spring on a ship that would be leaving from one of the Baltic ports.

'Money would have been preferable,' said Professor Gromeko sourly, but he acknowledged that they ought to be grateful. 'So we're leaving Russia, are we? Is that what it's come to?'

'I don't want to leave,' Tonya reassured him.

'We may not have a choice. The Reds are expelling people; I hear Milyukov and Kizewetter have got their marching orders, and Kuskova too. It's as bad as the old days.' He shook his head because it was mystery to him; but Tonya was thinking: if we leave – then what happens when Yura returns?

'We can't leave,' she said. 'I'll write and ask for money.' The thought of Yura distressed her too much for her to feel any embarrassment at putting a bald request for money to her cousin. 'He hasn't seen Masha – he may not even know that she has been born.' Then she told herself that he could not care: the civil war was over for practical purposes and Zhivago must have been released; he must have returned to Yuryatin; he would be living with the Antipova woman and her child. That was the unbearable part – not the separation, but to be unloved!

The house committee chairman had already read the letter with its foreign stamps and censor's marks. 'To maintain the reputation of our house for loyalty,' he called a meeting of the residents to be held in the hallway where Liubishkin had fallen to his death, and he invited a representative of the Cheka to attend. This man, a youngster in a leather coat, stood at the back throughout the proceedings and smoked.

'Comrades, you may want to know why we are here,' began the chairman, though everyone knew. 'What can I say? These last few months we have been nursing a viper in our bosom!' He corrected himself. 'I mean, vipers in our bosoms. I speak, comrades, of our fellow house-occupants Alexander Alexandrovitch Gromeko, formerly called a "professor", and his daughter Antonina Alexandrovna Zhivago.

'We are tolerant people. The fact that Alexander Alexandrovitch was a so-called "professor", and that his daughter was married to a so-called "doctor" did not prejudice us against them – provided that they displayed the correct attitudes and did not rely upon their past so-called dignity.'

'Get on with it, Josif Rodionovitch!' cried a drunk from the back of the hall.

'Yes – well – I'm coming to the point. What I want to know is, have they reformed? That's important, isn't it? Isn't it?' He paused for some sign of support. Put off by the absence of fervour, he floundered about. 'Antonina Alexandrovna's family were capitalists from someplace out east. That's important. And she has relatives in France

who are *international capitalists*. That's downright suspicious! She didn't tell us about *those*! And she writes to
them! And they write back! Yes! They want her and the
rest of them to go to France – leave Russia, abandon the
Revolution and live off the fat of the land with all the other
capitalists. It's not fair!' he added by way of summary.

As the chairman continued with a repetition of the
same charges under the false impression that this made
his eloquence more effective, Tonya studied the pinched
faces of the other residents and was struck by the slyness of
poverty. Why do they hate us? she asked herself, and was
overcome by sudden fear. What will happen if they throw
us out into the street? Sasha was still weak, her father too
old, her daughter too young. Alexander Alexandrovitch
was listening with a bemused look, having difficulty in
grasping that he was one of the criminals referred to.
Why do they hate us? But Tonya realized that the others
bore no hatred. They were attending to Josif Rodionovitch
with indifference, as if Tonya and her family had obtained
exit visas from the human race.

The meeting concluded with a unanimous vote that
the miscreants should be reprimanded as disloyal to the
house and their case referred to the authorities as bourgeois
traitors and probable spies. Then everyone went quickly
to their rooms, leaving Tonya holding her infant and her
father silently amazed at his circumstances. The Chekist
officer also remained in his remote position across the hall
by the door with its broken panes stuffed with rags. Tonya
wondered if he was there to arrest them. He was so slight
of build that it seemed improbable he could do anything
so forceful. But to balance his physical lightness, he had
an air of power – or perhaps the power was in the leather
coat the Chekists seemed to wear like priests' robes. How
odd it should be like that.

'I shouldn't let this business worry you,' he said at
last. Tonya thought she detected sympathy, but he went
on: 'You're all bought and paid for by your rich relatives,
and we'll make sure we deliver the goods.'

'You mean that we're to be expelled?'

He did not reply directly. Instead he tickled Masha under the chin with a gloved hand, then lit another cigarette. 'It's Josif Rodionovitch who should look out. We've got an eye on his blackmarket deals and we'll pull him in when the time is right. By the way, what does this Krueger want you for?'

'Want us for? I don't understand? He's a relative.'

'So what? What does he want a family of paupers for? He's a capitalist so there must be something in it for him.'

Tonya did not believe that. It was too crude a view of human nature. That had been her husband's complaint about the Revolution – not its principles, but the crudeness of its thinking and the baseness of its practice. Perhaps they were right and she was a traitor. If so, it was out of instinct since she had never thought much about politics. How young this man was and how smooth and well-fed his face. He was quite beautiful. By contrast, though not old, she knew she was withered and scrawny. It occurred to her that under the stress of hunger her periods had stopped. Along with everything else, her womanhood had gone. That, too. It would be sad if she could only find the tears to cry about it. Those monthly cramps and pains that she had kept secret from Yura, because her mother had told her they were a mystery from which men were excluded. How often she had wished they would go. And now they were gone, and she had never noticed – as if they were a lost trinket of no value.

When the exit visas came through, Tonya busied herself packing and obtaining provisions for the journey, which was the more difficult activity.

Josif Rodionovitch was arrested one night and disappeared. The old woman, Galina Mattveyevna, to everyone's surprise was elected head of the house committee, presumably because she was too decrepit to interfere. The atmosphere in the house became easier; people were helpful, and with their aid the family got ready for their journey.

There were letters to write. Tonya wrote at length one more letter to Zhivago in the hope that he had survived the civil war. It was a long letter and she could not entirely hide her reproaches. When it was finished she was not certain what to do with it, but in the end she decided to send it as before to Lara, whom she supposed to be still living in Yuryatin. If Yura had survived he would certainly return there and seek out Lara.

The letter said:

Dear Larissa Fyodorovna,

I am writing to you before we finally leave, after all the delays, to join our relatives in Paris. Enclosed you will find a message for Yuri Andreyevitch if he is still alive. Please give it to him – I am sure he will find you. Whether he will want to join us in Paris I do not know. I leave him with regret. We are being expelled by the authorities, but perhaps it is for the best: I must think of the children. Yura is a good man and I can see why he was attracted to a good woman; but it still puzzles me why he has abandoned us. Sometimes I think about him and I resent you for coming between us, but in my better moments I know that there was no evil intention and that in some strange fashion this must represent the will of God. Things have been very hard with us here in Moscow.

    May God bless you

    Antonina Alexandrovna Zhivago

With the letter Tonya sent a photograph of the family coloured by Liubishkin. In her baggage she packed the icon of Our Lady Of Moscow.

They left Moscow in the middle of March amid the first hesitant signs of a thaw. Before their departure Tonya insisted that they follow the old custom and sit down for a moment of silent prayer.

They travelled by train from Moscow through Lithuania

to the port of Memel in the company of other refugees with hopes or relatives in the West. A party of soldiers guarded them and kept them in a state of quarantine, as if they bore the contagion of treason.

For the most part they were willing refugees – officials, factory owners, rural gentry who found themselves useless and inimical to the new regime. But there were others, radicals and opposition politicians, who had lived in exile or prison under the Tsar only to find themselves still out of sympathy with the new government. They were the most pathetic. Having sustained themselves in the belief that they represented the people, they found themselves rejected by the Revolution. They were men without hope; but they had a certain decency and quiet dignity. By contrast, Tonya was repelled by the nervous arrogance of the others, the vengeful weakness and unreconciled hostility. They carried the burden of the old regime, smoked its cigars and even drank its wine, and kept up their spirits with boastful talk of revenge when the Revolution collapsed and the Communist *canaille* were swept aside by the resurgent forces of their holy tsar. Loyalty to the tsar was their bedrock of hope; even those who had despised Nicholas II while he lived. Meanwhile, outside the train, the Revolution clamoured at the windows.

This time Tonya experienced the palpable hatred of the mob, not the indifference that attended Josif Rodionovitch's manipulations. The thickness of a grimy windowglass separated two universes as the train halted at stations or coaling points, and starving peasants and fierce committees of workers and soldiers railed at her from the platforms. She thought: they don't know me. If we could talk it would all be different. They're just the same people that I shared a house with. Once we were able to talk, everything changed. In other moments she was less certain of the power of simple human contact and was left to wonder again: what did we do to them that they hate us so much? And again it seemed to her that she must have lived in a dream and that the waking truth had been kept at bay by the whips of the tsar's cossacks.

The journey was slow, as all journeys were in those days. At the border they were stopped for a full day while the suspicious Lithuanian officials scrutinized the papers of everyone on board and threw off those whose permits were not in order. It was a day spent in silence as each individual prayed that it would be his neighbour and not himself. Tonya understood only with difficulty that she was now entering a foreign country, for in the old days the Kruegers had had an estate near Kaunas; Tonya had visited it as a child and had picked berries on the ling-covered hills. Then it had seemed as much a part of Russia as the house in Moscow or the estate at Varykino. But apparently she had been wrong and Lithuania was not Russia and in the eyes of the inhabitants never had been.

The train was allowed to proceed, but now under local guards. Despite the hostility of these soldiers, the passengers began to relax. The Lithuanians were not Communists. When the reckoning came, they would fight alongside the Whites and help in the settling of accounts. The arrogant fantasie grew as the train moved slowly through bleak hills, then signs of settlement, fields of rye, meadows and then to the pine barrens of the sandy coast.

As they came to Memel the countryside changed and a German orderliness organized the fields with a neatness and absence of war. The train was stopped by French officials of the Allied Commission as they passed out of Lithuanian territory. Papers were examined again and finally they were allowed into the station. The platform was crowded with soldiers, Allied officials, representatives of relief organizations, and, like an exotic species among the drabness, men and women in fine dress and fur coats, fortunate aristocrats ready to welcome their relatives.

For Tonya and her family there was a short fat man in a dull business suit and a white shirt with a celluloid collar, a man with a pince-nez, a heavy moustache and oiled hair with a kiss curl slicked on each temple, who was left on the platform when the rest had cleared except for the porters and the railway officials. He came forward and introduced himself.

'Madame Zhivago? My name is Blanchard. I am the commercial agent of Monsieur Krueger and I have been commissioned to see to your well-being. Is this your baggage? All of it? I see – your recent time in Russia has evidently not been amusing. Well, we shall see what we can do.' He spoke French and showed some friendship behind his stiffness. He summoned a porter to take the bags, and outside the station engaged a cab to take them to an hotel.

'Are we in France?' asked Sasha as the cab jolted through the cobbled streets. He had a boy's interest and was familiar with the grey-blue uniforms and crested helmets of the French army, and in the narrow streets they came across parties of soldiers on patrol or lounging at the entrances to the *Bierstuben* smoking their aromatic *tabac brun*. 'Not yet,' Tonya told him gently and took in the signs on the shops in their queer German script, and the improvised direction posts and placards of military regulations which were in French. The world turned upside down – would it never end?

They found the hotel Zum Roten Hahn, an ancient building in a narrow byway called the Hahngasse. It had small windows like a myopic man and overhung the street; and jutting from above the door was the carving of a red cockerel which gave the hotel its name. Monsieur Blanchard attended to the formalities and escorted his charges to their clean rooms. 'I shall return tomorrow,' he informed them and bowed to Tonya at parting.

Two rooms had been provided. They were small rooms with truckle beds for the children, clean linen, fresh water and towels, but in their completeness and privacy Tonya found them frightening. Monsieur Blanchard had arranged that they should eat the house meals; they dined on *Eisbein*, cabbage and potatoes, and to their amazement found that they could not eat; their stomachs had adjusted to the meagre diet of Moscow. During the night Sasha was sick from the food and wet the bed. Tonya tried desperately to clean the mess before the maid arrived and, having used up the water in the pitcher, waited in panic for the maid's condemnation. When the latter arrived, she surveyed the scene calmly and then set about her work. She muttered, '*Verdammte Russen*' under her breath, but Tonya did not understand.

Monsieur Blanchard returned in the morning, still in his meek turn-out like a hired mourner. His news was that the ship, the *Ville de Dinant*, was still taking on its cargo of timber and supplies and would not be ready for some days. He advised caution in going about the town because of anti-Russian feeling among the inhabitants, and he gave Tonya a small amount of money for which he requested a receipt. Then he left, saying that he would come back with more news the following day.

Professor Gromeko proposed that they should all go for a walk. 'After spending so long on the train, I think that the children require fresh air.' He spoke with an air of authority which sat oddly with his threadbare appearance. Tonya agreed: it was in any case a good idea, but she also thought that her father needed the reassurance of being in charge. Since the collapse of their old world that had not been the case. The grand schemes of life had given way to the petty decisions of everyday existence; the hunt for food, for clothing, for hot water or an old cloth to stop a draught. Faced with that level of reality the professor had found himself inept; the habits of authority slipped and in even the large things he now deferred to Tonya. This morning, however, it was he who decided that they should go for a walk.

It was a grey spring day under a watery sky that imparted a slatey colour to the buildings. The streets had a muted sound of nothing much happening. The occasional cart rumbled past behind a pair of heavy horses; the occasional motor truck spluttered and pumped out sour fumes; the French soldiers patrolled in an easy-going, amiable fashion. Without any purpose the little party made their way towards the Kurisches Haff, and then found themselves suddenly standing on a narrow gritty beach and in front of them a grey expanse of water and a sky of mewling gulls.

'What is it?' Sasha asked with a mixture of excitement and fear.

'I could be mistaken, but I believe it's called *the sea*,' answered the professor archly.

'Don't tease, Father,' said Tonya, and the old man's smile crept out and he tousled the boy's hair. It was a faint smile, over and gone. He stared at his boots, where the sand was invading the holes, and then across the sad sea. The wind blew off the sea and caused a pinging in the rigging of a small boat pulled up on the beach.

'Across there is France,' he said inaccurately. He picked Sasha up. 'Can you see, my boy?'

'I think so,' said Sasha doubtfully.

'Of course you can!' said the professor. Tonya pointed the baby silently towards the water. 'Let's look for shells!' the old man exclaimed enthusiastically. So they did.

They scoured a length of beach after his grandfather had first shown Sasha what a shell looked like – as to which he had previously had only a dim idea gleaned from a book. They found a cockle, a shore crab and a pine branch stipped of its bark and cast up resinous and wormy by a storm. They watched the seagulls and the oyster-catchers and the rain clouds rolling from the West. And finally they turned for home and trudged back across the sand where Sasha found a small orange object lodged among pebbles.

'It's a piece of amber,' his grandfather explained.

'Is it valuable?'

'Higher than rubies!' said the professor and he held it up to catch its translucency against the white spot in the clouds where the sun was hiding. 'Did you know that sometimes a piece of amber can have a fly caught in it.

Look! Look! Here we are!' He pointed out a blemish and a piece of grit embedded in the stone and swore it was a fly. Sasha smiled and took his treasure, putting it away carefully in his pocket.

The rain caught them as they returned through the town. They were in one of the narrow streets and the rain came with a sharp wind and bounced off the rooftops. They took shelter in the doorway of a café. From the interior they heard noises and laughter. A group of people were sitting at one of the tables among a litter of coffee cups and plates holding the remains of cream cakes.

'Alexander Alexandrovitch!' shouted a voice. 'Don't stand there, come and join us!'

The professor turned to the speaker, then cast his eyes in embarrassment at his shabby clothes. Tonya recognized the man as Maxim Yuryevitch Golitsin, a landowner from the Minsk area who had been her father's chess partner on the train. He had shed his shabbiness and was wearing a solid worsted suit and carrying a polished walking cane. Two men of similar appearance were with him and a woman of striking beauty, dark and almond-eyed, wearing a sable coat open over a Worth creation. The faces of all four were locked in smiles, as if interrupted in something frivolous.

After further pressing, the professor agreed to take coffee. Chairs were brought up and Golitsin made the introductions. 'And this is the Countess Kalinowska, who had the foresight to leave before the Revolution and who is, for the present, my saviour and patroness.'

'I happened to be in Switzerland,' said the Countess lazily. 'My husband was sadly not so fortunate. He served with Yudenitch and was killed. But we must forget about these terrible things and look to the future.' Her voice was as delectable as her looks; she spoke Russian with a faint Polish accent and glided lightly over the words. Her beauty was of the dark Polish sort, her nose slightly pointed and retroussé. Tonya thought that their ages could not be far apart, but comparison was as meaningless as between different species.

'We are going to Paris,' said the professor clumsily.

'My dear, we are *all* going to Paris – Paris will be our beloved Russia in exile. At all events, until the Return.'

'And we *shall* return!' affirmed Golitsin, feeling comfortable on a glass of schnapps.

'Zhivago?' queried the countess. 'Are you a relative of Andrei Vasilyitch Zhivago, the millionaire? I knew of him in Switzerland, though of course I was too young ever to have met him.'

'He was my father-in-law,' Tonya admitted. 'But he was not a millionaire. He died poor.'

'Not poor,' said the countess in a tone that suggested that the idea of poverty offended her. 'I heard that there were financial difficulties – principally caused by his lawyers. But a man may have financial difficulties without being poor. It's a matter of being able to raise cash at the right moment. My own late husband had extensive estates, but when his creditors called demanding cash there was never any to be had. Ah, this is too depressing! We should concentrate on the fact that we have all survived! We shall regroup our forces and in due course attend to the Jews and the Reds – which are much the same thing.'

The conversation continued in the same vein. The rain stopped. Tonya grew tired of the countess's careful examination of her and her civilized contempt. Although Tonya had no regard for the Communists, she felt that they could not be dismissed so easily and the past simply restored. They could not have succeeded unless there was some weakness in the prized dream of the past. Surely there was something to be learned? This shallow conclusion depressed her and she wished she had given more study and thought to the subject. They finished their coffee, thanked their hostess and left the coffee house.

'I should like to go to church,' Tonya announced.

'Yes – well, I suppose the Germans do go to church,' said her father.

It turned out to be a Lutheran church, a severe red-brick building with an angular spire, so different from the churches at home. The interior was plain and whitewashed, without incense or images. Tonya found the long nave and the wooden pews unsettling by comparison with the Greek-cross shape of the churches she knew and the custom of worship on one's feet. The door creaked behind them and they walked hand in hand down the aisle.

The building was empty except for a cleric in a plain black cassock who was standing in one of the transepts busying himself over a pile of prayer books. He glanced round at the noise of footsteps echoing on the tiles. Recognizing the band of ragged Russians for what they were, he stopped his work and retired through a side door, leaving them alone.

Professor Gromeko remained standing, holding the baby and Sasha by the hand.

Tonya knelt in the aisle and tried to pray. She felt the pressure of the hard tiles. My knees are so bony. The prayers would not come; she could hear the words in her head but no-one was there. In the hotel she had taken the icon of Our Lady of Moscow out of her baggage and it had given her some comfort; but here God was absent. The building was so cold. I wish I had more clothes – a warm shawl. Mentally she reckoned up the items of the children's clothing like telling beads. It was difficult to wash them because she could not be certain they would dry before the ship departed. She was sure Sasha had lice. He denied it because he hated it when she combed through his hair and cracked the eggs between her thumbnails. Mary, Mother of God, protect us on our journey! Sasha was lying: he kept scratching his head. There's nobody there. They have taken my God from me. Masha's hair is too short for lice, but I shall probably get them. Lord have mercy upon us. Christ have mercy upon us.

In the streets the French soldiers watched her indifferently. She had ceased to register as a woman. She hurried the family away so that she would not have to bear that gaze. And now her God was taken away. It was too hard. Her head thumped as she struggled to grasp what it all might mean. But nothing would come by way of an explanation, only a glimmer of possibility.

She thought: it won't stop until everything has been stripped away from me.

Thinking this she caught sight of Sasha, who was skipping on the cobbles and dancing between the pools of rainwater.

After three days, the *Ville de Dinant* left Memel with its cargo of timber and its small freight of Russian émigrés cramped in the few passenger cabins. It battled on a grey sea through the spring gales and one day in April arrived in Dieppe. There, Tonya and her family were met by another of Aristide Krueger's agents, a one-armed *blessé* with a waxen face and a mustard-gas cough. He placed them in a hotel for the night and the following morning helped them on to a train to Paris. It was an uneventful journey; Tonya was struck only by the fat placidity of the land, the women working in the fields, the frequent villages, the fine straight roads between their avenues of poplar and plane. The French were civil enough, but Tonya had to excuse her appearance and explain that she and her family were not gypsies.

In the main hall at the Gare du Nord two men were waiting for them. One was a chauffeur in a grey uniform and lacquered boots. The second was a man of medium height, aged about thirty-five, and wearing a silk hat and a black overcoat with an astrakhan collar. He came forward, smiled a polite smile and introduced himself as Aristide Krueger. He kissed the children and shook Professor Gromeko's hand.

Tonya's first impression of her cousin was favourable. He had a familiar Slavic face with a snub nose and, when he raised his hat, showed a head of light brown curls. His teeth were even, his eyes bright, and he smiled in an easy way, looking comfortable with himself. The man inspired a natural confidence and Tonya responded to the unaccustomed warmth.

'Well, cousin,' he said, 'I can see that you've had a hard journey and I can imagine that things have been pretty bad in Moscow. Even here we hear stories. By the way, you don't mind my speaking French, do you? Fact is, my Russian is none too good: I speak it only to my father and he doesn't correct my mistakes. I'm afraid I must be an embarrassment to listen to.'

Outside the station a car was waiting. Krueger saw that everyone was loaded into it and instructed his driver to set off.

'Where do I begin?' he said when they were all settled. 'I'm sure you must be a fund of stories. Moscow! I've never been there – I've never even been to Russia. Your letters, they were so sad. You don't want to talk about it. I understand.'

'We were so grateful that you were able to rescue us,' Tonya answered woodenly. It was not the way she wanted to put it; the tone was wrong. She had lost the habit of conversation.

'Don't mention it. We are all family.'

'Are you married?' *No!* That was not what she wanted to say!

'I've never found the time. Perhaps I'm not the marrying kind? I'm afraid that there are no little cousins for Sasha and Masha to play with.'

'Where are we going?'

'To my father's house. He so much wanted to see his – great niece? – is it great niece? I find these family trees so confusing. Is it true that you're married to the son of Andrei Vasilyitch Zhivago, the millionaire?'

Gradually they left Paris and entered the suburbs. The conversation lapsed into occasional smiles of reassurance. Krueger cracked his knuckles and checked his watch. As the road emerged into a landscape of rolling wheatfields, the car turned off through a pedimented gateway and on to a long drive, an alley of horse chestnuts that were still bright with their candles.

'I should explain,' said Krueger cautiously, 'otherwise you may get the wrong impression. I mean about our family's position.' Parkland stretched away on either side of the drive; at the end, a large house with a high-pitched roof was visible. 'Our home here is an expensive relic of the past. The truth is that we can't afford it, but we keep it up largely for the sake of my father. Our business was terribly disrupted by the war – and then the Revolution more or less closed down the Russian trade. Frankly, it's a miracle that we've managed to keep going at all. I say this because appearances might make you think otherwise.'

'I know that we must be a burden,' Tonya answered. 'We are very grateful.'

'No,' he reacted sympathetically, 'you mustn't feel a burden. In any case, your present circumstances will last only a little while.'

'I don't see how things can change.'

'No? Well, there is the matter of your father-in-law's estate.'

'My father-in-law died bankrupt. He committed suicide.'

'Perhaps. But I understand that the former may not be the case. His affairs were in some confusion, but the situation was not necessarily hopeless – or so I've heard.' The car had arrived at the gravelled space in front of the house, from which a double set of steps swept in an arc to the main door. Krueger stepped lightly from the car and offered his arm. He said: 'We can talk about this later. I don't claim to understand these complicated matters. I've invited my lawyer, Maître Heriot, to see if he can clarify the business. The main thing,' he added, 'is that you are here and that you are safe!'

A manservant opened the doors and admitted them to an open hall that was hung with portraits and tapestries. Catching Tonya's look of surprise, Krueger joked, 'See what I mean? It's all appearances.' He removed his hat and coat and threw them to the servant. He was wearing an elegant grey lounge suit and a yellow boutonniére. He enquired of the man whether his father was available to welcome his visitors. 'He is with Maître Heriot,' came the answer.

Tonya's host suggested delicately that she might wish to refresh her appearance. He bade the servant show her to a bathroom. She took the children and followed to a room with green tiled walls and a basin with running water such as she had not seen in years, and there she was left in privacy. How cool it was, after the open road, here in the dimness on the shaded side of the house. How fragrant. A small bowl held broken petals of pot-pourri. She caught her reflection in the mirror. Yes, I do look like a gypsy. I have no business here. She washed her face, plastered Sasha's hair with water and wiped Masha's running nose. Then she sat for a while and breathed in the cool air. She must calm herself and make a good impression on Cousin Aristide's father.

They were taken to a large salon. The shutters were drawn on this side of the house and the air was striped with bars of light. In the shadiest corner an old man sat in a deep chair. Next to him a middle-aged, bearded man in black professional dress was sitting upright but composed with his hands folded tidily on his lap. Aristide Krueger was lounging by the fireplace and sprang to attention as they entered.

'Right! Are we clean and refreshed? I would make introductions but they seem so formal. My father has been expecting you, and Maître Heriot is here to – well, explain your position and your prospects.' The lawyer nodded respectfully. Chairs were offered and a drink. The butler brought glasses of sweet Marsala, pouring first for the old man and then his guests. Aristide helped himself to scotch from a decanter that was kept on a side table.

'Let me look at you,' said the old man. Tonya supposed him to be seventy or so. He had a thin pale face with skin that seemed drawn towards his nose like something striving for light. Tonya stepped dutifully forward with the children. She wondered if he detected a family resemblance, but the old man's eyes only confirmed her strangeness. She felt a flicker of panic and wondered: why do they want us?

The old man said nothing more. His mottled heavy-veined hand remained clutching Tonya's. A clock gave a deep resonant tock, the lawyer coughed, a glass chimed against a table and she could hear her father begging forgiveness for spilling his drink.

'My father,' said the younger Krueger, 'has asked Maître Heriot to attend.'

'Documents,' contributed the lawyer with an obscure smile.

'There are papers to sign. Lawyers will be lawyers, I suppose. Me – I don't understand it.'

'Is your husband alive, Madame Zhivago?' asked Maître Heriot. Tonya felt a sudden chill but it passed. Aristide Krueger gave her a reassuring glance. The lawyer repeated his question.

'I don't know, monsieur,' she answered hesitantly. 'My husband disappeared some two years ago. I have no idea where he is.' Maître Heriot pondered this reply.

'Would you be prepared to sign a certificate attesting to his death? I regret to ask this question, but it is of some technical interest. As the wife of Monsieur Zhivago you have a certain limited status. But as his widow – you understand?'

'I don't understand.'

'There is some property,' said the lawyer patiently. 'Possibly Monsieur Krueger desires to secure your interest in it. Strictly speaking, however, it belongs to your husband as the heir to his father's estate. Unless, of course, your husband is dead – in which case there are other considerations.'

'Don't be so gloomy, Anatole,' interrupted Aristide Krueger. 'Can't you see you're frightening the poor woman? Fact is, Cousin Tonya, that old man Zhivago, your father-in-law, left his affairs in a mess when he died. If he'd had a head for business he could have saved himself from ruin, but he hadn't and he didn't. Instead he had assets locked up all over the place, some of them here in France. If we could free them, then we could set you up pretty comfortably. That's what Anatole is trying to tell you.'

'In brief,' the lawyer confirmed. 'Of course, the undertaking is not without its problems. There are debts and claims to be settled, and ambiguities of title to be resolved. Your own status is equivocal; and then there is the complication affecting all Russian-owned assets, namely the repudiation by the Soviet government of certain railway loans that were floated here in the Tsar's time. But one can be hopeful – yes, hopeful.'

'Hopeful,' Tonya repeated, and tried to invest the word with hope. She realized how weary she was, how weary they all were: her children sitting intimidated and dispirited, her father gazing distractedly at the porcelain and the curtains in their heavy swags as if he had stumbled into a treasure house. Cousin Aristide was an attractive man and his father seemed a grave old gentleman, but they were strangers to her and she could find no family feeling. Were they trying to tell her she was a rich woman? How odd. She had got used to poverty, and of all her losses that of wealth was the easiest to bear. When the lawyer tendered some papers for her to sign, she declined and said that she and her family were very tired. They had proposed to her that Yura was dead. To put her name to this possibility was still beyond her. Cousin Aristide said he understood and patted her hand.

'I have arranged some accommodation for you,' Krueger said as he accompanied them back to the car. Something had disconcerted him and he was less lively than before. 'I'm afraid it's rather modest – a result of the times we live in, I'm sad to say. But I dare say you will make it homely enough. And there is an allowance settled on you. My father wanted to be sure that you were properly taken care of, and it's he who takes all the decisions.' He returned Tonya's look of enquiry frankly. 'He's a deep one, my father, even if he don't say much.' The old man had said nothing after his first request. He had sat listlessly in his chair holding Tonya's hand, and at parting had reached for a box on a side table and produced a chocolate for each of the children.

They drove back to Paris. The geography of the city meant nothing to Tonya, but the wide boulevards and splendid buildings in the mellow sunlight of late afternoon spoke of prosperity. Then these were left behind and they entered a series of mean streets of workshops, apartment houses, bars and seedy dance halls, finally halting before a crumbling house of four storeys where children played on the pavement. Silently Aristide Krueger got out of the car and invited his passengers to join him.

Krueger spoke to the concierge and instructed his driver to bring the bags. They ascended several flights of rickety stairs until they reached the topmost level under a dusty skylight. Krueger took out a key and opened a door into a large and sparsely furnished room.

'This is your home,' he said. It had a sad aspect of neglect and an atmosphere of dampness. It was furnished by a collection of shoddy items and a cold stove with a mound of ash spilling from it.

After a moment Tonya said: 'After Moscow this is the height of luxury. Thank you, cousin.'

Krueger tried to be cheerful. 'Home is where the heart is, eh? A bit of cleaning – a few more sticks of furniture – I'll see to the ceiling.'

'You've been more than generous.'

'Best I could do in the circumstances. I'm afraid the building is a bit of a Jews' nest, but I'm sure you won't let that affect you. Ah! – money! You must have a little money to be getting on with.' From his pocket he took a few francs and pressed them into Tonya's hand. He replaced the soft leather gloves he had taken off to use

272

the key, and began to make parting noises. Tonya stood with the children in the centre of the room and surveyed the dust. It would have to do. Cousin Aristide *had* been generous. It was better than life in Moscow. With effort the apartment could become their home.

Aristide Krueger left them and Tonya began wearily to set about her tasks. She despatched her father to find a pail of water, and planted the children in a corner to play in the rubbish. Mentally she moved the furniture and began planning a shape to their life. She felt vaguely the incongruity between the upheavals that had thrown down the past and the immediate problem of arranging where they would all sleep and what they would have to eat. She supposed that everything became reduced in this way to the practicalities of daily living, but it still seemed strange if this were the meaning to be distilled from so much suffering.

If only Yura were with her!

She thought of Lara and wished her well. She wondered what her neighbours were like. A noisy fight was going on downstairs and someone was yelling in Yiddish.

CHAPTER 12

THE WHITE COLONEL

In 1925, when he was ten years old, Sasha Zhivago witnessed the attempt to kill Colonel Menshikov.

At this date the family was still living in the apartment off the Rue Mouffetard owned by Cousin Aristide's father. The building, affected by dampness and disrepair, attracted only those who worked in poor and uncertain trades and a good number of people who lived there only in a general sense: they were rarely present when the rent was due and it was difficult always to be certain exactly which part of the building they occupied. Among the latter was Le Nain, the theatrical dwarf, who lived with his mistress, a tubercular singer from a *bal musette*, and who might be encountered on stair or corridor at any time, announcing himself by the smell of his cheap cigars whose glowing tips were visible at waist height in the darkness, far too low for a 'normal' person and erratic like the glow of a firefly. In Sasha's eyes there was something magical as well as sinister in Le Nain.

Shortly after moving into their rooms Tonya was approached by Cousin Aristide to perform a little service. Nominally it was unconnected with the payment of their small monthly allowance. 'You'd simply be doing me a favour,' he explained, 'or my father, to be more accurate.'

The favour was to collect the rents due on the properties owned by Krueger et Cie, which included the apartment house in which the family lived and some others nearby.

'You can see the tenants every day,' said Cousin Aristide. 'They would probably prefer handing the money to you rather than a rent-collector. And, of course, you could pass on their complaints.' He added that, speaking personally, he would have been too embarrassed to ask for this favour. But the idea had come from his father who, unfortunately, was less sentimental. Would Cousin Tonya help? Of course she would.

Accordingly, Tonya had undertaken the task. With little Masha she went around the apartments, knocking on doors, taking coffee and asking for money. She saw the Jews with their menorahs, the Russians with their icons, the Poles with their plaster figures of the Virgin: it seemed that each group had brought nothing with them but their religion, their cooking, and their ways of conducting family quarrels.

And once too, while Sasha happened to be with her, she came across a room at the head of some stairs, at the end of a passage and under a skylight, in fact scarcely a room but a place where brushes or junk might have been stored, which was occupied by Le Nain. The singer, who was rarely seen by anybody, was absent, represented only by her dresses. These were on hangers, garishly coloured and spangled but torn and darned, and the wooden floor beneath them was scattered with tarnished sequins like fingernails. The dwarf, however, was in residence and wore a smoking jacket, a flat straw hat, and grey mittens against the cold. Walking with his rocking gait, he welcomed them amiably, offered a seat, listened patiently to the demand for rent, and promised faithfully upon his honour as an actor to pay it when next he was in funds. But next time the room was empty and there was no sign of the man. Or perhaps, as Sasha suspected, it was not the same room, not even the same building; and Le Nain's room could only be found, as it were, accidentally: when recovering a lost ball or chasing a cat. The actor himself remained solid enough: smelling of cigars and drink and cheap cologne; singing vulgar songs and fighting with the police.

Tonya thought little of the dwarf and more of the women she asked for rent. She noticed their hair and dresses. While Paris went around bobbed and shingled and wore its dresses short, these women wore their hair and skirts long and modestly. The men generally went off to sulk or in a temper when Tonya called. The women tried to talk reasonably: 'Tea, Madame Zhivago?' . . . 'Thank you, Madame Grossmann' . . . 'My husband would like to talk to Monsieur Krueger' . . . 'I'm afraid Monsieur Krueger is terribly busy' . . . 'The roof is still leaking and the walls are damp. I'm worried for the baby' . . . 'I shall tell Monsieur Krueger.'

They were right. The roofs leaked, the walls were damp, the drains stank, the windows rattled in their rotten frames and the doors let in the draughts. Also the rents were too high, claimed the women. But in the end they paid. It was difficult to admit to another woman, especially one as mild as Tonya, that they could not manage their household finances; especially when they knew that Tonya lived in an apartment not so different from their own.

Tonya took the complaints to Cousin Aristide. He was always sympathetic. Sometimes, as she was counting out the money, he surprised her with a small posy of flowers or some bonbons for the children and she was embarrassed to go on.

'I agree,' he said. 'It is hard on them. I only wish I could do more. But the rents are very low, whatever they say. If they weren't, they would move somewhere else. But they don't.'

'What about the repairs?'

'Dear Tonya, I do what I can. But the truth is that the income from these properties is so small that I can't afford more repairs. As it is we lose money, if you can believe me. That's what my father says, and it's really his decision. I do all I can to persuade him, but he's the one with the head for figures.'

Tonya had not seen the older Krueger since that first meeting, but she had formed the unpleasant impression that he was a hard and grasping man, and pitied Cousin Aristide for having to act as his mouthpiece.

Colonel Menshikov was very religious. Each Sunday he was the first to arrive for the service at the cathedral of St Alexander Nevsky in the Rue Daru. Sasha's mother also made a point of arriving early, but the colonel was nearly always there before her. Sometimes he was alone and could be found staring at the iconostasis, oblivious to anything around him. More often, and particularly after the attempt on his life, he was with two male companions in trench coats, who, by contrast, were nervous and impatient and tended to watch the crowd rather than the priests. Normally, too, he was among the last to leave. At the end of the service he would remain in the same position, detached from the sociable hubbub that marked the close, and perhaps at the very end he would turn and Sasha could see his thin face and large upturned moustache; and his pale, painful eyes would scan the worshippers as if looking for the returning Christ or his next assassin.

'Is he very wicked?' Sasha asked his mother. He thought that this would explain why the colonel needed to spend so much time in church.

Tonya said that the colonel was a saintly man, a great patriot who had performed valiant deeds in the Ukraine during the civil war.

'Is that right?' Sasha asked his grandfather.

Professor Gromeko grunted noncommittally, and Sasha had an idea that the subject was more complex than first appeared. His grandfather resisted any conversation directed at the war. Tonya on the other hand, though ignorant of the details was always ready to tell Sasha how *We*, the Whites, were heroic, generous, daring, virtuous, etcetera, while the Reds were villainous murderers.

On the day of the shooting the service was over and the sociable crowd had spilled into the street and the sunshine, in no hurry to take a cab from the ranks that lined the Rue Daru at this time of day, as much because the cabbies were often Russians as because there were fares to pay. Among the motor taxis was the horse-drawn fiacre driven by Gromov and Sasha waved to him. Gromov had perhaps the last fiacre in Paris and made a precarious living by ferrying sentimental Americans who, always at the forefront of things, felt even at this early date a nostalgia for the era before the motor car.

The crowd had the air of an opera chorus: cabmen, waiters, diplomats, generals, seamstresses, ladies, mistresses. Sasha had noticed the difference from French churches where people of the same class went to the same places of worship and all looked respectable. He wondered why the Russians were different. They talked volubly and at length. They made appointments to meet at the various émigré cafés and restaurants. They told each other about jobs and apartments to let. They borrowed and repaid money. They repeated scandal.

The scandal was a thick, scummy, effervescent brew like the rich borscht for a party to which each villager was asked to contribute his share of mouldy beetroot and doubtful meat, but which always tasted wonderful and dangerous. The potage was doubly-spiced by the fact that many of the refugees had formerly been wealthy and powerful (and in some instances still were), and they felt their losses keenly. From their self-importance came the mass of petty jealousies that caused conflict, and the fantasies of power that replaced the power they had lost.

Tonya wasn't immune to the appeal of scandal. After Sunday service she would take her place on the pavement with the religious women, a small knot of respectably dressed persons who normally gathered around the bearded priest and blackguarded their neighbours. The latter consisted of several distinct groups. First: the Imperial connection, the various grand dukes and their households, who tended to leave quickly in their expensive automobiles. Second: the soldiers and diplomats, saluting each other and spinning plots. Third: the businessmen and financiers, imposing but of dubious honesty and known for a fact to contain within their ranks several Christianized Jews. And finally: the artistic and social crowd led by the impresario Diaghilev (whether or not he cared to attend), the most impressive in appearance and the most subject to criticism. Before the upheavals many of these artists had been atheists; but since then they had returned to the Church to worship, if not God, then the romantic ideal of Russia and its past, the Slav soul, the People, and the absurd embodiment of all of these, the martyred Nicholas II.

While Tonya was occupied in observing and listening and shaking off the attentions of her younger child, Masha, Sasha talked to his grandfather and kept an eye on his current hero, Gromov the fiacre driver. Then, without any warning, out of the sparkling, chattering, artists' group came a cry of recognition and there emerged the figure of a woman who came over towards them, still gaily throwing off streamers of words to the friends behind her. She was beautiful but of an uncertain age; her dark hair was fashionably bobbed, and her clothes were expensive and carried a scent that would linger when she had left. She smiled benevolently at Sasha and jogged Tonya's elbow to interrupt her unimportant conversation.

'Tonya Zhivago! It is, isn't it? How long? Three – four years? Not since the frightful time in Memel. So you made it to Paris with your wonderful children and gentlemanly father. Wonderful!'

It was Countess Kalinowska. Tonya did not recognize her at first because her appearance had changed according to fashion, but then the other woman's animation and attractively accented Russian brought back the memory. The countess went on at a lively pace:

'I really wasn't sure. I pride myself on never forgetting a face, but, my dear, that last time you looked so *ill*. And so *pauvre*,' she added, using the French presumably because it sanitized the idea for her. Ignoring the contrast between her own and Tonya's modest dress, she said: 'Well, anyone can see that you've been doing well for yourself. I was worried about you. I can say that now. In Memel things looked in such a bad way with you that I thought – well, I thought – I'm sure you can guess what I thought. My heart went out to you. It probably showed. But what can I say?'

What could Tonya say? She was taken by surprise and no longer felt certain of her recollection of Memel. Had the countess helped or humiliated her? She looked to her father, but the professor was offering the usual courtesies. Tonya mumbled:

'It's very nice to see you again. You look in good health.'

'Yes, I am. Do you often come here?' the countess enquired casually, with the suggestion that 'here' was a fashionable place to be.

'Every Sunday, and on the important feasts.'

'How good you must be!'

'I don't remember seeing you here before.'

'No, it's my first time. I'm a Roman Catholic, but I came with a friend – Golitsin, do you remember him? He was with us at Memel. He asked me to come because of the people one meets here, and I must say that it's all pretty much as it is in our church, except that our priests don't go in quite so much for beards. Your priests are all family men and look none too clean in their habits. Ours are unmarried, which makes them more mysterious and dangerous to know. Still the differences don't seem enough to make a fuss about. That's Golitsin over there.' She pointed out a well-fleshed man in late middle age, who was talking to some decorative young men in large hats and scarves.

Uninterested in what the other woman was saying, Tonya was struck simply by the attraction of her voice: the countess scattered her remarks with inconsequential lightness and laughter, like butterflies among flowers. How heavy I've become, thought Tonya.

'And you, have you become rich?' asked the countess, with an emphasis on the delicious *rich*.

'I don't know what you mean.'

'Of course you do! Your father-in-law's fortune. Has it come your way?'

'Oh, no. Anything he had was tied up in knots by his lawyer.'

'That was Viktor Komarovsky, wasn't it? I can see that. He was a notorious crook – utterly charming, but a notorious crook.'

'My lawyers are trying to unravel the business.'

'Yes, of course,' said the countess knowingly and Tonya thought for a moment that in her blithe tactlessness she would refer to the other claimants, old Zhivago's bigamous wife and bastard; but instead she asked, 'What on earth do you do for money? My dear, you're not *working*, are you?'

'No, I'm not working. We live on an allowance from my cousin Aristide.' Tonya closed the subject hurriedly, and out of politeness returned the enquiry.

'Oh, I get by,' answered the countess airily. 'Golitsin is a great help, out of regard for my late husband. We knew each other quite well before the war. That was why I was at Memel, arranging things for him. Unfortunately, he came out of Russia with absolutely nothing of his fortune, literally not a kopek. It was all invested in land and stolen by the filthy Reds.' She added: 'It was a great disappointment – yes. With no means of maintaining ourselves, we drifted apart. For a while I was working at the Paramount film studio. Do you know it? Opposite the racecourse at Vincennes. That was how I ran into Golitsin again. He'd been to the races. He owned a horse!

'Would you believe that two years before he had been

a complete pauper, and now here he was with a horse and an automobile! It seems that in France he has discovered his métier. In Russia things were so stultifying. Of course, he owned a lot of land, but that didn't give scope to his talents. But in France, well, that was different! He found he had a flair for stocks and bonds and things like that, and in two years he'd got his fortune back. Naturally we struck up our friendship again at once. And since then he's been a great help to me.'

To this Tonya could only murmur her pleasure that the other woman had been so lucky. But what she was thinking was that Lydia Kalinowska was one of those people who have no imagination when it comes to others. When a woman, or for that matter a man, has beauty and charm, whatever her moral qualities her company will be sought after: even now Tonya was hoping that she and the countess would meet again. And the countess showed insouciant amorality and unselfconscious egoism as if beyond conventional reproach. Describing her affair with Golitsin, she took for granted that her friends would approve her behaviour, since it was so clearly beneficial to her well-being and prosperity. She gave a little wave to Golitsin.

'He's looking for me, I must go.'

Tonya was not without curiosity.

'Who are those people he is with?'

'Oh, some of Diaghilev's young men, dancers. Golitsin has decided to patronize the arts. Look, I really must go. It's been wonderful to see you and we must keep in touch. And good luck with that little legal matter of yours.'

'Yes, we'll keep in touch,' said Tonya hopefully, and then, to Sasha's surprise, the countess stopped and gave him a kiss on the cheek. At that moment Colonel Menshikov came out of the cathedral and stood at the head of the steps, and a man on the other side of the street, who appeared to be doing no more than loafing among the trees, stepped forward and, taking a service revolver from inside his brown jacket, calmly fired six shots at his intended victim.

The fact that the attempted murder failed was put down by Tonya to the miraculous intervention of the Holy Virgin, but as the assassin was firing from a range of thirty metres, he was always unlikely to succeed with a pistol, and it gave the event a ritual almost dancelike quality. The would-be killer showed no urgency either in the deed or his escape but planted himself squarely and used both hands to steady the gun. And the colonel displayed a similar calm, reaching inside his own coat for a weapon and returning shot for shot with his attacker above the crouched and flattened crowd.

Of the onlookers only Sasha kept his nerve and resisted his mother's attempts to pull him to the ground. It was self-evident to him that he could not be shot and he was determined to observe the spectacle. So he noticed the assassin's coarse woollen jacket and blue canvas trousers, his thin hair and thin moustache. And he noticed, too, the easy loping stride with which the man ran away, which was quick but not forced, though the hobnails of his heavy boots struck sparks from the pavement.

When the shooting had stopped and order was restored and the colonel, shielded by a phalanx of ex-soldiers, was ushered to an automobile, the crowd speculated on the motives for the attack. There were two. The first was that there was a Bolshevik murder squad operating in Paris. This was absolutely known for a fact and required no evidence. Dolzhikov, formerly a gentleman farmer, swore to it. Some twenty years before he had written an article in a provincial newspaper supporting the Stolypin land reforms, since when he had been a marked man. Fortunately, for the same twenty years he had escaped death by the skin of his teeth.

The second explanation was that the colonel was the target of a Jewish revenge plot. During the civil war in the Ukraine, Colonel Menshikov had been engaged in certain activities against disaffected cosmopolitan elements of the population which were necessary and therefore praiseworthy, but which could not be spoken of in broad daylight or in front of the children.

'There are some here today,' said Anna Borisovna knowingly, 'who are Christians in name only, and whose ancestors dined on bread tainted with the blood of innocents.'

The other religious women nodded in agreement, probably without reflecting on the details of the charge to which they agreed. And, to her horror, Tonya found herself nodding in response to this cruel nonsense. Realizing her mistake she hurriedly pulled her father and the children away, and she saw that Gromov, the fiacre driver, was standing by his cab, holding the horse and beckoning to them.

'Good morning, Semyon Maximovitch.'

'Good morning, Antonina Alexandrovna,' answered the cabbie and he gave an ironic sweeping bow that made little Masha chuckle. 'May I offer you a lift home? My equipage stands at your disposal. And how are you, General Bonaparte?' he remarked to Sasha who was collecting shell cases from the pavement where the assassin had stood.

'Don't you have a paying fare?' asked Tonya, who couldn't pay.

'As you can see, no,' said Gromov cheerfully.

The police were beginning to arrive. The crowd was dividing between those who for one reason or another had best avoid the police and those who would claim to have seen everything. Gromov said:

'If we don't leave now, we'll be here all day while the police try to interview everyone. And I'm not losing anything: my Americans won't have woken up yet from last night's cocktails. I've got time to run you home and get back to the Hotel Crillon. It'll be a really bad day if I can't pick up someone there.'

When he got home Sasha changed and, taking the shell

284

cases with him, went downstairs to the Coëns' apartment and asked if Daniel wanted to play.

The Coëns had lived in the building since before Sasha arrived. In some way they were related to the Grossmanns. Both families were Russian Jews who had emigrated before the war during the period of the pogroms. Jakob Coën worked in the fur trade; his wife did garment alterations at home. The flat was always full of garment bags and at any hour of the day Sasha might run into a messenger from the furrier climbing the stairs, bringing or taking away the work.

The two families lived on good terms even though Tonya collected the rent. Jakob Coën was a vigorous, self-educated man; he and Professor Gromeko often sat and chatted for hours about the way of the world. On the other hand Sophie Coën had little free time. When she was not doing housework or shopping, she was working over the contents of garment bags. If Tonya wanted to talk to her she always had to go downstairs, never the other way round. There were other considerations too which kept relations between the two women at a more polite level. The rent, for example. And the fact that, while art and politics, which the men discussed, are universal, cooking and housekeeping when it comes to their particulars are not. Sophie had frugal ways and the leftovers of religious habits learned in the *stetl*; Tonya, however, had come from a comfortable, even wealthy home, and the forced economies of life in Paris had never become second nature. An instance was that Tonya was too embarrassed to argue with shopkeepers and finger the produce, while Sophie relished both. In short, the men met in the world of ideas where disagreements had no practical effect; but the women met at the level of behaviour and had to accommodate each other if life were to rub along.

Sasha and Daniel went out to play. In the Rue Mouffetard they hung on to cart tails. They went to the market place and hunted for interesting scraps and set one of their rat-traps made from broken crates and baited with bruised fruit, which never caught any rats. They looked for girls in their Sunday best and shouted insults at them.

'Look what I found today,' said Sasha. He showed Daniel the shell cases. 'These are from real bullets. I saw someone try to kill Colonel Menshikov.'

'Did he miss? He wasn't very good, was he?' said Daniel practically.

'You can have one,' Sasha offered and the other boy accepted without acknowledging any generosity. He had decided to resist asking about the attempted murder. This devalued it in Sasha's eyes and he put his remaining souvenirs away disconsolately. Daniel relented.

'I'm always bored when you go to church. Why do you bother?'

'My mother likes to go.'

'I don't see why she doesn't go on her own.'

They were on a patch of bare ground. Daniel drew a circle on the earth and they sat on a wall and pitched stones into it. Side by side they were very different. Sasha was taller, with light brown hair and a snub nose. Daniel had black hair shaved very close at the sides; his skin was sallow and the contrast caused his dark eyes to glitter.

'Why don't you go to church?' Sasha asked.

'Our lot aren't like yours. They don't have a church. There's another thing called a synagogue. They go there on Saturdays – haven't you seen old Fischbein?'

'You don't go.'

'My father isn't interested.'

'What do they do there?'

'Pray to God, I suppose.'

'What god? Is he the same one as ours? What's he called?'

'He doesn't have a name. If you call him by his name, you go blind and your hair falls out. What's yours called?'

'God.'

'That's not his name.'

'Yes it is.'

'That's stupid. "God" isn't his name, it's what he *is*. He's got another name. If you don't know what it is, it's probably something silly – like Maurice.'

They both laughed at the idea that God was secretly called Maurice.

Later Sasha asked:

'Why do your lot go to synagogue and not church?'

'Church is for *goyim*. Our lot are Jews.'

Sasha was stuck with that answer. 'Jew' was a term of abuse, he knew. It meant that you were mean with money and it showed in the size of your nose. Jesus and the disciples were also Jews, but they were a good lot, so he concluded that 'Jew' must be one of those words with two meanings. Which was Daniel? Probably the second. But in that case, why didn't he live in a house with a flat roof and ride a camel?

Religion was something that puzzled Sasha. Because his mother was religious, Sasha could not fail to be aware of it. Even when times were hard, candles burned before the icon of Our Lady of Moscow. He might have taken religion as a natural part of life – a universal given of a child's world, and so normal as to be beyond question. But he knew that this was not so. To take one case: the French did not go to the church in the Rue Daru. The latter was so obviously and entirely Russian. And now there was apparently something else that the Jews did. Except that Daniel's family did not.

'Why doesn't your father go to synagogue?' he asked.

'He doesn't believe in God,' said Daniel, and he was suddenly overtaken by a fit of laughing. 'He doesn't believe in – Maurice.' Sasha pushed him off the wall and they fell to fighting. Satisfied with cuffing each other they resumed their places and Daniel said: 'My father's a socialist.'

'What's a socialist?'

'You *are* ignorant, aren't you?' Daniel replied with an air of superiority. 'Socialists believe that everyone should be equal. People should share their property and things so that no-one is poor.'

Sasha thought this sounded fair.

'I think I'm a socialist too,' he said.

'Me too,' said Daniel. 'Have you got any money?'

'A bit. Why?'

'Give me half,' demanded Daniel quite reasonably.

Sasha was a Russian, a socialist, and he believed in God. He was also, secretly, a prince awaiting the call to his kingdom. This was not entirely fanciful: he knew of the existence of a mysterious Zhivago fortune to which he was in some fashion the heir. All princes were socialists – the good ones, at least – since they strove to be beloved of their people. If he really were a prince then he could make his people happy. It did not sound too difficult. In the early morning the *vidangeurs* could be heard clattering with their horses as they removed the night soil. And Sasha lay in bed and dreamed.

It was the year of the Exhibition of Decorative Arts. The Eiffel Tower was illuminated by a montage of swirling lights. Sasha was longing to see the gimcrack splendours of the exhibition by night, but his mother was nervous of the crowds and his grandfather was not interested. Because, in his view, the exhibition was vulgar and tawdry, Professor Gromeko failed to see that precisely those qualities would excite the boy.

One Sunday, when Gromov had again taken the family home in his cab, Tonya invited him into the flat for a glass of wine. Gromov had never been there before.

While Tonya arranged the refreshment, the fiacre driver sat politely in the professor's chair which he had vacated expressly. Gromov was wearing a heavy ulster and a bowler hat and this gave him an old-fashioned look; like a waxwork, thought Sasha, who had seen one.

'Have you been in France long?' asked Alexander Alexandrovitch. This was a standard question put by émigrés to each other. It usually led to a catalogue of personal horror stories which, in truth, were of no interest since the questioner had his own tales.

'Since 'twenty-three,' said Gromov, and accepted a biscuit from Tonya's hand.

'And what did you do at home?'

'I drove a cab.'

'Ah, I see.'

Sasha and Masha, in their Sunday best, watched their visitor. Masha, who was good at faking solemnity, offered a biscuit to her grandfather. Sasha was boiling with curiosity.

'Did you fight in the war, Semyon Maximovitch?' he blurted out.

The cabbie was drily amused. His flat, heavy-browed face cracked.

'Which one?'

'Any!' said Sasha, who was none too sure.

Tonya reproved him. 'You shouldn't ask questions like that.' But Gromov did not mind.

'I fought against the Austrians and then the Reds.'

'Where do you come from?' Tonya asked.

'Kiev.'

'Is that where you were a soldier?' Sasha pressed him.

'I was with General Denikin in the Crimea.'

'So did you come out through Constantinople?' enquired the professor.

'That's right.'

Then to everyone's surprise Gromov bared his right wrist and, with a piratical leer at Sasha, showed him a scar.

'I got that from a Red bayonet,' he said.

Sasha was entranced.

'Did you kill the man who did it?'

Gromov caught the flash of horror and embarrassment on Tonya's face and confined himself to a knowing look and a click of his tongue. He finished his wine and thanked the family. It was politeness that made Tonya ask about the state of his business: he had given his time to them.

'It's not too bad at the moment. There are plenty of tourists around because of the exhibition.'

This gave Sasha the chance to make his point. 'I'd like to see the exhibition!'

'Then I'll take you,' said Gromov.

'He wants to see the lights at night,' Tonya explained apologetically and refused the offer on Sasha's behalf. Though not handsome, there was something attractive about the fiacre driver's laconic manner. And, although the idea was not consciously in her mind, it was compromising to be under obligation to an attractive man.

Of course Tonya agreed to the expedition in the end, and Daniel was included as Sasha's friend. The trip to see the lights took place and the boys enjoyed it. But what they enjoyed more was the novelty of being together in a cab, the petting of the horse, and the bloodcurdling stories Gromov was now free to tell them. From this first trip the relationship with the cabbie developed, and from Tonya's point of view it was preferable that the boys were with Gromov than prowling the streets around the Place de la Contrescarpe. Of course they could not be with him all the time – not if he had a fare. But they could tend the horse when he was waiting, and if he found a passenger he would arrange a rendezvous in one of the cafés he frequented.

The Café Dantzig was near La Ruche, a collection of small, cheap apartments and studios arranged round a wine hall. The place was mostly occupied by artists. The Americans visited the artists; and Gromov ferried the Americans.

La Ruche was a haunt of refugees from the broken fragments of Eastern Europe. If the boys did not want a snack at the café, they could buy pumpernickel and sausages with horseradish sauce from the street vendors, and for amusement they played in the ruined garden and banged on the stove-pipes that issued through the windows of the studios, or went into the wine hall and admired its octagonal shape. It reminded Sasha of a beehive – a beehive that hummed with Russian voices. 'Gobble – gobble!' said Daniel, who spoke no Russian, only Yiddish.

Close by the Rue Dantzig were the slaughterhouses of Vaugirard. The butchers also used the café. Sasha was fascinated by these beefy men with smears of blood on their clothes. They came in gangs, so big they seemed to block out the light from the door. Sasha watched them drink their cheap red wine and joke tolerantly with the Russian artists and he sensed a comradeship between art and labour, which, like socialism, seemed a reasonable enough idea.

Little of this, however, was relayed to Tonya. Gromov, conspiring with the boys, told her of visits to the Rue Castiglione to collect Americans from the Hotel Continental and taking them to the art dealers of the Rue Boetie – which was something altogether respectable.

It was a rainy Sunday one day during that winter of their friendship with Gromov. Sasha had been to the Russian church, returned home, changed, met with Gromov, and now the three of them were waiting, sheltering in the cab of the fiacre while the rain pelted and sent rivulets pouring down the Rue Castiglione. Here, like a duck hunter hiding low in the water, Gromov kept a wary eye out for his American prey.

As usual the cabbie had been parked in the Rue Daru after the cathedral service; yet Sasha had noticed that he never went into the building.

'Why do you go to church?' he asked.

'It's somewhere to pick up business.'

'But you never seem to find any.'

Gromov grunted. It was true.

The day was a day for motor cars. Who wanted to take a cab behind a shivering horse? Today, the Americans, like ducks startled by the first gunshot, took flight out of reach in their large limousines.

'Should I ask people to use your cab?' Sasha volunteered. But the fiacre driver only laughed.

'Who do you know?'

Stuck for a name, Sasha said: 'Colonel Menshikov.'

'Of course,' said Gromov ironically, 'our hero – you would.'

'He carries a gun.'

'Everyone knows that. You forget: I was there.'

Abandoning their hopes for the day, they retired to the Café Dantzig where Gromov took a glass of wine and bought the boys a *menthe à l'eau*.

'Why do you think Colonel Menshikov carries a gun?' he asked.

'Probably he used to be a cowboy,' said Daniel, who was currently interested in cowboys.

'Sasha?'

'He's a hero – so he has enemies.'

'Who?'

'The Reds.'

'And who are his friends?'

'The Whites.'

'Which are you?'

'A White.'

Gromov tousled Sasha's hair and said wistfully: 'I suspect that's what you intend to be, isn't it, my little Alexander Yuryevitch – a hero?'

'If I can,' Sasha admitted.

Gromov finished his wine and went on rather distantly: 'You're right, Colonel Menshikov is a hero – another Strelnikov.'

'Who was Strelnikov?'

'Never mind. The point is that he's in danger; you've seen that for yourself. And who can he trust? The Reds have spies everywhere.'

Of course there was no question but that he could trust true-hearted boys like Sasha and Daniel, and staunch former soldiers like Gromov. The people he could not trust were the ambitious status-hunters who attended church and fawned on the Imperial family and the remnants of the White army command. That lot were riddled with traitors, said Gromov.

The boys volunteered to keep watch over the colonel.

Gromov pooh-poohed the idea. For Daniel it was a simple matter: he thought that spying was a good idea in itself, and he might as well spy on Colonel Menshikov as anyone else. But for Sasha it was something else: an act of fealty to a great cause. What that cause might be was still not clear to him, but it was instinctive in the Russian community and had something to do with history and loyalty, nobility and blood. He felt it and he knew that Daniel did not, and he was sorry for Daniel.

There were, however, practical obstacles in the way of giving help to the colonel.

The first was that nothing much was known about him, not even where he lived. Gromov could throw no light on this, though he agreed that, as a starting point, it would be a good idea to find out. The problem was that Sasha saw the colonel only at church, when the latter was with his two silent friends, and afterwards he was rushed into an automobile or escorted a few streets away by his heavily armed companions where he then took a taxi.

The second task was to learn more of who he was. Sasha asked his grandfather who gave him some further explanation. Colonel Menshikov had operated in the Ukraine with Wrangel and had been personally responsible for killing many Reds. Since killing Reds meant the same as killing flies but was more heroic, this answer satisfied Sasha.

Unfortunately, Daniel's father had a different story. Colonel Menshikov had fought with Hetman Petliura and had slaughtered a lot of Jews. Naturally this disturbed Sasha, but he remembered that Jakob Coën had not actually been in Russia during the civil war; so his information was second-hand and could be mistaken. Perhaps there were two Colonel Menshikovs? Sasha persuaded himself that this was the case. Daniel was indifferent. He was only interested in the excitement.

The answer to the problem of where the colonel lived was obvious. He should be followed. However, this was difficult for Sasha, since on Sundays he was with his mother as well as in his best clothes. Daniel came up with a solution.

On the following Sunday, Daniel waited in the Rue Daru until the service had finished. It was a bitterly frosty day and, as he came out of church, Sasha saw his friend on the other side of the street, red-faced, shivering and sheltering from the wind. Neither boy gave any sign of recognition and Daniel wore a muffler over his face to maintain secrecy. When Colonel Menshikov and his friends left, Daniel followed them.

That afternoon they met at the market place by the Rue Mouffetard. A pigeon was caught in one of their rat-traps. It was their first catch, even if they did let it go after debating whether to wring its neck – something they were each agreeable to, provided that the other did it.

'How did you get on?' Sasha asked.

'No luck. They got a taxi and I could only watch it as far as the Avenues des Ternes.'

This was not satisfactory. They decided not to report their failure to Gromov until they had worked out a better plan. Sasha came up with an idea. On the reasonable assumption that the colonel would take the same route, if Daniel positioned himself in the Avenue des Ternes, he could pick up where he had lost his quarry the last time and follow a little further. It was not a bad idea except that it was not always possible to spot the colonel's taxi among the others, and it was not true that he always took the same route. Sometimes he went to a restaurant, and on one occasion to a building in the Rue du Colisée. Sasha reported this last fact. It seemed definite enough to be important.

'Do you know what the building was?' asked Gromov wryly.

'No.'

'It was the office of ROVS.'

Sasha was too embarrassed to ask what ROVS might be. He had to ask his grandfather.

'It's the World Organization of Russian Soldiers in Exile,' the Professor explained, and on the next convenient occasion he pointed out its leader, General Miller, an elderly man with a moustache and pointed beard who resembled Tsar Nicholas II. This confirmed Sasha in his opinion that Colonel Menshikov was a hero associating with heroes.

Throughout the winter the boys plotted in stages the movements of their quarry. It was a tale of cold waits in the stolen shelter of café awnings, the shadow of frost-starred trees and windy corners; of wasted days when the colonel went to some other part of the city instead of home – indeed they could not be sure that the route they were trying to plot was home rather than the apartment of a friend or a restaurant or any one of a dozen other plausible locations. For the most part it was Daniel who did the work, though on occasion Sasha would find an excuse for not going to church. Then he, too, would take his post and add a street or two to the rough map they were forming. So much time, yet such a little distance covered!

They saw Gromov less. They came to the conclusion that their friend had his own secrets, though this did not disturb them in the slightest since they were of an age when secret societies have their maximum appeal. Generally, the fiacre driver was open with them; they sat at table with him in the Café Dantzig and listened as he exchanged gruff banter with the other Russians. But sometimes another man came, not a worker in blue drabs and beret but a character in a shabby suit, who wore celluloid cuffs and a straw hat and smoked cigarettes from a gun-metal case. This man would not come into the café even to keep warm. Sasha would first see him through the condensation in the window, standing in the street, pulling his jacket around him for warmth since he lacked a topcoat. Sometimes the man put his nose to the glass to peer inside. And then he would signal from the door and Gromov would leave his glass of wine and the boys for a few minutes to go – no-one knew where.

Then, in addition, one day Gromov took them in his cab to Auteuil and left them for half an hour to mind the horse. There was no pretence of taking or collecting a fare, and the very idea was a joke: Auteuil was a poor area where people thought about the price of shoes, not of cabs. It was very puzzling.

As spring came round they told Gromov one day: 'We've got something to show you!' He was polishing the brasswork on the cab and soaping the leather to remove the cracks and mildew of winter. The boys did not so much speak as sing the words, and he could hear the rat-tat dance of their excited boots on the paving and, when he turned, he saw their smiles and nudges.

'You know where Colonel Menshikov lives, don't you?' he said blankly. 'Okay, get into the cab and show me.'

It was a disappointing response, emotionless, when they had expected him to share their excitement. And frightening in an uncertain way because they were confronted by a stranger who seemed tired rather than glad to see them, who smiled narrowly and without humour, who rushed them into action to his own timetable without sparing them a few moments to relish their achievement. So they drove to Neuilly.

It was not so very far: a trivial distance for the months of effort they had put into the quest. Here they were now in a suburban avenue where the trees had still not broken into leaf and the houses hid behind stark branches and sour banks of yew and laurel. Daniel directed Gromov to stop by one of the large villas, but he insisted on driving on and tethered the horse to a tree in the next road, as if to underline the sense of danger. And, of course, it was dangerous. Colonel Menshikov was a dangerous man. People tried to kill him. From disappointment Sasha's spirits rose again and infected Daniel; and, while Gromov said nothing but merely sat in thought, the boys giggled and after a time burst into laughter and rolled around in the cab until Gromov told them sharply to stop and be sensible.

They retraced their route on foot and paced the wall that divided the garden of the house from the road. It was a high wall barred by an iron gate, through which the view was of untended flowerbeds choked with weeds and dried seed-pods rocking on dead canes, and a ragged lawn planted with yew trees as dark as poison. Beyond this was the house itself, a two storey building with a mansard roof of red tiles and an ochre stuccoed façade, overhung by a large maple.

Gromov grunted but otherwise said nothing. The house stood on a corner, so they walked the length of the other side and found a mound from which they could peek at the rear where there were outhouses and a dilapidated stable. The windows were shuttered.

It was a gloomy place, sullen and silent. Sasha was uncomfortable with it, but the dark hermetic stillness had a thrilling attraction. It seemed so right for Colonel Menshikov to live there. He was himself so lonely and mysterious that this house was exactly as it should be.

If only . . . If only what? Sasha felt that something should happen that would continue their adventure. But after inspecting the house, Gromov pronounced himself satisfied and drove the boys home. And he never mentioned the colonel's house afterwards.

During the next few weeks Sasha saw less of the fiacre driver. Gromov ceased to ply for hire on Sundays in the Rue Daru. Tonya remarked that he had probably decided that it was not worth his while since he rarely got a fare. The boys stopped their expeditions with him and never went to the Café Dantzig.

The only news came from Professor Gromeko. One evening he said: 'Guess who I saw today – Semyon Maximovitch. He wasn't in his fiacre. He was in a car with two friends.'

'Probably some taxi drivers,' said Tonya.

'I don't think so. The car wasn't a taxi; it looked quite

297

expensive. And his friends weren't ordinary workmen. They wore suits and looked quite well-to-do.'

The following Sunday was much as usual, though without Gromov. At church Sasha saw Colonel Menshikov and also Countess Kalinowska with her lover, Golitsin. The countess passed the time of day with Tonya, spoke a few trivialities and impressed Sasha again with her glamour.

The next day Professor Gromeko came home with a newspaper. Passing it to Tonya, he said: 'Look at this! They've killed poor Menshikov!'

'Oh, my God!' said Tonya and crossed herself.

'Oh, my God!' repeated little Masha and crossed herself too.

Sasha was stunned. He wanted to ask questions. Where? Why? How? But his grandfather was short-tempered with him when he tried, and his mother had lapsed into silence and tears.

Later Sasha retrieved the paper and cut out the clipping. He read it in bed that night.

According to the reporter, Colonel Menshikov had been shot by unknown assassins at three p.m. the previous day. Apparently, he had gone from the Cathedral of St Alexander Nevsky to the Russian Co-ordination Centre in the old insurance building in the Rue Malesherbes, in the company of two friends. They had stayed there for a quarter of an hour and then had lunch together, after which they had parted. The colonel's intention had been to take a taxi to his home in Neuilly.

It was surmised (said the report) that the colonel was followed. On the way back to his home, the taxi was stopped in a quiet street by a stolen vegetable delivery waggon blocking the road. The taxi driver had got out of his cab to investigate the obstruction. And at this point two men emerged from the gardens of nearby houses and calmly shot the colonel in the head, as he sat in the taxi, before making their escape on foot.

The police were making enquiries. A political motive was suspected.

Sasha screwed up the clipping and threw it down. He lay in bed staring at the ceiling, struggling to cope with his disbelief that fate could ultimately vanquish a hero like the colonel. How they had failed, he and Daniel! Despite their efforts to guard him. Sasha knew now where Gromov had been these last few weeks. He had been keeping watch on the colonel's house. But to no purpose! The assassins had not struck at the house. They had waited until the colonel was separated from his companions and then, like the cowards they were, ambushed him in a suburban street. It was almost unbearable for Sasha to contemplate!

Sasha sobbed in his sleep. In his dreams he saw the colonel's ascetic face. It was unexpressive and so, in its emptiness, expressed the pain and suffering of a man who had experienced everything. Sasha had seen that face before. In the icons of Christ the same face, empty of self, stared at the observer through open receptive eyes.

Colonel Menshikov was still a hero, but of another kind. A symbol of self-sacrifice.

The next morning, going to school, Sasha showed the newspaper clipping to Daniel.

'I know,' said Daniel. 'My father told me.'

He seemed unconcerned.

'It's terrible!' exclaimed Sasha, more emphatically than he wished because he could not understand Daniel's indifference.

Daniel shrugged. 'I don't care. My father still says that he was the same Menshikov who used to kill Jews.'

'Then why did you help us?'

'It was something to do.'

Sasha told his grandfather, though not the part about helping Gromov to keep guard over the dead man. He asked again:

'Did Colonel Menshikov kill Jews? Daniel says he did. His father told him. I thought the colonel was a hero?'

'He was,' said the professor. It was an unconsidered

remark. He saw Sasha's face and the unalloyed idealism that begged him not to break the illusion, though he went on to mumble something about 'hero' perhaps not being the exact word.

'But did he kill Jews?'

'He may have killed some. He was fighting against the Communists. Many of the Communists were Jewish.'

'Why?'

'Because the Jews were poor and the Tsar oppressed them.'

'I thought the Tsar was a good man?'

'He probably was. But he was foolish and ignorant. So are the Communists, for that matter. There are good men on both sides.'

The piece of moral relativism in this last remark was too subtle for Sasha and he suppressed it. He went to his mother and she, thinking only to comfort him, repeated the catechism of the émigré community. The Reds were completely hateful. They were demon-possessed and scarcely human. Anyone who fought them was a hero. Sasha was satisfied with this. He had been to see cowboy films – Will Hayes. He knew who the Indians were.

Meanwhile Gromov dropped out of sight. For weeks no-one saw him. Tonya mentioned the fact but then the topic was dropped. It was a mystery but only a small one, since the fiacre driver was not an important person. Only Sasha knew the truth: that Gromov had vanished because he would be the next target of the Red assassins. This was obvious since Gromov had been watching the villa at Neuilly and the assassins must have been doing the same. They knew who Gromov was and that he was their dedicated opponent. They would have seen his fiacre; the vehicle was distinctive and its owner's identity could not long be in doubt.

For the present, the police were having no luck tracing the colonel's murderers. Before the public lost interest there were a few inconclusive reports in the press and an editorial suggesting that the dead man's compatriots were not co-operating in finding the killers. It warned them against private vengeance. The professor explained this by saying that the newspaper was trying to excuse the incompetence of the police by blaming the émigrés.

The subject was naturally discussed at church. Countess Kalinowska delighted in the idea of private vengeance, and in Sasha's eyes the White officers began to look like conspirators. She said to Tonya:

'My dear, of course they know who did it! Proving it to the satisfaction of those pettyfogging detectives, however, is a different matter. And why should we bother? Have we Russians –' for this purpose she was Russian not Polish '– so far lost our manhood that we can no longer protect or avenge our own? We aren't talking about crime, we're talking about warfare. And in war there is no appeal to the courts!'

Sasha agreed.

So the summer arrived and the investigation dragged on to no effect. The countess voiced her frustration; then by degrees the subject lost interest for everyone except Sasha, who listened to every dark rumour that *Kontr-Razvedka*, the Whites' own intelligence service, was hot on the trail of the killers. He was still in a state of nerves because of his secret knowledge about Gromov and his worries for his friend's safety.

One day in August, a horse was found running loose in the Bois de Boulogne. A search discovered Gromov's fiacre together with blood and other signs of violence. Nothing else was ever found of the fiacre driver.

When the news broke, Sasha was appalled. The assassins had got his friend! He went down to the Coëns' apartment and took Daniel aside to their den in the corner of the market place.

He told Daniel what had happened. The Reds had killed Gromov.

'Don't be ridiculous,' said Daniel knowingly. 'It wasn't

the Reds who killed him, it was your lot, the Whites.'

'I don't believe you!' Sasha exclaimed. 'Why would they do that?'

'Because Semyon Maximovitch was a Red. He was one of the men who killed Colonel Menshikov. Why do you think he wanted to know where the colonel lived? Anyway, I don't care. Menshikov was a Jew-hater. If Semyon Maximovitch was on his side, he deserved what he got.'

'Liar!' screamed Sasha and he punched Daniel on the nose. 'Filthy Jewish liar! Liar! Liar! Liar!' And they rolled on the ground among the sacks and crates and vegetable waste, and Sasha kicked and scratched and bit, and, being the larger boy, forced Daniel into bloody submission.

Nevertheless, he believed him. Gromov had been a Red all along and had lied to him! Sasha was miserable at the perfidy of his friends. How could they do this to him?

He concluded that the Reds were like the Indians. Their treachery was limitless. His hatred of them was just.

CHAPTER 13

THE DANCING JESUIT

The murder of Colonel Menshikov caused only brief excitement. Hetman Petliura was shot in 1926 and General Kutiepov, the head of ROVS, vanished in 1930, both presumed killed by the Bolsheviks. And they were merely the more prominent among the Whites who were murdered or disappeared.

One day in March 1928, Tonya received a letter from Maître Heriot. The lawyer invited her to his office in the Avenue Macmahon, and she duly went.

Almost from the day she had set foot in France, Tonya had been involved in litigation concerning the Zhivago estate. The outlines of the story were simple enough – Yura's father had inherited a fortune: factories, buildings, even a bank; but, not having created this wealth, he treated it as inexhaustible and embarked on a determined path as a spendthrift and reprobate, pausing only once, in a fit of morality, to marry Yura's mother, whom he subsequently abandoned. His reckless career took him to many places, but in particular to France, which was the spiritual home of the Russian leisured classes. In France he met the two people who were to prove his nemesis. They were Alice Mercier, a beautiful woman of no particular fortune or position, who assisted him enthusiastically in wasting his money; and Viktor Komarovsky, the Moscow lawyer, who, as it happened, was in France negotiating railway loans. What Alice could not spend, Komarovsky tied up in an impenetrable network of bonds, trusts and front companies.

In favour of Komarovsky it had to be said that, while he was undoubtedly defrauding Zhivago, he had an eye for a shrewd investment and, sensitive to the political climate, he had placed much of the money abroad where, when the catastrophe came, it could not be expropriated by the Soviet government. Also, his fraud was in a way beneficial in that he preserved a significant part of the fortune from Alice's depredations so that he could plunder it himself at leisure, and his greed was of a steady, disciplined kind which meant that he consumed the income from his investments and not the capital.

There were two problems to be overcome, as Maître Heriot never tired of saying. The first was to discover the location of the fortune, which had been hidden by Komarovsky's legal devices and had lain in bank vaults gathering income, untouched since the Great War had put it beyond the Moscow lawyer's reach. The second was again attributable to old Zhivago's way of life. It was alleged that he had obtained a questionable divorce from Yura's mother somewhere on his travels, then gone through a form of marriage with Alice Mercier, and finally, that he had executed a will in her favour. Zhivago himself had repudiated the divorce and the re-marriage, and had apparently died in ignorance of the will, which was presumed to be a forgery. From the marriage to Alice came a son, now middle-aged, whom Tonya had never met and therefore thoroughly hated. Augustin Mercier-Zhivago was the rival claimant.

In the circumstances, with the disputed fortune situated in France and entangled in a thicket of obscurity, it was not surprising that Yura and his mother, living in poverty in Moscow, had not pursued their rights and that Yura had mentioned it to Tonya only as a comment about the tricks of lawyers and the ironies of the world. Yura had never been bitter about the fate that deprived him of wealth: it was, if anything, a joke. However, because of the fame of the Zhivago enterprises and their spectacular crash, the vague outline of the story was public knowledge both in Russia and, to some extent, in France. So, according to Cousin Aristide, his father had picked up the tale. It was old Krueger – again according to Cousin Aristide – who insisted that Tonya pursue the claim and provided the money that allowed her to do it.

Tonya hated her visits to the Avenue Macmahon. Although Maître Heriot was her lawyer, she always felt that she was being called to account for a crime. In particular, nothing good ever seemed to come from the meetings; she would be called upon to swear another affidavit or authorize another suit, drawing yet another party into the morass of litigation, and the most she ever obtained by way of comfort were the lawyer's complacent assurances that her claim was in the best possible condition and was making progress at an astonishingly rapid rate for an action of its size and complexity. And so the years had gone by.

In his office Maître Heriot was waiting in his sombre lawyer's weeds, wearing his undertaker's smile. But to Tonya's surprise Cousin Aristide was also there, reclining in an upholstered chair, smoking and sipping a glass of whisky-soda. He sprang to his feet as Tonya came in and embraced her warmly.

'We've got some good news at last!' he announced. 'Anatole will tell you what it is, but the upshot is that we've finally got some money out of the devils on the other side! This calls for a celebration! Let me get you a drink while Anatole gives you the story.' Carelessly he opened a boullework cabinet and from a selection of bottles poured Tonya an aperitif. Stunned by her cousin's enthusiasm, Tonya accepted and took a seat.

'As a result of the judgment of the Cour de Cassation,' began Maître Heriot in the indulgent voice of a professional, 'we have established your undeniable title to the Zhivago estate and resolved satisfactorily the nice legal point that has been the principal obstacle these several years.'

'Sure,' interrupted Aristide Krueger, 'but tell her about the money.'

'And – as Monsieur Krueger points out – we have recovered a portion of the estate, namely a parcel of bonds.'

'What does that mean?' Tonya asked.

'It means,' said the lawyer, 'some slight alleviation in your present financial situation, and the prospect – the very good prospect – of a material improvement in the future.'

'Come off it, Anatole, it means that dear Tonya is going to be rich!' said Aristide.

With some formality they drank to success. Tonya found it strange and unsatisfactory. In the years of waiting on this outcome she had built up a store of anger against her invisible opponent, and with victory it remained unassuaged. She wondered: what is it I wanted if not to win? Her religion stood in the way of examining her own motives. Some time in the past, unrecognized, her attitude to the case had changed. She was no longer looking for money. She wished to see Augustin Mercier-Zhivago destroyed in return for the grief and worry he had caused her. And that destruction had to be of the most physical kind that involved blood and pain. So it was no wonder that her victory at law left her at a loss. She felt faint, as if she had suffered a defeat.

Unconscious of this, Maître Heriot was continuing:

'Although there is cause for rejoicing, I would not wish you to disregard all prudence in your financial management. I shall, of course, send you a full account of the results from the action, but you should recognize that there will be deductions with respect to the costs of the litigation. And in addition – how shall I put it? – there is the matter of your living expenses, which have been defrayed to date by loan advances from Monsieur Krueger against the security of the estate.'

Tonya nodded and then realized slowly that the lawyer was telling her that all the money she had received from her cousins would have to be repaid. That was everything they had been living on for six years!

'I don't understand,' she began. But immediately she felt embarrassed at her own simplicity. She looked to Krueger. 'I thought the money you gave us was a gift?'

'Well, so it was, in a manner of speaking. I mean, if all this lawyer stuff had come to nothing, then you'd have heard nothing more of the money. And as for me, well, I never thought of getting it back, honestly. But the old fellow is different. Frankly, he can be a hard man and there's nothing I can do with him. But let's look on the bright side! Pour Cousin Tonya another drink, Anatole. After all, you *have* won, and there *is* money: in fact more than enough to square Anatole and my governor; plus a little bit over and maybe more to come. Isn't that cause enough to be pleased?'

'Yes, of course – I am pleased.'

Am I ungrateful? Tonya wondered. Without Cousin Aristide and his father we should have been destitute.

But against that, she thought of her years of humiliation collecting rents from poor people.

'I'm sorry,' said Krueger mildly. 'I hadn't expected you to be disappointed.'

The news of the family's good fortune spread. Visitors called to congratulate them. Countess Kalinowska and her lover, Golitsin, arrived in a large limousine and made their way up the unfamiliar steps to the apartment.

'Dear Tonya! I couldn't wait to tell you how glad we were to hear the good news!'

She introduced Golitsin. In Memel he had been a poor refugee. Now he was glossy and prosperous, a pillar of respectability in a morning coat and wing collar.

A second man was in the party, a younger man who

might be thirty years old: handsome in a long-headed, fair-haired way and fashionably dressed in a lounge suit and soft-collared shirt.

'I don't think you've met,' said the Countess affably. 'Alain was with us when we heard the news and just had to come round to see you. Alain, this is Antonina Alexandrovna, her father, Professor Gromeko, and – where are the children? I don't suppose it matters. Alain is a priest, would you believe it? A Jesuit, in fact, though I don't remember ever seeing him in his uniform?'

The Jesuit smiled. It was a modest, attractive smile with a touch of genuine humour. Tonya, who had been shocked at first by the sinister word 'Jesuit', found herself obliged to respond to it. He explained: 'In my work clerical dress can sometimes be intrusive. But I assure you, Lydia, I do actually possess the uniform.' He produced a silver cigarette case and enquired politely if he might smoke. Meanwhile, Countess Kalinowska was evaluating the room.

'Of course you'll be moving from here.'

The thought had not occurred to Tonya.

'I don't think so – not immediately. What we have won so far is not really so very much money. Perhaps later . . .'

'At all events, my dear, it won't take very much money to improve your appearance.'

'Lydia, you're being tactless again,' the Jesuit reproved her gently.

'Am I? Do you hear this, Tonya? My confessor and guide to polite manners. And I thought I was being helpful. I was only going to suggest that Tonya might require advice, and I suppose I know something on the subject of fashion. Poiret is finished, and Chanel is the thing. We could make an expedition to the Rue Cambon. And your hair – you must wear your hair shorter.'

'You're being very kind,' Tonya answered.

Golitsin had been sitting quietly, fiddling with a cigar cutter to no purpose. Glancing at him, Tonya felt that he was in some way angry: that he was bored and frustrated by the temperament of his mistress, yet at the same time unable to do anything about it. In the lull he spoke up and addressed Professor Gromeko with grave sincerity.

'Do you remember our games of chess on the train from Moscow, professor? That was a long time ago, wasn't it?'

'You've done very well for yourself, Maxim Yuryevitch.'

'Yes, I have. And I thank God for it – truthfully, I do. Lydia and I arrived here with virtually nothing, but with His help we have had some success.'

'I'm glad for you.'

'Thank you.' Golitsin's manner was very simple; his gaze was direct and his voice rather dull. Apart from his prosperous appearance he was an unremarkable man, and Tonya, recalling now the train journey, remembered that his conversation was tedious and reassuring. He went on: 'I can't take any credit. You know that you're lucky too, Alexander Alexandrovitch. Emigrés take care of each other. Antonina Alexandrovna's maternal relatives gave you assistance, and my Russian friends also helped me.'

'In what way?'

'Some of them were rich, but they weren't used to managing their own property. I was able to give them investment advice and that put my foot on the first rung of the ladder. These days I have a broader clientele, but one remembers how one got started. Do you know what you will do with your money once you have it?'

'It isn't something that we've thought of.'

Golitsin nodded. 'I understand.' He seemed lost in thought and then resumed, as though reluctantly: 'Well, I suppose I could help you. Normally I would charge a fee, but of course in your case it won't apply. Where's Alain?' he asked Countess Kalinowska.

'Oh, he's disappeared somewhere. He's always disappearing. He's positively the most mysterious of men!'

During this visit Sasha was with Daniel, up to mischief in the market. They had found a cigarette in an otherwise empty packet, cut it in two with Daniel's clasp-knife, and were smoking it as they wandered back to the apartment. They were being both brazen and secretive: smoking in the street where they were known; and cupping the cigarettes in their palms in case they were spotted. Adolescent courage was an uncertain quality.

Outside the house was a black and yellow limousine. Le Nain was hunched in the doorway, smoking one of his cigars and eying the car and the man standing with one foot on the running board. This was an elegant looking person who was taking the air with an amused and slightly distant expression.

'Some car, eh, Sasha?' grumbled Le Nain.

'Ah,' said the stranger, stepping lightly from the running board. 'So you are Sasha Zhivago? Pleased to meet you, Alexander Yuryevitch.' The Jesuit offered the boys his cigarette case. 'Here, take one of these. I'm sure they're tastier than what you've got. Then promise me not to smoke again.' It amused him to leave the boys stunned for a second, after which he said: 'I'm called Alain Duroc. I'm a friend of Countess Kalinowska. She's upstairs talking to your mother. If I were you, I'd stay down here – you'd only be bored. What have you been up to?' he enquired indulgently.

The boys could not resist the confidence of this overture. Even Le Nain, squatting on the step with his great chin resting on the breast of his greasy waistcoat, grinned evilly and nodded. And, before they knew where they were, they were telling the Jesuit all about their life in the streets, their escapades in the market, the rat-traps – and even about Colonel Menshikov.

Duroc was silent for a moment at this last point. Until then he had laughed and encouraged the boys, but now he detected the sorrow in Sasha's voice and responded with a concern that seemed to be unfeigned.

'So you tried to help him escape from his enemies? You were being rather brave, weren't you?'

'I don't think it was such a good idea,' said Daniel. 'He used to kill Jews.'

'That's what your father says,' retorted Sasha, who was reconciled after their quarrel but would not allow himself to be consciously persuaded. 'I don't see how he could know – not *really* know.'

'Does it matter?' said their new friend. He regarded Daniel curiously. 'I don't mean about the Jews – of course one shouldn't go around killing Jews. But forget about who Colonel Menshikov really was: it was your actions that were important, don't you think? After all, you did your best, didn't you?'

Sasha did not have a chance to reply; Countess Kalinowska was coming out of the door with Golitsin, saying, 'There you are, Alain!' and the Jesuit was making a bantering apology. But Sasha felt a flush of warmth and enthusiasm for this stranger who had become a friend. In one clear-thinking stroke he had removed the cloud of self-doubt that had troubled Sasha over the incident of the colonel. Sasha understood that it was the purity of his intentions that was important, and this was a revelation to him.

Afterwards Sasha told his mother of his admiration for the Jesuit. Tonya was touched by his naivety, and told him that Jesuits were trained to catch souls and that their sincerity could not be taken for granted. This was as much a warning to herself.

By degrees the situation of the family improved. After that first victory to establish title to the Zhivago estate, a series of manoeuvres by Maître Heriot began to bring in the property. By all conventional standards this was a cause for joy: indeed Countess Kalinowska and Tonya's other friends did not restrain their congratulations.

The price was paid in the office of Maître Heriot in the form of hundreds of documents, each subscribed 'the Widow Zhivago'.

'Please sign here, madame,' invited the lawyer.

'Here?'

'By the word "Widow" – yes there – by "the Widow Zhivago". That will do nicely. My pen I think? Thank you.'

'How can I be sure?'

'That you are a widow?' asked the lawyer, with a smile of encouragement. 'Please, madame, don't concern yourself. You are merely a *legal* widow. In your heart you may continue to hope.'

But hope reduced with each signature. For, surely, if Yura was still alive, God would not let her do this thing?

'Would you believe we've forgotten one? Please, madame, borrow my pen again. Just one – yes, there – just as before.'

Tonya wrote: Antonina Alexandrovna Zhivago; but her heart wrote: *the Widow Zhivago.*

At the beginning of 1929 they were able to move from their apartment in the 5th *arrondissement* to a house at Neuilly.

When it came to move they felt strangely reluctant. The final pangs of any parting are commonplace, but the move from a vermin-plagued apartment house to a villa in a prosperous suburb was more radical than most. It was in part a return to a world that they believed had been lost: but, in retrieving the material comforts of that lost world, they could not recover its psychological security. Their own history had taught them the fragility of the human condition. So, with all the appearance of prosperity, they occupied their new home with a poverty in their hearts; and fate or chance, however it might be named, waited at the door like a bailiff, ever ready to dispossess them.

Tonya had never felt at ease with the parsimony of life among the poor. Too often she had been dragged like a child at the heels of Sophie Coën, who pinched the flesh of chickens and haggled with stall keepers and good-naturedly encouraged Tonya to do the same. Yet, despite her unease, Tonya had grown used to her existence, and her poverty had at last seemed not merely a matter of lack of goods and comfort, but a sign that her life was following in its sinful fashion the way of Christ; and the move to Neuilly thus appeared at times to be a denial of spirituality.

In the weeks before the move Tonya spent more time with Sophie, as if she were fixing the experience in her memory. The professor too seemed to relish more than before the company of Jakob Coën. They were often together at the café, sometimes with Le Nain and his queer tales of theatrical life. The dwarf, with his unfortunate grimace and rolling walk, had hitherto been unconsciously shunned as a sinister figure, but at the time of parting he was admitted to his rightful place as part of what was being left behind. Behind his acid sense of humour and understandable readiness to see a real or fancied slight, he proved to be a sweet-tempered man, convivial and an accomplished singer of sentimental ballads. But the knowledge of his true character had come too late.

As for the children: Masha was generally unbearable. When she was not aping Tonya, she flounced around in new clothes and annoyed the other children. For Sasha it was otherwise. The arrival of wealth confirmed what he had secretly known. He was different, in some way favoured by the gods: the lost prince come into his inheritance. But that inheritance was not mere wealth. The money was just a token of his responsibilities, the mission he was destined to accomplish; the dragon he was meant to slay. And, because in this sense the change of fortune was more natural, Sasha was modest about it. He assumed no airs except a quiet confidence, and he wore no new clothes, preferring the disguise of a pauper. He continued to play with Daniel – in fact, one night they finally caught a rat, a ferocious beast that caused them to run away until it finally gnawed through the trap.

'Are you still a socialist?' Daniel asked provocatively.

'Of course.'

'Then what are you going to do with your money?'

'I don't know. In any case, I don't think it's really mine; I think it belongs to my mother.'

Daniel knew an evasion when he heard one; but, to be fair, he was not absolutely sure what he would do if he were rich, so he did not press the point.

Left to himself, Sasha decided at first that he would give the money away, and he had a dream of distributing largesse to grateful recipients. However, on reflection it became clear that such generosity would quickly reduce him to the same status as everyone else, and this was inconsistent with the obvious fact that he was different. In the end he compromised by deciding that he would retain his wealth but use it wisely and for the benefit of others – whatever that might mean. Socialism was a complicated business.

On the day of the move to Neuilly, Sasha got a shock. Their route took them down the quiet street where Colonel Menshikov had lived. He had to drive past the villa, which was shuttered and sparsely screened by winter trees, and he felt a shudder of horror at the recollection of the bloody day when the colonel had been gunned down by the fiacre driver and his gang of assassins. It had not occurred to him before that he would be living only a few minutes' walk away from the scene of his defeat.

To Sasha's eyes his new home was splendid. The house itself was almost as large as the whole of the apartment building off the Rue Mouffetard and, individually, the rooms with their fine plastered ceilings and gilded flambeaux seemed so large and magnificent that you could almost call it a palace. Masha thought so. She twirled her skirts in a dance across the empty polished floors and let out shrieks of pleasure as she opened each door.

Tonya's comment was: 'How on earth are we going to furnish it?'

'Darling, I'll help you,' said Countess Kalinowska, who had first found the property.

Sasha went into the garden. It came with a gardener,

a crabbed *blessé* with a gas-cough and a wooden leg, who nevertheless managed to keep it tidy. The boy found his grandfather and Golitsin by a small hothouse. Golitsin was smoking a cigar morosely, dropping ash into a large urn. In his dull way, he was explaining to his uninterested companion the Hanau scandal and the collapse of the Compagnie Générale Financière et Foncière which still troubled the financial press. Somewhere in this tedious recitation he observed: 'It's a fine property, Alexander Alexandrovitch, but it will take some upkeep.' Then, with a sigh, as though relieving himself of an unpleasant duty, went on: 'By the way, have you given any further thought to the matter of your investments? A fortune – even a modest one – can't be left to itself. It has to be managed. In the United States at the moment there's a boom going on. I don't suppose it will last, but while it does there's money to be made. Why don't you come to my office some day? We could stroll down to the Bourse together and you could see how it's done. Of course the place is a perfect madhouse, but insanity can be very stimulating. You're nervous? That's understandable: I felt the same at first, but one gets used to it.'

'I don't think I could get used to it,' answered the professor.

That was the problem – getting used to it. Countess Kalinowska and Golitsin had decided to take the family in hand. The countess took Tonya shopping: bought her clothes from Chanel, and furniture from everywhere. The most difficult part was having Tonya's hair cut and fashionably shingled. At home afterwards, Tonya stood in front of a cheval glass and studied the transformation. Carried by the enthusiasm of her friend, she was determined to like the change. She hated it. Later she got used to seeing the woman in the glass and rarely thought about it. But she experienced no pride or vanity. It was simply something that had to be gone through.

Professor Gromeko took Sasha to Golitsin's office in the Rue de Provence. They had an excellent luncheon and took a peek at the floor of the Bourse, which impressed Alexander Alexandrovitch without his being aware of it. He agreed to commit a part of the family's money to an investment in some Goldman-Sachs securities, which proved a wise move. Golitsin acted prudently and sold the securities for gold before the stock market fall which took place that autumn; and the family made a profit on the whole transaction, which was most satisfactory. And, in the meantime, Maître Heriot was busying away getting in more of the Zhivago estate.

As well as furnishings the family acquired friends, also brought to them by Countess Kalinowska and her lover. From her time in the film studio the countess knew several admittedly minor film stars and their followers who included an astrologer and an Iranian who preached the Bahai religion. Golitsin brought along actors and dancers from the theatres he patronized and the occasional politician whom he advised on financial matters. Tonya found herself giving dinner or cocktail parties for these gatherings without really knowing why or how it was that she had got into this situation.

A dinner party was held before their first Christmas at Neuilly. The house and garden were decorated with lights for the occasion and the drive was thronged with limousines and taxis depositing the guests. Tonya watched them from an upper window where she was still getting dressed. She had underestimated the timing of her preparations and Masha had shed tears and tantrums, insisting that she was to be dressed first and look positively her best. The children were to be allowed to mingle with the visitors before retiring to have dinner with the servants.

Lydia Kalinowska had been at the house all day. She had said: 'Darling, let me do the organizing and then perhaps you'll remember how these things are done.' Now she was welcoming the guests, greeting each one with casual intimacy as though she were the hostess, while Tonya, frozen by the panic of putting final touches to her dress, watched from above. A light rain was falling. In the garden the waxy evergreens glistened. The cars mirrored fat globules of light from the garden lanterns. The house filled with the murmur of voices and the countess's pleasant light laughter.

Was Tonya happy or not? She could not decide. She did not dislike these gatherings; nor was it that she was indifferent. On the contrary, she derived a sort of pleasure that events like this signalled the end of her long nightmare. She thought of Sophie Coën. The Coëns would not be coming; they had not been invited. What would it have been like if I had invited Sophie? What would she have thought? I wish I'd asked her. She couldn't have come. She couldn't have afforded a dress and wouldn't have accepted money to buy one. With difficulty Tonya had persuaded Sophie to allow her to clothe Daniel. It was necessary if Daniel and Sasha were to continue as friends that Daniel should not be shamed by his appearance.

Tonya was struck by the fact that her home had no feel of Russia about it. The guests would be comfortable because Countess Kalinowska had furnished it in the style of a superior hotel. Those objects that were Russian – the icon of Our Lady, a samovar, some old photographs – were few and would not have been out of place in an hotel that wanted to hint at a decorative theme. Tonya wondered sometimes what was left of her life in Russia: her religion and the custom of eating *pashka* on Easter Sunday. This party was not like those so long ago in Moscow. Her guests were not like the old Russian intelligentsia. They were people trying to get rich quickly out of the speculative boom. Even the Russians.

They had hired a small jazz band. The saxophone player was an American negro. Very fashionable. The women flocked around him: he was so handsome and virile. Tonya had not learned the new dances. She watched Lydia dance a Charleston with her tame Jesuit, Alain Duroc, who was so different from the grave, unsophisticated Orthodox priests of her childhood. Lydia had taken to the new fashions. Her skin was lightly bronzed. Tonya thought of her own skin, which had been proudly shielded from the sun by wide hats and parasols. The singer, Josephine Baker, was the rage in Paris. A pale skin was no longer valued.

Tonya escaped to say good night to the children. She found Masha still dressed and preening herself in front of a mirror. Sasha was in bed reading an adventure story. Even in his room she noticed the faint smell of cigars from below and opened the window. Behind her she heard Sasha say: 'Isn't this wonderful!' But when she turned round, his nose was stuck in his book and she could only kiss him on the top of his head.

Lydia had brought a friend – allegedly a princess, but in fact a Chicago millionairess married to a diminutive elderly Italian. The American drawled: 'Tony, this is swell. Parties in Europe are so much better than at home. You can get good liquor. Lydia told me about your coming into a fortune. You control your own money, is that right? I wish I did – well, maybe I do. I keep Carlo on an allowance. Daddy said that was a smart move. Lydia says you asked Max to manage your investments. That was a smart move too, unless you have time to follow the financial press. I used to take the tip-sheet from that Hanau woman – not bad: but lucky I didn't invest in any of her own stocks, huh? Put the lot into gold. If the price falls, you can always wear it, that's what I say.'

Why am I so restless tonight? Tonya wandered from room to room. In the study a card table had been set up. Her father was partnering Golitsin at bridge against a pair of politicians. Countess Kalinowska, in pale crepe de chine, was standing over her lover blowing on his left ear. During the few minutes that Tonya watched the game, two people came on separate occasions to talk to the financier. In each case Golitsin gave advice on some money matter, with a show of reluctance that seemed to make his opinion more valuable. Between times he paid little attention to the game, but conversed with the politicians in a low monotonous tone about loans to Czechoslovakia.

Tonya fled the card game, the dancing and the incessant talk of money. She ignored the offer of Cousin Aristide to mix her a cocktail, and went into the garden. There she found Antoine, the gardener, who had been dressed up as a flunky for the evening and was hobbling in the dim light of flares among the dead canes, clipping them and throwing them into a pile to be burned. Tonya felt ashamed to have asked him to shed his worker's blouse for a waiter's uniform. It exaggerated his limp and the stoop caused by his damaged lungs and deprived him of his dignity.

'That's enough for tonight,' she told him.

'What about clearing up?' he asked in a surly voice.

'I'll arrange it.'

'Whatever you say.' He pocketed a pair of secateurs and turned to go, leaving Tonya, still with her sense of shame, standing watching him until she noticed the chill and the fine rain staining her silk dress. A flare placed in one of the parterres flickered and went out. Still wanting to avoid her guests, she looked around for shelter.

A cigarette was glowing through one of the misty panes of the hothouse. The door was unlocked, the atmosphere warm and oppressive with the smell of a kerosene stove. At the far end, masked by fronds and foliage, Alain Duroc was quietly smoking. He said:

'You don't mind my being here, do you? Do you smoke, Tonya? May I? I don't think it does any harm to the plants.'

'I don't mind.'

Tonya looked for somewhere to sit without soiling her dress. She found a plain deal stool that Antoine used when tending the plants. Duroc had called her 'Tonya' for the first time, she realized. She felt something, but was uncertain what it might be. 'Why aren't you with the others?' she enquired.

'I'll go back shortly, but the Lord knows they are a tedious lot. Have you met the American woman, Princess

Wanda – Dolores – Gertrude – whatever? I overheard her talking to your cousin. She placed her hand over his while they were talking – which is always a bad sign. "Democracy in Europe is dead. The future lies with Communism or Fascism, and the real question is which one will let you keep your money? I mean: what has democracy done for France? Ten years ago there were twenty-five francs to the dollar and now there are fifty. You should listen to *Il Duce* – Carlo got me an audience with *Il Duce*. There's a man that has given Italy its self-respect – *and* your money's safe!"'

Tonya laughed at this impeccable impersonation.

'Are you sure you won't have that cigarette?'

She shook her head, then asked: 'Was she telling the truth?'

'Almost certainly. Even stupid people tell the truth, and Princess Wanda is far from stupid, merely confused about the meaning of money and short of interesting conversation.'

Tonya looked through the glass at the melancholy winter silence of the garden and for a minute or so neither spoke. The Jesuit lit another cigarette. Tonya began to wish he would speak again. She liked the sound of his voice, its attractive insolence, as if at all times he knew more than others. She had heard of the Jesuits: that they were worldly and at the same time sinister. Dressed for dinner and smoking his cigarette from a small ivory holder, Duroc was worldly; but his manner was too negligent and his voice too confiding to be sinister. He looked more like the matinée idol from a film – Tonya had seen one with Countess Kalinowska at the Marignan in the Champs Elysées. He could even dance. A dancing priest!

'Why are you smiling?'

'I was daydreaming – I had a picture of you dancing.'

He laughed.

'They're playing a tango now, can you hear it? Do you dance?'

'No.' Tonya regretted that she could not – not the modern dances. She had a moment of fear and desire that he would ask her to. The music was playing loudly and she could feel the rhythms.

But he made no advance, merely smiled, exhaled smoke and said: 'You should learn. I'm sure that Lydia could arrange lessons. If you learned, you'd feel more comfortable on occasions like tonight. That's what brought you out here, isn't it? Not boredom, as in my case, but the fact that these people make you uncomfortable. Poor Tonya! These past few months have been quite an upheaval, haven't they? Do you want to tell me about it?'

'How did you learn to dance?' Tonya asked quickly.

'I'm not sure – probably Lydia taught me. One of her lovers was an Argentinian.' He said 'lovers' without any sign of disapproval, rather he explained with sympathy: 'She had a difficult time when she first came to Paris. Apart from some fine clothes and a few pieces of jewellery, she had nothing. She lived with her Argentinian until Golitsin discovered his talent for making money.'

'Was she something to do with films?'

'I think her films were of a doubtful nature, made for a select clientele. Am I shocking you?'

Tonya nodded. The shock, however, was not one of disapproval – she was simply surprised at his frankness. He said:

'I suppose I should be more censorious, but the forgiveness of God is infinite. You understand me, don't you, Tonya? When I was in your apartment I noticed your picture of the Blessed Virgin. My first thought was that it was an image of mercy and forgiveness. Is it one of your ancient Russian icons?'

'It was painted by someone I knew in Moscow.'

'Then it's modern? So much for my knowledge of art!'

He enquired about the painter and Tonya told him of the photographer's colourist and his family dying by degrees around her. With the memory came tears, but unlike other men the Jesuit was not disturbed by them and Tonya felt under no obligation to suppress them, so that, when they stopped of their own accord, she was aware that they had formed an intimacy between herself and Duroc and that she could say anything to him. What she actually said was:

'Why has God allowed all this to happen – the war, the Revolution, everything?'

He teased her gently. 'Am I expected to know the answer to that?'

For a moment Tonya thought that she was mistaken and that, like any other man, he would not be responsive to her feelings. But he was thinking and then answered.

'When you were a child, did you ever suffer in order to learn a lesson? I once did something wrong and my father punished me by locking me in my room without dinner and forbade my mother to kiss me good night. Have you read Proust? No? Well, never mind.

'At the time the night seemed so long – so long – so lonely it could go on for ever. But of course it didn't. And I believe I learned my lesson. Now, of course, I recognize it as just one night among many. At the time it was my whole life. In retrospect, just a fleeting moment.'

'What was the lesson?'

'Not to break my toys in a temper, or something equally trivial. At all events that was the ostensible lesson to be learned – my father's lesson, if you like. It was superficial and I've forgotten the details; what I remember is the feel of that room, the shadows and the smells, and the revised image of my father who had visited me with this unexpected cruelty.' Breaking his narrative, he asked brightly: 'How do you propose to spend eternity?'

Was he serious?

'I've never thought about it.'

'I fancy playing cards for a while – but in the long run it promises to be awfully dull. Or do you suppose we shall be drawing on our experiences of life in order to understand the whole of God's intent and purpose? Could that be the lesson, that we have to suffer in order to learn? For, if that were the case, then our lifetime would be a brief lesson compared with the eternity in which we apply it.'

'Do you mean that we suffer as a punishment from God?'

'No, not as a punishment. If it were a case of punishment, we should expect to find some justice in it, but there isn't any: a poor Christian will suffer as much as a rich sinner. In fact, in my experience, rather more. But if our suffering is a lesson, an enrichment of the sum of our knowledge not for this petty existence but for the great span of true life hereafter, then, viewed from the perspective of eternity, our suffering will appear brief and hardly more than a memory of school.'

Tonya did not know whether any of this was true, but it seemed very fine. Any triteness was disguised by the attractions of the Jesuit's voice, its flow and cadence, and a happy choice of words. Fine speech is half the appearance of wisdom; the other half was beyond Tonya's unpractised powers to analyse thought and argument. She confused 'Is it true?' with 'Is he sincere?' And despite his light, almost flippant manner, she did not doubt his sincerity.

Alain smiled and from a silver case extracted another cigarette and fitted it to the ivory holder.

'Aren't we being serious?' he said. He struck a match, held it so that they could see each other, lit his cigarette, and blew the match out. He went on: 'I don't like discussing theology, but it's a weakness of Jesuit training. The Franciscans are much more sociable in that respect, but their Rule doesn't allow them to dance. The Dominicans are worst. They can be deadly dull, torture heretics, and have no dress sense – am I making you laugh again? Good! You should be in a mood to rejoin your guests.'

With the move to Neuilly, Sasha changed schools. No more playing with the boys of the Rue Mouffetard with

mice in their pockets, slings, stones and the other armaments of boyhood. No Daniel except at weekends and
holidays, by grace of delicate negotiations between his
mother and Sophie Coën that were designed to spare
each of them embarrassment. Professor Gromeko had
the idea of endowing a scholarship, which – naturally
– Daniel won, and this kept him dressed well enough
for participating to some degree in Sasha's new life. If
Daniel knew of this scheme, he showed neither gratitude
nor resentment. He hinted to Sasha that he was aware to
some degree that he had been helped by the Zhivago fortune. He commented wryly: 'Isn't socialism wonderful?'

The resentment was more Sasha's. At the *lycée* he
found himself with boys who had been brought up with
wealth since birth: boys who could ride a horse and play
tennis and even affected to learn golf; and who, in other
less definable ways, displayed their superior manners.

Sasha responded with a fourteen-year-old's truculence.
He claimed to despise the achievements of others and
maintained his non-conformity with his fists if necessary;
and at home he became gloomy and arrogant.

Tonya was summoned to the school to learn from
the headmaster that Sasha was a disruptive influence.
The headmaster belonged to the French anti-clerical tradition and disapproved of Tonya's evident religiosity. He
recommended rationalism and self-discipline. These were
universal, sovereign remedies and he left Tonya with the
problem of applying both. She approached her father.

'Boys grow out of it,' said Alexander Alexandrovitch
unhelpfully. 'Where is he now?'

'In his bedroom, reading.'

'There, things can't be as bad as you make out. What
does he read these days?'

'I don't know. I think it's a life of Alexander the Great.'

'His namesake,' commented the professor, and
chuckled.

What to do about Sasha? He raged about the house,
was disobedient, untidy, and not above hitting Masha out

of temper when he thought he could get away with it. Or, if he was quiet, he was obsessed with his books, reading of Alexander, Cromwell, Marlborough and Napoleon. What did it mean? On his wall hung a Russian Imperial flag given to him personally by General Skoblin of ROVS, who enthused over the boy's dedication to the White cause.

The headmaster recommended rationalism and self-discipline, and her father idly proposed benign neglect: but in each case Tonya was left to implement the policy. The men were complacent in having solved the problem by theory and regarded the practice as not so very difficult. Tonya was distraught with concern and could not concentrate since her mind was preoccupied with another problem.

She was in love.

Tonya struggled through the winter and the spring of the next year, conscious only of a distress which could not be explained simply by Sasha's surliness and Masha's precocious flirtations. She found that she was thinking of Yura again. It seemed odd that she had ever stopped, but the truth was that she had.

Yura was dead: Maître Heriot had killed him off in 1928 using a piece of paper as a weapon and Tonya's signature as the bullet; despatched him one afternoon in a quiet office over a glass of bitters; judicially murdered him so that the family could have access to his inheritance. Beyond this legal assassination there was no time and place to his death, no monument, relic or focus for mourning. This could have been the paradigm for the age of administratively convenient death that the world was about to enter, but that would be to attribute a foreknowledge that Tonya did not have.

What happened to you, Yura? Why did you leave me?

She supposed, in bitterness, that he was living with the Antipova woman; fathering bastards by the houseful;

deserting Tonya's bloodlessness for Lara's vigorous passion.

She did not believe this. She liked Lara – loved Zhivago – God help her!

In Yura there had been nothing so crude as lust. Whatever the explanation of his desertion and his attraction to Lara, it had never been that. In Lara there had been some fineness of soul, some spiritual beauty that Tonya herself did not possess. By comparison, Tonya was gross matter.

She did not believe this either. The spiritual and the physical could not be separated into boxes. In any case, admitting the attraction between Yura and the Antipova woman, what did it matter? By what right did Yura choose Lara over his wife? Tonya had done nothing wrong: on the contrary, Zhivago, after first meeting and falling in love with Lara, had fathered another child on his wife. Yura's exercise of his freedom had circumscribed hers.

She did not believe anything. Her mind was tormented with versions of reality that explained greater or lesser parts of what she knew to be true, and all of them foundered on inconsistency. Her ability to understand was limited because she herself was not without feeling, but passionless. Undistracted by passion, there were other things she could see clearly. Yura's longing for truth and beauty. His search for integrity. His love and concern for others. The great qualities of his art. All come to nothing because, in the face of his longing for Lara, he was incapable of making a moral choice, of keeping by his pledged word or fulfilling the duty he owed to his children. No casuistry could in Tonya's mind disguise the fact that Yura had behaved badly. There was no special code that excused him from the common virtues of life – neither art nor passion gave dispensation. Armed with the possibility of greatness, he had chosen moral mediocrity. And Tonya pitied him for it.

She longed for him or for someone.

At the Russian church she saw Alain Duroc in the company of Countess Kalinowska. He wore a pale grey suit and kid gloves and carried a cane and a soft hat which he held respectfully in front of him during the service. He was perfectly at ease and even made the correct responses to the Orthodox prayers.

'Obviously you're surprised to see me,' he said. They were in the Rue Daru enjoying a mild, early summer's day. For some reason the theatrical contingent was out in force and the tone of conversation with the mildness of the weather made the atmosphere quite giddy. Golitsin was making heavy conversation with Diaghilev's dancers, who seemed oddly taken with his humourless gravity. They were at turns shocked, amused, curious, fascinated, and showed their emotions with extravagant gestures as though still dancing. Occasionally the financier cast a glance at his mistress; as always, there was in his glance a note of anger and frustration. As for the countess, she was blithe and unaware that there could ever be criticism of her behaviour.

Alain said: 'You have no difficulty in understanding why Lydia comes here, but my position puzzles you. You are saying to yourself: how can a Catholic priest attend an Orthodox service?'

Tonya was embarrassed at her thoughts being uncovered, if only partially.

He continued: 'The fact is that you must regard our churches as partners in a long marriage, who have become fractious with age but still have an ancient affection for each other. It's a particular point with us that the Orthodox are *schismatics* not *heretics* – which, I admit, is a Jesuitical nicety, but we pivot on the head of such needles and I won't bore you with the difference. The thing is –' he finished with a smile '– I enjoy Orthodox services. And that's a good enough explanation for most things, isn't it?'

'I haven't seen you here before.'

'You didn't know me before. But I assure you I was here. I noticed you.'

'There was nothing to notice.'

'Wasn't there? You were among the first to arrive

327

and the last to leave, and you dressed yourself and your children with such simplicity. I'm trained to recognize simplicity, and I said to myself: "Now, there is a truly religious woman – what a pity she's not one of ours but one of theirs!"' He laughed. 'By the way, where are your children?'

'Masha is over there with my father.'

In her newest dress, Masha was flaunting herself before the other children. Alexander Alexandrovitch was talking solemnly with one of his fellow chess players, the major-domo from one of the large hotels.

'And Sasha?'

'He doesn't come any more – he refuses to come.'

Tonya was ashamed of her confession, but the Jesuit seemed to accept the situation as perfectly natural.

'How long has this been going on?'

'A month – six weeks.'

'Has he lost his faith?' he asked unconcernedly. 'Boys do. Perhaps he's become a socialist? I hope so. Everyone should be a socialist at some point: it proves one has a conscience.'

'He says he can see God in the sky and the trees. He doesn't see the need for churches.'

'Is that all? Well, that can be easily cured. I thought for a moment he'd become a Marxist. He used to have a Jewish friend?'

'Daniel Coën.'

'A lot of Jews are Marxist; it's understandable. But apparently that isn't our problem.'

Without thinking, Tonya asked: 'Will you – will you have lunch with us?'

She saw Alain examine her curiously and then search out Countess Kalinowska and find her hanging on Golitsin's arm, flirting with one of his actor friends.

'I was supposed to join Lydia. But to be truthful I'd rather dine with you. I can tell her I've been called to deal with a parishioner.'

Tonya was already regretting her invitation. 'You mustn't lie for me.'

'No? I'm a Jesuit – haven't you heard? I'm allowed to lie – not to mention murder and steal – in the interests of the Faith. Surely you've been warned? In any case, the world is my parish, so I can make my excuses and still preserve my innocence. If you leave now, I'll meet you at your car.'

So the family returned to Neuilly, with Masha on the way making outrageous eyes at the Jesuit, who treated her with good-humoured respect. Sasha was not in his room, and a search found him in the garden taking moody pot shots at the birds with a catapult.

'Alain!' he exclaimed on catching sight of the priest.

'You must say "Father Duroc",' his mother admonished him.

Sasha rejected the rebuke and almost insolently repeated the name.

'Alain will do all right,' said the Jesuit as he focused on the boy. 'How are you? It's months since I last saw you. I'm glad you remembered my name.'

Sasha laughed and then sulked.

'Lunch is getting cold,' said Tonya. 'Sasha, you must wash yourself.'

Masha preened. '*I* don't need to wash myself.'

'You must wash your hands.'

They went into the house. These days Tonya did not cook, and food had become a disconcerting magical event, arriving on the table almost unbidden and in inexact quantities so that it did not matter whether two or three more guests arrived. In fact, they frequently did. Golitsin often came, arriving unannounced and on his own for lunch. He would talk in a low voice about business to which no-one listened; and he seemed content, more than when Lydia was with him. Tonya felt that she was not in control of her own household and that she could do nothing about it. Something of Sophie must have rubbed off on her and she hated the waste. But today the excess was welcome because Alain had come.

Tonya went to her room while Alain and her father drank an aperitif. She removed her hat and examined her dress and stockings in the cheval glass. She smiled at herself. She arranged five versions of her smile and wondered which was the most attractive. The woman in the glass – the one created by Lydia – responded. Tonya sometimes felt that she could talk to that woman.

I am in love with a priest.

It was not necessary to speak aloud. The other woman nodded. She looked unconvinced. Tonya stared at her and saw the face behind the make-up. You could never disguise old eyes. The rest might be beautiful, but the eyes would peep out like prisoners. And, in this case, the rest was not beautiful, though it may once have been. So said the other woman. Tonya decided not to listen. She was Tonya, not this stranger.

In the dining room Alain was sitting with her father and the children. He was bantering with Sasha and smiled when Tonya came in. Immediately Sasha's face assumed a sour expression.

'Shall we eat?' Tonya invited.

'I should love to. And afterwards Sasha can show me what he is up to these days. Still making rat-traps?'

'Rat-traps?'

'Danny and I used to make rat-traps,' Sasha admitted defensively. 'But now I've made a squirrel cage. Antoine helped me. He's our gardener. He was wounded during the war.'

'Rat-traps,' Tonya repeated, and the thought crossed her mind: what had their poverty done to Sasha? But Alain intervened tactfully:

'I used to make them too – and damned difficult they are to make, unless you want to kill the beasts. If you take a rat alive, it can eat its way out of pretty well anything. Ever catch any, Sasha?'

'Once.'

330

'That beats my score!'

Was it tact, sensitivity or cleverness? In his melodious voice he turned the conversation to suit everyone's interest with a versatility and suppleness that were astonishing. He talked technical chess, gossiped about Coco Chanel, commiserated on the recent death of Diaghilev: fashion, finance, politics or botany, he could speak intelligently about any of them and seem enthusiastic for them all. And all of these elements were put together with invisible joins, so that a remark about fashion would illustrate a point in botany and Masha and the professor could both listen, entranced. And none more entranced than Tonya – unless it were perhaps Sasha.

At the top of the house was a room next to the cook's, a large neglected nursery with a deep linen cupboard to take large sheets and a window angled like a turret into the roof. There were finer rooms on the floor below, but Sasha had chosen this one for his bedroom. It contained half a century's jumble piled like the spoils of piracy.

'Come in.'

'Thank you.'

The Jesuit stood on the threshold and paused to look into the room at length, as if on the scene of a drama. Sasha said:

'Be careful of the floor, some of the boards have worn.'

'*Oui, mon général!*'

'Don't tease me.'

'I'm not teasing: I shall call you *mon général*, and you can call me – I don't know – what would you like?'

'Why *mon général*? I used to know someone who called me "little Napoleon",' Sasha was thinking of Gromov. 'What made you think of that?'

'An inspired guess, *mon général*.'

Sasha stroked his chin where a few wispy hairs had begun to appear.

'I'll call you Alain for now. Maybe I'll think of something else.'

They crossed the creaking floor. The light was breaking sharply through the window on to the faded wallpaper patched by the places where pictures had once hung and cast the long shadow of a disused gas-bracket. Sasha had not removed all the junk. He had kept those items which seemed to reflect the past inhabitants: a croquet mallet, abandoned when tennis became the fashion; a post card of the Eiffel Tower taken at the time of the Great Exhibition; an album of daguerrotypes; a stuffed owl; a bayonet, grenadier cap, and a soldier's knapsack made of hide with the hair still on it, all dating from the war of 1870; and candles, bundles of them, tied in string and shedding waxy flakes. To these he had added his books, his collection of French colonial stamps, a fish tank, a football, a foil and fencing mask, and a few incomplete jigsaw puzzles. In the corner stood a bamboo table and on it a record-player with a large papier mâché horn.

'I like it,' said Alain. 'It has – *atmosphere*! Do you have any records?'

A small stack lay under the table. It contained the '1812 Overture' and the old march, 'Veillons au Salut de l'Empire'.

'What, no dance music?'

'I can't dance.'

'Don't worry, I'll show you.'

'I don't want to.'

Sasha regretted that last remark. He felt foolish. He liked the Jesuit enormously and was conscious that his behaviour these days was boorish and ungrateful. But what could he do about it? He was forever being told to change his attitude and be polite; yet, however he felt, the words seemed to come out the same way and whatever he did to his appearance he looked like a lout avoiding the police. The fact that he could be rude to Alain quite contrary to his desires was proof that he was fated to be the way he was.

It was a frustrating world. His grandfather was becoming slow-witted with age. His mother seemed otherworldly (though lately she had perked up and become girlish, which was equally unpleasant). Masha, with her vanities and tantrums, would try the patience of a saint. And school! – it was a snakepit of pedantic masters and viciously snobbish boys.

The Jesuit was flicking through the books.

'Why do you read books about famous generals?'

'I don't know.'

'Have you read them all?'

'There's a big one about Napoleon – I haven't managed that one yet.'

'Your mother told me you were having problems at school.'

Sasha flicked his light brown hair out of his eyes.

'I can take care of myself.'

'Uh huh. You should read this book,' the Jesuit answered studiously. 'Read the part about Napoleon at school – at St Cyr. He was very lonely there. The other cadets made fun of him because his family was poor and wasn't French.'

'What did he do about it?'

'He studied. He proved he was better than the others.'

After lunch Tonya retired to her room. She always did this, otherwise she got in the way of the house running itself. She sat there with a book or some embroidery and heard the dishes clear themselves away. But today, after crossing herself in front of the icon of Our Lady of Moscow, she turned to a small mirror in a gilt frame and addressed the other woman.

'Did you see him handle Sasha? Isn't he marvellous?'

The other woman was sceptical:

'He's a Jesuit – and a Frenchman. They're both trained to be hypocrites to women.'

'He likes me!'

'Oh, I've no doubt he likes you well enough: your

333

religion saves him the trouble of converting you to Christianity, and his charm has got you halfway to becoming a Catholic.'

'Be quiet!'

'You're older than he is.'

'Be quiet!'

It was a false quarrel. Tonya knew that this love for the priest was purely a love in the imagination. She even recognized that it was not truly love, no more than the physical effort of sport is the same as real work. In her middle years she had again exercised her emotions and to her surprise they worked. If there were a man – a different man, not the priest – then there was still a heart there for him to capture. It was the waste of the thing that distressed her: the years when she was able to love and enjoy love, all thrown away. It was those years that Yura had thrown away, and they were never *his* years. Tonya knew now why she listened with polite boredom to so much of the conversation of the émigré women. They talked about the Revolution and the civil war as the great events that had reduced them to poverty and blighted their lives. She knew what they meant, but the force of this explanation had always something lacking. These great events had overturned the great backdrop of life and recast the scenes so that they were played out in poverty and exile instead of wealth and home. But it was her desertion that had left her without speech or purpose in the ordained plot of her life. And Yura had done it to her.

She decided to go upstairs to see what Sasha and Alain were doing. Mounting the stairs, she could hear them talking about the great French explorers. Sasha had a book on the subject; he sounded excited. She opened the door and said: 'Hello, you two.'

They turned from poring over Sasha's album of colonial stamps and both smiled the same smile, comfortable in each other's company.

Tonya examined the Jesuit's face and saw his love and dedication to the well-being of the boy. And she knew that he could never love her the way that she needed to be loved.

CHAPTER 14

THE KING OF ROME

'*En garde!*'

The two fencers touched blades and for a few seconds exchanged meaningless taps. Then Constantine d'Amboise made a simple beat attack and scored his first hit. Monsieur Autones made a pretence of consulting with the four student judges and awarded the point.

Sasha paid little attention. He was familiar with d'Amboise's style. It was domineering rather than marked by technical finesse. He was tall and indolently self-assured: not exactly a bully but achieving much the same effect by the confident assumption of superiority which was shared by all the boys except Sasha, who resented it and thought it undeserved.

'*En garde!*'

The bigger boy fooled a little, but his opponent took no advantage, so he delivered a disengage attack into the high line for his second point. This provoked a mild cheer from the sidelines, from the boys leaning on or swinging from the wall bars, and Lullien, his pleasant-tempered opponent, gave a shy smile as though to convey the idea that he was collaborating in his own defeat and should share in the praise.

'Get your back into it!' snapped Monsieur Autones. 'Pretend you're fencing, not waving a magic wand. Cover yourself!' But it was too late to shout a warning since Lullien was hit again and already walking off the piste looking for his spectacles which were handed to him. He joined in the hand-clap for the victor.

'Next! That's you, Zhivago!'

Sasha ambled to the piste, gave the salute and donned his mask.

'Drop him, Connie!' contributed a bystander.

'*En garde!*' Monsieur Autones declaimed, and as his opponent turned lazily from acknowledging his admirers, play was called and Sasha hit him neatly on the breast with the simplest of attacks.

'I wasn't ready,' d'Amboise complained. Monsieur Autones sympathized but could only shrug. 'That wasn't very sporting,' the former remarked to Sasha.

They returned to their positions. Sasha noticed that the other boys were all sitting or lounging at his opponent's end of the hall. Until the bout was called he had been sitting alone: not shunned, but ignored as someone who did not fit in and did not care to; but now, stinging under the taller boy's casual rebuke, Sasha decided that he was going to make the others take notice. Seeing that his opponent was standing off with his longer reach and considering what to do, he attacked with a vigorous *flèche* and struck home for the second time.

The third hit went to d'Amboise. Sasha was a victim of that longer reach and his own aggression had made him careless. Monsieur Autones called for order among the boys.

The fourth hit involved a disengage attack by d'Amboise which Sasha parried and the blade passed his flank without the point striking. However, the judge on that side called the hit, and Monsieur Autones, who was blind to the move, asked for the opinion of the other judge who confirmed it. Sasha waited, expecting that d'Amboise, who must know that the hit was invalid, would admit the fact, but his opponent had taken off his mask and was shaking his fair hair out of his eyes, content with the draw. Sasha did not bother to raise a fruitless objection, but retired to his corner and watched the rest of the match alone.

'You didn't like that result,' d'Amboise said. They were in the showers, half a dozen boys together, jostling and shouting in voices echoing off the white tiles above the splash of water.

'The hit was out,' Sasha told him evenly.

'Are you calling me a cheat?'

'Yes, if you like.'

D'Amboise gave a dry, puzzled laugh, not expecting this reply, but not apparently disposed to do anything about it. A hand taller than Sasha and well built, he could look to win any fight, but in the ordinary way his prestige came from his lazy unconcern and probably he was inclined to let the matter pass. But Lullien spoke up.

'You can't let him say that, Connie.'

'No, I don't suppose I can,' said d'Amboise, and would have struck out if Sasha had not caught his fist, twisted his arm, and caused him to lose his footing so that he sprawled on the shower floor.

The other boys piled on to Sasha and gave him a moderate beating until d'Amboise, back on his feet, stopped them. He grinned a great deal, and when the boys urged him on again, he merely laughed.

It was Golitsin who indirectly suggested that they should visit Nice. Over lunch in the garden of the Zhivagos' country retreat at Ozoir-la-Ferrière, under the magnolia which was in bloom, he happened to mention that he was going there on business.

'How long for?' asked Professor Gromeko.

These days Alexander Alexandrovitch lived for little else but his games of chess. His eyes were too weak to read. He had given up botany because arthritis made it difficult to stoop for specimens and the condition of his eyes made it near impossible to study them. He looked for warmth, wearing a shawl even on a mild day, and a little conviviality.

'A week – two weeks.'

'Why are you going?'

'To review investments with my clients. Some of them are still suffering heavily because of the Crash.'

Golitsin's clients on the Riviera were mostly émigré Russians. In Paris he handled the funds of substantial French investors, including the accounts of several ministers – or so the stories went, and the financier did nothing to discourage them.

Sasha paid no attention. He was resting between games of tennis. Constantine and Daniel were on the court. Glass in hand, he sat and watched Lydia and Alain. A door gave on to the garden, and inside the house they had rolled back the carpet and were dancing the foxtrot to a medley by Charlie Kuntz. Masha looked on anxiously. At twelve years old she was longing to wear make-up and learn to dance. Lydia was her heroine. Lately, Masha had put on a spurt of growth and was nearly as tall as her brother, in a bony way that was very fetching in a natural coquette.

'Why don't you learn to dance?' asked Tonya.

'Maybe I shall.'

'How many glasses of wine have you had?'

'Oh, mother,' Sasha answered complacently. Tonya knew better than to pursue this theme.

'Shall I arrange lessons for you?'

'If I ask Alain, I dare say he'll show me how.'

'That's my boy!' Golitsin approved, though he didn't himself dance and resented men who danced well. He was watching his mistress and the Jesuit and the charm of each over the other. 'It's a social asset,' he concluded.

Constantine and Daniel returned from their game, each slightly out of temper with the other. Their games were always one-sided: Constantine was too strong for Daniel, and in return Daniel pretended not to care.

'If you don't care about the result, I wonder you

bother playing,' Constantine remarked. He dropped his racket, stretched his long legs in a chair and shook a long quiff of fair hair from his handsome face. Daniel said:

'If it annoys you, Connie, then somehow it's all worthwhile. Sasha, will you pour me a glass from the spoils of capitalism?'

'Why do you have to pretend to be a socialist?' Constantine continued.

'I *am* a socialist. Why do you think I sponge on Sasha? How else do I reconcile my conscience?'

Tonya heard this remark, but when she looked at Daniel he had anticipated her and gave her a mischievous grin. He said:

'You're a socialist too, aren't you, Sasha? Thanks –' he tipped the glass that Sasha offered him to his lips '– well, aren't you?'

'I don't see anything wrong with socialism.' Sasha pretended to be bored. He looked away to the table where the loose petals of magnolia blossom lay among the remains of lunch.

'Well, I do,' said Constantine lazily. 'It's a ridiculous idea. It's un-Christian.'

'I'm not a Christian,' Daniel reminded him. 'I'm . . .'

'You don't have to tell me.'

'. . . an atheist. Did you think I was going to say Jew?'

'No, I knew you were going to say "atheist".'

'Well, I lied: I was going to say Jew, but changed my mind.'

'Don't quarrel,' said Sasha in a gentle tone as though his only objection was that the noise would give him a headache. He returned to his affectation of boredom, though in fact he was mulling over the complicated concept of socialism and wishing that his friends would change the subject and talk about girls.

Tonya listened to this exchange with the mild unease that occupied her these days. She had lost control of her house and seemed to be losing control of her children. No crisis had occurred, but Masha was in thrall to Countess

340

Kalinowska and Sasha to Alain Duroc. She supposed that she was too dowdy, unfashionable and unintelligent to hold any interest for her children. But it had not always been so – what had changed? It was not as simple as the bare fact that Sasha was seventeen years old. The change was in herself, or, rather, in her relationship to the world at large. She belonged to a different time – an earlier time, and served no function in this one. She wished that she were more like Lydia or her American friend, known jokingly as Princess Wanda.

'I need a drink!' announced Lydia coming out of the house, her face flushed with exertion. Tonya experienced pangs of unadmitted jealousy. The countess noticed Sasha cast a sidelong admiring glance in her direction and thought casually, and self-flatteringly, that a boy of his age should be taken in hand in the matter of sexual experience; though she did not seriously contemplate taking on the task herself. She asked: 'What are you drinking, Sasha? Ugh! Disgusting! Maxim, darling, fix me a whisky-soda – plenty of soda and ice. Remind me never to foxtrot with a priest: that quiet way of walking makes them natural lounge lizards.' She flung herself on to a seat and then perked up, pointing back to the room she had just left. 'Look at Masha – the little vamp! She won't give our *bon abbé* a rest. Ha! Your daughter's absolutely shameless, Tonya. A natural!'

The Jesuit had changed the record and removed his shoes to adjust to Masha's height, and he now took the slender girl in his arms to introduce her to the dance. Masha, however, was having none of her partner's stand-off hold, which he had adopted so that he would not tread on the toes of a beginner. Instead, she pushed her skinny pelvis against his as she had observed the countess do.

'See!' said the latter appreciatively. 'She's not going to let him push her around like a baby carriage. Ha! ha! Children! Don't you love them?'

Tonya tried to be unconcerned. What struck her about the incident was her friend's crudity. Her friend? Were they really friends? Tonya sometimes thought that the countess and her lover had merely insinuated themselves into her company. But all the world seemed to think they were friends, so she supposed that in some sense they must be. Certainly they were often visitors to the house at Neuilly. Golitsin claimed to have an apartment in the Rue Masseran and a house at Vincennes, but Tonya and her father had seen neither. When not at Neuilly they dined together on the financier's suggestion at the Ambigu, La Coupole, or the Boeuf sur le Toit, which were famous and fashionable and only added to Tonya's discomfort. So were they friends? They were so different.

Tonya asked her friend: 'Will you go to Nice, too?'

'I should think so – yes, very probably. I was there, what – two – three years ago? In 'twenty-nine. At the funeral of the Grand Duke Nicholas.'

'That was at Cannes,' Golitsin corrected her with a hint of testiness.

'It's the same thing. I don't know why you forever pick on the smallest points.'

'I'm a businessman, my dear. It's how I make my money: noticing small things that other people don't see.'

'Of course, Maxim is right. The grand duke died at Antibes, so the service was in the church at Cannes. If he'd been at his place at Choigny then the service would have been here in Paris and we could have all shared the treat. Marshal Pétain was there and so was the Duke of Genoa, not to mention a crowd of Romanovs. The end of an era, my dears!' sighed the countess and smiled winningly at the boys. Sasha felt his cheeks flush and glanced at Constantine, who was also enamoured of Lydia Kalinowska. Only Daniel seemed immune, brooding darkly over his glass of wine and water while the conversation discussed royalty. Lydia went on:

'The uncle would have made a better tsar than the nephew, even though the latter was a saint. At least Russia wouldn't have fallen under the influence of that German woman –' which was her way of referring to the Tsarina '– and then what might have been?'

This seemed to merit a moment's pious thought, even if the party had not been made torpid by the heat and food. But Tonya's actual thoughts were subversive. Had Lydia in fact attended the funeral? Golitsin had talked before about that particular visit to the Riviera, but outside of business he had mentioned only his winnings at the casino. Lydia was such a snob. She was quite capable of claiming to have been there when she had not.

Sasha on the other hand believed her, and he imagined the occasion to have been unutterably splendid: muffled drums, the corpse borne on a gun carriage, the favourite horse with its empty saddle being led by a faithful groom to a church decked in black crepe where the robed priests intoned the service. The vision was so vivid that it came to him almost as a recollection. It reinforced what everyone had told him since his infancy: that civilization and culture were dead and we lived in the ashes of their pomp and loveliness.

'I wish I'd been there,' he said. No-one replied, but his mother looked at him tenderly.

'I wish I'd seen the dresses!' said Masha, stepping out into the garden, while behind her the record-player played a jaunty number and Alain Duroc followed.

'This tune is too fast for our little girl,' he commented. 'Why is everyone so solemn?'

'We're tired,' answered Daniel sharply.

'Why don't we all go to Nice!' said the countess suddenly. 'After all, what is there to do in Paris? Tonya, you would look so much more attractive if you were a little *bronzée*. A touch of colour would make your face just a shade more interesting. Nothing more – just a touch.'

'Lydia is very taken by the musicians in these nigger bands,' Golitsin remarked acidly, though he said nothing against the suggestion.

'There are a lot of our own people there. Plenty of

conversation. Marya Yuryevna would have a chance to meet some genuine princesses and there are plenty of old soldiers to entertain Sasha. You'd like to go there, wouldn't you, Sasha?'

'It might be amusing.'

It might be amusing! The way that he spoke these days! Tonya stared at him critically, but he was distractedly brushing away a bothersome insect.

'Masha, you would like to meet a real princess, wouldn't you?' said the countess.

'Yes, please!'

The Jesuit was still in stockinged feet; he had emerged from the house carelessly swinging his shoes by their laces and he was now sitting down and putting them on. Sasha asked him:

'Will you be coming with us? To Nice with Lydia and Maxim Yuryevitch?'

'I dare say I could manage it.'

I dare say. So that was where Sasha had acquired the expression. Tonya wondered if it were the weather that was making her so sensitive? She was curious: how could Alain volunteer so readily to leave his affairs in Paris to go to Nice? But what were his affairs? She was curious as to the Jesuit's mission. To win souls for the Roman Church? Golitsin, apparently, had converted to Catholicism, but whether this was the effect of the Jesuit's preaching or the fact that his mistress was a Catholic was hard to say. In any case, there was no visible difference in Golitsin's behaviour. He still attended the Russian church in the Rue Daru and the countess and the Jesuit seemed to be content to accompany him. At times the lightness with which Alain bore his religion frightened her. And she had entrusted her son to him.

'Then I think it's all settled,' said Lydia Kalinowska.

'I propose we should visit Grasse tomorrow,' said Countess Kalinowska with her disconcerting habit of making suggestions on impulse, without any thought of the arrangements that might be necessary or the impact on the plans of others.

'I have to go over to Antibes to see the prince,' answered Golitsin with one of his vague but impressive references, 'but don't mind me. You all enjoy yourselves.'

'We shall,' Lydia replied, and, turning to Sasha, she asked him delicately to pass her the lotion she was using to protect her skin. Sasha obliged eagerly, and, leaning over, he detected the fragrance of coconut oil. Lydia was wearing a turban and beach pyjamas, her skin was bronzed, and she set off this effect with a vivid crimson lip rouge.

'Thank you, darling,' she cooed, and Sasha attempted to brush off any condescension with a glib piece of American slang, one of those expressions that last a year and then disappear.

'Shucks,' he said and smiled.

No-one else responded to the idea of visiting Grasse except for Masha, who was enthusiastic even if she did not know what for.

The boy who came with the villa emerged from the cool interior bearing drinks which he exchanged for the empty glasses. He was Sasha's age, but Sasha didn't notice him: in fact he was wishing that there were someone of his age to keep him amused. Constantine had gone to the country with his family, and Tonya had thought it inappropriate to invite Daniel, not because she did not want to, but because she was cautious of over-burdening the Coëns with causes for gratitude that might easily become resentments. So Sasha was limited to the company of Alain Duroc, but even Alain lacked enough variety to compensate for the lassitude induced by the heat.

'Won't it be hotter inland?' Tonya asked after a few minutes in which drinks had been sipped and conversation had dwindled to idle remarks such as how quickly the ice had melted.

'We shall be driving. *That* should cool us off. And the

air is drier, which is far less exhausting. And we shall be higher, in the hills.'

'But why go to Grasse?'

'The perfumes, my dear – Grasse is where they're made. And think of the flowers, Alexander Alexandrovitch: you would have the chance to study flowers that you don't see here on the coast.'

'Oh, really?' mumbled Professor Gromeko, who was increasingly deaf or vague, one could never be certain which.

'There won't be enough room in the car,' Tonya pointed out.

'I'm happy to remain behind,' said Alain.

'I'll stay with Alain,' Sasha conceded quickly.

Which is how it came about that four of the party went to Grasse and Sasha remained with the Jesuit in Nice.

Sasha was bored; he had been bored since the first day. The only diversions were occasional games of tennis, and these were unvarying. Either he thrashed Masha, which gave him a modest malicious pleasure the first few times, or he was beaten by Alain, who was as good at tennis as he was at everything else. In any case, it was too hot for the game, and after the excitement he became flushed and bad-tempered. Beyond that, he played *pétanque* with his grandfather, whom he was too ashamed to beat.

He was bored. He had started to read *War and Peace*.

Oddly enough, he was enjoying the book. He had reached that point in late adolescence when no book is too daunting, and massive nineteenth-century novels and experimental modern fiction are equally grist for the mill. He was alive to books and had no inkling that his literary stamina would wear off. He was idling in a rattan chair in the shade of a parasol, reading, when the hamper was packed into the open tourer and the expedition to Grasse got under way. The car had disappeared beyond a turning masked by a plane tree and pink oleander, and Alain, letting his waving hand drop, sauntered back towards Sasha and proposed that they wander into the town while the morning was yet cool.

Sasha had been into town with his mother and the countess. They went shopping to please Lydia, and visited churches to please his mother. She was attracted to the cool interiors and would stand studying the paintings and the altarpieces for so long that Sasha became embarrassed. It seemed to him that everyone must be staring: the prim English spinsters ticking off items in their guidebooks and politely saying 'excuse me' as they tried to get closer; the Americans sheltering from the heat, taking in the buildings at a glance while talking about money; the French schoolgirls in orderly files, shepherded by nuns. Only his mother seemed to suppose they were places of worship. Not even the inhabitants made that mistake. The clerics in their greasy soutanes either busied themselves tidying prayer books and candle stubs, like housemaids sweeping a parlour, or for a few francs acted as guides; but they did not display any religious veneration beyond an indifferent bob at the altar.

Now in the cool of the morning the sky was a limpid blue, and the sea, as they walked along the Promenade des Anglais, a veinous colour flecked with white reflections. On the pebbly beach a party of girls were playing a beach game; their cries of excitement at this still time of day had the hollow clarity of a choir, or of birdsong such as a lone blackbird singing on a chimneypot of an evening, so that Sasha was arrested by them and allowed Alain to walk ahead. He watched the girls and his senses were simultaneously overwhelmed by the carnal and the ethereal. He saw the tanned limbs and admired the soft wobbly chests, and all the time the voices sounded in melody and counterpoint as if the angels were singing to him.

They strolled along the promenade, the day grew warmer and gusts of hot air blew in their faces. They bore a resemblance as if brothers: both fair, though the Jesuit was fairer and a little taller. Duroc wore a light

347

tussore suit, and Sasha had deliberately bought a similar one, though of a slightly different shade. The Jesuit wore a panama.

At his suggestion they called at the Musée Massena.

'How can you be interested in Napoleon and not come here?' Alain asked with a laugh.

They walked the elegantly proportioned rooms; saw the pictures and souvenirs of his wars; overheard a pair of English ladies who had halted by a portrait of the Empress Josephine, one saying to the other:

'Of course, you do realize that Bonaparte was *divorced*. To my mind that says a lot.'

And the other: 'Henry VIII was divorced, Elspeth.'

The first adding censoriously: '*Not* the same thing! And in any case he was a bad king, which only goes to prove the rule.'

Sasha had read the biography of Napoleon. He knew of the boys of his own age, the 'Marie-Louises' who had fought for the Emperor in his last desperate campaigns. He knew of the son, the King of Rome, deprived of his heritage of glory to die of consumption in the stifling Austrian court; the son whose infant portrait was paraded before the Grand Army at Moscow; who gave hope to the Emperor in exile as he gazed over the bleak Atlantic ever awaiting the arrival of child and mother – in vain!

Alain seemed to interpret this mood. He gave an ironic but forgiving smile and said: 'Come, let's have a cocktail. The Negresco or the West End? Which do you prefer?'

After cocktails they walked to a bookshop in the Avenue de la Victoire and, leaving Sasha to stand outside and stare at the girls, Alain disappeared and emerged a few minutes later with a copy of *Le Rouge et le Noir*, which he handed to his companion. 'Present,' he said. 'Now, lunch!'

They ate lightly because of the weather, and drank only an aperitif and some mineral water. By chance, the English ladies had alighted on the same restaurant and were continuing their conversation in which each felt obliged to contradict every statement made by the other, and both seemed content.

'Joan of Arc crowned the dauphin at Rennes.'

'Reims, dear.'

'Rennes – and don't pronounce "Reims" in that French way, it sounds so affected.'

'Well, Rennes if you must, dear. And I suppose you'll be telling me *she* was divorced next. Pass me the Baedeker, and we'll see what *it* has to say on the subject – Rennes or Reims.'

Sasha and his mentor were silent for the better part of the meal. Sasha fiddled with his food. He was distracted by the girls who passed by in the street. It seemed to him these days that the world was full of girls, and apparently the English matrons thought so too.

'Everywhere one sees such *jolies filles*.'

'You really shouldn't try to speak French. I'm sure that "*jolies filles*" means tarts.'

'Now, that *is* a coarse word. I don't know how you can be so vulgar.'

'It's what my father called them.'

'Well I think that "*jolies filles*" means pretty girls, and it seems to me that your father's language leaves much to be desired.'

Alain leaned confidingly over the table and asked Sasha. 'Do you think there are so many "*jolies filles*"?'

Sasha nodded mutely.

'And you wish that you could talk to them, but you don't have the courage?'

'I don't meet many girls. If Constantine or Daniel had sisters, then maybe I would, but they haven't, so I don't. Mother doesn't socialize, so I don't meet the daughters of her friends. How is one supposed to meet girls? Dancing? Tennis? The girls I run into there seem – I don't know – slight?'

'What are you looking for? A great passion?'

'Is that unreasonable? Isn't that what everyone is looking for? If it isn't, then why are books written that way? Oh, I know that life isn't like that for everyone, but isn't it possible to rise above ordinary life?'

'Perhaps,' said Alain sympathetically and he called for the bill. As a coda to their meal the English ladies said:

'Fifteen per cent.'

'Ten per cent. In Baedeker it says ten per cent. You don't want the waiter to think you're a fool or an American.'

Now the sun was at its hottest. The light was so sharp that dust was visible on the palms. They had eaten too early and too quickly. The shops were closed, and the streets given over only to the foreigners: the English ladies looking for a bank; some Americans sitting outside a bar, drinking whisky-sours, bored and calling out to passers-by to join them; a carriage parked in the shade with the horse nuzzling in its feed bag. They turned into the cool of a quiet street shaded by plane trees and bordered by houses with closed shutters, secretive and respectable houses in which husbands were murdering their wives with poisoned tisane before donning their celluloid cuffs to return to serving at shop counters. Alain halted and knocked at the door to one of these houses, which was answered by an elderly servant woman.

'Madame Adélie is expecting me,' he told her, and she grunted and said that they should wait while she enquired.

'Someone you know? Business? A friend?' asked Sasha.

'After a fashion,' Alain answered with a breeziness that Sasha could not fathom.

They were introduced into a parlour that was every bit as respectable as the house, rather dark behind the shuttered windows and furnished with well-made but heavy and unfashionable furniture and a lot of pictures and ornaments largely of a sentimental character. A matronly woman of thirty or so with a plump but pretty face and a large bosom was waiting for them and, as they entered the room, before saying anything, she bowed her head to receive the priest's blessing, then examined her visitors closely and smiled broadly.

'So you're Maxie's friend, Father?'

Sasha gathered that 'Maxie' was Golitsin.

'Yes. He tells me you've known each other for a long time.'

'Oh, yes! Maxie and I have been friends for years. And these days he handles my stocks for me – he's clever that way, with the numbers and the money. Is this your lad? Now there's a silly question!' she giggled and extended a plump hand to be shaken. '*Enchantée*.'

They were invited to take seats, and Madame Adélie asked her servant to fetch coffee and offered her guests alcohol or a cordial, grenadine perhaps? On a small table by her own chair was a box holding sugary pastilles to which she helped herself, and it was these, Sasha supposed, that accounted for the scent of violets on her breath. When Alain asked for a glass of water she did not demur, but she said to Sasha: 'You should have a *digestif* after your lunch – a cognac?' and the cognac was delivered, though Sasha did not remember agreeing.

For a while the conversation was about Golitsin – 'Maxie'. Sasha learned that the financier had been pressured by his friends in the Government to produce some scheme that would ameliorate the lot of widows and wounded veterans. Their financial affairs were in a poor state following the devaluations of the franc and the collapse of prices on the Bourse. 'Well, Maxie, he won't do it, will he?' said Madame Adélie. 'You know how he doesn't like to get involved in other people's business. But they go on and on at him, the way they do, and in the end he agrees to do something, doesn't he?' The result was the Société Financière des Veuves et Blessés de la Patrie. Madame Adélie did not claim to understand the whole of the thing, and Sasha followed only a portion of what she said, but in outline it was this: by combining the savings of the widows and veterans, the *société* was able to buy government bonds on favourable terms, which gave a secure basis for their investment and left funds which could, for want of a better expression, be speculated in order to yield a high income. With all of this, and unique to the scheme, the *société* would put some of the money into its own workshops which, as well as producing profits for the investors, would provide employment to those same widows and disabled soldiers. The scheme was pronounced a marvel and would be put into operation in due course.

'Another cognac?' invited Madame Adélie cheerfully, and this time Sasha accepted willingly. She smiled with satisfaction and turned the conversation in his direction. Did he like Nice? How long was he staying? Was he still at school? Oh, but he seemed so much older! What were his interests? Not girls? Surely all boys of his age were interested in girls? She was a good listener and Sasha rambled on to someone who seemed interested in what he thought. He even talked about *War and Peace*.

Somewhere in these proceedings Alain slipped away.

'He did say something about having something to do, you mustn't have heard him,' said Madame Adélie. 'It's probably priest's work, and it's so hot outside you wouldn't want to go.'

Sasha found he did not care. Madame Adélie was so attentive, merry and full of laughter. Her plump face was pretty and dimpled.

'Here, what do you say, it's too hot? I'm going to change my dress. Help me with these hooks.'

She turned her back on Sasha with her head over her shoulder to look at him in a way that was very fetching. Sasha fumbled clumsily with the hooks, and she put her hands over her shoulders to stop her dress from slipping.

'I won't be a tick,' she said. 'Help yourself to the drink.' She left the room and Sasha heard her footfalls on the staircase. The old woman came in and cleared the dirty glasses, and, without asking, poured another cognac for Sasha. He drank it greedily and then sat down to wait. What he was waiting for he was not positive about. Certain thoughts had come into his head of a pleasurable but disturbing nature that he had difficulty holding on to. Then again, he was conscious that he was young and capable of misunderstanding situations that would be entirely clear to an adult. The measure of his confusion was that the thought that was uppermost in his mind was the fear that he would in some way be impolite.

Madame Adélie returned. She was wearing a loose robe of dark indigo silk with sprays of peacock feathers, and she had attended to her make-up; her lips were rouged and she had powdered her face that had previously been shiny with heat and good humour. She beamed at Sasha in the most natural and sympathetic way, so that he really did feel that, whatever she might suggest, it would be rude to refuse. She took his hand and cupped it in hers against her soft bosom.

'Now, you're going to like this,' she said. 'So don't go tense, and don't rush.'

When Alain returned to the house, he found Sasha sitting quietly in the parlour. He asked for Madame Adélie and the old servant said: 'She's upstairs, resting. She normally rests at this time of day, but if you go up now she probably won't have gone to sleep.'

'Are you all right?' he enquired softly of Sasha.

Sasha grunted. He was still drinking cognac and his eyes were vague.

The Jesuit accepted the invitation to see his hostess, climbed the stairs and found her in bed in a room with arsenic-green wallpaper and, on the wall, a picture of St Joan in a heavy frame: a room that smelled of jasmine and, faintly, of the chamber pot that was under the bedstead. Madame Adélie was wide awake and drinking a hot infusion of camomile.

'How is Sasha?' he asked.

'He's a sweet boy,' she said thoughtfully. 'But he's got some strange ideas. He told me he loved me.'

The Jesuit smiled and thanked her and went downstairs,

where he found Sasha standing and ready to leave, looking, in the circumstances, respectably sober if rather distant. They stepped outside, blinking in the sunlight, and commenced to walk back to the Avenue de la Victoire, where Alain said he hoped to find a taxi to take them back to the villa.

The air was beginning to cool. Shutters were open and life had returned to the streets. The two men, looking elegant in their tussore suits, attracted the attentions of the shop girls who looked up from serving their customers to follow them with their eyes. Alain could see why. Sasha was not obviously happy, but there was about him an air of transfiguration of which he was quite unconscious, so that there was no hint of vanity to disturb his beauty. But it passed – indeed, it lasted only a few minutes; and then the younger man looked melancholy and the Jesuit was also saddened. He thought of Adam and Eve, and the tasting of the fruit of knowledge, which brought enlightenment but also the shadow of death. These were fairly conventional thoughts for a priest, but like other conventional thoughts could seem lively enough when they fitted the reality they described. And evidently Sasha had been following a similar track since he said:

'It was a sin, Alain.'

'That's very true,' said the Jesuit gently.

'Then why did you arrange it?'

'Because sin is part of the human condition, unavoidable and only redeemed by the grace of our Saviour. You are of an age when you are bound to encounter women. I thought it was better that you shouldn't encounter them sordidly and in ignorance, or, worse still, blindly and brutally. Madame Adélie is a charming woman, don't you think?'

'Yes.'

'Good.'

'Have you ever been with a woman?'

'Yes, when I was at the seminary, before I took my vows. It was considered necessary. And in your case, aren't you glad?'

'Yes,' said Sasha. And he was telling the truth. Although his lovemaking had been clumsy and inexpert, and from the physical standpoint not wholly satisfactory, the softness and tenderness of women was a revelation to him. He was embarrassed now that at the height of his emotion he had told Madame Adélie that he was in love with her; but what he had said was not entirely ridiculous and Madame Adélie had not laughed. He had meant it and in a sense it was still true. That intimacy between them meant that he and she could never be indifferent to one another; and that disappearance of the barrier between them, that brief moment of oneness, even with someone who was otherwise a stranger, could properly be called love.

When they got back to the villa, they found that Golitsin had returned from Antibes bringing Princess Wanda and her husband with him. 'I just ran into them,' he explained. They were sitting on the terrace waiting for the cook to prepare dinner and for the party to return from Grasse. Golitsin was discussing finance with the princess, while the prince looked on uncomfortably like a man who wanted to borrow money. Sasha could not recall ever having heard the prince speak. He was small and dark, like a Levantine waiter, and seemed to attend on his wife in the expectation that she would give him a tip. Golitsin broke off his conversation to ask:

'Did you see Adélie?'

Alain acknowledged that they had.

'If you see her again, you might mention that I placed her money in the long-dated bonds as I promised. I trust she gave satisfaction.'

'She was charming.'

Golitsin returned to discussing his scheme for the widows and wounded war veterans, and Princess Wanda cooed and remarked: 'Of course in Italy that sort of thing has been taken care of by *Il Duce*. He said something of the sort to me at our audience, didn't he, Carlo?'

'Yes, *carissima*.'

'Who is Adélie?' the princess enquired.

'Just someone I know,' Golitsin told her.

Someone he knew.

It came to Sasha then that his visit to Madame Adélie had not been an improvisation by Alain, but something planned. He was not angry – since that would have meant being angry also with Adélie for whom he had most tender thoughts – but he felt deeply ashamed that his affairs could be discussed and plotted.

'I'm going to my room!' he said abruptly.

'Are you all right?' asked Alain.

'It's too late to ask, isn't it?' said Sasha in a tone that was intended to be meaningful, but in fact was just theatrical; and, as he left the terrace, from the interior of the house he could hear a brief squeak of laughter from the princess and he imagined that his shame had been explained to her by Golitsin. He went to his room, threw himself on the bed and sobbed with frustration.

He slept for an hour and, when he woke, it was almost dark. He changed his clothes, brushed his hair, and decided to comport himself with dignity. When he went down to the terrace, he found that the car had recently returned from Grasse, and Lydia and his mother were explaining how the day had gone.

'Smell! Smell!' cried Masha. She rushed up to him and stuck her neck under his nose. It smelled of a heady *mélange* of perfumes.

'Did you enjoy yourself?'

'It was wonderful, we went to the Molinard factory. Here, smell! Smell!'

'And Mother?' He thought that Tonya looked tired. Unused to the sun, she had allowed her nose and the tip of her chin to burn.

'Don't worry, Tony,' drawled the princess. 'You'll get used to sunbathing, and then you'll wonder why you haven't spent all your life doing it.'

Tonya smiled exhaustedly and lay down on a rattan

lounger. Alexander Alexandrovitch had not spoken to anyone but had simply found a chair and gone to sleep. The houseboy came on to the terrace and lit the lanterns, and already the moths were gathering. Countess Kalinowska was untying parcels and showing her purchases to the princess.

'Food!' cried the countess, who had a vigorous appetite.

The cook and the houseboy took steps to prepare a table, while Golitsin fixed cocktails.

Sasha had no appetite at all. He fancied that he caught Lydia looking at him slyly, and he knew that she, too, was a part of the plot. He moved away and found a corner out of the light, a place that like a turret was a vantage point from which it was possible to see the sea. Here there was a white bench and a small orange bush in a terracotta urn. He leaned on the stone balustrade and stared out at the water, which glittered remotely.

Again his sense of shame welled up inside him: that he was a boy who had to be taught lessons. It was this blow to his self-esteem, not any feeling that what he had done might be wrong in itself, that troubled him. Who knew? Alain, Lydia and Golitsin for certain, and probably the princess too. But his grandfather? His mother? Masha? – God forbid! From his place sulking in the shadows, every giggle or indistinct sound from the dinner table was a joke at his expense and every glance in his direction was replete with hidden meaning. It was unbearable! In an attempt at dignity he said airily: 'I'm going for a walk.'

'I'll come with you,' said Alain.

'I'd rather be on my own,' Sasha answered, and this gave him some satisfaction because the Jesuit looked pained.

He heard his mother protest, saying something about it being late, though in fact it was still early evening, and Alexander Alexandrovitch asked:

'What's the matter with the boy?'

'He's in love!' said Masha intuitively.

But he did not allow himself to be stayed. He put on

a jacket and took a stick and left them all to talk behind his back.

His walk took him vaguely in the direction of the sea. The air was warm and creaking with insect chorus and the rustle of palm fronds. Open carriages rolled along the Promenade des Anglais bearing Americans, and a gang of sailors from one of the yachts moored a little way off walked arm in arm, laughing and yelling. An Arab in a dark burnous mutely offered his brassware for sale. A Senegalese, his face so black that it was part of the shadows, sat on the pavement wearing an old tunic adorned with medals, begging for alms, so black and silent in fact that Sasha was momentarily afraid of him until he saw that the man had no legs and made no movements except to smile his ivory smile. And the sea lapped the foreshore and gently rolled the pebbles.

The sea was soothing. The yachts rode at anchor, displaying their riding lights in dribbles of colour on the water. On one of them a party was taking place: a rocket flared into the sky in a spangle of colour and a snatch of dance music reached Sasha's ears. A motorcade of open automobiles and shrill young people drove slowly down the promenade with horns sounding, and when it was gone the silence seemed more profound, soft as if the sea was breathing in its sleep. He saw the girl.

She was his own age, or perhaps a little older, and badly dressed though not shabby: a bottle-green coat with a faded velvet collar; a cheap cotton dress; cheap felt hat; cheap handbag. The hat hid her hair and permitted only a glimpse of her face, which in any case was mostly in darkness since she was walking along the pebbles. Sasha had no reason to suppose that she was beautiful. But he did suppose that she was beautiful – it was necessary to him that she should be so because his mood was melancholy and the sight of a lone girl so inappropriately dressed for a beach walk echoed that melancholy, and he attributed to her her share of disappointments and humiliations that would account for her decision to walk in the darkness and lose her thoughts in the sea.

Sasha took out his cigarette case. It was silver. Lydia had given it to him on his last name day. He lit a cigarette and the girl appeared to notice the light since she spared him a glance, and Sasha held up the lighter as if the feeble flame would help him to see her better. But she was not really interested in him, the flame was merely a distraction, and she turned to the water again and to Sasha's surprise put down her handbag and took off her coat.

'You'll catch a chill!' he shouted out. He was hoping that she would talk to him. He would have shouted anything that might have attracted her attention. However, she ignored him and instead began to walk slowly into the sea, until the water was lapping her knees and her dress was clinging to one side of her legs and on the other, floating like a lily pad.

'She's going to kill herself!' Sasha said loud enough for her to hear, but in his surprise phrased the words as if continuing the conversation he had wanted to have with her. 'No, don't kill yourself,' he said reasonably. If she walked out any further he was frightened that he would not be able to see her in the darkness.

He, too, was now on the beach and running across the pebbles towards the sea. But whether he was trying to rescue the girl or join her in her fatal intentions it was impossible to say.

CHAPTER 15

DANCING IN THE SEA

Katya married Shlyapin. The affair took place in Vladivostok before the couple went to Moscow to collect their papers and receive confirmation of Shlyapin's foreign posting. They presented themselves at a wedding-hall and went through the civil forms of registration and received a lecture on the significance of marriage within the socialist scheme of things. The banners of the federation hung on the wall beside a quotation from Engels, and a small pot of flowers stood on the registrar's table, and the registrar, who smoked throughout, tried to inject a note of sincerity into the proceedings. It was a weary sincerity as though experience had defeated past hopes; or so it seemed to Katya. But who was she to judge sincerity, when she was conscious of participating in a fraud? Despite her upbringing, she felt that she was party to a sacramental violation: even if the sacrament was not to God, it was none the less meant to be a true sacrament.

She wore a plain grey woollen suit and Shlyapin a dusty brown. Fraulein Buerli and Panov, the marine engineer, acted as witnesses, and afterwards they returned to the flat where there was no celebration, for there was nothing to celebrate.

It was, said Shlyapin, a business arrangement. Together they could get out of the country when individually they could not. And that is how it was discussed between them: drily, evasively, as if, following the formalities, they would shake hands and go their different ways, to meet perhaps as strangers in several years' time, struggle to recollect time and place, and finally enquire politely whether life had treated the other well.

For now there was the flat, where the railwayman, Kuznetsov, and his family had recently moved in and space was tight. Decisions had to be taken as to how this newly married couple presented themselves to the world. Between themselves they might agree that the marriage was a matter of convenience, but in the world of practicalities the marriage had also to be reduced to practicalities. Such as who slept where?

Beyond that vague sacramental unease, Katya was surprised at her own lack of feeling. It was inappropriate. She thought it must be false, an effort of will, and that if she were to let that effort falter, there would be an irresistible outpouring of emotion: yet she had little idea what that emotion might be.

In her imagination were two versions of her relations with Kolya. In the one, she was a child deprived of her mother; a sentimental schoolgirl who fantasized after the attentions of a handsome and charming man; a young woman who had been poised at the cusp of love and would have given herself generously to the man who would love her. Oh yes, she could love Kolya – had dreamed of loving him in those long-dead days of love, a month ago.

In the other version, Katya saw herself starkly: the daughter of a woman who had been mistress to her present lover; the wife of a man who had used her mother cynically and then discarded her for the convenience of the daughter. She thought it possible that Kolya might in fact love her, but his love had no faith or frankness in it, otherwise he would have confessed it instead of hiding behind the rational sham of their marriage. He reminded her of Viktor – not in his appearance or manners, which were very different, but in his perspective on the world and people, which regarded everything as mere instruments of desire and ambition, and nothing and no-one as having any value or integrity. This puzzled and grieved her because she did not know: were all men like that? A species of moral and emotional cripple, pulling the world's levers and reduced to tantrums when it failed to respond? Kolya – Viktor – even her father? She had read his affectionate letters from the Galician front, but also knew that he had become the monster Strelnikov. Only Zhivago had loved her tenderly; and he had relinquished mother and daughter for reasons that were unfathomable.

Kuznetsov, the railwayman, tactfully took his family out for the day, and his wife, Marya Pavlovna, tidied away the more obvious signs of their presence in the flat. Panov limped about the main room expressing himself satisfied as to the domestic arrangements; admiring in particular the curtain that divided the room between the two sets of occupants when necessary. This was a convenience, he pronounced: better than a wall since it could be put in place or removed at will; a mark of progress. Knowing the facts, he maintained the fiction of normality and, stroking first his paunch and then his grey beard, he said: 'Well, let's drink to the happy couple!' He had brought a bottle of vodka.

'We've nothing to eat,' said Katya.

'It doesn't matter. The point is the sense of occasion! You are the new Soviet man and woman! And, when he gets to France, Nikolai Afanasitch will be our window on the West!'

The old man's habit of speaking in clichés annoyed Shlyapin. He retorted sharply: 'Get out if you can't talk sense!'

'They're just expressions,' protested Panov.

'Expressions of the gibberish that passes for reason in this country.'

'You should be careful of what you say.'

'Or? Or?'

'Just – you should be careful of what you say.'

Katya intervened: 'You mustn't quarrel, please, don't quarrel. It's my wedding day.'

'I'm not going to quarrel,' said Panov in a dignified tone. 'I'll leave.'

'Don't leave.'

Panov softened but insisted: 'It's best if I do. I wish you well, Katerina Viktorevna – and you also, Nikolai Afanasitch. I may not see you again before you leave. Life . . .' He hesitated on the point of saying something pompous, and then smiled foolishly and sighed, 'Life!' He clasped Shlyapin warmly by the shoulders. 'Be good to her!' Then he hugged Katya closely and begged her to be happy. 'Come and see me sometimes,' he said to Fraulein Buerli, and then he left.

From the window Katya watched him walk for a while down the lane. She was touched for a moment by his affection. Then she caught a glimpse of her reflection in the glass: her own sentimental smile and the gloss of radiance. And she thought suddenly and coldly, what a shallow fool the old man was, a fool for being a friend of a crook like Viktor Komarovsky; a fool for regarding her marriage to Kolya as anything but a fraud – and herself an even bigger fool for being lulled for a moment into believing the same folly.

Panov had left his bottle of vodka.

'Don't get drunk,' she said to her husband.

Shlyapin ignored her and poured a glass.

'Ilya Tikhonovitch will be back soon,' said Fraulein Buerli with inappropriate gaiety. She began to arrange the curtain that divided the room so that the railwayman's children, Sergei and Varya, could sleep on the other side. Then she looked at the couch, formerly Komarovsky's, where Shlyapin had slept these last few weeks, and wondered if she were supposed to make it up.

Shlyapin turned from his drink and told her to leave it as it was. He stared at the bottle but was too self-controlled to drink any more; and at that moment there was a tap at the door and Kuznetsov shyly poked his shaven head into the room and asked: 'Can we come in?' to be followed by the children and Marya Pavlovna.

'Here – celebrate!' said Shlyapin flintily. He offered the bottle.

The railwayman's wife and children retired behind the curtain, but Kuznetsov accepted the drink and asked: 'Good day?'

'Marvellous!' said Shlyapin with a hint of mockery.

'Good – good. You can't beat married life. And you – I hear you're going abroad?'

'Yes.'

'Good, good.' Kuznetsov finished the vodka. 'Well, I'd best be going home. Good night to you all and – congratulations.'

He went 'home' through the curtain and no more was heard of him or his family except a rustling and a whispering of children. Fraulein Buerli extinguished the lamps except for one which was left burning on the small table. She said good night and retired to her room, the one she had formerly shared with Lara, leaving Shlyapin and Katya sitting in silence.

Katya thought: he doesn't know what to say to me. He can't even be insincere.

In any case, what was he thinking? It was frightening to realize that she was married to a man whose thoughts were a mystery to her: that she was trapped in a relationship in which she could not predict what would happen in the next five minutes. He might ignore her, or beckon her softly, or even use violence; and, as she considered each of these in turn, they were equally plausible. Was he burning with love, or lust, or anger, or coldly indifferent to her? Did she love him, hate him, or hold him in contempt? A mystery. All credible. All incredible. How calm I am. I am a turmoil of emotion. I can feel nothing. My mother felt this about Viktor – felt nothing – everything. There will be a fog tonight: the ships have started sounding their

horns. I hope Ilya Tikhonovitch isn't working the early
shift: he wakes the children and Varya sometimes cries;
and if I wake up I can't get back to sleep. My mother is
dead – my mother is dead. Lotte is saying her prayers.
He doesn't know what to say.

My mother is dead!

Shlyapin said: 'I'm tired.' He got up and went into
Katya's old room which the Kuznetsovs had considerately
vacated for the night. He said nothing of his intentions, not
betraying himself even by a look, but only by the briefest
of pauses at the threshold so that she might take note. She
heard him pour some water from the pitcher and wash
himself. At least his habits are clean, she said to herself,
unlike the Kuznetsov children who make the apartment
smell. And Lotte smells. But in her case, I don't know
what the smell is: not unpleasant, something to do with
age.

Katya too was tired. She had watched Kolya as though
a piece of theatre, interpreting the mime of his gestures.
And now it was with a surprise that she remembered that
she must decide which room to go into. So she decided
most coolly, practically and reasonably that she would
take her clothes off here and now while she considered
the problem; and she stripped to her shift.

The Kuznetsov children sniffled in the darkness and
Varya cried out: 'Pears!' Katya folded her clothes and
inspected them for tears and stains. A cart jangled past
the house and its swinging lanterns cast erratic shadows.

If he comes to me and tells me he loves me, I
shall love him and be a good wife to him.

I shall kill him with a knife like my mother tried
to kill Viktor.

My mother is dead.

Was she a creature of passion or reason? It was the
point Katya felt she had to decide, if indeed it were
a matter that fell within the realm of decision-making.
Surely I am what I am? But what am I? If Kolya should
touch me, then what would I be?

Her skin was quick to sensation, anticipating his touch, touched already by a ghost. Katya hugged herself for warmth and paced the little square of room on this side of the curtain, while on the other side, Varya whimpered: 'Pears!', and Sergei whispered crossly, 'Oh, do shut up!'

If Kolya touches me, I shall fall into his arms and it will all have been fated. I shall cease to be a person: I shall be an effect pretending to be a cause; forever trying to understand events and forever wondering what it was that I did. Can I resist him? Do I even want the burden of my life?

She placed her clothes on what had formerly been Viktor's bed and went to the door of Lotte's room. The old lady was snoring sloppily. With a shock Katya remembered that soon she would be leaving her, and she felt at the same time a great affection for this dear stranger who had come into her life – her birthday present, brought by Viktor – and a sense of shame that she could even consider abandoning her. It seemed self-indulgent for Katya to be concerned with the niceties of her own emotional life when Lotte was to be left old and unprotected to the chances of life in a country that was not her own. Or so Katya told herself, and she let her mind fill with images of the past and her love for Fraulein Buerli. It was a gentle evasion of the present.

'Katya,' said Shlyapin from the next room.

Katya froze. Despite all the changes, Kolya's voice had never lost its deep attractive qualities. He could not speak without her feeling the tug of it, and her mind went quickly round the same interminable cycle of arguments and her will was paralysed by her ignorance of her own nature and desires.

Mother – help me!

'Katya.'

She felt her body warming to her betrayal in its longing to be soothed and embraced.

If he calls once more, then I'm lost!

But he did not call, and Katya found herself standing

by Fraulein Buerli's bedside in the posture of a sleepwalker who had woken to find herself cold and confused of purpose. Hearing nothing more from her husband, she slipped into the bed next to Fraulein Buerli and kissed her softly on the temple. The old lady turned her head, still in her sleep, and smiled through her old lips that were crusted with spittle.

The next morning Katya told Shlyapin that she was prepared to live with him but would never truly be his wife. She was quite calm and the decision now seemed to her to be logical and easy. Shlyapin nodded his acceptance, but Katya thought that he hated her.

They went to Moscow and from there to Budapest; and one day in January 1932 they walked out of the Soviet mission and never returned. Agents of the mission ransacked their apartment and various of its members were interrogated and accused of complicity in the disappearance of the Shlyapins, but the fact is they were never found. The threats and punishments achieved nothing, but were administered none the less because the system by this time required that it should be so. There was also a matter of money that was missing. Shlyapin had forged sundry documents and bypassed the systems designed to prevent embezzlement; but the sum involved was not great and would not support the couple for long.

Shlyapin changed his surname to Safronov and with the aid of forged papers and bribes obtained a passage for both of them to France. First they went to Paris.

They rented a room near the barracks in the Rue Ortolan and looked for work. There was a White organization, RIS, which might have assisted them, but Kolya was certain it had been compromised by Soviet agents and preferred to act alone. He had no luck. The Depression was still in its deep phase and there was no work to be had, and, accordingly, after two months of vain searching, they decided to move to the Riviera while they still had money. They chose Nice because there was a Russian community that could give them aid. Initially they lodged in a house at St Laurent which had been founded to help poor refugees, but soon moved to a room in the Rue Gambetta near the Institution Alexandrino. The latter was a small Russian school in the Boulevard du Tzarewitch and Katya obtained a job there as a clerk. Kolya also found work. The enterprising White general, Lomnovsky, had founded a yoghurt factory and there was a vacancy for a labourer.

All of this sounds brief and, in a sense, was brief: brief in the way of short years filled with the long days of life suspended; days of detachment, slow and unmemorable so that the sum of their weariness would not amount to one good tale to amuse a child. Katya discovered the boredom of fear: that life and time were anaesthetized so that fear would not have to be contemplated. Looking back later on this period after her escape from Russia, Katya could not list anything done or learned that would account for the time spent.

She lived with Kolya at first because that was what the Soviet mission demanded, and then, at Nice, because Kolya had the only money until she found employment. But she stuck to her resolution to oppose any attempt by him to impose his will on her and, in the face of her opposition, he acquiesced with puzzlement and hidden anger. They lived as strangers forced by circumstances to co-operate; but for Katya this was not entirely negative because her very proximity to Kolya reminded her of her independence.

Katya responded to spring and the coming of summer in the way that is conventional and yet touches every human being as if unique to him or her alone, with a lifting of the spirits and a sense of hope and change. From her earnings she bought a hat, a coat and a dress. She would have preferred something light and more suited to the weather, but her clothes might have to see her through the winter, wherever she might be then. Still, they were new: that was the point! And they were hers, bought and paid for by herself. Also she had a bag, and in it she put a compact of face powder and lip rouge which she had purchased guiltily but was glad about.

She decided to go for a stroll in the evening. She was twenty years old, fair-haired, beautiful, and unconscious of her own beauty. This was not due to lack of vanity: she had enough to stand before the mirror and cup her hands around her hair to move it into different shapes, and smile and angle her face to guess how the world might see her. But she suspected the answer. She had seen herself in shop windows. A pale girl with refugee eyes, who wore cheap clothes.

Around the Port Lympia the restaurants were open and spilling yellow light into a sky turning through the lilacs and mauves of evening. On the castle hill the umbrella pines stood stark against the sky and insects trilled among the aloes.

On a night like this Katya could feel alive.

In the Place Massena boys hid in the shadows of the red arcades, visible by the glow of their cigarettes.

She could allow herself a sensual existence and admit the possibility of the thing she doubted most: the joy of living.

Along the Quai des Anglais the soft sea lapped the pebbles as a mother soothes a child with a hush, a breeze stirred the palms and the oleanders radiated a dusky sunset glow.

She wanted to mark the evening with some unconsidered foolishness that would express the anarchy of joy.

Katya walked along the foreshore and in her mind was nothing but the anticipation of that piece of foolishness, an expectancy that she could surprise herself like a kitten chasing its tail. On the promenade a man lit a cigarette. Katya saw his face rosy in the flame of a lighter. On an impulse, she put down her bag and took off her coat and began to walk towards the sea. She heard the man say something but paid no attention. She slipped off her

369

shoes. The water lapped around her feet and her toes curled to embrace the pebbles, while the water rose higher and swept the loose cotton of her dress and shaped it to a floating lily pad.

This, she thought, was a moment she would remember simply for its sensual delight. And the day itself would become one of the handful of days in a lifetime that are recalled not because of any event of obvious importance, but because the body is awake and every sense is acute, tingling with receptivity so that the world is more real than reality and the body is rooted deep in it. It would pass, she knew; and during the days of duller senses it would seem odd and inexplicable. But the possibility of this moment would define her as alive: become the touchstone of life.

Just then she heard a splashing in the water and felt a pair of arms clasp her about the waist, and a perfectly serious voice said: 'For God's sake, you shouldn't be trying to kill yourself!'

She turned and saw the earnest face of a boy, full of innocent concern, and he was saying: 'Well, I mean, you're beautiful, aren't you? And young. It's not right. You shouldn't.' He was panting and suddenly he laughed and then stopped. 'I shouldn't be laughing. Oh, I'm out of breath! Isn't it difficult, running across pebbles? I could have twisted my ankle. Are you all right? Can I let go of you, you won't slip or fall or . . .?'

He was still holding her by the waist, so close to her that they were off balance and it seemed one of them must fall; but then he took a step back and relaxed his grip gingerly; and now she could see him better. His face struck her first not as handsome but as amusing. His nose was small, broad and slightly upturned; his mouth, too, turned slightly upwards when at rest, and his eyes were mobile so that the whole of his face was particularly expressive. She could not see exactly in the dim light but she sensed that he was fair, and he was well made though only of medium height, slightly taller than herself.

'What on earth do you think you're doing?'

He was a stranger but she was not afraid of him. The irrational elation that had caused her to walk into the sea was still with her and it seemed impossible that this boy could mean her harm. He said rather crossly:

'I should think that was obvious! You could have drowned!'

'Don't talk nonsense.'

'What nonsense? You were trying to kill yourself. Maybe I should have let you.'

'I was not trying to kill myself. And you can let go of me.'

He turned and splashed his way back to the shore. Katya followed. She could not be angry with him. His manner made her laugh.

'You shouldn't laugh at me!'

That was too much! Katya could only laugh even more. Fortunately he seemed very good-tempered and joined in the laughing, though he interspersed it with complaints that she wasn't fair to him and maybe drowning was too good for her.

On the promenade a car had stopped and a man and woman stood by it. The man wore a tuxedo and a white foulard. The woman had platinum hair, styled in rigid waves, and wore a long salmon-pink silk dress and a small fur jacket. The man drawled, 'Kids,' threw his cigarette to the ground and got back into the car. The woman called out: 'Why were you dancing in the sea?' Her escort said in English, 'Forget the kids, Harry's waiting,' and she replied, 'I'm coming, honey.' Again she asked: 'Why were you dancing in the sea?' Then added, 'It's a really neat idea.' She went over to the car and got in beside her partner without waiting for an answer.

'Don't you think Americans are crazy?' the boy asked.

'We were the ones dancing in the sea,' Katya answered.

She thought: it must have appeared that way – and, almost, that was how it was. How else to describe it? And she was sad at the knowledge that the extraordinary reality of her perceptions this evening would cease and that tomorrow her senses would be dull and – worse – that this would be considered normal.

The boy said: 'You're Russian, aren't you?' He spoke a gentrified Russian with a French accent. 'Where are you from? How long have you been here?'

The veil was already drawing. Katya was conscious that her shoes were wet: her only good pair. The boy was unconcerned that his expensive suit was soaked to the knees.

'I'm from Paris,' he volunteered. 'We're here on a holiday of sorts. Do you live here? Let me take you home. I'll find a cab if it's far. Do you smoke?' He offered a cigarette. 'My name's Alexander Yuryevitch, but you can call me Sasha, I don't mind.'

'Katerina Pavlovna – Katya. You don't have to take me home.' She added: 'You needn't worry – I wasn't trying to kill myself.'

'Then what were you doing?'

'Dancing in the sea, like the Americans said. It's too complicated to explain.'

'I'd like to walk you home, anyway. It's dangerous for you to be out in the streets alone.'

Katya shrugged.

They walked and the boy kept up a pleasant banter. His mood seemed as elevated as hers had been earlier. He spoke with a gentle foolishness and confided in her in exchange for nothing. So she got from him a history of his life complete with a cast of characters she did not know, none of which was of great interest because each Russian émigré had gone through variations on the same theme and Sasha's account had the remoteness of hearsay, stories learned from parents. He did not mention his surname and she did not ask for it. She thought that he was intelligent and likeable, but innocent. There was a seriousness to him, but it was about God and life and meaning; a seriousness calculated to make a woman smile and think: I have a husband I don't love – what is your answer to that, Sasha?

'We're staying at the Villa des Capucins,' Sasha told her. Vaguely he indicated the hills. 'I suppose we'll have to call it the Villa Capuccino now – we've got Italians staying with us. Awful people! You'll like them.'

They were at the door of the apartment house and he was reluctant to leave her.

'Come and see us. Why don't you have lunch with us tomorrow? We haven't any plans. You'll take to my family. I can send a car for you.'

'How can you invite a complete stranger to your home?'

'I trust my instincts.'

'I'm married,' she said. There was a brutality in her tone. She wanted to rebut his confidence, which was so out of accord with her own feelings. Also, she felt she owed him the truth, and maybe even was curious to see what effect this would have on him. She had decided he was moonstruck. For her the magic of the night had fled, but not for this silly, touching boy. In any case, whatever her desires or intentions, Kolya was an unavoidable fact. She could see that Sasha was disappointed. He said valiantly:

'Oh, that's no problem. You must bring him along. Really, I insist! You're the only interesting person I've met in Nice. Please, Katya!'

She nodded slowly, but he saw her sad smile and needed to repeat his question and receive her answer several times before he was satisfied. Then he became unreasonably cheerful and said: 'So long, then. I'll see you tomorrow!' And again she had to agree. Then he left her and wandered off down the boulevard, looking back once or twice. Katya thought how optimistic and idealistic he was, and was sorry for him.

Sasha had been gone three hours, but the party at the villa had not broken up. It was sunk in pleasant lethargy after a hot and tiring day. Insects had gathered in a fluttering mist around the lanterns, and the still air was heavy with night-scented flowers. Masha had curled up in a chair and gone to sleep. Tonya was dozing. Lydia Kalinowska, Princess Wanda and Alain talked in low voices. Alexander Alexandrovitch and Golitsin played chess and chatted, while the prince leaned over and listened eagerly, as if the words were hanging from their lips like cigarettes and he was supposed to light them. In his slow, broken way the professor was saying:

'I remember a serf coming to my father. It was my name day and we'd eaten and were feeling very pleased with the world. He said: "Alexander Ilyitch, they've come to take my son for the army. He's good with the plough – how will we get the oats in? They'll shave his head and I shan't see him for twenty years, God bless me if I live so long. Help me, Alexander Ilyitch!" And my father did! Just because he was in a good mood. He saved the boy. But the point is that someone else's son was taken to fill the quota. So was it a good deed or not?'

'It's the way of the world,' said Golitsin without interest. 'Did he pay your father?'

'I don't think so.'

'Uh huh,' grunted Golitsin, as if he failed to see the point.

In his mood of distraction and elation Sasha was not concentrating, but then he thought: that isn't possible. The serfs were freed before grandfather was born. He must be repeating a story his father told to him. And it occurred to Sasha then how vivid the story must have been for it to have stuck in his grandfather's memory as if part of his own experience. Probably it had been told to him on his name day and the day had been so wonderful that the memory stayed. There were days like that, but you could never predict when they would happen.

Shortly after noon on the following day, Katya and her husband appeared at the gate of the Villa des Capucins and were let in by the houseboy. The heat of the previous day was repeated and every crevice of stone seemed to hide a lizard. Katya wore a pale green cotton dress and her legs were bare in white canvas shoes. Kolya wore a linen suit from which the stains had been sponged and carried in both hands a flat straw hat. With his small dark figure he bore something of the manner of a Portuguese compradore waiting on commissions for tea and spices; but this, too, was in part an effect of the heat and sunlight, which made the air milky and unreal.

Kolya knew everything. It was his business to know. When a new family of Russians took over the Villa des Capucins he had learned who they were.

Katya had arrived home. Her shoes were wet, her dress stained with brine. He asked her in his level way where she had been and what she had been doing, and she told him something of her encounter. For Katya to answer his interrogation was both a defeat and a victory. In his dark mood he was irresistible and dangerous to cross. But in answering him, she affirmed her defiance of his opinion by telling him of her meeting with a charming, foolish boy.

'He's the Zhivago heir,' Kolya told her. He was sitting quietly in the clothes he wore to work, a blouson and trousers in coarse indigo cloth. Katya could remember the first time he put them on, and despite herself she admired the fact that he was not brought low by the fall in his condition.

She knew nothing of the Zhivagos except the familiarity of the name, which might be coincidence. Kolya said:

'They owned a fortune in banks and factories. The grandfather wasted most of it, but there was money in France that he couldn't get his hands on. No-one knows anything much about the son except that he wrote poetry. The grandson came into the money a couple of years ago.'

Katya knew that Sasha's father had been called Yura – and now she knew that his surname was Zhivago. Coincidence? Of course it wasn't coincidence: even as she raised that possibility, she knew it was not true. Kolya also knew it was not true: he had known her mother and learned her history. Sasha was Yura's son! *Her* Yura, who was the nearest to a father that she could remember! It was a thought that made her dizzy – that frightened her as though her life had been touched by the finger of God, and that which was dead was resurrected!

'Katerina Pavlovna, may I introduce my mother?' Sasha had been drinking and was pleasantly merry. In the shadow of the palms Katya found herself before a woman in early middle age with a grave, gentle face; and in succession she was introduced to a girl who was Sasha's sister, an elderly grandfather, a handsome French priest, a beautiful Polish woman, a middle-aged Russian with a heavy, unpleasant manner, an American woman with striking, rather bony features, and a small, elderly Italian who seemed to be on the point of answering a question that was never asked. And with all of this was a confusion of names and explanations given gaily by Sasha, while Katya shivered in the shadow and heard nothing except her voice telling her that this was Yura's son.

'I told my mother we'd been dancing in the sea,' Sasha said.

'Was it really as silly as it sounds?' Tonya asked.

'I don't know exactly what Alexander Yuryevitch told you – but it was a beautiful evening. I suppose we were feeling – silly.'

Princess Wanda drawled: 'Well, to me it sounds romantic, especially when there's a husband in the picture. Dancing in the sea – can you really do that? Carlo —'

'*Prego?*'

'How does it grab you, the idea of shimmying in the briny?'

'For you, anything, *carissima!*'

'We could hire a band and put them on the beach. But isn't the beach full of pebbles? And the water must absolutely ruin your dress!'

'We weren't really dancing,' said Sasha. 'I don't know

exactly what it was we were doing. There was a bit of a misunderstanding.'

'You'd had too much to drink,' said the princess firmly. 'But that's no vice in a man. I always prefer mine with liquor inside them, they're so much more sociable. Speaking of which, Carlo, get me a drink, darling.'

Katya noticed that Tonya had deferred to the American's intervention and showed a puzzled tolerance, as if wondering why the other woman was there. So this was Yura's wife, before he and her mother had ever become lovers. Katya sensed an absence, a lack of something – she could judge Tonya cruelly without being aware of it: she was, after all, a stranger. She thought: this woman is good and loving and virtuous and – missing something, something indefinable. What is it? Do I have it?

Tonya was asking:

'How did you arrive in France? Did you come during the Revolution? I asked Sasha, but he couldn't tell me. I expect he spent his time telling you about himself, that would be fairly typical.'

'We were with the Soviet mission in Budapest. But we escaped.'

'Where in Russia are you from?'

'Vladivostok.'

'You have family there?'

'My parents are dead.'

'No brothers or sisters?'

'I had a sister.'

I had a sister! Little Tanya. I wished her away and then she vanished.

'You're crying,' said Tonya softly. 'I'm sorry, I didn't want to bring back bad memories.'

In another part of the garden Golitsin was talking to Alain Duroc and Lydia Kalinowska. Kolya knew that the financier might be a useful contact and therefore approached the group. Maxim Yuryevitch, in his guise of patron of the arts, was talking in his stolid way about ballet.

'The audience sees the ballerinas. Are they not beautiful? So light that one would think that they had no bodies. What an illusion! And yet – and yet – their feet smell terribly! Believe me, I know what I'm talking about. Of course, what can one expect? All that exercise, all that footwork. There they are: so beautiful! So beautiful! And their feet smell!'

Kolya took the opportunity of the pause to introduce himself. He made the point that, back home in Russia, he had been in business.

Golitsin studied him and answered:

'I hope you're not looking for financial advice? Anyone will tell you that I rarely give financial advice.'

They were called to table and the meal was served. Katya was seated next to her husband and opposite Sasha, with Tonya at the head of the table and the others disposed around it. Sasha proposed a toast: 'To new friends!' and it was drunk to wry smiles from Countess Kalinowska and the princess.

The latter seemed to be under the impression that Kolya, having recently lived in the Soviet Union, was a Communist; and, after praising Mussolini, *Il Duce*, she went on:

'I'll give you two reasons why what happened in Russia could never happen in the United States. The first is that it all depends on how you treat your Jews – because you can't have a revolution until the Jews have written a book about it. Every clever Jew has a vision and wants to lay down the law. But your Jews invented a political theory and founded a party, while ours made movies and set up film studios. So you got Karl Marx and we got Sam Goldwyn.'

'Who is Sam Goldwyn?' asked Sasha.

'Bless the child!' said the princess.

Alain Duroc asked: 'What is the second reason? You said there were two.'

The princess directed her reply at Kolya. 'Never argue with a Jesuit, Kolya. May I call you Kolya? Okay, so reason *numero due*: America is a land of individualists and private enterprise. Even the poor – what you call the toiling masses – don't expect to achieve anything except by their own efforts. So –' she said with a long breath '– when they can't take any more of it, they don't turn to revolution and the State, they turn to crime. In America we have our own dictatorship of the proletariat, but it isn't run by the Bolshevik Party, it's run by the Mob. And our Lenin is called Al Capone. The difference is that your Bolsheviks took over the State and since then haven't had a bean, but our mobsters took over business and are making a pile of money.'

Satisfied with this, the princess turned to discussing dresses with Lydia Kalinowska. Katya watched her and was curious at the self-confidence of the American woman and wondered if it were typical. Meanwhile, Golitsin engaged her husband in a conversation about the widows and wounded war veterans and their financial affairs, and explained how he had reluctantly taken on the burden of solving the problem, as a public duty.

Katya was watching Princess Wanda and Lydia Kalinowska when Sasha whispered: 'Lydia is Max's mistress,' and grinned mischievously. Katya looked at Tonya, who had not overheard. She reflected that her own mother had been mistress to Tonya's husband – how else could one describe her? And yet there was a difference of substance. Countess Kalinowska was vivacious and passionless. Lara on the other hand was – crippled by love? Again, how could one describe her? And how should Katya know, who had been a child and had a child's memory of Zhivago? It seemed to her then that 'mistress' was a word that hid as much as it explained: a word that avoided the question of why women loved men – or (which seemed to Katya more normal, thinking of her mother and Viktor, and herself and Kolya) why did women commit themselves to men whom they did not love?

Sasha had drunk a pleasant excess of wine. Katya found she could observe him dispassionately. He was engaged in a good-natured exchange with the Jesuit, who seemed to Katya aloof and ironical, but she had noticed that Tonya paid attention to him which was a sad fact if it meant, as Katya suspected, a hopeless sexual longing. The Jesuit was saying:

'Napoleon won his wars as much because he dominated his enemies morally as because he beat them militarily.'

'Napoleone was Italiano,' observed the prince wisely.

'You've read *War and Peace*, haven't you, Sasha? Do you remember the attitude of the Russians before the Austerlitz campaign?'

'He came from Corsica,' said the prince, 'which was also Italiano before the French stole it.'

'Half of the Russians regarded Bonaparte as an ogre. In fact they called him an ogre, which is a very sexual image, a fantasy of men as rapists. And the other half were already seduced by the glamour of him.'

'He was not an ogre!' complained the prince. 'He was of average height – *my* height.'

'After their defeat at Austerlitz all the Russians succumbed. Napoleon was fêted as the great emperor and there was a wild enthusiasm for things French. But note: *this was after their defeat!* It was as if the Russian aristocracy needed to be forced in order to be seduced.'

Sasha smiled at Katya over his glass of wine. 'What are you trying to say?'

Duroc laughed and said, 'I'm not sure I know! Perhaps that we should reconsider the history of nations as a sexual adventure rather than a political process.'

'What do you think, Katya?'

The question was unexpected and Katya had to consider. She had listened to the characters not the words.

'I think that you shouldn't talk so light-heartedly about women being violated.'

'Alain was speaking about countries,' Sasha protested.

'He was speaking about women,' Katya replied, 'considering countries as women.'

'*Essato!*' cried the prince. 'Beautiful France! Beautiful

380

Italy! We think of them as women and so we cherish them.'

'Or violate them,' said Katya.

'Nonsense,' said the prince. 'Our country is our mother! We do not let our mother be violated!'

Katya did not answer. There was a confusion in the subject. Were they talking about the relations between men and women or countries? She thought that the Jesuit was well aware of the ambiguity and distrusted him. Tonya was listening without contributing. To Katya she appeared unable or unwilling to control the Jesuit or her son. Yet it was not possible truly to describe Tonya as passive. According to the stories told by Sasha during their walk the previous evening, it was his mother alone who had organized their flight from Russia and worked to support them during their early years in Paris. There was a strength in her that was quite other than facile self-confidence. She was strong but different from those two self-confident women, the princess and Countess Kalinowska.

After lunch the party relaxed or strolled about the garden. There was a suggestion that they go for a drive, but in the heat of the day there was no enthusiasm. Katya took shelter from the sun inside the villa and found herself in a salon with the shutters drawn and bars of sunlight freezing the motes of dust. The furniture here was more luxurious than she had ever seen and she supposed it was antique.

'Do you own this villa?' she asked. Sasha had followed her from the garden, still wearing a straw hat against the sun. He had tipped this at a raffish angle.

'Max rented it.'

'The furniture is beautiful.'

'It's all right. We have nicer stuff at home.'

'Are you really so rich?'

'Fairly rich, or so Max tells us. He and Cousin Aristide handle the money.' Changing mood, Sasha said: 'It isn't right, is it, to be so rich? We used to be poor, so

I know what it's like. It puzzles me. I keep thinking that there must be a purpose to it all: something I'm supposed to do.'

'There isn't. It's just chance.'

'That's what Daniel says – he's a friend back home. He's a materialist, although he's poor. Shall I see you again? Max has finished his business and we're intending to return to Paris in the next day or so.'

Katya ran her fingers over the bombé front of one of the cabinets and scooped a fingertip of dust from the intricacies of an ormolu mount. She noticed on the floor the carcase of a large beetle that had been nibbled by a mouse, leaving the dry wing-cases like dead leaves. Sasha went on:

'How old are you?'

'Twenty – and you?'

'Seventeen. Do you like opera?'

'I don't know, I've never been. I like music: I used to play the piano and sing. Do you like the opera?'

'It's all right. Alain and Max are the opera fans. I go with them and Lydia, but Lydia only goes because it's the place to be seen.' He hesitated, 'I shall miss you.'

She turned to face him and said, harder than she intended: 'You'll forget me quickly enough.'

He curled the fringed end of the carpet with his toe and his eyes, now avoiding hers, became loose and unfocused.

'I'm in love with you,' he said. 'I fell in love with you when we were dancing in the sea – or whatever it was we were doing. Is that funny? I don't expect an answer, but I had to say it because I may never see you again. I'm frightened of life going by and never finding out what it is I'm supposed to do.'

'You're supposed to survive.'

'Do you love me?'

'No.'

She knew she was too abrupt, too cold. She knew the tone she wished to adopt, but it was like struggling to find a note that she could hear only in her head. He nodded.

'I guessed you would say that. But you will love me some day. I'm certain of that. It's Fate. I believe in Fate. It's the only way to explain what happens. I didn't deserve to be poor and I don't deserve to be rich: neither had anything to do with me. We didn't plan to dance in the sea, but that's what happened.'

Now she really was annoyed.

'You're talking romantic nonsense!'

Sasha shrugged. On the table was a bowl of cloisonné enamel holding an array of dried fruit. He took a handful of raisins and studied the brown wrinkled skins and dusty bloom. Matter-of-factly he answered:

'You needn't tell me I'm naive, everyone else does. But I'm intelligent – I know that for myself and no-one need tell me. Some day, if I live long enough, I'll become wise. Even now I think about things. I talk a lot to Alain, so I learn quickly. And I'm wise enough already to know that it's a shame to waste enthusiasm. Why do you seem so sad?' he asked.

'I'm not sad.'

'Yes, you are. I'm always cheerful, well, nearly always. But you seem sad. Is it wise to be sad? Sad people don't get things done. I intend to get things done.' He laughed: 'Provided I can find out what it is I'm supposed to do!'

Shrewdly he then said: 'You're sad because you don't love your husband. Why did you marry him?'

'In order to escape Russia.'

He was pleased. 'You could get a divorce. Here, America, Mexico – somewhere. I could talk to my lawyer.'

At that moment the door opened and Masha came in. She looked at them suspiciously and grinned. 'Whoops! Sorry!' she said and went out again.

Briefly Katya caught a flutter of his light-heartedness and smiled and he smiled too. But her rational mind was thinking: do I love him? and dismissing the idea – for if she had loved him she would not have been able to study the question so coolly. She examined the salon and its improbable luxury, and thought of going home with Kolya to her own rented room and the mundane days ahead that represented the reality of her life. These last two days were a fantasy and nothing was more fantastical than Sasha. But the matter had to be brought to a close.

'Kolya and I have got to leave,' she told him. 'You're going back to Paris and we're staying here. It's unlikely we'll meet again —'

'So you say.'

'— but I *am* grateful, Sasha. You've cheered me up. I'm glad you like me.'

'I'm in love with you,' Sasha repeated tolerantly. 'It's just a matter of time. Once I shave more often you'll treat me seriously. People like me put their hearts into things and then that's it, there's no going back.'

Katya shook her head. Then she noticed the piano in one corner of the room. 'Can I play it?' she asked.

'Of course.'

She went to the piano, raised the lid and tested the keyboard. The instrument was not as out of tune as she feared. She settled at it, and from her memory played one of the Schubert *Lieder* she had been taught by Fraulein Buerli.

This attracted the attention of the others, who came in from the garden and listened until she had finished. Then Princess Wanda said: 'Beautiful – but we can do without the gloomy stuff.' She asked to take over, and proceeded to knock out some jazz.

A taxi was arranged to take them home. It was evening. As they drove, Kolya said:

'The boy's in love with you.'

'What makes you think that?'

'Please,' he answered with lazy impatience, 'don't act as if I'm blind. He was making cow-eyes at you through lunch and followed you into the house. The question is: did he tell you? My guess is that he did. Some boys would

384

and some wouldn't, but that one wears his heart on his sleeve. Let me tell you something.' He leaned over and his dark eyes were opaque. 'I talked to Max Golitsin and he told me a story. Yesterday he and the priest arranged to take the boy —'

'Why do you call him "the boy"? He has a name.'

'— arranged to take him on a first visit to a prostitute. This is, apparently, an entirely respectable French custom. So, when he saw you on the beach – when you were dancing in the sea – he had just come from her.'

'I don't believe you,' Katya interrupted.

'Now here is the joke! He told the woman he loved her. He told her, and he told you – and, to be fair, he was probably sincere on both occasions. That's how it is with boys of seventeen. What was your answer?'

Katya made no reply. She was shocked: but more than anything it was the crudeness of Golitsin and Kolya that appalled her – that Golitsin should manipulate Sasha and then make fun of him; and that neither should see anything wrong because it was the way that men handled their softer feelings, by disparaging them when they saw them in others. Shlyapin went on:

'You told him that you didn't love him, didn't you? Don't be afraid to admit it if I'm wrong. Whom you fall in love with is your business. Once upon a time I might have cared, but when we made our arrangement, love wasn't part of it, was it?'

'It was you who told me that our marriage was just for form's sake!' Katya cried, overcome at the accusation.

'True. And you held me to that. When I offered you something more, you refused me.'

'Because you don't really love me!' Katya said scornfully. 'Oh, I'm sure you feel *something*, but it's all so overlaid with calculation that there's nothing genuine in it. You made a whore out of my mother and you want to make a whore out of me; and you pretend love so that you can live with yourself and deceive me. Well, I won't have it!' she shouted. 'I won't have you and I won't have Sasha. I won't have any man who feels a little sentiment and calls it love, because your masculine sentiment is self-regarding and never thinks what it may mean to the woman – any woman. You helped me when we were in Yuryatin, and I'm sure you felt oh so kind, oh so generous, and my mother and her little girl must have appeared *so* pitiful and grateful. But where was the real generosity? You helped us and you exacted a price from my mother – and when she became inconvenient and Viktor came for her, you were happy enough to get rid of her. What did you imagine? That my mother was *so* overwhelmed by gratitude that she fell in love with you? Well . . .'

'Well?' Kolya enquired with faintly contemptuous tolerance.

'She might have.' Katya paused and felt confusion in her mind. Who am I speaking of? My mother? Me? She continued:

'Yes – she might have. If you had truly thought of her and asked for nothing. If you had waited until she understood herself and what had happened between her and Viktor and Yura. But you never thought of that. You knew the facts, but you never considered how she might feel, or that there was a timing to her love and her needs that might be different to yours. You considered your own trashy little sentiment to be love, and, because *you* felt it, it had to be immediately gratified. And the result?' Katya halted and looked away from him. She had never articulated her contempt for men before and was surprised by it, though now it was clear and lambent and she wished only that her fierce emotion could drive the words like knives into Kolya. But instead she finished quietly, for the feeling was too great and she did not want to cry and give him the opportunity that any man would seize on: to ignore her simply as a creature of emotion.

He did not answer beyond a flicker of his lips in which Katya read a grim complacency and knew that, in his own mind at least, he had defeated her: that nothing she had said need be answered, or even considered, because it was a mere woman's reaction, devoid of any meaningful content. So he was able to change the subject confidently and say:

'By the way, Maxim Yuryevitch has offered me a job.'

'Has he?'

'Yes.'

'Good.'

She looked out of the window. To the west the sky was a deep rose stencilled by pine tops, and in the hush of evening could be heard a snatch of cheap song above the chirrup of cicadas. In the driver's mirror she caught a glimpse of her face. It was pale and hard, and the hardness frightened her because in it she could see a bitter future when all feeling was dead, reduced to pointlessness against a rock of complacency such as Kolya's. He, meanwhile, said nothing further, and she realized that he had assumed that, naturally, she would be interested in his affairs and enquire further. She obliged him because otherwise he would interpret her silence as petty sulking.

'Where?'

'Paris, of course. Max has a brokerage business and he's floating a new investment company handling widows' savings. He needs a reliable book-keeper.'

'So you'll be moving there?'

'As soon as possible. Will you be coming with me? I think we've already established that you don't have to. The question is whether you want to – if only to be near the boy.'

'I'm not in love with Sasha,' she said wearily, and again he did not answer.

She thought then that he was impervious to words – or, rather, that he could not interpret them as expressions of how she might feel. Instead, he turned them into echoes of his own thoughts. Now, for example, it was convenient for him to be jealous of Sasha because her assumed relationship would explain so much and do so in terms that would defend his pride. Her supposed love for a callow boy simply proved her emotional triviality and so, of course, that must be the explanation. That she denied it was irrelevant. Whatever she said, it was always possible for him to impute a tone or gesture that would confirm the opposite of her words. She saw clearly that he would make her dumb if she succumbed, and that even now he was posing a question, the answer to which – whether or not she would go with him to Paris – would be made to fit his preconceptions.

She laughed.

'Why are you laughing?' he asked sharply.

She shook her head and laughed again; and the voice in her head cried, I'm dumb! I'm dumb! But it was with an exhilaration: for if her words ceased to bear any meaning of their own, then he had given her the freedom to say whatever she wanted.

He was disconcerted.

'Well, are you coming to Paris?' he asked.

'Oh, I'll come to Paris – yes, I'll come to Paris!' she answered blithely. And because of this sudden change in her mood he found that, although the answer was the one he expected, he was not entirely certain what it meant.

'They are a charming couple,' said Lydia Kalinowska in a voice that affected to be pleasant while implying that charm was an overrated quality.

'She's a sweet kid,' said Princess Wanda, 'a bit too serious for my taste, but that's the way they seem to bring them up in Russia. Carlo, fix me another martini, darling. Now Kolya, I liked him too – but he's a crook. Max, you were talking with him: I hope you didn't promise him anything, unless, that is, he's your sort of crook. Well, Tonya, what did you think of Sasha's little friend?'

'I thought she seemed unhappy. I don't think she likes her husband.'

'Really? Well it *is* so difficult to like men – though one falls in love with them easily enough. And, as far as happiness is concerned, you have to belong to a culture that

388

believes in happiness: Italy for one, and the United States for another. Otherwise, what happens? You have all the conditions for happiness, but instead of being happy you wait for the sky to fall on your head, or maybe you shave your hair off as a penance since that's safer than having the sky fall on your head. People who aren't happy don't sincerely want to be happy.'

'You're in a philosophical mood,' said Alain Duroc.

'I'm always in a philosophical mood. It's just that my philosophy isn't as gloomy as the other sort, so people don't take me seriously. Also I'm a woman. If Jesus Christ had been a woman, then the Sermon on the Mount would have been put down as gossip and there wouldn't have been any Apostles.'

Sasha was still in the salon, picking over the piano with five-finger exercises. Now that it was dusk a bat had pursued an insect out of the pines and flown into the room where it was quietly circling the chandelier. He noticed Tonya enter but continued plucking at the keys. She picked up a book and sat down.

He played badly, but Tonya could recognize broken phrases from one of Schubert's *Lieder* transposed into a beginner's jingle-jangle timing. He was evidently sad and the reason was equally obvious. She might have spoken but she hoped that this mood would go the way of other adolescent sadness. What troubled her more were the remarks of the American woman. It seemed that happiness was only to be grasped by a sort of crassness, while unhappiness was a species of wilful folly.

'Did you like her?' Sasha enquired without turning or breaking off from playing. 'She isn't in love with her husband, you know. It was a marriage of convenience so that they could both get out of Russia. And it was a civil marriage. That doesn't count in the Church's eyes – you can ask Alain.'

Tonya switched on the lights and the bat shied from the brightness and hung itself from the drapes. She watched her son and felt for him, but was conscious of the absurdity of talking love to a seventeen-year-old boy.

'Yes, I liked her,' she answered and was then distracted by Countess Kalinowska coming in from the garden to say: 'Darling, it's time to get changed. Maxim Yuryevitch and Carlo have agreed that we can go dancing at the Negresco. Alain will partner you.'

Alain appeared.

'Not dancing in the sea,' he said, smiling, and lit a cigarette. Tonya felt the lightness he brought; but to look to him to share her thoughts on this occasion was in vain, since he merely added: 'Five minutes to change, and I'll drive.'

'You should go,' murmured Sasha. 'I'll be all right.'

'Are you sure?'

His lips closed in a thin line, then he said: 'It's all nonsense, isn't it? I wish I could play the piano.' He closed the lid over the keys. 'Yes, you ought to go; the holiday is nearly over. I'll give Grandfather a game of chess.' He approached the curtain and carefully scooped the bat into a cupped hand.

'Ugh!' muttered Countess Kalinowska.

'You shouldn't say that. They're warm-blooded and the bodies are covered in fur, rather like the mice I used to keep.' He stroked the creature's hideous head affectionately, released it through the window and then went out into the garden, where he could be heard calling to his grandfather over the noise of the cicadas and a gramophone record that was just winding to a close.

Tonya retired to her room to change. She crossed herself before the small icon she had set up on the dressing table and sat down before the mirror. She studied her reflection, the short hair she would never get used to and the face that told of wasted years.

'I liked her,' she repeated, and wished that she did not. She remembered the same wish she had made in respect of the Antipova woman. She had wanted to be her enemy and found that she could not be. The fault, if any, lay with Yura – and even of that she was not sure.

She liked the daughter as she had liked the mother. There was no mistaking the physical resemblance, and her names, Katerina Pavlovna, were the names she remembered.

She was certain that Katya was Lara's child.

CHAPTER 16

VERA

Vera Milkhailovna was named in the Russian fashion after her father Mikhail Semyonovitch Petrov. Sasha met her because Mikhail Semyonovitch was clerk to the Zhivagos' family lawyer, Maître Heriot. He had himself formerly been a lawyer and, before the Revolution, had had a notable practice in Kiev. Not surprisingly he found it difficult to study and re-qualify in France, but he obtained a position as a clerk, and he was valued because he was intelligent and diligent, and because Maître Heriot had a number of Russian clients.

The first meeting between Sasha and Vera was the result of her father's hospitality. He maintained the expansive Russian tradition of friendship even in his straitened circumstances, and his apartment in the 16th *arrondissement* was open house to a floating collection of soldiers, engineers, university lecturers, medical men and people of uncertain occupation, all in more or less of a bad way and happy to receive as little as a poor meal. There was no Madame Petrova. It was understood that she had died of influenza and the subject was not talked about.

Sasha still had occasion to call at the offices of Maître Heriot to sign papers or to collect his allowance, and even at this late date there was still litigation affecting the Zhivago estate. So he knew Mikhail Semyonovitch, who was a sociable man in his forties, slightly florid in complexion, with a goatee beard and spiky eyebrows. The man and boy often conversed in Russian while Maître Heriot sought papers. Sasha had mentally characterized him as an old-fashioned Russian, without being entirely certain what that meant. When, therefore, Mikhail Semyonovitch one day casually proposed that Sasha should accompany him home for a chat and some real Russian food, Sasha was sufficiently intrigued to accept. Only when he arrived at the Petrovs' apartment did he discover that no preparations had been made to receive him, that there was no guarantee of any food, that the general company was of a floating character, and that this was all quite normal.

'Come in, come in. This is my daughter, Vera – Vera, Alexander Yuryevitch, or Sasha to you. No, come in, take your coat off. This is Vanya – Vanya – Sasha. Vanya is a – major?'

'Road sweeper,' said Vanya.

'Major *and* road sweeper.'

'Major by calling, and road sweeper by occupation. Look, I'm just leaving.'

'Must you?'

'Absolutely,' said the military road sweeper, and putting on a large, shabby fur coat over his worker's overall, and tilting his greasy felt hat, he went out into the cold and wet autumnal night.

'There you have it,' said Mikhail Semyonovitch with a sigh. 'The Russian predicament.' He took off his own topcoat and handed it to his daughter while offering the same service to Sasha. 'You know, I can't think of a single person of my acquaintance who has made money since we came to France. Not one! The soldiers sweep roads, the admirals clean toilets, the nobility wait in restaurants – even useful people like engineers work as mechanics. What is wrong with us Russians? Emigrants of every other nation set to and create businesses, and before they know where they are they've made a fortune. But what businesses do we create? Restaurants! And most of those lose money and become insolvent within twelve months. Not, of course, that there aren't any rich Russians: but, such as there are, made their money before the Revolution and managed to bring it out with them. Or they're Jews – not that I've got anything against the Jews: fine people, many of them. Well, what do you think?'

There was a pan of soup warming on a gas ring. A rap on the door brought another visitor, who greeted his host with a mild hello and unceremoniously helped himself to the soup. Mikhail Semyonovitch did no more than wave a hand, murmur a name and say, 'Electrician and concert violinist.'

'We despise money,' said Sasha.

'I don't despise money,' said Vera drily. She had taken a seat by her father, and Sasha saw a strong-faced young woman of eighteen or so with brown eyes and brown hair, in no particular way remarkable but exuding a sort of ironic confidence. Sasha was struck only by her skin, which was smooth, and the fine down that extended below her hairiine towards her cheeks; and she moved her body as if her limbs were slightly oversized and had to be carefully folded if they were not to crease. No description could suggest that she was in any special way attractive, yet she was, though not beautiful.

Another visitor arrived. Sasha guessed that the Petrovs' home was a way-station for rootless men returning from work. This one was middle-aged and wore cuff-protectors on his shirt and a gold pince-nez. Again he missed the name, but caught the words: 'Bank clerk and Professor of Mathematics.' The visitor also took a bowl of soup and, ignoring his host, sat down with electrician-cum-concert-violinist and began to discuss the newspaper. The room was filled with piles of rusty newspapers, mostly in Russian.

Vera got up for a moment to fetch and pass round a plate of *pirozhkis*, and then sat down next to her father and said:

394

'Has my father explained that our failures are due to our concentration on our Russian soul?'

'I was waiting for you,' said her father indulgently. 'But it is what I would have said.'

'I'm bored with the Russian soul.'

'Why?' asked Sasha.

'Because we try to answer practical questions with metaphysics. There's no real mystery as to why we Russian emigrants have failed economically, and the explanation isn't our superior souls that make us aloof from materialism. Our Russia was economically under-developed, and what development we had was mostly in primary products such as timber and minerals, not manufacturing and commerce. We relied on foreigners and our own Jews and Germans to make our economy work. Those of us who escaped from Russia were aristo-crats, rentiers, officials and soldiers – in short: parasites. Charming and cultivated, no doubt, but still economically useless. So there is your answer to our lack of economic success in France. And it doesn't need any appeal to our fine Russian souls.'

Sasha enquired: 'Are you a Marxist?'

'Good God, no! I was only trying to put the Russian soul in its place, not deny that it exists. Are you a Marxist?'

'Don't insult our guest,' chided her father.

'Let him answer for himself.'

'No, I'm not a Marxist. But I can see that there is some sense in analysing societies structurally and not simply morally. Isn't that what you were doing in order to explain the character of our emigrants?'

'I was – but it's boring, too. Do you dance or go to the cinema?'

'The apartment belongs to an acquaintance of mine,' said Golitsin, 'Monsieur Aristide Krueger – you may have heard of him – I'll introduce you some time, Kolya. I admit it could be more comfortable.'

The building seemed indeed a queer place. Climbing

the stairs to the apartment they had almost stumbled over a drunken dwarf wearing stage make-up and a brocade waistcoat, who was lying flat out on a landing, smoking a cigar and singing a comic song. He had jumped to his feet, made a sweeping bow and accompanied them to the door while introducing himself: 'I'm *Le Grand Nain*. Do you get the joke? *Le Grand Nain* – hee hee!'

Through the grimy window, rattling in its rotten frame, Katya could see the bustle of the Rue Mouffetard: the financier's taxi, a furrier's messenger boy carrying a garment bag, two prostitutes and a slaughterman in a bloody apron.

'If you live up to your promise,' Golitsin was saying confidingly, 'then I have every confidence that shortly you'll be moving on to better things.'

'I hope to meet your expectations,' answered Kolya.

'You'll need time to move in, buy a few sticks of furniture and so on. Shall we say Monday in the office?'

'Tomorrow if you like.'

Golitsin raised his eyebrows and gave a patronizing smile. He said: 'I trust that your eagerness won't get the better of your discretion.'

'I can be very discreet,' Kolya told him.

Golitsin left with an exchange of compliments between employer and clerk.

'What am I to do?' asked Katya, surveying the damp, disused room.

'That's a matter for you. You could have stayed in Nice if you'd wanted to. I didn't insist you come to Paris.'

The comment was truthful and cruel. Katya was conscious that by accompanying her husband she had shown her dependence on him, and she knew that in his calculating mind he was turning her into a housewife.

'I'm going to look for work,' she said.

'I wish you luck. Do you intend to clean this place?'

'We can both clean it.' But in fact, having nothing better to do, Katya cleaned the apartment, went to the market and cooked dinner. Kolya was surprised and pleased. I have to find work, Katya told herself.

The following morning she knocked on her neighbour's door and introduced herself.

'I've moved into the next apartment.'

'Please, come in, come in!' said a cheerful Madame Coën. 'Daniel, make room for our guest.'

The apartment was full of furs and swatches of shot-silk lining material. A Singer sewing machine stood in the middle of the room and a youth, two or three years younger than Katya, was lounging in an old chair. In contrast to his surroundings, he was expensively dressed but careless of his clothes. His face was dark and unshaven and Katya's first impression was that he was bad-tempered and spoiled.

Madame Coën on the other hand was welcoming and talkative, though, after offering coffee, she had to apologize and ask if she might sew as they chatted. Katya supposed that ordinarily she worked alone all day and was glad of any company.

'Russian?' asked Madame Coën. 'You're Russian? I can tell the accent, but you do speak lovely French. Where did you learn?'

'I had a tutor.'

'So you were rich?'

'No, and I'm not rich now. It's a complicated story.'

'All our stories are complicated,' said Madame Coën and told hers, which was the familiar one of pogroms and cossacks; and, later, Katya felt ashamed that she paid little attention. Instead she drank coffee and contributed a few answers about her own history when forced to; but her thoughts were about the pressing need to find work if she was to maintain her independence against Kolya.

'What can you do? Can you sew?' asked Madame Coën.

'A little, but only very plain stitching and I've not done much dressmaking.'

'Never mind. It doesn't pay. Me, I don't know anything else. But it doesn't pay. Still, you're presentable. Can you type? Or perhaps you can learn to be a telephone operator?'

'I'm musical,' Katya said, not thinking that this was a useful skill, but demoralized at the thought that she had nothing to offer.

'Paris is full of musicians,' said her new friend. 'And the pay is terrible.'

Katya placed some small advertisements for work in the *tabacs* around the Rue Mouffetard. Returning to the apartment carrying two heavy bags of groceries, she came across Daniel Coën by the street door. He still contrived at the same time to appear indolent and serious, but today he had lost the sour expression that had struck Katya as unpleasant. In fact, she thought, he was a good-looking boy. Seeing her, he smiled and spoke.

'Those bags look heavy. Let me carry them for you.' He did not wait for an answer, but took them and together they began to climb the stairs.

On the way up they met Le Nain. The little man jabbed his finger at Katya and said sharply: 'You – I want a word with you! But not now. I'm in a hurry.' He disappeared downstairs in a whiff of brandy.

'He frightens me,' Katya said, though the fact was she was smiling.

'Oh, he's a good fellow,' answered Daniel thoughtfully. 'He's generous to a fault, considering that he has no money. And life has hardly treated him kindly, so why should he have a good opinion of it?'

'Does he live here?'

'It's difficult to say. He had a mistress who was a tenant. She was a singer, but she died last year. I think she was consumptive. Since then no-one knows where he lives and I don't suppose anyone much cares. He's only a dwarf and, unlike other human beings, they don't require food, shelter, love, affection or money. Have you got the key? This door always used to stick.'

Katya gave him the key. He shouldered the door open and stood back to let her in.

'Tell me,' he said. 'Do you know the Zhivagos?'

Katya was surprised. She viewed him cautiously.

'Why should I know the Zhivagos?'

'So you do. I thought so. Max Golitsin found you this apartment, didn't he? He's one of their friends. The Zhivagos used to live here.'

Daniel had followed her into the apartment and his intelligent eyes were appraising the arrangement she had made. He continued:

'Of course, in those days they were poor. Now they're rich. They bought me these clothes. They're always buying me things. I try to be grateful, and I suppose in a way I am. The trouble is they're good people, and good people stand in the way of destroying a rotten system because one doesn't want to hurt them. How can I join a revolution wearing these clothes?'

Katya was scarcely listening. It was a shock to her that the Zhivagos had once lived here. It increased her sensation of being bound to them. Daniel meanwhile showed no sign of leaving. He asked:

'Are you the woman Sasha met in Nice? He came back from his holiday with some story of this wonderful woman he had met.'

Katya became annoyed with him.

'Are you always so scornful of your friends?'

'Don't we always despise them? In any case, one can say whatever one likes about Sasha and he doesn't mind – really he doesn't. He's an idiot who thinks he's a genius, if that's the correct word. And the odd thing is that one half-believes he's right! Was it you that he met?'

'No, it was someone else,' said Katya.

Le Nain deliberately sought Katya out. She found him squatting on the floor outside her door. He gave her a malign look.

'So here you are at last. I've been waiting for ages. I told you I wanted to see you.'

'Here I am,' said Katya. She was nervous of opening the door in case the little man followed her in. 'What do you want?'

'I hear you're looking for a job.'

'That's right.'

'Jobs are hard to come by. You can't afford to be choosy. What are you prepared to do? I hope you're not one of those "nice" girls who don't like to get their hands dirty. I can't be doing with "nice" girls. And I don't normally like Russians – they're a lazy lot.' Le Nain seemed to choose his tone and words to be offensive and then wait for the reaction. He took the stub of a cigar from his waistcoat pocket, lit it and waved it around.

'I hear you're musical,' he said.

'Why do you want to know?' Katya returned his sharpness and he smiled.

'What do you play?'

'Piano.'

'Can you sing?'

'Yes.'

Unimpressed, he said: 'I can sing. I've got a fine voice, but the customers don't care. They think it's a miracle I can talk. Sing for me.'

'No.'

'Can you sing a jazzy, blues, nigger number? That's what they like to hear.' He stood up and swung his short legs in a walk around her, eying her and smoking his cigar. 'You're a good-looking piece, I'll give you that. I could have a job for you. The hours are late, the pay is bad, and the customers are scum. Interested?'

Suddenly Katya laughed, surprising herself as much as Le Nain. Disconcerted, he said:

'I hope you're not laughing at me. I won't put up with it!'

'No – no! I'm laughing at . . . I don't know what I'm laughing at.' Seeing he was still unsettled, she sat on the floor and brought her eyes level with his. She told him: 'Yours is the only offer of work I've had.' Her voice fell at this comment and the dwarf looked at her sympathetically.

'I used to have a partner,' he said. 'She was a tall person like you. She died, damn her. We had this act, her and me, sort of Beauty and the Beast – see? There was nothing funny about it, don't get me wrong. There *isn't* anything funny about this,' he added bitterly and tapped his legs. 'Well? What do you think? Are you prepared to give it a try?'

'I'd be glad to,' was Katya's answer.

Kolya was absorbed in his work. He had joined Golitsin with a certain confidence that he was a man of the world and knew most of what it was necessary to know. At the end of a week, he was thoughtful; at the end of two, excited. In the financier's business there was an alchemy that fascinated his new clerk, who set himself to study it. In this condition, he was inclined to ignore his wife and stay late at the office. So there was no difficulty when Katya went out one evening with Le Nain.

There had been no chance to practise. Le Nain dismissed the idea.

'It wrecks this sort of music. Anyway, the customers are too stupid to notice.'

He gave her the sheet music. She hummed the tunes. He corrected her.

'Speed it up. Watch me. Take your cues from me.'

They took a bus to Montparnasse and on the way her partner tried to enlighten Katya.

'Don't expect anything fancy. We're not stars, in fact we're not anything very much. If the customers don't like us, the manager will drag us off. If that happens, don't complain. Be nice and we may still get paid something.'

They got off the bus, and Le Nain weaved his way through some side streets, drawing Katya in his wake, finally finding the dim side entrance to a cabaret whose name she did not even notice. Once inside, her companion found the manager and his manner changed. He was pleasant and cracked inoffensive jokes with everyone he met.

'Nervous?' he asked.

'A little,' said Katya. But the nervousness was elation, not fear. It was not that she had any ambitions as an entertainer. The idea was absurd! Yet she felt the risk and delight of self-affirmation, and the bubbling joy must have been apparent for Le Nain said:

'Calm down. We're on in two minutes. On and off and we don't hang about. I put the customers off their drinks.'

Already they were being ushered through a door and on to a small stage that held a piano, and Katya could vaguely see a floor with some dancing couples, tables, and a bar, all nondescript and veiled in cigarette smoke and lights. Her companion urged her to the piano, and while she settled to it he treated the clientele to some coarse patter. Then she was playing and Le Nain sang.

He crooned. He sang beautifully, caressing the banal words. Six songs, each delivered longingly. And then off, and he was at Katya's side. 'Your turn.' He took her place at the piano and Katya, looking abashed, with her hands held in front of her, clasped on her simple dress, stood at the front of the stage and saw nothing but the spangle of lights cascading colour over the dancers. She sang her songs and afterwards remembered nothing of them.

When they had finished, the manager paid them in his office.

'Not bad,' he said to Katya. 'But take a tip from me: it's not opera. Your voice needs more tone. Do you smoke? You should start.' To Le Nain he said: 'Here's your cash, Marcel. Next week, maybe, again? I've nothing against the girl, but could you get a black partner? It's the fashion. Blame the Baker woman.'

Le Nain lit a cigar.

'The audience wants Americans. They're like gold.'

The manager nodded.

'You could be right. And you, girlie, remember what I said. Make it more husky.'

In the street Le Nain gave Katya her share of the takings. 'Can you find your own way home?' he asked. He reassured her: 'You did all right. Your voice is a bit high class, but we can work on that.'

'Thank you,' Katya answered. She held the dwarf's hands in hers.

'What's that for?' he snapped. 'It's just a job.'

'I needed a job.'

'Just so long as you remember that's all it is.'

He took his hands back and allowed her to kiss his cheek, and then turned on his small legs and in his jaunty fashion walked away. Watching him go, Katya still felt the sense of elation. She knew that it would pass, and that her work with Le Nain would become a wearisome round of brief appearances in cheap and unsavoury places. Yet it was a measure of her freedom.

The Christmas of 1933 found Nikolai Afanasitch Safronov with a position in the world, established in Paris these eighteen months and known among the brokerage houses and the Bourse as the right-hand man of the financier Max Golitsin, who had founded the Société Financière des Veuves et Blessés de la Patrie. On Max Golitsin – '*Le Grand* Max' according to the press – the Government looked favourably because he was assisting a section of the population, the widows and wounded veterans, who had been hard hit by the economic crisis. Since 1929 wages had fallen by a third and the monthly rate of business failures had increased seventy per cent. If these statistics were not widely known in detail, they were known in substance to every Frenchman nervous of his pension, his savings and his job. It was a nervous time because the Government appeared impotent before the catastrophe. And it was an equally nervous time because if democracy was supposed to embody the people's will, it had failed; for the people had never willed the destruction of all financial security. The forces of the Right and Left watched eagerly for the slip that would destroy this contemptible system.

For some, however, there was prosperity. With the success of the Widows & Wounded, Golitsin's chief clerk had justified the financier's confidence. He was rewarded. After only a few months he and his wife were able to move from their shabby apartment in the Rue Mouffetard into a new apartment furnished by that doyenne of contemporary taste, Lydia Kalinowska. Katya found employment teaching Russian and music, but refused to give up her partnership with Le Nain. Kolya told her that there was no need for her to work: he was earning more than enough for them both. Katya replied that there was every need for her to work.

That Christmas in the empty office by the silent ticker-tape machine, Safronov pored over the books of the Widows & Wounded and made such adjustments as seemed to him appropriate. These days he wore a suit with a waistcoat, and a fine shirt with sleeve-bands and cuff-protectors, and for reading had taken to a pair of tortoiseshell spectacles. His hair was oiled and parted and his lip covered by a handsome brown moustache. He was in every way respectable.

He was working on Christmas Day because the success of the Widows & Wounded demanded his attention and because there was nothing better for him to do at home. Among those few who knew him intimately it was reported that he had a wife, an intelligent but, in every sense, cold woman. It was known too that he had a mistress, but the latter felt obliged to be at home with her husband and children at Christmas. And so Safronov worked.

Shortly after noon the telephone rang and Kolya answered. The caller gave his name as Frossard and asked to speak to Max. Kolya knew Frossard to be the confidant of Joseph Garat, the parliamentary deputy for Bayonne and, like Golitsin, a well-known racehorse owner.

'I tried his home,' said Frossard, 'but he wasn't there.'

'He's at lunch with friends. I can't tell you where, but if you want to leave a message I'll pass it on.'

'This is urgent!' Frossard shouted in frustration.

'I'll pass that on too.'

Faced with such impossible calmness, the caller also became calm. He said: 'Look, I don't know how far Max is affected, but tell him that Tissier has been to see the sub-prefect and confessed.'

At this point in his career, 'Le Grand Max' had decided he could afford to throw a large luncheon party at the Hotel Crillon. With economy, he combined a gathering of his friends with his business associates and political contacts. The Zhivagos attended, except for Professor Gromeko, who was frail and preferred to eat lightly at home. Maxim Yuryevitch sat at the head of a table of about twenty persons and looked, as he always looked, grave and benign and slightly distracted when the subject of business came up, as though it were the last thing he wished to discuss. He was never tired of repeating that he never gave advice.

'It's so difficult since one hasn't all the facts. I merely make observations, and people are free to rely upon them as they choose. That way one never loses one's friends!'

This was thought to be witty, though Golitsin never gave indication that he regarded any of his remarks as amusing. His reputation came about accidentally from an obsession with his own affairs; so that he could make inappropriate comments and these would be taken for wit. In fact, his sense of humour was restricted to slapstick and burlesque. He enjoyed films by Charlot, and would occasionally slip away to the cinema of an afternoon in order to watch the little tramp.

Sasha sat with Vera on his right-hand side and Countess Kalinowska on his left. Lydia Kalinowska's mature beauty was now at its most brilliant. Glimpsing her in the hotel foyer Vera, with disconcerting directness, had said: 'She looks like a high-class tart. And I suppose that's in fact what she is.' She added: 'It's a way to make a living.'

'Would you do that?'

'If necessary. But only after trying other things. It's a short career and old tarts look pathetic.'

'There's nothing pathetic about Lydia.'

'She isn't old yet. But she will be. This is tedious, let's go in. Will the food be good?'

Vera never displayed affection. Instead, she spoke to Sasha always in the same unrestrained fashion, though whether this showed some special sort of trust he could not be sure. It was assumed by the world at large that there was an understanding between them. Sasha sometimes wished that Vera would enlighten him as to what that understanding might be.

Across the table sat Cousin Aristide. Sasha had an idea of interesting himself in the family's finances, which were managed by his cousin and Golitsin. It was especially necessary if he intended to apply his fortune in a useful way. With this in mind he had called once or twice at the offices of Golitsin et Cie, in the Rue de Provence, and had even visited the Bourse. On these occasions he had met Kolya Safronov again, but they had only spoken about business. Kolya had impressed him with his knowledge of the intricacies of stocks and bonds, but Sasha was lost in the subject and doubted he would ever grasp it. It seemed gross and materialistic.

They never spoke about Katya. Sasha had seen her only once since their time together in Nice. They had met at one of Golitsin's luncheons, and to Sasha she looked more lovely than before. The beauty of distress which she had worn at Nice was replaced by the beauty of self-confidence. She seemed happy to ignore her husband and observe the world with detachment. He was disappointed when she said casually that she had found some teaching and then enquired kindly about his studies and plans to attend the Sorbonne. He did not want her kindness. Kindness was a bonbon handed out to good children.

Golitsin was addressing the politicians on the subject of the Widows & Wounded.

'Of course the *société* has been a great success among the class whom it serves. But the difficulty is that, under the conditions of the times, their savings have been too small to undertake great projects, and, of course, for their security, have been invested mostly in government stocks. If we are really to do something for these unfortunates, we need to broaden our investor base: draw on the savings of clerks and shopkeepers and the smaller class of person who cannot do these things for themselves. Take the Czechoslovak loan: I am the first to say it would be too risky for the small people! But for the *société*? Quite another thing! The *société* spreads its risks and is always founded on the bedrock of the government stocks. Gentlemen, we need to move the *société* forward, and that can only be done if people will invest on your recommendations!'

He added that this was, naturally, purely a personal opinion. 'As the servant of the *société*, I am content for things to stay the way they are. You gentlemen set the objectives which you desire the *société* to meet – the alleviation of suffering among the unfortunates. I can merely make observations concerning the policies necessary to meet *your* objectives.'

The audience being politicians, and Golitsin being considered a wit as well as a clever financier, there was some uncertainty how to react to this speech. Countess Kalinowska supposed that it was intended ironically. She told a story:

'Have you noticed that we don't talk nowadays about the workshops for our dear widows and wounded? Max did set up a workshop in Nantes – dressmaking, I believe. But our widows proved too pretty and enthusiastic, and our wounded too lively and athletic, and the workshop was closed by the magistrate not so very long after it was opened by the prefect.' To Tonya she said: 'Darling, I wasn't referring to *all* widows.'

'I know – only the pretty and enthusiastic ones.'

'The truth is that it failed on financial grounds,' said Golitsin ponderously. 'Small-shop production doesn't achieve economies of scale.'

He then turned the conversation to the subject of the train crash at Lagny which had happened two days earlier and added to the stock of widows and wounded, though the latter were not war veterans.

'If the Government won't do anything for them, then perhaps the *société* can. A philanthropic gesture would add to our reputation.'

However, a philanthropic gesture would also cost money, and the gathering preferred to condemn the negligence and insensitivity of the Government.

'Have you noticed,' Vera whispered to Sasha, 'that even the politicians of the government parties are quite happy to condemn the Government?'

'Because they don't really believe they are governing the country. It's governed by something abstract called the system – and the system is as much a mystery to them as it is to the rest of us.'

Sasha was depressed that the political conversation was sordid or at best cynical, even when it came to the question of relief for the victims of the Lagny train crash. However, at that point, a waiter approached and asked to speak to Monsieur Golitsin. He indicated the door where a man in a topcoat and slouch hat was waiting.

'It's Kolya!' said Lydia Kalinowska, and added for the benefit of the others. 'He was invited, naturally, but he said he needed to work. The truth is that his wife refused to come.'

'Did she?' asked Sasha.

'She won't have anything to do with his business. She considers it beneath her. There's something offensively high-minded about that woman.'

Golitsin folded his table napkin and said: 'I'd better see what he wants.' He went to the door and the conversation continued in his absence. Sasha, however, stole glances in the direction of the door and noticed that the financier's heavy features showed unusual animation as he spoke to his colleague. Then he returned and announced politely: 'Troubles – troubles – the world is full of troubles, isn't it? Someone needs my help. It's Christmas and I suppose I should give it.'

* * *

In the afternoon, three days later, Sasha was in a café in the Rue St Jacques. He and his friends liked to pass themselves off as students, sit in the cafés near the Sorbonne and discuss politics and religion. Daniel was there, and Vera, and Danny's girlfriend Yvonne. The last-named was a striking blonde whose face had the pencilled features of a rag doll. She was fascinated by Daniel and sat closely to him with one hand hanging from his shoulder. Daniel made a point of being annoyed by this when he could remember, and from time to time brushed the hand away. His chin nowadays was blued by beard stubble. His manner was contemptuous even of his friends, and therefore declared him to be a serious man. Vera was asking him:

'Why do you say that democracy is finished?'

'I didn't say democracy was finished, only this democracy, the sort we have in France. Have you been to any of the cafés near the Palais Bourbon lately? They have signs up: "We don't serve deputies here"!'

'So the Government is unpopular: that doesn't mean that the system is finished. How else are we to make laws that have popular consent?'

'My God! Can't we see that your father is a lawyer!'

'Don't try to divert the argument into personal abuse. I don't have to defend my father. You have to defend your position on democracy. You have the talent of a demagogue: I can see I shall have to watch you carefully.'

'And tell your father so that he can tell the Sûreté.'

Vera gave him one of her sparse smiles. 'Answer the question.'

'Right. All right, then. Let's say – for the sake of argument, let's say that the people should consent to the laws. What are we to do if the issue between us is that you have stolen my property? If I'm to get it back, am I to ask the consent of the thief?'

'Go to the police.'

'And if the police are employed by the thieves?'

'Who are these thieves? Don't tell me – everyone except the workers; and in particular, the lawyers and the capitalists? You're a Marxist: I don't know why I bother to listen to you. Ah, well, go on – amuse me.'

Sasha intervened: 'Why are these people thieves? Most of them work hard. They earn their money. They don't use force to take it. You haven't made out your case that they are thieves at all.'

'What do you mean by "earn"? Do you mean they *deserve* their money?'

'I suppose so.'

'Morally?' asked Daniel. 'We are talking about morality not power, aren't we? After all, a burglar may work very hard breaking into a house.'

'Yes, morally,' Sasha agreed.

'Good, now there's something to talk about! Let's take the case of lawyers – with apologies to Vera.'

'I don't mind.'

'Okay. Now then, when you pay your lawyer – I don't know: five thousand francs? – do you ask yourself if he deserves it *morally*? Of course you don't. You may feel that the man is grossly overpaid, but if you search for another lawyer you'll find that his charges are more or less the same, because that's the market price. And the market doesn't judge morals. It tells you that an arms dealer is worth more than a nurse, and a landowner is worth more than his tenants, even if his morals are filthy. In short, the market tells you the state of economic power between the parties instead of physical power. But the two are at bottom the same thing: the exercise of force against the powerless.'

Vera asked levelly: 'What has this to do with democracy?'

'This!' said Daniel. 'Your democracy is just a way of setting the rules so that the use of economic power – the power of the rich – is legitimate, while physical power – the power of every brute labourer – isn't. And where physical force is legitimate, the rich use the market to buy it up, dignify it with the name of a "police force" and use it against the poor.'

'Nonsense,' replied Vera, but before she could go further, the door opened and Constantine came in. Astutely recognizing Daniel's cruelly complacent smile, she remarked: 'Don't think you've won the argument because we're interrupted.'

Constantine beamed broadly, kissed the girls, and asked, 'Am I disturbing something?' He put down the newspaper he was holding, removed his beret and ordered a drink. He then enquired: 'What news?'

'No news,' said Sasha. 'We were discussing politics. Daniel was expounding on the imminent downfall of democracy.'

'Well, I agree with him about that, except that he wants to hand power to the scum of the earth, while I want to give it to the bloody butchers of the working class. Anyway, why discuss theory when we can see the thing in action?' He indicated the copy of *Action Française*.

'Enlighten us, Connie.'

With relish Constantine said: 'Since you insist, I shall. Apparently, on Christmas Eve some petty administrator in Bayonne confessed to the sub-prefect that he had issued millions of francs' worth of forged municipal bonds. The bonds have been placed on the market by some fellow called Stavisky – anyone ever heard of him? No? Nor have I. However, this Stavisky is a friend of Garat, the local deputy, and also of Albert Dubarry!'

'Who's Albert Dubarry?' asked Yvonne.

'He owns *La Volonté*,' Daniel told her in his my-God-you-are-ignorant voice. 'For the record, he hates *Action Française*. Which, dear Connie, means that your story is just a squabble between newspapers.'

'Watch this space,' replied Constantine smugly.

Daniel left with Yvonne. Constantine asked Sasha insouciantly:

'Why do you have so much to do with that Jew?'

411

'Do you have something against Jews?'

'Me? Absolutely not! On the contrary, my question is: what do the Jews have against *me*? Whether they own a fortune and are screwing people for interest and rents, or are poor revolutionaries wanting to despoil the rich, they have a sort of resentment against the world. Take Daniel. You're forever giving him money, but he doesn't like you or thank you, or respect you for it: he simply resents the fact that you're rich and he isn't. That's all his ideology is, all his socialism. It's nothing more than envy.'

'But doesn't he have a point? That the distribution of wealth is morally meaningless?'

'Maybe it is, maybe it isn't, but notice how he focuses on the distribution of wealth as if that were the be-all and end-all of the world's problems. As if giving money to the masses would make them more moral. Having money certainly hasn't made me moral, even with the advantage of a better education.'

'What do you think?' Sasha asked Vera. She considered the point and said evenly:

'Constantine and Daniel are both alike. They take everything to extremes. One can't be certain when they're serious. In fact, they can't distinguish between argument and reality or rhetoric and real emotion. Boys are always posing. If they weren't decorative, I wouldn't listen to them.'

'Is that true of me, too?'

'Oh, I'd say that you were more confused than either of the others, but not so extreme.' She turned to Constantine. 'Is there really anything to this story in the paper? Isn't Pujo attacking Dubarry just because Dubarry is on the Left?'

'It depends who else is involved. The implication is that some of the ministers and deputies have been taking bribes to promote the forged bonds. Sasha should ask Max Golitsin or that friend of his, Safronov. It's the sort of thing they would know about.'

'I may do that,' Sasha said. 'In fact, why don't

we go there now? Aren't you curious to find out?'

'Can you do that?' asked Constantine. 'I mean, just breeze in?'

'Yes, of course,' answered Sasha, who considered the fact unremarkable.

They took a bus and walked and finally reached the Rue de Provence as daylight was fading and a flock of starlings swirled like smoke above the street, looking for its roost and chattering at a level to drown the sound of the traffic. On the way, between smiling at every attractive girl and removing his beret to reveal his fair hair, Constantine tried to enlist Sasha into the ranks of the Camelots du Roi, the youth wing of Action Française.

'I'm Russian, not French,' Sasha excused himself.

'What on earth sort of answer is that? You're a monarchist, aren't you? I've listened to your Russian friends and they're forever going on about restoring the Romanovs. So why not restore the Bourbons to replace this stinking republic of ours? What do you think, Vera?'

'I've no objection to bringing down a system that's so obviously failed, but it's romantic claptrap to talk of restoring the Bourbons. France needs radicalism, not priests and powdered wigs.'

'You mean someone like Herr Hitler and Signor Mussolini?'

'I'm not speaking in favour of them; but it's naive to suppose that any revolution of the Right won't be taken over by some energetic radical rather than left in the hands of an effete aristocrat. Your sort of legitimism went out with Metternich.'

'Then what's the point?' Constantine cried out. 'Who cares whether the Right or the Left wins, if the leader in either case is a miserable journalist or an ex-soldier with his backside hanging out of his trousers? If we're not inspired by a monarchy, then where is the inspiration?'

'In ideas,' answered Vera.

'Lord save me from ideas! They only confuse me. And you, Sasha – will you join the Camelots?'

'I'll think about it.'

Golitsin was at his office, closeted in his room and seeing no-one except his chief clerk. Sasha, in his amiable way, had got to know the switchboard operator and she told him that the office had been a madhouse these last two days. Constantine found this significant.

When Kolya next came out of Maxim Yuryevitch's office, Sasha introduced himself and his friends.

'You've caught us at a bit of a bad moment,' Kolya said. 'Still, we've got to take care of the customers, eh? And I could use a few minutes' break. Mademoiselle Lebrun, will you bring us some coffee?' He ushered them into his own room. Although he seemed a little worn, his manner was friendly and he maintained his smart glossiness. He offered cigarettes and asked: 'What can I do for you?'

'It's a matter of curiosity, really. Constantine thinks there's some sort of financial scandal brewing. And I thought: who better to ask than you or Max?'

Constantine explained: 'A chap called Stavisky has been selling forged bonds. *Action Française* is accusing the Government of being involved.' He added maliciously: 'Is that why you're so busy?'

To Sasha's surprise, Kolya took Constantine seriously. He answered: 'There may be something to the story, I can't say. But the rumours are unsettling the market. The situation is a problem for us here. The Widows & Wounded were thinking of making their own bond issue, but its success depends upon market confidence. The last thing we need is a lot of frightened small investors asking for their money back.'

'Surely you just pay them if they ask for their cash?'

Kolya grinned, 'If only it were so simple! But you have to remember that we don't have their cash. It's been reinvested, and we can't lay our hands on it at a moment's notice.'

The coffee came and while they drank it Kolya chatted pleasantly about matters he thought might interest them as students. Sasha thought: he's a funny little chap, but he knows how to handle people. He felt a pang that the other man had managed in some unfathomable way to tie Katya to him. In the abstract he resented Kolya's hold, but face to face with him it was impossible not to be charmed. Coffee finished, their host said:

'You'll excuse me, won't you, if I leave you and attend to dampening down the rumours and speculation.'

'He's impressive, isn't he?' Constantine commented when Kolya had returned to the ticker tape and telephones. 'He's not Jewish, is he?'

'You're obsessed with Jews,' Sasha answered. 'No, I don't think he's Jewish.'

'I'm not obsessed. I admire Jews, seriously I do!'

'He means in the same way that he admires a pickpocket who steals his watch,' said Vera wryly. She studied the financier's clerk through the open door and said, in her uncritical way: 'He's a crook. I should think that's fairly obvious. I'm surprised you don't see it. On the other hand, men pay more attention to power than morality, so perhaps it isn't so surprising.'

'How old are you?' asked Constantine.

'Eighteen. Why?'

'I had a bet with Sasha. I said you were wise enough to be ninety-seven, but Sasha said you were only forty and would grow out of it. So Sasha wins for being nearest.'

'Very droll,' said Vera.

'I said no such thing,' Sasha protested.

'You probably did,' Vera responded without anger. She had thought to draw the sting of the joke by her cool reaction, but the boys were laughing, and the office girls, who had witnessed the scene without hearing the details, shared a malicious sympathy with the boys, as though it were a good thing to belittle their own sex. And in fact Vera looked diminished.

Just then there came a tap at the glass panel in the main door and a pink face was visible through the milky frosting and the gold lettering, Golitsin et Cie. The office junior leapt to his feet from his high stool, adjusted his armbands, slicked back his hair with a palm-lick and rushed to the door.

And there was Katya.

'Hello, Katerina Pavlovna.'

Sasha was still laughing.

'Hello, Alexander Yuryevitch.'

Sasha was aware that they had addressed each other slightly formally: no 'Sasha' and 'Katya'. Was it fear of intimacy or merely a polite distance?

'May I introduce my friends, Constantine d'Amboise and Vera Mikhailovna Petrova.'

'I'm pleased to meet you.'

Whatever Sasha felt, she seemed to him to be quite undisturbed at their meeting. In fact, she disappointed him as she had on the other brief occasion he had seen her since the events at Nice. She was smartly though conventionally dressed in a pea-green winter coat and matching hat; her hair had been styled and she wore peach silk stockings. She was self-possessed and, he thought, striving to be unremarkable. She remained beautiful, but even her beauty was unremarkable. Once, Sasha had been shopping with Lydia Kalinowska, on a day when he was in a state of unfocused sexual arousal and she was feeling frivolous. She bought perfume and cosmetics in one of the shops along the Champs Elysées and Sasha had observed the assistants, who had also noticed him because he was well made and unselfconsciously pleasant. Their skins had been flawless, their eyes bright, their lips red and well shaped. It was odd how commonplace beauty could be.

Kolya momentarily left the telephone and greeted his wife with a routine kiss on the cheek. She said:

'I was on my way home, but I've lost my key. The concierge is away all day: she's gone to visit a relative in Beauvais. May I borrow yours?'

'Of course.' He slipped the key from his watch chain.

'Thank you. Shall I see you later this evening? Or

will you be working late?' To Sasha and his friends she said, 'Goodbye. I hope we'll run into each other again.' And with these words she would have left, but Sasha said quickly:

'We were just going to a café. If you have nothing else to do, you could join us.'

Vera, however, was still suffering from her humiliation. 'I have to go home,' she said.

Constantine gallantly volunteered to escort her.

'Sasha?'

She was staring at him not with petulance but a naked curiosity to see what he would do. Not intending to be cruel, he answered: 'I need to have a few words with Katerina Pavlovna. Can I call you tomorrow?'

'As you like.'

Vera and Constantine then left.

Katya had neither agreed nor disagreed with the idea that she and Sasha might take coffee together, but it was evident now that she must accept, and together they went into the street and to a nearby brasserie where Sasha ordered her a coffee and a brandy for himself and then sat back in his seat, wondering what he had done and why, but pleased that he had done it. And in itself this was enough to lighten Katya's mood, reminding her as it did of Nice and Sasha's invincible sweet temper. Thinking of Nice she remembered also Sasha's reckless declaration of love, which made her smile here and now, and her smile caused his to grow to a broad grin; and then she thought also of the girl to whom she had just now been introduced.

'I thought that Vera Mikhailovna was not pleased. Why did you insist that we have a drink together? We don't have anything to talk about.'

'I didn't have anything particular in mind. It was so long since I'd seen you that I thought – well, we have to talk. I don't much care about what.'

'I see, or I think I do. Is she your girlfriend?'

'I'm not sure. I think that she may be. She acts sometimes as if she is, and for that matter so do I.

On the other hand, she's brighter than I am, which isn't normally regarded as a good thing. Or it could be that she has a sharper way of expressing her opinions.'

'Do you mind her being brighter?'

'Not especially. I'm sure that if I were really interested in her I could convince myself I was more intelligent. Are you more intelligent than me?'

Katya laughed. 'How on earth would I know? We hardly know each other; and, in any case, how can we tell? You just implied that if one spoke well, one could be taken as intelligent.'

'My father was a poet.'

'I know.'

'You do? How? I thought I told you he was a doctor?'

Katya hesitated, uncertain that she wanted to hear about this. Zhivago was a personal memory; she knew him as well, if not better than Sasha – indeed there was no place for Sasha in her recollection of Zhivago, so that now it was as if Sasha were trying to steal him. She said:

'You must have mentioned it. Why? Is it important?'

'I'm not sure.' Sasha's eyes flashed humorously. 'Have you noticed that I'm always saying "I'm not sure"? The truth is there are so many things I'm not sure about. But do you see what I mean? All I have to do is stop saying "I'm not sure", and suddenly I'll be more intelligent! I do know what I mean about poetry: I was only unsure how to express myself.'

'And you meant what?'

'That my father must have been wise in some respects, otherwise his poetry wouldn't have been of any interest. After all, it isn't as if there were any great shortage of poetry. I even write the stuff myself though it's all drivel. I find it odd to think that my father was wise or in any way out of the ordinary.'

'What happened to him?' Katya asked cautiously, fearing that the question would unleash an attack on her mother.

Instead Sasha merely fiddled with his glass.

'I don't really know. My mother doesn't talk about him much. I think he was captured by some Red partisans during the civil war, and I suppose he was killed. At least, that's the official version. Our lawyers had him declared dead on that basis.' He rubbed his hair and looked distressed. 'It's difficult to take in – as if we killed him by having him declared dead. You look shocked?'

'No, no.' But Katya was shocked. Her Yura was the dead man who had come back from the war and taken Lara and her child to Varykino. Yet Sasha did not know of his father's return. This fact reminded her of little Tanya, and the pity of all the separations welled up in her: that a child could lose its past and the whole world. And in this case, she held a piece of knowledge like the knowledge of God: a knowledge of the afterlife. Should she tell Sasha? How would she even begin? They had known each other long enough that he would accuse her of deceit. Yet not to tell him was also a deceit. He was racked by a child's fear of slaying its parents and she was unable to dispel it. She felt then not love for him, but compassion. However, the two may be confused and Sasha detected the softening of her features and asked:

'Have you ever thought again about the time I said I was in love with you?'

She shook her head. If she spoke she did not know what she would say. He went on lightly:

'Am I being tactless? Love is tactless. It seems to bully its way into things, shouldering everything else out of the way. Well?'

'So you're still in love with me?'

'I'm not sure. Damn! I've said it again! I must remember not to. But I'm not, so there we are. I'm reserving judgement. You've changed.'

He demanded no answer but ordered two more coffees and glanced around the brasserie, nodding at acquaintances, always in the same pleasant way. Katya found his manner difficult because, though she was convinced that everything he said was intended seriously, he spoke so blithely. Now, for instance, he asked casually:

'Are you happy?'

'No,' she answered slowly.

'Contented?'

'Not contented, either. I accept things as they are. No – that sounds too passive. I mean that I see things as they are. I don't resent them. I'm not sentimental about them or the past. They form a starting point from which I work out each day. I've compromised with reality and mastered it at the level I can control. I've not bowed under it and I have no expectations of it.' This was hard to say because not deliberately thought out, and it was only politeness that made her ask: 'And you – what do you want?'

'I want to be a fool.'

'What?' She thought she had misheard, then realized that she had not. He was smiling winningly as ever and she laughed.

'Why do you want to be a fool?'

'Oh, it just seems like the thing to be. Most people are trying to be sensible, and they appear to be miserable failures, so there seems no point in imitating them. On the other hand, if one acts any differently from them, then one is going to be considered a fool. So that's what I'm going to do. Of course,' he concluded, 'I could be a fool pure and simple.'

The new apartment that came with Kolya's increased prosperity included a telephone. Le Nain called a few days after Christmas.

'I've got a booking at Le Tabarin,' he said. 'What do you think of that! A step up from the usual fleapits we've been playing.'

It seemed that a minor singer on the bill had gone sick and the management, at short notice, had agreed to engage the dwarf. This was on the understanding that he restricted himself to accompanying his partner on the piano, where his appearance could be decently masked.

'Well that's wonderful!' Katya congratulated him.

'It's not bad,' he purred.

'When is the booking?'

'New Year's Eve.'

'Oh, Marcel!'

'What's wrong?' snapped Le Nain.

'Kolya and I have another invitation. One of Max's clients.'

Le Nain must have been drinking since he grew angry and called her 'an inconsiderate bitch'. Later, he called back and made a grovelling apology. 'But it is important for me,' he told her. 'I know that you'll probably give up this line of work, but if I can get a job even as a pianist . . . well, you understand.'

He explained that the booking was for an hour at most, and in the early part of the evening when there would be few customers and they would not be paying attention. He could promise that the session would finish by ten-thirty. A taxi and Katya could be at the minister's entertainment well before midnight.

'How could you possibly agree to that?' said Kolya accusingly. 'What am I supposed to tell Max? With all this brouhaha over Stavisky we need the minister's support for the Widows & Wounded.'

'I couldn't refuse,' Katya answered. 'I owe Marcel too much.'

'For degrading you by dragging you through cheap cabarets?'

On the point of justifying herself, Katya decided not to. She did not feel defensive. She had stated her position and Kolya could accept it or not, as he chose. She confined herself to promising to attend the reception before midnight.

On the evening Le Nain was waiting at the back entrance to the club. Humbly, he said:

'I wasn't sure you were going to turn up. You look gorgeous! Is that your best party dress?'

'I shan't have time to change.'

421

'You're too good for this riffraff.' He rubbed her hand and kissed it. He urged her inside, speaking all the while. 'Lovely colour. Silk? We'll do half a dozen of our usual numbers, the slow ones. Have you been smoking like you promised to? You've been rushing; you should have a drink to calm you down.'

'Keep it bright and cheerful,' the manager told them. 'Times are depressing enough. What's the name – Marcel? I hope you don't need to read the music, Marcel, because – no offence – I don't want to have the lights on you. But you'll do all right, *chérie*, nice frock. Silk? We must be paying you too much, ha ha.'

The club was decorated with a few balloons and streamers, and a banner saying 'Happy New Year 1934'. It was too early to be full, and the guests were attending to their drinks and conversation. Katya and Le Nain took their places and she began singing to this uninterested audience.

She was part way through her fourth song when she noticed the entrance of two young men and their girlfriends. The boys she recognized as Sasha Zhivago and his friend Constantine. The party had been drinking and, although it was still relatively early, Sasha was boisterous and unsteady on his feet. Commanding champagne from a passing waiter, they took a table near the stage and began to converse noisily.

The song finished without applause. Distracted by the noise, Le Nain did not continue. Sasha was saying:

'Nonsense! The Holy Spirit proceeds only from the Father.'

'From the Father *and* the Son,' replied Constantine. '*Filiusque*.'

'The Roman Church added those words to the Creed!'

'Rubbish! They were always there, in intention at least.'

'Rubbish to you too!'

'We'll ask the waiter to arbitrate. Waiter! Does the Holy Spirit proceed from the Father and the Son or only from the Father?'

'Pardon, monsieur?'

'Another schismatic!' exclaimed Sasha and knocked his drink over. Ignoring the spill he leaned towards his partner and cooed:

'Vera – Verotchka – you tell us the answer.'

The girl replied calmly: 'The question makes no sense. What does "proceeds" mean? And how can anyone know the answer? You've had too much to drink.'

There followed an exchange about whether the boys had or had not drunk too much, during which Le Nain resumed his playing and Katya began a new song. All the while she kept an eye on the little group, astonished that they paid her no attention and did not recognize her. She admired the coolness and intelligence of the girl Vera. The behaviour of the boys she dismissed as idiotic.

Yet their idiocies were oddly in character. Hadn't Sasha claimed that he wanted to be a fool? Taking an unexpected break after the next song, she huddled with Le Nain in the cramped dressing area behind the stage where the dwarf smoked and a magician's assistant in a spangled dress was padding out her brassiere. This gave Katya time to wonder. What had the boys been talking about? A recondite piece of theology. Sasha reminded her of those strangely afflicted people who can perform mentally the most complex mathematical calculations but cannot read or understand the concept of money. In some societies they might be considered as touched by the Devil or by God. Katya, however, was more struck by their affliction, which prevented their talent from being put to any useful purpose.

'That Zhivago boy is going to the dogs,' remarked Le Nain scornfully. He examined the turnip watch he kept in his waistcoat. 'How are we for time? Ten o'clock. You'll get to your party before midnight.'

'Do you have any mascara?' asked the magician's assistant.

'Why don't you give the minister a miss?' suggested the dwarf. 'Come with me and Claudette here. We know a few places.'

423

'Thanks, but I have to go.'

The manager stuck his head around the door and called: 'Back on stage.'

They resumed their positions to find that Sasha and his friends had gone. Katya sang another few songs and then hurried to leave, Le Nain volunteering to accompany her until she could get a taxi. This was not easy because other New Year revellers were also looking for transport, and the dwarf kept urging her: 'Come and see how real people enjoy themselves instead of hoity-toity types like Kolya's new friends.'

'There's a taxi!' Katya cried as one came into view around the corner. 'I have to go,' she repeated to Le Nain and in a moment of affection kissed him on the forehead.

She was doing this when she caught sight again of Sasha's party. They were standing in the shadows on the other side of the road, the girls supporting Sasha, who was being sick.

After New Year the affair of the forged bonds issued by the municipality of Bayonne began to assume a higher prominence in the press, with *Action Française* setting the pace. The newspaper accused Albert Dalimier, the Minister of Colonies, of having promoted the purchase of the bonds, and produced two letters to prove the point. At the same time something of the history of the fraudster Stavisky was coming to light: in particular, that criminal proceedings had been outstanding against him for several years, but had been delayed by obscure processes within the law.

Curiously enough, both the Left and the Right found in this matter support for their respective positions.

Constantine, who was following the story in the press, telephoned to explain gleefully:

'Didn't I say that the affair would be laid at the door of this rotten government? Dalimier can't last, but getting rid of him won't solve the problem.'

Daniel was staying for a few days at the Zhivagos' and Constantine's call came through at breakfast.

'What do you think?' Sasha asked him.

'This Stavisky fellow can't have had his trial postponed for so long without the connivance of the police and the magistrates. For certain, it isn't the Minister of Colonies who has kept him out of gaol. Once their beloved police force comes under attack out of this affair, the Right will change its tune.'

It took Vera with her ruthless clarity to reconcile the contradictions.

'Robbery doesn't have any politics. I'm sure that Stavisky bribed both the Government *and* the police. So the Communists and the Leagues can each make what they want of it. The details don't matter – and certainly the truth doesn't. Stavisky will just be an excuse for an attack on the system.'

That Saturday saw Christmas Eve again, according to the Orthodox calendar. Presents were given and exchanged. Open house was kept, and Vera and her father called together with a major-domo-formerly-bishop, a car mechanic-formerly-physicist, and a boisterous man who claimed to have been an alcoholic in both Russia and France and asserted its merits as a stable occupation in uncertain times. They ate *pirozhkis* and mushrooms and *vatrushkies* and pickles. They drank vodka, plain and flavoured with berries or herbs. They sang carols by candlelight before the icons, and 'Bozhe Tsarya Khrani' before a portrait of the martyred Nicholas II. They read aloud a tale by Pushkin and told a story about Baba Yaga for the small children who were present. They swore undying love to each other – undying – undying – like Russia – undying – like Christ who died and is risen, truly risen.

Vera kissed Sasha in a dark corner, approaching him and crushing her breasts against him. She kissed him long and speculatively. Her face was flushed and her skin glowed. But her lips were dry, and after what seemed like an age of passion, she broke off suddenly and stalked away as if annoyed.

The following day they went to church. At Christmas even Countess Kalinowska was fervently Orthodox. Because Christmas with its evocations of past years was a reminder of all that had been lost, it could also be a time of ill-feeling. A favourite point of rancour was whether it was permissible for the Church in exile to acknowledge the Patriarchate in Moscow. The majority view, now represented by the Cathedral of St Alexander Nevsky in Paris, was that the Patriarchate was fatally compromised by the Bolsheviks. Tonya had her doubts on the subject for as long as the Patriarchate was correct in theological matters. Lydia Kalinowska, on the other hand, had no hesitations. 'Moscow is a contaminated well from which wholesome water may never be drawn. What do you think, Max?'

'I never give advice,' said Golitsin after a considered pause, as if the Patriarchate was wanting to invest money.

There was a gathering after church at the Zhivago house. Alexander Alexandrovitch was confined to his bedroom.

'He's dying,' said Countess Kalinowska to anyone who enquired. 'And the truth is, it's a mercy. His brain hasn't been clear these last two years.'

Tonya knew what Lydia was saying but, to anyone who asked, she said only that her father was not receiving visitors. In his lucid moments Professor Gromeko knew he was dying and was resentful, without feeling the need to be tactful. Tonya felt she had to protect him against the humiliation of senility or the loss of friends through an ill-timed burst of anger. She reduced the anger to religious terms. She thought he was angry because he would not fully admit his need for God at this time. He was angry because God had the temerity to place Alexander Alexandrovitch Gromeko in this mortal predicament, while all the time not existing.

As part of a tacit agreement with his mother, Sasha

broke away from the general gathering to visit the invalid. His grandfather was in a room lit only by the candles in front of the icons, besieged as it were by icons. His breathing was laboured. In the rest of the house songs were being sung.

Sasha crossed himself before the icon of Our Lady of Moscow. He knew the story of the photographer's colourist who had painted it and seemed to recollect its being done; but he knew too it could be a false recollection. Moscow was now so long ago that Sasha was no longer sure he was Russian. What did it mean to be Russian? If it was to have memories of the old Russian life, he did not have them. If it was to love the physical bones of a country – its shape, the play of light through the seasons, the cycle of buds breaking on the birch trees, the branches laden with catkins in the church at Whitsuntide, the blossom on the bird cherries, the forests and ripening fields of wheat, the snow – he did not have that, either. He knew only France with its fat land and intimate contours, its hot summers and mild rainy winters. He listened to adults in the hope of finding the essence of Russianness, and what he heard was fantasy and resentment: an endless poring over the past and a vision of the future that was of hatred and revenge. The adults talked of the Russian soul and compared it with the crass materialism of the French: even Maxim Yuryevitch, the reputed millionaire, described the French as gross in their peasant addiction to gold and lacking in any fine religious feeling. But what was this Russian soul? Sasha doubted it but did not want to let the idea go. If he had an image of himself, a programme for his life, it was to discover and refine that spark which was said to be present in every Russian and defined him as Russian. He saw that spark as one of sympathy and generosity – of love in short – and, though he saw it only with difficulty in the people around him, it was so attractive that he had to pursue it.

Now, in the dimness of the room, among the textbooks of biology and flora with the Cyrillic script on their

427

spines and the smell of their musty pages, he was with his dying grandfather, a representative of the old dead Russia, a learned man, gentle and kindly. If Alexander Alexandrovitch were to revive from his present illness, Sasha was resolved that, like a magician's apprentice, he would interrogate him for the secrets of the Russian life: the real life, undistracted by the myths of tsar and Holy Russia and the jingle-jangle panoply of émigré aristocrats and White colonels. He would ask his grandfather to explain to him the meaning of birch catkins and the ice at the turn of winter when it first formed across a running stream, grey and thin as gauze.

In the meanwhile, Kolya Safronov and his wife Katya had arrived. Kolya was still in his office clothes with ink on his cuffs and cigar butts stuffed into the pocket of his jacket. He had immediately gone into a private discussion with Golitsin, but everyone knew that it was to do with the Stavisky affair, as the matter was now being called. Countess Kalinowska was telling everyone in an offended moral tone:

'It's too bad of people to be prejudiced against Max simply because this Stavisky is also a Russian. The Widows & Wounded is a *patriotic* activity for France. Max has worked his fingers to the bone to help these unfortunates. Really people should be *forced* to invest as a matter of duty.'

However, it was known that among her audience, including those who claimed to agree with her, there were many who had not yet fulfilled their duty by investing.

Sasha came downstairs and saw Katya speaking with Cousin Aristide. Her hair had been elegantly cut and she was wearing a black cocktail dress. She was conventionally though not strikingly fashionable like Lydia, and he was disappointed. Why then did he want urgently to talk to her?

Tonya had been observing Lara's child, thinking of her in those terms. When Sasha moved in her direction, Tonya intervened to ask:

'How was your grandfather?'

'Sleeping.'

'Is that all you can say? Sleeping? You should keep him company.'

'I don't think he knew I was there.'

Tonya could not prevent him from talking to Katya. She searched for Vera, looking for her support, but could not see her. In frustration and anxiety she said: 'I'd better see to your grandfather, then. I just wish these people would go!'

Sasha helped himself to a drink and Cousin Aristide made way for him so that he could speak with Katya. She took him by surprise by commenting mildly: 'Your mother doesn't like me.'

'No, it's not that. I think she does like you. She . . . My grandfather is very ill.'

'I'm sorry,' Katya answered sincerely.

'He's old,' said Sasha, and added frankly: 'He may die. And I've never really talked to him.'

'About what?'

'Russia. What was it really like? Are the books correct? Tolstoy, Chekhov? Here I am, supposed to be Russian, and we're speaking French because I'm more comfortable speaking French.' Around them the hubbub of voices was mostly in Russian: the only other language being English, from a jazz record played by Lydia Kalinowska, who was dancing with Alain Duroc.

Katya did not like his speaking of age or of Russia. Suddenly she was reminded of Lotte whom she had abandoned when she fled. How appalling! How could she have forgotten Lotte, to whom she had sworn undying memory in her heart? The pang was sharp, but like so much else must be suppressed.

She said cruelly: 'Why are you interested? It's all romantic nonsense. We're all too concerned with the practicalities of life to worry about Soul.'

'I worry about it.'

'But you want to be a fool like Prince Mishkin. You told me so.'

429

'And you want?'

'To survive. I don't care whether I'm useful or wise – those are luxuries.'

Sasha asked impetuously: 'Why don't you leave Nikolai Afanasitch? He doesn't make you happy.'

'I don't expect to be happy. I don't even want to be in love. You love people and they die or go away. I was miserable as long as I tried to be happy with Kolya. Since I gave up that nonsense we have got along very comfortably. If I find someone who will make me more comfortable, then I shall leave him. It's a simple, rational calculation.'

'That's a terrible thing to say!' Sasha exclaimed.

'But it's how it is for most women most of the time. They fall out of love with their husbands and they live practical day-to-day lives. Men are slaves to sentiment, and much good it does their wives. None of their emotion is of any use in feeding, clothing and housing their families. And then men fall in love with their country or some great idea, and so they go off and fight wars and get killed. Their emotion is all self-indulgence.'

She was angry and trying not to be angry. She wanted to spare Sasha from her general contempt for men; though even that wish was to demean him as if he were a child. He had, she thought, no sense of the fragile compromises that bound the substance of life. He did not consider the danger to her of his efforts to deflect her from what he thought of as mistakes. Above all, it could never occur to him that her relationship with Kolya, for all its shabby self-interest, represented a victory over circumstances and not a defeat.

She asked: 'Are Princess Wanda and her husband here?'

'No. I think they're in Italy. Did you know that Prince Carlo is quite an important Fascist, a general or something?' Sasha laughed and his manner had become gay again. 'He seems so insignificant compared to his wife. They're an odd couple.'

'She adores him. He's a substitute for Mussolini.'

'I didn't know that. I thought he bored her. In fact he bores everybody. I've never seen a man so much ignored.'

'He does, but she's in love with his image and thinks the world regards him as a great hero and not as a small fat Italian. Lydia Kalinowska is in love with Maxim Yuryevitch for much the same reason. These superficial women are attracted by the surface of things. That's why they so often have bad taste.'

'Maxim Yuryevitch is very respected.'

'People think he's a crook. They respect him only so long as he doesn't get found out.'

At this Sasha's eyes switched to Golitsin, who was in a group with Cousin Aristide, Kolya and the usual politicians. Lydia was chatting with the fashionable women and his sister Masha, in a gorgeous frock, was listening attentively. There was a pause in the general conversation when Father Sergei called for attention and proceeded to recite a long Christmas prayer in Church Slavonic. When the blessing had finished, Sasha found that Katya had left his side and was no longer in the room. He had hoped to ask her when they might meet again.

At that moment Tonya came into the room. She was very pale and had been crying, but this in itself attracted no attention since she was hostess only by courtesy. Unable to address the whole gathering, she moved from group to group, waiting for a break in the various conversations. Then she told her guests apologetically that her father, Professor Gromeko, had just died.

Katya heard the news; and that night she cried over Fraulein Buerli, who would die and about whom no news would ever come.

On the day of the funeral it was cold and rainy. They sang 'Vechnaya Pamyat' over the open grave. Sasha shed tears and clutched the hand of the solemn but dry-eyed Vera. They sang 'Eternal Memory', conscious that memory was not eternal, and indeed could not be eternal or we should be borne down by inconsolable grief.

The wind blew and rattled the trees, and the few birds hopped with ragged feathers across the grass. The French, attending their own funerals, looked with distaste at the exotic, emotional Russians, and the latter, this time, returned their dislike.

The wind rattled the trees. What kind of trees? The mourners walked towards the motor cars. Sasha recognized the brittle elder, hung with swags of ear fungus. 'Come on, before it rains again,' said Cousin Aristide, who acted as marshal. And the other trees? He was not sure. 'Do we know who is travelling in which car?' Yew – willow – possibly, possibly. Small brown birds of uncertain species. 'You are all invited to the *pomeenki*.'

His grandfather had been a biologist. His father had written poetry imbued with a love of nature. And Sasha himself struggled to name the common hedgerow trees. Eternal memory. The naming of names, the stuff of memory was lost from generation to generation. How can I love Russia, when I can't name the flowers?

Sasha hated the wake. The mourners sang old songs and told old stories. They created the false Russia of exile, thinking that they were keeping alive the true. A tale of sentimental drunkards weeping over their dead mother. Eternal memory. Sasha waited until Vera and her father had left and then retired in disgust to his bedroom, where he spent the rest of the day.

He was angry with his grandfather for dying. He felt the guilty anger that the living have for the dead; for the dead always die inopportunely, before the things to be said are said, and the questions to be asked are asked; and, like thieves, they take away a portion of our memory; and their history, which is our history, is gone.

What was it like? What was it like? The dead do not say. Our memories are piled like grave-goods around them, the greedy dead: generations of memory, the sights, sounds, smells, textures of their stories. And for the exile it is worse, far worse: for the dead can steal our country.

Sasha prowled the upper floors of the house. He entered his grandfather's room, which was still impregnated with the chemicals of death. He fingered Alexander Alexandrovitch's textbooks; opened the case of biological slides and ran some under the brass microscope; examined the dry plant specimens and the curious contents of jars; read inscriptions in unknown hands. In a drawer he found an album of photographs with the studio labels gummed to the backs, bearing addresses in Moscow. Was it still possible to obtain 'Fine Portraiture in the Modern and Classical Style' from Oblomov & Son at 47 Minskaya Street? Were Klugman & Krestinsky still importers of German textbooks, 'Mail orders only – specifying half-calf or cloth binding'?

Among the photographs was one of Sasha's father, taken at the time of his betrothal to Tonya. The image gave his clothes the look of shabbiness, and his face an expression of bafflement. He stood with Tonya against a background of unnameable trees and was in every aspect of his appearance something other than a poet. Had he laughed and said, self-deprecatingly, that he always took a bad picture? Straightened his tie and asked: do you want me like this? Or like this? Was a bird (also unnameable as to species) singing in the treetops? And had they swayed in the wind?

Sasha sought refuge in a Maigret novel. He was in his room. Night had fallen when he heard a stone clack against the window glass. Looking out into the garden, he saw a dark figure trying to attract his attention by waving a cigarette lighter. He went downstairs and into the garden, where he found Constantine.

'What on earth are you doing here?' he asked. 'Come on in.'

Constantine stayed shivering in the darkness. 'I'll tell you, but I won't come in. Can we go into your conservatory? Oh, by the way, I'm sorry to hear your grandfather has died.'

'I don't know whether it's open. I haven't got a key, not on me.' But in fact the door was unlocked.

A storm lamp hung just inside. Constantine lit it. He held it up to his face and Sasha could see a graze and a livid bruise. Constantine giggled and fumbled for his cigarettes.

'My arm isn't too good either, but I don't think it's broken. Am I dirty?'

'Filthy.'

Inspection revealed a tear in his trousers and general dirt about his clothes.

Sasha asked: 'Who did it?'

'The police!' Constantine laughed. 'Could you help me with a light – my wrist seems . . . Oh, thanks!' He inhaled deeply. 'I was too busy turning a kiosk over and didn't see the swine. God, you should have been there, Sasha! But I'm scared of going home until I get cleaned up and I don't know if the police have my name. There were hundreds of arrests!'

In the garden was a pump. They filled a watering can and Constantine used a handkerchief to wash his face and sponge his clothes.

'How do I look?'

'Not exactly beautiful.'

'No? Well, it will have to do, unless you can lend me a suit. I promise to return it.'

'You're taller than I am.'

'Ah, well, I suppose I'll have to take my chances. The magistrates are patriotic, so I don't suppose anything really bad will happen if I'm caught.'

'What were you doing?'

'I was with the Camelots. We were protesting against the murder of Stavisky.'

'I thought he'd committed suicide?' Sasha had read the report. The fraudster had gone into hiding in a chalet near Chamonix and shot himself.

'Don't be naive. Stavisky was the only one who knew the full story. The Government had to have him killed to save itself. Dalimier has resigned, and you don't suppose he's the only minister involved, do you? They've arrested Dubarry, which only goes to show that the whole affair is a conspiracy of the Reds and the Jews.'

The following evening Sasha and Constantine were near the Boulevard Raspail. Sasha was meeting Daniel, Yvonne and Vera at their usual haunt, but Constantine was not going to the café. The Camelots were gathering at their rallying point in the boulevard with the intention of making a further demonstration against the Government, and he planned to join them.

'I told my father what happened,' he said. 'When it came down to it, I couldn't think of a plausible excuse. He knows my politics and all he had to do was read the paper to put two and two together.'

The newspapers had reported the riot: it was the second similar incident in three days. The right-wing Leagues had marched from the Boulevard St Germain into Place de la Concorde and attempted to cross the river to demonstrate in front of the Palais Bourbon. However, they had been stopped by the police and Republican Guard and fighting had broken out. As to whether the violence was started by the police or the demonstrators, and the relevance of the incident to the Stavisky affair depended on the politics of the newspaper. But all were agreed in disbelieving the official account of Stavisky's death.

Sasha asked: 'What did your father say?'

'He said, "Good for you, my boy! Anything that gets these scum out of office is justified." What do you make of that? Parents complain about us, yet they're so inconsistent! It's enough to make one stay at home and read a good book. Why don't you come with me?'

'I've promised to meet Vera.'

'And Coën?'

'And Daniel – yes.'

'Oh well, it's up to you, I suppose.'

When they parted, Sasha saw his friend join a group of other youths and they began singing:

> *Ça ira, ça ira, ça ira.*
> *Les députés à la lanterne*
> *Ça ira, ça ira, ça ira*
> *Les députés on les pendra!*

The street seemed filled with the berets of the Camelots and now and again the same cry went up:

'Let's hang the deputies!'

Was the Stavisky affair a conspiracy of the Reds and the Jews?

'It has nothing to do with the Jews, or the Reds, for that matter,' said Daniel. 'You don't suppose that it's the working class that's been investing in Stavisky's dud bonds, do you? Use your common sense! Since when has the Left been involved in financial manipulation? For one thing, we don't have the accountants.'

He had a copy of the *Canard Enchaîné*, in which there was a cartoon showing two men in evening dress walking arm in arm in friendly fashion. The caption read: 'Monsieur Chiappe feels Stavisky's collar'.

Yvonne this evening was lively enough to ask: 'Who is this Chiappe?'

'He's the Prefect of Police,' Vera told her a little bad-temperedly, as if embarrassed at her friend's ignorance. 'According to the paper he was a friend of Dubarry and knew Stavisky. The inference is that Chiappe was protecting Stavisky and preventing his trial from being heard.'

'That's what happens under this stinking system!' said Daniel vehemently. After this he no longer wanted to talk about politics. Instead he made amorous advances to Yvonne, who responded eagerly. Sasha looked to Vera, but she simply smiled.

They could not trust the buses because of the disturbances. There was confusion in the streets and knots

436

of rioters running to or from the demonstration. Here and there a squadron of Republican Guard sat in their capes on nervous horses, waiting for a command. Sasha was never short of funds and was happy to take Vera home by taxi. They had left Daniel and Yvonne drinking heavily.

Sasha was conscious that his relationship with Vera was evasively sexual. It was not that he was uninterested, but that her distance and ambiguity created a gap he found difficult to bridge. Under these circumstances a conversation about sex and one about politics are much the same thing. While they were waiting for a taxi, he asked:

'Do you think that Chiappe was protecting Stavisky?'

(*May I kiss you?*)

'Possibly –' she smiled '– who can tell? But I do know that this business is not simple politics, a matter of Right and Left. Stavisky was a thief: he didn't care who he worked with or whose money he stole. Action Française are against Dubarry because he's on the Left, but they support Chiappe because he's on the Right. Yet Chiappe and Dubarry know each other. It's not surprising: people like that make friends where they can. Chiappe must know a lot of people.'

Sasha had an embarrassing admission:

(*I want to touch your breasts.*)

'He's a friend of Maxim Yuryevitch. In fact, he's visited us several times. He used to flirt with Lydia Kalinowska.' Sasha could recall the Prefect of Police among the small group of Golitsin's friends who attended his parties and forever talked about money. Chiappe made a point of his elegant attire – so unlike a policeman. The cartoon of him in opera hat and evening wear was accurate.

Vera was amused. 'Did you know Stavisky?'

'It's possible. I can't remember. Max knows everyone, even the Communists.'

'That only goes to prove my point. It's the reason why the Leagues and the Communists are both attacking the

Government for the same cause. They can each twist the facts to suit their own case. The point is to bring down the system.'

'Isn't that what you want, too?'

They were still searching for a taxi, and Vera did an unexpected thing. She skipped lightly for a dozen paces or so and threw her arms and her face open to receive the cold night air. When Sasha caught her she was serious again and said:

'You absolutely don't understand me, do you? Never mind. Do I want to bring down the system? Well, this democracy of ours is rotten to the core, but I don't intend to demolish it: I'm merely an observer. But for us, any change is dangerous. Are you a French citizen?'

Sasha was surprised. 'Yes, of course. Cousin Aristide arranged it for us. Aren't you?'

She shook her head. 'A lot of Russian émigrés aren't. To become French, if it were possible, would mean admitting that we were never to go home. We're here as refugees, and that's the risk. If the regime is overthrown and replaced by a dictator, there's a chance that all foreigners will be forced to leave France.'

A taxi responded to Sasha's attempts to hail it. They got inside. Vera leaned against him in the darkness of the cab, and he supposed that he was expected to show some affection and so he ran his fingers through her hair. She allowed this but remained stiffly alert. Sasha decided that she was not indifferent to him even if this was all the demonstration of which she was capable. She said:

'I told my father I was going to the theatre with a friend.'

'Yvonne?'

'Don't be silly. Yvonne and Daniel aren't respectable: my father doesn't even know they exist. And he thinks that Constantine is a dangerous hothead – which is true.'

'Who, then?'

'You. You're respectable. My father has met you and thinks you're a polite, harmless boy. Also, he respects your money.'

438

Sasha did not know what to reply.

Vera examined her watch. She said: 'I'm eighteen years old. I think that at that age I should lose my virginity – what do you think? Have you ever been with a woman?'

'Yes.'

'Good. I understand it's painful the first time, but that afterwards it can be pleasurable even for a woman. Is that true?'

'Yes, I think so.'

She nodded and added solemnly: 'I don't want to become engaged. I like you, but I'm too young to make a decision. And at the moment all you do is live off your family's money, which may not last for ever.'

'That's true.'

Sasha redirected the taxi to an establishment that he and Constantine had visited several times under the tutelage of Golitsin. He discovered that, without the company of the financier, he was not recognized as a valued customer. However, the patron was willing to oblige him with a room. It was there that he and Vera completed their passionless consummation, and afterwards Sasha escorted Vera home. In the doorway of her apartment, she gave him a chaste kiss on the cheek, which pleased her father.

CHAPTER 17

RUBBISH AND NONSENSE

During those January days of 1934 the attention of France was focused on the Stavisky affair. Was it a scandal of the Left or the Right? The left-wing newspaperman, Dubarry, was arrested. On the other hand, Chiappe, the Prefect of Police, whose conservative credentials were impeccable, was impugned when the Chamber of Deputies appointed a commission of enquiry and proposed a reorganization of the police. Although there was a strong suspicion that Chiappe had directly or indirectly protected Stavisky, *Action Française* rushed to his defence, conveniently forgetting that it had itself first reported the affair and was still pressing for the culprits to be brought to justice. After the dismissal of the Minister for Colonies, the next to be accused was Raynaldi, the Keeper of the Seals.

'Chiappe is blameless,' affirmed Constantine. 'But in any case, who cares? We're moving towards a revolution and any tactics are fair. I like Chiappe. He has style! Did you ever see anyone who looked less like a policeman?'

They were at a dance hall with the girls, dancing to a jazz band. They drank too much and Sasha had a hangover the following morning which Masha was the first to point out, sneering:

'Who has been drinking too much wine, then?'

'You are drinking too much,' Tonya reproached him.

'No, I'm not. I have things on my mind.'

'Do you want to talk about them?'

'Of course not.'

He was struggling to understand the unsatisfactory relations he had with Vera. He was puzzled that he might have misconceived the nature of love and that the rational and bloodless exchanges between them were the sum and normality. In the nature of things, the particular leaked into the general and matters that at another time might have seemed simple were now also tainted with confusion. He was confused about politics and thought the subject more important to his happiness than it really was. It was obvious to him that the system was corrupt and should be brought down. The times called for a new Napoleon who could inject France with order and moral courage. But what was happening seemed to be no more than tawdry and cynical manipulation. France looked for a new Empire, but had found a new Directory.

Overnight a frost had gripped the garden. The yew tree stood as a dark sentinel over the white grass. The panes of the conservatory dripped from the heat inside. Sasha kicked morosely about the neglected areas, among the nettle and feverfew, the willowherb and dry web-hung stalks. Amidst the leaf-litter and empty snail shells he found a dead starling; he picked it up and examined its starspangled colours. The gardener, Antoine, moustachioed and wrapped in his blue overalls, watched from his hut and coughed his gas-cough.

Alain arrived. Sasha saw him through the window, speaking to his mother; and his heart lifted that here was someone he could talk to – and he was then depressed at the certain knowledge that Tonya was trying to suborn the Jesuit to her moral campaign.

'Sasha is drinking too much,' Tonya was explaining. 'I

can't control him. He has nothing to do. I've suggested that he work a little with Cousin Aristide or Maxim Yuryevitch, but he refuses. He has some idea that work is beneath him, that he's reserved for higher things.'

It seemed to her that the Jesuit looked at her tenderly – in a way that Father Sergei would not.

'He's a passionate boy. Wasn't his father a poet?'

'Yes. But Sasha has never shown any inclination.'

'No. Instead he wants to do something more difficult, absurd even. It would only occur to an adolescent boy that he could shape his life as if it were a poem.'

The Jesuit lifted Tonya's hands and held them. Tonya was conscious of how naturally the action came to him and of her own dry gestures. She knew that Yura's love for her had broken upon her lack of inner poetry. Perhaps that was what Lara had. And the woman who was never very distant from her thoughts – Lara's child.

Alain kissed her on the forehead. 'I'll speak to him.'

He went into the garden and found Sasha with his hands in his pockets lounging in conversation with the crippled gardener. The latter was content to accept a cigarette and return to his chores, leaving the priest and the boy to pace among the parterres. Inevitably, they first discussed politics.

'Will the Government fall?' Sasha asked.

'Certainly.'

'And will there be a revolution?'

'I doubt it. The Leagues are too disorganized to make a revolution. For a revolution of the Right to succeed it has to be led by a great man. Not necessarily a good man – he could be a tyrant. The leaders of the Leagues are too absorbed in petty squabbles and shabby dealing to accomplish anything great.'

'Then when will it happen?'

'Soon. Somewhere there is a new Napoleon, quietly studying mathematics or engineering, or who knows what? He can feel the stirrings within him, but is waiting for his opportunity. Why don't you work for your cousin or Max until the time comes for you to go to the Sorbonne?'

'They're only interested in money.'

'It's very important. The France of Louis XVI fell because the public finances collapsed. If the King had studied money instead of being a locksmith, he would have kept his head.'

Sasha laughed.

'I'm serious,' said Alain. 'Great men aren't made out of dreams. They have concrete talents. They know how to organize. They discipline themselves. Did you know that Herr Hitler is a vegetarian?'

'You approve of Hitler?'

'I approve of his single-mindedness. He broke a system that was as confused and corrupt as ours, because he was determined and he organized himself to do it. You shouldn't drink so much.'

'Russians are great drinkers!' said Sasha boastfully.

'Russians are great fools. The Tsar and Kerensky were both well-meaning men who achieved nothing. It took a determined Jew like Trotsky and a criminal like Lenin to make something of the country. The world should be spared Russian poets and dreamers.'

Later that day Sasha told his mother that he would speak to Maxim Yuryevitch and take a temporary job as a clerk to Golitsin et Cie.

On 27 January 1934, Chautemps' government resigned and Daladier was asked to form a new administration. He sought to broaden his base within the Chamber of Deputies, but the price of the Left's support was the dismissal of the Prefect of Police. This was unacceptable to the Right.

On 2 February, Daladier received a dossier proving to his satisfaction that Chiappe had indeed been involved with the fraudster Stavisky. Being astute, rather than dismissing the Prefect of Police, Daladier sought to move him out of harm's way by conferring on him the questionable honour of Resident General in Rabat. This proposition was put to Chiappe the following day. The latter complained that he was suffering from sciatica and declined to go to Morocco. The conversation took place by telephone on Paris' ramshackle system and resulted in confusion. Did Chiappe say that he would be 'in the street' demonstrating against Daladier's government or 'in the street', destitute after years of faithful service ('destitute' being an emotive rather than accurate term – Chiappe being rich enough for his needs)? At all events, the Prefect of Police was out of office. And on the next day, a Sunday, the Leagues demonstrated in force to support their abused hero.

Constantine was beside himself with anxiety and excitement. His father had had second thoughts about his son's participation in the disturbances and exiled him for his own safety to their house in the country. So Constantine missed the Sunday demonstrations and was living on rumour and the reports given on the radio. Sasha visited him for the weekend and, in order to work off their nervous energy, they went horse-riding.

Sasha rode in the dogged, competent fashion with which he did most things. He took his mount at a careful pace through the muddy lanes and the village and eased it into a trot when he was clear. By contrast, Constantine rode with rough flair and little skill; he was inconsiderate of his horse and indifferent to its nervousness. Having started bad-temperedly, he forced the beast at a gallop and seemed content to leave his companion behind.

This was rolling wheat country. Beyond the village the fields rose to a gentle height that was hazy in the damp February air. Here there was a stand of elms in which crows had made their nests. A breeze blew over the height and the birds took off into it, wheeled and returned to their nests in a quarrelsome mood.

When Sasha arrived at the trees, Constantine was staring distractedly into the aquatinted sky, where rags of cloud scudded before the wind. The gallop across the heavy earth had bespattered his horse with mud and the animal was in a sweat and restless under the rein.

'You should get off and calm him down,' Sasha suggested.

'Listen to them!' said Constantine. 'Don't they sound like politicians?'

'The crows?'

'Damn this horse! Yes, of course the crows. Politicians or women. In fact, just like my mother and my aunts! Is it going to rain? That's all I need! Do you like women? Or girls?'

'Yes.'

'Yes, rain, or yes, women?'

'I think it will rain. And yes, I do like women. My God, but you're in a strange mood.'

Constantine examined Sasha closely and answered abruptly: 'I probably am. Sorry.'

They dismounted. Beneath the trees the ground was littered with detritus from the nests: droppings, feathers, eggshells and dead chicks. In the damp places grew celandines, and cuckoopint was beginning to unfold in its secretive way, as if hiding and disclosing its sex.

'Why do you like women?' Constantine asked.

'I'm not sure. I know why I'm attracted to them, but I suppose that only confuses the issue. It's not obvious why we should like them, or them us. I think they understand more than we do?'

'What do they understand?'

Sasha grinned: 'How would I know? If I did, then they wouldn't understand *more*, would they? Do you like women?'

Constantine shrugged and replied dully: 'Well enough. But they're not as they appear. Whoever thinks that women are emotional is a fool.'

'Why do you say that?'

'Because their emotions – if you can call them that – are different from ours. Women never experience pure feeling. Anything higher, anything abstract has no appeal to them. Nature, country, art – all meaningless. Even religion. Think of St Catherine of Sienna. She wanted to

445

sleep with Jesus and get the Virgin to do her the occasional favour, nothing more. And that's because the emotions of women are all directed at relationships: fathers, brothers, sisters, lovers, what-have-you – not forgetting God. It's all tactics with them. That's why they're so changeable: first trying one thing and then another, whatever works. And behind every outburst their mean little minds are calculating the effect.'

He paused and gazed out over the countryside. The view extended over miles of dormant fields and a soft sky barred with shadows of rain. It was a sour day when winter is at its most characterless and miserable, but the boys ignored this in the cold air and buffets of wind. Instead they felt a dreaminess of well-being and made out of the grey landscape something of mystery.

Constantine said: 'Some of the earlier Christians believed that women didn't have souls.' He glanced at Sasha. 'I'm inclined to agree with them. Men have souls. Russians have – what's that word you use?'

'*Dusha*.'

'*Dusha*? *Dusha* – *dusha*! – Shower me in *dusha*! Oh, God! – Is Russia like this? Wheat? Isn't that what you grow?'

Sasha searched his memory painfully.

'I don't know. Sometimes I think I remember, but I can never be sure. There are birch forests, and firs, but that may be just something I've read. The cottages are made of wood – I think.'

'How can you love a country you don't know?'

'I'm not certain that I do love it. If I do, then it's the Russia I've got out of books.'

'Books!' exclaimed Constantine. 'I hate Russian novels. They're always trying to teach you something. And there aren't very many jokes.'

'I sometimes think that Russia isn't a place. It's words and images. It's . . . *dusha*! Have you ever been to one of our churches? The services are interminable. They numb you. Prayers, chants, incense, icons. After a while you forget who you are, where you are. You don't listen. You don't see. There's too much. Your senses retreat and you simply give in to the majesty. That's when you are touched by – God, I suppose.'

Constantine asked seriously: 'And that's how Russia is?'

Sasha was uncomfortable. 'Perhaps. I can't tell. It frightens me sometimes. It could all be an illusion.'

'Well, I believe in illusions,' Constantine answered firmly. 'I even believe in nonsense – in fact, the more nonsense the better! Did you know that Action Française supports the restoration of the Bourbon kings? I heard that, after this Stavisky business started, Pujo and some of the other leaders went to Brussels to see the Count of Paris and get the support of the royal family. Have you ever heard of anything more absurd? Me, I'm in favour of it. I know that the universe is all mud and atoms and that people shit and piss and rut like animals. But what good is all that rational knowledge to me? I want something that makes me come alive! Do you know –' he murmured in the face of Sasha's scepticism '– what the difference is between human beings and animals? No? No? It isn't intelligence or speech or culture or tools: the chimpanzees have all of those; the matter is only one of degree.'

'So what is the difference?' asked Sasha, smiling.

'It's nonsense! Animals are deadly realists. They eat, they sleep, they fornicate, they own no property and they believe only in what they can touch or see – in fact, a bit like the Communists. Only human beings believe in complete rubbish! No chimpanzee is in favour of the Bourbon restoration! So I am. At least, until I can find a better great idea.'

The shadow of rain crept across the muddy field and glistened on flints turned by the plough. In a second it was falling on the stand of elms whose bare branches offered little shelter. Sasha and Constantine stood with their backs to adjacent trees and the rain streaming down their faces.

'Wonderful!' exclaimed Sasha, licking the moisture from his lips.

Constantine made a mad dash out of the trees and capered in the mud before rushing back panting to resume his position.

'God, this is stupid!' he said joyfully.

'Long live the Bourbons!' cried Sasha.

'Long live the Bourbons! Down with communists, anarchists, republicans, chimpanzees, and all intellectuals whatever their colour! Long live rubbish and nonsense! Long live the Camelots and their jerry-built politics!'

'Rubbish and nonsense!'

'I think I'll get tattooed,' said Constantine. The rain had passed over. He let his head fall on his chest and shook his hair. 'I was in Marseilles once. The sailors there have marvellous tattoos. God, Sasha, but you're lucky!' he added morosely.

'Why?'

'Because you have your sainted tsar to believe in and a sporting chance that the Bolshevik riffraff will be overthrown and your people can go back to Russia. But what can I believe in? The Count of Paris!'

'And rubbish and nonsense.'

'That's true. What do you think of this Hitler fellow?'

'I haven't thought about him.'

'He seems to be doing the Germans some good. But he looks like a railway clerk. I don't know. What to do? What to do?'

He went over to the horses.

'We'd better take them back, get them dried off and rubbed down and their faces in a nosebag. Though I think that Tonnerre here is bound for the glue pot if he doesn't learn to do what I want. Whoa, boy! Easy – easy!'

Sasha calmed his own mount. Constantine seemed reluctant to leave. He said:

'We'll be friends for ever, won't we, Sasha?'

'Yes, I'm sure we will. Why not?'

'I don't know. Yes, I do! Because we'll become dull and respectable, and instead of rubbish and nonsense there'll be wives and families.'

'We can still be friends.'

'Not like this.'

'I don't see why not. I don't intend to be dull and respectable.'

'Nor me. I think I'll die young, if I can find something ridiculous enough to die for. Maybe God. I'm seriously thinking of becoming a priest. Don't look so strange. I didn't say I was going to become good or virtuous, merely a priest.'

Sasha was restraining his laughter. 'A tattooed priest?'

'Yes! With a splendid picture of the Blessed Virgin on my chest! And the Devil on my arse!'

They fell about laughing. Then, without warning, Constantine gripped Sasha by the shoulders, smiled at him beatifically and kissed him on the lips.

In silence they mounted the horses.

That Sunday, Katya and her husband dined with Golitsin and Countess Kalinowska at a restaurant on the Left Bank. Afterwards, they found themselves in a taxi driving along the Quai d'Orsay, which was crowded with youths. The Croix de Feu was demonstrating against the fall of Chiappe.

The day being cold, Kolya was wearing a homburg hat and a cashmere overcoat with an astrakhan collar. His complexion was naturally sallow and he still wore a moustache.

When the taxi was brought to a crawl to avoid hitting any of the figures who were spilling into the road and running among the cars, Kolya's appearance caught the attention of one of the youths. He pressed his nose against the window glass and then called to his companions.

'Hey, we've got a Jew here!'

A number of the boys broke out of the crowd and gathered around the taxi which was now forced to stop.

Kolya tried to urge the driver on, but he refused and abandoned the cab, leaving his passengers. The boys began to rock the cab, all the while shouting: 'Jew! Jew! Jew!' Kolya tried to ignore them. He stared straight ahead in silence.

'Jew! Jew! Jew!'

Katya could not maintain her husband's coolness. The suddenness of the assault on the car, the rattle and clamour of the boys, the irrational hatred in their faces terrified her. Without realizing that she was unconsciously adopting their prejudices, she shouted back: 'We're Christians! You fools, we're Christians!'

And as suddenly the attack ceased, the boys began to laugh and shake their heads as if amazed, and they wandered off down the road chanting their songs and fooling about in horseplay.

For a minute Katya and her husband remained in silence in the taxi. But then, the driver not returning, Kolya said calmly: 'We'll walk. We may find another cab.' They set out and Katya stumbled, finding her legs weak and her body shaking from the shock. Kolya took her arm firmly and escorted her to the pavement.

To her surprise, among the spectators of this scene was Daniel Coën. Smoking a cigarette he came over and asked: 'Is there anything I can do to help?'

Kolya did not know him despite their having lived in the same apartment house, but Katya, with a tremor still in her voice, briefly introduced them.

'You can find us another cab,' Kolya said briskly. To his wife he said: 'I promised to call on Aristide this afternoon. We'll be late.'

Katya shook her head and answered haltingly: 'I can't – I just can't.'

Kolya was looking at his watch. The action of the youths seemed to have made him more determined to meet his appointment, as if to prove how unaffected he was. Noticing this, Daniel volunteered:

'I'll take you home, if you like.'

'Will you be all right?' asked her husband. Pompously, he gave Daniel his card. 'Thanks for your help. If there's anything I can do for you, you know where to find me.'

Amused, Daniel pocketed the card and offered his arm.

They found a café and Daniel seated his companion and ordered two brandies. Faced by Katya's silence he made conversation.

'You're looking well. Life has obviously treated you kindly since the Rue Mouffetard. It must be a lucky apartment; once one lives there, one becomes rich. Le Nain still talks about you. He's found a new girlfriend, a great fat woman. She smokes and drinks like a fish; and picks him up and shakes him whenever they quarrel. They're very happy together.'

'I said I was a Christian,' Katya murmured.

'Oh. I wouldn't worry about that. Some of my best friends . . .'

'I'm not a Christian. I'm not anything.' Katya was shaking and sobbing with shame.

They drank their brandies. Daniel said:

'These demonstrations can be frightening. I was frightened myself, but the Party wanted someone to keep an eye on that lot and report back. There's a crisis in the offing.'

'It was like Russia – the Revolution. I thought I'd forgotten. I was very small.' Katya was astonished at her own reaction. Although it had been understandable she thought it showed weakness, and she had resolved never to show weakness in front of Kolya. She went on: 'Have you noticed that in a sudden crisis we react like children? It was the memory – the memory. If it had been something else – something I hadn't experienced before – then perhaps I would have behaved differently.'

Daniel listened sympathetically. He had no expectations of courage in others, no more than was needed to face the ordinary hardships of life such as that of his parents. Seeing Katya's determination to find a more than ordinary courage, he admired her for it. And for the fact that she was beautiful, though he made no mental connection between these two aspects of his appreciation.

Katya was made a little light-headed by the brandy. She felt an inappropriate obligation to be sociable. She asked Daniel about his history. He answered laconically while watching her with care. She nodded at each point, forgetting that she had heard most of the story from Sophie, his mother. When Daniel said he was a Communist, it sounded entirely reasonable. He might have said he was a mass-murderer and been received on the same terms. Daniel smiled, but with no lessening of his admiration for her.

'You are the girl that Sasha met in Nice, aren't you?' he said. 'I remember asking you once, and you denied it.'

Yes, she told him. It had been her. It was all silliness. How lightly she could say this! And then:

'I don't want to be loved!' she answered, distressed but suddenly sober.

'Why not?' asked Daniel as intensely as if he had proposed love, and half-aware of the fact and disorientated by not knowing how the conversation had come to this result.

'It's too cynical. No, that's wrong. I mean it's an illusion. Even sincerity isn't a test. We are all such self-deceivers.'

She shook her head slowly several times. Daniel did not like this. He had recovered from his own slight shock and saw a taint of hysteria in this quiet rhythmic gesture. Having normally no thoughts of love, and being of an analytical turn of mind, he looked coldly on her now.

But her fascination. Ah, her fascination! Even when he had taken her home and was returning alone to the Rue Mouffetard and mentally reporting to the Party on the activities of the Leagues today, her image intruded on his thoughts. She had said:

'Love is all chemistry and circumstance. Darwin and geography. Even your Marx could explain it better than any novelist. Boy meets girl. A thousand years of wars and economics explains why *this* boy meets *that* girl, and a few glands complete the transaction. Isn't it pathetic?' she asked, and repeated: 'Isn't it?'

Yes, it was pathetic. Daniel agreed with every word of her analysis, and found that he did not want to agree.

Katya found herself alone in the apartment. Her husband had not returned from his visit to Aristide Krueger. She put a record on the new radio-gramophone and sat in a new comfortable chair from which she could assess the art-deco splendour of the room. Yes, Kolya had been successful, and, more modestly, she was content with her teaching. They were prosperous.

The mob had called Kolya a Jew. He was not, though that hardly mattered. She had followed the story of the Stavisky affair in the newspapers without thinking that she would be in any way affected; but the behaviour of the hooligans had proved that nothing could be counted on as safe or stable and that even France – fat, rich France – rested on quaking foundations. She shivered at the recollection and poured herself a drink from the American cocktail cabinet that Lydia, on the advice of Princess Wanda, had insisted they instal. But now the drink made her melancholy.

What had she achieved beyond the comforts of her home, which the hooligans had proved to be as frail as anything in Russia? She remembered her mother and their first home with Viktor, the arrival of the captain and his Tatar horsemen, and the disappearance of Tanya – oh, Tanya! It was possible for everything to happen again. In her heart she felt a terror before the impermanence of things. And more: before the impermanence of people. Zhivago – Tanya – her mother. Love did not anchor them. A step through a door or round a corner and they could disappear into a world where she was not.

Another drink. A step to the window to peer into the street and see the passers-by on their way to their

453

own disappearances. Smooth her dress and think of how much it cost from her own earnings, not Kolya's, so no hostage there; and, if he didn't come back, what did it signify? That boy, Daniel Coën, had been attracted by her. He did not want to be, but she had seen that he was. However, each was too cautious to fall into the trap of mutual attraction. Unlike Sasha, who was by his own admission a glorious fool.

Her fingers scratched at fly specks on the glass. A handkerchief rubbed at grease marks.

But to give no hostage to another person, must she be barren? It seemed that there was no other way. Her sexuality was a traitor to her. She could feel it weeping like a fretful child, that has to be denied. A child that pursues the gaudy, the glamorous and the immediate. Of course it has to be denied. Sad, weeping child.

Kolya came through the door, cheerful after meeting Aristide Krueger and apparently unconcerned at the incident in the Quai d'Orsay. Katya saw starkly that his only object in life was to make money. No matter.

'I see you got home safely,' he said.

'Yes, I'm fine, thank you,' she answered coldly.

None the less she was glad to see him.

According to rumour, the Government was taking steps to protect itself. In the suburbs an armoury of machine guns and tanks was being assembled. The spahis and Senegalese troops were being mobilized.

'They'll turn the niggers on their own people!' Constantine sneered.

On the Monday evening Constantine appeared at Sasha's house and asked for a bed for the night.

'What are you doing in Paris?'

'I couldn't stay away. My father doesn't know I've left. The Leagues have ordered a big demonstration tomorrow. One more push and we'll bring down the whole rotten mess! You must come!' he urged. 'For one thing, you can make sure that I don't get into trouble. If you're there, I shall be as demure as a virgin.'

Sasha agreed. There had been so many demonstrations that he could not allow them to pass without his witnessing at least one. They kept their intentions secret from Tonya, who accepted it as quite natural that Constantine might stay.

The great riot of 6 February 1934 unrolled in an accidental fashion as though, at the point of decision, neither Right nor Left could face the prospect of forcing the issue. Until 6 February, *Action Française* had promoted the riots which brought down the government of Chautemps only to replace him with the equally odious Daladier. But none of the disturbances was likely to destroy the hated system unless it resulted in the seizure of the Palais Bourbon and the key ministries and was accompanied by a definite plan under which the leaders of the Right were available to exploit the success and form a revolutionary government. This had not been the case at any time in January. On 6 February, few of the leaders of Action Française or the other Leagues were with the units they nominally led and no communication network had been created to allow them to control events. Had the Palais Bourbon been taken by the mob, no-one would have known what to do with it. Like Tolstoy's great men of history, the leaders of the Leagues ordered the demonstration because their followers required it; it would have happened whether they had ordered it or not; and it unfolded in a manner that bore little relationship to their orders or intentions. Accordingly, the Leagues deployed in a ring at various distances from the Palais Bourbon, each largely ignorant of the location of the others so that co-ordination was impossible. In addition, a huge, disorganized mob, having received no orders, gathered in the Place de la Concorde and the Tuileries gardens. And beyond this, the Communists and their supporters grouped on the Champs Elysées between the Rond Point and the Grand Palais, with the object not of fighting their opponents in the Leagues but of joining them in the assault on the Palais Bourbon.

The leaders of Action Française rightly anticipated that any attempt to storm the Palais Bourbon from the direction of the Place de la Concorde would be blocked by police and troops at the bridge between the two. They therefore gave verbal orders for their main force to assemble on the Left Bank, in the boulevards St Germain and Raspail, from where they would advance on the War Ministry in the Rue Ste Dominique. Furthermore, they dispatched a small party of Camelots to observe events at the Hôtel de Ville, where the Jeunesse Patriotes, with an eye to the precedent of the Commune, contemplated proclaiming the overthrow of the Republic.

These orders were not carried out, nor could they be, since no staff-work existed to communicate them to the supporters. The greater part of the Camelots remained ignorant of their leaders' intentions and joined the general mass in the Place de la Concorde.

Constantine had been at his parents' house in the country and so did not know the designated assembly points or the time when the demonstrations were supposed to start – though the latter, too, was outside the control of the leaders and would occur spontaneously once a critical mass of rioters had collected. The Chamber of Deputies was fixed to sit at three o'clock in the afternoon to hear Daladier present his cabinet. In so far as any factor dictated the timing of the riot, it was the common desire of both deputies and rioters to eat a good lunch.

Over lunch Tonya commented: 'You seem very excited about something.' The boys exchanged secret smiles. Dimly suspecting that something was wrong, she asked: 'Have you told your parents that you are staying with us?'

'They know,' Constantine lied solemnly.

'Do you have some plans for the rest of the day?'

'Just messing about,' said Sasha.

Once in his room, he said: 'I hate telling lies to my mother.'

456

'Really?' was the answer. 'I lie to mine as a matter of course. People who ask questions they aren't entitled to must expect to be lied to. In any case, "messing about" is more or less what we'll be doing, so strictly, you didn't tell a lie.'

'Do you intend to be a Jesuit when you become a priest?'

'Jesuits don't lie. They merely bully the truth into a corner and argue until it surrenders. Do you have a knife?'

'What for?'

'Self-defence.'

Sasha was alarmed. 'I thought the idea was just to watch and stay out of trouble?'

Constantine was in an unreasonable mood. The uncertainty he had displayed when they were horse-riding had gone. The prospect of action had created an unreflective arrogance, a vanity even: he was combing his blond hair in front of the mirror and applying brilliantine.

'So we are. I said *self-defence*. You don't think that the Government is going to sit passively by, do you? What are you going to do when some big nigger soldier swings out of the trees and hits you with his club?'

'Run, if necessary,' said Sasha jokingly but firmly.

'Oh well, suit yourself.' Constantine produced a knife from his pocket. He opened the blade and admired it. Reassuringly he said: 'Don't worry, I don't really intend to use it. I'd be too scared. We're only doing this for a laugh. Rubbish and nonsense, eh? If a nigger soldier comes for me, I guess I'll just have to let him cook and eat me.'

Even so, Sasha was nervous. He was not frightened at the prospect of the riot, but like a soldier on the point of battle was wondering: how did I get here? What is the point of this? He felt at the same time an invincible desire to be there and the irresistible pressure of circumstance that would have forced him there even against his will. He remembered Prince Andrew, who had thought to turn the tide of battle at Austerlitz by seizing

457

the flag and advancing at the head of his regiment; and Napoleon, who had grasped his opportunity at Toulon. It was the characteristic of great men that, in the tumult of history, they recognized the defining moment in the chaos of events.

'You look thoughtful. What are you thinking about?' asked Constantine.

'Rubbish and nonsense,' Sasha replied. 'Shall we go?'

Constantine wore his beret and tucked into his pocket a brassard with an enamel badge that would identify him as a Camelot. He would put the armband on later. For the moment he suspected that in the confusion they might come across bands of Communists whom it would be wiser to avoid. Sasha carried no such insignia.

They took a bus a little distance, but public transport was disrupted by the disturbances so the boys continued on foot. The sky was full of grey lowering clouds and it would soon be dark.

In the Champs Elysées they came across the first of many gatherings. Under the aegis of the Communists, the Association Républicaine des Anciens Combattants was assembling behind its banners, demanding fair treatment for veterans. Instinctively the middle-aged and elderly ex-soldiers had formed ranks. They had dressed to display their pride. Their chests were armoured with rows of medals. Here and there among them Sasha could see the one-armed and the pale gas-victims and recognize the former officers and the cocky NCOs. There he is, a jaunty sergeant with thick moustache, who cajoles the others into line. Here limps a lieutenant of artillery with an artificial leg. And now see the broken-down *poilu*, who has been fodder first for the trenches and the unemployment queues, and now for the demonstration, and in a few years' time for the grave. The ex-soldiers are serious men and quiet. The catcalls are from the rowdy knots of Camelots who, like Sasha and Constantine, are making their way to the Place de la Concorde.

Traffic was now thin. The respectable citizenry avoided

the crowds of youths, but their faces showed awe and in many cases sympathy. Some of them gave money. Others voiced support. 'That's it, lads! Show the swine who are the masters!'

Constantine shouted:

'See! France is behind us! Long live France!'

The Camelots, now coalescing into larger groups but still incoherent, began a ragged chorus of their version of 'Ça Ira'. There was a great deal of laughter and good-natured banter. Crowbars and clubs began to appear and were dragged rattling along the pavement. A cheer went up when a kiosk was overturned.

By now the sun, which had been scarcely visible through the clouds, slipped below the horizon; the lamps were lit and a flock of starlings wheeled into the darkening sky. The Place de la Concorde was filling with a mass of people and a bus was burning by the obelisk. Gangs of youths swarmed over the terrace of the Tuileries, tearing up railings, benches and stones.

Having never experienced anything quite like this before, Sasha supposed that the mob shared some common plan that was unfathomable to him. He was squeezed against Constantine in the crush. Across the river he could see lights of the Palais Bourbon where the deputies were in session, and he supposed that the demonstration was moving in the direction of the bridge; but this movement, if it existed, was lost in the swirls and eddies within the mob itself so that, though he firmly desired to witness the happenings at the bridge, Sasha found himself driven towards the American embassy at the other end of the square. Pressured by the mass, the two boys became separated.

The crush by the embassy eased and the movement of the riot seemed to reverse. Where, before, Sasha had been pressed into the dense throng, it now opened up, and the square, instead of being packed, appeared spacious except by the bridge. Yet no-one had left: on the contrary, at every moment more people were arriving and the din of yells and chants was increasing. Sasha could not understand this phenomenon: this physical expansion and contraction that was unrelated to the numbers involved; nor the cries and noise which seemed to come from people other than those that he could see. In fact, where he was standing the demonstrators were in a relaxed, even playful mood, ignoring the distant mêlée with the police and instead standing in groups, chatting and smoking or listening to orators; even reading newspapers by the light of the burning bus. Yet this, too, was temporary.

At the bridge the police and troops were firing shots into the air. Sasha heard them as a dull crackling, remote and of no importance, but they provoked two opposite movements: a retreat of rioters from the bridge and a rush towards the bridge of those who were angered or wanted to see what was happening. And the sense of space, of which Sasha had been conscious only a moment before, vanished and he was stifled again by the weight of bodies.

New reinforcements arrived. A body of youths from Solidarité Française, who had assembled by the Opéra, entered the square from the Rue Royale and scattered with the bulk rushing towards the bridge. At the same time a drift of people came from the Rue de Rivoli, some of whom were injured. Sasha collared one of the new arrivals, who was exhausted and happy to pause and talk.

'We were at the Hôtel de Ville,' he said, 'but nothing much was happening; so we tried to cross the river at the Pont Solferino. But the police were ready for us. I saw dozens of people getting beaten up, and God knows how many dead.' He spoke quite evenly and then suddenly burst into angry tears. 'Bastards! Bloody murderers!' He wandered off, brandishing a stave, and the last Sasha saw of him he had halted to double-over and vomit and someone was shouting furiously: 'Not on my shoes, you idiot!'

Sasha was aware that he was not moving. He had been buffeted and spun round, crushed and released: but he remained in the same spot. He thought: I'm not here. This has nothing to do with me. In the darkness he could see the pulsations of the mob, but none of the movement, the shouts and cries, the explosion of firecrackers being thrown at the horses of the Republican Guard, the shots, had any visible relationship. Shots rang out and the mob did nothing. Silence, and the mob was retreating before nothing. It surged forward in response to no urging from its leaders. It ignored specific calls to attack. Now it was moving as a body towards the bridge. Next it was breaking into parts and the parts seemed self-contained, as if nothing that was happening had anything to do with them.

A second bus was on fire. The rioters had smashed the windows and put a torch to it. This was close to the American embassy (windows alight and the faces of prim attachés pressed against the glass) where Sasha was standing, but he did not notice it happening! It was already burning when he became vaguely conscious that he could read the slogans on the banners that had earlier floated like dark angels in the air. That explains it, he told himself, observing the bus without reflecting on the fact that it had been destroyed without his seeing it.

The veterans he had seen hours before in the Champs Elysées now arrived in a disciplined column. They looked at the riot but ignored it. Sasha could see the scorn on their faces. Intent on presenting a petition at the Elysée Palace, the column turned out of the square and advanced up the Rue Royale, harassed by the police but offering no violence. Sasha watched it go and so saw also for the first time that the Naval Ministry was ablaze and the firemen were trying to control the flames. Coolly they went about their work, paying no attention to the riot. It was as if scenes from different stories had become mixed: the disturbance in the square, the street jammed with the dense marching ranks of the veterans – and the firemen working.

Sasha decided to move closer to the bridge, where he could see better the object of the demonstrators. At this point in the confused rhythm of the riot it was possible to stroll across the square. Beyond the actual mêlée with the police, *gardes mobiles* and Republican Guard, exhaustion was settling on the rioters. Even those intent on joining the affray did not hurry. They walked. Those that had staves or pieces of railing trailed them or bounced them on the stones like a child beating a hoop. If invited they were happy to stop for a smoke or a chat; and then, as if workmen finishing a break, they shouldered their weapons and set to the task again.

Sasha looked for Constantine but could not see him. He halted. Here, closer to the centre of the tumult, he was surrounded by figures running to or from the mêlée or throwing missiles from a distance. He looked back at the fires by the obelisk, the American embassy and the Naval Ministry, and at the swirling pools of humanity. He saw now the accidental drama and choreography: a scene that was stage-lit by chance, in which the actors formed patterns that were unintended but were patterns nonetheless. He thought: how pointless – and how beautiful!

The veterans in their advance on the Elysée Palace were blocked by police and *gardes mobiles* and driven towards the Rue Richelieu. Thwarted and aimless, they drifted back towards Place de la Concorde. Daniel Coën had been among the band of Communists who had accompanied the former servicemen; but after reaching the Rue Drouot, he too made his way to the square, pausing only to sit and rest a while in the Tuileries gardens. Then, with no particular purpose, he pushed his way through the loose knots of people towards the bridge. It was as he was doing this that he saw Sasha.

'You look as if you're in a daydream,' he said, tapping Sasha on the shoulder.

'Oh, it's you. How are you? How are your mother and father?'

'I can't hear you!' Daniel shouted. A cry had gone up.

A Republican Guard had been thrown from his mount and the horse was running loose.

'I said: how are your mother and father? I haven't seen them in ages.'

'They're fine. And your mother?'

'Fine.'

'What are you doing here?'

'Just watching. I came with Connie.'

'That doesn't surprise me. These Fascist swine are about his size. But I thought you were a socialist?'

'I don't know what I am.'

'An effete bourgeois. Do you have a smoke? I'm so short of money I have to sponge cigarettes wherever I can. It's called Communism. And a light? Thanks. Hey! Who do you think you're pushing?' he snapped as someone brushed past heavily.

'Sorry,' apologized the stranger. He wore the armband of the Camelots and noticed Daniel's Communist badges. He asked Sasha: 'I don't suppose you could spare me one too?' Sasha gave him a cigarette. He lit it and inhaled deeply. He looked to the bridge and said, as if making a scientific assessment: 'One more push and I think we can shift those bastards. Then we'll have a few deputies swinging by their necks before the night's out. Well, see you around.' He trotted off towards the front.

'What a waste of time,' commented Daniel. 'They don't realize that history is set against them. If they win tonight, it'll only be to deliver the revolution to us on a plate.' He stubbed his cigarette. 'We can't hang around here. Fancy overthrowing civilization with me?'

'Why not?' Sasha laughed.

The two boys let out a loud ululation and began to force their way towards the head of the bridge.

Sasha had expected that here, face to face with the police and Republican Guard, the riot would display some purpose and order. Instead he saw the same confusion, but conducted at a furious pace like at the stirring

463

of an insects' nest. Instead of a co-ordinated attack by all the forces of the demonstrators, a body of youths would collect; then, as soon as it was large enough to sustain its own courage, it would charge the barricade, preceded by a volley of rocks and other missiles, and then retreat under pressure of water jets, gun fire and baton charges. The effort of resistance would draw out the defenders in a counter-charge on foot or horse; and, as this reached the mass of the rioters, so it too would lose cohesion, the horses would be panicked by firecrackers and flying stones, the police would find themselves outnumbered and exposed, and they too would retreat – an action which only encouraged the rioters as they regrouped. Between these sporadic mêlées, parties made forays to hurl more stones or to collect the dead and wounded who lay in the roadway.

Daniel looked about for a group to which they could attach themselves for the next assault. Sasha, seeing the dim silhouettes of men and horses, thought only: I'm here. It's not what I expected. But this is where France's destiny may be settled. He too looked about, but he was searching without knowing it for that mysterious person whose presence this night was fated to inspire the mob, so that it would carry the barricade and sweep on to the Palais Bourbon. He saw Constantine.

Constantine was squatting on the ground. His face was obscured by night but he recognized Sasha by the faltering light and said simply:

'They broke my damned arm. My right arm. They broke it! What am I going to tell my father? They broke it!'

Sasha had to stand aside as a gang of youths chanting slogans rushed up out of the darkness and flung themselves at the barricade. When they were gone, Constantine had mysteriously disappeared, but five minutes later Sasha saw him again, holding his broken arm as if nursing a baby, and being pursued by a horseman. The latter swung at Constantine with a baton, missed, then wheeled his horse and cantered back to his own lines.

Constantine ran on into the square and was lost to sight.

Daniel had attached himself to a band of veterans and Communists. They were fewer than the Camelots but more disciplined. Seeing them, Sasha was reminded of the Emperor's Old Guard and thought in the detached way that had affected him all night: this is it! These are the men who will storm the Chamber of Deputies. A new Empire will be proclaimed tonight and I shall witness it! And still he was looking for that mysterious figure who was Destiny. In the scurrying crowds of youths in berets and shabby suits, carrying their staves, rocks and lengths of pipe, he searched for the one who like Christ wore about his head the nimbus of glory.

From the square a mass of Camelots, hooting and yelling, was advancing towards the bridge. Daniel and his grim Communists and veterans fell in with them, and Sasha joined his friend at the head of the left-wing column. He saw Constantine yet again, still nursing his broken arm, but leaping and cavorting among the Camelots. His eyes were feverish and he was shouting in a voice pitched almost at a scream: 'Madmen of the world unite! You have nothing to lose but your sanity!'

Preceded by skirmishers who pelted the defenders of the barricade with an artillery of rocks, the rioters were pressed by the constriction of the bridge into a dense phalanx. From the direction of the barricade came a return fire from hosepipes and a rattle of shots, some in the air, and some at the attackers. One or two of the latter fell, and the head of the column might have halted but the weight of numbers drove it forward.

Half a dozen Republican Guard now made a sortie. The hooves of their animals drummed on the stones; but even before they reached the mob one of the riders was unhorsed by a flying stave, and the others fell back under a barrage of missiles. This foray by the horsemen prevented any further fire from the barricade and the mob rallied.

So close to the enemy, Sasha could still see little of them. He was in the press of the mob several ranks behind the leaders. In his imagination, battle was a panorama in which everything was laid out with the clarity of a chessboard on which the power and purpose of each piece was known. But here and now, so close to the decisive moment, everything was chaotic and obscure. He felt the security of companionship and the elation and glory of the hour as the fluttering banners swayed high; but mixed with this was an oppressive dread, a certainty that he would die. No! He would live for ever! Fear, shame, excitement, glory – no thought or emotion was whole or pure: each carried its opposite as a shadow; and each drove him forward as if emotion of any character was a fuel. Onward! Now the mob is almost on top of the barricade and the skirmishers are already grappling with the police. Yet Sasha can see only the vague shapes of the Republican Guard and feel the swaying of the mob under the pressure of the struggle. He participates only as each molecule in the sea drives the waves on to the beach, but he is not in the wave. The noise is terrifying: shots, the whinny of horses, shouted commands, firecrackers, the crackle of falling stones like hail, jets of water, the clatter of hooves, the smack of staves against shields and helmets, screams, sobbing, victory cries, groans, chants of 'Long live France', the 'Internationale', 'Ça Ira'. The veterans among whom Sasha finds himself are transfigured by hatred: some of them are screaming; he hears insults about the *Boches* as if they are bayoneting Germans. It is impossible any longer to be detached or to have any emotion that is different from the common emotion of the mob, which has no name. Sasha too is in a fury. He yells abuse at criminals, Fascists, Communists, Germans – at every indefinable object of hatred that the universe can contain. He claws his way forward, determined that he will be foremost among those to carry the barricade. Now! Now! This is the moment!

With comrades on either side, Sasha scales the barricade

and is face to face with the dense mass of police and *gardes mobiles*. In front of him a young officer has lost his kepi. Next to the officer a young policeman calmly strikes out with his baton whenever a rioter comes within reach. This young man has short hair and a classical, almost Roman face. He is small, dark, intense. On his uniform jacket is a medal. He is proud. See him strike out! He smiles a thin smile of pleasure, self-contained, undisturbed. A man who is acting well and anticipates promotion.

'No!' Sasha cries out. 'It can't be like this! This is wrong! You're on the wrong side! The wrong side!'

The young policeman stares at Sasha and his self-confidence is so complete that he is not even curious at the meaning of these words addressed to him.

He looks like Napoleon.

He raises his baton and strikes Sasha with full force over the head.

Sasha falls back unconscious and is carried to the rear.

CHAPTER 18

REASON AND ROMANCE

'The art of revolution,' said Alain Duroc, 'is to control the mob, not to be part of it.'

They were at Vincennes. Golitsin's horse, Fleur de la Russie, had just won his race and the financier's party had retired to take champagne after welcoming the victor in the winner's enclosure. On such an occasion, in particular on a sunny day when the colours are as bright as bunting, all conversations are frivolous, including the serious ones. For example, the military uprising in Spain, which looked to be turning into a civil war, could be dismissed with a disparaging remark about the Spaniards: everyone knew what they were like and no-one could expect anything better of them.

In fact, the Jesuit's remark was a comment on the riots in Paris two years before. Lydia Kalinowska had drawn the comparison to events in Spain. 'Here we confine ourselves to a civilized riot – and that only after the Count of Paris has given his permission.'

It was an open secret that Sasha had been involved in the February riots. He had been brought home concussed by the earnest Jewish boy, Daniel Coën, but otherwise had not suffered much. Even the moral results were muted.

His injuries prevented Tonya from reproaching him, and his sister, Masha, tempered her normal scorn with admiration for his daring. Maxim Yuryevitch indicated his approval and Lydia was positively enthusiastic: nothing was so wonderful or so idealistic as to risk death to bring low the scum who were ruining the flower of civilization, *la belle France*. Lydia could be Polish, Russian or French as the mood took her.

Only Alain hinted at any reservations.

'A mistimed insurrection can ruin the hope of change for a generation. The supporters of order, who were your natural allies, are frightened at the disorder you created. Now nothing except war is going to change France and save it.'

'I've grown out of riots and revolutions,' said Sasha.

'Has he, Vera Mikhailovna?'

'I shouldn't think so,' answered Vera sceptically. 'He's sincere enough, but like a man with a hangover who thinks he will give up drink. Now that he's studying philosophy at the Sorbonne he thinks he's getting wiser, whereas he's only finding more elegant reasons for making bad decisions.'

'Is that right, Sasha?'

'Probably,' Sasha admitted cheerfully. 'Who wants another drink?'

It was difficult to avoid the subject of Spain. It was almost the only story in the press, and provided new reasons for abusing the Government. Lydia was saying loudly:

'If that frightful Jew, Blum, drags us in on the Republican side, I don't believe the country will stand for it. Max, how many drinks have you had, darling? Do take it easy.'

Golitsin was looking red-faced and leaden despite his win. He glanced at his mistress with withering contempt and said:

'If only that were the case. But the day after the Cabinet agreed to stop exports of arms to Spain, our friend Blum was at St Cloud and the crowd cheered him to the echo, despite the fact that arms for Spain was what they wanted. There's a lot of support for the Republican cause.'

'Only from the rabble, darling, only from the rabble. Thinking people support Franco and the Church. But you're right to distrust Blum. He only agreed to the arms embargo under pressure from the British, and they only insisted out of hypocrisy, not principle. The mob knows that his sympathies are with the Reds.'

Tonya disliked the talk of war in Spain. She remembered too acutely the civil war in Russia. It astonished her that the others – Lydia, in particular – could discuss it so casually and suggest that it was in some way justified by the Spanish government's alleged crimes. More distressingly, they seemed to have a painless recollection and could speak plausibly of conflict as a surgical operation against a diseased body, with no intimation of death or destruction. Yet she could not voice her concerns. Instead she said feebly:

'What a beautiful day. Do we have to talk about politics? The sun is shining and our horse has just won a race.' She smiled kindly at Katya. She always smiled kindly at Katya, because it was her duty. It would be wrong to allow her feelings about the mother to influence her attitude to the daughter. And the two were not alike. When they had met in Nice, Tonya had been frightened of the other woman, thinking that she shared Lara's dangerous passions. But she had been wrong. Katya had become elegant, restrained, and calculating – indeed not a very pleasant person at all. Tonya could afford to smile at her.

Hearing Tonya, Katya thought: she's a trivial woman hiding behind religion and avoiding the issues of life. Lydia may be vulgar, but nothing frightens her. Men can destroy women like Tonya, but Lydia is invulnerable. Which of them better represents our sex?

A nudge at her elbow and Kolya was offering her

a glass of champagne. He removed the splashes from his hand with a silk handkerchief and then regarded her from beneath the brim of his panama hat.

'So hot,' he murmured. 'What were you thinking?'

'That I should rather be Lydia than Tonya.'

'A fairly obvious choice.'

'Not so obvious. They're both incomplete. I don't admire either of them as women. Tonya is a victim of men, and Lydia is a parasite on them. Neither makes much sense on her own. Why do you prefer Lydia?'

'Because if I can't have love, I'd rather have cynicism. I don't want some vapid creature hanging on to me out of need. Lydia at least has the honesty of a whore. I can respect that.' He gave a small, narrow smile.

Lydia was talking about something or other; her voice was so melodious and the substance so slight that one often ignored the content. And her gestures too were sweeping and expressive. Like a piece of gauze thrown up into the sunlight and hanging slowly in the air, thought Katya. And she thought too of her own barren sexuality and suppressed the fleeting thought that affection was worth buying on any terms.

'What will she do when she's no longer beautiful?'

'Trap a fool like Prince Carlo before he has time to notice. Or miss her opportunity and become poor, old and ugly. Who cares?'

Katya looked at her husband. The completeness of his cynicism was almost admirable and he did her the courtesy of not hiding it from her. She thought of how he proclaimed his support for the insurgents in Spain; but in fact, until the embargo, he had been involved in selling aeroplanes to the government side. He made a deal of money in the process.

She never accepted money from him. Though she had given up her cabaret singing with Le Nain, teaching work provided her with funds. From her earnings she clothed herself in the style that Tonya considered so chic. Kolya provided an apartment, and in return she was his companion when he entertained potential investors in the Widows & Wounded.

Golitsin was now saying proudly: 'I survived the Hanau scandal, the Wall Street crash and the Stavisky affair! And my investors have always made money! Why shouldn't they have confidence in me?'

'Darling,' said Lydia, 'we all know that you're the greatest financier in France. But why do you have to make so much noise about it? No, don't have another drink, I really think you've had enough.'

Golitsin swayed unsteadily and said: 'People should be forced to invest in the Widows & Wounded. It's too important to the country. It's their duty to invest.'

'Of course it is, Max. But where should we be if we all did our duty? Why, I'd have to get a job!'

Sasha was conscious of Katya's presence, but he was with Vera and so forced his attention on to the next race, though he saw not the race but the play of colours in the overpowering sunshine: the bright silks of the jockeys, the dust-laden air, the stillness of trees in a natural torpor, their leaves too thick with green, as if tired of summer.

Whenever he was not at his studies – and he was an indifferent student, too popular and sociable – he was with Vera. In his mind he turned over periodically the idea of asking her to marry him. He found her appearance and her quirky intelligence attractive, and supposed that this was the better part of love, if uninspiring. She was also sexually quite enthusiastic, though always as if she were trying to get to the bottom of it, understand its nature. Sasha always feared that one day she would announce in her blunt way: 'Well, that's that! It's a waste of time when you think about it, isn't it?'

But what was the alternative? He remembered that magical evening in Nice when he had fallen in love with Katya. He told himself that it was rubbish and nonsense. He had tried on the few occasions when they met to revive the sensation of intimacy, but she was unresponsive. He

472

felt that she had considered love and rejected it as a delusion. She had reached some sort of accommodation with her husband and that was enough for her – or, if not enough, it was the only thing of substance that the world offered.

'She's beautiful, isn't she?' said Vera.

'Who?'

'Katerina Pavlovna. You were staring at her.'

'Was I?'

'Yes. You always do, whenever you see her.' Vera's eyes returned to the course. 'God, isn't horse-racing dull? There's some interest the first time, but once you understand it, what's the point?'

'What's the point of anything?'

'Another dull question. Look at Maxim Yuryevitch.' She tugged Sasha's arm and pointed out Golitsin, who was clearly very drunk; and by him Lydia Kalinowska was smiling and contriving surreptitiously to knock him into shape, like a salesman dealing in shoddy goods. 'Max is finished,' Vera declared. 'His Widows & Wounded is going to collapse and there'll be a scandal, just as there was with Stavisky, except that this time there won't be any riots.'

'Why not?'

'Would you riot again?'

'No.'

'Neither will anyone else. The riots achieved nothing except to frighten everyone, including the rioters. They were just a fashion, and nothing is as boring as last year's fashion.'

Sasha scarcely noticed the decline in activity at the Société Financière des Veuves et Blessés de la Patrie. In the press little attention was being paid to financial news. The rebellion in Spain and the intervention of the Fascist powers had raised the spectre of a general European war. At the Sorbonne the students had divided into two camps; some of the more adventurous had even abandoned their studies and gone to join the armies.

When Sasha called at the office in the Rue de Provence, he found only the typists and the clerks and they were unoccupied and gossiping. The telephone switchboard had been disengaged because there were too many callers. The ticker tape was working but the messages were ignored and the tape was coiling in white snakes in its basket.

'Can I help you, Monsieur Alexandre?' asked the senior secretary. He was treated as a member of the family – Sasha suspected they thought he was Golitsin's son.

Sasha fiddled with the desk furniture. 'Did you know that your phones are out of order? I want to chat with Monsieur Golitsin about our investments.'

'Monsieur Golitsin is not in, as you can see. Neither is Monsieur Safronov.'

She was a dark-haired spinster, who had worked for Maxim Yuryevitch for years. Her eyes and her mouth held secrets. Sasha lit a cigarette.

'Things seem very quiet.'

'The season,' she answered noncommittally.

Sasha noticed from the shelves that many of the files had been removed. But the desks were empty. Through the frosted glass of the door to Kolya's office he saw darkness. The shutters were drawn and had been left undisturbed. Kolya had been working at night.

'No point in waiting, I suppose?'

'None. Shall I take a message?'

But Sasha had no message to give. He had come merely to relieve a disquiet he felt.

The staircase was blocked by men in mackintoshes and slouch hats who were ascending. They stopped Sasha.

'You anything to do with this Golitsin outfit?'

Sasha nodded.

'Back upstairs with you then.' They bundled him back into the office, and doffed their hats. The leader said to the secretary:

'Police. Is your boss in?'

474

'He's not expected today.'

'Know where he is?'

'He didn't leave a message.'

'We've got a warrant to search this place.'

The secretary nodded, unsurprised.

'Don't anybody leave.'

There were half a dozen detectives. They searched the general office and the rooms of Golitsin and his chief clerk. They collected the files, and threw them into a hessian sack. They ransacked drawers for diaries and notepads. They took the ledgers. The office girls enjoyed this: they collected in the doorways to watch the progress of the search and giggled and talked among themselves. Sasha lit another cigarette and smoked it nervously. He knew that he had nothing concrete to fear from these men; but he did worry irrationally that they, too, would think that he was Golitsin's son and that it would be impossible to prove otherwise.

'And you, son, who are you?' they asked Sasha.

'I'm one of Monsieur Golitsin's clients.'

The detective whistled. 'I'm impressed! Which are you? A widow or a wounded?' He laughed and the others laughed with him, including the office girls. 'Well, whichever, you've just lost all your money, son. Unless, of course, you happen to be a lawyer. The lawyers are going to have a wonderful time!'

They took Sasha's name and address.

Golitsin had fled. No-one knew where he was. Lydia Kalinowska, in tears and looking smartly beautiful, came to see the Zhivagos.

'Tonya, I'm destitute!' she pleaded. 'I have my clothes and the rent of our apartment is paid to the end of the month. Otherwise I have nothing!'

Tonya cried in sympathy. She thought: what has happened to this silly, shallow woman is what was to be expected. But she still cried because she had allowed Lydia to become her friend. The crying was good for them, and at the end they could dab their eyes and address practical matters.

'I'm sorry,' Lydia apologized. Because Sasha was there she was trying to be alluring. He had noticed her perfume. Even her distress, which he supposed was genuine, could not stand in the way of her duty to be attractive.

'We could help with money, couldn't we?' Tonya volunteered uncertainly.

Sasha nodded.

The countess asked: 'But aren't you ruined too?'

'I don't think so,' Sasha answered. 'We didn't invest in the Widows & Wounded. I told Maxim Yuryevitch I didn't want to.' Sasha did not know why. It was a feeling. At bottom he had not trusted Golitsin since the affair with the prostitute in Nice. He wondered whether Madame Adélie and her small savings were involved in the catastrophe. It would be a pity. He remained fond of her.

From the press it appeared that it had all along been known that Maxim Yuryevitch Golitsin was a crook. Instances of his dubious dealings could be quoted: for example the Czechoslovak loan. It seemed that no-one but a fool could have been taken in by him. As for the Société Financière des Veuves et Blessés de la Patrie, it had always been a fraud. The workshops in which the needy would find employment, which had been one of the scheme's attractions, had never existed except for the disreputable business in Nantes. Studies were produced which showed that the small savings and pensions of poor widows and veterans could, from the beginning, never have covered the scope of Golitsin's activities or generated the lavish returns he promised, which was why he constantly needed to draw more investors into his net. In fact the fraud was not even clever. The financier had robbed the investors in order to pay fictitious profits on the *société's* stock and finance his own luxurious lifestyle: a scheme so old-fashioned that the newspapers could point to a dozen examples of the same thing.

In short, the matter was crystal clear and always had been.

And yet it happened, thought Sasha. History was transparent, yet it was executed by blind men. Therefore there were no lessons to be learned. People who ignore history are condemned to repeat it. People who study history are condemned to repeat the history of the ignorant. Even a great hero like Napoleon could not master events. In the glory of his coronation, when he seized the imperial crown from the hands of the Pope, his doom was foretold in a gesture.

Unlike the furore surrounding the Stavisky affair, the newspapers handled the collapse of the Widows & Wounded in a knowing, academic manner. Even *Action Française* could not excite itself over yet another financial scandal. The press was concerned with the war in Spain.

'You know, of course, that Max is Jewish?' said Lydia Kalinowska. 'His real name isn't Golitsin, it's Goldstein. All his estates in Russia were the result of mortgages that he had foreclosed. He was a money-lender.'

'I had no idea!' said Tonya. 'I thought – I thought you didn't like Jews?'

'Why on earth did you think that? In any case Max had converted, and they say that baptism washes away all sins. The truth is that I was a fool for love!' Lydia meant that hers was a love such as had never before been seen in the world. 'And now I don't know what I should do. My life is ruined.'

'We'll help you.'

'You're sweet. Perhaps I should go to Spain. So many people are going to Spain. I could be a nurse.'

'Do you have any experience?'

'What experience does one need? No matter, it was only an idea. A nurse – a whore – what am I fit for?'

'I'm sure there are lots of things you could do.'

'I won't work in a shop!' Lydia said decisively, then hesitated. 'Unless, perhaps, hats or dresses or maybe flowers . . . Oh, I don't know!'

Whatever her worries, she was calmer, even cheerful. She began to recite a list of her other friends: 'I wonder how much they've lost in the Widows & Wounded? Perhaps they won't talk to me? They're not all as kind as you.' Sasha could see that she was mentally reckoning the favours she might ask. 'I must go,' she said at last. 'Wanda and Carlo are in town. I believe Carlo may be going to Spain with the Italian volunteers. I must see them.'

'You will come again?' Tonya asked. 'I was sincere when I offered help.'

'Of course you were,' said Countess Kalinowska and kissed her. 'By the way, could you lend me the cost of the taxi fare?'

It was difficult to discover the exact financial situation of the family. The police had impounded all the papers of Golitsin et Cie and closed the office. There was money in the bank, but beyond that only uncertainty. Sasha felt obliged to take up the burden of the family's financial affairs and he approached Cousin Aristide. The latter replied in his languorous way:

'I'm the wrong person to ask about money. I always take the advice of my father.'

Old Krueger must now be ninety, Sasha thought. Cousin Aristide said: 'My own affairs are in a mess because of Max. Money is very tight. But I'm sure it will come right in the end. You didn't invest in the Widows & Wounded, did you? Wise man! I like to think the best of people, but I have to conclude that Max was not entirely honest.'

'Your cousin will be all right,' Daniel said when they next met with the girls in their usual café. 'He's into armaments.'

'Are you sure?' Sasha was astonished.

'That's how old Krueger made his money: selling arms to the Greeks during the Turkish war and also to the White Russians. This business in Spain will make him a fortune. I can't see the embargo standing in his way. You have to admire capitalism!' he concluded with ironic enthusiasm.

Sasha was worried for Daniel. The latter's nervous energy seemed bottled up in a suppressed anger. He smoked continuously. His gestures seemed a collection of nervous tics: rubbing his forehead, shaking a dark lock of hair from his face, stroking his chin and moustache. Yvonne, normally so careless, looked as if she had been crying.

'What's wrong?' he asked.

'Nothing's wrong!' said Daniel, energetically shaking Yvonne's affectionate hand from his shoulder. 'Everything's clarified. I'm throwing up university and going to Spain.'

Sasha tried to be dismissive. 'Everyone's talking about going to Spain, as if it were a day trip to Paradise. All problems simplified and solved. You can't give up university,' he added seriously.

'I can't go on would be more like the truth. How can I stand by with what I believe in, and watch a crisis of history?'

'Is that a criticism of me?'

'No – no! But my situation is different: I'm a Communist and a Jew. I can't be just an observer. I have to have some kind of *moral* existence.'

'Don't I?'

'Yes, but you have to find your own. The situation of the bosses and the workers is clear: we fight! But you're Prince Charming. I've no idea how you fit into the story. In your own crazy way you claim to be a socialist. Now is the time for you to discover what that means.'

'It never meant slaughtering people.'

'We didn't start the slaughter. Mola, Franco and that crowd rejected democracy. Hitler and Mussolini are helping them. Someone has to defend the Republic!'

'Why not the Spaniards? It's their war.'

'It isn't their war! This is a conflict of ideas, of visions of the world. Ideas have no frontiers. Don't you see? This is a struggle for the human soul!'

Vera laughed drily. Daniel shot her a venomous look to which she was indifferent.

'How will you go?' Sasha asked.

'There's an office in the Rue Lafayette. They're recruiting volunteers. I've already made enquiries.' Daniel paused and then urged softly: 'Come with me!'

Sasha was appalled. The stark thought of fighting frightened him, as well as the idea of leaving his studies and his family. He was ashamed. He would have said something about his mother, but Vera spared him this feebleness. She said, careless of any reaction:

'Stupid.'

'What?'

'I said that the war is stupid: the people who join it are fools, and your so-called conflict of ideas is a conflict of idiocies. Your idealism bores me.'

Daniel began shouting something back, but it was impossible to argue with Vera because she felt that nothing merited a response, all arguments were pointless, and that one might agree or disagree with her as one chose. She merely explained her opinion without any effort to persuade. A waiter came over and told Daniel he must be quiet or leave. When Daniel had fallen into silence Sasha asked her:

'Why is it all stupid?'

'Because, whatever their glorious ideas, the fighting will push both sides to extremes. Anything that is fine or beautiful or liberal will be destroyed. The Republic, even if it wins, will destroy itself and be taken over by monsters and terrorists. It's so obvious that I don't know why I bother to tell you.'

Sasha took Vera home. She was more than usually silent. He asked her what was troubling her.

'You'll go to Spain,' she answered, 'with Daniel or with someone else.'

'Of course I won't,' he said, and tried to pitch his voice so that it was joking. 'I agree with you: it's all nonsense.'

'You're a fool,' she told him bitterly.

Sasha thought: she really is fond of me. It was one of his pleasant characteristics that he was surprised to be liked. With her face slightly flushed and her eyes bright, he marvelled at how beautiful she could sometimes be. He dismissed her criticism because, of course, he would not go to Spain.

'Can we go away somewhere,' she asked, 'just for a few days? The weather is so lovely. Perhaps we could go to Deauville?'

'Why not? What will you tell your father?'

'That I'm going with you. I'm twenty-one. He knows I'm not a child.' She was amused. She kissed him. She said: 'You're so shallow!'

Sasha laughed and she laughed too. She said:

'See! You don't even care. I scratch away at the depths – and there are no depths!'

Sasha was unconcerned. He knew that his good nature hid depths of thought and feeling. How could it be otherwise?

They kissed again and Sasha went home.

Alain Duroc maintained an apartment in the Rue d'Alsace. The Jesuit, in his peculiar way, did not associate with other priests. His duties were mysterious, though vaguely supposed to involve evangelizing the Russian community. Some people thought that he was a spy for the Sûreté or the Vatican, but whatever the case his accomplishments and cultivated manner gained him easy access to any home.

Sasha had been to Alain's apartment on many occasions. Over the years they had spent much time together, even going on a walking holiday in the Auvergne. The apartment was the place where Alain's vocation was apparent. It was small, the walls were painted white and the furniture was sparse and functional. In the main room an altar was set up on a deal table, but even these instruments of religion were of the kind that might be carried in the field by an army chaplain.

Alain welcomed his visitor in his usual friendly manner.

'Excuse the mess. I'm packing for a move, but I think I can still offer you a drink. I have a bottle of *marque* somewhere, if that's acceptable.'

The apartment had been stripped of its pictures; the altar had been put away, leaving a bare table on which were the remains of a plain meal. Two trunks stood in the middle of the floor, one of them open and in the course of being filled. Alain emerged from the kitchen with two glasses.

'Your good health!'

'Yes – and yours.' Sasha was puzzled. In his shirtsleeves his friend looked very domestic and there was about him an indefinable tenderness so different from his normal detachment.

'Cigarette?'

'Thanks.'

Alain extended a light. 'A bad business about Max,' he said. 'I prayed for something better, but I feared as much. Have you and your mother lost money?'

'I don't think so. But I'm sorry for those who have. Lydia came to see us. She was left destitute.'

'Lydia will survive.'

'Probably.'

They remained standing. Sasha examined the room and was surprised that everything that represented his friend could be contained in two trunks.

'Have you found another apartment?'

'Another drink?' From the kitchen Alain continued: 'Lydia came to see me too. She wanted money, of course. She thought that the Church should provide it. Apparently, living with Max is to be considered missionary work. Would you believe that when she came to see me she wore a veil – a black veil?'

482

'She said that Max is Jewish.'

'I don't think that's true. Here's your drink. Good health again! Lydia is simply angry with Max and thinks she can abuse him by calling him a Jew.'

'Where are you going?' asked Sasha.

Alain placed his drink on the table, and the tenderness which Sasha had observed was in his eyes. 'I've been ordered to Spain,' he said.

They each took a seat. Sasha examined his friend and felt bereft. He asked:

'Why are you going to Spain?'

'The Church is in danger there.' Alain smiled: 'You must remember that I'm not just a lounge lizard, I'm a priest – even if a bad one.'

'Everyone is talking about going to Spain.'

'Who, for example?'

'Lydia. I know it's nonsense and she'll never go: but the thought had crossed her mind, as if there were something magical about the place. Daniel Coën has volunteered to fight for the Republic.'

'Poor boy.'

'He wanted me to join him, but of course I shan't.'

'No, of course not.'

Sasha thought that Alain did look and sound like a priest. He seemed transfigured – clarified. No longer cynical and witty, he appeared humble – a working priest in humble surroundings. Sasha thought: I've misunderstood. He was always like this.

In the open trunk was a Spanish phrase book.

'Do you speak Spanish?'

'A little,' said Alain. 'I shall have to brush up. Do you have any Spanish?'

'None at all. Are you going to give me your blessing?'

'If you like. Certainly, before I go.'

'Yes, and you must see my mother.' Sasha paused. 'Why Spain? What is so important about this war?'

The Jesuit considered the question at length. Indeed Sasha thought he would not answer: he offered another drink, another cigarette, posed another couple of questions about Tonya and Sasha's sister, Masha. Then he began slowly:

'There has been a struggle waged for the human soul these two hundred years. I am not speaking of the medieval idea of Good fighting Evil in all its obvious gothic guises, but about modern man as we understand him. Let's call the parties to this struggle the forces of Reason and Romance.

'Reason claims to elevate man, to shake from him the fetters of ignorance and superstition. By its powers of experimentation and analysis, human reason will uncover the real nature of the universe: its physical laws, the psychology of man, the structures of his thought and society – and at the end tell us what is the moral significance of our lives and, if you like, reveal the mind of God.

'There are two flaws in the approach of Reason. The first is that it ignores the effects of sin. In fact, it constitutes a sin, because it glorifies humanity's pride in its own attainments. This is, perhaps, a religious point and I'll pass over it. The second flaw is that the status given to Reason rests on a fallacy, on assumptions for which there is no basis. It assumes that man is a reasonable animal, that the universe is susceptible to rational analysis and that man is powerful enough to control those things that he discovers. It is an act of faith to believe that these things are true – one which is all the more unreasonable because we know that man is not reasonable; that his ability to discover facts is tainted by his values and prejudices; that his interpretations are distorted by his fears and desires; and that he cannot control even that which he understands.

'And – at the end – for all its claims, Reason diminishes man. In every real sense he ceases to exist. His behaviour, his desires, emotions, insights no longer belong to him. He does not own them. He does not initiate them. He is merely the effect of chemical, physical and social forces. If I desire to go to Spain, it is not *my* desire that drives

484

me, but the product of the forces that dictate that, at a particular point in history, Spain has an irresistible significance that will draw to it men of a certain age and social class who share a certain stock of ideas and are driven by a certain combination of political and economic pressures. Where am I in this? I am nobody, a bubble on the surface of the water that has no existence apart from the currents that move the water.'

Alain paused and smiled as if to say: this is pompous stuff. He sipped his drink and meditated over his cigarette. Sasha sat transfixed by every word, not because the words or ideas were original or well expressed, but because they were addressed to him and came with heartfelt sincerity. He felt them with the force that every convert feels and that is incomprehensible to the observer who sees not the prophet transmitting fire to the soul, but the shaman and charlatan chanting incantations over his bag of magic bones.

'You are a Romantic,' Alain resumed softly. 'Don't be ashamed of that fact. The Romantic is conscious of his own soul, its individuality and integrity, and that it is less than and confronted by the greatness and mystery of creation. This is a consciousness of man's fundamental freedom, but it also contains the humility of weakness. It is therefore a base from which he can be receptive to the majesty and grace of God.

'In his weakness the Romantic strives to be a hero. He has so much to conquer and is master of so little. He is a hero because he knows that his task is hopeless but he will attempt it at all costs. By his striving he affirms all man's possibilities; and by his failure he affirms the greatness of God.

'I do not mean, Sasha, that the Romantic is necessarily a good man. He will fail because his resources are poor and he is beset by sin and the thousand illusions that Rational men deny. But he is not guilty of the pride that makes him so self-sufficient that it excludes the possibility of God's grace. His humility makes him an open vessel into which it is possible to pour love.'

Two days later, Alain left for Spain. The family gathered at the Gare d'Austerlitz to bid him farewell: Tonya, Masha and Sasha, and also Lydia Kalinowska, who wore a veil and a black dress and looked like the young widow of a rich man who has been disappointed in her inheritance.

Tonya could not accept that the Jesuit was leaving her. She felt still the barren sexual love that the priest had first inspired in her. Poor thing that it was, she had clung to it in her imagination through the sterile years and now it was exposed in its emptiness. She was deserted. Alain had loved her only with his remote priest's idea of love: so abstract, so passionless – so useless. She presented herself to him with her face uplifted and her arms by her side.

'You don't need my blessing,' he said lightly. 'You're a good woman, Antonina Alexandrovna.'

He made the sign of the cross over her.

Embrace me! her heart cried out.

'God be with you.'

Embrace me!

Lydia Kalinowska raised her veil, rushed forward and kissed him. He clambered the steps into the carriage and took a seat by the window. The train was about to leave and the carriage was full of passengers, so he had to push and make excuses and arrange his baggage and thus had no time to spare even a backward glance for Tonya. And then the train was leaving.

Embrace me!

Sasha embraced her and in this position they watched the train depart.

Daniel left for Spain the same day, but Sasha was unable to see him off.

Kolya had not fled with Golitsin. He waited at home until the police came to arrest him and take him in front of the examining magistrate. He maintained that he was innocent of any crime and volunteered to assist the authorities with their enquiries. He was, he said, simply Golitsin's chief clerk. He had kept the books and signed the cheques, but had never been consulted as to the payments and investments made on behalf of the *société*. As to the *société* records, Madame Lebrun swore that they had been removed in her absence during the weekend before the scandal broke. Whether this was done by Golitsin acting alone or with his chief clerk could not be proven. However, with the files presumed destroyed, there was no evidence against the latter and he was released.

As the investigations into the financier's affairs continued, it became apparent that his frauds were not confined to the Widows & Wounded. The bonds representing the Czechoslovak loan were examined and pronounced to be forgeries. Other securities were discovered to be fraudulent or non-existent. In short, there was a growing belief that the wreckage of Golitsin et Cie was total and that nothing could be saved of the monies invested with the company.

Sasha and his mother received an invitation to attend the offices of Maître Heriot. They found Cousin Aristide waiting in the anteroom. He sprang to his feet and seized both Tonya's hands.

'Darling Tonya,' he announced, 'we are all going to have to be brave. Max has ruined us!'

Tonya was pale and composed, fearing the worst. Sasha had been studying the financial press and had prepared her. She asked:

'Are your own losses considerable?'

'Whatever Max had.'

'We didn't invest in the Widows & Wounded. Sasha told Maxim Yuryevitch specifically that he was to invest in – what are they called?'

'Government stocks and good quality shares,' said Sasha.

'It makes no difference,' said Cousin Aristide. 'Any funds which were managed by Max have disappeared. I can't tell you how sorry I am. My father – he is prostrate at our own losses.'

'How much have you lost?'

'Everything we had with Max.'

'The apartment houses you own? Your factories?'

The older man answered cautiously: 'I can't say exactly how much. My father has always managed the business.'

'How old is your father?' Sasha enquired coolly.

'Why do you ask that?'

Sasha shook his head. What did it matter? The money had come like fairy-gold and disappeared like trash. If it weren't for his mother and Masha (who could not be told) he thought he would be glad to be rid of it. Perhaps then he could focus on some purpose to his life, if only a purpose driven by necessity. What annoyed him was Cousin Aristide's specious commiseration.

Tonya, too, was not overcome by distress. Her thoughts had first turned to practical matters. What to tell Masha, who was now sixteen and interested in nothing that was not vain and frivolous? How would they live?

'I'm sorry that you've lost money too,' she said.

'Oh? Oh, that's good of you, Tonya!'

She thought for a moment that her cousin was about to cry. She disliked his emotionalism. A middle-aged man whose good looks have turned to fleshiness, who wears a dove-grey suit and hat, and carries a handkerchief of lilac silk and a shagreen walking stick, cannot expect his emotions to be believed.

Maître Heriot invited them into his office. Cousin Aristide helped himself to whisky and water from the tantalus and lounged in his normal easy fashion.

'I've told dear Tonya the story,' he said, 'so you can tell us the worst, Anatole.'

The lawyer was relieved.

'I don't know exactly what Monsieur Krueger has explained, but the situation, certainly, is very poor.'

'How poor?'

'Not good. There is some property left that was never

488

in the hands of Monsieur Golitsin. There is some money in the bank, and I hold some bonds which were given to me several years ago as security for my fees. You have a house in the country – I'm afraid Monsieur Golitsin mortgaged it, but there will be a little left when it is sold. The house in Neuilly is rented and you will not be able to maintain it. However, it is furnished and if the furniture is greater than your future needs, some of it can be sold – the Louis XV commode, in particular, will fetch a good price. The car must go. The horses too. I'm pleased to say that your debts are insignificant, and as to Monsieur Alexandre's fees and expenses at the Sorbonne, it may be possible to arrange a scholarship.'

Tonya nodded with the intensity of one who does not understand what is being said, and at the end she asked:

'What does this really mean for us?'

The lawyer exchanged glances with Aristide Krueger, and Sasha was momentarily ashamed of his mother, at her ignorance. Then he thought: but what did I do to avoid this catastrophe? I should have seen it coming. I was given a chance to understand Max's business and never really took it. Maître Heriot answered:

'You will have to move to a cheap apartment and severely reduce your standard of living. If you do that, then it is possible for you to live within the income from your remaining funds, assuming that you do not wish to work. The main problem will be the cost of Monsieur Alexandre's education. At this time of year the majority of scholarships will have been taken up. It would certainly help your affairs if Monsieur Alexandre were to quit his studies for the next academic year.'

'Sasha must complete his education,' said Tonya.

'No, mother,' Sasha interrupted. He told her gently: 'It won't be a sacrifice to give up the Sorbonne for a year. I'll find something to do. I won't be a burden on you.' To the lawyer he said:

'Thank you for your advice.'

'It's the least I could do.'

'Look on the bright side,' said Cousin Aristide. 'This will make a man of you. And if it's a job you need, old chap, I can have a word with my father.'

'That won't be necessary.'

'It's no trouble.'

'It won't be necessary,' Sasha repeated.

Sasha did not return home immediately with his mother. His anger and despair were too great and he felt compelled to redeem himself by doing something practical. Therefore he told her he intended to go to Max's office. He had a futile hope that among the office papers he would find something to help the situation. That the office would probably be closed and the papers in the hands of the police, he did not consider.

The weather was out of harmony with his thoughts. Paris was in bright September sunshine, softer than in the height of summer, gently golden. The weather and Sasha's indefatigable optimism eased his mood. He began to persuade himself that there was something noble in the sacrifice of his education and that there was something he would be able to do. He would take a job of some kind – he was not sure what, but he felt he must be qualified for a clerical position somewhere; and who knows, he might be able to rise from this and retrieve the family's fortunes. He had in mind the law, or finance – in fact, if he took either of these courses, he might be able to understand what had happened to Golitsin et Cie and salvage something from the wreckage. He fondly imagined himself as an advocate demolishing his adversary's case and recovering the lost monies.

On the other hand, his new freedom gave him an opportunity and he was troubled that he might throw it away by entering a humdrum profession. Great events were happening in the world, and surely it could not be coincidental that the wealth, that had been a drag on his powers of decision like a drug, had now vanished, leaving him clear for action?

Mulling over the alternatives took him to the Rue de Provence, where he recognized the figure of a smartly dressed middle-aged woman standing uncertainly on the pavement outside the narrow door which led upstairs to the offices of Golitsin et Cie.

'Madame Adélie?'

'Monsieur Alexandre?'

'I never expected to see you here in Paris! How are you? What's brought you here?'

Madame Adélie was still plumply pretty, but in her street clothes had the matronly air of a woman who might run a respectable hat shop. She smiled and offered her cheek to be kissed and said gaily:

'Oh, I was in Paris and one reads so many things in the papers one doesn't know what to think. And Maxie, though he's a villain, isn't so bad as people make out. I thought I'd drop in on him and chat things over.'

'Max isn't here,' Sasha told her. 'The police are looking for him.'

'Oh? Well, I'm sure it will all blow over. Max will have a story that explains everything, *chéri*, he always does.'

Sasha took her hands and said seriously: 'Max is a crook, Adélie. He's ruined my family.'

The woman flinched but came back brightly: 'Finance is so complicated, isn't it? Maxie once explained it to me. It all depends on movement. It's like juggling balls. You only ever have one ball in your hand and you can never have two. But it doesn't matter as long as you keep on juggling. Do you follow? He's probably out of the country. In Czechoslovonia, most likely – he was always going on about Czechoslovonia. I'm glad you're here: we can both go up together.'

Sasha gave her his arm. She was anxious to talk.

'You've become more grown-up, more gentlemanly. Do you have a little friend?'

'Yes.'

'I bet she's pretty – prettier than your poor Adélie. I've

got out of the business, you know? I run a little lodging house. Maxie arranged it for me. Isn't this business in Spain terrible? Even with money worries it makes you realize when you're well off. And so many poor boys going there, good-looking boys, it seems a shame. Ah, here we are!'

They were standing before the door, staring through the frosted glass into the office of Golitsin et Cie. No lights were on. A pale, nacreous daylight filtered through the glass. The door was unlocked.

'Hello?' Sasha called. 'Is anyone here?'

'Who is it?' answered a voice, and Katya came out of Maxim Yuryevitch's office. 'Oh, it's you, Sasha, and . . .'

'May I introduce Madame Lossec. This is Madame Safronova.'

'Charmed,' said Adélie gushingly.

'Is anyone else here?'

'No,' said Katya. 'I came to collect some papers for Nikolai Afanasitch, but almost everything has been taken by the police.'

'How is he?'

'He was arrested, but they had to let him go. Now he's helping the police.'

'That's good,' said Madame Adélie. 'But as I was saying to Monsieur Alexandre, Maxie isn't such a bad man. It's very difficult to understand a business as complicated as his. If he was left alone, I'm sure that everything would come all right. You don't know where he is, do you?'

Katya shot a concerned glance at Sasha.

'Madame Lossec was one of Max's investors,' he explained.

'I'm sorry.'

'Oh, there's no need to be sorry, *chérie*!' said Adélie. 'I'll get by until this blows over. You do get by, don't you? Isn't this place dirty?' she added, running a finger over a dusty desk by the silent ticker-tape machine. She took a seat on the high stool where the book-keeper had once sat. 'Mahogany,' she said, admiring the desk. 'That's quality.'

'Why have you come?' Katya asked.

'I had an idea I could find some useful information. I see I was being stupid.' Sasha cast his eye sadly over Madame Adélie and continued: 'We're all a little crazy, the investors.'

'Have you lost money? I understood you didn't invest in the Widows & Wounded?'

'It isn't just the Widows & Wounded. Max stole or lost everything. We've been ruined.'

'Dear God! I didn't know.'

He was going to say: why should you have known? But then he thought, bitterly: but of course she should. She lived with Kolya. He could see she wasn't living on a clerk's salary. Look at her clothes, how stylish and expensive, and her make-up and hair, so perfect. She read his thoughts.

'Kolya is innocent,' she said.

'Please, Katya, don't disappoint me. I can forgive a lot – I have a lot to forgive myself – but don't ask me to believe the incredible. I knew that Max and Kolya were greedy and unprincipled, but I was lazy and spoiled. For me it doesn't matter: I didn't deserve to be rich, and maybe now I'll do something useful. But for my mother to face hard times again is criminal. And Masha is so frivolous, I don't know what she'll do.'

'Are you blaming me?' Katya asked.

Sasha shook his head. He looked at her and she seemed naked to him. Her arms were by her side. Her face was so absent of any contrived expression that it was plain. If he had raised his arm against her, he knew that she would not have resisted. And he felt nothing.

'You've been less than perfect,' he said at length.

'Should I have been perfect?'

'I was unreasonable, but perfection was what I wanted. That night at Nice, when I found you on the beach, I thought I had stumbled into my lost domain. You were so beautiful. You had no history. I thought I was in love, but of course it was pure egotism – trying to make an ideal out of a living woman, trying to treat you as if you were no-one except what I fashioned in my imagination. I had no right.'

Madame Adélie, rising from her chair in a state that resembled drunkenness, pointed at a map on the wall and asked:

'Where is Czechoslovonia?'

Katya showed her.

'So small! What did the Czechoslovenes want my money for? Do they have a lot of widows and wounded?'

'I don't think the loan was for the widows and wounded,' Sasha said gently. 'And the Czechs didn't get it. Max stole it.'

Madame Adélie was crying silently. She batted her hands against her side as if cold. Noticing the two young people she smiled and asked: 'Is this your little friend?'

'No,' answered Sasha.

'Oh? You seemed to be talking so seriously and – you know – in *that* way. You speak so beautifully, Monsieur Alexandre. Doesn't he speak poetically, mademoiselle? And you, *chérie*, your accent is so lovely. Where is it from?'

'Russia,' said Katya.

'How mysterious!' cried Madame Adélie and burst into tears.

Katya rushed to her and took her in her arms. She smelled a strong perfume hiding a body that was none too clean, but embracing and soothing the other woman, she thought: this is what it means, Max and Kolya's fraud. And she felt tainted by it. Of course Kolya was a criminal! She had always known he was a criminal. From the beginning, his charm, his good looks, his concern, his protestations of love had all been fraudulent! And Katya had sheltered behind him, thinking that, because he had never been her lover, she had preserved herself from him. That was the pitiful measure of her integrity: she had adopted the most bourgeois and conventional of forms and thus persuaded herself that she was honest.

'I must go,' said Madame Adélie, pushing Katya away. 'So much to do – lawyers to see – go to the bank. When do you think Maxie will be back? I suppose he takes a long luncheon: probably he's entertaining. What a man he is! So cunning! He'll turn the tables on everyone, just you wait!' She dabbed her eyes with a scented handkerchief. 'Well, I'll leave you two lovebirds. Yes, I must go, I've so much to do.'

She refused any offers of help. At the end she was dignified. Sasha and Katya watched her go down the stairs to the street, and then they were left with each other. Katya said:

'I must go, too. There's nothing here. Are you going to stay? I have the key.'

Sasha looked about him at the office that was so strangely empty of papers: at the clerk's high desk, the ticker-tape machine, the disconnected switchboard, the ink wells, blotters and pen wipers.

'Shall I see you again?' he asked.

'That's highly unlikely, isn't it?' she answered almost brutally. 'Everything has changed; there's no reason to meet again.'

'You're probably right.'

'Of course.'

Sasha felt in his pocket and produced a cigarette and a lighter covered in mother of pearl. His lips formed a thin smile.

'Max gave me this,' he said. 'He bought it in Nice that time. I think I'll keep it, as a souvenir.' His eyes turned to hers. He noticed the flush of her cheeks. 'I have no hard feelings against you,' he told her.

She bridled. 'You have no reason to.'

'All right – if you like.' He tried to be his bright self, the Sasha everyone was fond of for his good nature. 'By the way, you don't have to marry me any more! Sorry – I know you're eager to – but I release you from your promises.' His voice dropped: 'I don't love you. That must be a relief. I probably never did.'

Katya made no answer. She told herself angrily that she was glad to be rid of his follies. His love had been shallow and despicable. And now even his forgiveness, however sincerely felt at this moment, was like all masculine emotion: a thin, transient sentiment – self-regarding in its assumption that there was something to forgive. She was angry that he felt entitled to a response to this emotional trash.

Sasha took Vera to Deauville for the weekend as he had promised. He knew that he could no longer afford to, but he had discovered that it was always possible to find excuses to avoid petty economies. He would not admit to himself that he did not want to be there when his mother arranged the move from the house at Neuilly; or that, while he strolled along the boardwalk in the September sunshine, she was selecting furniture for auction.

Travelling on the train, he explained the change in his circumstances to Vera.

'You were so careless that sooner or later someone was bound to rob you,' she said. Sasha realized that this was her odd kind of sympathy.

She had gone to some trouble for the visit, buying a new dress that went very prettily with her colouring. Deauville was empty of visitors except for some yachtsmen and late English tourists, the latter of an especially dull sort, and Vera, handsome rather than beautiful, was striking. The English, who looked like invalids or co-respondents in a divorce case, managed to be offended and offensive at every turn and brought out everything that was most sullen and uncooperative in the French.

Watching an English couple complaining that the weather was unreasonably cool and that they must have words with Messrs Thomas Cook, Vera took Sasha's arm affectionately.

'This isn't like you,' said Sasha with surprised pleasure,

placing his hand over hers.

'I was listening to that couple and their petty argument, and thinking how impossible it was ever to quarrel with you.'

'It's nice of you to say so, though I'm not sure it's a compliment: it makes me sound like one of those supine husbands dominated by his wife.'

'I don't believe that anyone else could lose a fortune and be so even-tempered about it.'

'That's the effect of six terms studying philosophy. Not that I'm any more philosophical, but my brain is so addled that when anything happens to me I ask myself: ah – but is it *real*?'

He looked away from her and out to sea, where a group of white-sailed dinghies lay on the horizon beating against the breeze and a man in a rubber cap and stout blue costume was swimming determinedly.

'What are you going to do?' Vera asked.

'I haven't decided. I have to stop being a burden on my mother. Perhaps I'll be able to get a job, but I'm not sure. Cousin Aristide offered me something, but I don't trust him; he and Max were very thick. Daniel has gone to Spain. So has Alain. Connie talks of going, but Connie talks of everything from being a monk to robbing banks. He went on holiday to Germany and is very impressed by Hitler. Should I go to Spain? No, of course not. They talk about it as if it were some mythic battlefield in which Good and Evil meet in cosmic conflict. But what are Good and Evil? If only I could be sure!'

They took several turns up and down the boardwalk, giving way to a family man escorting his children on to the beach. The man evidently came from the city and treated his annual visit to the sea with the same seriousness as his annual confession. He wore a heavy woollen suit and a tie. Vera watched him indulgently. Sasha sensed that there was a softness about her today, but it struggled with her natural angularity. As if to be difficult she said:

'I simply can't understand this enthusiasm for Spain.

497

It annoys me. It's so obvious that neither side will achieve its aims or anything commensurate with the sacrifice.'

'But isn't the struggle itself worthwhile? Are we always to compromise? Perhaps we are marked as human because we resist the inevitable.'

'Romantic nonsense,' she answered mildly. The breeze was whipping foam off the waves. Nearby was a flagpole from which fluttered the red flag of Normandy. A seagull was positioned at the pinnacle and alternately preened itself or scanned the sea with its ruthless eye. Vera shivered. She turned to Sasha and gave him a pitiful look.

'You have no idea what I'm like, do you? You suppose without thinking that I have feelings similar to yours, and that the difference between us is merely the degree of our response to particular situations.'

'Aren't all feelings universal?'

Vera laughed. 'You have a talent for profound obviousness! Don't you see? I'm bored and empty! I live in a world in which everything is clear, mechanical, predictable and obvious, and yet everyone else seems to treat it as an object of deep mystery.' She paused, then said slowly: 'There – is – no – mystery! The answers to all the questions that trouble you are in fact simple, and fundamentally uninteresting. There is no God. The universe has no purpose and operates as a machine. Human beings are animals and act by instinct. Morality is an illusion. Why do I even bother saying this? Why study something which is meaningless? Why try to change something that is governed by forces that are beyond our individual power?'

'So you despise me?' Sasha asked her.

'You fool! I love you, as far as I'm capable of loving anybody. When you open your mouth and say stupidities; when you embark on one piece of idiocy after another; every time you enthuse over something valueless; when you laugh or cry or scratch your head because everything is so complex and confusing to you, I feel a rush of joy and life, as if it were me who could do and feel those things.'

'Then marry me,' Sasha said to her.

Vera shook her head. 'You don't love me. In fact, you think you're in love with Katerina Pavlovna. But the truth is that you're only in love with the idea of being in love; and perhaps that's as far as it will ever be with you, I can't tell.'

The family man was pitching boules in the sand. The swimmer had returned to the shore and was walking up the beach removing his cap. Strolling back from a café, the English couple argued about how much they had paid and the value of the franc; and the seagull descended from its perch and was tugging at a dead crab.

Katya chose not to think too closely about her encounter with Sasha at Golitsin's office. In so far as she did, it was her anger that she focused on and not her guilt. So she was able to spend the next few days in a semblance of normality.

Kolya was occupied with two things. He had to see the police several times to explain what he knew of Max's business, and for the rest he was out and about in cafés and brasseries, now seen talking to a sleek Spaniard and now to a German reputed to be the agent of Krupp of Essen. There was talk of armaments and the Spanish war.

Three days later a report appeared in *Le Jour*. The fraudster, Max Golitsin, had been murdered by one of his ruined investors. Madame Adélie Lossec, the widow of a war hero, whose means of livelihood was a small *pension* in Nice, had placed all her savings with Golitsin et Cie and lost them in the crash. She had come to Paris to demand justice of the criminal and traced him to a house near Passy owned by an associate, one Aristide Krueger. An argument ensued during which Madame Lossec produced her deceased husband's service revolver and shot at both men. Golitsin had died of his wounds. Krueger escaped injury, but was now in custody. Why – asked *Le Jour* –

had the police themselves not discovered the fraudster's whereabouts?

Katya had no-one to talk to. She saw the words written starkly on the page and she had no-one to talk to. Instead she could think only of the poor distracted woman and knew of her own tacit complicity in the disaster that had befallen her.

She rose from the table where she had been reading and looked about the apartment she shared with Kolya. Its very tangibility filled her with a physical horror. The comfortable chintz-covered seats, the radio-gramophone, the American cocktail bar Kolya had installed on the advice of Princess Wanda were the plunder from his crimes. She could see them now for what they were: the vulgar rubbish that a flashy crook like Kolya would buy; absurd in their pretensions to style and luxury; as fraudulent as he was and sickening to look upon.

It was impossible for her to stay in the apartment. She put on her coat and fled, and for an hour or more she walked the streets until finally, out of weariness, she went into the Ambassadeurs cinema in the Avenue Gabriel. There she saw a romantic film and a newsreel about the events in Spain and another film, a comedy about a bank clerk who tried to return to nature; and after seeing the romantic film for a second time, she emerged and found that it was evening, and that the film had made her cry.

She walked. Daylight was fading; everywhere she saw pigeons flying in to settle on the buildings and the pavement was collecting the first leaves of autumn. September was a poignant month, suggesting happiness passing but still capable of being retrieved, like the summer not quite gone. A soldier in a greatcoat was playing a concertina. At his feet was a tray of ribbons and buttons.

How ridiculous to cry at a film! And not even a good film. The dry-eyed shop girls pointed at the screen and laughed. Some boys jeered at the newsreel, which was of war preparations made by the Republicans and pictures of damage wrought by the insurgents. Pain, whether from love or war, did have its funny side. It was entirely sane to laugh at the suffering of others, for the alternative was unbearable.

But I cried, thought Katya. A barrier came down and I cried at suffering that was completely artificial. It was a marvel to her and frightening. She was terrified that some day she would be able to see the suffering without the need for artifice. As she walked the humdrum streets in the pleasant air of evening, she heard the false romanticism of the film's music, and saw a calvary of faces. She thought how graceless suffering was, how unredeemed; and she prayed that the insistent swells of cheap melody would cease and that she would be left with the balm of indifference.

She arrived home in darkness, but it was not her home as she knew it. She had no sense of being *in* the world. It had become remote and reified like a theatrical set, and the casual objects ignored in everyday life had the intrusiveness of props which the audience waits for the actors to handle. A panic swept over her. How was it possible to live in this too solid world, where even the air, fragrant with dew and damp earthiness, was no longer simply to be breathed but must be observed? How could she move, when each step, each swing of the arm, the lifting of a hand to turn a latchkey, the closing of the clasp on her purse, lacked spontaneity but had to be considered and watched closely so that she should not depart from the mental script? Still more did she fear speech.

'Hello,' said Kolya. (Observe how he sits – neat – small – upright – wearing sleeve-bands.) 'Where have you been?'

Katya considered the danger of saying anything, curious what it might be.

'I went to the Ambassadeurs.'

'Good film?' (He turns a page of the papers on the table in front of him. Figures are written on them. The paper rustles. The copy of *Le Jour* lies where Katya left it.)

'It was very silly.'

(Searching her memory for the customs of these occasions, she remembers that on coming into the apartment it is usual to remove her coat and hat. There is a place to hang them.)

'You don't normally go to the cinema. Was there something special or were you bored?' (He is playing the character of an affable man. He smiles readily. Probably he is conscious of having escaped the consequences of his crimes and is untroubled.) 'Are you all right? You look cold.'

'I'm fine. There is a little chill in the air. I see you're working. Have you eaten? I haven't cooked. I'm not hungry. Would you like an aperitif?'

Katya studied the alien form of the American bar and steeled herself to go to it and produce a cocktail according to one of the princess's recipes, which she gave to Kolya. She could think of no customary action to perform next, and so stayed at the bar as if waiting for a customer. She asked in a tone which she could not herself interpret:

'Have you read the newspaper?'

He did not look up.

'Is there a report of Max's death? The police mentioned it to me when I saw them this morning. Max was stupid to hide at Aristide's place, but then he never had much intelligence.' Now he turned round. 'Does that surprise you? It shouldn't. People like Max rely on blind faith in their own ability. It wouldn't surprise me if he really believed in the Widows & Wounded and thought it would work miracles even when he was robbing it blind. Why are you still standing?'

'Sorry. I'll sit down.' Katya looked for a chair and contemplated the mechanics of sitting. Did she normally cross her legs at the ankles?

'As for Madame Adélie, the poor widow, she was a whore from Nice that Max used to see. He introduced Sasha Zhivago to her. She was his first love even before he met you, my dear.'

Katya had worked out the process of sitting down. She now had to remember to listen to Kolya. That was what one did when people spoke. And make appropriate replies. Was this appropriate?

'Is there anything left?'

'Out of Max's affairs? I suppose, now that he's dead, I can tell the police where he hid his money. But they'll find precious little. Max wasn't rich. The irony is that he ruined himself, too. He was speculating with the funds, trying to get a higher return than he promised his investors. If he'd succeeded, then none of this would have happened. The fact is that he was very good at getting people to place their money with him, but he really didn't know how to make a sound investment.'

From her mental agenda of possible responses Katya tried to select one. Should she quiz Kolya about his own involvement? Should she reproach him? She decided to stay silent. To talk to him was futile. (Look at him now – he doesn't care. He returns to his papers. His eyes are tired and he wipes them.)

'There's money to be made in Spain,' he said with satisfaction. He rubbed his eyes again, put his papers in an orderly bundle, stood up and stretched himself. 'I think I'll go to bed. Tomorrow I'll give the police a call. When I tip them off as to the location of Max's cash, I'll be their blue-eyed boy. Are you going to bed? Are you sure you're not ill?'

He left the room. Katya heard him going through his nightly rituals. The sound of a bath being drawn. The night breeze rattling the shutters. The rattle of the elevator and a voice bidding good night. The lights faded at a fluctuation in the current and came bright again and a sheet of paper, placed carelessly, slid from the table and floated to the floor.

In this too tangible world Katya was afraid to move. She suspected that the carpet would crackle like ice beneath her feet and the air would be so thick that she would have to swim through it. Her thoughts were noisy. She could change them like radio channels but never turn them off. It was unbearable.

She had never known before that her conscience could be a physical burden, but now she could feel it wrapped close about her like leaden cloth. (Look, I'm lifting my arm – feel the weight – ah! it's hardly possible.) Her neck turned like the turning of ill-oiled gears and her eyes made a camera's slow traverse of the room to the door where Kolya, complacent, washed, perfumed, wearing a silk dressing gown came out, said something and went into his bedroom. The light went on. The door half-closed, leaving a crack of light.

Katya's thoughts were worked over as each mental word was deliberately placed:

I failed to become truly free. I turned all feeling into cynicism. I have lost any capacity for love. What expiation can I make? What grace can be extended to me that will make me whole again?

Kolya reclined against the comfortable pillows of his bed. He smoked and read, and, occasionally, put down his book and contemplated his future. He had escaped from the Golitsin debacle with a comfortable sum in his own bank account. His dealings with the Spaniard and the German promised more profitable opportunities.

He could hear noises from the next room: Katya undressing. His thoughts turned to her, and tonight they were tender: he could never entirely lose the tenderness he had first felt for Lara's child. If only she had responded, he would have loved her.

The first Spanish deal would return a million francs. He needed to speak to Prince Carlo. Who was the right contact to tell him of Italy's needs for Spanish iron?

The bedroom door opened and Katya appeared naked against the light. Kolya was stunned. He had never seen her naked and her beauty was even greater than he had imagined. How unearthly she looked; expressionless, disengaged; it seemed impossible that a human being could embody beauty in so abstract a form.

She advanced towards the bed and placed her hand upon his.

'I'm going to sleep with you tonight,' she said. 'And tomorrow I shall leave you and it will all be over.'

BOOK THREE

Life From Death

CHAPTER 19

THE BUREAU OF NOTHING IMPORTANT

Sasha was woken not by the chiming of Cathedral bells but by the palatal snore of José's asthma. The bells were the signal to get up; the asthma, however, intruded a half-hour earlier with the regularity of a clock. Sasha lay listening to its flutings and pipings while the morning light broke through the jalousies and swept up the dust, thereby saving the landlady the trouble and dishonour of sweeping it.

He used the earthenware chamber pot. Doña Rosa was proud of this instrument. When Sasha bought it one day, she made a point of showing it to the neighbours as proof that her three young lodgers were gentlemen.

As each person responds to different stimuli, so Sasha's use of the pot woke Miguel, and the latter's groan and habit of opening the day with a tale of prayers on his rosary woke José. Sasha washed, José fingered his socks, sniffed them and speculated on a change, and Miguel smiled like an angel until, putting his thick spectacles on his nose, his eyes became myopic puddles of glass and his smile, as if burdened by the weight of the spectacles, turned down.

'Breakfast?' proposed Sasha, after pouring the dirty water from basin to chamber pot. And, as always, this was agreed.

'Why do we always go to the same place?' complained José as they dodged a donkey in the narrow lane leading from their quarter of the city to the square in front of the bishop's palace. 'It's not even convenient for the office. Well, is it? Convenient for the office?' The walk made him breathless; his method of progress was one of pauses and short bursts of running at a waddle to catch his companions.

'Do your boots hurt? Is that why you walk like a duck?' enquired Sasha.

'Ho, ho! Why do you always say the same thing?'

'Why do you always complain about where we take breakfast?'

'I've missed early Mass again,' said Miguel with the resignation of a sinner.

'You always miss Mass,' was the answer.

'But it's not a sin of intention. I *intend* to go to Mass every day.'

'And I *intend* to make love to a woman every day,' said Sasha. 'But we're both failures.'

'Ho, ho,' repeated José drily. Ho, ho indeed.

In the Plaza Anaya Sasha blinked in the sunlight between cathedral and palace. He could never get used to the sudden transition from shadow to sunlight, the staginess of it. In the cool and shady Rua Mayor soldiers sat outside the cafés, stretching their arrogant legs into the paths of passing nuns.

'See!' panted José. 'We could have breakfast here.'

But he always said this and they never did. Instead they breakfasted in the Plaza del Coralillo, in the shadow of an arcade of iron columns, where a tall, blond officer strolled past them and entered the Romanesque door of a small church that gave on to an angle of the square.

'Will the Fat One be at the office today, do you

think?' asked José, earnestly. Because of his asthma and his heavy, flat-footed build he was always worried that the army would discharge him.

'Why should he be?'

Their commanding officer was a likeable, easy-going man, fat and one-eyed.

'He seemed excited about the *Koblenz*.'

A small German freighter, the *Koblenz*, had landed its cargo of war materiel at Corunna. There was a discrepancy between the manifest and the reported delivery.

But Sasha was too lazy to think of German freighters. Instead he said:

'I'm sure I know that fellow.'

'Who?'

'The one who just walked past. Look, I'll be back in a minute.'

'Are you trying to get out of paying?'

'Ho, ho.' Sasha was already out of his seat and directing his steps towards the church. Inside he found a few women and a smartly dressed officer on his knees before the altar. The baroque reredos stood in rich contrast to the simplicity of the rest of the interior.

'Connie?' he asked hesitantly.

The young officer turned round and a smile of surprise and delight grew on his handsome face.

'Sasha! Dear God, it's Sasha!'

'Connie!'

The two men embraced and for a moment Constantine let his head rest on Sasha's shoulder. Then, pulling apart, he said abruptly:

'Well, I suppose Salamanca is as likely a place for you to turn up as anywhere else.'

'And a church is as good a place for you. What are you doing here?'

'Oh, I'm making a round of the churches. Today I'm praying to Our Lady of Occasional Cowards, and tomorrow to Our Lady of Compliant Generals; and, in a week or so, when I've done the rest, I shall go to the cathedral and pray to Our Lady of Absolute Gibberish. But, my God, I am glad to see you!'

'Yes,' said Sasha, overcome. 'And I you. But I meant: what are you doing in Salamanca? Have you had breakfast? I've got some friends outside.'

'I'd love breakfast. I went to early mass. And as to Salamanca, why am I here? Yes, why? Why is one doing anything in war? It's a mystery to me. I thought one went out to kill people, but apparently not. Most soldiers stay as electricians or drivers or clerks or whatever they were in private life or at all events, not very much different. Apparently the Spanish army needs wastrels and layabouts, so I've responded to the call of duty.'

Sasha wanted to laugh at his friend's eccentricities, but confined himself to squeezing his hand affectionately. He said:

'You've grown a moustache.'

'Yes. Do you like it?'

It was reddish and had been waxed.

'Breakfast?'

'Lead on!'

They returned to the square and Sasha introduced Constantine to his two colleagues. Constantine, in quirky Spanish, treated them to his exuberant personality. When, tactfully, they had gone to the office, leaving the friends alone, he said:

'Nice fellows, aren't they? How is your Spanish, by the way?'

'Like a cow.'

'Mine too. Where is your barracks?'

'Not barracks – office. Do you know the Calle San Pablo?'

'I don't know the town at all. I only got in yesterday. So you're working in an office? I'm impressed! I've never met anyone on the general staff.'

'Not exactly that. We call ourselves –' Sasha hesitated over sharing the joke '– the Bureau of Nothing Important.

There's just the three of us running it, and our commander. He's an old Africanista, so I suppose that's why they gave him a job. He was in the Rif and an Arab shot his eye out. It's an astonishing injury. Apparently, with one eye he can't read at all; so he excuses himself from all paperwork.'

'But what exactly do you *do*?'

'Let me think. Last week we scoured the province for replacement horses and this week we're distributing blankets to the poor. Why us? After all, the cavalry have their own remounts department and the Auxilio de Invierno pass out the blankets. Answer – I'm damned if I know! We're the Bureau of Nothing Important, and that, I suppose, explains everything.'

Walking towards Sasha's office they halted opposite the Plaza Colón.

'That's it.' He pointed to a nondescript building. And beyond the quiet garden and statue of Columbus, he indicated across the square the Civil Guard barracks beneath a stone archway inscribed: *Todo por la Patria*.

'We don't have a telephone. They keep a chair for us. We take two-hour shifts to sit and wait for calls on their telephone. Do you want to come in?'

'No, I can't. Where do you live?'

'In the *barrio* de Santiago. I share a room there with José and Miguel. It's by the river, but you wouldn't like it; it's an awful slum. The senior officers have taken the best places. Where are you staying?'

'In some hotel or other. I'm only here a few days.'

For an awful moment it seemed they would not meet again. Then Constantine said brightly:

'What am I to call you, Don Alejandro?'

'I think Sasha will do. I'm only a corporal. And you? I still can't recognize all these insignia. Are you a Carlist?'

Sasha knew that the Carlists were eccentrically monarchist. It had surprised him at first to discover that the Nationalist side was divided into various factions more or less at odds with each other, while still uniting to fight the Republic.

'I'm a provisional officer – or permanent corpse, as the saying is. I'll tell you about it later.'

'Are you on the staff?'

'I'm attached to a general – but only a tiny little general, that is to say more important than God but less important than Franco. Isn't the sun bright? How do they put up with it?' Shading his eyes, Constantine lit a cigarette and stared about him. Above the dappled shadows of the plane trees he noticed the stork's nest, a crazy structure sitting on the belfry of the church next to the Civil Guard barracks. He asked:

'What do you do for entertainment here?'

'Sit in cafés and stroll about. The truth is it's rather dull. The situation with girls is hopeless. If you talk to one, she becomes your *novia* and you have to marry her. There's a cinema, the Teatro Moderno, and a few good cafés in the Calle del Prior.'

'Dancing?'

'I've seen some dance halls in the Cuesta del Carmen; and the Germans spend their time in the *barrio* Chino, but it's not to be recommended.'

'I heard there was an officers' club.'

'Only for captains and above – not for humble corporals.'

'Oh, I think we could get in,' said Constantine, and Sasha believed him.

In fact, Sasha found two girls who were happy to accompany the two boys to the officers' club. Dolores and Mercedes, typists at the military headquarters in the episcopal palace, were pleasant young women who wore modest, long-sleeved dresses in the style favoured by the conservative taste of the regime. They spoke no French. Constantine, who made a fine impression in his uniform, joined them at a café in the Plaza Mayor.

'I see you found some girls,' he commented offhandedly.

'I thought we could have some fun. Are you sure we can get into this club?'

'My general takes me everywhere. There won't be a problem.'

'What's he saying?' enquired Dolores, who was the more forthcoming of the two. 'Why doesn't he speak Spanish?'

'*No hablo Español*,' said Constantine, which was not true. Indifferent to the girls, he stretched his elegant legs and stared vaguely across the public garden where the usual evening crowd was strolling and chatting. From the belfry over the town hall a monarchist flag hung limply in the warm still air.

Caught between the girls and his friend, Sasha tried to make conversation.

'You didn't actually tell me what you are doing, Connie. Are you really on the staff?'

'Yes. I'm the tall fellow at the back. Do you follow? In the photographs of the famous, there's always some tall chap in the background, whom nobody knows. Well, that's me. It's a very important job.'

Sasha tried to translate, but the girls failed to see the joke. Constantine continued languidly:

'My general likes to have tall fair-haired young officers at his side.' He raised an eyebrow. 'Lord knows why.'

'Have you seen any action?'

'Not exactly. My general follows about ten kilometres behind the army. We have a large car, courtesy of our German allies, and we drive around terrorizing the peasants. My contribution to the war effort is prayer. The artillery fire the shells, and I pray that they hit the enemy. What about you?'

'I'm stuck in my office. Neither José nor Miguel are fit for active duty, and being a foreigner is considered a sort of disability. We have a major in charge of us, when he cares to be. Franco seems to have a soft spot for old campaigners who fought in the Rif and so he finds odd jobs for us to do. It isn't what I imagined when I volunteered. I had a vague idea of being a hero – in fact, I half-expected to be dead by now. But after a spell at headquarters one loses one's enthusiasm. I think these days I'd be too frightened if I saw the enemy.'

They left the Plaza Mayor, the boys in front and the girls, somewhat listlessly, behind. Sasha enjoyed the sociability of these Spanish evenings: the public *paseo*, the bars with their bright yet secretive interiors, the spill of light from cafés on to the dark narrow streets. The officers' club was in a gothic building close by the Cuesta del Carmen. The narrow ground-floor windows were barred and the building was in darkness except for a lighted doorway. A sentry stood at duty. After a few words from Constantine they were admitted.

Having been previously excluded from the club, Sasha had supposed that it must be exciting. In fact, it proved to be a narrow smoke-filled room, overcrowded with officers and one or two women with, at one end, a small stage and a gramophone operated by an ordinary soldier. The latter changed the records at intervals and desultory dancing took place, the men partnering each other as there were so few women. On the walls were film posters and pieces of propaganda: *España, Una, Grande, Libre*; *Por la Patria, el Pan y la Justicia*; and other familiar slogans.

Forced together, standing as a little group of four, Constantine said morosely: 'Well, this is fun!'

'What's he saying?' asked Dolores. 'Why doesn't he speak Spanish? It's rude.'

'Tell the bitch to shut up,' said Constantine casually. 'By the way, I should have asked: how is your mother? What was her reaction when you decamped to Spain?'

'Oh, she's well,' answered Sasha guiltily. 'She supports Franco and the Church, naturally. But you can understand that she didn't want me to come here. As a matter of fact we quarrelled.' He tried to shrug his shoulders insouciantly. Failing, he said more intensely: 'She wouldn't understand that I couldn't stay at home, financially ruined, eking out a penny-pinching existence as a draper's assistant or whatever.'

'That's women for you. They see only the personal

and the concrete. Though, to be fair to my mother, she was reasonably understanding of her "darling". It was my father who flew into a rage. But you don't have a father.'

'No.'

'Cigarette?' Constantine seemed to notice the discomfiture of Dolores and Mercedes. 'Would you like to smoke?' he asked in Spanish.

'Spanish girls don't smoke,' said an offended Dolores and Constantine's face became blank as he snapped his lighter shut.

'To be frank,' he returned to Sasha, 'I never expected to see you here. I don't mean here in Salamanca – it seems perfectly reasonable that in this place one is sooner or later going to run across everyone that one knows on our side. I meant that I had half an idea you might have joined the other side.'

'What on earth made you think that?' asked Sasha, astonished. 'I've never been a Red.'

'You kept company with that Jew, Coën, and he most certainly is a Red. Do you hear from him?'

'Of course not! Our mothers still see each other, but it's difficult for mine to write about Daniel; one has to read between the lines. I understand he's well.'

'And Vera? I really thought you were going to marry Vera. I'm glad you didn't. There was something cruel about that girl.' Constantine thought for a moment and added: 'You know, I've never understood why men are regarded as beings of intellect and women as creatures of passion, when it's so absolutely clear that matters are precisely the other way round. What did happen to you two?'

'We just drifted apart,' Sasha answered, not wanting to talk about it. After Vera's avowal of love and refusal to marry him he had decided not to see her again. And she had been right: he had not been in love with her. When he thought of her at all, it was with a puzzlement that their relationship had been such as it was.

Noticing the girls, Sasha volunteered to get them a

drink. From being bored they were now taking a lively interest in the other officers; this was reciprocated in an exchange of glances with the younger ones. Sasha was disappointed that Constantine showed no interest in Mercedes' dark-eyed beauty. For himself, he would have liked to know Dolores better.

Returning with drinks, he cast his eyes towards the door.

'I could swear,' he said to Constantine, 'that I just saw Princess Wanda. That would be too much of a coincidence!'

'Fate – I believe in Fate.'

'You believe in rubbish and nonsense.'

'Of course. Where is she?' He glanced over his shoulder and saw a bony-faced woman of a certain style hanging on the arm of an Italian captain. The latter was handsome in a Roman way and definitely not Prince Carlo.

Pushing his way through the crowd, Constantine cried: '*Principessa!*' and, stooping, seized her free hand and saluted it with a kiss.

'My word, it's that boy, the crazy one!' replied the princess without any hint of surprise in her tone.

'Your slave!'

'Paolo,' she addressed her escort. 'This is Constantine. The mad one. I told you about him. Paris? The Zhivagos? I had an idea that he would turn up in Spain one of these days, but I didn't know he was here.'

'You are the son of the millionaire?' enquired the captain politely.

'Not me. You mean Sasha – who, dear *principessa*, is even crazier than I am.'

Sasha had made his way to the group. Princess Wanda offered him a cheek to be kissed.

'This is Captain Marchesi,' she said.

'It is you, after all!' Sasha exclaimed with pleasure, as though the princess were his dearest friend.

'I don't know why you're so surprised,' she answered levelly. 'If it were anywhere but Salamanca, perhaps. But since Franco's headquarters is here and Spain has become the biggest bazaar in Europe, one must expect to come across old friends.'

'Is the prince with you?'

'Of course. And, before you ask, we're only here for a few days. Carlo is escorting a trade mission. Have you met anyone else we know?'

'No.'

'I saw Alain Duroc in Burgos and I hear that Kolya Safronov is in and out of Spain all the time. Arms sales, mostly to the Reds. I don't suppose his heart is in it, but business is business. His wife has left him.'

At the thought of Katya, Sasha passed on quickly. 'Lydia – do you hear from her? My mother and I saw her after Max died.'

'She's living with Kolya. I gather there was a touching scene when she went to him for help – he knew where Max had hidden the money from the Widows & Wounded. She used to be ten years older than Kolya, but of course these days she's two or three years younger than him.' She turned to the captain and said in Italian. 'Get me a drink, darling. Martini, if they have such a thing.' To Sasha she said: 'Whatever happened to Kolya's wife after she left him?'

'I don't know,' Sasha told her.

When they left the club, in a more mellow mood after several drinks, Constantine suffered the attentions of Mercedes, and Sasha was able to walk with Dolores. Though repressed by the exaggerated conventionality of Spanish life, especially under the high moral tone set by Franco, she was, Sasha suspected, a lively and intelligent young woman. Being reminded of Katya made him more attentive to his companion. It was, he told himself rationally, absurd to continue his adolescent fascination with a married woman.

In the darkened streets they came across small parties of *regolares*. Harassed by the Civil Guard and the military police, the young Moroccan peasants, swarthy and unshaven and wearing tarbush or turban, looked alien and bereft. Denied women or entertainment, they gathered in dark places and held dark conversations in Arabic, breaking off shiftily to stare at any passers-by with intent, hollow eyes. Their presence made Dolores shudder and cling to Sasha.

'Why have you come here?' she asked him.

'I don't know what you mean. To fight for Spain.'

She seemed annoyed.

'All you foreigners. None of you have come here for the sake of Spain. You are simply continuing the fights of your own countries. Italian Fascists fight Italian Communists. White Russians fight the Reds. We poor Spaniards have to put up with you all. Why don't you leave us to our own quarrels?'

'Don't you like us?'

'Yes, I like you. But not as soldiers. If it weren't for all the weapons that Germany and Russia are sending, maybe this war would be over.'

'But then Franco might lose.'

'Yes,' she admitted. 'I wouldn't like that. If the other side won, it would be the end of Spain. All their ideas are from abroad. Marx, Bakunin, jazz music. Think instead of all our beautiful churches!'

They had halted in the Rua Mayor from where the cathedral could be seen darkly. A string of mules ambled down the street. A cart was being unloaded. A Civil Guard with a carbine slung over his shoulder was checking someone's papers while his partner smoked.

The girls lived in different streets, so the two couples split up and Sasha walked Dolores to her home. He did not kiss her, knowing that she would think of him as her *novio* if he did.

The cargo shortage from the *Koblenz* was a mystery most probably explained by theft or general confusion at the docks in Corunna. However, Major Ruiz, the one-eyed fighter of the Rif, disliked the Germans and believed that he could lay the crime at their door. To the surprise of his subordinates, he came into the office and proposed that they should lay the result of their investigations before Franco himself. It was, he inferred, a matter of international importance. That said, the fat major and his three bemused and somewhat fearful assistants, buttoning their uniforms and examining their boots, made the short walk from the Calle San Pablo to the bishop's palace.

Of the three, Sasha was the most blithe. He had looked out of his window that morning on to the river and seen washing spread out across the bushes, goats grazing among the rushes and irises, and the torpid flow of the water lapping the islands in its midst. Doña Rosa, barefoot and smiling thin-lipped like an elderly murderess, had noticed and commented gaily that he was in a good mood. There was no question that she liked him the best of her lodgers.

The generalissimo's Moorish guard was posted outside the palace and a flow of people entered or emerged into the sunshine. It was, Sasha thought, a modest building from which to organize a war: softly gold in the morning light, it looked more suited to the home of a provincial mayor, and the swagger of flags and guards could not change its amiable character. In the public area of the ground floor a throng of military men of all types was gathered. Franco himself occupied the first floor and his staff worked from the second. Among the soldiers, the red-bereted Carlists and blue-shirted members of the Falange, Sasha noticed two civilians formally attired in black frock coats and accompanied by a squat Italian officer in a uniform of light sand colour with varnished boots. They were talking volubly to attract the attention of one of the aides. Pushing through the crowds, Sasha accosted the officer.

'Prince Carlo?'

The officer turned. His face, which Sasha remembered as plump and friendly, was stern and seemed strangely that of a man used to command.

'Signor Alessandro – yes? Wait, wait.' The prince was watching the marble staircase, where a German general was descending followed by a train of lieutenants. He marched through the crowd, descended the steps to the square and waited for the door of his car to be opened.

'I hate that man!' remarked the prince. He said something in Italian to his colleagues. 'He has managed to see Franco.'

'Who is he?'

'Faupel, the head of the German legation. Did you notice his smile? That is bad news for us. The men with him are from HISMA. They hope to rob the Spaniards and call it trade. Ah!' He shook his head and tried again to harass one of the generalissimo's aides to gain an interview.

In the press of people clamouring for the right to see Franco, Sasha had lost sight of Major Ruiz. He found José standing by the door, panting, and, coming up the steps, an officer in a Carlist uniform followed by Constantine who was carrying his bag.

'Hello,' said the latter. Nodding in the direction of the interior, he said, 'I suppose it's the usual confusion in there? It must suit our dear generalissimo to have all these suitors for his attention. Good for his self-importance. I wonder if he needs someone tall and blond to stand behind him and hand him pens?'

'I've just seen Prince Carlo.'

'Really? He must be having a hard time. The stock of the Italians isn't so high in Spain these days. My general was highly amused by their defeat on the Guadalajara.'

'Why are you here?'

'To ask for more supplies. Bullets or prayer books, one can't be sure which. The Carlists are slightly cracked where religion is concerned. They'd have us on our knees in sackcloth and ashes, whipping ourselves and begging God for victory. And quite right, too.'

Above the general brouhaha, Major Ruiz was insisting on his right to present his findings to Franco.

'That's my chief,' said Sasha, 'I'd better help him out. How long are you going to be here? We ought to fix up something before you leave to join your unit again. I enjoyed last night. In the end did you like Mercedes?'

'She was all right. Look, I don't know how long this business will take. Why don't you leave a message at my hotel? Maybe we can take a boat out on the river or go riding.'

'I'll do that.' Sasha pointed out the prince. 'There's Carlo. Don't you think he looks impressive in his Fascist uniform? I always thought of him as a complete nonentity, a short, fat Italian with nothing to say for himself; but now I'm not so sure. Yes, well. I'll send a message to your hotel and you always know where my office is.'

'The Bureau of Nothing Important.'

'The very same.'

From Miguel, Sasha learned that the confusion at the bishop's palace was due to Faupel's insistence on seeing Franco.

'I heard that one of his airmen went into the *barrio* Chino looking for entertainment and was found in a scandalous position by the Civil Guard and arrested.' Before the war, Miguel had been a seminarist and had a prurient interest in sex. Normally pleasant, he sniggered when he spoke of it. 'Faupel was trying to get the man freed.'

Sasha thought it more likely that Prince Carlo was right and that the German had been talking to Franco about trade. But at all events, his visit had disrupted the day's planned appointments and there was nothing to do but make new ones and leave. José and Sasha were pleased since they were entirely unconvinced that their business of the cargo shortage was anything more than trivial and they preferred to forget about it.

To his mild surprise, on his way across the Plaza Anaya, Sasha found himself approached by the prince.

'I have a message,' said the latter. '*La principessa*, she invites you to come and see us, and also bring your friend d'Amboise.'

'That's very kind of you both.'

'Old friends,' said the prince doubtfully, and Sasha could see why. He was still struck how Prince Carlo had been transformed into someone purposeful.

'Where are you staying?'

'Capitano Marchesi will explain,' answered the prince. He snapped his fingers and an officer came to his side. Sasha recognized him as Paolo, who had been Princess Wanda's escort the previous evening. The prince left his aide to deal with the matter of directions, while he joined the frock-coated civilians and wandered away. Paolo gave directions to a commandeered farmhouse about fifteen kilometres outside Salamanca, along the road to Peñaranda de Bracamonte.

'What happened between you and Mercedes after Dolores and I left you?' Sasha asked.

'Nothing at all. She confirmed my first impression that she had nothing to offer either intellectually or sexually.' Constantine could excuse himself from any more elaborate response by the fact that he was driving the open-topped staff limousine lent to him by his complaisant chief and bowling down the Peñaranda road scattering peasants, goats and chickens.

Sasha knew he would get no better response and also that it was a lie. After taking directions from Captain Marchesi, Sasha had returned to the bishop's palace and managed to see Dolores in the room she shared with the other clerks and typists. Instead of welcoming him as he expected, she had been very cool and he could not persuade her to take coffee or go anywhere alone with him. However, in a moment when she thought no-one else was paying attention, she whispered vehemently: 'Your friend is an animal!'

'You weren't – I don't know how to put this – improper with her?' he asked Constantine. 'You know how traditional Spanish morality is, especially where it concerns women.'

'Those two were hardly traditional Spanish women.'

'Do you mean because they work? I don't think that necessarily changes anything. You can't assume —'

'What do you think I assumed? I was a perfect gentleman. You know that I can make myself very attractive to women when I take the trouble.'

This last comment was true. Constantine was often very popular with women, though Sasha had noticed that his appeal was more commonly to somewhat older ones such as Lydia Kalinowska and the princess. This popularity did not seem to influence his generally contemptuous regard for female qualities.

Their speed was reduced by troop movements and military traffic, which were throwing a fine dust up into the face of the morning sun, so that at times the sky seemed a white bronze with a glitter of mica particles. The fields, sown for wheat and sunflowers, lay flat to the horizon, broken only by odd stands of ilex.

Stragglers from the columns were relieving themselves among the plants. Without other cover they hid in the natural anonymity of their faces, so that they were happy to stare and be stared at, and this, with the ritual posture of squatting and the public arena, gave the act of defecation a strangely sacramental quality. Constantine cheered and blew the horn whenever they came in sight.

Beyond Peñaranda, beyond Avila and the mountains, the road led to Madrid and the front, but save for the stragglers and a *tercio* of legionaries marching on foot, burdened in the sunshine by their undiscarded winter campaign dress, the road was empty of soldiers though not of war. For kilometres an unending line of supplies and supports crept at a walking pace: carts loaded with sacks of flour, rice and chickpeas, sutlers' vans, mobile forges, ambulances, ammunition wagons; equipment for sappers, engineers, bridge-pontoons, radios; gasoline carriers, water carriers, trucks loaded with blankets, tents and kerosene stoves. Although some of the transport was motorized, most of it was pulled by long spans of draught animals advancing under the whips of the teamsters. When there was a breakdown, the carts were pushed into the fields to await repair. Sasha and Constantine came across animals grazing among the growing crops, their masters waiting patiently by the roadside, barefoot and mending their *alpargatas*.

The car became stuck in this line and had to proceed at the same pace. After initial impatience, Constantine mused: 'Do you suppose that anyone is actually doing any fighting?'

'What sort of plane is that?' Sasha pointed to the sky, where a machine seemed to browse slowly among the clouds. 'Ours or theirs?'

'A Savoia – ours. Have you been *anywhere* where there's been fighting?'

'I once went through a village where the church had been burned and the priest shot, or that's what I was told. Are you sure it isn't a Junkers?'

'It could be. What did you see?'

'Nothing. We went through on the train. A few slogans had been daubed on the wall of the station and I saw a couple of buildings that had fallen down or been shelled, but who could tell which? At the best of times this is a run-down country.'

'Do you want to see action?'

'I don't know.'

'I do. I want to get myself killed – provided I'm there to watch the funeral. God, this is a bore! If we turn off here, we may be able to get ahead of the convoy.'

They were at a junction where an unmetalled lane met the highway. Constantine yanked the car off the main road and accelerated between the fields of sunflowers, leaving a cloud of dust behind him. However, beyond a small farm the lane gave out at a bend in a broad river, which they supposed was the Tormés.

'Damn!' cried Constantine. 'Shall we turn back? Why bother?'

'Prince Carlo is expecting us.'

'The devil take Carlo and his cow-faced wife.' Constantine got out of the vehicle and paced up and down the river bank. It was obvious that there was no crossing. He picked up a fallen branch and slashed at the rushes extending from the shallow bank.

'What shall we do?' Sasha asked.

In the middle of the stream was a broad, flat island, surrounded by reeds and iris and covered with stunted ilex and acacia. The sky was still white and marbled with cloud, but the water reflected a deep vegetable green, stirred by nothing but fish snapping at flies.

'I intend to swim out there,' said Constantine. He began at once to strip off his uniform. Then, naked, he plunged into the river and swam briskly the short distance to the island. A minute later Sasha saw him leaping and waving among the undergrowth. 'Come on in! Come on in!'

'Don't be stupid!' Sasha shouted across. 'We're already late.'

Constantine did not reply except to give a Fascist salute and then march up and down the bank in a goose step.

'Damn you,' murmured Sasha, and he too stripped off and made the short swim.

On the other side, he found Constantine on his knees praying. Seeing Sasha, the latter looked up and grinned.

'You're a madman,' Sasha said, still annoyed.

'Quite likely,' Constantine answered, unconcerned. 'But at least I'm a thorough-going madman. I don't expect everyone to love me for it under some pretence of innocence. You need to grow up, Sasha, and become completely sane or crazy. What are you now? A philosopher or a child? I can't follow which. Do you remember rubbish and nonsense?'

'Of course.'

'Well, I've finally found their perfect embodiment: Carlism!'

Sasha knew little about Carlism except that the Carlists

supported Franco and their stronghold was in Navarre. They were also stridently Catholic and reactionary. Whenever Sasha had occasion to attend church, the *boinas rojas* of the Carlist militiamen were prominent among the worshippers. Sasha found that Spanish Catholicism made him uncomfortable. It was riddled with death and virginity in a way that bound the two together. Looking now at Constantine, he saw suddenly that this might have a shameful appeal to his friend; and, for the first time and briefly, he felt a frisson of disgust. Constantine, however, had got to his feet and was standing by the water's edge looking upwards through the trees as a flight of Savoias passed high overhead on the way to bomb Madrid.

Sasha realized that Constantine's eccentricities were beginning to bore him and that, oddly, the feeling was reciprocated. Mechanically he said: 'So, tell me about Carlism.'

'What's to tell? It's the most absurd movement that ever was. Apparently it goes back a hundred years to the Don Carlos who was the uncle of Isabella II and fought a couple of unsuccessful civil wars to try to win the throne. Why anybody should care these days, God alone knows. And what makes the thing more ridiculous is that, as far as I can make out, the Carlists are monarchists without a king, since their claimant appears to have died. Do you follow? They're fighting in favour of an illegitimate king who happens to be dead!'

Constantine spoke as if he was trying to inject, if not enthusiasm, at least humour into his tale of nonsense. But instead he became melancholy and distracted, picked up a handful of pebbles and threw them singly into the water. 'Of course, I'm in favour of Carlism,' he added. He looked up again at the sky where the bombers were still passing. 'That'll be us soon. This – this peace is all false! Something will happen and it will be horrible!'

'I think the Bureau of Nothing Important has enough work to see me quietly through the war,' Sasha answered.

'I've told you that I'm supporting Carlism. What about

you? Why are you here? Don't tell me that you admire the Lord of Hosts, Prince of Peace, His Pot-bellyness, Generalissimo Franco?'

'No, I don't.'

Perversely, Constantine asked: 'And why not?'

'Because all Franco wants to do is perpetuate a regime of landlords, priests and businessmen in a sort of mirror image of Marxism, as if he wants to prove that Marx is right. If that's all his crusade amounts to, then it isn't enough. Not for me and not for Spain. Within nationalism and religion, the State has to have a social message: it has to offer something to the poor.'

'You're sounding like a Communist again.'

'No, I'm not. That's precisely what I'm *not* doing. Franco and the Reds are both promoting class conflict and they'll each fail because, in the long run, social classes cannot be suppressed, still less destroyed. If the Right is going to succeed, it has to be idealistic: it has to have a radical social programme that integrates the classes and reconciles the workers to the regime.'

'You've been reading Don José Antonio,' Constantine said with some amusement. Sasha admitted that he had studied some speeches of Primo de Rivera and agreed with them. In fact, he had been touched by the idealism of the Falangist leader and the tragedy and nobility of his death in a Republican prison.

'Then you're a Fascist,' said Constantine.

'I suppose I am. It's a perfectly respectable thing to be.'

'Who said it wasn't?'

'Then why smile?'

'Oh,' said Constantine airily. 'I suppose because your idealism is even more absurd than my Carlism, since you fool yourself that it can actually come about in this world.' The smile stopped abruptly and he stared fiercely at Sasha and said: 'I believe in ignorance, obscurantism and meaningless ritual. Left to myself I would wipe out the whole of verminous humanity.'

'And leave what?'

'What? Yes – what? I think I would leave a choir of angels singing "Te Deum Laudamus". And *nothing* there to hear them!'

'We were expecting you earlier,' said Princess Wanda, adding in her American drawl: 'Not that it matters.'

'There was a lot of military traffic on the road,' Sasha explained.

'I know. And it doesn't seem to make any difference if one travels at night. That's war, I guess. A glass of wine?'

Prince Carlo was asleep. All the Italian officers were asleep and expected to wake up at four or thereabouts. The ordinary soldiers dozed under the acacias, played cards or wrote letters home. Outside the walls of the farm, which enclosed shade-giving trees and formed a nest of coolness, the shadowless plain simmered in the sun. It was still the early part of the year, only April. Sasha thought that in summer, in the south, the heat must be unimaginable. But what did he know of Spain?

The princess had applied cold cream to her face against the sun. On the table beside her were a pair of small gold spectacles and a copy of the *Christian Science Monitor*.

'You've missed lunch. You could still take an hour's siesta. You look . . .'

'We've been swimming,' Sasha told her.

'I remember you once danced in the sea.'

Obscurely bad-tempered since their swim, Constantine said: 'I think I will take that siesta.'

The princess waved him away. Sasha said:

'That seems such a long time ago.'

'It was with . . . Katya Safronova? That's it, Katya! I'd forgotten. I had a picture in my head: so vivid, yet for the life of me I couldn't think who the woman was. I suppose she wasn't important – to the image, I mean. To you, I guess, she would be important. And there I was, the other night, talking about her and how she had left Kolya and whatever happened to her – all the time forgetting that you might have been interested in her. I'm sorry.'

'It doesn't matter now.'

'I suppose not.'

Princess Wanda cast her eyes about her listlessly. Sasha thought that in this heat he and she seemed the only things truly alive; the soldiers seemed no more active than a dog scratching for a stray flea. The house, whose walls were powdery with an ochre distemper that contributed its dust to the dust of the yard, was blind-eyed behind its shuttered jalousies. A few yuccas had been planted in the dust, and mimosa and oleander. Returning her gaze to her guest, the princess said indifferently:

'I'm going to make a pile of money out of this war, see if I don't. But who cares, eh, Sasha?'

'I was talking to someone. She said that the foreigners in Spain didn't care about Spain. They were just continuing the conflicts of their own countries.'

'She's a smart girl. On the other hand, nothing's that simple. If I perform an altruistic act like fighting for Spain, I satisfy my desire to do it. So does it cease to be altruistic and become selfish? You can quote me on that: it isn't original.'

Through the gate Sasha could see the path that joined the farm to the Peñaranda highway. It was difficult to judge the distance across the plain. One or two pines and ilex trees in the middle distance might have marked it. It was near enough for the motor vehicles to be audible; the sky immediately above the horizon was orange with dust. So the sensation of war was as palpable as a heartbeat, there to be felt whenever attention strayed to it. Sasha was conscious of its latency and tension.

Prince Carlo had woken early. He did not come outside. Instead he applied himself to work. Sasha could hear him bawling out the captain and had enough Italian to realize that he was issuing precise and detailed commands. Only logic told him that it was the prince: nothing in the voice suggested the diffident man who had once followed in his wife's shadow. And this thought brought Sasha to reconsider what Princess Wanda had said. She would make a pile of money out of the war. He had treated the remark as a vulgar Americanism, consistent with his general prejudices and his previous opinion of her. Then she had added: 'But who cares?'

What to make of that little coda? Did it suggest that in fact she was a sentimental woman whose materialism was more a habit than a conviction? She had, after all, remembered that he had danced in the sea and the fanciful image had stayed with her. Sasha had to accept the possibility that he had been mistaken both about the princess and her husband.

Coming through the door, the prince noticed his guest. He said rather stiffly: 'So you are here, Alessandro. Good. Forgive me if we do not talk, but I have work to do.' Captain Marchesi and the two frock-coated civilians followed. The group sat itself where it could best find shade and Prince Carlo demanded iced water. When the soldier bringing it spilled some, he struck him. 'Fool! Get a cloth!'

A paper had been knocked from the table. Sasha picked it up and read: 'Società Anonima Finanziere Nazionale Italiana'. He replaced it and turned his eyes on the soldier, who seemed a heavy-jowled peasant.

'It's about the mercury mines at Almadén,' said the princess. 'We're trying to get our share of the concession, and Franco, naturally, is trying to resist. Really, Carlo,' she remarked to her husband, 'you shouldn't hit the men.' She smiled at Sasha and, lifting her hand to screen her eyes from a shift in the position of the sun, she said: 'This is not my idea of war. Do you know, I think that's the first violence I've seen.'

They drove back slowly to the city. The traffic, which on leaving had seemed so heavy, now seemed negligible. Instead, the flow of vehicles and men was in the opposite direction, as if the front had reversed itself and the troops who had been needed in the morning to attack Madrid were now needed to defend Salamanca. They came across a company of *requetés* bivouacked in a wheat field. One of them, recognizing Constantine's red beret, sprang out of the gloom and flagged the car down.

'Captain . . . Sorry, sir. My mistake. I thought you might be our officer.'

'What's wrong?'

'We've got separated from our tents and rations. Our captain went back to look for them. Have you seen him?'

'No.'

'No luck, *amigos*!' shouted the soldier into the darkness, and a cry came back: '*Hombre*! Does nothing go right in this damned army?'

The men had a priest with them. He was wearing marching boots, puttees and a short army blouse over his soutane. When he appeared, Constantine, to Sasha's astonishment, leapt out of the car, knelt and asked for his blessing.

'My blessing? Yes, all right. *In nomine patris* . . . Did you catch any sight of the cart with our rations?'

'He hasn't seen them,' said the soldier.

'Damn!' said the priest.

It was nearly midnight when Constantine returned the car and they went to a café in the Plaza Mayor. José and Miguel were at their usual spot. Conversation was still about the Italian defeat at Guadalajara. It amused them to tell stories of their ally's discomfiture. On the other hand, there was an air of tension. The Civil Guard were present in force, moving in pairs through the evening crowd, checking papers. A few nights before there had been trouble at the Falangist headquarters and cadets from the Pedro Llen school had broken into the building to restore order. Next there had been a disturbance at a pension in the Plaza Mayor itself and the bodyguard of a Falangist leader had been killed. These incidents were followed by arrests. Tonight the Civil Guard were picking out for particular attention anyone wearing Carlist insignia or the blue shirt of the Falange.

Without any obvious cause, Constantine seemed to have become drunk. While watching the leather bicornes of the Civil Guard bobbing among the seated customers of the cafés, Sasha heard him speaking as though in confidence to Miguel, but in a loud voice.

'I had this friend – naming no names. A Communist, though you wouldn't think of it to look at him, one of the milk-and-water Reds who can wreck everything because you think that no-one so apparently decent could possibly hurt you. He fell in love with a married woman. I use the term "married" loosely since the ceremony was a civil one, in fact we only have her word for it that there was a ceremony at all. So let's call her a whore, shall we? My story is about a Red in love with a whore.' Seeing Sasha, he said in calm and deadly drunkenness: 'I'm talking about a friend. Do you want to listen?'

'No,' said Sasha angrily. He found it difficult to believe that Constantine was telling this story and it was his incredulousness that stayed him from any further action. Constantine continued determinedly:

'This Red was a fool. He believed in love and ideals. I know you're going to say that Reds are the sons of Satan and don't believe in love and ideals, but in actual fact you're wrong. Being a Red is about misplaced love and ideals; don't believe all their nonsense about materialism.'

He had lapsed into French, which only Sasha could follow clearly. The others, who at first had listened, turned their attention to the radio in the café, which had blared an anthem and Franco was beginning to speak. At this the tables emptied and those who could squeezed into the interior. Some of the men stood solemnly.

Sasha was alone. He could see that around the square the same scene was being acted. But in the public garden the strollers had heard nothing and continued their *paseo*. Among them he saw Dolores and Mercedes.

Franco was announcing the dissolution of the Falange and the Carlists and the merger of their supporters into a new party of which he would be the leader. Among the listeners there was consternation and then snatches of song – 'Cara al Sol', 'Oriamendi', 'El Novio de la Muerte' – until one dominated the others and the crowd as a whole was on its feet singing.

Or so it seemed to Sasha. Later, José said that the people seemed unenthusiastic and that among the supporters of the old parties there was much resentment. He did not recall the singing or the salutes or the *vivas* for Franco. But in Sasha's version, the anthems were ringing in his head as he left the empty table. He walked over to the two girls and spoke to Dolores. Mercedes turned and stood aside.

He said:

'Hello. How are you?'

'What? Oh, it's you. What are you doing here?'

'Excuse me? I'm with Constantine.'

'Hah!'

Dolores turned away and scooped Mercedes under the arm and they walked away through the garden, looking as ridiculous as two girls can do who stick together, love and hate together. Puzzled, Sasha followed. He put away thoughts of Constantine, seeing what another man might not have seen: that behind the ridiculousness there was pain.

'Dolores?'

'Go away!'

'What's wrong?'

'Go away!'

But she stopped, and Sasha, so earnest, was now too stupid to realize that she was attracted by him, despite whatever made her angry. He was watching Mercedes, who was crying. Around her the boys were laughing at her, cadets and young officers out for the evening and looking hopelessly for the girls that convention denied them. He pressed Dolores.

'Don't be silly, you must tell me what's wrong!'

'Ask Constantine!' she answered.

'Connie? What about Connie?'

He looked back to the café and fancied he saw Constantine among the singing cheering crowd.

'He tried to rape her!' said Dolores.

CHAPTER 20

THE FOUNTAIN WITH CARYATIDS

The two women nudged each other with pleasure as they examined the goods in the window of Tomàs Collomer, a jeweller's shop in the Paseo de Gràcia, that had recently felt confident enough to display its wares again, after a period of months when the anarchists had been liable to ransack the shop at any show of luxury. Now, except for the tape across the glass to prevent it from shattering, one could almost believe that things were back to normal.

On the corner a shoeshine boy had set up business and a soldier was sitting to have his boots polished. Katya had been vaguely aware of him, but only when she turned her head to say something to her friend did she recognize him.

'Daniel?'

The soldier looked up from his newspaper. Dark and good-looking in the slightly dangerous way of a man who stares too long, his face was aquiline and pinched as though he had recently been ill. He wore a uniform, not unusual in itself, that was neither for combat nor smart enough for a staff post. Katya had seen similar uniforms. They belonged to officers who organized transports and the billeting of troops. His expression changed to a smile.

He folded the paper and dropped a few coins into the hands of the shoeshine boy.

'Katya! I had no idea that you were in Barcelona!'

She smiled delightedly.

'I knew you were here. Your mother wrote to me. I went to the Voroshilov barracks looking for you, but no-one had heard of you.'

'I was at the Pedrera, they should have told you that. But I'm astonished to see you. I never thought . . .'

'That I would come to Spain? No, it took me by surprise as well!' She laughed, as did her friend, and Daniel thought fleetingly that this was not the Katya he knew. She seemed merry. She said: 'Let me introduce Maria. We work together. This is Daniel Coën. I've mentioned him before.'

'*Bon dia*,' said Daniel, which only provoked more laughter. They seemed bubbling with it.

'Maria isn't Catalan, she's an Italian, a foreigner like me! But seriously, it is good to see you, Daniel. I never thought I'd want to see people I knew from Paris, but here you are and it's wonderful.'

'You seem very cheerful.'

'Yes, I am. Grotesque, isn't it? In the middle of a civil war, I find myself as happy as I've ever been. I should be ashamed.' But obviously she was not. 'Look, we have some errands to do. We can walk? The fact is that we shouldn't be here, we're far too busy, but we had half a mind to see a film.' Further down the street, below the Fénix insurance building, was a cinema.

'What are you doing?' Daniel asked. The women were walking arm in arm, taking pleasure in each other's company. Although they were each wearing drab, blue, oil-stained *monos*, the effect was raffish and attractive. Maria was very pretty, black-haired, black-eyed, with an olive complexion and a small overbite; when she was not smiling, her teeth rested prettily on her bottom lip as if she were always about to speak. The women were obviously very fond of each other.

'Doing? We're trying to buy supplies.'

'No, I meant here in Barcelona?'

'We're not always here. We run an ambulance between Barcelona and the front. Maria is a nurse. Would you believe I'm a driver and mechanic? No? I find it incredible, too. Kolya taught me to drive, and as to the mechanical part, the Spaniards seem to believe that all foreigners are geniuses with machinery. Isn't that right, Maria?'

'Katya is a wonderful mechanic!' said Maria.

'Are we taking you out of your way?' Katya asked.

'No, I'm going to the Hotel Colón. As a matter of fact, if you ever need to find me, I suggest you leave a message there rather than at the barracks.'

The Hotel Colón was the Communist headquarters.

'Why there? Are you in Barcelona permanently? Don't you have a unit? I heard that the Fifth Regiment . . .'

'I've been invalided out of the army,' Daniel answered quietly, and Katya realized that there was something wrong with his left arm. The sleeve of his khaki *cazadora* was folded and pinned beneath the elbow. She had, in fact, noticed this on first meeting him, without attaching particular significance: it was one of those small but unsettling differences, like a change of hairstyle, which alter appearances without the cause always being evident. She exclaimed:

'You've lost your arm? I mean – oh Daniel, I'm sorry!'

It was Daniel's turn to smile with a shade of irony. 'I've got used to it.'

'But how?'

It seemed to Daniel that she was concerned but not distressed. Most people would be embarrassed, yet she was not. He supposed she must be habituated to the sight of the wounded.

'I did a spell of training at Albacete and then they sent me to Madrid. It was during the big rebel attack on the University City, when we were throwing in every man we could, even raw recruits. I was struck by grenade fragments.' He swung the stump from the shoulder and

539

tried to sound encouraging. 'See, I haven't lost all of it, just the forearm. What's left is still quite useful. I can carry a parcel under it.'

They were in the Plaza de Cataluña. Katya was waiting for a tramcar to pass before crossing to the central garden.

'This is as far as I go,' said Daniel.

'You? . . . Of course, I was forgetting where we are.'

Draped with red flags, the Hotel Colón was only a few steps away.

'The Party found me a political job.'

'You haven't thought of . . .'

'Going home? No. What use would I be? What work could I find? Here at least there is something I can do, something with a purpose.'

'Yes . . . I can see that.'

They remained standing for a moment among the press of passers-by. Katya was thinking how obtuse she had been: his sallow face showed no trace of the sun; she imagined him working in an office. He asked:

'Where are you staying?'

'The Hotel Jardín. Do you know it?'

'No, but I can probably find it.'

Katya smiled wryly. 'Six of us share a room.' She turned to her friend. 'Is it six, Maria?'

'Six, maybe eight.'

Apparently the overcrowding was a joke.

'We're all ambulance girls. We spend half our time at the front ferrying casualties from the clearing stations. No-one is exactly sure how many of us are sharing our room, since we're never all there at the same time.'

Daniel also found the notion amusing. He had a mental picture of a room full of women and drying underwear. He supposed, rightly, that the Hotel Jardín was a dingy pension somewhere in the *barrio* Gótico.

'In that case, perhaps I'd better not call on you.'

'No, probably not. But we could go to the cinema. I told you I enjoyed films.'

'I like them too.'

'Then that's what we'll do. Is that agreed?'

It was agreed and a time and place fixed. Then Katya said that she must be going. Daniel, too, had urgent business, but he waited and watched as the two women dodged the tramcars and supply trucks to cross the square. He lost sight of them somewhere in the central section among the trees and monuments before they reached the top of the Ramblas; but he noticed that, once out of his company, Katya and her friend held hands and talked again in pleasant intimacy. He saw the swing of their hair and hips, and the way that, in talking, they inclined their heads one to another as though passing secrets.

He remembered a woman who had been melancholy and disappointed, and wondered what had happened to her.

'I thought you said he was sinister, a bit of a fanatic?' said Maria. From time to time she had looked back and, once, waved and giggled.

'That was how he struck me,' Katya answered. 'He used to appear so dissatisfied and resentful. And in those days I thought that all Communists were sinister fanatics.'

Maria's eyes twinkled. She was a Communist. That was why she had fled Italy, and, ultimately, why she had come to Spain.

'Well, he doesn't look sinister now. And that arm, neither of us noticed it. He doesn't wear it like a disability. It makes him look distinguished, a man with a history. I just hope –' she added '– that nothing else has been damaged. Nothing vital, if you understand me.'

'You are vulgar!' Katya jostled her friend playfully.

'Of course I'm vulgar. The working class is famous for vulgarity. It is our contribution to culture. And I don't care. What I said is true. I don't mind about his arm so long as he is a proper man.'

But, thought Katya, he has changed. He isn't softer, but he seems more at ease with himself. Spain has done that for him, as it has for me. Clarified us.

In the Ramblas, not far from the square, was an old pharmacy with a façade of brown and green tiles. Maria went inside to investigate the stocks. Katya turned the corner into a small side street where a linen drapers hid beneath a dark arcade. The shop, El Indio, had some cotton remnants which she bought for bandages. On the opposite side of the street was a patisserie.

'A treat,' she told Maria, handing her a pastry. Maria had acquired a bottle of ammonia.

'Where's yours?'

'I wasn't hungry,' said Katya. She had given hers to one of the child beggars who haunted the pastry shops. Maria accepted the explanation. She ate her gift with animal pleasure. Katya asked her: 'Did you find anything?'

'Only this,' she said, indicating the bottle of ammonia. 'There's another pharmacy further down. Let's try it.'

There they found disinfectant and a quantity of aspirin.

'Well? Now what? Try somewhere else?'

'Tomorrow. I need sleep.'

'I don't know about sleep: I need to wash my knickers. And my hair, for that matter.'

'You are vulgar,' Katya repeated with a smile. Arm in arm they returned to the Hotel Jardín.

In the Plaza del Angel the windows of the numismatist's shop were patterned with tape in a manner that was almost artistic. Someone, identifying coinage with capitalism, had painted a slogan on the wall: *Proletarios de Todos Paises! Unios!* But these days it was permissible to wash such slogans away and pretend that life went on. A man might even wear a hat and tie.

Daniel arrived by tramcar down the Via Laietana, a depressing commercial street that Katya thought seemed intimidated by its buildings. They had agreed to meet in the Plaza del Angel because the café there was convenient and reasonably cheap. He was dressed in the same military blouson as earlier and, on this occasion, one of the common *gorillo* caps with a red star worn fore-and-aft in a sporty fashion. Katya had wanted to wear her only dress, but that afternoon, unthinkingly, she had decided to have her hair cropped against lice before returning to the front; and, when she put the dress on, her face had seemed gaunt. So she wore a clean blue overall.

'Are you as jolly as you were this morning with your friend?' he asked. He had noticed the hair without noticing, recording mistakenly that her face seemed more serious. Katya disabused him by grinning.

'So you really are glad to see me again?' he said.

'Yes, though I know what you mean. In strange places, people one doesn't know well, or doesn't particularly like, suddenly seem like old friends – I'm sorry, that sounds tactless.'

'I understand. And it happens that I agree. Do you want another drink? I can't remember: do you smoke?' He took out a pack. 'We have a system, a rota. Each of us takes it in turns to queue for a ration. You don't? I had an idea – didn't Le Nain once try to persuade you to smoke? Something to do with your voice.'

'Yes, he did! Good God, I'd forgotten.' Katya shook her head, both pleased and embarrassed at the recollection. She had in fact tried and hated it. 'How is he?'

'Oh, he's fine! He has a new act – he hit on a new idea. He dresses up and parades around the stage looking like Mussolini. A dwarf who looks like Mussolini! Can you imagine it?'

'He should do Franco. Franco is shorter.'

'That's true! On the other hand, I suppose the joke is in the contrast.'

They fell silent, but it was an enjoyable silence. Katya reflected that Daniel was the first man with whom she felt wholly comfortable, and wondered whether it was some particular quality of his or a change in her own nature. At last he proposed that they should go to the cinema, if that were the object of the evening's entertainment. After some discussion they agreed on the Poliorama.

There was a Russian drama and an American comedy, and the newsreel was heroic and misleading. Afterwards, stepping out into the night, they heard nearby, from a café close to the Hotel Falcón, a group of POUMistas singing a revolutionary song. The young men and women were sitting beneath the plane trees on the central promenade. One of them had an accordion. They sang with feeling, even beauty, but Daniel pulled Katya away and they walked in the other direction down towards the quayside.

'Why did you do that?' she asked.

'They annoy me. This isn't the time for revolutionary postures. There's a war to win. Look, I don't want to talk about politics.'

'In Paris you always talked about politics.'

'In Paris there was nothing else to do. We could afford to be purists. Here we have to be realistic. The Party isn't looking for a revolution. The conditions aren't right. We're happy to collaborate with the bourgeois democrats. As for singing, I leave it to Maurice Chevalier.'

He gave a sudden laugh.

'What's funny?' asked Katya, ready to share.

'I just remembered something. When we were kids, Sasha Zhivago and I had a joke that God was called Maurice.'

'Why Maurice?'

'I've no idea! Maurice . . . ? No, I can't recall.'

They both laughed and repeated: 'Maurice! Maurice? Ha! Maurice!'

'Do you have any news of Sasha?' Daniel asked. 'I haven't seen or heard of him since last September, before I came here. My mother has written nothing. I half-expected that Sasha would write himself.'

'Then you don't know?'

'Don't know what?'

'That he's in Spain.'

'Since when?' Daniel exclaimed.

'I don't know exactly – four or five months? He left Paris a few weeks before I did.'

'Then where is he? Which militia did he join? I can't believe it! I asked him to enlist with me, but I never expected that he would come.'

Katya realized that he was genuinely ignorant, and could think of nothing but to tell him. He had stopped walking when she first said that Sasha was in Spain and turned to face her. Her hands had gone out to touch him. One hand rested on his right forearm. The other had reached for the left and found nothing. He could feel her reaching clumsily for nothing, and took both her hands in his one good hand and asked what was wrong.

'Sasha joined the rebels,' she said. 'That's probably why your mother hasn't told you.'

'The rebels?' He was shocked. No, it wasn't shock, she thought, but a sort of resigned anger as if it were something expected but not accepted. He said gloomily: 'It's Constantine and that damned Jesuit,' and added, incongruously, 'Would you like a drink?'

They were by the Café de l'Opéra. It was possible to get wine, though not coffee, and the waiter volunteered slyly that he could supply Lucky Strike cigarettes for ten pesetas, which was a day's pay. Daniel resumed bitterly:

'I have never met such a fool as Sasha! Why does everyone like him? Why does he have to be liked? It's crazy but even now, if I met him, I'd probably throw my arms around him.'

'It's because he likes other people,' said Katya. 'He believes the best about them. He sees their point of view. I think he even pities them.'

'He's Sasha Zhivago, not Jesus Christ! And, even so, how could he fight for Franco?'

Katya shook her head. She recalled the night in Nice when Sasha had stumbled across her and thought she was going to kill herself. Immediately he had befriended her, a stranger, and taken her to his family. There was something completely indiscriminate about Sasha's affections. It would be impossible ever to feel that he was exclusively committed to one person. And there was something

545

demeaning in being the object of goodwill without ever being required to deserve it. Perhaps that was why she could not love him.

Seeing Daniel so angry at the folly of his friend reminded Katya of her own lack of childhood friends. During those years with Viktor he had managed to contrive a situation in which her only company was that of adults. It was a horrible thought that he had wanted her to be adult, and surrogate for her mother; and, in the end, that was what she had become, taking care of his household after the disappearance of her mother.

'Katya?'

'I was drifting off, thinking about something else.'

Daniel, preoccupied with Sasha, picked up no clues that he had stirred distressing memories. Recognizing this lack of insight, Katya smiled wryly. Thinking he was at one with her thoughts he was saying:

'I think you're right. Sasha lacks any moral discrimination. If he likes you, he thinks you must be good and decent and any ideas you hold must be worth considering. He goes beyond being liberal. Any moral proposition seems to him to be good, as long as one holds it sincerely.' He laughed and Katya thought that his laughter added a bright humanity to his serious face. He said: 'It's ironic, isn't it, that Sasha of all people should have studied philosophy! It's almost enough to make one believe in God! The joke is cosmic! But that's philosophy for you. It merely gives you a vocabulary for your confusion, a formal structure for idiocy.'

In the mild evening people were still strolling along the Ramblas and chatting under the plane trees and the hanging banners of the political parties, red for Communist, red and black for Anarchist. When they rose from the café, Daniel took Katya's arm in his and they walked together. Katya was pleased by the casual gesture of intimacy. It was so obvious to her that, for now, her companion's thoughts were filled with Sasha and politics – a point as to which she was mistaken since Daniel was thinking intensely about her, and his taking of her arm had been anything but casual.

On the left of the street, before the square, was a fountain. A child was drinking the water, and Katya, looking at the child, noticed the fountain and, without at first knowing why, was transfixed.

'Well?' prompted Daniel.

'What? Oh, sorry, I was looking at the fountain. There was something about it. Don't you think it's beautiful?'

The surprise had gone. In fact Katya felt happy.

'It's all right. Yes, it's beautiful if you like,' Daniel answered. He paused and asked in a voice that showed his wonderment at her transformation: 'Who are you? Whatever happened to the woman I knew in Paris?'

Katya answered gaily:

'I don't know. What do you think? How am I different?'

'You're happy. What a thing to say! But it's right, I suppose. In Paris you were, if not exactly miserable, composed. I didn't like your composure. It seemed – what's the word – glued together out of bits that didn't fit. I would have said that you were a person who wasn't made for happiness.'

'I would have said the same,' said Katya thoughtfully.

Her gaze had lingered over the mysterious fountain.

'Let's go and have a look at it,' Daniel proposed.

The fountain stood on a curved pedestal and was covered by a dome topped by a cluster of dolphins. Four caryatids supported the dome and on one side water poured into a scallop shell. It was made of iron and had been there for perhaps fifty years, an unremarkable piece of street furniture.

Katya studied the four female figures and murmured: 'The caryatids!'

Daniel said nothing but watched as she ran her fingers over the curves of the fountain; and for a moment she seemed a part of the group as if it had come alive and marvelled at its own life. Her fingers left the fountain yet

547

her face retained something of the serenity of the figures, and then she smiled and said:

'When my mother and I lived in Yuryatin, there was a house opposite ours. I don't remember it exactly – I was very small – but there were caryatids built into the stonework. I saw them every day, women made of stone – and they supported the building.'

'Yes?'

Katya shook her head. 'How does anyone explain her childhood?'

'You were happy there?'

'Oh, yes!' she replied enthusiastically. 'It was the only time in my childhood that I was happy! My Uncle Yura came back from the war and we lived there and at Varykino. It's all impressions. I can't describe it to you. But, yes, we were happy.'

'Who was Uncle Yura?'

'He loved my mother,' Katya answered softly and then suggested: 'Why don't we go dancing?'

Daniel was taken aback and could only say: 'With this arm?'

Katya grabbed him and he suffered himself to be manoeuvred into a dancing position.

'I see nothing wrong with that,' she said firmly.

'Don't be silly. We can't dance in the street.'

'In the street! In the sea! Even in a dance hall! Come on, I know one!'

Katya pulled and Daniel found himself following helplessly behind her, marvelling still at the joy that was in her. And she, too, was thinking how changed he was and that the sinister qualities she had once suspected in him had gone. It did not occur to her that Daniel was perhaps only mirroring her own excess of life, and that in reality nothing had changed with him except that his former attitudes were now deeper and more considered.

In a city at war but not actually under siege, there is no shortage of dance halls. They differ from those under conditions of peace in that they are more gay and more poignant. The banal melodies are more haunting and the words more full of meaning – indeed the very songs that are the facile lies of peace become true in war, the song-writers true philosophers. Can you dance? See the black American volunteer (from Birmingham, Alabama via Chicago and the Communist Party) who can now dance the stately *sardana*. See the poor Catalan labourer, down from his dirt farm near Monistrol to fight for land, who now foxtrots to a tune by Cole Porter. See the girls in cotton frocks or blue overalls, scandalously free from their suffocating families, embracing in dance men who are strangers to them, who have not been properly introduced, who will steal a kiss yet never become their *novios*. There is much happiness in war. Visit a dance hall.

And afterwards walk.

Walk, and tonight the moon will shine and the air will be soft and the fragrances sweet: or, if they are not, every variation on these themes will itself be full of delight. For tonight folly occupies our bodies, and common sense, like a drunk, is dragged in our shadow and changes size and shape and wanders crazily across the walls at every passing light; and we can be forgiven for distrusting so unreliable and inconstant a thing as sense. Or so it seems as we pause to light a cigarette or fasten a shoe, or even to talk about the night itself, using such language as makes our shadow of sense hide in the dark. For language itself has become foolish, and makes no apologies.

Caught in the light, the shadows of Katya and Daniel were thrown across a wall, like caryatids supporting the roof.

In a small and smelly square of darkness stood the Hotel Jardín, by a church that had been wrecked by workers in the social revolution that followed Franco's uprising.

'Why don't you come up?' said Katya leading Daniel by the hand.

'May I?'

'Why not?'

Up the stairs and into the small room which eight female ambulance crew (more or less) shared as occasion demanded. But tonight there was no-one there: even Maria, following her own vigorous sexual appetite, had found alternative lodging.

By candlelight, the power being cut, Daniel saw the piles of linen, bandages and medicines stacked between truckle beds and bedrolls, and the revolutionary posters, and even the rosary that had no place being there.

'Have you bought this stuff yourself? I remember you saying something about shopping for supplies. Surely the Government provides everything you need?'

'I spend Kolya's money,' said Katya. She sat on one of the creaking beds. Daniel did not read her movement as an invitation. In the confines of the room shadows were small: shadow and body nearly one. 'I don't feel guilty about it.'

'But I thought you left him?'

'I did. He still makes me an allowance. He has many faults, but he isn't a vindictive man.'

Daniel accepted this as true, but except for a passing thought that Kolya was a fool, he made no further enquiry. It did not occur to him to compare Kolya's obsession for Katya with his own fascination for this woman. He supposed, like many men but few women, that his feelings were unique. And what could he learn from another man that would not expose his vulnerability?

Instead he paced the room, fingering the objects under the fiction that he was interested in the minutiae of this woman's life; that he really cared about her day-to-day concerns; that he was about to leave.

Katya did not suppose for a second that he would go. She had not in particular planned that it would be this way, but from the moment that they had danced together she had asked herself: shall I make love with this man?

She looked at him. Seeing that he loved her – whatever

that might mean – she made the strange discovery that a man who loves, as distinct from one who merely desires women, has to be seduced. How else could she explain his reticence?

They had created between them a tactile space. The movement of her finger in the air caused his hand to recoil. His breathing, not especially close to her, made the hair on her neck quiver. Taking her courage, Katya kissed him on the lobe of his right ear as his face was turned away, ostensibly as he studied something in the room. He shuddered and then suddenly returned the kiss and just as quickly enveloped her in his arms. It was a movement that was too possessive – frighteningly so, as if he had misunderstood her intention, but also irresistible. She had been prepared to spend a little of the love that these last few months had welled up in her from unknown sources. In his urgency he seemed to demand it all, and, in her own need, it was not possible to be moderate or calculating. He said:

'You are the most astonishing woman.' And, as if angry at himself: 'What is it about you?' He released her sharply.

He removed his jacket and in a very mundane way looked for somewhere to hang it. The stump of his amputated arm was closed in a cuff of padded gauze.

'Not pretty, is it?' he said cruelly. He seemed too angry to desire her. He waggled the stump like a flipper. 'Not pretty. No.'

Was he bent on repelling her? Not if his eyes were truthful. Had she touched a nerve of distrust and self-disgust? This was quite possible.

He stared away again and she extended a hand to rest on his shoulder and her fingers caressed his throat and turned his face to hers. His hand now took hers and placed it around his waist. He gave a small sigh, scarcely more than a click in the throat, and his eyes closed.

Katya wanted to laugh. She was not mocking him. She supposed this must be what joy felt like.

The next day Katya and Maria had to drive to Lérida and then spend two weeks ferrying casualties from the clearing station at Monflorite to Sietamo and loading trains with wounded for the hospitals of Taragona and Barcelona. After that, in their old Hispano Suiza ambulance, which Katya repeatedly had to repair, they returned to Barcelona with wounded for the Santa Cruz y San Pablo hospital.

In the meantime she had been reading Maria's newspaper, the *Mundo Obrero*, which contained increasing Communist invective against the POUM, a Marxist party inimical to Stalin. Hitherto she had attached no particular importance to this. The quarrels between the various parties of the Left that supported the Republic were of little interest to her. She gathered that the POUM and the anarchists wished to continue the social revolution that had broken out during the previous summer and led to the church burnings and the taking over of some industry by the workers in an outbreak of class resentment. The Communists, in alliance with the bourgeois parties and in the name of anti-Fascist solidarity and a Popular Front government, were opposed to this. They were matters as to which she had no opinion: it was not a narrow point of ideology that had brought her to Spain. However, the charged atmosphere that had first politicized the country and divided it between Nationalists and Republicans continued to work even within those groupings. In the Nationalist zone, Franco had resolved the situation to his satisfaction, in April 1937, with the forced amalgamation of the Falange and the Carlists. In the Republican zone, however, the situation was otherwise: no single party had Franco's advantage of domination over the armed forces.

Catalonia's traditions contained a strong anarcho-syndicalist element that owed nothing to Marx and was opposed in principle to government. In contrast, the Communists were by inclination authoritarian and centralizing. Prior to the uprising, the influence of the Communists had been negligible, but during the war it had increased considerably, mainly for two reasons. The first was the enormous prestige of the Soviet Union, which had provided materiel in significant quantities when the democracies stood aside. The second was the discipline of the Communists, which appealed even to the middle classes when the latter were confronted with the alternative of disorder and revolution. Now it was May and the situation within the Republic was still unresolved.

On the morning after her return, and after a sleep of exhaustion, Katya paid a visit to the Hotel Colón. She intended little more than to inform Daniel that she was back in the city; and if anything were to develop from that, then so it would. In her new freedom Katya was beyond making plans.

Daniel met her in the lobby. Having no Party card or explicable business, she was not allowed to go further. With him was a Spaniard, introduced merely as Pedro. The latter asked: 'Are you a Communist?'

'She's a sympathizer,' Daniel told him. To Katya he said: 'Well, we can't stay here. I know somewhere where we can get coffee.'

On the way he asked her about her visit to the front and she told him merrily about the problems of the old ambulance: at one time they were towed for five kilometres by a team of mules.

'And the front itself?' he asked earnestly. 'Doesn't that depress you?'

There was an obvious answer to that: a tale of blood and pain and a confession of distress. But Katya thought it over and to her own surprise discovered that it was not true. She told Daniel so.

'Have I become callous? I don't think so. In fact, I think I feel things more intensely than I've ever done. Everything is so vivid. But I don't feel pain – no, that isn't true: I feel pain but it doesn't seem to disable me. There doesn't seem to be the room for it that there was before. When I see the poor wounded men I feel sorry for them: but I think also, there's something I can do for them, something useful. That's where the difference lies. Before, I was a spectator, screening myself from suffering so that it wouldn't become too acute. Now I can engage with it and I know honestly that I have played my part in limiting it.'

If Katya had been able at that moment to read Daniel's thoughts, she would have been disappointed. The intensity of his gaze reflected his fascination with her every physical sign, even the small flush of emotion that had coloured her cheeks. But as to her words, they struck him, probably rightly, as a conventional reaction to suffering that any doctor or nurse might have; and therefore of no particular interest. He forgot how unoriginal human beings are and that even a commonplace idea or sentiment, when recognized for the first time, can be imbued with freshness and force. In any case, she had misunderstood his question. It had been directed not at her feelings but at her impression of morale at the front, which seemed to him more important. The confusion, however, was buried in the mutual pleasure of seeing each other again. Then Katya asked:

'Why did you tell – Pedro? Was that his name? – that I was a Communist sympathizer?'

'Because you are, aren't you?'

'No. I had too much experience of Communism in Russia.'

'Then why on earth are you here?'

He was annoyed in the most petty way, namely because he had been contradicted. But Katya could only laugh and say:

'Would you believe that Lydia persuaded me?'

'Lydia Kalinowska? I should have thought that she supported Franco?'

'She does!'

'But . . .?'

'How could I support a movement that was nothing more than mindless authoritarianism and self-interest disguised by piety and cant? Whatever was opposed to it

554

had to be better. I don't support the Communists, but the Republic is more than Communism: it is *better* than Communism.'

Daniel shook his head. 'Because it has the support of good people? Is that what you're telling me?' His voice held patronizing disbelief. 'My dear girl, Good has been smashed by Evil throughout history. If we hoped to make progress through the efforts of good people we should still be eating corpses. Read your Marx. Progress is through the development of objective social structures, not the moral vapours of reformers.' He seemed to recognize his self-righteousness and his voice eased. 'But I don't want to quarrel with you. You can be here because of some quaint fancy, if it pleases you. The fact is that you are here, and I'm glad. Is that enough?'

It was enough not to quarrel. Beyond that, Katya intended to be cautious. She saw quickly how Daniel would take silence as consent, would assume her agreement with any position he adopted, and dismiss as intellectually lightweight any alternative reasons she might give. And if she were to put these points to him, he would disregard their merits by the same methods of argument. Katya had not broken with her husband to fall into a familiar trap.

In the café the waiter wore a white shirt and addressed her using the formal *usted* rather than the informal *tu*. These were small signs that the camaraderie of the revolutionary days was over. Katya had no particular longing for revolution and did not believe in the perfectibility of man. But she could regret the downfall of hope. She noticed Daniel checking his watch. She said:

'I'm taking up your time?'

'How long are you in Barcelona?'

'Two or three days. What would you like to do: go to the cinema or go dancing again? Maria has fallen in love with a huge Yugoslav – a monster! We could form a foursome. Do you work on Sundays? If you have tomorrow free . . .'

'Do you know what the date is?' Daniel asked. Katya had to think.

'The first of May.'

'Precisely. Haven't you noticed anything? There are no signs of demonstrations and parades by the workers.'

That was true. In fact the city seemed quieter than normal. Daniel explained: 'The UGT and the CNT have agreed to call off the usual processions.' The UGT and CNT were the socialist and anarchist trade unions. 'The situation here is so tense that fighting could break out at any time.'

'Why?'

'Because it's what Franco wants. You don't suppose that there are no Fascists in Barcelona, do you? Franco has *agents provocateurs* scattered throughout the city, and the whole POUM organization is nothing but a smokescreen for Fascist disruption.'

Katya was sceptical that the POUM was controlled by Franco, but was not inclined to dispute the matter. She was familiar with Communist paranoia. It was often intended to do no more than unsettle the population. What disturbed her more was Daniel's seriousness. She tried to deflect it.

'Assuming that a coup isn't staged tomorrow, I thought that we could go with Maria and her big Yugoslav . . . Now what is his name?'

'I'm not free tomorrow,' Daniel told her. 'It doesn't mean I don't want to see you. But there really is a crisis, believe me.'

'I believe you.'

'Good girl.'

Katya flinched. But Daniel did not notice, and his failure hurt her because it meant that his instinct to trivialize her was beyond his conscious reach. For all that she felt his deep affection for her, she saw that he posed as profound a danger as Kolya had, and that the difference between them lay in the crimes into which they would draw her as their tacit accomplice.

556

Should she fight him to establish herself? Where were the tools for such a loving fight? Already he had paid the bill and risen to his feet, and, his dark face smiling its unwonted smile, he was enquiring without interest how she would spend the day and saying he must go; kissing her hand; promising further kisses in his tender eyes. It seemed to her that he did not realize that there was a battle to be fought, and she doubted her ability to bring this realization to him. The gulf of misunderstanding between men and women was beyond the power of uncertain language to bridge. When the meaning of words was not fixed and attitude or prejudice could turn clear text into its opposite, then women must proceed by persistence and subversion, if they were not to be dominated by the overt power of men. Men hated them for it. And women did not understand why.

During the night there were shootings, and the secret police, the SIM, cruised the city in their cars, arresting enemies for their secret prisons. On the following day the chief of police and the Civil Guard raided the main telephone exchange and seized the censor's department on the first floor, while the anarchist workers, on the second floor, shot at them down the stairs before a truce was arranged. Spare ammunition was fired off through the windows of the limestone building and a crowd gathered in the Plaza Cataluña.

This was not a coup, or the world would have known and been prepared. Rather it was a stone dropped in the pool of tension and its effects were felt in delayed and attenuated rings, so that in some outer parts of Barcelona it was possible to believe that the disturbance was nothing more than the excitement of riffraff and *provocateurs*; newspapers appeared and the tramcars ran more or less on time. On the day itself, in the *barrio* Gótico, no more than a kilometre away from the Telefónico, it took some time for news of the incident to arrive. But then, in ripples radiating from the Plaza Cataluña down the Ramblas and through the working-class *barrios* either side, shutters went up on windows, sandbags miraculously appeared, and cobblestones were prised out of the streets; political banners blossomed in gorgeous reds and black, and, on the towers of ruined churches and the domed roofs of hotels, snipers armed with rifles scouted the streets for movement.

Such was the variability of this current of tension in its pools and eddies that Katya and Maria, buying food in the vegetable market, stepped out into the Ramblas and found an empty tramcar stranded in the road and, up towards the Poliorama and the square, cars abandoned by their drivers who now dodged between plane trees and news kiosks, while at the lower end traffic moved and people went about their business.

'What do you think is happening?' asked Maria. She was unable to take seriously gunfire that was limited to a few hollow shots, like a farmer potting vermin.

It was impossible to tell. A truck full of young anarchists waving banners, hooting and yelling and armed to the teeth, came past at speed, and a patrol of Assault Guards routed cowering civilians out of doorways and checked their papers. It seemed to Katya not another uprising but a parody in which elements of war and peace intermingled, and civilians bought groceries while snipers exchanged fire among the rooftops; and so strong was this sense of anomaly (she was holding a bag of vegetables and clutching her change) that there seemed a chance that the militiamen, recognizing it, would feel ridiculous and go home.

Creeping a few hundred metres, keeping to the cover of the buildings, and then exercising caution in crossing to the east side of the Ramblas itself, they found no obstacle to walking back to their room at the Hotel Jardín. Here the small tradesmen – *pâtissiers*, *chocolatiers*, booksellers, cutlers, haberdashers, milliners – had put up their shutters but were still tentatively open for business and encouraged to be so by Communist and Civil Guard patrols. The slogan painters had come out and the young men, brave, excitable, louche, sly, loitered the narrow streets and waited on events. Katya and Maria reached their room and decided to mend clothes until a call came for them if they were needed.

The night was punctuated by random shots, the blare of a car horn, the rattle of running feet. In the morning Maria said:

'Well, I suppose we'd better find some work to do. It looks like they've forgotten we're here. Or maybe they think they can't get a message through.'

'Concha needs a fuel pump,' said Katya. 'Concha' was the name given to the old Hispano Suiza.

'Yes? Then let's see if we can find one for the old lady.'

They went out and discovered that the city was quieter. The shops had closed. From the direction of the Ramblas machine gun fire could be heard. Most of the fighting was there and in the other avenues and their offshoots around the Plaza Cataluña. The reason was the simple one that the trade unions, the political parties and their respective militias had occupied the various hotels and commercial buildings as offices, and at the outbreak of trouble had rushed to defend them. They were in close proximity to each other and hence more threatening and threatened. Yet outside of this area an eerie calm reigned, punctuated only by irrelevant shots that seemed almost a sport in their pointlessness.

In such circumstances they walked. It was a long way to the large military hospital in the hilly Vallcarca district where Concha was housed and they received their orders; but it was oddly pleasant to stroll hand in hand along the empty avenues and exchange inconsequential chatter, or pause to examine the faded painted stucco of a building or the play of light among the pines and plane trees. Katya was struck by the ability of normality to survive in the interstices of war and mock it. So the morning was more beautiful because the fighting could be heard in insubstantial echo, yet here was nothing but ordinariness stripped of people: ordinariness in its grime and banality to be studied and appreciated. A newspaper kiosk plastered with posters. The tram tracks delineating the streets like an artist's lines of perspective. The overhead cables, now strung straight, now hanging in swags: black lines against a white sky; insulator pots like the black bobbled fruit of the plane.

'Good God!' said the doctors, on seeing them. 'Good God!' said the mechanic. 'I suppose you'll want that fuel pump fixing?'

'I'll fix it,' said Katya. There were some old vehicles that could be cannibalized for parts, and after much work, with the day wearing on, it was done.

'Can you get down to the Hotel Colón?' asked the ambulance despatcher. 'They're collecting casualties there.' Katya drove back into the city centre with Maria and a *practicante* in the back of Concha.

Perhaps there was an amnesty for ambulances. They were able to drive and park unmolested at the back of the hotel. In the lobby, the walking wounded were smoking and telling their stories to each other. The *practicante* was left to attend to them and give emergency attention to incoming casualties. The stretcher-cases were loaded into Concha by Civil Guards and Communist militiamen. Katya made two journeys like this back and forth to the hospital. On the last journey the tyres were shot out: so she had to leave the ambulance among the other abandoned vehicles in the Paseo de Gràcia and seek refuge in the hotel. There the talk was of artillery. So far the fighting had been with small arms and grenades, but there was a fear and a thrill at the possibility that the Government or its enemies might bring up some 75-millimetre field guns.

She found Daniel in the loading bay behind the hotel, organizing militiamen. These were despatched at intervals to support a skirmish line among the trees and monuments in the square or into side streets and alleyways as raiding parties against buildings held by the POUM and the anarchists.

'Have you eaten?' Daniel asked.

He went with her to a canteen established in an elegant former restaurant. Among the columns and chandeliers, the disorder and filth, they ate a mush of beans and chickpeas. Daniel smoked his Lucky Strike cigarettes. He had not shaven and his face was fierce. He carried a pistol in a leather holster.

Katya said something about tragedy – the fighting was a tragedy. It seemed obvious to her, but Daniel reacted strongly.

'It's necessary. The air needs to be cleared. The Government can't fight a war with these divisions in its rear. The anarchists have to be put in their place and the POUM dissolved.'

His friends interrupted with rumours: the Durruti Column and the 28th Division were marching on the city; President Companys had resigned; someone had found an old 77-millimetre Krupp gun and shelled the Telefónica. Some of this was evident nonsense: from the Hotel Colón the Telefónica could be seen across the square, standing pale grey and undamaged in the sunlight.

'I can't fight,' said Daniel. 'It's frustrating.' He laughed and waggled the stump of his left arm. 'I practised throwing a grenade and fell over! It's a question of balance.'

A call rang out for volunteers for the next raiding party and a group of diners wiped their lips and mess tins and left in a clatter of boots and guns. Daniel remained seated.

'You're seeing more action than I am,' he murmured bitterly.

'I don't really see action. The clearing stations aren't in the front line. Sometimes we're bombed, but the bombs miss us. That's one of the peculiar things. People seem to be injured by chance. Sometimes there's an air raid and we get no casualties, and then there will be a flood of injured and we have no idea what caused them. And they don't seem to know either. A lot of the cases are through sickness – dysentery. These men have never seen the enemy.'

She saw he was not listening. His mind was mulling over the ideal of war. Disappointed that he was not in the streets fighting the POUMistas, he would still bear his disappointment for the excitement of being a spectator.

He mopped out his mess tin with a piece of bread and stood up. He was dressed in the paraphernalia of war but had a fountain pen clipped to the pocket of his green blouson.

'How long will this go on?' Katya asked.

He shrugged. 'A day or two. Neither side is organized for this fight. It wasn't planned.' Revealing his thoughts he added: 'We prefer to arrest our enemies. The real struggle will be decided in the prisons.'

In the lobby Maria broke from a small group of nurses and pounced on Katya.

'I've got a job for us to do!' she announced mischievously.

She had volunteered the two of them to make a foray into the middle of the square and recover two wounded men. They would be accompanied by four Assault Guards who would give covering fire and carry the stretchers.

'Look what they've given us!' She produced two trench helmets of an old German pattern, big as buckets and too large to wear on their cropped heads. She held one to her breast. 'We can use them to cover our *mammelle*.'

'You're a madwoman,' Katya told her.

'Very likely. Kiss me for luck.'

They kissed, and Katya thought: this isn't at all funny. But how can one treat it seriously? Particularly when their danger was of no interest to anyone else. Katya looked about the lobby. Squatting on the reception desk, a militiaman was cleaning his rifle with a rag dipped in olive oil. Another was sighting his weapon on a hanging light and soundlessly mouthing: 'Bang! Bang!' Boxes of ammunition were being carried from cellar to roof. A boy of sixteen was approaching individuals in turn, scrounging for cigarettes. A sense of her own unimportance came to Katya and she wondered if that was what courage amounted to: that one adopted the valuation of others in respect of oneself. It felt so. She contemplated the possibility of her death and could not imagine it as a sacrifice, but only as an accident and not worth bothering about: as if, indeed, it were the death of someone else.

After the dark interior of the hotel, the square glittered. The small group of men and women dashed across the carriageway towards the central gardens. If anyone was shooting at them it was impossible to say. Bursts of gunfire had become so habitual that one ignored them unless a ricochet or splinter came one's way. Lying behind a stone balustrade was a man with a chest wound and under a nearby tree another whose leg was badly injured.

Katya helped Maria to staunch the blood so that both men might be moved. While she was doing so, she noticed another stretcher party – anarchists, she supposed from the colour of their kerchiefs. Each ignored the other.

It was on the return journey that Maria was shot by a bullet probably aimed at the Assault Guards. She said nothing but pitched violently forward on to the road and lay unmoving.

'We'll come back for her!' shouted one of the men. However, Katya fell to her knees. She murmured: 'Darling – don't worry – darling – can you hear me?' There was no response but Katya pretended to hear one. 'That's it, darling, they'll be back in a moment. What did you say?' She recollected the discipline of her calling and with tears streaming down her face began to go through a learned routine of first aid, until discipline itself was exhausted. Then she folded over and nuzzled the body as an animal will do its dead mate.

From the hotel came help. Assault Guards, nervous and ready to shoot, creeping like Red Indians around a corpse. And with them, like men thrown out of a bar, militiamen who had been lounging in the lobby; who were smoking and fastening their trousers, but as alert as law-breakers might be, who were keeping a sharp eye out for the police.

They dragged Katya screaming into the hotel and afterwards brought in the body.

The events of 4 May marked the crisis in Barcelona. Compromises were reached, the composition of governments was changed, and a cease-fire was gradually implemented. Maria was buried. Four women carried her body to the grave.

Katya experienced something that was difficult to admit: the coarseness and vulgarity of grief. She cried in public, got drunk, and fought another woman in a bar. In short, she behaved like a man; which is possible in war.

The hospital allotted her a new nurse. Her name was Isabel and she was Spanish; and her arrival confronted Katya with the choices that death and grief impose. Isabel was a fat girl of only moderately good temper, with a hatred of the countryside in which she was brought up. Like many fat people, she could move on small feet with a sway and poise as if dancing ballet. The question for Katya was whether she could have the joyful intimacy that she had had with Maria: and the answer was that she could. It was shameful, the callousness of life towards death. Katya often thought so as, on lonely nights, driving Concha along the black winding roads of the sierra, to the jolting springs and the jolting stars, she exchanged an affectionate smile with Isabel. Guilt at the death of Maria lay black on her heart, as did a sense of her own moral worthlessness. But how easy it was to forget. Stopping on the road to get water and directions from soldiers bivouacked at twilight in the fields, the two women shared jokes with the men and drank *aquardiente* when they could get it. Katya was often drunk when she drove. During the period that she mourned Maria she was selfish, thoughtless, extravagant, loving, guilt-ridden, vulgar and callous. In her madness she gave freely to beggars, even the fraudulent ones.

Daniel was not there to console her in her grief. Time did not allow it. She had to repair Concha and get her back on the road and then the call came to return to the front. Instead she was left only with dreams of Daniel, dreams that she knew were absurd and sentimental but which were vivid and tactile. She knew how false sentimentality could be: a dross of emotional small coins from which no fortune could be built. But, reduced to emotional beggary, how necessary to her those small coins were; how treasured; how inflated.

She walked again in her gallery of ghosts: her father, Zhivago, Lara, Fraulein Buerli and, always, Tanya (in drink, *little* Tanya). And now sweet Maria had joined them.

Yet time passed, and as a result of Communist manoeuvres, the government of Largo Caballero was replaced by that of Negrín. The war went on, summer came, and Katya returned to Barcelona.

The May crisis had been a mere symptom, an eruption on the surface of the disease that was working within the body. The Republic was vulnerable because, despite the good and liberal instincts of its politicians, it was exposed to the Communists supported by the Soviet Union, its only significant ally. The other democracies deserted it. They screamed that the Republic was Communist, and made it so by abandoning it to the Soviet Union.

However, their very success was a problem for the Communist. Spain had its own vigorous left-wing tradition that owed nothing to Stalin. It was these socialists and anarchists who carried out a social revolution in Republican Spain after the military uprising. It was they, not the Communists, who frightened the British and French; but the latter were too stupid or prejudiced to recognize the difference.

The Communists were therefore in a trap. They were identified with revolutionaries whom they did not support. Yet, in giving their real support to the bourgeois parties to suppress the revolutionaries, they increased their own influence and prominence and thus still alienated Britain and France. Even Stalin could not reconcile these contradictions.

But to understand this is to misunderstand Spain as it was experienced by its people and to misunderstand Katya. For beyond the politicians, intellectuals and dogmatists, people were willing to recognize the generous spirit of anyone who would sacrifice his or her life to oppose tyranny. It was possible to disagree with Communism and admire the Communist one knew as a friend.

This was also true of the Fascists. The charm and generosity of Don José Antonio were recognized by his opponents up to the moment that they shot him. Within the Falange there was a section that genuinely promoted the welfare of the poor. Don José Antonio Primo de Rivera was a Fascist who loved people.

But now it was June and Barcelona could offer that joy of Mediterranean cities, the ability at every turn to set the deep shadow of the buildings against the sharp glories of the sun; and the plane trees and acacias were in leaf, and their dappled, fugitive shadows also softened the remorseless splendour of light.

Katya and Isabel still shared with the other women the room in the Hotel Jardín. These days the chance opportunity allowed to Katya and Daniel did not exist. Isabel did not like men. Since they did not, in general, like fat women, they were poor creatures of poor judgement. She was prepared to make exceptions, but two things, in her opinion, remained constant. The conversation of men was stupifyingly dull (they appeared to think one was interested, when one was silent merely because they talked louder or butted their way into a woman's conversation). And they were smug at a level that defied any attack. Indeed one could not even trust a man who agreed with one's point of view. The nearest a man came to *sincerely* conceding defeat was when he said: 'I know that I'm right, but you do as you please.' This confession was limited to the few men who were eloquent. Nor could one trust a man who understood women. He knew only enough to be dangerous. Isabel was prepared to describe in intimate physical detail what these dangers might be.

Somewhere in her history, Isabel had had a dead baby, grown angry with peasant life and become an anarchist. She claimed to have shot a priest. On any point of detail she was capable of telling lies, but she believed in the lies and they were true, if not of her. Her history was terrible and it made both Katya and Isabel laugh. Katya told her own history as they drove half-drunk during the long nights. It was also funny.

Barcelona appeared as a city of good order. There were changes but one would have to be acute to notice them. For example, *La Batalla*, the newspaper of the POUM, had vanished from the kiosks. And the party militias were less in evidence and the regular police more so. The Communist newspapers were strident in their denunciations of the POUM. Daniel refused to discuss the subject except in the terms used by the press. On all other matters he could be sweetly reasonable.

'I've received a letter from my mother,' he told Katya.

'That's wonderful! Is she well?'

'Yes, she's fine, and so is my father. The interesting part is that she has news of Sasha.'

'I thought she couldn't write about Sasha because of the censorship?'

'Well, one has to read between the lines a little, but apparently he has a quiet staff job somewhere in the rear; my mother doesn't say, but she means Burgos or Salamanca, I suppose. Don't you find that a joke?'

'What?'

'That, of the three of us, it's you, the woman, who is closest to the fighting.'

'It's just a matter of chance. I didn't want to be close to the front.'

'That's the irony. I do! Even though last time it cost me an arm.' He looked at the letter again. 'She says something about Safronov too. Do you want to hear about it?'

Katya nodded. Kolya was one of the least things that disturbed her.

'Apparently Lydia was having his child, but it miscarried. She was too old, I suppose. How old do you think she is? Thirty? Fifty? I've always thought of Lydia as beautiful, but never as young. And the idea that she could ever have a child strikes me as bizarre. Don't you think there's something about her that makes her a failure as a woman?'

Katya thought the comment astute. She remembered a conversation:

'I once asked Kolya what would happen to Lydia when she got older. He said that she would marry a fool like Prince Carlo.'

Daniel laughed. 'And now she's living with Kolya! That's marvellous!'

Katya thought how unpredictable human relations could be, and how full of compromise. Here she was now, with a man who made her come alive but whom she distrusted. Yet she had once said to Daniel that love could be explained by Marx and Darwin.

'You once said something to me,' he was saying. 'What was it? Love is all glands and economics? It seems a fair explanation of Kolya and Lydia. Money and sexual attraction.'

The following day Katya made one of her expeditions to buy additional supplies, using her allowance from Kolya. At the head of the Ramblas there was confusion outside the Hotel Falcón. Civil Guards were posted at the door and Communist militiamen were carrying boxes of papers to a truck outside. She asked Isabel:

'What do you think is going on?'

'I'll find out. You wait here.'

Katya went into the pharmacy and bargained for some plasters and lint. When she came out she found Isabel red-faced and angry.

568

'They've banned the POUM!' she exclaimed. 'There are arrests going on all over the city!'

Katya tried to find Daniel at the Hotel Colón, but there was confusion at the Communist headquarters. Paranoia was in the air and those she spoke to were more interested in her papers and her background than in answering her. Seeing one of Daniel's colleagues, the man called Pedro who had once enquired if she were a Communist and been told that she was a sympathizer, she requested him to confirm her credentials.

'Do you know where Daniel is?' she asked him.

Pedro was in a hurry.

'He's at the Convent of San Juan,' he told her.

She had to ask Isabel about the Convent of San Juan. Clearly it was no longer functioning as a church, but she could think of no reason why Daniel would go there.

Isabel's face showed fear.

'It's a prison – a secret prison run by the SIM.'

For one terrible moment Katya thought that Daniel must have been arrested. Then she realized that that was nonsense. It was the POUMistas who had been arrested and the Communists who were their gaolers. Daniel was one of their gaolers.

And what else? Secret policeman? Torturer? Murderer?

CHAPTER 21

DEATH BEFORE BREAKFAST

After the shooting of prisoners, the priest went for his breakfast.

The prisoners were Juan Moreno, day labourer, José Avilo, sharecropper, Antonio Naranjo, goatherd, and Eugenio Martínez, schoolteacher. All four professed to be socialists, which was the political colour of the village. Three of them received the last rites and were reconciled to the Church, but the fourth, the schoolteacher, maintained that he was an atheist and made a long speech about Proudhon. The firing squad – who had known the men during their imprisonment and had no taste for the task – in the face of Martínez's speech, shot them out of annoyance and boredom; making a bad job of it and leaving their lieutenant to put a bullet through each head and the priest to confirm the deaths.

This took place by a dry stream, with the prisoners standing on the stony bed and the firing squad on the bank. The bullets raised white dust from the stones and powdered the grey-green agaves. The sky was a brilliant blue and the oleanders a vivid pink.

The corporal arrived in Málaga on an evening train.

During the journey the carriages had often been halted for long periods in the sun, and it was a pleasure to step out of the airless interior on to a cool platform and find the sky black and glittering with stars.

In the station, an office dealt with troop movements. The corporal, in green khaki, carrying a blanket roll and wearing a *gorillo* cap with a red tassel, joined a queue and finally saw a bored railway official, who checked his papers and told him that there was no train to his final destination, but there was a motor bus leaving at dawn or thereabouts. The corporal was left to spend the night on the platform with the other displaced soldiers, disturbed by the periodic patrols of the Civil Guard and the military police.

In a tavern he was able to buy a piece of bread and a glass of wine. The bus was late and almost empty. An old lady, a *recovera* who had sold her basket of eggs in the city, slumbered on a back seat. A young man, in a good suit, sat next to the corporal and made conversation. He had been to Málaga to visit a whore and was still drunk. It emerged that he was the son of a village boss, a *cacique*, who had fled at the time of the revolution and returned with Queipo de Llano's army. He had a car, he said, but could not get petrol. The corporal, tired, did not pay much attention, but he could not fail to notice the young man's complacency. The latter said:

'I'm not angry with the peasants. At bottom people are all the same. In their shoes I fancy I would have burned the church and murdered the landlords, too. Of course we have to shoot them for it, to keep them in their place – but to be angry, what's the point?'

'Don't you object to the injustice?' asked the corporal.

'Injustice? Where's the injustice? If someone wins a lottery and I don't, do I complain of the injustice? No, I don't. I regard life as a lottery, and more to the point, so do the peasants. I do no injustice to them because I do no more than they would do to me if the positions were

571

reversed. Life's a lottery,' he repeated. 'I won and they lost.'

The young man went to sleep. His tussore suit smelled of perfume and spilled wine. His hair was oiled and he had a moustache drawn like a pencil line.

Outside the bus, with its broken windows, it was light and still in the cool of the morning. The road wound up terraced hillsides against the pine-green edge of the sierra. Once the bus stopped and the driver got out to urinate against the wheels. Once it stopped simply because it stopped, and the passengers got out and wandered among the agaves and mulberry bushes while the driver muttered imprecations at his vehicle.

The corporal's new friend suggested they play cards. He had a pack in his pocket. He would even lend the corporal the means to bet. During the card game he went into detail about his life – the money he had gambled; the times he was drunk; his motorcycles; his stingy father; women. He took a perverse pride in the meaninglessness of his life. The point, it seemed, was to be free. Any purpose in life represented a commitment and a limitation on freedom. He went on to explain, in a way that the corporal had heard so many times from fellow soldiers but still found repellent, that all women were whores.

'*Hombre*, it's true! There isn't one of them that won't lie on her back and open her legs.' He excepted his sainted mother and sisters. 'And what for? Not money. I've screwed women for the price of a drink or a cinema ticket or a bunch of flowers. They use sex as a bait to trap a man. Women can't stand freedom. It goes against the grain with them. I put it down to biology: the need to get a man to bring up their brats. But there it is; they can't stand freedom. That's why it's women who support dictators and religion.' He added that he also supported Franco and the Church, but that was on rational grounds: the need for an ordered society.

The terraces were planted with olives, and here and

there an irrigated patch grew cabbage, lettuce or chard. On dry land the peasants tried to extract a crop of wheat every four years. Wooden ploughs barely scratched the surface. Ploughing and re-ploughing, the labour required was immense and the returns poor. Fields had been stripped of their vines by landlords for whom the trouble of managing peasants was not worthwhile. Grudging or barren, the land lay white and dusty, and liquid in the heat shimmer.

The village was entered by a narrow cobbled street of whitewashed houses with tiled roofs. The driver signalled his arrival by blowing his horn and stopping in a small square with a fountain where barefoot women washed their laundry. A fig tree offered shade. A burnt-out church stood on the east side and a burnt-out *casa del pueblo* on the west. In front of the tavern sat a priest in a dusty soutane and biretta, eating his breakfast. A monarchist flag hung from the town hall.

The corporal descended alone from the bus. He deposited his bedroll on the ground and, shading his eyes from the sun, looked around. An unshaven Civil Guard emerged from the town hall and enquired as to his papers and purpose in visiting the village.

'I've been asked to interrogate a prisoner,' said the corporal.

'We've shot all the prisoners,' said the Civil Guard. He shrugged his shoulders. 'You'd better speak to the lieutenant.'

'Where is he?'

'Search me. Speak to the priest.'

The corporal dragged his bedroll to the tavern where the priest was sitting with his back to the square. A cough and the priest turned around. It was Alain Duroc.

'Hello, Sasha,' he said.

'Alain.' Sasha dropped the bedroll and the two men embraced. As they pulled apart, Sasha thought that his former mentor looked older and careworn in his dusty clerical dress.

'Take a seat,' said the priest. 'Have you had any breakfast?'

'I've eaten, but I haven't slept much. Is there any chance of closing my eyes before we get down to business, or is it a matter of urgency?'

'It isn't urgent. There's a bed for you here in the tavern. I'll tell Lieutenant Torres you've arrived.'

'You want me to interrogate a Russian?'

'How is your mother?'

'My mother? She's well. Angry with me – not "angry" but something else – there's a word for it. But surely she writes to you?'

'Regularly,' was the answer, and the Jesuit looked wistful. 'And she tries to tell me the truth, but such a narrow focus is distorting. I'd understand her better if she lied occasionally.'

A few olives and some barley coffee appeared. Sasha allowed an interlude in which questions were asked such as: how was the journey from Málaga? And: aren't the buses terrible? Such rickety things! He said:

'I wasn't sure whether I would find you here. My orders weren't clear. I understood you were in Burgos?'

'And you were in Salamanca?'

'Yes.'

The Jesuit twisted his neck slowly, like a cat cleaning the fur on its back. The gesture served no purpose except to relieve tension. And with the insouciant air of a cat who had satisfied himself in that regard he said:

'I was in Burgos, but I asked for a posting closer to the front. And for my sins –' a brief smile '– it was granted. This isn't the time to chat, is it? You look exhausted.'

'Give me your blessing.'

The Jesuit looked at Sasha as if searching for a trace of irony. He gave the blessing and then returned to his breakfast. Sasha went into the tavern and found his miserable room decorated with a picture of Franco cut from a newspaper.

*　　*　　*

574

The lieutenant was a middle-aged man, pale-faced, squinting as if short-sighted but wearing no spectacles: a man in most respects undistinguished, but who would stand out in a crowd because he would feel uncomfortable in it, or indeed anywhere else. He lacked a sense of physical space, or timing, or aptness, or humour. Without making the normal enquiries as to name, unit and the discomforts of the journey he said:

'So you've come to help us liquidate the scum, eh?'

'Do you want to see my papers?'

The lieutenant bit his lip and after a pause said in a bluff manner: 'Put them on the desk. Paperwork for the pen-pushers, eh? And fighting for the soldiers?'

Sasha was uncertain if the questions invited answers or what any answer might be.

'So . . .'

'Yes?'

'Ha! Seen much fighting?'

'No, sir.'

'Good.' The lieutenant hesitated and changed his manner to inquisitorial. 'You're not Spanish?'

'No. It says so in my papers. I'm a French citizen.'

'But you speak Russian? Where did you learn?'

'My family is Russian – émigrés.'

'Communists?'

'Of course not.'

'Good.'

The lieutenant smiled slyly so that Sasha anticipated a new line in questioning: about railway timetables or books.

'I only speak Spanish,' said the lieutenant.

Should Sasha say 'Good' or 'Bad'? He tried a non-committal grunt.

'You are educated?'

'I broke my studies at the Sorbonne.'

'The Sorbonne is – where?'

'Paris.'

'I have not been abroad.'

'He's a whimsical fellow, your lieutenant,' said Sasha to Alain Duroc that evening after the Jesuit had conducted Mass. 'For the life of me I couldn't work out why I was here: to interrogate some Russian or have the lieutenant interrogate me?'

'He's one of those people who are natural caricatures. One can describe their mannerisms but have no idea about their interior life. Does it even exist?'

'Doesn't confession make that clear?'

'I can't speak about the lieutenant's confession. But, considered abstractly, their sins are either dull or lurid and in either case have a fictional ring to them.'

They had agreed to walk. The village was in darkness except for patches of light that here and there revealed intimate tableaux of life: the basket-maker weaving esparto grass; the baker loading pine cones and brushwood to fire his oven; a woman cleaning wax from a child's ear, twisting and licking the corner of her apron and soothing the wriggling infant. Here they could smell rosemary burning with the brushwood, there the fumes of a lime-burner's kiln. A stick thwacked the back of a mule. Its panniers creaked. A tethered goat strained at its rope and tap-danced on the stones. Strolling with the priest, Sasha reflected that here was a perfect night and that, in other times, he might have walked with a girl and the night would become fixed in their memories. He thought of the night when he and Katya had danced in the sea. He was persuaded that they had really done so, and had forgotten all the elements of chance and misinterpretation that had led to his holding that surprising stranger in his arms. He knew that they had truly danced, swinging through the shallow water in unalloyed joy. He had held her in an embrace, and here on this hillside, among the moon-reflecting glimmer of olive trees and the smell of rosemary burning, his hands could feel the smooth slide of her cotton dress and his arms her gentle weight.

'What have you heard of our friends?' Alain asked.

'I saw Connie in Salamanca. I don't know where he is now. I think he went north for the Basque campaign.'

'How was he?'

Sasha told the Jesuit something of Constantine's visit. He could not avoid conveying the faint repulsion that had affected him at his friend's eccentricities.

'He says he believes in God or Carlism or rubbish and nonsense – that's a joke between us. He makes me laugh, but all the time I feel that he has a hatred of belief. He hates reason and he hates faith. What else is left?'

The priest did not reply directly. Instead he said: 'I saw Carlo and Wanda in Burgos. They told me they'd run across you.'

'Yes. I spent an afternoon and evening with them. Carlo has become a Fascist hero, I could hardly recognize him.'

'He's taken up a field command and Wanda has returned to Italy.'

'Oh?' Sasha paused. Staring up the hillside he saw, like moving stars, the flares of esparto torches flickering along the terraces as the peasants irrigated the fields; and from the darkness they heard a *'Buenas noches'* as the water bailiff checked the channels and made sure the peasants claimed only their fair share. Sasha went on: 'Wanda puzzled me, too. I thought she was a hard, cynical woman, but she took me by surprise. Her guard slipped and I thought I saw a softer person.'

'You're being sentimental,' said Alain.

'I suppose I am. I can't think now what persuaded me to become a soldier. I don't agree with the Republicans, but I don't hate them. And I don't look forward to death – I'm frightened of it and I expect it. When it happens it will be pointless and unheroic. I'll be a chance casualty of a bomb blast or dysentery.' He laughed. 'Please God, I don't die on the toilet! Anything else, but not that!'

They took a turn at the dry bed of a stream, where the bodies of unsanctified rebels lay in fresh graves among the oleanders. Alain said:

577

'Katya Safronov left her husband – but I suppose Wanda told you that? Safronov is doing something in the arms trade. Lydia lives with him. Of course, she denies it to her priest so that she can still attend Mass and make confession. Would you believe she wrote to me and told me so? I wrote back and said that the sacraments were invalid if taken in a state of sin, but I don't suppose she believes me. It's obvious to her that she has to live with Safronov if she wants to live in her accustomed state, and it would be unreasonable of God not to recognize the fact. And who knows? She may be right. Katya is in Spain.'

He halted and looked at Sasha, but in the darkness neither could see the other's face. Sasha saw only the shifting stars and heard the old men in the fields hooting to each other like owls and the thin trickle of water in the irrigation channels.

'She joined the Republican side,' Alain resumed. 'Lydia wasn't certain, but thought she might be in Barcelona, working as a nurse. Lydia naturally resents her, since Katya is young and beautiful, while these days Lydia is merely handsome, if fascinating in her own way. She makes a point that Katya's marriage, being civil, is invalid in the eyes of the Church; and so Safronov is free to marry Lydia. She was never married to Max. On the other hand, there is a suspicion that the death of her first husband may be one of Lydia's pleasant fictions. Doubtless she expects God to help her out of that problem, too. In her letter she asked some pointed questions about annulment.'

Sasha murmured: 'Katya in Spain!'

'Why are you laughing?'

'What? Was I? I was thinking of one of life's ironies.'

'Do you want to talk about it?'

'About life's ironies? Good God, no! There's nothing original to say. And the same is true about war. There is nothing original to say about it – or, at least, not for me.' Sensitive to the irony, Sasha spoke lightly. Indeed, he even felt cheerful with the bitter cheerfulness that recognition of one's own errors can bring.

So Katya was in Barcelona – as remote as the moon! He admired the bravery that had taken her there. His generous mind could not suppose any other reason, and certainly he could see no obvious connection with her separation from Kolya. But to be in Barcelona while he was here in Andalucia! What wonderful folly that he had so misread her as to suppose that she would admire him for joining Franco's army!

'You seem in a curious mood,' Alain observed.

Sasha grinned. He said: 'A few years ago I told someone that I wanted to be a fool. I meant it as an intellectual conceit, thinking that folly was a disguise for wisdom in a world full of fools.'

'And?'

'I just discovered that I am a first-rate fool. The genuine article!'

'Are you comfortable here?' asked Alain. Sasha had opened the shutters and in daylight the room above the tavern had a dusty attractiveness. It was the case that poverty in sunshine looked less poor. Sasha, this morning, had put on a light summer uniform. The priest still looked shabby and had not shaven.

'Why is the prisoner here and not in Málaga?' said Sasha.

'There were so many prisoners after last February's offensive that there wasn't room in the city to house and feed them all.'

'But a Russian – I assume you mean some sort of Red commissar – surely military intelligence would want to interrogate him?'

'We don't know for certain that he is a Russian. He's hardly said ten words since he was captured. Lieutenant Torres would like the kudos of presenting his superiors with a prize, but he won't do so until he's sure what he's got.'

Sasha shaved himself from a basin of cold water without the benefit of a mirror. Today there was no bus and no activity in the square. He was conscious how quiet the village had been since his arrival.

'Why didn't you interrogate him yourself, Alain? You speak tolerable Russian. In any case, he probably speaks some Spanish. If he isn't talking, then it's because he doesn't want to talk. I don't see what I can do about that; I'm an office boy, not a torturer. Do you have a name for him? Can't anyone in the village tell you who he is?'

'He was wounded when the Reds retreated, and was billeted here. No-one knows him. I think they're telling the truth. According to his paybook, his name is Francisco Ruiz González. I would put his age somewhere in his forties. And if you want to know why I didn't interrogate him, it's because it gave me a chance to see you again.'

Sasha had finished shaving and was wiping his razor.

'Me?'

'I was able – or, rather, Lieutenant Torres was able – to ask for a Russian translator. I gave him your name, knowing you were in Salamanca.'

'Pass me my boots, will you?' Sasha asked. He was amused. 'I understand that. But why all this trouble to see me? Thanks.' He accepted the boots and began to put them on.

'Because I'm your spiritual pastor. Because I have obligations to your mother. And it was a chance to see an old friend.'

'Then I'm much obliged. I mean I'm pleased, yes, pleased.'

Sasha pulled his boots on and laced them. He enquired if it were possible to get his laundry done. Listening to Alain, he thought how meek the priest's manner had become. All traces of the Jesuit's urbanity, except in occasional patterns of speech, had gone.

'What was the noise I heard this morning?' Sasha asked. 'It woke me up. I hope it doesn't happen every day.'

'Not every day. We shot a prisoner. His name was

Gil Cortes. He was an itinerant blood-letter, so he said.'

'Dear God,' Sasha murmured.

'To quote you: there is nothing original one can say about war. And yet one is always surprised to find that things happen exactly as one is taught to expect. Even one's own reactions are so predictable that one suspects that Jansen was right about free will. I'm being slowly destroyed, Sasha,' he concluded calmly. He stood up, walked to the window and stared out into the square. Sunlight and shadow divided him equally. He asked: 'Do you have a cigarette? I understand that on the other side they have a shortage. Poor souls, they must go into battle very nervous and bad-tempered.'

While Sasha fumbled for a packet in his bedroll, the Jesuit remarked: 'In the bullring they kill the bulls in the afternoon, in broad daylight when everyone can see. Here we have death before breakfast, done in private like performing our ablutions. It's appropriate since we are cleansing the nation. They call it *limpieza*.'

Alain turned around with tears in his eyes and proposed that Sasha talk to the putative Russian.

The prisoner was a man of medium height with brown hair turning grey. His skin had a lifeless appearance, as though spider webs had been laid across it: the skin of a man who smoked heavily. The eyes were pale and vaguely milky, and set in leathery pouches. The lips were the colour and texture of bruised fruit. He had been denied a razor and wore a beard that had been trimmed inexpertly by someone who did not care. He rose to his feet at the sound of his visitor's arrival.

'Having a good day, are we?' asked Lieutenant Torres, adopting the amiable manner of a country doctor. The prisoner returned a silent gaze of scornful curiosity without any trace of anger.

The room was a simple cell with a metal cot, a chair and a Bible. It received no natural light; instead an oil lamp hung on a bracket beyond the bars. Scrupulously clean, the cell still smelled of excrement. Lieutenant Torres took the chair and Sasha stood beside him.

'My colleague –' introducing Sasha like a consultant '– speaks Russian. Oh yes, we know you're a Russian all right!'

The prisoner now examined Sasha, scanning the surface for its uses and dangers and uninterested in the person behind.

Having played his surprise card ineptly, the lieutenant was at a loss what to do next. His discomfort appeared more acute than that of the prisoner.

'May I speak to the man alone?' Sasha enquired. 'If he does speak Russian, you may not be able to follow the interrogation. I'm sure you have important things to do.'

The lieutenant agreed eagerly and Sasha was left alone with the prisoner.

The latter raised his pale, cobweb face. He seemed to Sasha to be a patient man, and indeed Sasha knew this to be so. He wore the grimy blue *mono* in which he had been captured. The insignia had been removed, probably by the prisoner himself, and his captors had taken his boots, so that now his horny feet were exposed naked.

'Cigarette?'

Sasha held out the pack and the man inclined his head to accept. He coughed on first smoking, took out the cigarette and studied it. Sasha took hold of the other's right hand and rolled back the sleeve of his battledress. The prisoner stared at his forearm as if it were an object apart, but did not resist.

'You got that scar fighting for the Whites,' Sasha said in Russian. He waited for an answer. 'At least that's what you told me, Semyon Maximovitch.'

The prisoner's milky eyes examined Sasha's face again but they seemed inward-directed, self-searching.

'Is that your name: Semyon Maximovitch? Semyon Maximovitch Gromov? It used to be, a dozen years ago, when you drove a fiacre in Paris.'

Sasha waited, thinking: he must talk to me. If I continue, then he will dominate me as he did when I was a child. After a long pause, the prisoner said in a hoarse, unused voice:

'It will do.'

'Alexander Alexandrovitch.'

'Ah!' A breath and then silence. The stub of the cigarette dropped on the floor where it burned until Sasha placed his boot on it. 'There was another kid . . .'

'Daniel.'

'Daniel – I remember.'

'You called me . . .'

'Sasha – Sasha – Zhivago.' Gromov thought long and deep then asked: 'How's your mother?'

'Well.'

'Good . . . She is a good woman. And your grandfather and sister?'

'My grandfather died. My sister is well enough.'

Gromov was content and said no more.

There seemed in his voice and his movements an ache. Sasha asked:

'How is your wound?'

'I wasn't wounded. I was sick – dysentery, I think. Don't worry, I'm fine.' He tried a smile, revealing gaps in his smoke-stained teeth. 'Another cigarette? Thanks.' He lit it but seemed as unused to smoking as to anything else, though the nicotine gave him a small life of nervous energy and he stirred in his seat where before he had been still.

'I thought you were dead,' Sasha told him. 'After you shot Colonel Menshikov, everyone thought you were dead. Your fiacre was found in the Bois de Boulogne. There were bloodstains.'

'Some of your White gentlemen formed a death squad and came after me. They killed one of my friends.'

'You betrayed my trust in you.'

Gromov shrugged. 'Menshikov was a Jew-hater and a monster. The feelings of a small boy didn't weigh much

583

against those facts. I was sorry then, and I'm sorry now – is that what you want to hear? But you got over it. You look well, but I'm sorry you're on the wrong side. You used to have ideals.'

'You think that our side has no ideals?'

'No, you probably do. More's the pity.' Gromov looked at Sasha and then lay back and stretched out on his cot with his eyes closed. Like a corpse, Sasha thought, and realized that the other man regarded himself as already dead. And this is a seance. Sasha remembered Lydia Kalinowska's secret predilection for seances and her assertion that that was how Max Golitsin (dead Max Golitsin) got his stock market tips. It was, he thought, the explanation of his own deadened reflexes on seeing his old friend. He was in mourning, talking not to Gromov but muttering over the bier of his own memories. Why was it like this? Memories of the fiacre driver and memories of Alain who was dying inside. Cigarettes instead of flowers.

'I have to ask you some questions about your presence in Spain,' he said. 'Are you a Soviet military advisor?'

The prisoner raised one eyelid.

'Go to hell.'

'Do you have a political mission?' Sasha asked patiently.

'Do you?'

'Can you confirm if your name is Semyon Maximovitch Gromov?'

'I have no name. If I ever had one, I've forgotten it. Gromov? I used to know a Gromov. He died.'

Sasha had armed himself with a pencil and a notebook. He looked at the notebook now and saw the blank page. He wrote: Interrogation of Francisco Ruiz González. Gromov said:

'They're going to shoot me, Sasha. It's just a matter of time. I've got nothing to tell them and the only question is whether they torture me first before they find that out.'

'Tell me before they have a chance to torture you.'

'They'd torture me in any case.'

The older man was now lying so as to face his

interrogator and Sasha felt raked by his remorseless gaze.

'My only hope is that your fool of a lieutenant will shoot me. Do you understand? Tell him I'm not a Russian, just some poor mute Spaniard. Get him to shoot me!'

Gromov rolled over again and lay with his face to the wall.

In the hour before dawn the tramcar rolled down the darkened street carrying a cargo of ghosts, striking sparks from the overhead cables like spectral flares. Four men sat in an American sedan under the plane trees and discussed their business.

'For the last time, Pedro, are you happy with the car?'

'The engine keeps misfiring.'

'I know it keeps misfiring; I could feel it all the way here. The question is: will it start when it needs to?'

'Maybe.'

'*Hombre!* What kind of an answer is that?'

'It's a "maybe" answer. It's a machine! Who knows what a machine will do?'

'You want a horse? I should go out and find four horses?'

'The car will start,' said a consolatory voice with a foreign accent. 'And if it doesn't, then we simply walk away. Who is going to stop us?'

'Time?'

'Five-thirty.'

'It's cold.'

'You move faster in cold weather.'

'But the car may not start.'

'Mother of God!'

The door, squeezed into the narrow space between the bakery and the haberdasher shop, opened and the *portero* stood on the sill yawning. Three of the men got out of the car and pushed their way past the old man.

'Keep your mouth shut, uncle,' said Jaume, the youngest. Jaume was barely seventeen.

They ascended the stairs to the second floor. Salvador

led. He was the oldest and the heaviest: a dockworker. They called him 'Viga', the girder. He could shoulder or kick down a door with one blow.

The third man was one-armed.

The stairs opened into a landing with doors leading off into the apartments. The landing was not lit. The ceiling held a fitting from which bare wires protruded. Viga struck a match to identify the doors and light himself a cigarette. He was nerveless. He often laughed, but not because of nerves. It was just that he was enjoying himself and had been since the revolution started. Jaume also laughed, but in his case it was nerves. The one-armed man did not laugh.

'This one,' said Viga.

'Are you sure?' Jaume asked. He always asked: 'Are you sure?'

'*Hombre*, I'm sure!'

'Okay, let's go in,' said the one-armed man, and Viga grunted and kicked down the door.

The occupant of the apartment was a doctor. You did not have to be sharp to know: his certificate hung on the wall and there was a small oak cabinet with the bottles and vials that doctors use, a shelf of books that doctors read, and a tray of the knives and instruments that you need only if you are a doctor or a torturer. And he looked like a doctor, even when coming out of his bedroom in his underwear, fixing round-rimmed glasses on his nose.

'Fancy coming for a ride?' asked Jaume. This was the part he always liked. The question fell flat. The doctor spoke only Castilian and Jaume had to repeat himself slowly as if describing symptoms, and even afterwards the doctor seemed uncertain, not knowing if he were being called out to his death or a difficult childbirth.

They allowed him to dress. In his wardrobe was a respectable suit, and in his drawers a nest of wing collars in tissue paper and a pot of English hair pomade. But he had got out of the habit of these things and instead put on some workmen's trousers, a collarless shirt, and *alpargatas* on his feet. These clothes annoyed Viga.

'Look at him,' he sneered. 'He doesn't dare let people see what he really is.'

'Do you want me to change?' asked the doctor mildly. 'Do I need to pack more things?' He showed the first signs of panic. 'Oh, I must bring my shaving salve! I have an allergy.' At the top of the stairs he began to shake violently and felt he must apologize. The one-armed man and Jaume carried him under the armpits down and into the street where Pedro was waving the crank handle, grinning and admitting that the car would not start.

On hearing this, the four men relaxed their guard, and their prisoner, after a moment of hesitation, took it into his head to run. The one-armed man was the first to draw his gun, and with two shots he brought the doctor down, but still alive so that it took Viga to finish him off just as Pedro managed to start the car.

'Good shooting, Gary Cooper,' said Viga to his companion and he smiled because he was a sincere man, who liked to be liked. 'Okay, *vaqueros*, let's be going!' he added, as a tramcar went past and the ghosts inside pasted their noses to the windows to stare.

They walked to the dry stream as the birds were stirring, the prisoner, the corporal, the priest, the lieutenant, and the firing party of six. They did not march but walked easily, like labourers saving their energy for work and the heat of the day; and in the same fashion the soldiers carried their weapons like tools as suited the comfort of each man.

The bank was steep and the prisoner was helped down and then positioned on the rocks in the bed of the stream. The priest offered even now to hear the man's confession and give him the sacrament, but the man declined without rancour. The priest clambered back to the top of the bank and there began to read silently from his breviary. The lieutenant tendered the blindfold and the prisoner refused, but he accepted the cigarette. He seemed to concentrate on this and did not look at his executioners; instead his head rested to one side with his eyes down, as if interested in an insect crawling among the stones. The soldiers rummaged in their cartridge boxes, looking for some well-made bullets among the doubtful ones (even so, one rifle was to misfire), and, having loaded these, they waited tensely for the order. 'Fire!' cried the lieutenant, which they did. And fortunately their aim was good and the prisoner collapsed, and died quite neatly and without fuss.

The corporal, who took no active part, was for this reason able to take the role of the observer, and even tell himself that it was not really happening. Such was his detachment that he could study a lemon tree growing a little way off and then look back, thinking: isn't it over yet? In fact he was able to take the motorbus to Málaga and, with stops and changes, the train to Salamanca in such a state of calmness that he felt content with himself. He knew he was a true soldier even though he had seen no other action.

Two nights later and for many nights after that, he had to be slapped awake by his roommates to bring him out of nightmares that were more vivid, real and filled with violent emotion than the event itself had been – or had seemed to be.

The corporal became transformed. He believed that his own identity had died with that of the dead man, and that this breathing thing that remained was a mere husk of reflexes. With care and concentration, it was possible to articulate the husk and fool others into thinking that it was a whole man, but the corporal, of course, knew better. Reflecting on this state of affairs – and he could reflect quite calmly since he was undistracted by emotion or the other trappings of real personality – he decided that the situation could be resolved, and the whole man reunited, only by going to the front and getting himself killed as soon as possible.

Returning to her room at the Hotel Jardín on a mild July evening, Katya found a small, neatly formed man in a straw hat and pale blue seersucker suit, sitting at his ease and talking to Isabel and Iñez, another of the ambulance drivers, a pretty girl with a stammer and quiet on that account.

'Hello, Katya,' said Safronov.

'Kolya has brought us some coffee,' said Isabel, 'real coffee, not the other stuff.'

'It was nothing.'

'Thank you all the same,' said Katya, putting down her bag and running her fingers through her hair out of habit on coming in from outdoors. She saw at once that Kolya had already made himself one of the exceptions in Isabel's general distrust of men. Her face was glowing. As for Iñez, she had no opinion of men, having been limited by a strict upbringing and her speech impediment. 'Have you been here long?'

'About an hour.'

'I meant in Barcelona.'

'I arrived two days ago. I had to see Companys on business between the Generalidad and my firm.'

Companys was president of the Generalidad, the government of Catalonia.

'Arms?'

'Business.'

'Iñez, are you going to make us a cup of Kolya's good coffee?'

'C-c-certainly.' Iñez was always glad to help. She took the bag from Isabel's lap and went out to the communal kitchen that served the residents.

Katya thought that her husband seemed very comfortable with himself; but he always did. It crossed her mind that he had sought her out to ask for a divorce so that he could marry Lydia: but that anyone would marry the countess, rather than simply live with her, struck her as implausible. Still, here he was.

'How did you find me?'

'Through the bank where I pay your allowance.'

Did he mean to terminate her allowance?

'Isabel tells me that you use it to buy additional supplies for your ambulance.'

'I told Kolya how grateful we were to him – how grateful we are to you,' Isabel added, using the familiar *tu*.

'Yes, we are grateful,' Katya said neutrally. 'I try to put your money to good use. I hope you approve.'

'It's a matter for you.'

'I tell people that it's your money. You have a reputation as a benefactor. Perhaps Companys has heard of it.'

'I'm flattered.'

Katya examined him for any sign of physical tension and found none. She studied herself and noted only curiosity and perfect emotional indifference.

'You speak very good Spanish.'

'Like you!' interrupted Isabel. 'You both seem to have a gift.'

'Life is obviously treating you well,' Katya went on. 'And everyone else? Do you have any news?'

'I don't see many of our old acquaintances. Aristide was brought to trial as a result of the Widows & Wounded. I gave evidence against him and he was sentenced to two years' imprisonment.'

'And you?'

'I had an understanding with the prosecution. I'm an innocent man – that's official. Do you have any news?'

'Daniel Coën is in Barcelona.'

'The Jewish boy, the one who lived next to us in the Rue Mouffetard?'

'He's a Communist.'

Kolya was uninterested. He asked if he might smoke and gallantly offered cigarettes to Isabel. Turning to Katya he said:

'I thought we might have dinner together. Say at ten?

Isabel says you're not due at the front for another two days. Look, I can't stay for coffee, I have an appointment, but shall we agree on ten? I think my allowance to you entitles me to dinner, doesn't it?'

Katya understood the reference to her allowance as a delicate allusion to his power. And she thought again of the lack of frankness that characterized all his actions, and his unwillingness to commit himself without first understanding the relationships of power and his position in them. But she agreed, curious as to why he so evidently wanted to see her, and feeling unthreatened and confident in herself despite the danger he posed.

Iñez returned with the coffee after he had gone, and had to be reassured that she had not been too slow or done anything wrong. Isabel took her cup and glided about the room in her fat elegance.

'So that's your terrible husband!' she said. 'He doesn't seem so terrible to me. For one thing he's short – good-looking, but short. I can't imagine him beating me up. In fact, I think I could give him a hard time – or a good one!' She laughed and swung about with her beautiful movements. 'Go and have dinner with him. Enjoy yourself! And who knows?'

Kolya knew a restaurant and had influence. It was possible to eat in the style of their prosperous period in Paris. In her commitment to her work, Katya had become guilt-free in other matters and did not care where the food came from, or that there were child beggars watching the restaurant from the shadows of the acacias. To be able to bear a measure of suffering in others was a mark of sanity if not of refined morality, and on another day she might address the problem of beggary like any other problem to be solved. Kolya was at his most amiable, which was very amiable.

'When we were talking about old friends, I forgot about Wanda and Carlo. I saw Wanda in Paris. She was buying little luxuries and shipping them off to Spain – Carlo was already here with a trade mission, I think.'

'How are they?'

'That's the joke, or the mystery. The war has turned Carlo into a Fascist hero – or beast, if you prefer. I suggested, as politely as I could, that it was all a sort of circus act, buffoonery in uniform. But Wanda says that isn't the case. Carlo is informed on the subject he has to deal with, or takes the trouble to inform himself. He's become a master of organization and is a tyrant over his subordinates. The result is that Wanda can't handle him. She tried flirting with one of the junior officers, and Carlo packed her off home to the family *palazzo* with an instruction to go barefoot and raise *bambini* and generally keep out of trouble until the conqueror returns.'

Katya laughed over her glass of wine. She was enjoying herself. Yes, how beguiling he could be when he set his mind to it! It was in such a manner that he must have entertained Lara all those years ago at the Cherry Tree restaurant in Varykino. He had what the Americans called glamour, she thought, an attraction of surface. His voice had lost none of its deep, thrilling resonance. But now she felt under no obligation to defend herself. She had broken free, and could enjoy him as an exotic and curious animal.

Mistaking her pleasure for an awakening involvement, he felt confident enough to change the subject.

'How long do you propose to stay in Spain?'

'I haven't thought about it.'

'You should. This is a war, not a career. Sooner or later it will end – probably sooner, if pressure mounts to send the international volunteers home. And what will be left for you? Nothing. Not even your friendships: they'll scatter to the four corners.'

'I recognize that. I've learned to be able to lose people.'

'What does that mean?'

She thought: he really doesn't know! We lived together for five years and he understood so little.

'It doesn't matter,' she answered. She could even smile wryly. This relaxed him and he felt able to expand his thoughts in the pompous way that seemed invariable with confident men. He leaned back in his seat and wiped his mouth with his napkin. Katya was distracted by a car going past with four men inside. Whenever she saw such a sight she wondered: was it Daniel taking someone for a ride, as the popular expression was? She had no evidence that he was engaged in the round of secret arrests and murders beyond a slight and possibly accidental connection of his name with one of the SIM prisons at a date when all was confusion and he might plausibly have been anywhere. But the thought was a worm in her heart.

Kolya was saying:

'The Republicans are going to lose this war.'

'Really? That should please you. Your sympathies, I'm sure, are more with Franco.'

He probably dismissed this as her natural acidity and not expressive of a serious point. Even his warning was mild.

'Don't say that – not here – not even in Russian. But if you want the truth, it's immaterial to me who wins, except in terms of my business. Franco supports capitalism, which is good, but I can do without all the flummery of religion and national crusade, "*Dio Patria y Rey*".'

'But why should the Republic lose? It has the support of the Soviet Union.'

'You've not become a Communist, have you?'

'No. But what I said is a fact. Why should the Republic lose?'

'Because the Soviet Union can't afford for the Republic to win. That would antagonize the British and the French. The best Stalin can hope for is to prolong the conflict until there's a general European war with Britain and France as his allies. Hitler and Mussolini aren't under the same constraint. They accept the need for a general war sooner or later, and it would suit them to have a Spanish ally before that happens.'

He fell silent, recognizing that he had allowed himself to be distracted from whatever was the direction of his thoughts, the purpose of this dinner. Katya was prepared to wait. Let him continue under the illusion that he was in control, since the alternative was inconceivable to him. He could imagine only female stubbornness, not principled resistance.

Kolya ordered brandy and offered the waiter a tip to go into the street and buy cigarettes from one of the beggar children. He told the man to leave the child with the small change and then looked at Katya, knowing that he was virtuous.

'I'm concerned about you,' he said warmly.

'How is Lydia? I understood she was living with you. Why didn't you mention her before?'

The question caused a flutter in his equilibrium.

'You've heard that she and I were living together? Well, it's true, we were.'

'Yes?'

Uncertain if she knew about Lydia's pregnancy, he decided to confess.

'Lydia had a miscarriage. You didn't know?'

'Poor Lydia. Was the child yours?'

'Probably.'

That 'probably' was the best one could say about Lydia and Katya was prepared to forgive him for it. Retrieving his humour, Kolya said:

'We weren't getting on well together. The miscarriage was the last straw for her. Afterwards – you know Lydia – she had a fit of religion: she thought she looked attractive as a penitent. These days she's living with Wanda in Italy. Can you imagine the two of them together?'

Katya shook her head. He pressed his mockery of the countess, thinking to entertain her.

'They've probably filled Carlo's *palazzo* with Fascist gigolos. *Bellissima contessa! Bellissima principessa! Mm! Mm! Mm!*' He kissed the back of his hand.

'Señor, your cigarettes,' said the waiter obsequiously. Katya had grown unused to this class of service and did not like it. Kolya did not notice. He lit a cigarette and smoked it with a nervous complacency, content with his own performance but unsure how it was received.

Katya, however, was thinking of Lydia. It was too easy to adopt Kolya's picture of a house filled with attractive young men; and Lydia, attiring herself in penitent's weeds and admiring her figure in front of the mirror, was all too plausible. She existed for others as a caricature, never entirely real, and certainly incapable of real thought or feeling. But she had lost a baby; Katya, aware of her own barrenness, could not forget that. Lydia in despair, knowing that at her age she would never have a child; Lydia abandoned by her lover and seeking the comfort of another woman; a *palazzo* occupied by two lonely women on the brink of middle age, fretting each other with petty annoyances and the endless repetition of their woes: these were also possibilities.

'Why did you want to see me?' Katya asked.

'I want you to come back to France with me. This place is a fantasy. It can't last. I can take care of you.'

'You know how it was between us. What's the point?'

She wondered if he could bring himself to say he loved her: if, in fact, he did love her in his fashion. But whatever he said, she was resolved it would make no difference to her. His dishonesty and need to manipulate created an unbridgeable gulf between them, one so deep that he could not see it. He was incapable of regarding her as anything other than an appendage to his life; and the essential woman, who resisted him in the struggle for her own identity, would never be more to him than a stubborn and unreasonable female, the butt of jokes in bars and men's clubs.

'I see,' he answered. He made no threats, merely ordered the bill and paid it promptly as if in a hurry for another appointment.

'You'll come to see reality,' he told her coldly. Katya saw the foresight and calculation in his reply. He would rely on circumstances to reduce her.

She noted that he could not bring himself to say he loved her.

Concha was laid up at the military hospital, streaming oil, with Katya underneath her, carrying out the repair.

'I love to see a woman working,' said a voice. 'Cooking, cleaning, bringing up the children! Hello, Katya.'

Katya rolled from under the old ambulance and, blinking in the sudden light, saw Daniel grinning at her.

'Your feet will get sunburnt.'

She looked at her bare feet, which had been sticking out. Daniel continued:

'You didn't let me know that you were back in Barcelona. I had to find out for myself. How long are you here?'

'I should have gone to Lérida yesterday, but Concha won't leave.'

'A sentimental vehicle.'

Katya wiped her hands on a rag; an oil smear appeared on her forehead as she tried to brush a lock of hair out of her eyes.

'You've let your hair grow again.'

'Isabel will cut it before we go to the front.'

'You haven't explained why you didn't get in touch. You can still reach me at the Hotel Colón.'

'I've been busy.'

'And I have nothing to do. Come for a walk with me.'

'Now?'

'Why not? You've already overstayed your leave. This is Spain. Do you think anyone minds much if you repair Concha today or tomorrow?'

There was about him this morning something irresistible and Katya was not inclined to resist. After her dinner with Kolya she was willing to borrow Daniel's cheerfulness and pretend that it lacked complexity. They made the short but strenuous walk up the hill to the Park Güell, reaching the top in the naked heat of the sun which forced them to seek shelter under the pines. Stretched out below, the city shimmered blue, with domes like jellyfish floating in the mists of a placid sea.

This was Daniel, whom Katya distrusted for his dark, intense nature; whom she suspected on flimsy evidence of being a killer. He was picking up a handful of sandy soil and letting it trickle through his fingers. He could not look at her without smiling.

'So Kolya expects us to lose the war?' he said. She had told him something of that night. 'Well, he may be right. For good or bad Spain's fate lies with foreigners: in fact, there are times when it's difficult to believe it's the Spaniards' war at all. What stupefying arrogance: to take over a whole country in order to fight our quarrels! Ha! And he wanted you to return to France with him? Will you go?'

'Of course not.'

'Why "of course"? We're running out of time here, we foreigners. At heart we're all romantics and the war has exhausted its romance. From now on it'll be simply a case of pushing bodies through the killing machine.'

Removing his *gorillo* he swatted at a fly that had settled on his leg.

'I'm thinking of leaving. They'll probably permit me to because of this.' He raised the stump of his left arm. 'I don't know what I'll do afterwards. Journalism? The Party will find me a job.'

'What has brought about this change of heart?'

'Would you believe that you have?'

'Me?'

'Yes. Don't look so surprised! I haven't changed my opinions or become disillusioned by war. I still believe in the inevitable processes of history, grimly grinding on. But I thought that, for a while, they could grind on without me.'

'I don't see how I've caused your decision.'

'Don't you?'

And, of course, she did. For a moment she thought that Daniel was going to confess a mooncalf love such as Sasha Zhivago had proposed at Nice; but that was a fanciful supposition. Daniel's love – if it were love – would

597

be of a graver kind. Today his manner had reverted to a certain boyishness, but behind it she suspected a driven soul. Where Sasha's generous spirit was broad and encompassing, so that his opinions and affections were a ragbag of incompatibles, Daniel had the mentality of a ruthless reductionist, whose ideas were fundamentally simple and tested by the consistency of their logic and not the observation of their effects. She feared that Daniel's love was a sinister embrace.

Yet, to be loved at all! Katya felt exhilarated, so that she was frightened he might make an explicit proposal. What would she say? Today she no longer had that sense of self-control that allowed her to face Kolya. If that was inconsistent, so she was inconsistent and knew it. In fact it was a marvel to her, feeling as she did here and now, knowing *this* Katya and her longings, that she had been able to oppose Kolya's strong and calculating will. How was it possible to feel strong and self-contained against one man, yet weak and needful against another, and this when each of them represented a danger to her? For she had no faith in Daniel. His egoism might be of a different and more attractive kind than Kolya's, but it was one that would allow no true equality and might be more damned and dangerous in its narrow concentration. But to allow herself to love! Perhaps that was Daniel's attraction: not his love, but the opportunity to give release to the pent-up love in her own heart, that mewed, starveling child who wailed against her barrenness, who disturbed her slumbers like the memory of Tanya. Who, like a child, craved for touch and immediacy, warmth and sensual delight.

But then she was saved, not by any act or desire on her part, but by a certain masculine pride and fear of rejection, so that, looking at her, Daniel saw only himself and the risks his rational mind would not accept. And he did not see a woman pregnant with longing.

'We'd better get back,' he said.

They returned to the hospital.

*　　*　　*

That night Daniel and Katya slept in separate beds in separate places. Katya dreamed of Lydia Kalinowska. She was profoundly affected by that absurd woman who had emerged from the world of caricature into that of reality. She saw herself in later years, suffering the fate of single women, no matter how beautiful, who cease to be human in the sight of others, and who, where they once had character, now merely have ridiculous mannerisms. Katya saw herself the object of every sly joke, the stranger at every party, who must be talked to kindly and introduced to men with quaint, angular manners, who would have strong opinions on the ultimate trivialities: pets, politics and the meaning of life. But, worse, while this woman gossiped about important nonsense and ignored trivia such as a badly made dress and over-elaborate jewellery, she would feel within her the suppression of her real life and a pregnant absence, tangible yet not there, the child unborn. Lydia had lost her child and Katya had lost Tanya, her baby sister. Neither was the result of a deliberate act, but where children are concerned there are no accidents. We love and hate them too much. The loss of any child, under any circumstance, is an abortion from the womb. Katya dreamed of Lydia crying because she had murdered her baby.

Daniel dreamed of killing people. He slaughtered the rich, the Jew-haters, the complacent ignorant. He felt the surges of hatred and anger and their release that comes only in dreams. He killed Sasha, and the only difference was that Sasha understood why he must die, and accepted death as he accepted everything else. Daniel shot Sasha out of loving necessity and cried as he did so. In a flash of insight, he recognized his own jealousy, and knew that Sasha forgave him.

Into this holocaust of resentments his softer nature from time to time intruded. He pictured Katya and his admiration and great tenderness for her swept away his anger. He saw her as an escape from his crimes. A man in love and loved could not be a monster. He wanted her arms to enfold him when he returned from his work as history's henchman. He wanted her kisses to obliterate the horror, and her breasts into which he could bury his head and its secrets. Above everything he wanted it all – the undefinable 'all' – to cease.

He woke early from a restless night and, in the turquoise dawn, washed his face from a pitcher of water that stood on a table. He dressed with the nimble technique he had learned in mastering his disability. His jacket and his unloaded gun lay on the bed. He would finish dressing and go for breakfast at a nearby café. At the door came a knock.

Daniel went to the door, thinking it might be Jaume and Viga with the car. Instead two strangers with pistols forced their way into the room and pinioned him expertly against the wall. They spoke rapidly, in coarse Catalan, but Daniel understood them well enough.

'We've got a little *cochecito* outside with the engine running. This time, you bastard, it's your turn to take a little ride!'

CHAPTER 22

THE WORLD ICE THEORY

Along this section of the front, under wind and rain and scudding cloud, the two armies sat on the crests of opposing ridges two thousand metres apart, well out of range of the poor marksmanship of either side. While battles had raged elsewhere, here the two thinly manned lines had dug trenches where the depth of soil allowed, and otherwise sat for months in scrapes or fox-holes faced with barriers of rocks, observing – or, more accurately, ignoring – each other.

In the valley lying approximately halfway between the lines was a small, abandoned farmhouse which had been hit by occasional shell or mortar fire but was still a substantial ruin, and a spinney of ragged pines that grew bent by the prevailing wind. Isolated and dominated by the hills, the farm had no significant military value, but sometimes housed a sniper, and in fact did so today since the sniper had just shot the Kid.

The Kid was sixteen, an illiterate who had come down from the sierra, from goatherding, esparto gathering and charcoal burning, to see the glamour of the world in the shape of the armies. His habit was to range the hillside and the valley, armed with a sling, and gather brushwood or hunt hares; and, ordinarily, this was a safe enough activity. Except that today, as he was bringing back a hare, clambering over the rock faces and waving to his comrades, the sniper got him with a neat shot to the head.

'The bastard must be in the farmhouse,' said Gerónimo laconically, as the Kid's body was borne down the communications trench to the rear.

'And I suppose we'll have to winkle him out,' said Sasha. When they heard the shot they had rushed to the trench and climbed the firing step to peer out. Seeing no movement except the wind whipping the grass, they sat down and Sasha replaced his heavy helmet with a cap. 'It's a shame,' he commented. Then: 'Let's get back to work.'

'Yes, Sergeant.'

Sasha was supervising the filling of a field latrine and the digging of a new one. The work was going slowly since it was raining and the men were hindered by their waterproof capes. Uncomfortable with any distance between himself and those he commanded, Sasha helped out with pick and shovel and talked to Gerónimo the while.

The latter was a miner from Asturias. He was squat and muscular; his arms and head bore small coal-dyed scars. Unlike the others, who smoked, he had the miner's habit of chewing tobacco and raw onions when he could get them. His teeth were a deep brown and his breath smelled foul, but he was good-tempered and hard-working, and Sasha liked to encourage him since he set the pace for the others. He made little secret of the fact that, before the war, he had been a socialist: in fact he had taken part in the uprising of 1934. His presence in the Nationalist army might have been regarded as an anomaly, if it were not that many of the men were in the army simply by way of being in the rebel areas at the time of the revolt, and would have been equally content to fight for either side or none. In the case of Gerónimo, he had been disabled by an accidental roof-fall, and by the time he had recovered, Asturias had fallen to Franco and he was a soldier in the generalissimo's army. He showed no particular distress at this, and was prepared to shoot at the Republicans for so long as they were shooting at him; and, being a disciplined man, it did not occur to him to desert.

Possibly in order to clarify his own ideas, Sasha tried to talk politics with his companion. His hope was to persuade the miner that Fascism, as represented by the ideas of José Antonio Primo de Rivera, had a genuine social programme that would appeal to working men. In short, that it represented an authentic socialism within the context of an integrated national society: a socialism without class conflict. Gerónimo listened patiently and agreed that there was much to be said for a society without conflict, and it was a pity that Don José Antonio had been killed. 'But I can't stand priests and lawyers.' His wife was religious, and he had once had a dispute about the inheritance of a cottage from a brother killed in the mines.

Lieutenant Ramírez came waddling towards the new latrine from the telephone shack. His cape was streaming with rain, drops hung from the tassel of his *gorillo*, and his boots were white with limestone mud. After the customary salutes, he said:

'Zhivago, I want you to take some men and capture the farmhouse.'

'Very good, sir. When?'

'I leave the details up to you.'

'Tonight, sir?'

'That will do.'

'Very good, sir.'

The lieutenant was a pharmacist in civilian life. When he had gone, Gerónimo said:

'And I can't stand shopkeepers either. I once had credit from a shopkeeper when I was out of work. But apart from priests, lawyers and shopkeepers – oh, and landlords – there's something to be said for Fascism.'

The night was moonless and cloudy, the wind blowing and the rain falling. 'We'll break our necks,' said Gerónimo.

'I'm sorry about the Kid, but I don't fancy breaking my neck for him. If he was still out there, wounded, it'd be different.'

'We still need to get rid of the sniper,' Sasha reminded him.

'He's probably cleared off home. He must reckon we'll be after him.'

'Will one of us have to stay in the farmhouse?' asked Pepe.

'The lieutenant didn't say so,' answered Sasha. Pepe was the best shot in the company and had done sniper duty when the situation was reversed, but he did not like doing it. The farmhouse was too far from the lines to be supported easily, and on the last occasion he had fled for his life when the Republicans made a night raid.

'We'll get wet through,' said Gerónimo. They would have to leave their burdensome capes, which made too much noise.

'Maybe they'll relieve us if we pull this one off. Think of the chance of a warm bed!'

Six of them, carrying their Mauser rifles and a couple of grenades apiece, slipped from the trench and made their way down the winding path that led from the ridge to the valley floor. This part of the exercise was familiar though difficult enough in the dark. The path in fact led directly to the farmhouse, but it had to be assumed that it would be covered by the sniper, and the latter was regarded as having supernatural eyesight. Even though they had an experienced rifleman in their party and he was an ordinary fellow, snipers in general were regarded with dread. There was an inhuman malice in their ability to pick off men at will, and, because one could never be wholly prepared for them, this seemed a devilish quality.

On either side of the path they advanced at a crouch. The ground was a bare red earth sown with white rocks, clumps of thyme and other scrub. The rain had activated every spring and rill, and between the gusts of wind they could hear the tinkle of running water and feel it sucking at their boots. Ahead was the house, only a couple of hundred metres away, whitewashed and faintly glimmering, its roof gone and interior burned out: most of them knew it from other raids; even Sasha had been there once.

Accordingly, there was a routine. Gerónimo and two of the others fanned to the left, and Sasha with Pepe and one other took the right. It was impossible to be wholly silent, but with attention to the wind, particularly here, close to the trees, they could mask the noise. The worst part was by the building itself, where the scrub gave way to naked rock and on a quiet night a boot could sound as loud as a shot. But tonight there was wind, rain and mud.

They broke into the house simultaneously from each side, Gerónimo and Sasha flashing torches as they did so. It was empty.

'He's been here, though,' said Gerónimo. By the window that faced the Nationalist lines were cartridge cases, a heel of bread and some cigarette butts. In the corner, urine splashes and a pile of turds.

'Okay to smoke, Sergeant?' asked Pepe.

'In the corner where you can't be seen.'

'Mind the turds,' said Gerónimo. 'Unless they're yours from last time. What do we do now? He isn't going to come back in a hurry.'

'He could still be out there. In the trees, maybe.'

'Quite likely. But what can we do about it? The house is one thing, but the trees are another. If we get split up, we'll end by shooting at each other. I've seen it happen.'

Sasha went to the door at the rear and looked out on to the enemy side of the valley. The crest of the ridge was dim against the clouds and here and there a faint glow marked a fire. He had no opportunity to decide anything further since at that moment there was an explosion and he was blown back from the door in a shower of earth.

'Mortar fire!'

'It's a trap!'

Without orders the men scattered from the house into the night, only Gerónimo staying long enough to grab Sasha by his soaking blouson and drag him behind. Another mortar shell exploded squarely in the building and a light machine gun opened up from a hundred metres or so. Belly-down in the sodden mud, Gerónimo asked:

'You all right?'

'Yes – yes, I'm fine.'

Gerónimo laughed. 'Clever sods, aren't they? You've got to admire them for it. Please God our side don't take it into their heads to shoot back.'

In fact, a couple of artillery rounds whistled overhead and exploded somewhere harmlessly on the hillside. But by then the raiding party, in ones and twos, frightened and bad-tempered, was well on the way back to its own lines. Sasha and Gerónimo were the last to arrive.

After the execution of Gromov, Sasha had volunteered for the front and in the process became mysteriously transformed into an infantry sergeant. He had been in a state of profound depression and had sincerely hoped that he might be killed. However, he had discovered that for most soldiers, most of the time, it is quite difficult to get killed, and that, even when opportunity arises, there is an instinct for survival that unreflectingly overrides any contrary intentions. In addition, it became apparent to him that, like the Kid, most soldiers are as surprised by death as any civilian walking blindly in front of a tramcar. Disease, shellfire or a sniper's bullet takes them randomly, unexpectedly and without glory and, since what Sasha had in mind was a form of suicide and expiation, to die suddenly and unshriven was repellent to him. So, bit by bit, his natural good spirits reasserted themselves and unwittingly he began to think positively about life again. He was marked by the death of the fiacre driver in a different way. It made him calmer, more reflective and, conscious of his own follies, the folly and fanaticism of others moved him to a profound pity.

Lieutenant Ramírez was a provisional officer. Aged thirty or so, he was slightly overweight and harassed by the burden of office. His pharmacy was in one of those small Spanish towns that form independent worlds only tenuously connected to the rest of Spain. For men of his kind, wider culture was represented by the sermons of the priests, the editorials of highly political newspapers, and the café conversation of similar men who thought they were exchanging ideas. He worshipped Franco.

Sasha was curious about the lieutenant, and the latter regarded Sasha as his friend (calling him 'Zhivago' instead of 'Sergeant'). He had a love-hate relationship with intellectuals – 'so-called' intellectuals, as he styled them – and viewed Sasha as an intellectual because he spoke foreign languages and had attended the Sorbonne, even if he had not graduated. He wanted at the same time to use Sasha as a sounding board for his attacks on intellectuals and also impress upon Sasha his own credentials as a serious thinker. His thoughts included elaborate cosmologies of an unorthodox nature.

During Sasha's first spell of relief from the front line, the lieutenant, having explained that off duty they were permitted to be more sociable, took him to a café in the city, bought him a drink, and began to set forth his ideas about the war.

'It's all caused by the Jews,' he said.

'The Jews? I don't see how that can be. Spain has hardly any Jews – in fact I'm not sure there are any Jews here at all. Didn't Ferdinand and Isabella drive them out?'

'The Catalans.'

'They're not Jews.'

'That's what you think.'

'Well, I don't have an opinion, but I've never heard anyone suggest they are Jews.'

'That's hardly surprising, since the so-called historians

are Jewish. But, just consider, which part of Spain is nearest to the Holy Land? Where is the first point that they would land if they came to Spain?'

'Catalonia?'

'*Precisamente!* So now you see the appeal of Jewish Marxism for the Catalans!'

'I'm beginning to.'

The lieutenant had a decisive argument.

'Barcelona!'

'Yes?'

'Don't you see?'

'Not exactly.'

'Hah! Call yourself a student of languages. *Bar* is Hebrew for "son of". *Bar*-celona! See!'

When Sasha explained this to Gerónimo, the latter said he understood the point and thought it quite possible. After all, the Catalans were famous for being hard-working, calculating and grasping – in fact not like Spaniards at all. On the other hand, he did not think that socialism was a Jewish philosophy. Christ was a socialist, though the priests told lies on the subject. As to whether Christ was Jewish, he could not say, but thought it unlikely.

On the next occasion, Lieutenant Ramírez expounded on deeper stuff. He asked Sasha whether he believed in the World Ice Theory as discovered by the philosopher-scientist Hörbiger. Sasha answered that he was unfamiliar with the subject.

'That's because it isn't taught in your conventional universities,' said the lieutenant. 'There's an extraordinary narrow-mindedness among so-called intellectuals. If an idea doesn't fit into their preconceived theories then they won't consider it, and – worse – do their best to suppress it. If I wanted to teach the World Ice Theory at their universities, would they let me? Of course not! Yet, if I, as a man of only fair education (not poor, you understand) can grasp the World Ice Theory, why can't they? Refusal to consider other people's hypotheses isn't scientific!'

He went on to explain, as far as Sasha could gather, that the planets, other than the Earth, were made of ice; that space was in fact filled with ice; that the sun was wholly or largely made of ice, and that its apparent heat was simply the excitation of molecules in the Earth's atmosphere. The Earth would fall into the sun in the reasonably near future.

The day after the night raid on the farmhouse Sasha and his men were relieved and allowed into the city. Eating a poor meal of stew and chickpeas in a restaurant in the Calle Tozal, Sasha was surprised to find Lieutenant Ramírez approaching him with a new, slightly deferential air. He took a seat, asked if he might share Sasha's bottle of wine, and began, secretively:

'I've heard a story about you, Zhivago.'

'Good or bad, sir? If it's bad, it's likely to be true.'

'What? Oh! Ha ha . . . Is it true that your father is a millionaire?'

'My father's dead.'

'But he was a millionaire.'

Sasha debated about giving an honest answer, but guessed that the lieutenant had a moderately reliable source.

'My grandfather was very rich, but my family lost everything in a financial swindle. Why are you interested?'

'Oh, someone mentioned it to me.'

'Someone I know?'

'A brother officer – French – name of d'Amboise.'

'Connie!' Sasha could not believe the fortunes of war that had brought them together again. 'Where is he staying?' He pressed the lieutenant for an answer and the latter, being good-natured, directed him to an hotel near the civil governor's residence; but, on the way, he heard a cry from a café beneath the colonnade in the Plaza Torico and, turning round, saw Constantine, looking fairly drunk, in the company of some other officers.

'Hullo Sasha! *Amigos*, let me introduce Alexander Alexandrovitch Zhivago, who is a fine fellow but, for some

609

unaccountable reason, not an officer. How are you, my boy?'

'I'm fine. I just heard you were here.'

'I was talking to some queer little chap, a lieutenant. Is he yours?'

'It sounds like him. He is a bit odd, but well-meaning. What on earth has brought you here? When did you arrive?'

'Yesterday.'

'Are you still with your general?'

'I've moved to higher things. I'm with the commissariat in Burgos and allowed to use the telephone. I handle the materiel of war, its very sinews: boots, plasters, laxatives, and the other stuff, the one that stops you. I'm here boot-counting.'

'And when must you leave?'

'Tomorrow. The Minister of Boots requires my attention. The economy of the Third Reich is geared to the production of boots and requires only my report before it goes into action.'

'Then there's only this evening?'

'Fear not, drink up – oh, you haven't got a drink. *Amigos*, a drink for my friend!'

A glass was brought and filled with spirits. Then Constantine's companions, recognizing he was otherwise occupied, wandered away and they were left alone.

'So, what news? Mother? Sister?'

'They write. The letters take a while to get through, but they're both well. And your family?'

'Fine. My father is proud of me since I've managed not to get myself killed and look like ending the war as a general or something. Any other news? Did you know that Wanda and Lydia are in Italy?'

'Alain said something to that effect. Did I mention I saw him? No, of course not, I haven't seen you since April.'

Constantine's face assumed a solemn expression, which, for a second, Sasha assumed to be his usual facetiousness.

'Well? Tell me the joke.'

'It's not a joke. I thought you would know. Alain is dead.'

'But how?' Sasha was stunned.

'He shot himself. I haven't said that right. He had an accident, cleaning a revolver. There was a suspicion . . . you understand . . . a suspicion.'

'Dear God.'

'Yes – well – you were fond of him.'

'He was my . . . I suppose spiritual adviser is the expression. At times he was like a father to me. Alain dead! I saw him four or five months ago in Andalucia. He struck me then as very strange, but he was oppressed by the war, by . . . the things he had to do.'

Sasha thought of the execution of Gromov and the Jesuit's tears. Had Alain really killed himself? How close had he, Sasha, come to killing himself? It was a strange possibility and one he had not considered. He had been depressed to the point of wanting to be killed: but to kill himself? No, it was something that had never occurred to him. Perhaps his vanity and capacity for self-dramatization had saved him. He had never envisaged death without an audience: spectators to his final effort to be a hero. 'I must write to my mother,' he said, wondering how he could possibly tell her.

'Let's get drunk!' Constantine proposed. So they did.

Constantine continued to prattle with his usual levity, and Sasha laughed with him. Then, to his surprise, Sasha felt ashamed. What was he doing? Constantine had ceased to interest or amuse him. Their friendship seemed to have no more than the pointless quality of habit, from which nothing new could emerge.

In the course of the evening they returned to the café where Sasha had begun with Lieutenant Ramírez. The latter was still there, and with the true monomaniac's sense of time he ignored the condition of the two younger men and continued where he had left off as if nothing had intervened.

'I asked about money, Zhivago, because I'm looking for investors for a little idea of mine. You know that I'm a medical man, and I can say from my own experience, as well as extensive reading, that there is only one source of illness in the human body, and that is the retention of toxic and necrotic matter in the digestive and excretory tracts. And for that there is only one sure and certain cure.'

'Is that right?' asked Sasha whimsically. Feeling he should show informed interest, he enquired: 'And what is it, this universal cure?'

'Colonic irrigation!'

Constantine burst out laughing.

'It is *not* funny!' insisted the lieutenant. 'I have invented a new model enema, and I'm looking for capital to put it on the market after the war.'

Just at that moment Gerónimo and Pepe came into the café, beating a white powder from their caps. In his drunken state, Sasha was fascinated by this and moved to the door, followed by Constantine. He rolled aside the loose blackout curtain and stared into the night. Snow was falling, the first he had seen in Spain. It was falling slowly, and in the café someone had put a record on the gramophone. It was playing a waltz. The snowflakes seemed to fall in patterns, one-two-three, one-two-three, soft and glittering.

Sasha was made melancholy-happy by the mix of old friendship, drink, the news of death, and now the snow, which suddenly reminded him of his childhood in Russia and the bittersweetness of that time, when, very small, he had travelled on a train through the winter to Yuryatin in the company of his father, mother and grandfather. The complex overlays of emotion disturbed him in their contradictions, but – possibly only because of drink – they seemed to reflect a unity of a mysterious kind.

In the meantime others had come to the door and were making various remarks of a prosaic nature about the snow: that it would be good or bad for this or that. Lieutenant Ramírez said:

'We'll need to dig out a path for the food truck.'
And Sasha answered:
'Maybe your World Ice Theory is true.'

The hills and the valley lay covered in snow. Gull-grey, the sky was heavy with more to come. The air was tangy and snapping with brushwood fires from the trenches.

From the slit between the brim of his helmet and the buttoned-up collar of his cape, Sasha, standing on the firing step, peered across the valley. On the far ridge men, small and black as ants, were foraging the slopes for fuel. In the still morning the plumes from their fires rose in smoking columns.

'You can take the helmet off,' said Gerónimo. 'There's no-one in the farmhouse.'

'How do you know?'

'He'd freeze to death, and there's no point in him lighting a fire since we'd know he was there.'

This morning the farmhouse, which under other conditions was white, stood as a blackened ruin next to the starkly drawn pines.

'It seems warmer this morning,' Gerónimo remarked. 'Why is that? Why is snow warmer than frost?'

'The World Ice Theory.'

'What's that?'

'I've no idea.'

Leaving two men to guard that section of trenches, Sasha wandered off with Gerónimo to the rear where a football match was going on in a farmyard and bets were being placed. Several spectators commented that it was warmer now that snow had come, and Gerónimo explained that it was the effect of the World Ice Theory. Sasha watched the game for a while and then went searching for food and a place where he could take off his gloves and read a while.

It seemed to Sasha that the army was obsessed by human excrement. Soldiers talked about it all the time and the officers continually emphasized the need for hygiene and latrine discipline. As evening fell, Sasha was called to the bunker occupied by Lieutenant Ramírez.

'The Moors aren't using the latrines,' said the lieutenant brusquely.

A company of Moorish *regulares* had been brought up the day before to occupy the next section of the line.

'Is it our problem?' Sasha asked. 'Shouldn't their own officer order them?'

'You know my views about toxic and necrotic matter.'

Sasha wondered if he wanted the Moors to be given an enema for the sake of their health.

'In any case,' said the lieutenant, 'they're not confining their activities to their own section. I went to the canteen and found turds in the next field. And tomorrow we're due for inspection. Also, how do we know that we shan't be in that section on our next spell?'

'What do you want me to do?'

'Go to their officer and ask him to make his men use the latrine.'

'Wouldn't it be better if it came from you directly?'

'I've got paperwork to sort out.'

That night there was a little moonlight and a frost giving a grey glimmer to the snow. Between the two sections of trench stood an outcrop of white rock defended only by a few fox-holes which were currently unoccupied. The untrodden path was deep in snow and Sasha was concerned at the dampness soaking into his puttees. But he could see the lieutenant's point. Like molehills or small cairns, deposits of turds lay scattered on the snow. He came across a Moorish sentry wearing a knitted helmet and a *chilaba* and asked to see the company commander. He was shown to a dugout where a European officer had managed to instal a stove of sorts and was sitting in his jacket.

'Excuse me, sir. I bring the compliments of Lieutenant Ramírez.'

'Do you? What does he want?'

'He points out that there is an inspection due tomorrow,

and requests you to order your men to use the latrines instead of performing their ablutions elsewhere.'

'Sorry, I can't do that.'

'Why not?'

'Because, Sergeant, whoever dug the latrines wasn't thinking of my men. They won't shit in the direction of Mecca, and that's final. And I can't dig another latrine until the ground softens or they give us some picks.'

'I'll tell my lieutenant.'

'Do that.'

The officer sat back on the packing case he was using as a seat and squinted at the small area of Sasha's exposed face. Easing a little, he said:

'You're a foreigner, aren't you?'

'Yes, sir.'

'Didn't I see you the other night? I was drinking with another foreigner, a headquarters type, Captain . . .'

'D'Amboise.'

'That's him! Is he a friend of yours?'

'Yes.'

The officer laughed. 'He's a madman! He claimed, straight-faced, to be the son of a cardinal. He said his father was keeping the job for him until after the war.'

'That sounds like Constantine.'

Looking around the dugout, Sasha saw a picture of the other man's pretty young wife, and next to that a copy of the Koran.

'Ah, you're looking at that, are you?' said the officer. 'Well, you have to have some knowledge of it if you're to control my men. Give them an order that's against their religion and they'll cut your throat. But, as for cleanliness – forgetting the shit business, which I've explained – they're very clean. Their religion demands it. Cutthroats and murderers, but very clean.'

Sasha turned to go, but the other man stopped him.

'It's a cold night out, Sergeant. Would you like a drink?'

He had a bottle of brandy and poured two measures into tin cups.

'I can see you're an educated man. Can you imagine how it is for me, commanding these boys? For that's all most of them are, just kids. And ignorant, you wouldn't believe how ignorant they are. Some of them still think they're in Morocco. They slept on the boat and never noticed the sea – not that they have much concept of the sea, some of them. They think that Franco is the Sultan of Fez.'

Sasha finished his drink.

'I'd better be going.'

But the officer was lonely.

'Come and have a look at them. It'll be something to tell your children. Are you married, by the way?'

'No.'

'You have a *novia*?'

'There's a girl I'm in love with,' said Sasha, thinking of Katya but really trying only to be agreeable.

'I'm married,' said the officer, adding embarrassingly, 'but my wife seems to be infertile.' Sasha tried to dismiss the thought with a joke.

'My lieutenant is a pharmacist. He thinks that all illness is caused by poor bowel movements. He recommends daily enemas.'

The other man failed to understand.

'Does he? I'll think about that. Maybe my wife should try it.'

The wind had got up and was blowing flurries of snow. In a hollow nearby, a group of half a dozen *regulares* had lit a small fire and were sitting around it, most of them boys under twenty and one older man with a lined face and a grey beard. They wore a mix of capes and *chilabas*, woollen helmets, red tarbushes and turbans. Stitched on their *chilabas* was a white crescent. They were listening intently to the older man.

'Carry on,' said their officer indulgently.

The man began to recite – or sing, Sasha was not sure which except that there was a guttural music to the sound, a rhythm, a rise and fall. It was not beautiful;

the sound was too unstructured to Sasha's unfamiliar ear, but it seemed instinct with a beauty waiting to be formed, the formation of which would occur as the listener gave himself.

'What is he talking about?' Sasha asked.

'He's reciting the holy Koran.'

'He knows all of it?'

'No, I shouldn't think so. But a fair amount. They learn it by heart. It's pretty much all they learn.' The officer nodded and smiled encouragingly at his men. 'Murderous-looking bunch, aren't they? Yet you'd think they'd hardly given up their mother's milk.'

Sasha found them disconcerting. They had boys' faces and curious eyes, but the faces were masked by beards where possible.

'Do you understand Arabic?'

'I manage. The same might be said of you. You speak good Spanish.'

'You're a professional soldier?'

'Yes.'

'What is he saying now?'

> *'Your Guardian Lord*
> *Is God, Who created*
> *The heavens and the earth*
> *In six days, then He*
> *Settled Himself on the Throne.*
> *He draweth*
> *The night as a veil*
> *Over the day, each seeking*
> *The other in rapid succession:*
> *And the sun,*
> *The moon, and the stars,*
> *All are subservient*
> *By His command.*
> *Truly, His are the*
> *Creation and the Command.*
> *Blessed be God, the Cherisher*

It sounds rather like the Bible, doesn't it?'

'Yes, it does,' said Sasha thoughtfully. 'Well, I must be going.'

'Another drink, Sergeant? No? All right. Tell your lieutenant I'll get a latrine dug as soon as I can.'

'Not facing Mecca.'

'What? Oh, ha ha – definitely not! Not facing Mecca!'

Sasha walked away, leaving his companion to muse over the strange men he commanded. He left the hollow and found himself in swirls of wind-blown snow. Knowing that around him hundreds of men were bivouacked, he felt intensely alone and, in the silence of his thoughts, considered the scene he had just witnessed, the World Ice Theory, the death of Alain, and the departure of Constantine. It was particularly difficult to think about the last two. He wondered if he would ever see Constantine again, and thought not, though he could not have given a reason. Why was he not more distressed at Alain's death? Again he could not say, except that he was becoming used to life's relentless stripping away of attachments.

Having wandered from the path and lost his bearings, Sasha looked back and saw, some distance off, the glow of the fire lit by the Moorish soldiers. Still the snow was stirred by the wind and, unable to settle, it hung in the air. Here it caught the reflections of the fire, and, over the hollow where the group of boys gathered like shepherds at the Nativity, was suspended a dome of golden light.

The shellfire began before dawn, breaking in a cacophony of explosions over the Nationalist lines. Sasha sheltered in a trench in a state of abject and impotent terror, hunched like a foetus, his hands over his ears as protection against the noise and pressure waves, his helmet tinkling with a continual rain of earth and fine debris. The barrage continued for an hour, then ceased abruptly; and at this point the Nationalist soldiers, dazed and frightened beyond any capacity to think, rushed and jostled in mad confusion to the firing step. This unreflecting action was drilled into them as the difference between life and death: for the barrage was the prelude to an enemy attack. Under its cover, the soldiers would have advanced and, while Sasha loaded his weapon and slipped a bullet into the breech, the man who would kill him might even now be only a few paces away with rifle and bayonet poised.

Except that it was not like that.

As Sasha, Gerónimo, Pepe and the others – stumbling and pushing, fumbling with their weapons, holding helmets in place in the fear they would fall off, like clowns in a silent movie – took their firing positions, they saw not a dense mass of the enemy about to fall on them, but a ragged line, scarcely a line at all, wading through the snow a thousand metres away. Swathed in capes and greatcoats hung with mess tins, water bottles, cartridge pouches and the other rattling paraphernalia of war, their heads masked in woollen hoods, crested helmets, felt hats and caps, bundled and bagged and tied with straps and strings, the attackers appeared as an uprising of tramps and derelicts who had struggled in alcoholic confusion into the dazzling, snowbound daylight.

On the Nationalist side a machine gun began to fire. Taking his cue from this, Sasha fired also. None of this seemed to have any direct effect; yet the enemy, for some unconnected reason, in the same bemused fashion in which it had attacked, halted and began to retire: some of the men leaping over the snow, others ploughing through it, still others lifting the skirts of their greatcoats and walking like fastidious women concerned at getting wet.

'Well, we saw that lot off,' said Gerónimo. 'But where did they all come from? I thought there weren't more than a couple of thousand of them along the whole of this front?'

In the valley, black bodies stuck out of the snow and a Russian tank, keeping its distance, wandered back and forth like a taxi plying for hire. In the direction of the city, artillery rumbled. Some Katiuska bombers passed overhead with an escort of Ratas.

To their surprise a hot meal arrived, together with a priest. The latter was dressed in a biretta and soutane, with a khaki pullover covering the soutane and his skirts tucked loosely into a pair of riding breeches. He had two boys with him, carrying a gold cross and a censer; and four old men, black as mourning, laboured under the burden of a statue of the Virgin. In a jolly mood, the priest distributed blessings and took confessions from soldiers who knelt in the snow, holding their helmets clasped to their breasts like wedding bouquets.

In the later afternoon, as light was fading, came another attack. This was supported by a couple of tanks but was beaten off like the first. This time, however, there was less artillery support to the Nationalist lines and, behind them, Sasha saw a glow of flames. The attacks by aircraft continued throughout the night.

'Zhivago,' said Lieutenant Ramírez, 'get your men on their feet and ready to move in five minutes.'

'We're retreating?'

'A realignment, that's all.'

'But we held them off.'

'Not everywhere,' said the lieutenant. 'Five minutes.'

'Yes, sir.'

Night still had several hours to run, but no-one was sleeping for the drone of aircraft and thunder of guns. The horizon was lit by flashes like summer lightning, and a cold moon, wrapped in a halo of ice, glimmered over a sharp frost.

The narrow road was jammed by a battery of howitzers and they, in turn, were held up by no-one knew what except that from somewhere ahead came a whinny of draught horses. On either side of the road men drifted like wraiths in the snow, and a mounted officer on a spirited horse coursed up and down the line calling for order and discipline and shouting unit numbers, only to be greeted by jeers and catcalls. In fury he cried out:

'Name – yes, you there! Name!'

'Go to hell!'

'Don't tell me to go to hell! I'll know your face!'

'You'll know my arse!'

'Do you call yourself soldiers of General Franco?'

'To hell with General Franco! And the Pope, too!'

Angry and ashamed, the officer turned his mount and cantered away, leaving the men trudging slowly in the darkness, buried in their capes and helmets, unknown, even to each other.

'Pablo?'

'Who?'

'Sergeant! Where's the sergeant?'

'Any idea where we're going?'

'Don't push! Mother of God, stop pushing!'

'I'm hungry.'

'I want a shit.'

'God, it's cold! My fingers are solid.'

'Who's heard this joke before? Shout out who's heard this joke before – the one about . . .'

'God, it's cold!'

Thus for two hours, marching a little distance, no distance at all, but far enough to place them in an unfamiliar landscape with the configuration of the hills changed and the location of the enemy uncertain. There on the exposed ground they scooped out holes in the snow and thin scrapes in the earth, and lay sleeplessly. And in the morning they found that their alignment was wrong in relation to the expected direction of attack, so that the fox-holes and rudimentary earthworks had to be dug again.

'Where are we?' asked Gerónimo.

'Close to La Muela, I think.'

'What does that mean?'

'That we're surrounded, but I could be wrong.'

'I hear that Lister is on the other side. He a tough

hombre, a Communist. If I were on the other side, I think I'd join the Communists. You need the discipline if you're going to win.'

'I thought there'd be a longer barrage before they attacked. I expected days of it.'

'They probably haven't got the shells. In any case, all the guns do is chew up the ground.'

It was a guess that they were near La Muela. Their present location was a hill. It commanded the country, an expanse of dazzling barrenness, so white and bright that it was difficult to look at.

Gerónimo rolled over on his back. On his chin a thick stubble was white with rime and his eyes seemed red and lidless. His breath came out in clouds. He said:

'Look at that sky! It looks like a sheet of ice. Did you notice the moon last night? It had like a rainbow around it. They say that's caused by ice crystals.'

'They're right.'

'They are? What do you know!' Gerónimo whistled. He rolled over again. Snow clung to his cape like fur. His helmet had a grey sheen of ice like the bloom on a grape. 'This Hörbiger you mentioned, he's a scientist?'

'After a fashion.'

'And a German?'

'Yes.'

'So he'd know about this World Ice Theory, if it's true?'

'It's rubbish.'

Gerónimo laughed: 'It can't be all that much rubbish if a German believes in it! It stands to reason that there must be something to it. You said yourself that the moon is made of ice.'

'I said no such thing.'

'And look at the sun today. There it is, shining away, and here we are – freezing.'

'Dear God,' cried Sasha, 'here they come!'

Up they came, in their shambling lumpishness, a khaki swarm accompanied by a hail of mortar and artillery fire. Sasha emptied his rifle in their direction, scarcely bothering to aim, and then scrabbled for ammunition in his cartridge box. Gerónimo, more at ease, fired at leisure, and between rounds shouted above the noise more questions about the World Ice Theory. Pepe, the marksman, told off his count of dead men like rosary beads: 'One – two – three – no, I missed that one, he fell over, stupid bastard.' Hour after hour, it seemed to Sasha, with no let-up except a certain animal rhythm, a collective breathing in and out by the enemy.

And at the end he was still alive, with the sensation of having taken part in a miracle. His ears were numb with cold and deafened. His fingers frozen and senseless. His shoulder bruised with recoil. And around him, in pools of watery snow, lay the cartridge cases that had fallen hot from his rifle.

The movement was not a rout, rather a drifting to the rear of cold and hungry men. Commands were given which would explain this phenomenon to historians, but few of the soldiers could remember any orders. They retreated because they had fought well against superior numbers and it seemed the obvious thing to do. For Sasha it was a stroll in dreamlike exhaustion across a high and windy land, with here a cottage, its roof weighted with rocks against the wind, and there the spoor of a fox traced in the snow. He chatted to Gerónimo and Pepe. He kept long silences. Most often he smiled a crazy smile and admired the sky, its subtle greys, the iridescence where it hid the sun. And then he was looking down from the steep white escarpment of La Muela and before him was a city on a hill dominated by its ancient *mudéjar* towers. He descended the escarpment and crossed the narrow valley floor, the single-track railway, the vegetable gardens and the bridge. Once inside the town he met again the familiar officiousness of men who directed traffic, took roll calls, and allocated billets.

Sasha and his men were given an artisan's workshop of some kind, situated near the ancient walls. A family lived upstairs. Downstairs was a large room whose ceiling was supported by a wooden pillar and beams that showed adze marks. It was filled with billets of wood, half-shaped staves, iron hoops and nails, lumps of wax, pieces of cut and uncut leather, dust, shavings, a smell of tallow and olive oil, a magazine picture of the generalissimo, a portrait of His Holiness from which a sacred medallion hung. Snow was heaped against the stone walls and on the tiled roof.

'Now this is what I call homely,' said Gerónimo. 'Look at all this wood! We can make a fire and get ourselves warm.'

They made a fire and sat around it in the filth of their damp and steaming underwear. They turned out the seams of their clothes and cracked lice eggs between their thumbnails. Another time Gerónimo sat in his blouson, naked from the waist down, and combed crab-lice from his pubic hair. Pepe, nervous and prudish, groaned: 'Must you? Do you have to do that?'

'I like doing it,' answered Gerónimo with a grin of his brown teeth. 'It's the only thing to be said for lice, that hunting for them is fun. What do you think, Sergeant? Have you got kids?'

'No.'

'I have, one, a little girl. She gets lice. Well, kids do. So I say to her, "Come to Papa," and she does, good as gold. Don't kids have beautiful hair? I put her on my knee, and I comb through her hair. She loves it! I comb through her hair . . .' he mused. 'Every time I find a louse, she gives a chuckle. We call the adult lice *pioyos* and the eggs *llendres*. She says: "Are they *llendres* or *pioyos*?" If we find *pioyos* they go on my score, and if we find *llendres* they go on hers. There are more *llendres* than *pioyos*, so she always wins.'

'Do you have kids, Pepe?'

'I can't afford a wife.'

'What do you do for a living in civilian life?'

'I was a sacristan. And some of the time I used to teach.'

'Are you a socialist?'

'No. Socialism only leads to anarchy. The best years for me, if you ask my opinion, were in Don Miguel's time. He opened the country schools. There was a chance then for peasant children to get an education. That's when I got my certificate and did a bit of teaching.'

'So you support Franco?'

'I support order. In Don Miguel's time there was order. I don't mean tyranny. Don Miguel was a soft-hearted man, a human being. He liked good food and wine and women. But if there was a threat to order, he could be hard – but only just hard enough.'

Gerónimo stood up. By the flicker of firelight he put on his trousers. He said:

'How long have we known each other? Three months? And you never told me you were a teacher.'

'It was none of your business.'

'It's just that this World Ice Theory that the sergeant has been going on about, has me intrigued. What's your opinion? Is it true?'

'I don't know,' said Pepe shortly. 'And I don't think the likes of you and me are entitled to have an opinion about it. When those who know better than us put it into the text books, then it'll be true.'

'Why aren't we entitled to an opinion?'

'Because we haven't the education to allow us to understand – excepting the sergeant. That's the trouble with socialism and foreigners and Protestants, and Jews worst of all. They think that everyone's entitled to an opinion and everyone's opinion is worth the same. Well, it isn't true. Most people are stupid and have to be told what to think or they get crazy ideas.' Pepe hesitated then apologized to Sasha: 'I wasn't including you when I said what I said about foreigners. Obviously there are exceptions. I don't want you thinking that I have blind prejudices.' And it was true that, despite their political differences, he was on good terms with Gerónimo.

By Christmas the Republicans were inside the town,

advancing by rifle, bayonet and grenade in bitter house-to-house fighting. The defenders retreated to the southern districts, to the civil governor's office, the Bank of Spain, the seminary and the convent of Santa Clara. Lieutenant Ramírez's platoon of infantry was scattered in the fighting, and during this period Sasha was in the company only of Gerónimo and Pepe. Other soldiers were known to exist, but they were mostly seen as fleeting shapes among the ruins, except on one evening when Sasha found a small group cooking potatoes in the ashes of a fire. This was the only hot meal he ate for five days.

On the day after Christmas the sound of nearby fighting drew them out of the workshop and into the narrow street. They discovered that the enemy was barely a hundred metres away, engaged in a close struggle with a party of Nationalists barricaded in a radio repair shop. The attackers were trying to suppress the defenders with rifle fire, under cover of which small groups made forays with grenades. Sasha realized that the fall of this position would mean the next attack would be against his own, and so, with only a vague idea of tactics, he tried to lend support to the repair shop with oblique fire from the street while Pepe sniped from an upper window. This was apparently effective until nightfall.

'Thank God that's over,' said Gerónimo when no nearby shots had been heard for an hour (shooting and explosions from other parts of the town were continual but none of the three men paid much attention). 'Well, Sergeant, what do you suggest we do now?'

Sasha did not know what to do, and it astonished him that the others had any confidence in him.

'What about some food?' he suggested.

'That sounds like a good idea. Where do we get some?'

'Pepe.'

'Sergeant?'

'Will you go and look for some? See if you can find a canteen or a field kitchen, otherwise get what you can.'

An hour later Pepe returned with some dried figs,

a few grams of uncooked rice, and a handful of beans. They chewed on the figs and Gerónimo filled his helmet with snow, placing the beans inside in the hope that they would soften. The rice they kept until they could make a fire to boil it.

'Talking of which,' said Gerónimo, 'we could do with getting inside and making a fire or we're going to freeze out here.'

'I don't know. If we don't cover the street, there's every chance of a raid and then we'll be trapped like those poor devils –' meaning the defenders of the repair shop who, he imagined, must be surrounded, otherwise it was inconceivable that they would not have fled. Gerónimo bowed to Sasha's superior knowledge of war and they decided to pass the night in the street where they improvised a barrier of rubble, tiles and broken timbers.

During the night Sasha was disturbed by a terrifying tap on the shoulder, but it was only the old man who lived above the workshop. The latter apologized.

'My wife and I are leaving,' he said. 'Can I ask you to take care of the place? You couldn't find somewhere else to fight, could you? This place is all I've got. There's another house over there. It's empty. The owner has a daughter in Caudé, so if his house gets destroyed he's got somewhere else to live.'

'Where will you go?'

'We'll probably find shelter in a church somewhere.'

'Well, good luck to you.'

'Thank you. Oh, and you too.'

Just at that moment a section of the sky lit up. Someone had fired a flare which floated in the snow-stuffed clouds like the Christmas star. By it Sasha was able to see the old man clearly and also his wife, who showed her grief according to her own sad limitations, a sort of crossness as if her husband had mislaid his socks. He noticed that Gerónimo and Pepe had both gone to sleep. It seemed incredible! Sleeping, despite the fact that they were blue with cold and shivering. Then he remembered that he too had been asleep and dreaming, first of his mother and then of Katya. He and Katya dancing in Nice. But, instead of a beach, from the Promenade des Anglais a field of snow stretched as far as the horizon and it was in this snow that they danced. Yet they were not alone. From the promenade a crowd, basking in sunshine, watched them with horrible complacency, and – still more horrible – across that vast field of snow, men, who a moment before had been corpses draped in greatcoats, woollens and the khaki rags of war, rose in pairs; and they also began to dance two by two in a ponderous peasant waltz made fat and lumpish by scarves and pullovers, boots and puttees. And the music rose in volume and quickened in tempo so that these bodies of dead soldiers, with the stateliness of drunkards, quickened their vile parody of dance, and they kicked the snow up higher and denser, in star-bright flurries, thickening until the air was a grey opacity and Sasha found himself, arms outstretched, dancing alone, and Katya lost, calling his name distantly from somewhere beyond the veil of snow.

'Wake up! Damn you, wake up!'

Sasha shook and kicked his two companions until, groggily, they came to life.

'What's up?' asked Gerónimo.

'It's no good. We're going to die out here. We've got to find shelter and get warm.'

They went into the workshop, kindled a small fire from the stocks of wood, and there warmed themselves. Exhausted, they forgot about cooking the rice.

In the morning Sasha woke cold and hungry around the ashes of the fire. He noticed that the shooting around the radio repair shop had ceased. He woke Gerónimo and Pepe and they crept into the street. From the makeshift barricade they glimpsed the enemy infiltrating nearby buildings. Sasha told the others:

'We can't stay here. Without support, we'll be cut off like those other poor devils, and we're low on ammunition.

I propose we pull back until we make contact with our own troops.'

Neither of his companions objected, but Sasha felt ashamed that his decision was motivated as much by cowardice as by rational considerations. He feared that when he rejoined Lieutenant Ramírez he would be humiliated for losing contact with the rest of his platoon, and for abandoning a defensible position.

There were friendly troops only two streets away. The distance was not great, but Sasha had discovered that in house-to-house fighting there is a radical change of groundscale, and that a hundred metres may acquire as much significance as a kilometre in the open battlefield. Finding the officer, Sasha enquired as to the location of his own company.

'I've no idea,' he was told. 'Organization above the level of ten or twenty men doesn't mean much under these conditions. I'm simply hanging on here. I've very little notion of the overall picture.'

Sasha saw that the men were trying to bar the street with furniture faced with earth and rubble to absorb the impact of bullets. They seemed filthy and demoralized, but their officer was of a different character, excited, eager even.

'Where have you come from? *Hombre*, you look half-dead!'

Sasha told him where they had spent the night, though he did not know the street name. The other man said:

'If it's any consolation, you were wise to pull out. I don't think there's anyone else forward of this position. In fact I wouldn't be surprised if they've pulled back to Ensanche and there's only us this side of the viaduct. If you'd stayed you'd have been surrounded and killed for sure. I suggest, Sergeant, that you and your men remain with us. As a group we can give enfilading fire if the enemy tries to pick off these houses one at a time. That gives us a chance to hold him.' Seeing that Sasha was discouraged, he added: 'The *Caudillo* isn't going to let the Reds take this town. He lifted the siege of Toledo and he'll do the same for us. It's all a matter of hanging on.'

Sasha returned to his two companions and told them that they would stay. He noticed, without finding it remarkable, that he was limping on his frozen feet. They drew some ammunition and dry bread from the small stock of supplies and were allotted a house to defend. This one had belonged to a teacher with strong religious convictions, to judge by his books. The owner had fled, or possibly was fighting elsewhere. The advantage of the house was that it had a cellar where they could shelter against artillery fire.

Given the proximity of their positions, Sasha had expected that the enemy would press his attack. However, the latter proved cautious, suspecting snipers and booby traps at every turn, and advanced only slowly. Possibly the enemy had problems of his own in respect of cold, exhaustion and supplies. Chilled and frightened, Sasha and his two friends discussed this among other things, from films to football, and between times drifted in and out of a febrile doze, troubled with dreams.

In the ruins of one of the houses a fire was lit. As evening fell, with the enemy still relatively inactive (though the sound of fighting from other parts of the town never ceased), the Nationalist soldiers emerged from their burrows. Someone had found a sack of potatoes and these were baked in the embers and eaten greedily. A question was asked:

'Why did he lay off us today?'

'It's just chance. I could hear him giving it hot and strong to some other poor beggars.'

'Maybe Franco and some reinforcements are breathing down his neck. He may have had to withdraw men to face them.'

'Please God you're right. But it's no joke trying to relieve a siege in this weather. It's murder on the transports.'

'I don't like the look of that sky, and there's a wind

getting up. The temperature is dropping and we're in for more snow. Mother of God, I'm freezing!'

'That's it – cheer us all up!'

Sasha, too, thought that the weather was deteriorating. On the other hand, he was sure that, behind the immediate din, he could hear the sound of artillery somewhere north of La Muela, which might mean that reinforcements were on the way. The situation appeared to him to be a race between the weather and the relieving force. Regardless of the activity of the enemy, he detected signs of frostbite and exposure among the men and suspected that many would die of these. He gave no thought to his own condition. It did not occur to him that the detachment with which he observed the other men was the result of his own dangerous state, or that the hollow-eyed gazes that sometimes met his, were weighing up his shambling, shivering appearance and marking him too for death.

Within the house there was no more fuel and to light a fire was in any case dangerous. They huddled in silence against the bitter frost. When the attack came at dawn the next day, it was sudden and ferocious. Pepe, who had a vantage point on the upper floor, was killed when a mortar shell came through the roof and blew apart this section of the house. Also, from somewhere, the enemy was sweeping the street with a heavy machine gun, and grenade parties could be heard making progress from house to house. Sasha had grown attuned to the sound and rhythm of this form of attack: the explosion of the grenade muffled by the walls of a room, then the one or two shots that seemed invariably to follow.

He had ceased to take any active steps in defence of himself, though he kept his rifle beside him out of habit. It was the effect of cold, hunger and exhaustion, but in his light-headed state Sasha had concluded that he must be a coward. He found this a curious and unexpected aspect of his character but was convinced that it must be so since, by

contrast, Gerónimo had become bad-tempered and energetic, muttering dark curses and abuse and making brief
expeditions into the street to fire a few rounds before the
machine gun drove him inside. Neither man spoke to the
other.

Since he was apparently soon to die, Sasha set about
the preparation of his soul. He had an idea that this should
be done methodically, like the filing of paperwork; and
so, while the fighting grew noisier and closer, he tried to
reckon up his sins and wished he had pen and paper with
which to write them down. Unable to concentrate for long
on any one subject, his thoughts drifted to the theology of
confession. He remembered Alain once saying to him that,
in extremis, a man might make confession to his horse.

'No horse,' he murmured.

He looked around for some worthy object and his
eyes lit upon his right boot, which was still covering a
numb and frozen foot. He stared at it and it seemed to
become detached and independent of him. Opening his
blue, cracked lips, he addressed it wryly.

'Boot? Will you hear my confession, Boot?'

With an effort of will, he managed to waggle his
foot. He grinned.

'Good.'

Satisfied, his thoughts wandered again. He saw Katya
as she was that night in Nice: not the cynical creature
she had later become. He realized that that single night
had become more significant than he had ever supposed,
for into it was compressed all the love for a woman that
would ever be allowed to him. He tried to recapture it in
his imagination but it eluded him at the most basic level.
Had they really danced, or was it all a mistake? He could
feel his arms around her again and even the motion of their
bodies in relation to the waves. But had they danced? Had
she responded as he had to the shock of sensation when he
held her? Had she felt the same thrill of certainty?

Distracted again, he spoke to his boot.

'It is six months – six months – since I made my

last confession, Boot? What do you say to that? Are you a forgiving Boot? Are you the Boot of the Living God?'

He tried to move his foot again.

'It was cold last night. Were you cold, Boot?'

A cough racked his body and drew the attention of Gerónimo who was at the door shooting into the street and yelling imprecations. But nothing was said by him. Sasha's mind continued to wander.

'Since my last confession I have been guilty of cowardice and folly.'

The folly he could not regret was that which had caused him to fall in love with Katya. Above all others it had given him joy, and now it gave him a sort of peace. How curious – he thought – that life was explained only in such moments, and for the rest consisted of sleep and humdrum routine, experiences common to all men like interchangeable parts. He was convinced that he loved Katya, for if he did not his life had been truly meaningless.

He meditated on dancing. The folly of dancing. Swinging in great circles through the spray of sea and snow. Clasped in a wordless embrace. Smiling and understanding that each loved the other. That *was* how it had been. One-two-three, one-two-three. He remembered that there had been music. What was the tune? One-two-three. And Katya said: 'I love you.' He recalled that too.

He glanced at the doorway and saw Gerónimo sitting in it. The other man's chest was spread with a great red stain. His face held a rictus smile. Sasha stared at his boot. He tried to move it and could not.

'Got nothing to say for yourself?' he enquired. He could make out the image of a face from the pattern of eyeholes, laces and creases in the leather, but he could not animate this mute countenance.

He wondered if he truly existed in the mind of God. Sometimes it was difficult to believe so from the way that God disposed of His creatures. He wondered if there were an impassible God, who, in His search for knowledge of His infinite possibilities, imagined the suffering of His imagined creatures, and, like an artist unconvinced of the reality of his creation, discarded each imperfect draft and sketched new versions of suffering in each generation. Was it so? And, if it were, would suffering cease if we could persuade Him that we truly suffered?

CHAPTER 23

EL NOVIO DE LA MUERTE

On New Year's Eve the Nationalist Relief Force reached the low limestone ridge, La Muela de Teruel, from where it could shell the city. A blizzard broke out which lasted for four days and left the sierra deep in snow. Artillery fell silent; machines froze. Along the road to Valencia, Republican supply vehicles were halted in their hundreds.

The old ambulance, Concha, was abandoned between Teruel and La Puebla de Valverde. Katya and Isabel, swathed in greatcoats and woollens but still chilled to the bone, struggled through the snow to Valverde and found lodging in a school that had been thrown open to refugees from the stranded convoys. These included casualties from the fighting who had been on their way to the hospitals in Valencia. For the duration of the blizzard, Isabel nursed the wounded and Katya performed the humble tasks of cleaning the improvised ward, laundering the linen and cooking. When it was over she worked herself to exhaustion in the snow-clearing parties as, by degrees, the road was re-opened. Two days after the end of the blizzard, they found Concha again and spent another day digging her out and putting her in a state to be driven.

The convent and hospital of Santa Clara fell on New

Year's Day. The defenders were dead. The Republicans captured the civil governor's residence on 3 January. On 8 January, the Nationalist commander in Teruel surrendered and the whole city was now in Republican hands. The civilian population was evacuated. In the meantime the Nationalist relief force established itself in a position to besiege the city and the battle continued through snow, frost, wind and a bitter winter.

Though the besiegers continued to tighten their grip, the road to Valencia remained open and it was possible to evacuate casualties. Katya and Isabel found themselves ferrying cargoes of wounded and supplies between the two cities down the road from the mountains. These journeys continued without let-up for about a month, during which time the heights of La Muela were lost to the enemy, who then crossed the River Alfambra at a weakened section of the Republican front, causing enormous losses of men and materiel. On their last journey to Teruel the two women found a strange town occupied only by soldiers, among whom were the disorganized remnants of units that had fled the defeat on the Alfambra. The Nationalists were shelling the town.

'So where do we stay tonight?' asked Isabel.

The street was choked with rubble. Fires flickered in the ruins of a tailor's shop, and dummies lay about like mutilated dead. They stepped over the fallen masonry and poked among blackened household effects belonging to the tailor who had formerly lived above the shop. A mattress gave off a smell of smouldering feathers. Bolts of cloth and half made-up suits lay in a tangle of kitchen utensils and domestic furniture.

'Why didn't anyone tell us?'

On earlier occasions they had shared the shop with other nurses, the owner having been evacuated.

'Perhaps it's only been destroyed today?' Katya suggested. She found a bar of soap, pocketed it without thinking and examined the light bulbs to see if they were intact. This searching for essentials she did not consider to be looting. Isabel had taken a towel and some buttons.

'I don't care!' cried Isabel. 'I'm cold, I'm tired and I'm hungry!' She looked about her and finally at Katya, and sobbed: 'I want a bath. A *warm* bath. I smell.'

'I know, darling.'

'Well do something about it!'

'I shall. We'll find somewhere.'

They left Concha and walked, meaning to return to the hospital and make enquiries. Isabel apologized for her outburst but continued:

'What I would really like to do is wash my hair. Look at it! It's like tarred rope. I knew I should have cut it, but I have beautiful hair.'

'Yes – beautiful.'

'Beautiful hair. And the rest of me is fat and ugly!'

'You're not ugly,' said Katya consolingly.

'Are you laughing at me?'

Katya realized that she was smiling at her friend's petulance.

'Go on! Enjoy yourself! Laugh!'

Katya laughed and, after a moment's hesitation, Isabel laughed too. She wiped her eyes and, hand in hand, they walked on.

Near the Plaza Torico, in the ruins of what had once been a public building to judge from the shattered cornices and stumps of classical pillars, was a cellar with the entrance marked by a board and a sign: *Cantina*. Noise, laughter and the sound of a record-player were coming out of it. It seemed odd, from another world, in the fading afternoon lit by the flare of fires.

'I don't remember this place?'

'I don't know. I'm too tired.'

'I'm hungry and I'd like a drink,' said Isabel.

Inside there were only men, and a cry went up:

'Whoa! Look at that! Women!'

Men came over to introduce themselves. They had the ragged look of soldiers too long in the field: filthy, unshaven, smelling and bleary-eyed. Isabel returned their invitations with coarse good humour, and Katya was amused by the vanity of the men. There was not one of them who did not think himself attractive in his mud-stained greatcoat, with the soles peeling from his boots.

A kerosene stove had been improvised from oil drums. The food was a soup of tomato, bread and garlic, or a mess of beans with some scraps of mutton. These, together with cigarettes and damp uniforms, created a dense fug in which the oil lamps glowed with hazy luminosity. The tables and chairs were of caissons and ammunition boxes of various sizes, a narrow channel of water ran down the middle of the cellar, and, incongruously, a filing cabinet stood at one end where it was used to support a gramophone. The latter played a strange medley of records: Viennese waltzes, ragtime, American crooners, Argentinian tangos about love and death, sung by men who had been killed in brothels.

Katya and Isabel helped themselves to bowls of soup and found a table where the men made space for them. Despite her tiredness, Katya noticed and felt flattered. Isabel whispered:

'I don't like them, but I fancy one tonight. Imagine all that warm flesh! Wouldn't it be comfortable?'

Katya adopted the idiom of her friend:

'But look at them! They're filthy and there's no meat on any of them.'

'Beggars can't be choosers.'

'They're frozen to the bone.'

'We can warm each other up. I want . . . I want to exchange dirt, to exchange smells! I don't even mind if he's got lice! I want . . .' In a second Isabel switched from being merry to being sad and muttering filthy oaths under her breath. She said: 'Oh, God, I want . . . I want . . .'

A soldier came over and asked Isabel to dance. With a shock Katya realized that, by contrast with her own cropped head and gaunt features, Isabel was the prettier one. The soldier, who looked as though he had acted on a wager, looked also as if he did not know what to do; but, taking courage, he seized his partner as if she were a dangerous but respected lioness, and the two of them, buried in their greatcoats, which by necessity kept them at a decent distance, swayed around in no particular relationship to the music, while the soldier's friends laughed.

In this interlude a man came to the table.

'May I sit with you?'

He was, Katya thought, about sixty years of age – though in war men look above their years. His face was thin and drawn in vertical lines, his hair grey and he wore a thin grey moustache. But his carriage was lithe and active, and he had bright eyes and facial muscles that were quick and expressive. He smiled a great deal and, like other people who smile in a certain way, with sympathy, he was attractive despite his superficial qualities.

'I don't recognize you. Are you one of our nurses?'

'No. I drive an ambulance.'

'You're not Spanish. French? No, not French.'

'Russian. But I've been living in France for several years.'

Katya liked his voice for its calmness.

'I'm called Ignacio Peralta García,' he said. 'I asked whether you were a nurse because I'm one of the doctors.'

'Katerina Pavlovna Safronova.'

'People call you what? Comrade Safronova or Katya?' He smiled. 'Are you in this salubrious spot for long?'

'We're returning to Valencia tomorrow with some wounded.'

'I'm disappointed.'

'We'll be coming back,' Katya volunteered, and immediately felt foolish. She looked at Isabel, who was draped over her soldier and grinning peacefully. The other men, tired of their sport, had returned to chatting and eating and, when a shell exploded nearby causing the oil lamps to swing, paid scarcely any attention.

'Your friend is also a driver?' asked Dr Peralta.

639

'A nurse. She travels with me.'

'She seems to have found someone to make her happy. Tell me, what brought you to our poor country?'

'I was looking for something useful to do with my life.'

'Just that?'

'Yes.'

'Are you a Communist?'

'No. Are you?'

'I'm not a Party member, but you might say that I support their general aims. I believe in social reform and in winning this war, and I don't see how either is going to be achieved without the discipline of the Communists.'

Katya was uncertain where this conversation was leading. She turned her eyes to the doctor's hands, and noted their fineness, and that, like the hands of most men, they had not aged in the way that a woman's hands do. He wore a masonic ring similar to one worn by Kolya and Viktor before him. Immediately it made her distrust him, though there was no other reason for distrust.

'I have grandchildren,' he said frankly. 'My wife died of breast cancer five years ago.'

Katya saw that he wanted clearly to establish the age gap between them. She might at this moment have mentioned that she had a husband, and thus contributed her own measure of distance. But that would lend Kolya a significance he no longer had for her and would be dishonest. She forgot her distrust in curiosity.

He went on: 'I've found that age isn't what I expected it to be. I don't mean that I still feel young – I'm too conscious of the changes in my attitudes. But I still feel alive. That's what surprises me. When I was twenty, I thought that people over forty were dead. Oh, they walked around and acted as though they were alive, but I didn't regard them as if they were *really* alive: more that they imitated being alive. And then I became forty. It was a shock!' He laughed.

The room fell silent. Aircraft could be heard passing overhead and the thump of bombs a little way off. When it ceased, someone broke the silence by singing 'Hijos del Pueblo' until he was told to be quiet and a record was put on the gramophone, a jolly tune.

'I have to be going. Isabel and I need to find a place for the night. The house we normally stay in has been destroyed.'

'There are nurses at the casualty station. They sleep nearby and, I'm sure, wouldn't mind giving you space on the floor for one night.'

'Our things are in the ambulance, and we ought to move it.'

'Is it nearby?'

'Not too far.'

'I'll escort you there. It isn't safe to be alone. Since the last battle the town has filled up with stragglers. They have no officers and are living by looting.'

Katya called to Isabel, who reluctantly left her soldier. Her face was glowing, and the demoralized woman of an hour earlier had gone. Katya introduced Dr Peralta and explained he would accompany them. In her excitable state Isabel shot Katya a knowing look.

After the raid new fires had started and the town was lit with a febrile light. This time Katya noticed the dark figures flitting in the shadows and felt afraid and glad of company. They passed a party of field police, and, in a narrow street of pottery workshops, came across a number of vehicles that were being marshalled into a convoy.

'Is there going to be a retreat?' she asked.

'Probably. The Fascists are already on the north edge of the town, and there's a chance they'll cut the Valencia road. Where is this ambulance of yours?'

In the darkness it was difficult to see, and the configuration of the streets seemed to have changed. The entrance to the street where Concha had been left was now blocked by the collapse of a building, and fires were burning along its length. In the midst of this, the old ambulance was burning too.

'Well, that's just wonderful!' exclaimed Isabel. 'Now we're stuck here!'

'Come with me,' said the doctor. 'We'll sort you out for tonight, and in the morning we'll see what we can do about arranging transport.'

'We've got nothing,' complained Isabel. 'Not even soap and a towel.'

Katya felt in her pocket for the piece of soap she had found earlier. She showed it to Isabel. The latter looked astonished, then laughed, and soon all three were laughing as they wandered arm in arm to the casualty station, ignoring the calls and sexual propositions that came from shadows hiding in the ruins.

That night was spent in a cellar shared by twenty nurses and *practicantes*. It was lit by an oil lamp; on the wall hung a sliver of mirror glass in which Katya was able to see herself.

The face of an older woman looked back at her. It was grey, the eyes were red and staring, and the hair was an ill-cut stubble. Katya realized that it was a face that a sixty-year-old doctor might approach without any risk of vanity.

The morning came with a bombardment of renewed intensity and fresh influxes of wounded to the casualty station. Under this pressure Isabel had no option but to go with the other nurses. Katya said she would look for a transport that could take them back to Valencia. She was able to find vehicles aplenty that were about to quit the town in the incipient retreat, but in their urgency they had to go straight away. Katya was unwilling to leave without Isabel, and Isabel could not leave until a decision was taken to evacuate the casualty station.

Katya saw Dr Peralta. He was resting between surgery, smoking and chatting with one of the *practicantes*. The rumble of guns did not appear to disturb him. Seeing her, he exclaimed:

'Katya! What, still here? I thought you would be

gone this morning and I should never see you again, like so many pretty nurses in my life. If you're still here this evening, we could perhaps meet at the *cantina* again? Assuming that the Fascists haven't blown it to pieces. In which case, no doubt, some enterprising soul will have taken steps to open another one.'

'Is there anything I can do to help?' From being used to the shellfire, Katya was experiencing one of the periodic panics that affected people subjected to the stress of a prolonged time at the front. Conscious of this, she needed an activity to distract her.

'Are you sure you're in any fit state to help?'

'I can clean and cook. I'm not a nurse.'

The doctor thought for a moment and then laid his hand on her shoulder in a manner that was intended to be reassuring.

'There is something you can do,' he said. 'Not here. We have some Fascist prisoners – sick and wounded. They're in a fairly bad way. Don't misunderstand me: they haven't been mistreated, but naturally we've been giving most attention to our own men.'

He gave her directions to where she might find these prisoners. It proved to be in a church, a building that had survived largely intact, though around it the houses had been reduced to rubble.

The church had been ransacked by the Republicans when they first captured the town. Many of the pews had been broken up and taken, probably for fuel, the statues of the Virgin and saints defaced. The altar was bare of ornament and an attempt had been made to set fire to the reredos. The building was open to the weather through the shattered windows, but some heat was provided by a cast-iron stove. About a dozen prisoners huddled around this stove, and others lay on filthy palliasses strewn about the floor among rubble and glass. They were unwashed and for the most part wearing their weather capes and winter uniforms, sometimes over filthy pyjamas. Many were in bandages or plaster, but none appeared to be seriously wounded though some were feverish.

'They're the last,' said the *practicante*. 'At one time we had over a hundred in here. You should have seen it: like a gypsy camp. We've evacuated the others.'

'The place is a disgrace,' said Katya.

'Foreigner, are you?' answered the *practicante* wearily.

'Why don't you clean it up?'

'If you don't like this, you should see the latrines. Look, comrade, I don't have the staff. I thought that was the point of your coming here. And don't think I don't try. But every time a shell lands – even if it misses us – we get more shit blown in here. Understand?'

Katya understood that the man was tired and frightened. To argue with him was pointless.

'Do you have brushes? Buckets?'

She was shown to a room and a small closet where cleaning materials were kept. Returning to the body of the church, she began to sweep up the debris and broken glass. The prisoners watched her listlessly, none volunteering to help. The air filled with fine plaster dust as she worked in the grey light. There was no sound except the sweep of bristles and the scratching of glass fragments on the stone floor. In the dark corners of the side chapels, overlooked by smoke-blackened pictures of Dominican saints, were heaped piles of mouldering human waste.

'I'll try to mop the floor,' she told the *practicante*. He was smoking and dropping ash where she had cleaned. 'Do you have any disinfectant?'

'Don't waste your time.'

'What about the latrines?'

'They're a lost cause. You really don't want to see them.' He pointed to an oil drum. 'They do it in that, and we roll it out every morning – don't tell me it's unhygienic. I'll tell you what you can do: give a hand with the cooking.'

Some maize was being boiled up into a gruel in which floated pieces of fat and a few beans. A cauldron of this was carried by the *practicante* and one of the guards and

644

placed on the altar. The prisoners formed an orderly line, each with his own mess tin. The *practicante* was a wit. As Katya ladled out each ration, he said: 'This is my body given for you . . .' until he got bored and began to talk to the guard about the weather and the state of the Nationalist advance into the suburbs.

When the line had been fed, Katya attended to the prisoners still lying on their straw mattresses. She went to each in turn with a pannikin of gruel and encouraged him to eat it. With a touch of vanity, or perhaps sentimentality, she had expected to receive a measure of gratitude for the food, but she met only hollow-eyed stares, first at the food and then at her face, except from a few, the chirpy ones she knew would survive. They gave her a look that was frankly sexual and could still manage a lascivious smile.

That left one man. Katya had noticed him while sweeping. He stood in one of the dark side chapels, with his face in shadow and his forehead pressed against the brickwork. In the hours that she had been there, he had not moved except to transfer his weight from one foot to the other. He was draped in a mud-spattered weather cape, and wore his steel trench helmet as if expecting at any moment to be shelled. He had no boots and his feet were swathed in dirty bandages.

Katya tendered a pannikin of gruel and tapped the prisoner gently on the shoulder. 'You should eat,' she said. He made no response beyond a tightening of his shoulders. His arms were wrapped in front of him. 'Please eat,' she urged. Around her she could hear the sound of coughing, of spoons scraping in mess tins, and the patter of dust in the aftermath of a shell. 'Please!' But no answer came. She placed the pannikin on the floor and left, intending to ask the *practicante* what she should do next.

A few minutes later, while collecting the mess tins for washing, she noticed that the prisoner in the chapel had changed positions and was now squatting, contemplating the food. She could see his face, and it was that of Sasha Zhivago.

Sasha! The first emotion Katya felt was an incredulous joy. It was as if he were inexpressibly dear to her, as dear as any loved one: indeed as if he were a dear husband or brother given up for lost after a long journey to a strange country from which no news comes; who now appears on the doorstep, with his travels packed on his back, surprised that his letters have not been received. If she had been told that she had merely liked Sasha but never loved him; or that, on the last occasion they had met (which was at Max Golitsin's office after the fall of the Widows & Wounded), she had been angry with him, she would have had to search her memory, for it would strike no chord of present feeling. It might be said that she felt the inflated regard held for any familiar person after we have been long separated from home. Or, more briefly, that her emotion was a combination of chemistry and circumstance – an analysis of love she herself had once maintained. Whatever was the case (and Katya did not care, or even pause to consider causes), she was at first stunned and then flooded with loving recollections of a boy she had once met, a boy so full of romance and folly that it seemed impossible that such a person could have existed or that there were times and places where such things were allowed.

But this was no boy, and such things were not allowed. Katya remembered that she had seen the figure of a shell-shocked soldier, hiding from the light. And that was what she saw now: a huddled figure with grey skin and lips like scrapings of tallow, who could not face the decision of whether or not to eat.

'Sasha?'

His dull eyes looked up from the problem of eating.

'Do you recognize me? Katya?' she said in French.

'Hello, Katya.' He looked at his feet, then back to her, and his cracked lips formed a half-smile. 'I've lost my toes. Look! No toes! Frostbite,' he added seriously, and began to sob.

Katya lifted him and he hobbled to a darker corner of the chapel where they would be unseen. She removed his helmet so that she could see him clearly. He looked pained and puzzled. Katya wanted to cry, but she told herself that she must not. Taking the pannikin, she brought the food, spoon by spoon, to his lips, and, relieved of the decision, he ate impassively. While he did so, Katya unbound the dressings from his mutilated feet, quelling her revulsion, and was relieved to find that they appeared free of infection.

'What will I do?' he asked.

'Give up football? Become a clerk?' Katya was uncertain if her tearful attempt at humour would work, but Sasha had always been so full of high spirits.

'Yes – I suppose so. I never played football. What shall I tell my mother?'

'She'll understand.'

His gaze drifted to the church. The grey light was failing, and the prisoners were squatting, hunched in their capes, like pigeons at dusk. The artillery barrage continued in its dull way somewhere else in the town.

'Franco's men will be here soon,' he said.

'I think so.'

'Will the prisoners be shot?'

'No – no, of course not!'

'I want to go home. I've had enough of fighting.' He looked at her as if unsure of her identity. 'Is it you?'

'Yes.'

'Good.' He hesitated. 'I've not been very good at war. I'm not a hero. In fact, I think I may be a coward. Isn't that terrible?'

'No.'

'Good.'

Of his own volition Sasha now picked up the pannikin and spoon, and greedily he scraped at the remnants of gruel.

'It's good,' he said. 'I've been tired and hungry –

and cold. This is warm. I've been frightened to eat. My bowels have been bad. It exhausts you. But this is good. Is there any more?'

Katya left him for a minute to go to the kitchen and refill the pannikin from the last dregs of the cauldron. The *practicante*, eyeing her, said: 'You seem to be taking a lot of interest in that one.'

Katya answered him shortly: 'He's ill. You'll have a corpse on your hands if he isn't fed properly.'

'Who cares about one more dead Fascist? Do you know what will happen when they retake this town? It'll be a massacre!'

'That's not my business.'

The *practicante* shrugged. He said bitterly: 'I hate you damned foreigners. This war would have been over long ago if it weren't for you.'

'You should be on the other side.'

'I would have been. But when the rebellion broke out I happened to be on the wrong side, in Valencia. Now they'll probably accuse me of mistreating their men and shoot me.'

'Then let me feed this one, and maybe they won't.'

She returned to Sasha. She found him dozing, but hearing her approach he woke up and gave her one of his sweet smiles.

'I feel better already,' he said. 'Or am I dreaming? You can't really be here.'

'It is me.'

'Yes, it is!' he answered, and began to cry in long breathless gasps, until Katya took his head in her arms and nursed it to her breast.

As night fell she was forced to leave, promising to return in the morning. The air was full of dust and the smell of burning. The sky droned with aircraft. Shells fell and machine guns rattled insistently. In the streets, glass from a thousand shattered windows sparkled so that at times it was like walking on stars.

She found Isabel asleep and did not disturb her. From another nurse she begged clean bandages and antiseptic ointment, forcing her to go back to the casualty station to get them. Stooping at the doorway, Dr Peralta entered the cellar.

'So you're back,' he said. 'I'm glad you're safe.'

'How long is all this going to go on?'

'A day or two, no more. By then the road will be cut and anyone left here will be a prisoner. We're starting to evacuate the casualty station. Perhaps you will leave tomorrow.'

'What will happen to the Fascist prisoners?'

'Why are you interested? I suppose they'll be left behind. We don't have enough transports for our own men.'

'Will they be safe?'

'Safe enough, I should think. Perhaps the officers will be shot. It's not my decision.'

He was a naturally confident man, Katya thought, but had now reached an age where his confidence with younger women had ebbed. He asked:

'Have you eaten? Why don't you come to the *cantina*? We can even have a drink.' He had a bottle of surgical alcohol.

The sound of gunfire and explosions was now almost continuous. It was odd to think that bitter fighting might be going on only a few streets away. Walking was achieved in short rushes at a crouch, as though under a low ceiling.

In the *cantina* there was no music playing. Sheltering from the guns, soldiers crowded into the cellar and squatted, playing cards, smoking or talking. All conversation was about evacuation and retreat. It remained possible to get food.

'What will you do when you get back to Valencia?' asked Dr Peralta.

'What?' Katya was thinking of Sasha. The immediacy of his suffering had displaced her from her context. She could think only of minutiae: of dressing his wounds and

649

making sure he ate. 'Oh, I shall wait for orders, I expect. And you?'

'I have no idea.' The doctor asked a question that had been burning him: 'Do you have a husband?'

'No – I'm sorry, I mean yes. We're separated.'

'What are you thinking of? I had an idea you were thinking of him. Something is troubling you, Katya.'

She could not tell him. She dared not tell him. But she noticed how tenderly he looked at her. She felt intensely vulnerable. Something these last few months had opened in her so that love, affection, sympathy leaked in and out of her, and mingled and separated and flowed into wrong or different channels, all independent of her conscious will. She was becoming, she suspected, as confused as Sasha had been, who had no powers of discrimination. Irrationally, it was a thought that made her gay.

'No, don't worry! Really, don't worry.'

'Now you're cheerful!' He was puzzled.

'Am I? Ah, well! I am . . .' I am what? I am hopelessly vulnerable to love. I am inconstant, unfaithful. I am truthful, without illusions. Barren. Capable of bearing fruit. There is a joy in life. I could cry for Sasha. How attractive you are despite your age. At another time . . . I thought once that love was narrow and focused on one person to the exclusion of all others; yet now I am awash. I am a madwoman!

'You need to rest,' said Dr Peralta.

'Yes, I think I do.'

In an afterthought, she said to herself: I used to be armoured against love. How can I have changed so much? What happened to me? It was a marvel to her that so much inconsistency could be harboured within one body, or that any thread of continuity could explain the transition. Then, in a revelation, she realized that she felt as she supposed an adolescent girl might feel: or as she should feel, whose years of adolescence had been blighted by Viktor and Kolya. How absurd! How gloriously absurd!

At that moment the table where she sat with the doctor was approached by a stocky man with a broad face, high cheekbones and slightly turned-up nose. He was thirty-five or so and wore a peaked cap with a red star among its insignia. He brought with him a zinc tin holding soup and an enamel cup filled with wine. Nodding to the doctor, he introduced himself to Katya. 'Gómez. And you, comrade?' Despite his name, he was undisguisedly a Russian.

Katya guessed that he was a Soviet 'advisor'. She knew that many of these provided genuine military and technical advice, but her caution was instinctive. Dr Peralta appeared to know him.

'Mikhail, let me introduce Katya.'

'Katya?' said the newcomer, and he regarded her narrowly though without hostility. 'You're Russian?' he asked. She nodded. 'Excuse me. I'm surprised. There aren't many Soviet women here. What is your function?' He was speaking in Russian.

'But I'm not from the Soviet Union,' Katya told him. She knew that if she had completely denied her Russian origins, he would have pressed her with questions until the lie was exposed.

'Don't speak Russian,' said Dr Peralta. 'You know I don't.'

'I'm sorry, Ignacio.'

The doctor had given her a breathing space, and when Katya looked at him, she saw a certain blankness and civility in him. She was grateful for the warning.

'So –' said Gómez '– how do you come to be in the West?' The question was framed generally. He was not interested in Spain but in her earlier history.

'My parents came from Kiev in 1904.'

'You're Jewish?'

'Yes.'

He said something that Katya could not understand, but she nodded and he continued until, of a sudden, he stopped and Katya saw that she must make an answer. And that the language he spoke was Yiddish.

Dr Peralta said: 'Are you leaving tomorrow, Mikhail?'

'Why?'

Katya realized that, in his urge to save her from her mistake, the doctor had made one of his own. He had admitted the possibility of defeat.

'You know how it is. My people are being evacuated. One tends to assume that everyone is going.'

'No decision has been made in my case.'

'I can see that you'll be needed for a while yet.'

Another man came to the table and Gómez was called away. Dr Peralta was relieved. He said:

'Mikhail really isn't a bad sort. By the way, are you really Jewish?'

'Do you mind?'

'Dear Katya, I shouldn't care if you were a Hottentot! But shall we go? I think we should go.'

They left, and, in the darkness and the barrage, Katya was terrified and clung to her companion. In the cellar where the nurses were camped she found Isabel still sleeping peacefully. Without undressing, Katya lay down on her own cot.

Before going to sleep, she was able to consider her position briefly. She thought of Sasha and how she had felt a great compassion for him, and then of Dr Peralta who, despite his age, was able to quicken a response in her. She thought how irredeemably trivial her emotions were, but this caused her no distress. It seemed to her that she was on the brink of some great understanding, yet she had no apprehension of what that understanding might be.

Beyond the cellar, the Nationalist army moved to advance its position by night. It fired a barrage of brilliant white flares; for a time sky and earth were reversed, and the sky itself was as white as a field of snow.

'We can leave today,' said Isabel. 'There's a convoy

planned for three o'clock. I don't suppose it will be on time, but there's a fair chance we'll get out.'

Katya sat on the edge of her bed. She was cold. All emotion had gone and she felt she was reinventing herself from day to day, which perhaps explained her frenetic changes of mood. This troubled her. That it might be the effect of stress and external circumstance did not occur to her. She thought (at least at this moment) of the mind in its integrity, operating according to the laws of its internal processes.

'I have to go somewhere,' she said. 'I need to see the Fascist prisoners.'

'You're joking?'

'I have to go,' said Katya.

'What on earth are you thinking of? The Fascists are about to capture this place. You're a foreigner and a woman. If they capture you, you'll probably be raped and murdered!'

Around them, the women who shared the cellar were packing their few belongings. Some were ready to leave, but for the moment that was impossible; the shells were now falling so closely that, after each explosion, they could hear the clatter of earth and shattered stones above them. In the intervals they maintained a tense and frightened silence.

Katya pulled her friend aside into a damp corner where there was no-one except a single distraught woman, who was sitting on her coat with her hands over her ears, sobbing uncontrollably. Katya whispered:

'I know one of the prisoners.'

'What? *What?*'

'Be quiet! It's Sasha Zhivago. We've talked about him.'

'You must be insane!'

'I can't simply leave him.'

'Don't be stupid. His own side will be here any moment. He's about to be rescued.'

Katya hesitated over voicing the full extent of her fears. Then she said:

'There's a man in Teruel. He calls himself Gómez, but he's a Russian. I think he's a political advisor, but he may also work for the SIM. Do you understand me? He will have details of all the prisoners, and before the town is abandoned anyone who is identified as an officer or a class enemy or a foreigner will be shot. Isabel – please – *please* – don't shake your head. You *know* these things happen!'

'On your feet!' said a masculine voice from the door. There was a lull in the shelling. The women filed up the steps and, once in the daylight, stared about in wonderment at the transformation wrought by the artillery. Buildings which had already been ruined were reduced to debris. Fires burned everywhere. The air was thick with masonry ground to fine powder.

'Kiss me goodbye,' said Katya. She clasped Isabel close to her.

'I shall never see you again.'

Katya tried to laugh. 'Don't be melodramatic!'

An officer was trying to take a roll call and give directions to the transports, anticipating that the party would become scattered if the shelling resumed. Katya noticed with peculiar horror the dead pigeons, perhaps a dozen of them, scattered like blue-grey garlands, apparently uninjured. Isabel was speaking, but she could think only of the birds, destroyed by an unintelligible cruelty. Then Isabel, too, hugged her and kissed her cheeks before drawing back. And the women in their drab blue overalls, like so many pigeons, were leaving; picking their way among stones and rafters, rubbish, stink, rottenness and fire.

In its final agonies, the town had become shapeless. Familiar buildings and the pattern of streets ceased to have meaning amid waste and ruin. Even light itself seemed to have lost its variety of colour and become reduced to greyness. Through this desolation of entropy, Katya sought out the church where the Nationalist prisoners were held. On the way she passed parties of soldiers moving forward in small groups to defend the wreckage of a house or shop, isolated men wandering in confusion or hiding and staring on the world with feral eyes, and transports manoeuvring erratically around obstacles of rubble and masonry. The vehicles were crammed with listless soldiers abandoning the town. From the livelier ones came catcalls:

'*Hola! Señorita!* Come with us!'

'*Chiquita*, don't be frightened! We'll keep you safe and warm!'

'Give us a kiss! We're lonely!'

Katya came across a body lying in the dirt. It was that of a boy of twenty with dark eyes and bad teeth, his lips shrunken and curled back like a snarling dog. Frost covered his face like sugar on candy. Katya did not want to look at him, but she was forced to turn him over and then to lift his dead weight in her arms as she removed his greatcoat and cap. When this was done, she closed his eyes and turned him face down to the ground.

The guards and the *practicante* had fled the church, but the prisoners remained. Where else was safer? The men had allowed the stove to go cold. In their fear and demoralization, all solidarity among them had gone. They cowered in ones and twos against columns, altars and the corners of side chapels, as seemed best to each man. Only one was excepted, and that was Sasha. Tottering on his injured feet, he hobbled from painting to painting of saints and martyrs, and stared at each as if amazed.

'Sasha?'

Katya had approached within a few metres of him and he had paid her no attention, though his wandering gaze must have crossed hers. He now looked at her curiously.

'Katya?'

'Yes.'

A hand stretched out to touch her, touched, recoiled as from a flame, touched again, and, slowly, the fingers embraced her forearm.

'It is you! You are real!' he said weakly.

'I'm real.'

655

He gave a long sigh. 'Ah! Thank God!'

Katya supported him under the arms so that he could sit on the floor without falling. His incredulity also affected her so that she was asking herself: am I here? Is this a dream? The church was as grey as a dream, the daylight as pale as sour milk.

The successful act of sitting seemed an achievement to him, and he smiled. He gripped her forearm again in reassurance, relaxed his grip and patted her. He said:

'I wasn't sure. I've had . . . visions!'

'We must go, Sasha.'

'Wait – wait! Don't you understand? I've had visions!' The thought of movement appeared to distress him. He looked into her eyes with singular intensity and announced: 'I died!'

Katya did not know what to do. Nothing had prepared her for this! The obvious assertion that he had not died would be almost frivolous in response to the force behind his statement. He said nothing more. The church echoed to the shuffling of feet, and soldiers, as at the resurrection of the dead, peeped from the shadows of tombs and altars.

'Tell me.'

'I died!' he repeated. He considered for a moment, then began in a voice that was lucid but elevated above his normal tone: 'Do you remember Prince Andrew Bolkonsky? *Think!* He died of the wounds he received at the battle of Borodino. I was reading the book that time – when we were in Nice.'

'I remember.' After the beach and the dancing in the sea, during the walk back to her apartment in the Rue Gambetta, he had prattled on about literature among other things. He was reading *War and Peace*. He admired the character of Prince Andrew. Katya had tried to explain to him that the true hero of the novel was Pierre Bezukhov and that Prince Andrew's life was fundamentally a failure; but Sasha only laughed and said: 'You should give me lessons in literature!'

'When he was struck by the shell fragment, his first thought was a passionate desire to live. He was conscious of the smell of wormwood, and the grass and air.'

'Yes?' crooned Katya. Sasha looked at her accusingly.

'It isn't like that! Tolstoy was a liar! Prince Andrew was dying, but Tolstoy couldn't let him just die; he couldn't let him despair; he had to say something *sentimental* and life-affirming!'

He was shivering. Katya held him close to her, ignoring the curious eyes of the other prisoners. Sasha showed no physical response. He continued:

'I was cold. And I wanted to die. Anything was better than that coldness. My friends were dying around me and I wanted to die, too.' He was crying but, though Katya held him and soothed his face with strokes of her hand, he remained rigid and angry. 'I felt death coming. It was stealing up on me, like a wave of coldness sweeping from my feet to my heart. And then . . . and then . . . my heart went thump – as if I'd been hit by a blow to the chest. No, no! I can't describe it! A thump! No! It stopped! My heart stopped! And I thought: this is the last sensation I shall ever feel. Let go of me! Leave me!' Furiously Sasha shook her arms from him. He shouted out into the echoing vault of the church: 'I died! I'm a ghost! Aah! Aah!' His last breath was prolonged near to a scream, and, with its cessation, he slumped forward with his eyes open but insensible. And at this moment Katya felt not compassion but horror and panic, so that her instinct was to jump to her feet and flee this church that was filled with despair. She was saved by one of the other prisoners, a small cocky man whose determination to stay alive was evidenced by the two greatcoats he wore, one slung as a cloak on top of the other. He shuffled over in his *alpargatas*, glanced at Sasha, then at her, and said:

'He's a bit cracked, that one, if you get my meaning. Want a hand? What are you doing with him? It isn't as if any of us was going nowhere.'

'Get him to his feet,' Katya said.

'As you like, *señorita*. Whoops! Ha! Heavy, isn't he? Hmm! There's a lot of weight in skin and bone. Mother of God! *Hombre*, can't you stay on your own feet and get off mine?'

The stranger slipped Sasha's arm from his own neck to Katya's. Sasha now appeared to be conscious. He was smiling mildly.

'Help me to get this coat on him!' Katya ordered, and the prisoner obliged. He examined the Republican cap with its red star, but made no comment, only placing it on Sasha's head.

'Sweethearts?' he enquired. 'Is this one your *novio*? I don't know why you bother. Franco himself is coming through that door any moment.' He shouted to the others: 'Isn't that right, *amigos*? Our little *Caudillo* will be here in a second?'

'Yes!' came the answer from unseen voices scattered throughout the dark interior of the church. There was a rhythmic banging of mess tins; then a tenor voice began to sing the legionary anthem: 'El Novio de la Muerte'.

Katya took a hesitant footstep, praying that Sasha would follow. He stumbled forward, unresisting, and his feet did not give way. 'Look at those two,' said the other prisoner and laughed. 'The Lovers of Teruel!' He joined in the anthem, and the other voices came in one by one as slowly Katya reached the door and opened it to the daylight. 'El Novio de la Muerte', they sang – 'The Betrothed of Death'.

In the narrow street in front of the church was chaos. Men scuttled like vermin over the ruins. Loot was carried or abandoned. Arms were collected or dropped. In the damp air smoke drifted, and figures drifted in and out of it, now grey and uncertain, now lit up vividly by the fires. Amidst them one group moved purposefully. Katya recognized Gómez leading a party of half a dozen soldiers towards her.

Seeing her, Gómez asked: 'What are you doing here?'

658

'I am an ambulance driver. I'm helping to evacuate the wounded.'

He examined her doubtfully. His eyes scanned Sasha.

'Wait here,' he told her. He posted one of his men to guard the entrance, and, with the others, went into the church. In terror, Katya obeyed him and waited in the expectation of his return and the unmasking of Sasha as an enemy prisoner. She felt dizzy from the smoke, the weight of Sasha supported by her shoulders, and the sight of gibbering humanity in its abject desire for escape. Sasha was whispering to her.

'No – be quiet!' she answered him without listening. His voice insisted:

'Russian!'

'What?'

'He spoke to you in Russian!'

But of course he had. He was a Russian. What did Sasha mean? It came to her then that the guard placed by the door might not have understood the command. He was probably a poor Spanish peasant or worker, ignorant of any foreign language. But what if she were wrong?

She moved again, slowly. She did not look back. Step by step, still supporting Sasha, she made her way down the steep lane, manoeuvring as best she could around the debris. At each step she heard Sasha issue a little grunt of pain, a sigh, a stifled cry. It seemed to her that she would never reach the bottom; and, beyond that, what was her goal? To walk to Valencia in winter, bearing this crippled man? Tears sprang into her eyes, her throat was choked by the bitter smoke, and the weight was almost more than she could support; but, despite the hopelessness that oppressed her, she forced herself to go on, and at last she turned a corner into a street she recognized, close by the Plaza San Juan and the wreckage of the civil governor's residence. Here a line of vehicles was being loaded ready to leave.

The engines were running. Coldness kept the fumes from rising and the air was blue and sour. It appeared that it was materiel not men that was being loaded. By contrast to everything else she had seen that morning, here there was a sense of order, and an officer with a clipboard was making some effort to control the situation. 'Up there! No! There! Stow it safe.' There was something ridiculous in his calmness, that was heightened by the fact of a stream of men, worn out and ragged, flowing past the trucks on either side.

'Can you help me?' Katya asked. 'This man is wounded. We need transport.'

'Try the ambulances.'

'He can hardly walk.'

'It's not my problem, comrade, I've got stores to shift.'

'*Please!* I'm begging you!'

'Don't beg. I can't take you and that's the end of the matter. I don't want to sound cruel, but I'm trying to save military assets, not liabilities.' He looked at Sasha, who had lapsed into a daze again after the stress of movement. 'Your friend is going to die,' he said.

'He can be saved!'

'I doubt it.'

Looking at this man who, in ordinary circumstances, she suspected could be decent enough, Katya became aware of the scale of the catastrophe of which this was but one moment. The Republican defeat was total. The toll of casualties and prisoners would be huge. The scale exerted its distorting effect and the fate of any individual was insignificant. Viewed through this distorted perspective, the facts might be as the officer claimed, and the stores loaded on the waggons of more value than the lives of two people. She was too tired to argue the point and time was in any case subject to the same distortion, and the fate of individual lives merited at best a moment's consideration. On the trucks the men were tying the loads down.

'I'm a driver-mechanic,' Katya said quickly. 'How many do you have? Do you believe you can reach Valencia without breakdowns?' She had found her tongue and was speaking a language that the man could understand. He hesitated.

'How do I know you're telling the truth?'

Katya held out her hands to him. He could see the calluses and ingrained oil stains, if he wished to recognize them for what they were. But did he? In any case, how important to him was an extra driver?

A joker on the truck cried out: 'Come on, Lieutenant, you can take her to the cinema next time we're here!'

'All right – all right. Just a second,' he answered sharply. In truth, an extra driver was not important to him. But she had given him a reason, an explanation for what would otherwise be an irrational decision; and he liked to think he was a rational man.

'Very well,' he said at last. 'Get on board. Help them up, lads!'

Hands reached down, and faces that had looked on them bad-temperedly when they were an obstruction to departure, now became friendly to fellow travellers.

'You're a lucky pair, and no mistake!' said the joker cheerfully.

Katya did not answer. Sasha lay exhausted on top of the loaded waggon and his feet were leaking blood.

CHAPTER 24

THE LOST DOMAIN

Harassed by the Nationalist Air Force, its Heinkel and Savoia bombers, its Messerschmitt and Fiat fighters, the Republican army retreated towards the plains of Valencia and Castellón. Broken amidst the red earth and white rocks of the weather-scoured high sierra, dead among the olives on the stony terraces of the few small *pueblos*, the defeated abandoned their vehicles and pack animals. In the midst of this, Sasha lay on the truck and told jokes.

Katya found herself in demand. The road was jammed with vehicles at every bridge or turn. Engines overheated, axles and suspensions broke, crank cases were smashed by rocks. She repaired, improvised, cannibalized vehicles beyond repair; and, when all else failed, put her shoulder with the men or harnessed the mules to push or drag the wrecks from the highway. And when she returned exhausted, she would find Sasha regaling his companions with a joke or a story, and he would turn his feverish eyes on hers and ask gaily: 'Is everything okay?'

Without her affection towards him being diminished, Katya thought how alien he was. She remembered him dimly as a child, and then as an adolescent, full of an adolescent's passions: but, whereas adolescents become adults, Sasha had been transmuted into something else. As the convoy crawled forward at night by the lights of the trucks and the fires of troops bivouacked among the scrub and patches of snow, Sasha expounded to the half-dozen men sitting on top of the vehicle and the other dozen trudging in their greatcoats alongside. He told amusing tales of life in Russia and Paris; he told a joke (the one about . . .); he explained how the Demiurge, seeing the idea of the world in the mind of God, fashioned it from crude matter as a man might make a diamond from sand (the joke about the Catalan who inherited a fortune and . . .); he explained the World Ice Theory. The men treated him like a holy madman.

Katya was terrified that he would reveal himself as a Fascist.

The speed of a convoy is dictated by its length, the slowest vehicle and the obstacles on the road. To increase its speed of movement the column divided. Katya's vehicle (which she was now driving) was sent with others by a side road towards Castellón. The passengers changed, the able-bodied being replaced by the wounded. The wounded sometimes died. By degrees, through accident, breakdown and the vagaries of command, the column further divided, and Katya found herself driving on an empty road in a vehicle holding, in addition to its cargo, Sasha and two other men, both of whom were dead.

'Where are we, do you think?' Sasha asked.

They had come to a halt in the middle of a plain extending southwards. To the north, in a haze, hills lay covered in pine and streaked by crags of limestone. On the plain grew groves of almonds and vineyards. In the sunlight the new tops of the almonds glowed russet, speckled with the green of buds, and the soil was bright gold.

'Beautiful!'

'I think we're somewhere north of Tarragona,' said Katya wearily. She tapped the last can of fuel. 'A few

663

more kilometres and then we're finished unless we can find some more.'

Sasha was unconcerned. In the sunshine the sickness that had marred his face seemed to be lifted. He stroked his hand across the reddish-brown beard he had grown. He asked:

'Where are we aiming for? Valencia? Barcelona?' He got down from the cab and scanned the horizon, shading his eyes. Returning to Katya, he said: 'If we report to the army, I'll be shot. I can't explain myself as a reluctant conscript who deserted Franco as soon as he could. I'm a foreigner. By definition I'm a volunteer.'

Katya had given little thought to the practicalities of the future. She had considered everything in terms of immediate problems. Sasha was right of course. He would inevitably be unmasked if they went to Barcelona.

'How are you feeling now?' she asked.

'Sane again.' He smiled.

'How sane?'

'A little bit. Fortunately, not very much. But I'm right, aren't I? We can't go to Barcelona.'

'You're right.'

'Good. How far can we get with our present fuel?'

'Twenty or thirty kilometres.'

In tangles among the ragged stands of tall cane, early vetches grew blue and lilac. Cheerfully light-headed, Sasha hobbled from one clump to another, picked flower heads and pulled them apart with childlike curiosity. Returning to Katya he asked:

'What do we have on board?'

'I don't know.'

'Where is everyone else?'

'Gone.' Katya had buried the last of the dead the previous day at dawn, when Sasha was still asleep. They had been in the hills somewhere, and she had dug a shallow scrape, then covered the corpse with dry branches of rosemary and a cairn of white rocks.

They agreed that it would be good to know what

they were carrying. Under the tarpaulin they found burlap sacks containing rice, flour, beans, and lentils.

'We're a travelling grocery store!' said Sasha.

For the rest, the load comprised machinery of various kinds, artillery breechblocks and engine parts, coils of wire, some telephone equipment. Sasha said:

'We could live for months on this stuff.'

'And then what?'

'I don't know. Maybe the world will end.'

Listening to his craziness and sensing the dullness of her exhausted responses, Katya wondered if, between them, they represented any sort of sanity. Sasha was still speaking.

'Before the war, land was being abandoned because it was uneconomic for the landlords to farm it. Even now that the peasants have taken over, there must be cottages standing empty. All the young men have been taken off to fight.'

'What are you suggesting we do?'

'Find a place and stay there.'

'Just stay there?'

'For a while – only for a while. We can see what turns up.'

Katya shook her head, but she agreed that they needed to find shelter, if only for a day or two. Revived, Sasha exhausted her with his nonsense. She wanted to sleep. That would be enough, she felt. And afterwards they could plan.

She woke up on a bed of straw and broken tiles. The night was full of stars, visible through the broken roof. A small fire burned untended in one corner. Stepping inside under the low door, Sasha said:

'Awake? Are you hungry? I've boiled up some rice.'

'Where are we?'

'Don't you remember?'

She remembered vaguely: a small ruined cottage on a slight rise of ground, standing amid the arid wreckage of a vegetable garden. By the house was a quince tree. In her exhaustion she had picked up a piece of fallen fruit and stared fascinated by its strangeness: large as an apple, green as a lime, with waxy peel like a lemon. Then she said something mundane like: 'I'm going to get some sleep.'

'Here – eat.' He passed her a pannikin of rice and watched her eat as she had formerly watched him. He said:

'I've taken the tarpaulin off the truck. If I can drag it on to the roof, I can weigh it down with stones and it should keep the weather out.'

'You intend to stay here?'

'Why not? Eat up. I've made a start with unloading.'

She joined him outside. In the clear sky the dusty orange moon hung low and large. The earth, which in the morning had been bright and golden, now shimmered like a still sea freighted with dark sails of almond, cypress and pine. An owl was hunting mice among the brakes of cane.

'This is where we've come to,' said Sasha obscurely. Standing on the back of the truck, he heaved at one of the gunny sacks and deposited it on the ground before pausing for breath and to stare at the stars. 'There's water,' he added. 'A well. I need to clear some rocks out of it. I haven't found a stream. Perhaps that's why this place was abandoned. Too dry.' He swung down and picked up one of the sacks to carry it into the cottage.

In the far distance an oil lamp made a point of light to mark a village. Behind the cottage, the hills rose to crags that glimmered pale in the moonlight. The night was silent except for Sasha shuffling inside the house and the crackle of wood burning.

Why not here? thought Katya. What else is there for me to do? Who wants or needs me? Having eaten, she felt pleasantly melancholy with the night. Unlike the reproachful day, which pestered her with tasks to perform, it soothed her and demanded nothing. Why not here? Was it really so impractical?

'Can you lend me a hand?' asked Sasha, lifting the next sack.

Of course it was impractical to her rational mind, or indeed to anyone's except Sasha's.

'Are your feet all right?'

'My feet? Ah, my feet! What an unheroic wound!' He laughed. '"Tell me, Papa, what happened to you in the war?" Oh, it's a terrible story, my son. My toes dropped off! Yes, they're okay for the moment. In fact, they're not the problem. This silly walk of mine seems to be doing something to my knees and hips. Does that make sense?'

'Yes.' Katya did not want to disturb the peace of the night with labour. She said: 'Leave the unloading until the morning.'

'If you say so, but I need to hunt for something to keep us warm. I have a recollection of seeing some blankets.' He sprang back on to the truck, and continued to mutter to himself in the voice of the supposed child: '"Where are your toes? Have they rolled under the furniture? In the morning we must buy some new ones at the toe-shop. Mother will stitch some labels on them so you don't lose them again."'

'Stop it! You're making me laugh.'

'Am I?' Sasha threw down the blankets. 'Good.'

The fire died to glowing embers. Sasha said, musingly: 'I'll have to build some sort of oven. We can't afford to squander fuel at this rate. I have some ideas about it, based on what we used to do in the army. Where do you suppose people get their fuel from? The sierra? Brushwood? Esparto? The economy of these villages must be dominated by shortages of fuel and water.'

Katya was amused by the misplaced concreteness of his thinking. He had moved on to questions of fuel and water while she was still asking herself: is this the right thing to do? Which was not a question to be answered this evening, when reason was seduced by their arrival through mysterious byways at this lost domain. When she turned to look at Sasha again she could not see him. In the darkness were visible only the red ashes and the stars seen through the door-way.

'Thank you for saving me,' she heard Sasha say.

'I couldn't do anything else.'

He shuffled. She could not see what he was doing. With a shock she felt his fingers clasp hers. He asked:

'Do you love me?'

'No – I don't think so.'

'Ah.' The fingers released hers, and that too was a shock. He was saying: 'That sounds reasonable enough. It's the toes, I suppose?'

'What? Your toes?' She paused. 'You're joking again, aren't you?'

'I thought you'd never guess.'

'I can't see you smile.'

'I thought perhaps you'd lost your sense of humour. At that point I almost fell out of love.'

He had said that he loved her. There was the nub of her practical problem. How could she stay here with this man who said he loved her?

'Do you still love me?' she asked.

'I think so. Of course, I could still be a bit crazy. Why don't you love me? Everyone else does.'

'That's a very vain thing to say.'

'Is it? It was a comment based on observation. I didn't suggest that I deserved to be loved: in fact I can think of all sorts of reasons for the opposite – including being a fool and having no toes.'

'Be quiet about your toes!'

'Very good, madame.'

Oddly, not being able to see him, she was much more aware of his physical presence. She could hear his small movements dislodge fragments of tile or crush the straw; his breathing was audible; and she could smell him, not always too pleasantly. He went outside to relieve himself, and she heard him urinate.

These sensations were reciprocated. Earlier Sasha had noticed a spot of blood on the trousers of her *mono* and supposed she was menstruating. Her hair was unwashed and smelled of sebum. She had singed the soles of her *alpargatas* against the fire and he could smell the burned esparto rope.

Without their touching, there was between them a profound intimacy of sensual relations, wrapped in the night as if it were a blanket. Their wariness and uncertainty made each of them alert to the other so that one might detect the smallest of signs that expressed something thought but unsaid; or, in the air, a slight change in body temperature volatilizing a bead of sweat. It was a comforting conversation, a series of wordless questions and responses.

Sasha had read Proust (in the brief interlude of life bounded at each end by the ability to read only detective stories or similar). Now, in the silence, he followed his own train of recollection. Smells are more evocative of memory than images or sounds. From the smell of this woman here and now, he remembered another woman during another war: his mother giving birth to Masha when he was four or five years old. Forgetting that Katya was not party to his thoughts, he asked:

'Was that you? The little girl?'

'What?'

He had to explain the little he recalled of life in Yuryatin. He told Katya about the beautiful midwife who attended Masha's birth, and the midwife's little girl – well, *big* girl in fact, since she had been three or four years older, and a good head taller than little Sasha. The girl had sat Sasha down with a book and tried to teach him to read.

'Why should you think it was me?' asked Katya.

'I don't know. Perhaps you look like the midwife.'

'Can you remember her so clearly?'

669

'You sound surprised. Why?'

'Because . . .'

Katya knew that she must decide whether and what to tell him. It occurred to her that she had never been honest with him about the connections in their pasts and, in trying now to decide, she was conscious of a sense of shame. This was not a casual embarrassment at never having spoken before, but a deep and burdensome shame about her own history, though its particulars and origins were obscure to her. To think of it, even in concept, was painful. To speak of it, even more so. Yet – so it seemed to Katya now – it was the existence of this burden of shame that in the past had prevented her from responding to Sasha with anything but disdain and detachment. It was curious and frightening; and only by talking of it could it be uncovered and known. She must decide and begin.

'It was me,' she said. 'I lived in Yuryatin with my mother. She was a nurse.'

They spoke slowly and at length, though with little sense of the passing of time except that when, for a breath of air, they stepped outside in the blackness, the distant oil lamp was extinguished and the sphere of stars had rotated and glittered with a fresh pattern.

To her astonishment Katya discovered that Sasha knew nothing. He had never heard of Lara or Strelnikov or Komarovsky. His father and mother had been blissfully happy. His father's disappearance had been as a common casualty of war. That he had been alive as late as 1929 (when Tonya was having him declared dead) was incredible.

Yura – who was this *Yura*? Who was this woman, no relation of Sasha, who could talk of his father, using his first name, and whose memories of him were as affectionate yet more extensive and detailed than Sasha's own? It was wrong, Sasha felt. *Wrong!* She had appropriated his father, stolen him like a thief and enjoyed him more completely than Sasha ever had. And what was more, she had kept silent about her theft so that every exchange between them had been tainted by the undertone of her mockery and deceit.

'We have a sister,' Katya told him. 'Her name is Tanya. Your father was her father and my mother was her mother.'

'What does that make us to each other?'

'I don't know.'

A sister! No sooner raised into life then killed off again by Komarovsky. Sasha was still struggling with this stunning revelation when Katya tried to explain her own role in Tanya's disappearance, the letters from her father, the letter from Sasha's mother to her own, that single flash of hatred of her little sister which had magically caused her to disappear.

In his distress, Sasha cried angrily:

'Don't be stupid, of course you didn't cause Tanya to disappear!' He wanted to strike at her: that she could be so self-indulgent as to worry over that piece of nonsense, while with words she had torn down the history of his life and rebuilt it into something alien and unrecognizable. Of course she could not love him when at every point he was a humiliated creature in her eyes. His own folly towards her was so comprehensive that even he found it scarcely credible.

And Katya? Did she find the source of her shame? Yes, here and there, for it was not one thing. She was ashamed of deceiving Sasha. She was ashamed of her part in Tanya's disappearance, while recognizing the difference between cause and symbol. But, above all other things, she discovered that she was ashamed of her mother, and this was the most bitter shame: to find herself despising so much that was beautiful and good. For, as she told her story, it seemed to her that Lara's relations with Komarovsky had not been inevitable but were the product of weakness; and her liaison with Zhivago and their betrayal of Tonya and Katya's own father had been contemptible. It seemed to Katya that life and, still more so, love were not forms of art, to be considered good if they were beautiful. To be in love was not the same as to be good, and, whatever guilt they had felt at times, Zhivago and her mother had made that confusion in their actions if not in their thoughts. Sasha understood this too and reproached Katya for it.

Above all the sins that were rehearsed on this bitter night, this was the one that represented Katya's unmoveable burden: that she was Lara's child.

In the morning they woke in opposite corners of the small room and looked at each other in wonderment, as if at a stranger. So alien were they that it was difficult to speak, there being no certainty that they shared a language. Even gestures seemed curious, each adopting a politeness lacking all intimacy.

After half an hour of this, during which she washed at the well and surveyed the bright day, sharp with blue and gold, Katya decided that this condition of things was not supportable. She would go to the village, explain her situation and get transport to Barcelona or Castellón, whichever was nearer. Sasha could stay or leave, as pleased him. She looked for Sasha, meaning to explain the choices open to them, and found him by the quince tree. He too had picked up one of the fruit, as Katya had the previous day, and was trying to understand it. Hearing her footsteps on the small stones, he turned and smiled at her.

'Are we speaking to each other?'

'Yes, of course.'

He put the quince to his nose, sniffed it, then rubbed his thumb over its waxy surface.

'I think what I meant to say was: is it possible to speak without hurting each other?'

'If we try.'

'Yes. I think we should try.'

'I'm willing.'

'Let's go for a walk.'

They walked towards the village, through the almonds. They circled to the higher ground where the fieldstones had been walled to form terraces, and there they knocked olives from the trees. They examined the house more closely and found beneath it the stabling for the animals, now empty of anything but dried dung.

Katya was quiet in his company. He was, she thought, wide-eyed and still a little mad. He seemed intent on something. He halted her at last and said:

'Katya, last night we said difficult things to each other. I don't think that anything else could ever be as hard between us. I have no particular command of words: but, despite everything, I do truly love you. Is it possible for you to love me?'

During the course of their stroll Katya had come to expect these words because there was nothing that Sasha was incapable of saying if it reflected what he felt; and his capacity for feeling the extraordinary and the inappropriate seemed limitless.

'Love is just chemistry and circumstance,' she answered softly.

'I know all that. And literature is just ink and paper.' He studied her for a moment and then sighed. 'I can't wait around for an answer. I always was impetuous. You do love me, I can see it.' He held out his hands so that they touched Katya on the upper arms, and briefly she looked at each hand and tried to recognize its corresponding sensation of touch. She thought to herself that love was not meant to happen in this way with this man and that between them every circumstance of history and character was opposed. He drew her to him and kissed her; and still she thought that her objections were valid. She returned his kiss, still misleading herself that she was irritated with him, but, instead of irritation, she felt flooded with the warmth of his sweetness and dearness.

But he was quite mad, she told herself. Yes, quite mad. A fool with scarcely any skills of practical use. She did not doubt that she loved him, but she was surprised that love could be so completely unreasonable.

In fact it was unreasonable on both sides. From resisting him, from holding him almost in contempt, Katya became avid for her lover. When he pottered about their piece of land, trying in his inept fashion to clear it and make things grow, she would sneak up behind him and put her arms around him. Or, finding him moving a rock from one place to another, she would make him put it down, take his hands and cup them to her breasts.

For his part Sasha responded eagerly. He was unselfconsciously physical, capable of limping around the cottage naked except for a pair of *alpargatas*. His body was strong and well muscled; Katya loved to watch him wash it. And as for his good humour, it seemed to grow to excess. In the midst of his tender endearments he was capable of telling a joke at quite the most inappropriate moments. He was an enthusiastic but disconcerting lover.

They had been living in the small farmhouse for about a month when, one morning, they saw a man carrying a gun. He was walking quite openly along the path and the gun was a sporting rifle carried in the crook of his arm. In years he was of indeterminate middle age, and he was dressed in coarse overalls and wore a red stocking cap.

'Good morning to you, friend,' said Sasha, planting himself where the man would have to pass him. 'Are you on your way somewhere?'

The stranger halted. He hesitated as if reckoning up his words, then said:

'I had a mind to come and see you. Down in the village we were expecting you to call on us, but you didn't. Where are you from, Castille? Or are you some sort of German?'

'France.'

'I've heard of that place. Do they speak Castilian there?'

'No.'

'Ah. That explains the accent.'

The stranger did not seem disposed to go. He had seen the truck and was curious about it.

'We don't get many of them around here. I've seen one or two in Montblanc, and I hear that Tarragona is full of them. They don't strike me as terribly practical. With one of those, you're stuck on the roads, and even then the roads have to be good, like the one between Tarragona and Lérida. Maybe in Germany you have good roads. What's your name?'

'Sasha Zhivago.'

'Sa-sha Zhi-va-go.' The stranger chuckled. 'You have to get your tongue around it, don't you? Say something in German for me.'

Je ne parle pas allemand.

The stranger was amused. 'I can half-recognize that. There are some folk who speak Catalan and it sounds like that; though it doesn't, not around here.'

Katya, seeing that the stranger bore no obvious ill will, came out of the house.

'This is . . .'

'Valentí – Valentí Feliu.'

Katya offered some olives in one of their two pannikins. Feliu grinned and accepted. Examining his face, Katya concluded that he was ordinarily good-natured. His skin was a deep brown and more wrinkled than she could remember seeing in a man before. His fingers had horny nails and he used one to split the olives and extract the stone.

'Are you planning on staying here?' Feliu asked.

'Yes. Does anyone mind?'

'No, not as long as you stay in your boundaries. We can walk round them and I'll show you. That's why I've come.'

'Are you a farmer yourself?'

'A few vegetables, a few *fanegas* of wheat. In the off season I make rope or *espardenyas*. No-one is interested in this place. Is your water running?'

'Yes. Why?'

675

'This time of year it's normally fine. But in July and August . . .' He rocked his hand to indicate uncertainty. 'Two years out of three. You can't grow anything here if you don't irrigate, and you can break your back and still lose your crop. I see you've already got some vegetables in. Good, good. Well, those boundaries, are we going to walk them?'

'What? Yes – of course, let's do it.'

They set off with the sun still low and cool and the air flecked with petals of almond blossom. As they walked, Feliu pointed out features of the boundaries which seemed clear enough to Sasha. In any case, he was thinking to himself: there's more than enough here. There must be *hectares* and *hectares* (*hectare* being a word he knew, though its area was uncertain). Problems preoccupied him: what do I grow? Wheat, I suppose. We can't live on almonds, olives and a few cabbages. Where does one get seed from, or a plough? He looked at his new friend and wondered if he could overcome his embarrassment and ask these questions. The other man was stooping occasionally to take a handful of earth and crumble it in his fingers. He said:

'Masia always was greedy.'

'Masia? What's Masia?'

'This – here – your farm. That's its name.'

'Oh. And what do you mean by "greedy"?'

'It wants water and sweat and fertilizer and even then it doesn't want to give back. That's why it was abandoned. The landlord tried to find a sharecropper and even agreed to take only a quarter, but no-one was interested because the water is too unreliable.'

They walked up the hill to find the higher boundary. Sasha's companion remarked:

'You don't walk too well. Have you been wounded? That truck and the mess tin your wife gave me olives in, they're from the army. Did you desert?'

Sasha was put out by the question. He had never thought of himself as a deserter. He answered:

'No. I got separated from my unit in the retreat after the battle.'

'I heard something about a battle. I gather we lost.'

'Will you turn me in to the authorities?'

Feliu was offended but not angry. 'Why should I do that? I can see you've done your bit. In any case, I don't see that you Germans are obliged to fight for us at all; so you can hardly be a deserter in the ordinary sense, can you?'

Having reached the higher boundary, Feliu pointed across the plain and to the further hills.

'There San Quentín. Ten kilometres, maybe. I live there. Over there – you can't see it – Montblanc. And in that direction, a long way off, Lérida.'

A breeze had got up and on the lower slopes almond blossom was blowing like a blizzard. Sasha could hear his companion explaining something to him, something that was probably important given Sasha's level of ignorance, but all he could think of was the almond blossom and, indeed, this country which was so beautiful. In such a place couldn't a man be simply happy?

However, when Feliu had left with many expressions of good will, and Sasha walked back to the cottage, where the breeze had dislodged the tarpaulin that he had weighted insufficiently so that he would have to perform the chore over again, he was oppressed by the enormity of the task that he had undertaken and the paucity of his own resources. Depressed, he told Katya:

'This isn't going to work. I'm not a farmer. I don't know the first thing about farming. We don't have any seed or animals or fertilizer. I was mad even to think of living here.'

'Of course,' she answered. She was blithe to a degree Sasha did not recognize. 'But does it matter? We have the supplies in the truck and can grow a few vegetables. That should be enough for several months or a year. And afterwards, why shouldn't we simply leave?'

'Leave? Yes, I suppose we could. We leave now or we

leave later, what's the difference? We'll be happy enough, won't we?'

'I think so,' said Katya and he was satisfied with that. In fact, relieved of the burden of earning his living, he made quite a success of his vegetable garden and spent the rest of his time wandering in the hills to no particular purpose.

A week after their first meeting with Valentí Feliu, Katya told Sasha that she was pregnant.

Sasha went down into the village. He found a small square flanked on three sides by an arcade under which were a bar, a communal store and some artisans' workshops. On the fourth side stood an ancient stone building decorated with armorial carvings and surmounted by an open gallery under the roof from which, behind delicate columns, the square could be viewed in the comfort of air and shade. It was now the *casa del pueblo*, hung with the banners of the Republic and plastered with various official posters. Next to it the women of the village washed clothes in a stone trough. He asked the way to the home of the ropemaker and was given a civil answer by one of the women, but how strange it was to be regarded with curiosity, almost with awe.

At the bottom of a narrow dusty lane he found a stone cottage with room underneath for stabling animals and living quarters above. Behind the cottage was a yard, and in the yard was Valentí Feliu. The ropemaker wore about his waist a thick coil of esparto twine which he was feeding into a wheel, but on seeing his visitor he broke off from his work.

'Well, I didn't expect to see you,' he said. 'Even though everyone knows you're up at Masia, I didn't expect you to show your face here.'

'Why not? Isn't it safe?'

'It's probably safe enough as long as you're prudent. What brings you to the village?'

'We need salt and oil. I have some money.'

'There are shortages, but I can arrange something. Let me get you some wine.'

The ropemaker went into his house and returned with wine, cups and a plate of olives. Sasha meanwhile looked about the yard. Standing in the open was the wreckage of an old horse-drawn diligence, its yellow paintwork almost blistered away by the sun and its canvas roof in shreds. Leaning against it were a number of stilts. He asked:

'What are those for?'

'Them? We used to use them in the fiestas. The custom was for someone to act the part of a giantess, I forget why. I've half a mind to burn them as firewood. What about you? How is Masia treating you? Still got water?'

'Yes. I'm like Candide: I just tend my garden.'

'Candide? Is that the name of your woman?'

'She's called Katya.'

'I see. Nice name.'

They sipped the wine and ate the olives. Neither man seemed inclined to do anything else. Sasha found himself comfortable in the ropemaker's undemanding company. He sat down and stretched his legs and blinked at the sun. Feliu asked:

'Are you married to your woman?'

'No. Why do you ask?'

'I noticed she didn't wear a ring. I'm not married either. I prefer to take my women where I find them, though it's difficult here. Is it easy in your country?'

'Easier than here, I expect.'

'Ah,' said Feliu. Sasha sensed the deep curiosity of an intelligent but ignorant man, the curiosity which had driven him to pay his first visit to Masia. The ropemaker went on: 'It was partly the priests. I could never face the thought of turning up with my woman in front of a priest. What business of his was it what we got up to? I wanted to love my woman and be done with it.'

'You didn't like your priest?'

'He was all right. But he was fat when the rest of us

679

were thin. And whenever there was a dispute, he took the side of the *cacique* against the people. We locked him up when the revolution came, but he escaped. He's probably fighting for Franco.'

Feliu stared at his wine.

'We used to have a lot of land, I can't remember how many *fanegas*. I'm speaking of my grandfather's time. We held our land according to the life of a vine. If the vine died, we lost our land. What kind of justice is that?'

'The vine died?'

'There was a disease. It killed all the vines. These days we use American vines and they don't get the disease. So it was all a matter of luck. That's all it was: luck, not justice. The landlord tried to turn us into sharecroppers but we weren't interested. My father worked and saved and bought a little land, not enough but something. My brother went to the Basque country to build ships. I haven't seen him in thirty years. That's how it is with poor people.'

The ropemaker volunteered to accompany Sasha to the communal store since the shopkeeper spoke only Catalan, which Sasha understood poorly. On the way he continued to talk. His conversation was about priests, poverty and hardship, and how were these things abroad? What does he want? wondered Sasha. I can't explain these things to him. I don't even understand them myself. He felt ashamed that he had once been rich.

'Do you know anything about machines?' asked Feliu.

Sasha smiled and shook his head. 'I was a student of philosophy before the war. Katya knows a little. She was a mechanic.'

'Your woman!' exclaimed Feliu. His face cracked with laughter and he beat Sasha on the shoulder affectionately. 'You Germans, you're incredible!'

During the summer the ropemaker visited Masia several times. Sasha, whose days were spent in the easy task of tending his vegetables, was happy to go with his friend up into the pinewoods and the sierra. Katya, her face glazed with the gloss of pregnancy, contented herself on these occasions with sitting in the shade and dozing over the contemplation of her own body and its changed condition, which she had thought would never happen to her. Once the ropemaker shot a wild boar. Katya accompanied the two men as they carried the beast into the village, and joined in the butchering, the pickling and brining, the making of hams and sausages. She accepted wine and was cheerfully drunk. When Valentí proposed that she take a look at the broken olive press, she agreed.

The whole village took an interest in this event. It was evening and the people were freed from their work. Holding lamps and candles, they came like altar boys following a priest to the yard where the olive press stood. It consisted of a large stone crushing wheel which was turned on a vertical axis by the force of a mule. Attached to it was a hopper into which the olives were fed. Now it was in darkness, but by the light of a taper Katya, who had to be encouraged forward giggling under the influence of alcohol, saw that the main axle was broken. Disappointed, she said:

'You need a carpenter or a wheelwright.'

'I know that,' said Valentí, stroking his chin. 'I thought maybe . . . you know. Our carpenter went to join the army. Never mind, we can get someone from Montblanc to come and fix it. There's no rush.' He put his arm around Katya as, with Sasha walking cheerfully alongside, they returned to his house while the villagers dispersed to their own homes. 'Watch out for the stones. Thank God there's a moon tonight, so at least you can see them.' The stones were set like stars in the path whose dust was blued by moonlight. 'You mustn't catch cold. You have the baby to think of.'

They stayed the night at the ropemaker's house, all of them sharing the same room. Over a last cup of wine Valentí apologized:

'I'm sorry if I embarrassed you over the olive press.

681

I wanted to give you a chance to shine in front of the people. But it doesn't matter. They like you all the same for trying. In Spain it doesn't matter if you fail.'

'I'm sorry I'm not a carpenter,' said Katya, now tired and sleepy.

'It's better to be a car mechanic. There's no money in being a carpenter in a poor place like this.' Valentí paused: 'Mind you, there'd be no money in being a car mechanic, either. The only car I ever saw around here belonged to Don Alfonso – I'm speaking of the *cacique*, not the king. He had one in Don Miguel's time. It was a Studebaker. I think that's a German car, so you've probably come across it. Your farm, Masia, belonged to Don Alfonso. My grandfather's farm belonged to Don Alfonso's father. He left the village. They say he went to Barcelona to live in a brothel. I mean Don Alfonso, not my grandfather.'

'Good night, Valentí.'

'What? Oh, yes, good night.'

Later, when all three were on the point of sleep, the ropemaker's deep voice sounded out of the darkness.

'The Studebaker is an American car, and you two are French, not German. Ha! You thought I didn't know that, didn't you?'

In Sasha's eyes Katya waxed more lovely with every day that passed. He was entranced by her; he could hardly bear for her to be out of his sight. The glow of her skin, the roundness of her swelling belly, even the faint blue veins pressed to the surface of her body fascinated him. Katya loved him, but she found his constant attentions wearing. She told him to take himself off into the sierra and trouble nature or God instead of her. Sasha went away for a week and came back smiling but in a more reasonable frame of mind.

'I've started writing poetry,' he told her. 'My father was a poet.'

'I know.'

'Of course . . . Yes, of course.'

682

Katya heard no more of the poems. She remembered Yura writing on a table in the house at Yuryatin, but she saw no evidence of Sasha doing the same and supposed that he was working secretively. In the end she asked him.

'Are you still writing? Why haven't you shown me your poems?'

Sasha did not answer directly. Instead he invited her to sit upon his lap and amused her by asking questions about her pregnancy and talking about the nights he had spent on the sierra under the summer skies.

'The only problem is that all the walking is making my hips hurt,' he grumbled, adding: '"A hip injury from which I had suffered until that year had made me fearful and unhappy."'

'What?'

'It's a quotation. I don't know if I've got it right or even what book it's from. It just came into my head one night when I was sleeping. I'd been walking all day and my hips hurt.' He laughed. 'But I'm not fearful or unhappy! On the contrary, my life with you is blissful.'

'And the poems?'

'Oh, the poems! I've forsworn poetry. A son should never imitate his father. I'll write a book on philosophy instead: Everything I Have Ever Learned About Wisdom. I expect it to be quite short.'

In the autumn they went gathering mushrooms. Her pregnancy well advanced, Katya pottered flat-footedly among the pine needles and broken stumps. They returned with baskets of *rovellós* which Katya proceeded to string and dry so they could be used throughout the winter. Others she made into a soup, which she offered to Valentí when he turned up one day in a two-wheeled cart with a canvas roof.

'What brings you here?' she asked. 'And why have you come in that?'

'To take you to San Quentín. It's too far for you to walk in your state. That's if you want to come,' he added.

683

Katya could tell he was being sly.

'The fact is,' he admitted, 'we've come by some film. We're not sure what it's about. It could be a comedy or something to cheer the village up. And we've got a what-do-you-call-it, one of those gadgets you need to show a film?'

'Projector.'

'That's the fellow. We've got one of those, too.'

'What about electricity? You'll need that, and the village hasn't any.'

Valentí grinned. 'That's where you're wrong. We've got the generator that Don Alfonso used to have at his place. We liberated it during the revolution, but since then there hasn't been much call to use it.' He hesitated: 'Well, if the truth be known, there is no-one who knows how to make the thing work.'

'Shall we help them out?' asked Sasha.

'I think we should,' said Katya, touched that she should be asked.

Valentí was delighted. He had only seen a film once before. That was five years ago in Montblanc.

On the way to the village they saw the grapes being gathered. Like poppies waving in a field of wheat, the red caps of the men bobbed among the green vines. Valentí said the harvest would be poor. There wasn't enough labour because of the war. Asked about the war, he said:

'It seems there's some big battle going on Gandesa way. I don't know if it's the same one that was going on in the summer.'

'Who's winning?' asked Sasha. Gandesa was west of the Ebro, in territory captured by Franco's forces in the spring. These days he had forgotten his Fascist past and wanted a Republican victory. He never considered how he had come to this change of mind.

The ropemaker did not know.

'But we could do with a few victories on our side,' he said. 'It beats me why we keep on losing. Franco's lot are

684

just a bunch of priests, *señoritos* and darkies. You'd think they wouldn't have the stomach for a fight. It's a mystery to me.'

They arrived too late for Katya to examine the generator, and so had to spend the night at Valentí's house. In the morning she went to the *casa del pueblo* where the machine had been set up on the ground floor. She had it moved outside, explaining that the exhaust fumes made it dangerous to use indoors. This observation impressed the villagers.

It was strange to work in the street, in open view of the people, with mules clip-clopping past carrying great panniers of grapes. The consensus among the crowd was that she must be well fed for the task, and plates of food continually appeared until they had to be refused. The general opinion of the older women was that, once the generator started up, Katya would undoubtedly go into labour. It was well known that the shock of these things could bring on childbirth and that the babies were the irritable kind who never gave you a moment's peace.

Fortunately for Katya there was nothing wrong with the generator that cleaning and oiling could not cure. When she had finished, the assembled villagers applauded. When the machine coughed into life, Katya did not go into labour. This was explained by her being a foreigner and used to machinery. It was the same with the girls who went to Barcelona to work in the textile mills, and it proved you could get used to anything.

It was decided to show the film in the gallery under the roof, where the evening air would cool the spectators. A cable was accordingly run.

'Are we ready?' asked Enric, the clogmaker, who had procured the film and the projector. He was a tiny man, scarcely bigger than Le Nain, with a ferocious reputation as a drinker and fighter. But for now he was deferential, even gentlemanly. 'Will the baby be all right? Can you operate the machine?'

The whole village was present, a hundred people or

more, sitting on benches expectantly. Uncertain of the occasion, some had come straight from the vineyards and sat with bare arms stained with grape juice; while others were dressed as if for a wedding, the women in cotton frocks, the men in boiled white shirts and with oiled hair so that they looked like nervous gangsters. Enric took his position at the front where a sheet had been improvised as a screen. Beside him was an upright piano and a single oil lamp with a globe of white glass, and his shadow, like that of a giant, filled the gallery. He began:

'Yes. Right. Quiet now, everybody. I'm not used to this. You'll have understood, comrades, that I've been to Tarragona. Actually I took my cart to Montblanc and caught the bus. I sold some of my stuff and you'll be pleased to know that I got good prices there because of the shortages. A word about the war, yes. There's a big battle going on and it seems we're winning. But I have to say that we're well out of it here, yes. Things are pretty bad in Tarragona, a lot of soldiers and wounded, and things very crowded. But the battle is going well, yes.' He thought for a moment and then said: 'By the way, comrades, I'm sure you'll join me in thanking our comrades from Masia for fixing all this equipment so that we can watch the film. So without more ado, I give you – the film!'

Abruptly he doused the lamp and a murmur went up.

'Light for the cameraman!' shouted someone, and a candle was brought to Katya so that she could see.

'I've no idea what's on these films,' Katya whispered to Sasha. The reels were unmarked. She took one at random and loaded it. Sasha squeezed her hand. 'It'll be all right,' he answered.

But in fact it took five minutes to make ready, though no-one seemed especially concerned. Tired at the end of the day, the villagers were content to chat and relax in the comfortable darkness. Sasha went over to the parapet and leaned on it, staring between the columns over the glimmering roof tiles at the silhouettes of cypresses and

686

the starry sky. He thought to himself: if only I were a poet, what could I say about all this? He found Valentí by his side with some wine. The ropemaker said:

'She's a fine woman.'

'Yes, she is.'

'The child . . .'

'Yes?'

'When it's born . . . if you want it baptized. You understand me?'

'Of course. Look, we're about to begin!'

The first reel appeared to be part of a Soviet documentary about the gathering of the harvest in the Ukraine. It showed the fields of waving wheat extending to the horizon, the heroic peasants (filmed close with their monumental heads against the sky like badges of hope), the lines of mechanized harvesters stretching as far as the eye could see, the trucks of grain, the silos, the barges, the river loaded with its freight of grain. From the spectators came muted cries: 'Ah! Look at that! Would you believe it? The size of those fields. Is that fertilizer they're using? My God, look at those machines! And they say it all belongs to the peasants. Can you imagine how rich they are?'

When the reel was finished, the oil lamp was lit again, the men began to smoke and an excited discussion started. Enric the clogmaker approached Katya. His face was glowing, but he had a concern.

'That was good,' he said. 'Very impressive. But there was no sound. What do we have to do about sound? Do we need a record-player or something, so we can hear the voices?'

'All we have is a projector,' Katya told him. 'It's an old one. There's no sound system.'

'Right . . . right. So no sound? Right. Let's see how we get on.'

The second reel also appeared to be from a Soviet film. It began part-way through, without titles, so that no-one knew its name or what it was about. It seemed to be a historical drama set in the eighteenth century.

There were scenes in a palace, where a bewigged king, dripping with ribbons and orders and surrounded by servile priests, commanded the flogging of peasants. The film then switched to a cossack host of handsome men sweeping on their horses across the plain.

'Wait a minute!' shouted Enric, standing in front of the screen and holding up a hand. 'We need music for this! Who can play the piano? Come on, comrades, surely someone can play the piano?'

Sasha had moved to stand by Katya. As she watched over the projector, he stood behind her with his hands gently around her waist. He said:

'Why don't you play? I can keep an eye on this.'

'Must I?'

'We can't spoil their enjoyment.'

Katya went forward, feeling the eyes of everyone on her. Enric proclaimed: 'Our comrade from Masia will help us out again. She's a foreigner, you know. Is this international solidarity or what? Here, comrade, sit down, take your time.' He leaned over and whispered: 'Play whatever you like, something stirring to make the blood move, yes?'

There was no music. Katya tried some of the piano keys speculatively and achieved a result more or less in tune. A stool was brought to her and she took position, nodding gently in the direction of Sasha. He started the projector again.

The screen flickered white and black, then settled with the cossacks again. After a little hesitation Katya began to play. Sasha fancied she played part of the earlier section of the '1812 Overture', the passage which to his ear was suggestive of Russia's vast expanse. The scene shifted to something dramatic in the city (St Petersburg, perhaps?) and he heard some notes of Beethoven. Then Mozart. Then Chopin. Watching the screen and searching herself for a response, she was improvising, moving with elegant transitions after initial uncertainty, from one composer to another; transposing key; repeating themes

688

where none had been repeated; paraphrasing another's music in a glorious pastiche of variations. It wasn't possible, he thought. She could not sustain her imagination, the technical virtuosity, even the physical effort for want of practice. She would slip. A melody would slide into discord. A crescendo would fail at its height and she would slam the lid down on the piano and sit frozen. It was not possible!

The villagers fell silent before this force. The men who had been lounging by the parapet smoking and talking, extinguished their cigarettes and pocketed the butts or threw them outside so that the burning tips described glowing parabolas against the night sky. Children sat hushed on their mothers' knees. The mothers stared at the screen so that their faces, ordinarily so bronzed by the sun, were pale in the reflection.

I've seen this before, thought Sasha, or read about it: but I can't remember where. A strange fête in a place that one has only found at the end of a mysterious journey. Where did I read about it? 'Returning from Toulon, he had met her one evening, distraught, in one of those gardens at Bourges that they call *les Marais*.' Sasha was shocked that the words of a book read so many years before came back in so lively a way to the tip of his tongue. He reminded himself: he (who?) fell in love with her, just as I fell in love with Katya. Who was it that fell in love? I feel dizzy. Is it some chemical in the film?

He rose from the projector, thinking that he really must get some fresh air. Valentí was still standing by the parapet, recognizable only with difficulty by the nacreous reflection. Eating olives, he remarked soulfully:

'Beautiful. A man might face a priest with that one. What a talent! She plays the piano and repairs cars. What's wrong, Sasha? You don't look well?'

'I just need a breath of air.' Sasha leaned with both hands on the stonework and gulped the air. He stared below into the dust of the square, and then across the rooftops to the vineyards beyond. A mule had come loose from its tethering and was browsing in the lane. A night bird called.

This is better! he told himself. I was losing my senses. Something in the film. And that projector gives off quite a bit of heat. He turned his attention to the audience again. Look at them! They're entranced by her. It's an experience they're not used to, trapped to the earth in poverty as they are. It's astonishing!

'Is today a fiesta?' he whispered urgently to Valentí.

'What? What sort of a question is that?' was the puzzled answer. 'Yes, as a matter of fact it is. Saint somebody-or-other. Why?'

A strange fête in a mysterious domain. Where was it? I can't remember. Am I simply thinking of that evening in Nice and the following day when Katya came to the villa? I was already head over heels in love with her.

'Oh, nothing. It doesn't matter. Yes, she is beautiful.'

'You're a lucky fellow.'

'Luckier than you can imagine.'

'I can imagine a great deal.'

All eyes were now focused on the screen and even Sasha, distracted by disturbing recollections, turned his gaze on the images of courtiers in their brocade and periwigs, their powder and finery. Dancing. They were dancing in a great hall of columns, mirrors, chandeliers and servants. Katya was playing a waltz and her timing was so perfect that the dancers on the screen moved in time to her music as if she were conjuring them.

'I am luckier than you can imagine,' Sasha repeated.

'Ah, the power of love!' said Valentí with amused irony. 'Hey, where are you going?'

Sasha was walking to the front. No-one paid him any attention. He reached Katya and one of his hands fell softly on her shoulder. She turned and the music stopped.

'Sasha?' she enquired.

'What's going on?' said someone.

'Hush! Watch the film. The pianist needs a rest.'

'What do you want?' asked Katya cautiously.

'Dance with me again.'

'What!'

'Dance with me again. Here and now.'

Sasha extended his hands and lifted her from the stool and pulled her to him. In front of the screen was a space before the first row of seats, and Sasha led her there. He held her in his arms and took the first step of a waltz, murmuring: 'That's it. With me. One, two, three! One, two, three!' He swung her clumsily in a circle, she big with child and he hobbling on his injured feet. 'One, two, three,' he repeated. 'One, two, three.'

'Madman!' she whispered.

'Thank you.'

'Idiot!'

'Such compliments.'

'We'll be thrown out of here.'

'They need us to work the projector.'

The film had moved to a scene of snow. A droshky was skating across the snow. A man and woman, wrapped in furs, giggled and talked in the back. More snow. A house among birch trees, its roof burdened with snow. Peasants standing in the snow while an orator addressed them. Snow and the shadow of children falling on the screen. Some of the children, seeing the grown-ups dancing, had left their seats and also came to the front where they were fooling around or shyly partnering each other in imitation of Sasha and Katya. The adults, after their initial surprise, were smiling and laughing. Sasha and Katya, glimpsing their faces, joined the infectious laughter until it was too much for them and they could dance no more.

Then they stopped. One by one the children stopped, too. The laughing faces folded into grinning contentment. What a sight! The things these foreigners will do!

'Bravo!' said Valentí as they returned to their places. 'Are those the sort of tricks you get up to in France?'

691

'Yes. And in Spain?' answered Sasha cheerfully out of breath.

'Oh, Spain! In Spain it's normal. A Spaniard can do anything that he wants to do. Dance, make love, fight a civil war, all three together. It's the law of God!'

CHAPTER 25

THE FALL OF BABYLON

December came and Katya's time was due. Valentí came to stay at Masia for a few days, saying that he had nothing better to do. When Katya went into labour, he got on his mule and went to San Quentín, returning in a two-wheeled cart with the midwife. The latter seemed a competent woman. She drove the men out of doors and left them kicking their heels among the almonds under a dull violet sky where the moon was visible even in daylight.

'What will you call the baby?' asked the ropemaker.

'Alexander, if it's a boy,' said Sasha. 'After my grandfather.'

'Not your father?'

'No,' answered Sasha thoughtfully. 'He was called Yuri – I think that's Jorge in Spanish.'

'I knew a Jorge. He was a cooper in Montblanc – may still be for all I know. What if it's a girl?'

'We haven't decided.'

'What's the name of Katya's mother?'

'Larissa – Lara,' Sasha answered reluctantly.

'Lara – I like that. What about that for a name?'

'I'm not sure.'

They had barely discussed names. The subject was

burdened by memories and obscure resentments. In due course Tonya would have to be told and a name wrongly chosen would be a reproach against her. Not Lara – certainly not Lara.

'You'll be leaving soon,' Valentí said as though it were a fact.

'Why do you say that?' asked Sasha, thinking the remark an accusation.

Valentí smiled reflectively. He said:

'My friend, this place has been a fantasy for you. You're no farmer. You've been living on the supplies in your truck, and they're almost gone. Maybe Masia could give a living to one of us poor devils who knows this land, but you . . .? It would break you. And why spoil a fantasy? You should think yourself lucky that this thing has happened to you.'

'Your people have been good to us.'

'Yes? Maybe. Don't count on good will. You have amused them and also given them a little help. But where are the relatives whom you can really depend on when there are troubles? Who will you go to when the water fails and your crops die? Who will protect you when the Fascists come?'

'You think they are coming?'

'For sure. I've been to Montblanc. They get news there. They say that the big battle on the Ebro is lost. The war is almost over. If all the stories are true, the Fascists will be here inside the month. And then what? Torture? Shootings?' Valentí paused and seemed to come to a decision. 'I lied to you about our priest. He didn't escape. Enric and I, and a couple of others I won't mention, we took him out one night up on to the sierra, and we shot him. Everyone knows we did it.' He shrugged. 'What can I say? He was a bad man, Don Alfonso's nephew. Even so I wish we hadn't done it, but back then, during the revolution, we were angry. Some priests were burned in their churches or crucified. At least we didn't do that. We gave him a drink and let him say his prayers. He

694

was a man all the same. He had a housekeeper. We left her alone, but she knows we shot Don Jordí. I suppose we could shoot her too, but what good would it do?'

'Were there many killings?' Sasha asked. He thought of Gromov, the fiacre driver, shot before breakfast. His own sin.

'A couple of Civil Guards. They weren't from around here, and I don't feel so bad about them. They should have stayed in their own villages like decent men instead of going to another village where they could act as they pleased because they had no reputation to protect. Ach, it's all been a waste of time! The revolution – the war – all a waste of time, because no-one really knows how to change things. Instead of making guns, the Government should have brought electricity to San Quentin. Now that would have made a difference.'

The midwife came out of the house and announced that it was all over. The child was born, a fine boy. The mother was well.

'Alejandro!' proclaimed the ropemaker.

'We must see them,' said Sasha.

The midwife accompanied them back to the house.

'What are you going to do about milk?' she asked. 'You haven't thought about that, have you? You think your wife is a cow and will produce milk on demand. Let me tell you: all women aren't like that. Then what will you do? Probably you'll be lucky, though you don't deserve it. She's a strong woman. You can't judge by the size of the breasts. Some big women are good for nothing. But my guess is she'll be fine.'

In the house Katya was lying on a makeshift mattress on the earthen floor. The baby, still with traces of vernix about him, was in her arms. Looking about the room, at the furniture made from packing cases and the roof of tarpaulin, Sasha thought: this is all I have done for her. Reduced her to beggary in the home of a cripple. Without detecting his change of mind, from desiring to stay here he felt an urgent need to leave. They *must* quit Spain. It had reduced them to this condition and made them think that poverty was a virtue. It was full of insensate anger and dark secrets, so that your friend might be a murderer and you would not know. Yes, they must go.

'Your son!' said Katya. 'My child,' she smiled feebly. 'I never expected a child. Never! Never!'

She began to cry.

Sasha felt transformed by the child. He was victim of the amiable illusion that this purely biological process had in some way endowed him with maturity and wisdom. In conscious moments he could be grave, at which times he would talk to Katya seriously about the future: the necessity of leaving Spain as soon as she was fit to travel with Alessi (as his son was affectionately known). At other times he might be found on the roof, adjusting the tarpaulin after a buffeting by the weather. Then he could be seen staring towards San Quentín across a landscape of golden earth and almonds which had lost their leaves and assumed again a delicate russet. And in those moments he sensed the everyday mysticism of life, which is less than a knowledge of God and little more than the joyful but mundane experience of happiness.

Katya found her milk. Her baby thrived. Perhaps because she had taught herself never to expect motherhood, every aspect of her son, from his suckling at her breasts to the cheesy smell of his evacuations, filled her with an inexpressible sensual delight. She would say: 'You're good enough to eat, yes, good enough to eat,' and kiss his bottom or his wriggling toes; or perhaps: 'Who's a little man, then? Is it sore? Mummy will put oil on it and you'll feel better.'

They entered a stage of love when each was self-absorbed and yet unselfish. Sasha would speak to Katya and she would think, as though addressing the baby: who's that speaking? Is it Papa? Is he speaking to us? As if we care! What does he know? And Sasha for his part, full of love and complacency, thought: she's become a sort of animal, wrapped up in the responses of her body. She hardly thinks at all. And yet she used to think all the time, forever observing and judging things. It's incredible!

Four weeks went by and it was raining when Valentí, draped in an oiled cape, arrived on his mule. His face was grim, but on seeing Katya and Alessi he could only grin and coo and offer a finger to the baby. To Sasha he said: 'It's time to go for a walk.'

'Now, in the rain?' asked Sasha obtusely.

Valentí grabbed him brusquely under the arm.

'Outside!' he said. 'Getting rain on your head will water your brains!'

Rain crackled off the tarpaulin and the men's capes. Valentí was wearing wooden clogs against the mud and these were loose so that each step sounded plop, plop. The ropemaker's eye for weather and its implications distracted him. He looked at the grey clouds as if mentally converting clouds into crops. Then he said:

'It's all over with us, the Government. The Fascists are on the move again. There's fighting north of Borjas Blancas on the Lérida road. How far's that from here in one of your fancy cars, an hour? I swear I've heard guns at night when it's quiet.'

'They may be halted,' suggested Sasha. 'How long did we hold them on the Ebro, six months? The Government may not know how to attack, but it knows how to dig in and defend.'

'Everything's falling apart,' Valentí answered. 'Enric went to Tarragona again. The people in the cities are living on lentils, not enough to feed a chicken. Nothing works. The factories are closed. They scarcely have electricity. The SIM are everywhere, arresting people whose faces they don't like. Do you follow me? It's finished! Over!'

'What will you do?'

'I don't know. Change my name? Take to the hills? Wait until I get myself shot? It's not your concern. I'm

697

a single man and an old one at that. Maybe I'll take my gun and shoot a few Fascists before they get me. It doesn't matter.' He seemed genuinely unconcerned in a way that Sasha, experienced in self-dramatizing heroism, found surprising. He could never be like the older man. Valentí said: 'You have to leave. You've known that for a while, but now it's urgent. Maybe the Fascists will be here tomorrow, maybe they'll be held for a month. They say Lister and the Communists are still fighting, so there's hope, but only for a little while.'

'When should we go? How?'

'Today. Now.'

'I can't move Katya!'

'On my mule.'

'Can't you come back tomorrow with your cart?'

'It isn't mine. I borrowed it.' The ropemaker ran his fingers through his thinning hair and shook the rain from them. He said: 'Look, I don't know how to explain this. For the village you no longer exist. You are too dangerous. People want to forget you were here, just as they want to forget who shot the priest. I can't ask my friend for his cart.'

They went back into the house and Sasha could think of nothing but to tell Katya: 'Valentí thinks it's too dangerous for us to stay here. The Fascists will arrive at any time. We have to leave today.'

'If you get to Tarragona,' said Valentí, 'you should be able to find a bus or train to Barcelona. Do you have any money?'

'Enough.'

'There's been inflation. I'll give you some.'

'Valentí . . .'

Katya was taking the baby from her breast. Looking at her, Sasha wondered whether she understood and, even when she spoke, he thought that she must be speaking automatically. She said practically: 'We don't have many possessions. We can go quickly.'

Had she been planning this? Had her appearance of

motherhood deceived Sasha? She smiled at Alessi, but when she looked at the men her eyes seemed ruthlessly calculating.

In fact her mind was in turmoil. But the ruthlessness was real enough, if only a fraction of her thoughts.

Are we really going? Yes, of course. I knew we would. I told Sasha from the beginning that we couldn't stay. It's all been a fantasy, and we'll look back on it and feel ashamed.

And to Alessi, silently:

Don't worry, mother's darling. I'll take care of you. Wrap you up warm. All cosy. Mama won't let anything bad happen to you.

She caught sight of Valentí as if seeing him for the first time, his face so burned and wrinkled by the sun, his eyes yellowed and clouded, his fingernails square with hard ridges. She felt, without at first knowing its origin, a terrible sense of loss. She thought: I haven't wished him away! He isn't like Tanya. He won't disappear like my mother or Daniel. And yet I shall never see him again in my life. We'll swear to remember each other always and meet in better times, but we never shall meet. There will be only memories.

Sasha gathered clothes and waterproofs and a military satchel into which he scooped some dry rice and lentils and a few olives. He inserted a quince from the tree that had first bedazzled him with its mysterious fruit and then closed the bag. Katya was changing Alessi and dressing him warmly. She was asking herself: can I sit on a mule? I'm not fully healed. She had broken off from feeding and her breasts felt hard with milk. It's all right, she told herself: I can feed him as we ride; it'll be cold but that doesn't matter, though I hope the rain stops. Oh, how my breasts ache!

'Ready?' enquired Valentí.

Sasha was replacing his *alpargatas* with munition boots and stringing a pair for Katya which could be slung over the mule for the time being.

'That looks like a Fascist cape,' said Valentí.

Sasha saw that he was right.

'Yes. It's waterproof. Our own greatcoats let the rain in.'

'Let's get the mule loaded.'

'Yes, let's.'

On the horizon a sliver of blue marked the sky, though here the rain lashed them. 'This rain will pass,' said Valentí. He drove the mule with a stick. The yellow earth seemed lighter than the grey clouds.

'I shall never be able to eat almonds without thinking of here,' said Sasha.

Valentí looked at him curiously. 'Don't you grow almonds in France?'

Sasha laughed. 'I don't know!'

'I thought they grew everywhere. What about wheat?'

'We have wheat.'

Rain streaming down his face like tears, Valentí laughed: 'Bananas! Do you grow bananas? I've heard of them, but I've never eaten one.'

Sasha did not answer, and they proceeded in silence.

It was evening when they reached San Quentín. Valentí went into his house briefly and came out with some money and a sausage which he stuffed into Sasha's satchel.

'It's from the boar I killed.'

He took hold of the mule's harness.

'Are you coming with us?' Sasha asked.

'For sure. As far as Tarragona. I can't afford to lose a good mule.'

'Can't we catch the bus at Montblanc?'

'There's no gasoline for the bus. Come on, we must go.'

They continued at walking pace, passing through Montblanc sometime during the night when the rain had stopped, halting in the shadow of its ancient walls to rest the mule, feed Alessi and eat themselves.

On the Tarragona highway they were the only traffic on foot, but between the long silences, military convoys approached them, travelling in the direction of Lérida to reinforce the line beyond Borjas Blancas. Even now the vehicles bore the banners and slogans of victory. Finally, sometime after midnight, they crept from the road and dozed for a few hours under the almonds.

Towards noon the following day they reached Tarragona. Sasha was not familiar with the city. Would there be trains or buses to Barcelona? He noticed queues, drabness and despair, and knew for certain that the war was lost. Yet this no longer seemed important. He felt elevated above the conflict, able to see it as a purposeless struggle. He regarded this as a moral insight instead of a mere effect of tiredness or, worse, the luxury of a foreigner ultimately relieved from the consequences of the war. There was no cruelty in his perception, but he still believed in the possibility that his thinking could rise above chance and circumstance. Meanwhile they found the railway station and there were indeed trains running to Barcelona, though neither times nor tickets could be promised. How long to wait? An hour – a day. At least in the crowd and confusion of refugees the police could not operate efficiently, which was fortunate since they had no papers except for Katya's army paybook. Even Sasha's weather cape, when folded, went unnoticed.

And there was Valentí.

'I've never seen so many cars and trucks,' he said. And: 'I must go back home.' He smiled and winked at Sasha. 'I lied about the mule, too. It isn't mine. I only have a half a mule. But what Spaniard can admit to owning only half a mule?'

'I shall miss you, Valentí,' Sasha told him, speaking from simplicity of feeling.

Valentí said brusquely: 'Go back to France and get rich for both of us.'

Katya could not speak. She passed the baby to Sasha, and, extending her arms, drew the older man close to her so that her head rested on his shoulder. Again the sense of loss. Would losses never end, the little deaths when people said goodbye or, as seemed to happen, did not say goodbye? She knew what he would say. Her terrible power of reason had divined it to its uttermost banality. He said:

'We'll remember each other, yes? And in better times, who knows? We'll see each other. I'm sure.'

The line of the Ebro was breached. By 17 January 1939, Tarragona, Montblanc and Borjas Blancas had fallen to Franco. The farm at Masia and the village of San Quentín were occupied by the enemy. Barcelona was a chaos of refugees and demoralized soldiers. Industry was shut down, food was scarce, the public services operated intermittently if at all.

When Katya and Sasha arrived in the city an air raid was in progress. Unopposed, Heinkel bombers were bombing the port. These raids were so frequent that, after a while, people ceased to pay attention. In nervous crowds they discussed food or the general situation, while behind them plumes of smoke rose from the direction of the sea and oily smears marked their faces like black tears.

They went to the Hotel Jardín in the *barrio* Gótico. Katya hoped to find Isabel there but she was not. The other nurses and drivers, now a dozen of them jammed into the small room, said that Isabel had been seen at Tortosa only a month or five weeks before, so there was hope. After discussion, they took pity and agreed to accept Katya and the child, but said that Sasha must fend for himself.

There was no accommodation to be had for him. The squares were filled with refugees camping. Shops were closed and money was valueless. A pervasive fear of the SIM made everyone cautious. It was believed that they and the Communists were engaged in carrying out final acts of vengeance, shooting private enemies and the last remnants of the POUM. Sasha was left to walk the streets and sleep in doorways and, for half an hour each day, to see Katya and the child.

Hunger and his sense of non-involvement in the war made him light-headed. It was impossible to focus on anything for the city itself lacked even visual stability. He ceased to see trees and buildings and the physical bones of the place: rather he saw movement everywhere in the ebb and flow of people. Crowds ran to the subway to shelter from the air raids or to catch one of the few tramcars. Queues formed at shops but, expecting nothing, they would break up at the slightest rumour and re-form elsewhere. Even the masses, camped in sullen desperation, heaved and chattered like a hive of insects. And no-one spoke to him. He had become invisible.

The Fascists reached the Llobregat, a river a few kilometres west of the city. The Government and the Communist chieftains fled to Gerona. No-one could tell the exact moment of the Nationalist army's arrival, and in anticipation the first Fascist and monarchist banners began to appear at windows and balconies as Falangistas and others of the Right, who had been in hiding or had suppressed their opinions, felt it was safe to venture forth.

He saw a slogan painted upon a wall: 'Long Live Death!' the cry of the Fascist legionaries. He sat on the ground to study it.

The world, in its transmutation from stability to movement, had also replaced objects with symbols. It was scarcely possible for Sasha to look at anything without making associations with other things read or seen in the dim recesses of memory. Seeing the writing on the wall he thought: Babylon has fallen! The edifice of pride in ideals, hopes and achievements, which had nourished the spirit of the war, was now crumbling. The barbarian was within the gates. Sustained by this commonplace notion, which yet seemed to him a revelation, Sasha dragged his way in filth and rags about the city.

Of course he tried to find transport to escape. But he had little money (if that were worth anything) and no claim on anyone. How could he queue for a train – today, tomorrow, who knows, comrade – without Katya and the baby by his side? Katya was unwell. Her milk was failing. She softened rice in water and by chewing, and fed it as a gruel to Alessi, who cried and complained and then fell uncannily silent so that she wanted to shake him to make him cry.

'Do we walk?' he asked her, not wanting to decide.

'How far is it?'

'A hundred and fifty kilometres.'

Could they walk so far?

One by one the women began to slip away from the Hotel Jardín.

'We'll leave tomorrow,' they agreed.

The morning came and they panicked at the prospect of carrying Alessi unprotected on so great a journey. Katya reported her milk a little easier. If she could feed the baby for a day he would be stronger. A second day came and still she had milk though she was herself feeling desperately weak. *Strengthen him! We must strengthen him!*

'We have to go!' Sasha insisted, drawing on reserves of resolution. On that third morning he had been out in the streets, even as far as the bullring in the Gran Via, where, standing in the shadow of its *mudéjar* ornaments, he had witnessed a seemingly endless column of refugees and a jam of trucks and cars.

Katya conceded. Nothing else was possible. They must go now.

There was nothing to pack except warm clothes for the baby and a few handfuls of rice and lentils which they lacked the means to cook.

'Let's go! Let's go!' Katya cried as though Sasha were being unreasonable and holding her back. What a laggard he was! How useless!

They walked to the Gran Via. Everywhere Fascist flags had now appeared. They ignored the flags and instead bickered.

'If we can find transport for you and Alessi,' he told her, 'you must go on without me. Someone may take a woman and a child, but they won't take me.'

'Don't talk nonsense!' Katya retorted. 'We must stay

together.' Although Sasha annoyed her, she felt possessive of him.

As a truck passed them, Sasha snatched Alessi and ran after it, holding the child up high like a trophy. He yelled: 'Take the woman and the baby! Not me! The woman and the baby!'

Katya caught up with him and took Alessi back. She turned on Sasha furiously, almost screaming. 'Don't ever do that again! Never! Never!' After a bitter silence she said practically and calmly: 'We mustn't run. We'll exhaust ourselves.'

They walked through Badalona and El Masnou. The road followed the railway and the shore. On the left, low faces of red stone hemmed the overflow of people. On the right, tall stands of *caña* grew down to the beach where the refugees spilled off the road to cook, relieve themselves or camp. By night they had reached Materó, where the town had filled up and people bivouacked along the pavements or by the railway line in the hope of jumping on to a slow-moving train. The dark hours were passed dozing restlessly. Moans, cries and the wailing of children prevented true sleep. Alessi pressed, greedy and fractious, against Katya's breast.

The following morning they passed through Arenys de Mar. They were trapped in a mass of mules being driven forward by the refugees. An aircraft of the Condor Legion dropped a bomb and, miraculously, for five minutes the road was clear except for mules grazing at the edges.

The red stone turned to golden sandstone and pines, and the land broadened to a plain several kilometres wide. They could see the road ahead, marked by a line of telegraph posts. It seemed a living thing, so thickly was it packed with humanity.

No longer did Katya and Sasha speak to each other. Alessi could cry for an hour and Katya did not hear him. She felt her individual consciousness merge with that of the mass. She walked at a certain pace because it was their pace. She could not stop walking because they could not stop walking. She had no sensation of hunger, merely a light-headedness.

Small vegetable gardens bordered the road near Malgrát. The refugees poured across them and stripped the produce. Dusk was marked by bonfires as the field shelters of dry canes were burned. Katya found space by one of these fires and boiled up a mess of rice and lentils and a few cabbage leaves. Sasha, still restless and unable to bear the sight of Katya's misery, went for a walk down the length of the fields where a line of motor vehicles stood parked for the night.

Two men sat on the running board of a car, arguing over a bowl of beans. One said:

'The Generalidad should have suppressed the anarchists in 'thirty-six. The amount of production we lost in those early months when we still had raw materials and Franco had not got the Fascists organized would have won us the war.'

His companion objected:

'Be realistic. The objective conditions weren't right. The masses had to vent their anger. The revolution was a necessary precondition to orderly mobilization.'

Standing before them like a penitent, wearing his Fascist cape regardless of who might see him, Sasha asked:

'Can you spare some food, comrades?'

'Go away.'

'I have a wife and child.'

The second man looked up. He scanned Sasha's face with what seemed like sympathy, but still said: 'Don't bother us.' To his friend he said: 'The mistake was to give the militias their head. It was impossible to co-ordinate an offensive when every man thought he had the right to vote on whether to fight.'

'Isn't that the same point? The masses had to convince themselves that they needed order before they could work or fight.'

706

Babylon has fallen, thought Sasha. He looked along the line of cars, seeing the web of frost along their roofs. A mule browsed among the cabbage stalks, and still a trickle of people marched in the hope of escape.

The River Tordera flowed as a narrow stream in a wide rocky bed. It was possible to wash and fill canteens. Katya sat here for an hour and fed Alessi with breast milk and rice gruel. She washed the rags that bound him, having little hope that they would dry. It was not possible to change him. His watery defecations poured down her *mono* and froze.

The land rose to hills covered with pine and fine yellow broom. Fires were lit from the broom and a little cooking and drying could be done. On the descent it was possible to see the snow-capped Pyrenees in the remote distance. This started a rumour that the French had barred the main road and that the frontier would have to be crossed illicitly by mountain paths. Hearing this, Katya hugged Alessi to her. She thought: dear God, it isn't humanly possible. We shall die.

Sasha's contribution was to deny himself all food. He lost concentration. At times he could be quite practical. He collected brushwood for a fire and broom to make a windbreak. At other times his mind wandered obsessively over the theme of Babylon's fall, which seemed to him to have some world-revealing power. He tried to imagine a life without ideals. He wondered if there were some other system of belief that had not been brought down in the ruin of that great city. The mountains became a metaphor for his own ignorance. In the face of the disaster he was humbled.

Gerona was stuffed with refugees. They camped by the river under the plane trees. Here an attempt had been made to set up canteens and it was possible to get soup. The rumour had now changed to concern about the

Nationalist pursuit. It was close behind the column but delayed by the wreckage of the flight and the road strewn with abandoned vehicles. Even so the town would fall on the morrow. No rest could be permitted.

The following day they crossed a plain of arable fields, olives, vines and cypresses. Sasha's feet began to weep a watery ichor which dried like honey on his bindings. He exchanged his boots for *alpargatas*, sitting down to put them on. When he rose, he wandered off across the fields until Katya pursued and caught him.

'Where are you going?' she asked.

'To France.'

She led him gently back to the road.

At Figueras he sat and wept. For several hours the column passed and showed no curiosity at the sight. Katya left him to rest. Clutching the baby, she bobbed in and out of the line begging food, and returned with some potatoes which they ate raw. She contemplated the road to the frontier village of Junquera. It rose into hills of pine and cork oak, with the mountains now close. The thought of those mountains dominated Katya's mind. They could not be crossed! It was impossible to face the heights and the snow in their present condition. Looking about her she saw that others, too, were giving up the struggle. Then a child went past, pushing an old man in a perambulator. Pausing she asked:

'Is it far?'

'Not far,' Katya said encouragingly.

'My grandfather is asleep,' said the child. She stared at Sasha, then added: 'My father is a tram driver. He's very important.' She leaned forward with her arms outstretched and the upper part of her body almost parallel to the ground and in this position pushed the perambulator forward.

Sasha looked up from his dreaming. He smiled and said: 'When I grow up, I want to be a tram driver. Come on, let's go.' He stood up and cupped Katya's face in his hands. He said: 'How can we let it end like this? Are we worth nothing?' All the while he smiled.

At Junquera the frontier was open and they were permitted to cross into France.

CHAPTER 26

A NEGOTIATED PEACE

They camped in vineyards and burned the vines. They slept in the open or the wrecks of the trucks that had brought them to France. They slaughtered the donkeys and mules that had shared their burdens, but more of the sociable beasts always appeared. The French ignored them. Squadrons of spahis, cavorting on their stallions, yelled in Arabic like Franco's Moors but kept their distance. Parties of Senegalese, black faces under red tarbushes, patrolled a loose perimeter. The sun burned them during the day, and the nights were bitter.

Katya struggled to feed her mewling baby with her own milk. Sasha, too slow to catch the mules or forage far, hopped and hobbled from group to group begging scraps – 'For the baby, comrade. Thank you. And you, comrade? For the baby. Thank you.' Gaunt and mad-eyed, smiling like an importunate drunk, he accepted abuse and food alike. 'Go to hell!' 'Thank you, comrade. For the baby.' Watching Katya and his son, nestled in an earth scrape by the small fire of vine branches he had gathered, he thought of himself, in his crazy way, as man the hunter and provider. And while he slept, Katya took the baby and slipped away. 'For the baby. Thank you, comrade.'

She cupped her breasts, searching for the least sign of fullness, and gritted her teeth as her child nuzzled at her cracked nipples.

The French separated them. This was done not from cruelty, but for administrative convenience. What else could be done? Refugees by thousands were scattered over the countryside about Perpignan with their herds of abandoned pack animals, eating up the land like a barbarian host. In vain Sasha asserted his French citizenship, but his name and lack of papers told against him.

'But what will happen to my wife?'

'Don't worry. She'll be in the hands of the Quakers.'

'Where will they take her? When shall I see her again?'

'Arrangements will be made.'

'What arrangements?'

'Calm down.'

'I am calm, damn you! You're taking away my wife and child!'

'We'll meet in Paris,' said Katya.

'Yes – yes! Go to my mother!' Sasha urged her.

'I can't – not without you.' Even now, thought Katya, he did not understand how she would appear to his mother: he could not grasp the anguish he would bring with the joy. 'The Rue Mouffetard. We have friends there. If I can't find a room, I'll leave a message there.'

'Yes! Yes! That's it!'

'I love you,' Katya told him.

'What? I can't think. You love me – I mean: I love you.'

He thought: how feeble I sound. Love? All the world is in love, but I shall die if I don't see her again. I have no choice: I have lived and breathed her so that she is life and air to me. I have no words to express her dearness.

Limping behind the truck, he shouted: 'I love you! I love you! Keep safe! Keep safe!' until the sand churned up by the wheels began to choke him and the vehicle turned at a bend where the sun glowed red through the dust and a clump of mimosas was in bloom.

*   *   *

He was taken to the camp at Amélie-les-Bains. Twenty-five thousand men were there. It was one of the smaller, better camps: by the pinewoods near the snow-covered peak called Canigou, so that it was possible to gather branches under the watch of the *gardes mobiles* and have warmth against the cold nights. And, behind the football ground, where six thousand camped, flowed a rocky stream where men could bathe waist deep in icy water. But then, as will happen, they polluted the stream and the camp became riddled with disease. Sasha himself became sick. He shook and ranted and survived. His eyes glittered. In moments of confusion it seemed to him that God was trying to pare away his body until he became a thing of pure spirit. He began to think of God as the enemy of mankind.

This torment of mind and body lasted a month until, at the end, Sasha's claim to be a Frenchman was accepted. He was given a set of clothes and a train ticket by a charity; and with these he set out to find Katya and his child. Nagging his heart was the fear that, in her need, she might have turned to her legal husband, Safronov.

Katya found that a group of English, American and Swiss Quakers had established a charity to aid refugee children. They gave her rest and fed her child. Then, learning that she was a French citizen, they put her on the train at Perpignan, supposing that in Paris she had a family. After the long journey, she arrived at the Gare d'Austerlitz, from which she had set out for Spain more than two years before. The city was in sunshine and the trees had come into that period when their leaves are fresh, pale and translucent and the streets are dusted by fallen blossom. Though lifted by the sight of places she held dear, her spirits were weak. She felt her emotions at all times near the surface, as likely to be touched by the smell of a restaurant, or the rattle of a train in the metro. She had not expected this. Grown so used to the necessity of strength, she had forgotten the weakness of exhaustion.

Off the Rue Mouffetard stood the decayed apartment house in all its familiarity. She climbed to the Coëns' flat, finding the broken stairs in their familiar places. But at the door a stranger answered. No, the Coëns no longer lived there; had been gone about a year; no, the woman could not say where they had moved to.

Katya turned from the door to find Le Nain haunting her footsteps.

'So you've turned up again!' the little man said accusingly. Today he was wearing a red velveteen waistcoat and a black tail coat which trailed the ground.

'Hello, Marcel,' she answered softly and patted her child, who had been startled by the sharp voice.

'Don't "Hello Marcel" me! Where've you been? You never visited. You never wrote. You look terrible.'

Katya stooped to give him a kiss on the cheek.

'I've been in Spain.'

'Now stop that!' He wiped the kiss away. 'So, Spain – that explains a few things. Whose is the kid? Yours?'

'Yes.'

'Is Safronov the father?'

'No.'

'Then who did it to you? I'll kill the swine!'

Katya laughed gently.

'Don't laugh! You know I don't like it,' said Le Nain. Calming down, he asked: 'Do you fancy a drink? You look as though you need it. I've got some good brandy – well, bad brandy. Or you could have coffee. Take the weight off your feet. I suppose the father is some smooth-talking devil who's already married?'

'He's Sasha Zhivago.'

'Ah! Your morals are getting terrible,' Le Nain added piously. 'To be fair, I always expected you'd leave Safronov. I never took to him. What about that drink?'

The dwarf was living at the top of the house in what seemed to be a low space under the roof, entered only by a hatch. The room had no natural light and smelled of tobacco and stale food. When Le Nain switched the light on, Katya saw a confusion of dirty clothes, unmade bed, unwashed cooking utensils, theatre posters, greasepaint, empty bottles by the dozen, and an array of stage costumes distinguished by the truncated legs of the trousers.

'Sorry about the mess,' he apologized nonchalantly. 'I'm living on my own at present. Eulalie left me.'

'I didn't know Eulalie.'

'No? After your time, I suppose. She was a tall woman. Lovely voice but a terrible boozer – worse than me! We used to fight all the time. Of course, she had the advantage of height, but –' he winked '– you should see the bruises on her knees!'

He cleared a space and began hunting among the empty bottles. Very tired, Katya sat down. The baby started to fret and suck at the clothing above her breast.

'Just a second for that drink,' called Le Nain. He turned, hearing the infant cry. 'You look done in, *chérie*. What's up with the kid?'

'He's hungry.'

'Ah – then you'll want me to leave. That's all right.'

Katya shook her head. 'I'll manage,' she said, 'if you don't mind.'

'Me? Ha-ha! Me!' He was blushing, and in his surprise and delight simply sat down, while Katya turned aside and unbuttoned her blouse so that she could put her baby to the breast.

All that day they talked, Katya and the theatrical dwarf. Or, rather, Katya talked: telling him of her break with Kolya, her decision to go to Spain, the terrible events there, her love for Sasha. Could she talk about love? 'You can talk to me about anything, *chérie*. People in the profession are forever falling in and out of love: men and women, women and women, men and men. And talk! They do nothing else. Me, I just listen.' So Katya talked. What had happened to her reserve? Her cynicism? Overcome by the mystery of her own emotions – indeed

714

by the only mystery of abiding interest: the relationship between men and women – she needed to talk in order to fix her inconstant self, the floating thing she had become that seemed to have no connection with the Katya of her own history. Le Nain chuckled, grunted, snorted, picked up the baby distractedly and, without thinking, paced the room, rocking him on his twisted hips until he was free of wind. For once Le Nain appeared happy.

'So where will you go?' he asked. 'To Sasha's?'

'I don't know. I don't want to see his mother until Sasha returns.'

'The Coëns? Did you ever see their lad? He was in Spain.'

'Yes,' Katya answered painfully. 'I saw him in Barcelona.'

'He's not come back yet.'

'He disappeared.'

'Another goner, I suppose,' Le Nain answered without detecting the hesitant inflection of her voice.

He became bad-tempered again and banged about among the junk, claiming that he had some bread and smoked sausage: would Katya like some? Frustrated with this, he murmured:

'If you can't get yourself sorted out, you can always spend the night here. Only one night, mind. No funny business, you understand? It's up to you.'

'Thank you,' answered Katya softly.

'Here! Stop that! No crying! I won't put up with crying – or laughing.'

In fact, Katya stayed several weeks in Le Nain's room. She found him considerate, and deeply tender towards her child. He got drunk only twice, and on both occasions slept on the stairs.

On his release from the camp at Amélie-les-Bains Sasha, too, returned to Paris. On the train he felt furtive, like a burglar breaking into a house: for, to his astonishment, France had become a foreign country, richer and more well favoured than he could recall from any of his memories. Where Spain was a land arid and sparse to its rocky bones, here the hills had such fatness of vegetation that it rolled and flowed like water. Vineyard, meadow, pasture, tilled field; beech, elm, oak, coppiced willow reflected in still pools; chicken, cattle, pigs; byre and barn. The light itself was fat, if that were possible; the sun rose, softened by veils and gauzes of mist; and spring rain fell in streaks upon the carriage windows.

He carried his blanket roll to the dim landing outside the Coëns' apartment and knocked on the door. A pale woman answered him cautiously.

'They've gone. They cleared out. Réné, how long since we've been here? Twelve months?'

'Have you seen my wife? She may have been here some time in the last month.'

'Skinny woman with a baby?'

'Yes.'

The question evoked a prurient interest and the answer a smug satisfaction. The woman said:

'There's someone of that description living upstairs with that old drunk, Stumpy.'

'Le Nain?'

'That's the fellow. What are you doing letting your wife live with the likes of him? It isn't natural.'

Sasha found his way to the top of the house and stared with disbelief at the hatch that marked the door to Le Nain's home. He thought: no wonder I never knew where he lived. He remembered his childhood and how the dwarf, like a fairy-tale character, had had a magic habitation that could never be found when one looked for it. 'Is this where Katya is?' He was afraid to knock. This was not Spain but a different world, about which nothing could be presumed. That Katya had truly loved him in that far country and remote time, he did not doubt: but that in *this* world, disfigured and undeserving, he might still be loved, seemed implausible. Katya had never ceased to say, even in their endearments, that love was all chemistry and

716

circumstance. And now the chemistry and circumstances had changed. Sasha had expected his longing to turn to joy at this moment, instead of which, he felt shame.

In the end he did knock on the door. From behind it came small domestic sounds: a pan being replaced on a gas ring, a cup being rinsed in an enamel bowl. Then the noise of bolts being drawn. Katya was there, she saw him and stepped back in silence to admit him through the low hatch.

He found himself in a small room that was kept clean and tidy, though a little exotic because of the posters and the dwarf's costumes. A baby, naked except for a tiny vest, was lying on a mat, trying to suck its toes. The air bore a cloying smell of cheese and fruit.

'I was changing him,' said Katya.

'He looks a little sore.'

'There are creams I can use. His skin is so soft and it goes that angry red colour, but I think it upsets us more than it upsets him. How was your journey? Did you travel overnight?'

'Yes. I'm tired but feeling better now I've seen you and our little Alessi. Is your milk still coming?'

'Yes.'

'Not too much, I hope. Do you remember the lumps –'

'– in my breasts. It was painful that first month when I had too much milk.'

'Mastitis,' said Sasha abstractedly. 'That's what they call it when there's an infection. I asked. There was a doctor in our camp. He said it was the right thing to do, to suck the breasts in order to express the excess milk.'

The baby cooed. Without windows the attic room was warm. A cast-iron stove in the middle of the room, anchored to the roof by a crazy flue-pipe, gave off heat.

'Comfortable,' Sasha said approvingly.

He was aware that she was behind him and that, since that momentary glance of recognition, he had not looked at her. Behind the infant smells were others in a heady concoction: patchouli, cigars, coffee and cheap

717

brilliantine. In the dim light the colours and textures were at once rich and subtle: burgundies and deep greens, flashes of scarlet; velvets, brocades, fluid silks; and here and there a sparkle of gold thread. Sasha felt dizzy.

'Why haven't you looked at me?' Katya asked. Sasha was not certain if he could detect annoyance in her voice. At this moment, he could think of no reason why this woman should love him. Their past lovemaking seemed to him irrelevant, an exchange between different people. Far from their past intimacies, with this woman he lacked even a language. Her fingers touched his neck.

'Kiss me,' she said.

Sasha turned, wondering if he would even recognize her. He asked:

'Do you still love me?'

Katya was looking at him and he realized that he too was a revelation to her, and that, abandoned by him to find her way here, bereft of her first flush of beauty and encumbered by a child, she also had been racked by anxieties. When she kissed, her lips were dry and tentative: they were implicit with the possibility of parting. He felt a void opening between them. He said:

'I've been so frightened. Everything has been stripped from me. I have no money, no job, no particular talents. Does love have to have a rational basis? If it does, I'm a lost man. I have nothing to offer you.' He looked for a chair. 'May I sit down? These damned feet of mine are good for nothing.'

'Why are you being so formal with me?' Katya asked.

Sasha sat down. His feet seemed greasy in his shoes. He wondered if his injuries were still leaking fluid.

'I'm trying to give you choices. How can I presume anything? What happened in Spain was between different people.'

To Katya his smile seemed infinitely sad. He gave a brief laugh in a shy way.

'I feel like an adolescent,' he said, 'approaching a girl I barely know but have only admired. Do you remember the flutters and the heartache? It isn't like *being* in love, but *falling* in love again. Don't you think that's silly?'

He waited on her judgement and in the meantime removed himself by studying the child. He was right, Katya thought. We are free of obligation to each other. In this light, it was possible to consider him coldly. She thought of the asymmetry of love. It was never experienced in the same way or to the same degree of intensity. They talked of love and did not even mean the same thing. For Sasha, she suspected, she would always be a mere focal point for his universal compassion and generosity. And for herself? After her long deprivation, she wanted an animal passion, possession, exclusivity. In her need for love there was something pitiless. Perhaps she needed a measure of his pity.

She thought how foolish he was to leave his fate to the ruthless analysis of a woman. What a risk he had taken! In the coldest corner of her heart she thought how, like Kolya though for different reasons, he could be made to appear contemptible in his weakness.

Is this me thinking? Is this what I have become?

She remembered an occasion when love had been something different. Who was the person who had given herself to Daniel without any second of regret either then or later? Had she supposed then that Daniel had regarded her with the same abandonment of spirit and self that she had showed to him? There was an asymmetry of love, but within and not only between people. It was a spring to be guided and channelled, not a flood sweeping everything before it.

She decided to love Sasha because she could choose not to love him. And, having made this decision, the debate in her mind passed like the passages within a dream and she could not remember any alternative. It was inconceivable not to love him. His every appearance, gesture, word, folly was inexpressibly dear to her.

She took his hand in hers, and he, knowing that she loved him, embraced her wordlessly.

In the shabby cast-offs given to them by the charities, they were shunned like gypsies by the passengers on the bus and metro. Their response to these sour faces and disdainful glances was to hold hands tighter, nudge each other, and even giggle.

To Sasha's surprise his mother and sister were no longer living in their modest apartment. Instead a forwarding address had been left with the concierge. This directed callers to another address in Neuilly. Neuilly – a place of memories from the days of the family's prosperity. It was not difficult to find: a pleasant, modern apartment block decorated with Egyptian motifs, where the tradesmen's boys leaned their bicycles against railings cast like stands of papyrus.

'You go up,' said Katya.

'Me? Do you mean on my own? Surely you're not frightened of my mother?'

'Of course not! Oh, dear Sasha, you can be so obtuse! It'll be a shock to your mother just to see you alive. You must recognize that it won't be easy for her to meet me.'

'And the baby?'

'The baby is my defence. Don't worry, I'll be all right.'

He left her, taking the cage lift that rose between flights of marble stairs whose banisters were patterned with a series of royal cartouches. Though Katya had proposed that he go alone, she half-consciously resented that he had attachments other than to her and their child. For his part, Sasha could only wonder at what miracle had wrought the change of fortune, even speculating that Cousin Aristide had made a restitution.

The door was answered by a maid. Flustered, like one of the wounded veterans who in his childhood had sold dubious cosmetics and curious patented inventions from door to door, he asked to see the mistress of the house.

A strange woman came to the door. She was wearing a silk robe of a vivid geometrical pattern. She was very pretty and blonde and in the early stages of pregnancy. Sasha recognized her, but only in the vague way that he might know an actress whom he saw in the street. Indeed there was something of the actress in this young woman, a desire to appear attractive to him even though he was a person of no significance. Only slowly did he appreciate that she was his sister.

'Masha?'

She was a little short-sighted, but vanity forbade her to wear spectacles. Peering at him, she gave a little squeak and then cried: 'Sasha? Oh, my God, it's Sasha! Mother! Mother! Philippe! It's Sasha! He's here!' She threw her arms about him and smothered his face with kisses.

In the door at the end of a corridor appeared an older woman, and, behind her, less distinctly, the figure of a man. Tonya's hair was greyer than Sasha remembered, but otherwise she was his mother. The changes were in himself. He did not know if he was a boy or a man. As for his mother, there was a certain chic about her that, in France, might be normal, but which seemed to him so odd after the poverty and restraint of Spain. A sense of his own awkwardness vanished when Tonya melted into his arms, crooning: 'My son! My son!'

He was introduced into a smart living-room and the maid was despatched to get refreshment. Masha, flaunting her pregnancy, announced:

'This is my husband. Yes, my husband! I'm Madame Bonnet-Leclerc! What do you think?'

Philippe Bonnet-Leclerc was a man of about Sasha's age, though looking older on account of the unlit pipe gripped in his teeth and the Scottish tweeds he wore. Despite which, he was a good-looking man of the type who might be the juvenile lead in a drawing-room comedy. He said little beyond 'Hello', and thereafter studied his new brother-in-law with a pleasant curiosity.

'When did you get back?'

'How was Spain? Is it as exotic as it sounds?'

'Oh, Sasha, you look so ill!'

Sasha was overwhelmed with questions, and the fact that he did not answer one made no difference to his being asked another. It seemed that the time allowed to him was only enough to answer a casual enquiry about a holiday. He thought: it must be me. I've become very sensitive and don't understand how ordinary life works. They're delighted to see me; it's just me who doesn't grasp the intensity of their feelings. They don't know how to ask the questions I want to answer. In any case, I don't want to answer them now, because something is wrong. It was his mother in particular who disappointed him. He could not resist the mental accusation that she had become 'smart', in the same way as this apartment, so fashionably decorated, with its little statuette of an athletic young woman made of bronze and ivory, or the cocktail cabinet, banded of light and dark woods.

'I've brought someone with me,' he told them.

'A friend?' asked Tonya.

'Bring him up!' urged Masha.

Philippe was of a practical turn of mind. He enquired: 'Do you need a hand? With luggage or anything? I only ask because you look as though you've just got off a train or something.'

'No. I arrived yesterday. These are the only clothes I've got.'

'I can probably kit you out. You look about my size.'

'I'll only be a moment.'

Sasha left them and went down in the lift to the lobby where he found Katya sitting on one of the marble steps dangling the baby and, walking across the lobby, making an expensive echo with the heels of their shoes, a couple who were silently shocked, as if on discovering their neighbours were Algerian.

'How are you?' he asked.

She seemed to him frightened and diminished. Each saw in the other the passing thought that the renewal of their love, only the previous day, had been a charade.

'Hold me!' he said, anticipating her words. He clasped

Katya and their child fiercely, protectively. He told her: 'It was horrible. I can't explain. My mother is here. Masha has married. They talk in an imitation of speech. I'm sure they mean what they say, but the words are all subtly wrong. And the timing. We seem to be talking out of time. Do you suppose it's always going to be like this?'

'Not all the time,' Katya answered. 'But sometimes – yes.' She rocked the baby, who was becoming unsettled. 'It isn't going to be a success, this meeting, is it? But, then, it never would be. Did you tell them I was here?'

'I said I had a friend with me. They assumed you were a man. I suppose they thought of war comrades, the friendship of the trenches. Perhaps that's what's wrong: their thinking is so conventional.'

'Let's walk by the stairs. I want time to be calm.'

The staircase was depressingly full of smartness: painted in subtle pastels, dusted in gold and silver, with panels veneered in burr walnut, lights like fans of mother of pearl, and long windows barred with bronze acanthus leaves. Sasha brightened the moment when he said: 'Here we are – the returning orphans! Do you think we've been in a fairy tale?'

'If we have, then I'm the villain in boots, with a big hat and a feather.'

That remark was not like Katya. They exchanged glances of a softness and intimacy they had not given since their reconciliation.

And now they were at the door.

Katya and the child were admitted with a degree of surprise and caution but no recognition. They were introduced into the drawing-room where Masha and Tonya sat like ornaments. Sasha wanted to explain, but the correct forms of language escaped him. He tried:

'Mother, this is Katerina Pavlovna Antipova.'

Not too indelicately, Masha said: 'I thought you were Kolya Safronov's wife?'

'You can consider her as my wife for as long as she'll

723

have me. And this is our son. He's called Alexander, after our grandfather.'

'Lord, these Russian names!' said Bonnet-Leclerc cheerfully. 'No wonder no-one reads Russian novels nowadays.'

Tonya rose stiffly, her face unreadable. Katya thought: she must hate me. Advancing, Tonya looked at the child tenderly. She asked: 'May I hold him?' She did not look at the mother. Instead, taking the baby to her seat, she occupied herself putting the knuckle of her little finger to its mouth and letting it clasp the fingers of her right hand.

'Philippe is in his father's business,' said Masha gaily. 'Bonnet-Leclerc? Do you know the name? They do machine-made lace —'

'Oh, more than that!'

'— and lots of pretty embroidered things.'

Philippe said: 'What are your plans, Sasha?'

'I haven't made any.'

'We're branching out. Into military wear. You know: braid, lanyards, badges.'

'Do you think there's going to be a war?'

'I'm certain of it. The English are driving in that direction since their guarantee to Poland, and we're being dragged along in their tail. Do you want to sit down?'

'Thank you. My feet. I've been injured,' Sasha said without thinking.

Tonya looked up as if shot.

'You've been wounded!'

'No, Mother. Nothing. It was nothing. I spent my time at Franco's HQ in Salamanca. Don't worry.'

'Talking about the future,' said Philippe, 'I can give you a few tips, if you're looking for work.'

'That's kind of you.'

They left. Or rather, they were got rid of with every politeness, like guests who have mistaken the date of a dinner engagement and for whom everything has been improvised to maintain the fiction of expectation and convenience. Hosts and guests realize that there is a lot to talk of, affections to be renewed, and much that is genuine and human: but this is not the time and place and we are not prepared for these things. Except that the reality here concerned not hosts and guests, but mother, son, daughter, child who were linked by long absence, deep memory, love, resentment. There would in any case have been an ambiguity of language and gesture in dealing with this freight of emotion, and the unexpected timing of Sasha's return only compounded the situation and reduced the reunion to bare intelligibility.

Sasha left his mother with words of love and longing unspoken on his lips, and Katya, insensitive in her own maternal egoism, could only trouble him by saying that he had ignored her when she was excluded from the gathering, and had talked trivialities, and had adjusted himself to his mother and not to her – all of which he frankly admitted to be true, though it vexed him to be told so and he could find no way to reconcile the irreconcilable. Was it possible to love his mother and his wife? Katya, at her most coarse and greedy, denied that it was. At her most loving, she insisted that everything with his mother must be made clear and that it would be horrible for a daughter-in-law to come between mother and son.

On another occasion Sasha went to see his mother alone and found her alone. He told her that he knew all about Katya's history – about his father, Lara, Komarovsky. He explained rationally that any objection to his relationship with Katya was the fruit of unreasoning emotion. He even told her – God forgive him – that he understood her point of view.

At this interview, Sasha appeared shabby and defensive. Tonya seemed narrow and vindictive. They would have quarrelled except that Tonya, in a parting gesture, returned to him a baby's napkin that had been left behind, washed and ironed by the maid. This piece of material was the catalyst to the language that allowed them to talk to each other. And at the end they were reconciled – not agreed, but prepared to bear their differences.

Tonya prayed to Our Lady of Moscow. She thanked God for the salvation of her son. She begged relief from the memory of her sufferings. She asked for the grace that would allow her to treat Lara's child as her true daughter. But, beyond her prayers and unrecognized by her charitable nature, she noted with satisfaction that Katya had lost her beauty: that her face was marked by hardness and the experience of suffering.

They found a small apartment and, with the help of his new brother-in-law, Sasha obtained a position as a clerk with a lawyer's office. He completely abandoned any intention of continuing his university studies. Instead he could be seen, morning and evening, in respectable bourgeois dress, walking to the bus with the stiff-legged gait he was forced to adopt because of his injuries, a pale young man in his middle twenties with a face that was drawn and serious but ready to smile at the least encouragement. Life had an enjoyable banality. It was a pleasure and an achievement to save up and buy a radio. In the evenings they listened to songs by Suzy Solidor and Charles Trenet.

Philippe and Masha were a sociable couple. They often invited Sasha and Katya to have dinner at home or in a restaurant. On these occasions Tonya, the doting grandmother, took care of the baby. She avoided her daughter-in-law.

The men talked politics. Philippe was of the moderate Right. He spoke of the needs of capital and business. Sasha continued, with difficulty, to try to explain that within Fascism there was a genuine social message, a hope for the poor, a chance of social reconciliation behind a national ideal. Katya listened and was forced to conclude that, on this as on so many other matters, her lover's thinking was irredeemably second-rate.

Sasha decided that he would qualify as a lawyer. He bought a correspondence course and brought home textbooks, and while Katya sewed or played with the baby, he sat at a polished table covered with an oilcloth to prevent heat marks, and attempted to study. However, the fact was that he did not have the concentration required for prolonged study of the law, and preferred to read Maigret novels or philosophy. He read accounts of Plotinus and Porphyry, Masilio Ficino, Pico della Mirandola, Giordano Bruno, and Irenaeus's attacks on Carpocrates. When Katya asked what it was that he found so interesting, he talked about Platonic ideals, Hermes Trismegistus, Sophia and the Demiurge. He gave her the books, convinced that, with her sharp intelligence, she would understand. And Katya understood well enough. But it seemed to her that the philosophers were constructing frameworks for the unknowable, merely romancing with ideas. In short, philosophy was principally a game; and it was therefore scarcely surprising that it was chiefly men who engaged in it.

To her surprise, Katya found her domestic life congenial. Only occasionally was she ashamed of this fact, and on such occasions, perhaps sparked by some difficulty with the baby which frightened or frustrated her, she complained bitterly that her life was becoming stifled and her mind rotting. Whenever she did so, Sasha readily agreed with her. He was proud of her natural quickness and talents, and genuinely upset if she felt that he was thwarting her development. He proposed that she visit Le Nain regularly for the sake of his stimulating company. It did not bother him when she went to hear the dwarf sing or do his comic turns, or if she accompanied him on the piano in a low cabaret. Only Masha was disturbed. She thought that Katya brought a disreputable tone to the family.

As for their love, it entered a phase of quiet contentment.

Sometimes they played a game. It is called *Why do you love me?* and all happy couples play it.

'Why do you love me?' Sasha asked. 'I've never

understood.' He put down his books and the fountain pen he had been refilling. Katya turned from ironing (they had a new electric iron, which was run on a flex from the ceiling light), smiled and answered thoughtfully:

'Because you are kind, gentle, sensitive, considerate, forgiving, generous, helpful, amusing, hard-working – and a complete fool.'

'Oh? Not because I'm strong, decisive, dominating and heroic?'

'No, none of that.'

'You didn't say that I was handsome.'

'Because you're not, or not remarkably so.'

'Oh!'

'And me? Why do you love me?'

'You – I love you because . . . I can't say. I only have to look at you and . . . I find everything about you . . . Oh, get back to your ironing, woman!'

'Oppressor!'

'Communist!'

In September the expected general European war broke out. In October Masha gave birth to a son whom they called Alexandre, in the French manner but also after her grandfather, Professor Gromeko. Technically a single man, Sasha was subject to conscription, but he failed the medical inspection. His work became busier because his fellow clerk was called into the army.

On the day of the christening (in a Roman Catholic church – Masha having converted on her marriage) Sasha and his brother-in-law discussed the political and military situation. Philippe blamed the English for forcing France into a war in the fatuous and impractical defence of Poland. Sasha, despite anything previously said by him to the contrary, stated that the Fascist ideal had lost its way and that henceforth he was a supporter of the Third Republic. He was particularly disparaging of those young men who had volunteered for the forces. 'Heroism is nonsense!' he said vehemently. 'In practice it means committing yourself to an extreme. Romantics are always willing to destroy themselves and don't mind destroying others in the process. There is something cruel and vain about those who set out in advance to be heroes.' Philippe replied that some men were called by a noble ideal: he himself would have volunteered 'for France', if his family commitments had not prevented him. Both men were agreed that the Maginot line would hold off any attack by the Germans and that a negotiated peace could be expected in six months or so.

In the meantime, Katya located the Coëns. She approached some of the furriers for whom they worked and obtained their address. They had moved only a few streets from the Rue Mouffetard. She went to see them.

'Hello, Katya. Please, come in.' Sophie Coën seemed to Katya to have aged a great deal. Probably she was little more than fifty, if that, but she was grey, lined, and worn. She offered a glass of wine and a biscuit. 'My husband isn't here.' Unenthusiastically, she added: 'This is a surprise.'

Katya took a seat by the Singer sewing machine surrounded by furs and swatches of silk lining. Sophie brought wine for her guest only, and sat herself by the machine, begging to be excused if she continued to work. In what followed, the clickety-clack of sewing punctuated the conversation and the silences.

'Daniel wrote about you,' she said, 'in his letters. He was fond of you.'

'I was fond of him.'

'Did the Zhivago boy come back from the war?'

'Yes.' Katya decided for the moment against telling Sophie of her present situation.

'Good – I'm pleased for Tonya. She wrote to me – did she tell you? The letter was forwarded, but I didn't reply. At that time both our boys were missing. But what could we have talked about? My husband blamed Sasha for joining the Fascists. Seeing Tonya would have made him angry. Me, I always supposed that Sasha had his reasons.

He was always a good-hearted boy. When did you last see Daniel?'

'In June or July two years ago. We were in Barcelona.'

'His letters stopped about then. I can't think why. He wasn't close to the fighting – not since . . .' She peddled furiously and the stitches rattled like machine gun fire. 'There are camps in the south – so I'm told – for the Spanish refugees. I've made enquiries, hoping that he might be among them. Of course he isn't. He could be a prisoner with Franco, but I understand that the Fascists shoot all foreigners. Is that right?'

'I don't think so.'

'I think they do. Especially Jews. So I have to accept that Daniel is probably dead.' She stopped her work. She took the garment, held it up for examination, folded it and placed it aside. 'It's hard to accept, without a body or any firm news. And he's an only child. That makes it harder. I couldn't have any more. Because of women's trouble . . . you know? Down there.'

Sophie's quiet and dignified pain left Katya speechless. She could think selfishly only of how to escape from the palpable mourning. And afterwards she felt guilty that she had behaved so politely and given the older woman nothing of compassion or comfort that would help assuage her grief. Indeed, she wondered why she had visited Sophie. Was it not out of a species of egoism, a desire to purge herself of the residue of her relationship with Daniel? But for her own selfish concerns, how else could she have been so unprepared for an encounter whose outcome was so predictable?

The truth was that she had never tried to come to terms with what had happened in Barcelona. Had she really loved Daniel? Not wishing to think about this, she had never given serious consideration to his probable death: he had merely, in some vague way, dropped out of her life.

When she saw Sasha that evening, she was angry with him for his stupidity. Despite all his amiable qualities, she despised him for the false heroism, romantic nonsense and intellectual weakness that had led him to espouse a cause so meretricious and contemptible as Fascism. No-one had a right to be so stupid! It was unforgivable.

She was shaken too in her sense of the uniqueness of her love for Sasha. Not only was it not a great love in the sense of fiction (a notion about which she was sceptical, thinking it an affectation), but it was not the unique love of which she was capable. It was self-evident that she could have loved someone else – perhaps Daniel – perhaps even Kolya if circumstances had been only slightly different. Thinking of Daniel she remembered the dark and dangerous qualities that had so frightened her. But she remembered too his internal struggle against cruelty and his search for tenderness, and she wept. Sasha found her like this, crying in the bedroom when he was looking for a change of clothes for the baby.

'What's wrong?' he asked. 'What have I done?'

'Nothing.'

He might have accepted that, thinking no more of it than the vagaries of a woman's tears, and, in fact, he was under pressure to get back to the baby. But something stayed him.

'No,' he said. 'I must have done something. If it were anything else you would have told me about it.' He knelt and took her hand. 'Darling, have I done something stupid? You can tell me. Forgive me for it, whatever it is.'

He had to return to the baby without an answer. He picked the child up and went back to the mother. He stood in the doorway, rocking the child on his hip. He said:

'Do you remember the days when I wanted to be a fool?'

'Yes.'

'I thought it was a route to wisdom. Well, here's the only piece of wisdom I ever discovered. It's this: mankind is invincibly stupid. If we can't be forgiven for stupidity, then there's no hope for us. So now, do forgive me.'

But Katya could not forgive him that day. She was too confused by memories of Daniel, by the thought of other loves and the other Katyas she might have been.

In the morning she found a note written by Sasha and left in the kitchen (of all places!) among the bills and recipes.

It said:

Père Alexandre's Recipe for Love
Take the following ingredients and mix continuously:
Contempt, Compassion
Chemistry and Circumstance
Sentiment, Forgiveness
Reason and Romance
Trash, Transience
Wisdom, Folly
Rubbish and Nonsense
Chance and Chimpanzees

CHAPTER 27

LIFE FROM DEATH

There was no negotiated peace. In the summer, as Alessi was toddling around the furniture and beginning to speak a French in which odd words of Russian were mingled, the Germans attacked. The French army collapsed under the onslaught and the roads streamed with refugees. In the chaos of the defeat, the Government abandoned the capital. Paris was declared an open city.

Even before the radio announcement, on the previous day when rumour was of German aircraft bombing gasoline storage tanks on the outskirts of the city, Philippe and Masha had decided to flee. They had the advantage of a motor car, though the roads were jammed with peasant carts, bicycles, perambulators and people on foot. Sasha had gone to Neuilly to discover their plans. Tonya begged him to come, too, if only for the sake of his family. He refused. He could remember the sufferings of the retreat from Barcelona and was convinced that it was safer to stay. The Germans, he said, were civilized. If the Government did not defend the city, there would be no fighting. In this he was to be proved right. Philippe admitted as much some months later when the family had returned. 'But then, you have so much experience of war,' he added in a note of admiration. This was part of a conversation when Philippe was trying to persuade his brother-in-law to take a 'realistic' view of defeat and its consequences.

But for now Paris took on an unearthly beauty. For a summer's evening the boulevards were empty of people and traffic. The stones of the buildings glowed with the setting sun; the monuments enacted the still drama of their statuary to empty amphitheatres where only the rustle of leaves applauded. Insisting that on this evening they should go for a walk to quieten their fears, Sasha led Katya and their son past shuttered shops, and there heard sounds that would not be heard in those streets again: a carpenter sawing wood somewhere in a cellar; a seamstress in an upper room, working on her machine; a man – place unknown – striking a match.

And then the Germans arrived in their motorized columns and it was raining. They brought discipline. They recalled the population to its duty. They ordered Paris to be gay and saw that it was done. Various parades were held, but Sasha did not watch them. He pitied the soldiers for their sickening adoration of glory. What did Sasha do during the Occupation? He got a bicycle, and worked.

For the most part the Germans did not steal. But, by levying a contribution for the maintenance of their army and by fixing an overvalued exchange rate for the Reichsmark against the franc, they were able to obtain by purchase the advantages of plunder. Shops were stripped of luxuries by the victors and, even in the early months of the Occupation, shopkeepers, with their stores of rationed goods, obtained a dominance over everyday life. Sasha and Katya obtained an 'A' card for their own rations and an 'E' card for those of their son. In October 1940 rationing was still a novelty and, when they were invited to a dinner party to celebrate the first birthday of Masha's boy, Sasha had to ask: 'Do we bring our rations?'

'Of course not,' said Philippe. 'We're going to a restaurant.'

The celebration took place at the Aiglon, a luxurious restaurant in the Rue de Berri, where a small band and an accordion player entertained the guests, the menu was printed in German as well as French, and Wehrmacht officers were well represented among the diners.

'You seem uncomfortable?' Philippe observed.

'How can you afford these prices?' asked Sasha. Although his brother-in-law was a pleasant fellow, his manner could be condescending.

'Oh, I think that's a problem you can leave with me.'

'Obviously!' replied Sasha, determined to be cheerful and enjoy the food. But when it came to eating, though he was hungry enough, he felt ashamed.

Tonya led the conversation to the subject of the children. Masha had adopted the enthusiasm of motherhood without the labour, for which she had a nanny. The talk was banal enough, but to Katya it seemed as if they were speaking of different experiences. In particular, Masha seemed unaffected by the practical problems of feeding and clothing her son.

'How are you finding the Germans?' asked Philippe.

'How? I don't really have anything to do with them. An officer – a general or something – came to see us because he wanted to buy a château. Other than that, a law firm like ours has little reason to see them. They seem polite enough, though one hears stories.'

'They like to have a good time, but that's to be expected with so many young men.' With his pipe and his 'responsibilities', Philippe did not like to be considered young. Masha deferred to him with a certain amusement, as if he were a rich, middle-aged lover – like Max Golitsin or Prince Carlo. 'The Moulin de la Galette is about their level. They like girlie shows. But there's no harm in them.'

'If you say so.'

'I do. I regard myself as a realist. France has lost the

war. You don't think the English are going to save us, do you?'

'I suppose not. No, it doesn't seem likely.'

'Then one must draw one's conclusions. Patriotism has a different meaning under these conditions. Have you listened to Marshal Pétain on the radio? No-one could accuse him of lack of patriotism.'

On the way home, a long walk through the silent streets of the strange new Paris lit blue by shaded streetlights, Katya said uneasily: 'That meal cost over a thousand francs a head!' Both knew well that in a normal restaurant one might ordinarily eat for twenty or thirty francs. 'Where is Philippe getting his money from?'

'I'm not sure that I want to know.' Sasha took her arm under his. He made a comment about the night: it was peaceful, it was beautiful.

'Oh, you don't want to believe ill of anyone!' Katya said acerbically.

'As always, you are absolutely right. "Judge not that ye be not judged."'

'That's a piece of moral laziness.'

'Quite likely.'

There followed a familiar exchange along the lines of 'What am I to do with you?' which, as always, ended in a kiss. Not that Katya had changed her mind. She continued to think that Sasha's limitless tolerance was a vice. However, for the rest of their walk home they talked of meat and milk and eggs. These days it was desirable to have relatives in the country. Sasha wondered if Philippe had any.

A hard winter came – the first of those that were to characterize the war – and fuel was scarce. Snow fell and, with the diminished traffic, lay almost undisturbed except for the tracks of bicycles. Muffled in snow, Paris lay silent.

'I wish I had a pair of *valenki*,' said Katya.

'*Valenki?* Did you ever wear them?'

'Of course. Remember, I was twenty years old when I left Russia.'

Sasha searched his memory. He could not remember wearing felt boots in winter. He examined Katya and their child more carefully. Did they look Russian? What did it mean: to be Russian? For him Russia had died with his grandfather. *Valenki?*

They were frightened when little Alessi got whooping cough. He lived. To keep warm they reached an arrangement with their neighbours. They would pool fuel and heat only one room at a time, alternating between apartments. This was quite convivial. They played cards and read each other's books and listened to André Claveau joking in *Cette Heure est à Vous*, or detective stories on Radiodiffusion Nationale. Like the victim of an exotic vice, suspecting others but never certain, Sasha wore leg bindings under his trousers to keep warm at work, and layers of strange woollens when at home. Katya found army surplus underwear (no longer needed in the absence of an army) and cut it into women's underwear, grey in colour and of dubious taste. At night they wore bedsocks in brightly coloured hoops, knitted by Masha in a fit of maternal industry.

'Your problem,' said Philippe patronizingly, 'is that, at bottom, you're a conventional person. You work within the system and don't use it.'

On Sundays, whenever possible, they wrapped up warm and cycled to Neuilly. Alessi travelled on an improvised carrier and enjoyed it. It was odd, in the Champs Elysées, to see a woman pushing a sack of potatoes in a perambulator, young German soldiers in their greatcoats admiring the sights, and level snow in places where snow had never lain. The point of these visits was to get a meal 'off the ration' from Philippe's mysterious supplies. The disadvantage was that Sasha had to listen to his brother-in-law's moralizing, and Katya had to bear the baleful stares of Tonya, and Masha's inconsequential chatter.

Sasha defended himself.

'I work as hard as I can. These are difficult times. When the war is over I expect to complete my legal studies and have my own practice.'

Overhearing him, Katya wondered wryly what legal studies he meant, since in the evenings he read philosophy and cheap fiction, listened to the radio or played with his little son.

'That isn't what I mean, and you know it. Look,' said Philippe, 'come into the next room and I'll show you.'

The next room was Philippe's study, though instead of books it held accounting ledgers, hunting trophies and mildly pornographic prints. Such literature as there was, was represented by copies of *Le Matin*.

'Here!' Philippe held out a cardboard box, one of a number. Sasha opened it and found some silk lingerie in a nest of tissue paper. 'You can have it.'

'I don't think it would keep Katya warm.' Sasha smiled and in fact felt rather proud. 'These days she's entirely practical.'

'Well, suit yourself. I've got some silk stockings and cosmetics, too. No? Tell me something: are you in the RNP or the PPF by any chance? I'm not recommending them, in fact the Germans rather despise them, but you used to be a Fascist before the war. I'm interested in where your sympathies lie.'

'Are you a black marketeer?'

Philippe fiddled with his pipe and lit it.

'Not exactly. I'm more interested in the wholesale end: cement, beef carcases, you name it. My customers are the Germans, so it's all more or less legal. I work with some friends. We have an office in the Rue Pétrarque. A few other fellows are in the same business, you might say it's almost respectable.'

'Why are you telling me?'

'Frankly, because Masha asked me to. And, to be fair, I could use the help. It would put an end to your present

738

miserable existence. You understand why I asked about
your politics? France needed the invasion like a shot in
the arm after years of neglect. Of course I want to get rid
of the Germans as much as the next man, but that's only
going to be possible as Germany's ally, not its enemy.'

'You want me to collaborate with the Germans?'

'I regard it as an alternative way of working for France.'

Sasha promised to consider the offer and they returned
to the other room. He caught a glance from his mother and
supposed that she knew of Philippe's plans, and he wondered what she thought. Then he reflected that Philippe
had not raised the matter in Katya's presence: indeed had
avoided doing so. Was it because, in his brother-in-law's
estimation, it was a subject unfit or too complex for
a woman, or because he considered that Katya would
object? The affair beguiled Sasha. On the way home,
as they were cycling slowly in the darkness, trying to
avoid being pitched into the snow, he told Katya what
had happened.

'And you didn't answer him?'

'I wanted to talk to you first.'

'Why? Isn't the answer obvious? We're not collabor-
ators.' Katya was tired and spoke testily.

'No. On balance that's what I thought. I'll tell him so.
Do you mind if we walk a while? My feet. The pedals.'

They pushed their bicycles. Their son dozed in his
carrier. In the snow each footfall sounded with a crunch.
A frost was forming a crust over the snow, the sky was
clear and the stars brittle. Sasha tried to describe the night.
He was feeling mellow for some reason and, without being
conscious of it, trying to frame his words at a sub-level
of poetry, as people commonly do when affected by a
moment of beauty. Out of harmony with him, cold and
annoyed in the vague way that Tonya's deliberate kindness
always annoyed her, Katya asked:

'Why "on balance"? On balance you're against collaboration?'

'What? Is that what I said? I wasn't thinking about

Philippe in particular. He's a pleasant fellow, but nothing more than a well-mannered crook. I was thinking of collaboration in general.'

'So on balance collaboration in general is wrong?'

'Probably.' Sasha stooped to pick up snow and form a ball. He threw this at a street kiosk. Laughing, he said: 'Wouldn't you think that after Teruel I'd hate the snow? But the truth is that I love it! Look how beautiful it is! Not white but . . . mother of pearl!'

'Why only "on balance"?'

'Oh, it just doesn't seem to me that the conclusion is obvious. I'm against collaboration, but I may be wrong.'

'How can you say that?'

'Well, if Germany wins this war – which seems likely – France will have to be reconstructed in some fashion or other. There's no such thing as a vacuum. And from a practical point of view I don't see how that can be done except by collaboration. Certainly collaboration will happen. And if it isn't done by the good people, it'll be done by the crooks. It rather depends on what kind of France you want.'

For a while they walked in silence. Then Katya asked:

'Do you have no instinctive moral reactions? Reactions that don't depend on an analysis of right or wrong? Don't you just *know* some things are right and others wrong?'

'Yes . . . I mean: I think so.'

'For example?'

Sasha considered for a moment. He said: 'I think hatred is wrong. If I reach a conclusion that means I have to hate someone, then I need to pause and think about it.' A little later he added: 'Why are you still angry with me? I've just agreed with you to turn down Philippe's offer, and that collaboration is wrong.'

On the way home they were stopped by a policeman and asked to show their papers. Katya noticed that, in going slowly through his pockets, smiling, apologizing and finally wishing the man good night, Sasha showed not the least resentment, fear, or even concern, but seemed inwardly distracted as though mulling over a point of philosophy.

Katya realized then that she was in love with a man whose thought processes bewildered her.

It was inevitable that the Germans would register the Jews and shortly afterwards force Jewish shops to display a sign to that effect, though some poor souls, thinking they deserved better of their country, also displayed medals and photographs of uniformed men from the previous war to make their patriotism evident. Some months later, the first arrests began. The Jews were taken to a camp at Drancy for holding until their deportation.

An exhibition entitled 'The Jews' opened at the Palais Berlitz. The film, *Le Juif Süss*, showed at all the cinemas. In the metro one could notice shabby Jews, forced by circumstance to look like their caricatures (and hence have no inner life), entering the final carriage. Between three and four in the afternoon, they haunted the empty shops where scraps and rags were graciously permitted to them.

Katya thought of the Coëns. She went to see them and found them still in their apartment and still permitted their trade, which was not among the prohibited professions. All in all they seemed well, and able to refuse charity. Katya could persuade herself that things were not too bad and that the restrictions were no more than inconvenient. Having made this moral gesture, Katya ignored the developing situation without any sense of callousness.

In any case, the conditions of life were deteriorating and constant effort and attention were needed to procure the bare necessities. Plundered by the occupiers and destocked by the ordinary exigencies of war, the economy of France faltered. The quality of the food ration became poorer. France hungered amidst her own largesse, and, in the streets so strangely emptied of cars, could be heard the clack of wooden shoes.

During this period, the spring of 1942, Katya ran into

Le Nain again, struggling to ride a child's bicycle along the Rue de Rivoli.

'Marcel!' she called out from beneath the awning of the shop. The dwarf stopped.

'Ah!' he said. 'You catch me at a disadvantage, madame. Normally all meetings are arranged by appointment through my secretary.' He seemed in a good mood, and prosperous as things went in those days, wearing a blue suit and a beret that covered his greying curls.

'How are you?'

'I shall have to consult my doctor before answering that question. Expect a press release from my agent. How is my godson?'

'He's well.'

'Taller than me?'

'No.'

'And not as good-looking, either, I'll wager. You look . . . elegant. Yes, elegant! The health regime introduced by our friends across the Rhine has given us all better figures and a certain classic simplicity of dress.'

'What are you doing for a living?'

'Thriving, as you can see. But seriously, I sing numbers between the acts at a girlie revue in Montmartre. The *Boches* seem to love it. And now, Madame, pray put me down.'

Katya saw that, in embracing her friend, she had forced him on to his toes and that passers-by had begun to stare and step aside. Becoming aware of this, Le Nain apologized to Katya and, turning on the spectators, in his old sharp manner snapped:

'What's up with you? Can't you tell the difference between a dwarf and a Jew? What? What? No? I'll tell you what! Yes! I'll tell you. You can always recognize Jews. *They're tall!* Do you hear me? Tall!'

He looked at Katya.

'You know,' he said, 'you look tall enough to be Jewish.'

*　　*　　*

That spring the Germans introduced the regulation banning Jews from shopping except at hours when it might be expected that stocks of any desirable items had been sold. Katya went to see the Coëns again.

'How are things?' she asked.

'Hard,' said Sophie. 'Food is hard to find and there's not much work. Look –' she indicated the collection of shabby suits and coats awaiting alterations. 'Rags! People aren't buying new clothes.'

Katya made no promises but she went to see her brother-in-law.

'You want food for a Jewish family?' Philippe asked.

'They're really very nice people,' Masha contributed winsomely, 'even if they are Jews.' She was blooming under a second pregnancy and this had filled her with good will. Her husband smiled at her indulgently and, in his measured way, said:

'Very well, to please you, darling. But you must understand, Katya, that my name is not to be associated with these gifts.' He thought for a moment and added: 'What about fuel – either for yourself or your friends? I might be able to arrange something.' Which made Katya think that Philippe was not entirely a bad fellow.

During the month that followed, Katya made a couple of expeditions of this nature.

On a fine evening in June, Katya was looking out on the street when she saw Sasha riding home on his bicycle in the erratic way caused by his injuries. He appeared to have attracted the attention of the local children, who were dancing about him, calling names which she could not hear. When he came through the door, dressed in his usual make-do fashion with his trousers tucked into his socks and carrying a small cardboard suitcase tied with string to hold his papers, he seemed upset. He burst out:

'There's been a big round-up of Jews! One of the girls at our office has disappeared. Apparently they've all been carted off to the Vel' d'Hiv'. Damn the Germans!'

Katya could scarcely reply. Her eyes were fixed on the

badge he was wearing over his left breast. It was a yellow Star of David, prescribed for Jews to wear as a mark of their shame.

'Where did that come from?' she asked.

'This?' Sasha took it off. It was only a piece of gummed paper. 'Oh, I was so annoyed that I felt I had to do something!' Frustrated, he said: 'It was a gesture – just a gesture.'

Katya saw that where, on the real badge, the word 'Jew' should appear, Sasha had written 'Lawyer'.

'Just a gesture,' he repeated forlornly. 'Obviously a joke. I didn't have the courage to do more.'

The next day Katya returned again to the Coëns' apartment. She did not know herself what she had in mind. In the event, when she got there, she saw a man loitering on the stairs. He wore a short, belted leather jacket and a beret, and, almost unheard of, dropped the stub of his cigarette instead of keeping it for re-use. Katya did not doubt that he was a member of the French Gestapo, the *Carlingue*.

'Good day, madame,' he introduced himself. 'May I see your papers?'

Katya showed them and the man pawed through them.

'Do you know the family who lives here?'

'No. I'm just visiting my sister-in-law.'

'Who is . . .?'

Katya hesitated, dry-mouthed. But then the man was called away by a colleague and she was left standing by the door, her hand supporting her from the post. Her skin felt cold. Her breathing was irregular. Forgetting her errand, she staggered down the stairs to the street.

Katya never went back again to the Coëns' apartment, and she made no enquiries as to the family's whereabouts.

On a rainy night in February, a man arrived at the Zhivagos' apartment building by car, a fact unusual in itself and enough to cause faces to be glued to windows. The passenger was appropriately prosperous, a neat man in a long belted camel-hair coat, who had a small moustache and slicked-back hair. He entered the house and knocked at the door of the Zhivagos' apartment. Katya answered it and found herself face to face with her husband.

'Are you going to invite me in?' Safronov asked.

'I . . .'

'You weren't expecting me, I know. Hello, Sasha.'

'Kolya.'

'And *this*!' The visitor had taken in the room at a glance and now beamed at the child. 'This must be your son!'

He was here – uninvited and unwanted, but here within the walls of her home. By this fact alone Katya felt that he had established his dominance; and, though she expected no violence from him, he frightened her.

'Have you come far?' she asked. 'Where are you living these days?'

'Paris, Vichy, Bordeaux, nowhere in particular. Business demands that I spend most of my time in hotels, though I've bought an estate in the Périgord – only a small one.' He smiled.

He removed his coat, shaking off the few drops of rain. Beneath it he wore a well-tailored suit. Katya thought he had put weight on; his face was fleshier and not especially attractive, rather the contrary: the skin pitted and somewhat florid.

'Being in Paris, I thought I would drop in on you.'

'Insincere as always,' answered Katya to remind herself and him of their past. She looked at Sasha and he was unfathomable. She said: 'I'm afraid we can't offer you any refreshment. These days we don't run to it, not even a glass of wine or a piece of bread.'

'I understand. May I sit down?'

'The shortages don't seem to be affecting you. Yes, do sit down. In fact you look very well. Perhaps we could offer coffee, not real coffee: made from acorns or barley or something. Would you like some?'

Safronov took the comfortable though threadbare chair

by the radio where Sasha normally sat in the evenings. Katya moved to where Sasha was standing by the kitchen door with their son framed between his legs. The positioning was consciously defensive. She was convinced that in some fashion or other Kolya intended to attack her life. Again she looked at Sasha and again his thoughts were beyond her grasp.

'I gather you're working in a lawyer's office,' Safronov said to Sasha, adopting a patronizing tone. 'I won't make a mystery of it: your brother-in-law, Bonnet-Leclerc, and I have business together. He gives me titbits of information. I was pleased that you sorted yourself out. I was never sure – well, never sure you'd make a go of anything. Forgive me if I say it, but being so rich so young seemed to spoil you for anything sensible or useful.'

Katya noticed that Sasha was plucking at woollen threads on the mittens he often wore about the house these cold days. She looked at her own grey knitted stockings, and her pale ivory hands which were beginning to acquire the blue translucency of age. She and Sasha were, she thought, an unattractive pair, of negligible interest to the outside world. Why should they interest Kolya?

Sasha asked:

'Why have you come to see us?'

'Katya concerns me. I worry about her. Is that unreasonable, given that I'm her husband? Believe me, I've not come to cause trouble, only to give a bit of advice and some help.'

'What sort of advice?'

Behind her husband's civilities, Katya detected an intensity in him that she had not known before. It was as if this encounter represented for him a final opportunity to retrieve something. It reminded her of other times, other occasions in her childhood, but for the moment she could not fix on them. He was meanwhile explaining:

'The Germans are going to lose this war. Are you aware of that?'

Sasha answered: 'I don't think about the war. I just

746

try to take care of my family.' He looked at the child and asked Katya: 'Will you put him to bed while I talk to Kolya?' He spoke to Safronov: 'Or is it Katya you want to speak to? In which case, I'll see to him.'

'I don't want to go to bed,' said little Alessi clinging fretfully to his father's legs.

'You must, you must. It's late.'

'How old is he?' asked Safronov.

'Four. Katya, will you take him, or shall I?'

'What I have to say is for both of you.'

'I'll see to him,' said Katya. She picked her child up and carried him to their bedroom, promising: 'You can sleep in our bed. There, isn't it bigger and more comfortable?' Moments later, while she was undressing him, Sasha came in.

'Let me do that.'

'What? I thought you were talking to Kolya?'

'No. I can't – I mean, I'm not the one he really wants to talk to. You must face him, Katya.'

Irritated, Katya asked: 'Are you frightened of him?'

'No, of course not.' Earnestly, he added: 'But he has things to say. He has rights.'

'You mean he has a point of view and we must always listen to the other person's point of view,' Katya retorted contemptuously. 'Well, I ask: *why?* Why do I have to listen? Here, take him.' She handed his son to Sasha. 'Papa will get you ready. Don't wet the bed, darling. It isn't yours.' She returned to the other room where Safronov was placidly reading a newspaper.

'What do you want?' she demanded brusquely.

'Is Sasha joining us?'

'No. Now tell me what you want and then go.'

After a second of hesitation Safronov said sadly:

'Don't I deserve better of you than this? No? Ah, very well.' He looked about for an ashtray and asked if he might smoke. He lit a cigarette and commented that the neighbours were playing the radio loudly: was that always a problem?

'The walls are thin.'

'Yes?' He looked now to the door of the bedroom where Sasha was telling a story. He checked his watch. Beginning again, he said: 'The Germans are going to lose the war. And, as they lose, there will be greater resistance in the countries they occupy and the Germans will become increasingly violent. You can expect arrests, hostages, executions and so on. I'm sure you understand this, Katya, but I doubt you've thought what it means. No?'

He paused. Superficially he was smoking his cigarette, knocking ash into the tray and removing a strand of tobacco from his lower lip. But to Katya it seemed that he was struggling with a subject quite different from the present one. However, he continued:

'Sooner or later the Gestapo will get round to dealing with veterans of the Spanish war. They must have the names of those who were in the camps at Perpignan, and it's quite likely that they obtained further lists from the Soviets. Stalin has no liking for the international Communists who fought for the Republic. Are you following this? It can only be a matter of time before you and Sasha are arrested!'

Now Katya understood well enough where she had experienced this scene before. Viktor had come to Varykino to separate her mother from Yura. He had returned to remove her from the home of the three sisters. In each case he had armed himself with threats of what would happen if his advice were not taken and had used his dominance of reason and character to obtain his will.

Sasha had come back into the room. Katya felt him behind her. He touched her shoulder and gently kissed the nape of her neck.

'Go on,' he said to Safronov mildly. 'I heard what you said.'

'Is Alessi settled?' Katya asked him.

'He's awake, but I think he'll go off soon. Did you give him a drink? I gave him one. I hope he doesn't wet the bed. Do you remember last time? It took days to dry the mattress,' he explained to Safronov.

Safronov had finished his cigarette. He played now with a pair of soft kid gloves which he held on his lap.

'Come with me,' he said. 'Things are still easier in the south than they are here. I have friends, contacts. If I'm right about the way things are going, I can make arrangements to get us to Switzerland or Portugal.'

'All of us?' asked Katya.

'Yes,' affirmed Safronov, looking straight at Sasha.

'Shall you go?' she asked Sasha. She supposed he would detect her irony. Contemptuous herself, she expected Sasha to display contempt and anger, instead he shook his head. 'But I won't stop you. There's a lot of sense in what Kolya says.'

Sense. Yes, there was sense in what Kolya had said. Reason in all its treachery was capable of leading to appalling conclusions supported by inescapable logic. But that Sasha could admit even the possibility that they might part pushed Katya towards a sudden and unforeseen abyss. *How could he?*

To the astonishment of the two men, Katya, who had displayed a self-control tinged with anger, burst into tears. She shouted: 'You decide! You decide!' and fled into the kitchen.

'Katya!'

Alessi had heard the cry and was already at the door of the bedroom, complaining: 'Mama! Papa!'

Sasha followed on Katya's heels, telling his son: 'There, there, go back to bed.' He found Katya supporting herself against the sink. She looked away. He touched her. She looked at him. In that moment she experienced again the flash of hatred which had once been so effective in disposing of Tanya. She knew that according to his strange lights he thought he was acting for the best, but she saw only his contemptible weakness and his blind willingness to sacrifice to the unearthly principles that activated his soul. Alessi had come into the kitchen and was clasping her legs, screaming frantically: 'Mama! Papa!'

'Stop it!' she shouted at the child.

Confused, Sasha said: 'I love you! I do love you. You've misunderstood.'

'Oh, be quiet!'

She grabbed Alessi, picked him up and rocked him almost cruelly. Unconsciously she held him away from his father.

'Madman!' she shouted at Sasha. 'Fool! Idiot! Madman!' She rushed from the kitchen into the room where Safronov was sitting peaceably. He raised an ironic eyebrow, and Katya thought: yes! I'll do it! I'll go with Kolya. I may as well kill myself, but I'll go with him. I can't stay with Sasha. What is he? Is he human?

But she did not go with Kolya. She was stayed by a coldness that overcame her, yet was not the effect of reason. Indifferent to what might become of her, she felt a revulsion towards Safronov that, at his worst, Sasha did not inspire in her. Her husband and Viktor Komarovsky had become compounded into everything that represented the power and manipulation of men and she refused to be compelled to a decision dictated by them.

How had it been for her mother? Katya could remember her unforgiving thoughts. Yet what choices had Lara had when confronted by the power of Komarovsky and her abandonment by Zhivago? How had she been able to resist when burdened by her guilt: her surrender to Viktor as a girl; her betrayal of Katya's father and of Tonya? Katya now felt an anguish that was not her own: a burden of generations falling on her. Even if Sasha by his renunciation were to make her life a desolation, she would not concede to Kolya, for that would be to render life meaningless. She was not her mother. Katya believed herself stronger, clearer in her thinking, more acute in her moral analysis: so that she would not accept the guilt of another's failings in the way that Lara had felt herself tainted by Viktor's crimes.

Kolya said merely:

'Well?'

Go!

Katya did not say: go! She was distracted by the most mundane of things: a wriggling child. She had to take Alessi to the bedroom and try for ten minutes to soothe him, tell him a story and persuade him that everything was all right. And when she returned to the other room she found both men there, and her feeling was not hot anger, but cold resentment that they had driven her to this, and a disappointment in Sasha that was beyond words.

She told Kolya: 'Get out.' She was tired. She turned to Sasha.

'I can't explain,' he said. He meant not that she would not understand but that he, too, did not understand.

Safronov stood up, angry, confused. He knew that he had lost; but that he had lost to such a pitiful specimen as Sasha Zhivago was bitter and incomprehensible to him. And from this woman, who was capable of so much that was greater! It was almost beyond belief!

'I'll go,' he said. He picked up his coat. 'You're both fools,' he told them.

When he had gone, Katya could only look at Sasha and think: we must go on. Life must go on. There's Alessi to consider. She wondered if she still loved Sasha and decided that she did. But how strange love was! How far beyond her previous imaginings.

Someone must have denounced Sasha and Katya because two nights after Safronov's visit they were arrested though they had done nothing wrong. Perhaps it was Safronov who betrayed them. But with all his failings he had never in the past been vindictive.

There was nothing remarkable about the circumstances of the arrest. In the small hours of the morning they heard a noise at the door to the apartment from the landing but, before Sasha could slip into his dressing gown and answer, the door was broken down and half a dozen men entered the main room. Simultaneously in German and French, a brief document was read over at the same time as Sasha was being spun around and handcuffed and Katya and Alessi routed out of the bedroom. The substance of the document was that, under various regulations of the occupying power, it was essential for the well-being of the State and to suppress criminal and gangster elements, that Alexander Alexandrovitch Zhivago and Katerina Pavlovna Safronova be taken into preventive detention. Various other things were said relative to the formalities of the arrest, but it was difficult to catch these since, to her subsequent shame, Katya screamed almost continuously from the time Alessi was taken from her arms until she was bundled down the stairs to the waiting van.

Sasha, on the other hand, retained a measure of calmness. He insisted that he was a French citizen. He demanded sight of the piece of paper authorizing the arrest. He asked for particulars of the charges and maintained that he and Katya were innocent of any wrong-doing. In short, he acted as though the affair were a matter of reason and law, and could therefore be discussed and clarified if only these policemen would not be in such a hurry. He, too, was thrown into the van, and after him followed a bundle of clothes and an instruction to change if he wanted to be warm.

'The handcuffs,' he said. 'I can't change my clothes if my hands aren't free.'

Four of the men – two French, two German – were also in the back of the van. They exchanged words among themselves, then one of them said:

'All right. But remember we have guns.'

He unlocked the cuffs and Sasha threw his arms around Katya. He pulled her close to him. Her body seemed to have collapsed as though she were unconscious, but she was speaking, softly repeating: 'Alessi! Alessi!'

'What about my son?' asked Sasha.

'Arrangements will be made,' said one of his captors.

Sasha lunged at the man, but was parried easily and struck in the face with a small leather-bound cosh. 'Now, calm yourself down,' said the man. 'Take it easy and we'll be easy with you. Think of the lady. Why don't you get changed? You may not have a chance later. I'm afraid there's not much we can do about the lady. She'll have to wait.'

'My son!'

'Look, if it's any consolation, you're not the first. We have procedures for these things. He'll be taken care of.'

'Alessi!' moaned Katya.

'Keep the woman quiet, will you? It doesn't do any good.'

'I'll try,' promised Sasha, and he held Katya even closer, though her coldness gave him no comfort.

Where was she? he wondered. Not here. Not with me. She acts as if she doesn't know I exist. Where are we going? I can't see. I wonder if they'll split us up? I suppose they must.

'You're pissing yourself,' said their captor.

Sasha looked down.

'I'm sorry.'

'That's okay. It happens. It's as well you didn't change first. If you've finished, wipe yourself, take off your pyjamas and put on your pants.'

But Sasha could not. To do so he would have to release his embrace of Katya and the thought of that was unbearable.

He thought: I'm saying goodbye. We'll never meet again. I'm trying to say I love you and she doesn't even recognize me. This isn't what I expected. I thought we'd grow old together.

The men were saying among themselves: 'Look at his feet. How did his toes get like that? Do you think he's been arrested before?' But Sasha was thinking only: we shan't grow old together. We shan't say goodbye. I can't remember if I kissed Alessi before Katya put him to bed. He wouldn't sleep. Did he know?

'Where are we going?'

'Wait and see.'

What was the last thing we said to each other? I can't even remember if we said good night before bed. She was still angry with me over that business with Kolya. I didn't want her to go, but if she'd gone with him she would have been safe now.

'How long?'

'Twenty minutes, maybe.'

I want to think of her and nothing else, but, my God, I'm so frightened. Will they kill me? Torture me? Why have I been arrested? I've tried to stay out of trouble.

'Cigarette?'

'Thanks.'

Are you awake, Katya? Why are your eyes closed? We're saying goodbye and you can't even see me. I'm frightened. I think I'm about to die and I want you to tell me one last time that you love me. Don't play dead. Don't pretend. Tell me! Tell me! *I'm frightened!*

Sasha was taken to the Gestapo building in the Avenue Foch. Katya was left in the van with the two Frenchmen. This was a development so unexpected that Sasha had got out of the vehicle and was standing in the cold night air before he realized that the doors at the rear were closing again. He rushed back, and the German escort, thinking he was making an attempt to escape, hit him with a pistol butt. He fell to his knees with his fingers and chin over the back of the van, so that he could, for a second, glance into the interior before one of the guards kicked him away and pulled the doors closed.

'I love you!' he called out.

Did she hear him? In that last glimpse had he seen her emergent from her state of shock, and had she recognized him? Had they parted with her still angry after the business with Kolya? What were the last words of affection that had passed between them?

For a week he was mistreated by the Gestapo in

their routine fashion. Then, since it did not take the Germans long to ascertain that their prisoner was genuinely ignorant of any important matters, they lost interest in him. However, having been classified as a Russian, he was disposed of as such and sent to the Channel Islands where Soviet prisoners of war worked in slave battalions building fortifications for the Reich. Sasha joined one of these gangs. There were many deaths from starvation and maltreatment.

Under these conditions, and given the other things that had happened to him, it was not surprising that his health deteriorated and his state of mind became confused. Lying freezing in his filthy bunk, he spent many hours reflecting on his last days with Katya, working and reworking every scene. Unable to accept the brute reality of their parting, that it could happen at such an ill juncture in their love, he searched for a moment when they had each had a premonition of what was about to happen and so had sworn their love and been reconciled. A very few times he found in his memory a recollection of that moment. They were in the kitchen, or the bedroom, or perhaps listening to the radio. And, by a glance, each had recognized in the other the ineffable and unbreakable bond of joy they had created between them.

More often, however, Sasha found nothing, for the reason that it did not exist. The truth was that, though they had loved each other, those last days had been marked by peevishness and disappointment. Realizing this made Sasha weep inwardly.

Retreating from such painful memories and from the tangible pain of his surroundings, Sasha wondered what it was that had brought him to his present predicament. Although he could accept the contribution of external agencies such as the Germans, it seemed to him that in substance he had brought himself to this place. After all, there were millions of Frenchmen who were not there, and that must mean something.

What had he sought that might be found here? Knowledge – *scientia gnosis*? Certainly not heroism, something which he had abandoned so long ago that it was difficult to credit that he had once believed in such nonsense. Whatever it was, it was somehow bound up with folly.

At odd moments he did not believe that he was entirely a fool. A lot of the time of course he was. But occasionally . . . occasionally. There was a species of folly that was an attempt to take Truth, as it were, unawares. He wondered if that were the point. He wondered if he would be vouchsafed a glimmer of Truth before he died. That he would die soon he did not doubt, nor did death in itself trouble him. But to die in ignorance and unreconciled, that was the unbearable part, ultimately more unbearable than his separation from Katya and his son. That separation he had cast into forgetfulness as a spirit of transcendence gripped his cold and hungry body, as if it would pluck him out of it.

One morning in the autumn, Sasha and his fellow prisoners were trudging on foot to the place of their labours. They were in a deep lane with high banks topped by hawthorn hedgerows such as characterize the islands: lanes that thread their way secretively with scarcely a view beyond the banks, except that now and again two lanes join and a stone-built farm stands like a fortress at the junction and a patch of sunlight breaks the shadows.

Leaves and fruit had fallen, and the cold and bandaged feet of the Russians churned the damp brown porridge of mould and mud, sloes, acorns and hawthorn berries. Their lungs breathed in the mist. Their eyes scanned for crab apples and milk cap fungus.

Weak and distracted, Sasha paid little attention but he felt himself immersed in a strange russet glow, a halo of mist touched by the sun. Looking down to his feet he could see individual hedgerow fruits, bruised and decaying, eaten by worm and mould, but still intact in the mud and grass among the broken twigs. Concentrating on this – this revelation, as it appeared to him – he stopped walking and in some fashion or other (he was not sure how) got his face and eyes down to the ground so that he could study it more closely. All the while his companions dragged their feet past him and a guard brought up the rear, snapping and chivvying in German. Among the voices Sasha heard one say:

'I was in Spain. According to the Spaniards, it takes an hour before you can see the soul in the face of a dead man.'

'What sort of a soul do you think he has?' asked another.

'I hardly knew him. I heard he was a nice fellow. A bit mad, but decent enough.'

After that the voices became faint and Sasha's senses could focus only on the fallen berries inches away from his eyes, and his thoughts ranged over things he had seen or read which might help him explain this phenomenon. As they did so, he became conscious that the particulars of the fruit, the marks and blemishes, were no longer visible to him; indeed the red hawthorn berries seemed not like berries, but spots of blood reminding him of the spots of menstrual blood he had noticed on Katya's *mono* that night in Spain when they had fallen in love.

Then for a second Sasha thought he saw, behind the corruption and blemish of these berries lying in the mud, the beauty of the imperishable idea they embodied. And for that brief span he sensed too the presence of an indwelling God, a true God behind the dross of time and matter, yet one in whom he could no longer believe.

At a building in the Rue de la Pompe, Katya was treated to the unspeakable abuses of the *Carlingue*. Finding no particular crime in her, they shipped her off to Germany to perform forced labour in the armaments factories of the Ruhr. She remained there until liberated by the advancing Allies and during this period had no news of her son or of Sasha. The state of shock that had affected her at the time of her arrest transformed itself into a numbness of fear and exhaustion in which the unbearable had to be borne because there was no alternative. Prior to her arrest Katya would have said, with facile conviction, that she would die if she were ever separated from her son. She did not die. Instead, perhaps in the same way that her mother had coped with the loss of Tanya, she killed her son in her own heart and hid the grave in dark corners of oblivion. In fact, if any time were the worst for her, it was when a party of smiling Americans brought medicines and rations and opened the gates of the compound where the slaves were held. For at that moment, when Katya was freed to think of her son, she felt the force of her murderess's conscience. Though it was true that she had not caused or willed their separation, she knew she was responsible for the destruction of his memory within her, and for this her guilt was bitter.

In May 1945 Katya returned to Paris. Finding her own apartment let to new tenants, she went to see Sasha's family at Neuilly. They were still in residence. Indeed it was Tonya, looking older and greyer but still handsome, who opened the door.

'Yes?'

'Don't you recognize me?'

'Katya? Katya, oh my God!' Tonya held out her arms and the two women fell upon each other with tears and kisses. Behind them scampered children, three of them, a boy and girl belonging to Masha, and Alessi. Though he was taller and two years older, the physical changes in him were not so very great, and the softness of infancy, which Katya feared he would have lost, was still there in his face. He said nothing, but seeing Katya flung himself into her arms almost hurting her with the force, and she found to her surprise that he was heavy and she was too weak to carry him.

They went into the salon. It was as remembered, though a little shabbier. Philippe and Masha were at home and all around tears and cries of joy greeted the visitor. 'This is wonderful!' Katya found herself saying repeatedly, smiling, and dabbing her eyes. But it was not wonderful. In fact she felt very little beyond a deadness, a lethargy and an awful fear that this was how it would be for ever, and that for the sake of Alessi she would have to bear with an imitation of life in which she would smile or cry to order.

'You're pregnant again?' she remarked to Masha when a certain calmness had been restored and Katya felt obliged to ask about what had happened since her arrest.

'Yes!' said Masha gaily. 'I've discovered that I'm suited to being a mother. Who would have thought it? In fact I've even got rid of the nanny. Actually she left. The war has meant that one simply can't get staff.'

Katya looked at Tonya and saw the glow of pride and joy in her grandchildren. Uncharitably she thought: this is her revenge on me and on my mother. How old is she now, fifty-five, sixty? After all these years she is happy, but my mother is dead and I am destroyed.

'Do you have any news of Sasha?' she asked.

'We think he's been in the Channel Islands,' said Philippe. 'They've only just been liberated, but we expect news any day.'

They did expect news, and had no especial foreboding. However, Sasha did not return from the war and no record of him was ever found except that he had been among the Russian prisoners.

When Sasha failed to return, it proved impossible for Katya to continue to live with the rest of the family. Apart from practical considerations of space, it was clear that she could not share a home with Tonya. Although Tonya did not overtly blame Katya for the death or disappearance of her son, she became increasingly carping and critical, and Katya caught her studying Alessi and herself, Lara's child, with strange intentness. At times Katya even felt a little fearful. In her darkest moments she even suspected that Tonya posed a physical danger to herself and her son.

Moreover, matters were not easy for Philippe and Masha. There were suggestions by malicious persons that

Philippe was a criminal and collaborator, and though he cleared himself of these charges there was a period when life was tense. He even abandoned his pipe for cigarettes.

She moved with Alessi to an apartment of her own and found work, first as a clerk and then as a teacher of Russian and music. At the school was a colleague, Pierre Mollin, who taught French literature. He was, like Sasha, a man of middling height and pleasant but unremarkable appearance. In 1940 he had been in the army and was taken prisoner, and had passed the war years in Germany. None of his experiences had destroyed his wry sense of humour.

He was unmarried. Over the months Katya and he became friends. She introduced him to Alessi, who found him good fun, and Pierre seemed to take to the boy and was happy to engage in rough-and-tumble play on the carpet of Katya's apartment.

Katya continued to visit the family at Neuilly, primarily for the sake of Alessi who was fond of his grandmother and cousins. On one of these occasions, Tonya handed to her an unopened letter bearing a postmark from Lyons and a date in September 1943.

'I forgot about it,' she explained briefly. 'You were away, and I put it in the drawer. Do forgive me.'

Katya felt faint on seeing the familiar handwriting of her husband. This is what the letter said:

Dearest Katya,

Will this letter ever reach you? If my fears are justified, then I doubt it ever will. So why write? Because I need to relieve my thoughts and require at least the fiction of another person to whom they may be addressed.

Why did you refuse to come with me to Vichy? Did you suspect my motives, and, if so, why? When have I ever behaved towards you other than to protect your interests? I brought you out of danger in Russia. I took care of you in Paris. When you went to Spain I watched over you and sent you money when you needed it. In return for which I have received nothing but your coldness and contempt, except for one inexplicable night before you left me.

Does this sound like a complaint? I suppose it must. But do I not have reason to complain? From first knowing you in Vladivostok (I ignore your childhood) you have been a mystery to me. It has always been inconceivable to me that my kindnesses towards you should be so cruelly rejected.

Write to me. Explain to me. I pray that you are safe, and also your child, even though he is not mine.

Your affectionate husband,
Kolya

Katya destroyed the letter and kept the news to herself. She thought that it was emotionally self-indulgent and supposed it had been written when Kolya was drunk and his affairs were not going too well, otherwise he would not have risked the letter in the hands of the censors. On reflection it still seemed to her that her reasons for rejecting her husband were obvious and justified. He was insincere. He had tried always to take her when she was vulnerable. Whatever he might think, there was no love in him, and what he conceived of as love was no more than a horrible fascination.

And if she were wrong? It was too late to reconsider or at this date burden her conscience with more guilt. For among the titbits of news that from time to time arrived, was the report that Kolya had died in 1944. He had been involved in some sort of ring for smuggling fugitives to Switzerland and, when it was broken by the Gestapo, he was shot. It was impossible now to ascertain if his motives were mercenary or patriotic. The Resistance claimed him as their own. In later years, in a small village near Lyons, a plaque was put up to his memory and a street now bears his name.

Despite the company of her son and the friendship of Pierre, the year after the war found Katya a lonely woman in her thirties. She detected a hardness in herself and foresaw a life of bitterness and regret. She asked herself: had she ever been truly capable of love? Thinking of the men she had loved or who had loved her: Sasha,

Daniel and Kolya, she was struck again by love's asymmetry. In timing, intensity, meaning and exclusivity it was never the same for two people, who yet proceeded under the fond illusion that it was. But to forgo love was unbearable.

She considered Sasha. He lacked all moral grandeur, even of the monstrous sort that is the stuff of tragedy. Instead, he offered the world and Katya a general kindness, effective enough from day to day but useless in its broader influence: a benevolence supported by wrongheaded, mediocre thinking. Knowing this, she had brought herself to love him for his weaknesses as much as his strengths. Yet how could their respective emotions be considered equal? In her recognition of his weakness had she not always had a hard and cruel reservation? When had she mourned him?

When Pierre Mollin offered to marry her, late in 1946, Katya accepted and it was done. She was very fond of him and he was a good man, kind to her child. Even Tonya, hiding whatever secret feelings she might have, congratulated her on her wisdom, if only for the sake of Alessi. The following year, at the age of thirty-five, she bore a daughter whom she named Marie-Isabelle after her dear Spanish friends.

Over the years that followed she heard news of various other friends and acquaintances. Princess Wanda left her husband after his return from Spain as a Fascist hero. She went home to Chicago and ran the family meat-packing business. As for Prince Carlo, he stuck by his doomed leader and, after Mussolini was rescued by the Germans and founded his puppet state in northern Italy, he became chief of police in one of the cities. He was hanged by partisans in May 1945.

Constantine did not come home after Spain, but was believed to have survived. In some fashion he became associated with the Nazis, probably as a result of his contacts with the Germans during the civil war. In 1950 he was said to be an importer in Argentina. In 1955

762

he was reported to be a priest. Thereafter nothing more was heard.

Katya met Le Nain on several occasions with decreasing frequency. With age, the dwarf lost his voice and his work as a cabaret artist. He died in obscurity, reputedly of drink.

Of them all, Lydia Kalinowska may be said to have made a success of her life. For a period during the war she was mistress to Aristide Krueger, until his death in a motor accident. Thereafter she married an elderly deputy of the Fourth Republic, becoming in due course a political widow famous for her salons and eccentric humour. She died, full of honours, in 1972.

One winter evening, when her daughter was seven years old, Katya attended her school where the children were putting on one of the little entertainments which so charm parents. Sitting on a bentwood chair with Pierre and Alessi next to her, she watched as Marie-Isabelle and the other children, in pinafores and paper garlands, danced to a folk tune played on an upright piano. The room was dimly lit by candles and the crepe decorations glowed red and green and fluttered to the rhythms of air and music.

Sitting next to her son and husband and watching her daughter's clumsy but winsome steps, Katya felt the pride of any parent. And she felt too, not for the first time, that this was a moment that would not be recalled for the significance of the event, but for the unalloyed joy and well-being that flooded her soul.

For no particular reason, Pierre leaned over and kissed her on the ear, and she smiled at him, and he enquired:

'Are you happy?'

'Yes,' she answered.

'Do you love me?'

She squeezed his hand.

Seeing Alessi, who was grinning and then murmured something to Pierre who returned his grin, she thought of Sasha. Was it not Sasha who had taught her to take and treasure these moments of folly? Was it not Sasha who by his generosity of spirit had given her the possibility of taking joy in life? It was, she felt at last, possible to mourn him, for mourning was not to be feared. He was Sasha: to be mourned in folly and joy, with a light heart, with love in fact.

There were, she thought, so many who had died. Life had been harsh to her and to all the others. Yet love in all its asymmetry had filled her not once but again and again, and still had the capacity to bring meaning to her life.

This moment would go, but others would come for her and for her daughter. Marie-Isabelle, imagining herself a great ballerina, clumped about the stage transported by the music and the light. She smiled fixedly. Her eyes glittered with pleasure. She nudged and winked and whispered to her friends.

'What does she think she's doing?' asked Pierre. 'What does she think she's doing?'

Dancing in the sea, thought Katya. She's dancing in the sea!

THE END

ZADRUGA
by Margaret Pemberton

In Belgrade, in the balmy spring of 1914, neither of the royally related Karageorgevich sisters had the slightest presentiment of disaster. Seventeen-year-old Natalie was enjoying the danger and secrecy of friendship with young nationalists, eager to free their lands from Habsburg domination. Katerina, her less volatile sister, was deeply and secretly in love with Julian Fielding, a young English diplomat.

Then, when accompanying their father on an official visit to Sarajevo, Natalie inadvertently plunged their lives into chaos as she found herself caught up in the assassination of Franz Ferdinand. As the Austrians demanded her extradition Natalie had no choice but to flee the homeland she so passionately loved. She chose to leave in a manner that was to prove catastrophic – as the bride of Julian Fielding, the man her sister loved.

0 552 13987 4

LEGACY OF LOVE
by Caroline Harvey

Charlotte was the first – wildly beautiful, wildly frustrated – who married her soldier husband solely to escape from the claustrophobic respectability of Victorian life in Richmond. When she reached the British lines in Kabul she was bewitched and fascinated by the exotic world of Afghanistan – and by Alexander Bewick, the scandalous adventurer who aroused an instant response in Charlotte's rebellious heart. As the city of Kabul turned into a hell of bloodshed and misery, Charlotte was forced to choose between her devoted husband, and her reckless lover.

Alexandra lived – always – in the shadow of her legendary grandmother, Charlotte. Reared in a gloomy Scottish castle by a mother who resented her, she finally had to reach out and try to create a life of her own.

Cara had inherited the wildness, the passion, and also the selfishness of her great-grandmother Charlotte. Smouldering with resentment because she had to help care for her crippled mother when her friends were all joining up at the outbreak of the Second World War, she finally found, as the tragedies of the war began to erode her life, that she also had the courage of Charlotte – a courage that was eventually to bring her happiness.

Caroline Harvey is a pseudonym of the award-winning writer Joanna Trollope.

0 552 13872 X

THE LADY OF KYNACHAN
by James Irvine Robertson

An epic novel of the '45.

Not long after he inherited the highland estate of Kynachan, young David Stewart was shown, in a dream, the image of his future wife. When, at a ball in Perth, he saw the beautiful Jean Mercer – the woman of his dream – he proposed at once, determined that she should become his Lady of Kynachan.

The marriage was passionate and happy, and Jean learned to love the life of the Scottish Highlands. But when Prince Charles landed in 1745 and summoned his men to follow him, David Stewart, a devoted Jacobite, went to fight for the Cause, perishing on the field of Culloden with all the men of Kynachan save one.

As the British government ruthlessly set out to destroy the Highland way of life, the Lady of Kynachan summoned all her courage, her wit and strength, to build a new life for herself, her children, and the people of Kynachan.

Based on the lives of James Irvine Robertson's own ancestors, and beautifully evoking the life of the Highlands in the eighteenth century, *The Lady of Kynachan* is a story of romance, tragedy, and hope reborn that recalls *Gone With the Wind*.

'Exciting . . . A romantic novel of rich appeal'
John Prebble

0 552 14298 0

A SELECTED LIST OF FINE NOVELS AVAILABLE FROM CORGI BOOKS

THE PRICES SHOWN BELOW WERE CORRECT AT THE TIME OF GOING TO PRESS. HOWEVER TRANSWORLD PUBLISHERS RESERVE THE RIGHT TO SHOW NEW RETAIL PRICES ON COVERS WHICH MAY DIFFER FROM THOSE PREVIOUSLY ADVERTISED IN THE TEXT OR ELSEWHERE.

☐	14058 9	**MIST OVER THE MERSEY**	*Lyn Andrews*	£4.99
☐	14049 X	**THE JERICHO YEARS**	*Aileen Armitage*	£4.99
☐	13992 0	**LIGHT ME THE MOON**	*Angela Arney*	£4.99
☐	14044 9	**STARLIGHT**	*Louise Brindley*	£4.99
☐	13952 1	**A DURABLE FIRE**	*Brenda Clarke*	£4.99
☐	13255 1	**GARDEN OF LIES**	*Eileen Goudge*	£5.99
☐	13686 7	**THE SHOEMAKER'S DAUGHTER**	*Iris Gower*	£4.99
☐	13688 3	**THE OYSTER CATCHERS**	*Iris Gower*	£4.99
☐	13977 7	**SPINNING JENNY**	*Ruth Hamilton*	£4.99
☐	14139 9	**THE SEPTEMBER STARLINGS**	*Ruth Hamilton*	£4.99
☐	13872 X	**LEGACY OF LOVE**	*Caroline Harvey*	£4.99
☐	13917 3	**A SECOND LEGACY**	*Caroline Harvey*	£4.99
☐	14138 0	**PROUD HARVEST**	*Janet Haslam*	£4.99
☐	14262 X	**MARIANA**	*Susanna Kearsley*	£4.99
☐	14045 7	**THE SUGAR PAVILION**	*Rosalind Laker*	£5.99
☐	14002 3	**FOOL'S CURTAIN**	*Claire Lorrimer*	£4.99
☐	13737 5	**EMERALD**	*Elisabeth Luard*	£5.99
☐	13910 6	**BLUEBIRDS**	*Margaret Mayhew*	£4.99
☐	13904 1	**VOICES OF SUMMER**	*Diane Pearson*	£4.99
☐	10375 6	**CSARDAS**	*Diane Pearson*	£5.99
☐	13987 4	**ZADRUGA**	*Margaret Pemberton*	£4.99
☐	13636 0	**CARA'S LAND**	*Elvi Rhodes*	£4.99
☐	13870 3	**THE RAINBOW THROUGH THE RAIN**	*Elvi Rhodes*	£4.99
☐	14298 0	**THE LADY OF KYNACHAN**	*James Irvine Robertson*	£5.99
☐	13545 3	**BY SUN AND CANDLELIGHT**	*Susan Sallis*	£4.99
☐	14162 3	**SWEETER THAN WINE**	*Susan Sallis*	£4.99
☐	13299 3	**DOWN LAMBETH WAY**	*Mary Jane Staples*	£4.99
☐	14296 4	**THE LAND OF NIGHTINGALES**	*Sally Stewart*	£4.99
☐	14118 6	**THE HUNGRY TIDE**	*Valerie Wood*	£4.99
☐	14263 8	**ANNIE**	*Valerie Wood*	£4.99